THE CLASSIC ADVENTURES

AYESHA: The Return of She
BENITA: An African Romance

THE CLASSIC ADVENTURES

AYESHA: The Return of She
BENITA: An African Romance

SIR H. RIDER HAGGARD

NEW ORCHARD EDITIONS
Poole · New York · Sydney

This edition published 1986 by New Orchard Editions Ltd
Robert Rogers House
New Orchard
Poole, Dorset BH15 1LU

Copyright © 1986 New Orchard Editions Ltd

ISBN 1 85079 043 4

Distributed in the USA by Sterling Publishing Co. Inc,
2 Park Avenue, New York, NY 10016

Distributed in Australia by
Capricorn Link (Australia) Pty Ltd
PO Box 665
Lane Cove, NSW 2066

Printed in Great Britain by
Bath Press Ltd., Bath, Avon.

AYESHA

THE RETURN OF "SHE."

By H. RIDER HAGGARD.

" Here ends this history so far as it concerns science and the outside world. What its end will be as regards Leo and myself is more than I can guess. But we feel that it is not reached. . . . Often I sit alone at night, staring with the eyes of my mind into the blackness of unborn time, and wondering in what shape and form the great drama will be finally developed, and where the scene of its next act will be laid. And when, ultimately, that *final* development occurs, as I have no doubt it must and will occur, in obedience to a fate that never swerves and a purpose which cannot be altered, what will be the part played therein by that beautiful Egyptian Amenartas, the Princess of the royal house of the Pharaohs, for the love of whom the priest Kallikrates broke his vows to Isis, and, pursued by the vengeance of the outraged goddess, fled down the coast of Lybia to meet his doom at Kôr?"

DEDICATION.

TO ANDREW LANG, ESQ.

MY DEAR LANG,—
The appointed years—alas! how many of them—are gone by, leaving Ayesha lovely and loving and ourselves alive. As it was promised in the Caves of Kôr, *She* has returned again.

To you therefore who accepted the first, I offer this further history of one of the various incarnations of that Immortal.

My hope is that after you have read her record, notwithstanding her subtleties and sins, and the shortcomings of her chronicler (no easy office!), you may continue to wear your chain of "loyalty to our lady Ayesha." Such, I confess, is still the fate of your old friend

H. RIDER HAGGARD.

Ditchingham, 1904.

AUTHOR'S NOTE.

NOT with a view of conciliating those readers who on principle object to sequels, but as a matter of fact, the Author wishes to say that he does not so regard this book.

Rather does he venture to ask that it should be considered as the conclusion of an imaginative tragedy (if he may so call it) whereof one half has been already published.

This conclusion it was always his desire to write should he be destined to live through those many years which, in obedience to his original design, must be allowed to lapse between the events of the first and second parts of the romance.

INTRODUCTION.

VERILY and indeed it is the unexpected that happens! Probably if there was one person upon the earth from whom the editor of this, and of a certain previous history, did not expect to hear again, that person was Ludwig Horace Holly. This, too, for a good reason; he believed him to have taken his departure from the earth.

When Mr. Holly last wrote, many, many years ago, it was to transmit the manuscript of "She," and to announce that he and his ward, Leo Vincey, the beloved of the divine Ayesha, were about to travel to Central Asia in the hope, I suppose, that there she would fulfil her promise and appear to them again.

Often I have wondered, idly enough, what happened to them there; whether they were dead, or perhaps droning their lives away as monks in some Thibetan Lamasery, or studying magic and practising asceticism under the tuition of the Eastern Masters, trusting that thus they would build a bridge by which they might pass to the side of their adored Immortal.

Now, at length, when I had not thought of them for months, without a single warning sign, out of the blue as it were, comes the answer to these wonderings!

To think—only to think—that I, the editor aforesaid, from its appearance suspecting something quite familiar and without interest, pushed aside that dingy, unregistered, brown-paper parcel directed in an unknown hand, and for two whole days let it lie forgotten! Indeed, there it might be lying now, had not another person been moved to curiosity, and, opening it, found within a bundle of manuscript badly burned upon the back, and with this, two letters addressed to myself.

Although so great a time had passed since I saw it, and it was shaky now from the author's age or sickness, I knew the writing at once—nobody ever made an "H" with that peculiar twirl under it except Mr. Holly. I tore open the sealed envelope, and sure enough the first thing my eye fell upon was the signature, *L. H. Holly*. It is long since I read anything so eagerly as I did that letter. Here it is:—

"MY DEAR SIR,—

"I have ascertained that you still live, and, strange to say, I still live also—for a little while.

"As soon as I came into touch with civilisation again I found a copy of your book 'She,' or, rather, of my book, and read it—first of all, in a Hindostani translation. My host—he was a minister of some religious body, a man of worthy but prosaic mind—expressed surprise that a 'wild romance' should absorb me so much. I answered that those who had wide experience of the hard facts of life often found interest in romance. Had he known what were the hard facts to which I alluded, I wonder what that excellent person would have said?

"I see that you carried out your part of the business well and faithfully. Every instruction has been obeyed; nothing has been added or taken away. Therefore, to you, to whom some twenty years ago I entrusted the beginning of the history, I wish to entrust its end also. You were the first to learn of *She-Who-Must-Be-Obeyed*, who from century to century sat alone, clothed with unchanging loveliness in the sepulchres of Kôr, waiting till her lost love was born again, and Destiny brought him back to her.

"It is right, therefore, that you should be the first to learn also of Ayesha, Spirit and Hesea of the Mountain, the priestess of that Oracle which since the time of Alexander the Great has reigned between the flaming pillars in the Sanctuary, the last holder of the sceptre of Hes or Isis upon the earth. It is right also that to you first among men I should reveal the mystic consummation of the wondrous tragedy which began at Kôr, or perchance far earlier in Egypt and elsewhere.

"I am very ill; I have struggled back to this old house of mine to die, and my end is at hand. I have asked the doctor here, after all is over, to send you the Record—that is, unless I change my mind and burn it first. You will also receive, if you receive anything at all, a case containing several rough sketches which may be of use to you, and a *sistrum*, the instrument that has been always used in the worship of the Nature goddesses of the old Egyptians, Isis and Hathor, which you will see is as beautiful as it is ancient. I give it to you for two reasons: as a token of my gratitude and regard, and as the only piece of evidence that is left to me of the literal truth of what I have written in the accompanying manuscript, where you will find it often mentioned. Perhaps also you will value it as a souvenir of, I suppose, the strangest and loveliest being who ever was, or rather, is. It was her sceptre, the rod of her power, with which I saw her salute the Shadows in the Sanctuary, and her gift to me.

"It has virtues also; some part of Ayesha's might yet haunts the symbol to which even spirits bowed, but if you should discover them, beware how they are used.

"I have neither the strength nor the will to write more. The Record must speak for itself. Do with it what you like, and believe it or not as you like. I care nothing who know that it is true.

"Who and what was Ayesha, nay—what *is* Ayesha? An incarnate essence a materialised spirit of Nature, the unforeseeing, the lovely, the cruel and the immortal; ensouled alone, redeemable only by Humanity and its piteous sacrifice? Say you! I have done with speculations who depart to solve these mysteries.

"I wish you happiness and good fortune. Farewell to you and to all.

"L. HORACE HOLLY."

I laid the letter down, and, filled with sensations that it is useless to attempt to analyse or describe, opened the second envelope, of which I also print the contents, omitting only certain irrelevant portions, and the name of the writer, as, it will be noted, he requests me to do.

This letter, that was dated from a remote place upon the shores of Cumberland, ran as follows—

"DEAR SIR,—

"As the doctor who attended Mr. Holly in his last illness, I am obliged, in obedience to a promise that I made to him, to become an intermediary in a somewhat strange business, although in truth it is one of which I know very little, however much it may have interested me. Still, I do so only on the strict understanding that no mention is to

"'My mind is made up, so talk no more.'"

be made of my name in connection with the matter, or of the locality in which I practise.

"About ten days ago I was called in to see Mr. Holly at an old house upon the cliff that for many years remained untenanted except by the caretakers, which house was his property, and had been in his family for generations. The housekeeper who summoned me told me that her master had but just returned from abroad, somewhere in Asia, she said, and that he was very ill with his heart—dying, she believed ; both of which suppositions proved to be accurate.

"I found the patient sitting up in bed (to ease his heart), and a strange-looking old man he was. He had dark eyes, small but full of fire and intelligence, a magnificent and snowy-white beard that covered a chest of extraordinary breadth, and hair also white, which encroached upon his forehead and face so much that it met the whiskers upon his cheeks. His arms were remarkable for their length and strength, though one of them seemed to have been much torn by some animal. He told me that a dog had done this, but if so it must have been a dog of unusual power. He was a very ugly man, and yet—forgive the bull—beautiful. I cannot describe what I mean better than by saying that his face was not like the face of any ordinary mortal whom I have met in my limited experience. Were I an artist who wished to portray a wise and benevolent but rather grotesque spirit, I should take that countenance as a model.

"Mr. Holly was somewhat vexed at my being called in, which had been done without his knowledge. Soon we became friendly enough, however, and he expressed gratitude for the relief that I was able to give him, though I could not hope to do more. At different times he talked a good deal of the various countries in which he had travelled, apparently for very many years, upon some strange quest that he never clearly defined to me. Twice also he became light-headed, and spoke, for the most part in languages that I identified as Greek and Arabic ; occasionally in English also, when he appeared to be addressing himself to a being who was the object of his veneration, I might almost say of his worship. What he said then, however, I prefer not to repeat, for I heard it in my professional capacity.

"One day he pointed to a rough box made of some foreign wood (the same that I have now duly despatched to you by train), and, giving me your name and address, said that without fail it was to be forwarded to you

after his death. Also he asked me to do up a manuscript, which, like the box, was to be sent to you.

"He saw me looking at the last sheets, which had been burned away, and said (I repeat his exact words)—

"'Yes, yes, that can't be helped now, it must go as it is. You see, I made up my mind to destroy it after all, and it was already on the fire when the command came—the clear, unmistakable command—and I snatched it off again.'

"What Mr. Holly meant by this 'command' I do not know, for he would speak no more of the matter.

"I pass on to the last scene. One night about eleven o'clock, knowing that my patient's end was near, I went up to see him, proposing to inject some strychnine to keep the heart going a little longer. Before I reached the house I met the caretaker coming to seek me in a great fright, and asked her if her master was dead. She answered 'No'; but he was *gone*—had got out of bed and, just as he was, barefooted, left the house, and was last seen by her grandson among the very Scotch firs where we were talking. The lad, who was terrified out of his wits, for he thought that he beheld a ghost, had told her so.

"The moonlight was very brilliant that night, especially as fresh snow had fallen, which reflected its rays. I was on foot, and began to search among the firs, till presently just outside of them I found the track of naked feet in the snow. Of course I followed, calling to the housekeeper to go and wake her husband, for no one else lives near by. The spoor proved very easy to trace across the clean sheet of snow. It ran up the slope of a hill behind the house.

"Now, on the crest of this hill is an ancient monument of upright monoliths set there by some primeval people, known locally as the Devil's Ring—a sort of miniature Stonehenge, in fact. I had seen it several times, and happened to have been present not long ago at a meeting of an archæological society when its origin and purpose were discussed. I remember that one learned but somewhat eccentric gentleman read a short paper upon a rude, hooded bust and head that are cut within the chamber of a tall, flat-topped cromlech, or dolmen, which stands alone in the centre of the Ring.

"He said that it was a representation of the Egyptian goddess, Isis, and that this place had once been sacred to some form of her worship, or, at any rate, to that of a Nature goddess with like attributes, a suggestion which the other learned gentlemen treated as absurd. They declared that Isis had never travelled into Britain, though, for my part, I do not see why the Phœnicians, or even the Romans, who adopted her cult, more or less, should not have brought it here. But I know nothing of such matters and will not discuss them.

"I remembered, also, that Mr. Holly was acquainted with this place, for he had mentioned it to me on the previous day, asking if the stones were still uninjured, as they used to be when he was young. He added also, and the remark struck me, that yonder was where he would wish to die. When I answered that I feared he would never take so long a walk again, I noted that he smiled a little.

"Well, this conversation gave me a clue, and without troubling more about the footprints I went on as fast as I could to the Ring, half a mile or so away. Presently I reached it, and there—yes, there—standing by the cromlech, bareheaded, and clothed in his night things only, stood Mr. Holly in the snow, the strangest figure, I think, that ever I beheld.

"Indeed, never shall I forget that wild scene. The circle of rough, single stones pointing upwards to the star-strewn sky, intensely lonely and intensely solemn : the tall trilithon towering above them in the centre, its shadow, thrown by the bright moon behind it, lying long and black upon the dazzling sheet of snow, and, standing clear of this shadow so that I could distinguish his every motion, and even the rapt look upon his dying face, the white-draped figure of Mr. Holly. He appeared to be uttering some invocation — in Arabic, I think—for long before I reached him I could catch the tones of his full, sonorous voice, and see his waving, outstretched arms. In his right hand he held the looped sceptre which, by his express wish, I send to you with the drawings. I could see the flash of the jewels strung upon the wires, and, in the great stillness, hear the tinkling of its golden bells.

"Presently, too, I seemed to become aware of another presence, and now you will understand why I desire and must ask that my identity should be suppressed. Naturally enough I do not wish to be mixed up with a superstitious tale which is, on the face of it, impossible and absurd. Yet, under all the circumstances, I think it right to tell you

that I saw, or thought I saw, something gather in the shadow of the central dolmen, or emerge from its rude chamber—I know not which for certain—something bright and glorious which gradually took the form of a woman upon whose forehead burned a starlike fire.

"At any rate, the vision or reflection, or whatever it was, startled me so much that I came to a halt under the lee of one of the monoliths, and found myself unable even to call to the distraught man whom I pursued.

"Whilst I stood thus it became clear to me that Mr. Holly also saw something. At least, he turned towards the Radiance in the shadow, uttered one cry—a wild, glad cry, and stepped forward ; then seemed to fall *through it* on to his face.

"When I reached the spot, the light had vanished, and all I found was Mr. Holly, his arms still outstretched, and the sceptre gripped tightly in his hand, lying quite dead in the shadow of the trilithon."

The rest of the doctor's letter need not be quoted, as it deals only with certain very improbable explanations of the origin of this Figure of light, the details of the removal of the body, and of how he managed to satisfy the coroner that no inquest was necessary.

The box of which he speaks arrived safely. Of the drawings in it I need say nothing, and of the *sistrum* or sceptre only a few words. It was fashioned of crystal to the well-known shape of the *Crux ansata*, or the emblem of Life of the Egyptians ; the rod, the cross, and the loop combined in one. From side to side of this loop ran golden wires, and on these were strung gems of three colours, glittering diamonds, sea-blue sapphires, and blood-red rubies, while to the fourth wire, that at the top, hung four little golden bells.

When I took hold of it first, my arm shook slightly with excitement, and those bells began to sound—a sweet, faint music like to that of chimes heard far away at night in the silence of the sea. I thought, too — but perhaps this was fancy—that a thrill passed from the hallowed and beautiful thing in my body.

On the mystery itself, as it is recorded in the manuscript, I make no comment. Of it and its inner significations every reader must form his or her own judgment. One thing alone is clear to me—on the hypothesis that Mr. Holly tells the truth as to what he and Leo Vincey saw and experienced, which I at least believe—that though sundry interpre-

10

tations of this mystery were advanced by Ayesha and others, none of them are quite satisfactory.

Indeed, like Mr. Holly, I incline to the theory that SHE, if I may still call her by that name, although it is seldom given to her in these pages, put forward some of them, such as the vague Isis-myth, and the wondrous picture-story of the mountain-fire, as mere veils to hide the truth, which it was her purpose to reveal at last in that song she never sang.

THE EDITOR.

CHAPTER I.

THE DOUBLE SIGN.

HARD on twenty years have gone by since that night of Leo's Vision—the most awful years, perhaps, which were ever endured by men— twenty years of search and hardship ending in soul-shaking wonder and amazement.

My death is very near to me, and of this I am glad, for I desire to pursue the quest in other realms, as it has been promised to me that I shall do. I desire to learn the beginning and the end of the spiritual drama of which it has been my strange lot to read some pages upon earth.

I, Ludwig Horace Holly, have been very ill; they carried me, more dead than alive, down those mountains whose lowest slopes I can see from my window, for I write this on the northern frontiers of India. Indeed, any other man had long since perished, but Destiny kept my breath in me, perhaps that a record might remain. I must bide here a month or two till I am strong enough to travel homewards, for I have a fancy to die in the place where I was born. So while I have strength I will put the story down, or at least those parts of it that are most essential, for much can, or at any rate must be omitted. I shrink from attempting too long a book, though my notes and memory would furnish me with sufficient material for volumes.

I will begin with the Vision.

After Leo Vincey and I came back from Africa in 1885, desiring solitude, which indeed we needed sorely to recover from the fearful shock we had experienced, and to give us time and opportunity to think, we went to an old house upon the shores of Cumberland that has belonged to my family for many generations. This house, unless somebody has taken it believing me to be dead, is still my property, and thither I travel to die.

Those whose eyes read the words I write, if any should ever read them, may ask— What shock?

Well, I am Horace Holly, and my companion, my beloved friend, my son in the spirit whom I reared from infancy was— nay, is—Leo Vincey.

We are those men who, following an ancient clue, travelled to the caves of Kôr in Central Africa, and there discovered her whom we sought, the immortal *She-who-must-be-obeyed.* In Leo she found her love, that re-born Kallikrates, the Grecian priest of Isis whom some two thousand years before she had slain in her jealous rage, thus executing on him the judgment of the angry goddess. In her also I found the divinity whom I was doomed to worship from afar, not with the flesh, for that is all lost and gone from me, but, what is sorer still, because its burden is undying, with the will and soul which animate a man throughout the countless æons of his being. The flesh dies, or at least it changes, and its passions pass, but that other passion of the spirit— that longing for oneness—is undying as itself.

What crime have I committed that this sore punishment should be laid upon me? Yet, in truth, is it a punishment? May it not prove to be but that black and terrible Gate which leads to the joyous palace of Rewards? She swore that I should ever be her friend and his and dwell with them eternally, and I believe her.

For how many winters did we wander among the icy hills and deserts! Still, at length, the Messenger came and led us to the Mountain, and on the Mountain we found the Shrine, and in the Shrine the Spirit. May not these things be an allegory prepared for our instruction? I will take comfort. I will hope that it is so. Nay, I am sure that it is so.

It will be remembered that in Kôr we found the immortal woman. There before the flashing rays and vapours of the Pillar of Life she declared her mystic love, and then in our very sight was swept to a doom so horrible that even now, after all which has been and gone, I shiver at its recollection. Yet what were Ayesha's last words? *"Forget me not . . . have pity on my shame. I die not. I shall come again and shall once more be beautiful. I swear it—it is true."*

Well, I cannot set out that history afresh. Moreover, it is written; the man whom I trusted in the matter did not fail me, and

"'At one point she paused, and I looked downwards.'"

the book he made of it seems to be known throughout the world, for I have found it here in English, yes, and read it first translated into Hindostani. To it then I refer the curious.

In that house upon the desolate seashore of Cumberland, we dwelt a year, mourning the lost, seeking an avenue by which it might be found again and discovering none. Here our strength came back to us, and Leo's hair, that had been whitened in the horror of the Caves, grew again from grey to golden. His beauty returned to him also, so that his face was as it had been, only purified and saddened.

Well I remember that night—and the hour of illumination. We were heart-broken, we were in despair. We sought signs and could find none. The dead remained dead to us and no answer came to all our crying.

It was a sullen August evening, and after we had dined we walked upon the shore, listening to the slow surge of the waves and watching the lightning flicker from the bosom of a distant cloud. In silence we walked, till at last Leo groaned—it was more of a sob than a groan—and clasped my arm.

"I can bear it no longer, Horace," he said—for so he called me now—"I am in torment. The desire to see Ayesha once more saps my brain. Without hope I shall go quite mad. And I am strong, I may live another fifty years."

"What then can you do?" I asked.

"I can take a short road to knowledge—or to peace," he answered solemnly. "I can die, and die I will—yes, to-night."

I turned upon him angrily, for his words filled me with fear.

"Leo, you are a coward!" I said. "Cannot you bear your part of pain as—others do?"

"You mean as you do, Horace," he answered with a dreary laugh, "for on you also the curse lies—with less cause. Well, you are stronger than I am, and more tough; perhaps because you have lived longer. No, I cannot bear it. I will die."

"It is a crime," I said, "the greatest insult you can offer to the Power that made you, to cast back its gift of life as a thing outworn, contemptible and despised. A crime, I say, which will bring with it worse punishment than any you can dream; perhaps even the punishment of everlasting separation."

"Does a man stretched in some torture-den commit a crime if he snatches a knife and kills himself, Horace? Perhaps; but surely that sin should find forgiveness—if torn flesh and quivering nerves may plead for mercy. I am such a man, and I will use that knife and take my chance. She is dead, and in death at least I shall be nearer her."

"Why so, Leo? For aught you know, Ayesha may be living."

"No; for then she would have given me some sign. My mind is made up, so talk no more, or, if talk we must, let it be of other things."

Then I pleaded with him, though with little hope, for I saw that what I had feared for long was come to pass. Leo was mad; shock and sorrow had destroyed his reason. Had it not been so, he, in his own way a very religious man, one who held, as I knew, strict opinions on such matters, would never have purposed to commit the wickedness of suicide.

"Leo," I said, "are you so heartless that you would leave me here alone? Do you pay me thus for all my love and care, and wish to drive me to my death? Do so if you will, and my blood be on your head!"

"Your blood! Why your blood, Horace?"

"Because that road is broad, and two can travel it. We have lived long years together and together endured much; I am sure that we shall not be long parted."

Then the tables were turned and he grew afraid for me. But I only answered: "If you die, I tell you that I shall die also. It will certainly kill me."

So Leo gave way. "Well," he exclaimed suddenly, "I promise you it shall not be to-night. Let us give Life another chance."

"Good," I answered; but I went to my bed full of fear. For I was certain that this desire of death, having once taken hold of him, would grow and grow, until at length it became too strong, and then—then I should wither and die who could not live on alone. In my despair I threw out my soul towards that of her who was departed.

"Ayesha!" I cried, "if you have any power, if in any way it is permitted, show that you still live, and save your lover from this sin and me from a broken heart. Have pity on his sorrow and breathe hope into his soul, for without hope Leo cannot live, and without him I shall not live."

Then, worn out, I slept.

I was aroused by the voice of Leo speaking to me in low, excited tones through the darkness.

"Horace," he said, "Horace, my friend, my father, listen!"

In an instant I was wide awake, every nerve and fibre of me, for the tones of his voice told me that something had happened which bore upon our destinies.

"Let me light a candle first," I said.

"Never mind the candle, Horace; I would rather speak in the dark. I went to sleep, and I dreamed the most vivid dream that ever came to me. I seemed to stand under the vault of heaven, it was black, black, not a star shone in it, and a great loneliness possessed me. Then suddenly high up in the vault, miles and miles away, I saw a little light and thought that a planet had appeared to keep me company. The light began to descend slowly, like a floating flake of fire. Down it sank, and down and down, till it was but just above me, and I perceived that it was shaped like a tongue or fan of flame. At the height of my head from the ground it stopped and stood steady, and by its ghostly radiance I saw that beneath was the shape of a woman, and that the flame burned upon her forehead. The radiance gathered strength, and now I saw the woman.

"Horace, it was Ayesha herself, her eyes, her lovely face, her cloudy hair; and she looked at me sadly, reproachfully, I thought, as one might who says : 'Why did you doubt?'

"I tried to speak to her, but my lips were dumb. I tried to advance and to embrace her—my arms would not move. There was a barrier between us. She lifted her hand and beckoned as though bidding me to follow her.

"Then she glided away, and, Horace, my spirit seemed to loose itself from the body and to be given the power to follow. We passed swiftly eastward, over lands and seas, and—I knew the road. At one point she paused, and I looked downwards. Beneath, shining in the moonlight, appeared the ruined palaces of Kôr, and there, not far away, was the gulf we trod together.

"Onward above the marshes, and now we stood upon the Ethiopian's Head, and gathered round, watching us earnestly, were the faces of the Arabs, our companions who drowned in the sea beneath. Job was among them also, and he smiled at me sadly and shook his head, as though he wished to accompany us and could not.

"Across the sea again, across the sandy deserts, across more sea, and the shores of India lay beneath us. Then northward, ever northward, above the plains, till we reached a place of mountains capped with eternal snow. We passed them and stayed for an instant above a building set upon the brow of a plateau. It was a monastery, for old monks droned prayers upon its terrace. I shall know it again, for it is built in the shape of a half-moon, and in front of it sits the gigantic, ruined statue of a god who gazes everlastingly across the desert. I knew, how I cannot say, that now we were far past the furthest borders of Thibet, and that in front of us lay untrodden lands. More mountains stretched beyond that desert—a sea of snowy peaks, hundreds and hundreds of them.

"Near to the monastery, jutting out into the plain like some rocky headland, rose a solitary hill, higher than all behind. We stood upon its snowy crest and waited, till presently, above the mountains and the desert at our feet shot a sudden beam of light, that beat upon us like some signal flashed across the sea. On we went, floating down the beam—on over the desert and the mountains, across a great flat land beyond, in which were many villages and a city on a mound, till we lit upon a towering peak. Then I saw that this peak was loop-shaped like the symbol of Life of the Egyptians— the *crux ansata*—and supported by a lava stem hundreds of feet in height. Also I saw that the fire which shone through it rose from the crater of a volcano beyond. Upon the very crest of this loop we rested awhile, till the Shadow of Ayesha pointed downward with its hand, smiled and vanished. Then I awoke.

"Horace, I tell you that the sign has come to us."

His voice died away in the darkness, but I sat still, brooding over what I had heard. Leo groped his way to me and, seizing my arm, shook it.

"Are you asleep?" he asked angrily. "Speak, man, speak!"

"No," I answered, "never was I more awake. Give me time."

Then I rose, and going to the open window, drew up the blind and stood there staring at the sky, which grew pearl-hued with the first faint tinge of dawn. Leo came also and leant upon the window-sill, and I could feel that his body was trembling as though with cold. Clearly he was much moved.

"You talk of a sign," I said to him, "but in your sign I see nothing but a wild dream."

"It was no dream," he broke in fiercely; "it was a vision."

"A vision, then, if you will; but there are visions true and false, and how can we know that this is true? Listen, Leo. What is there in all that wonderful tale which could not have been fashioned in your own brain, distraught as it is almost to madness with your sorrow and your longings? You dreamed that you were alone in the vast universe. Well, is not every living creature thus alone? You dreamed that the shadowy shape of Ayesha came to you. Has it ever left your side? You dreamed that she led you over sea and land, past places haunted by your memory, above the mysterious mountains of the Unknown to an undiscovered peak. Does she not thus lead you through life to that peak which lies beyond the Gates of Death? You dreamed——"

"Oh! no more of it!" he exclaimed. "What I saw, I saw, and that I shall follow. Think as you will, Horace, and do what you will. To-morrow I start for India, with you if you choose to come; if not, without you."

"You speak roughly, Leo," I said. "You forget that *I* have had no sign, and that the nightmare of a man so near to insanity that but a few hours ago he was determined upon suicide, will be a poor staff to lean on when we are perishing in the snows of Central Asia. A mixed vision, this of yours, Leo, with its mountain peak shaped like a *crux ansata* and the rest. Do you suggest that Ayesha is reincarnated in Central Asia—as a female Grand Lama or something of that sort?"

"I never thought of it, but why not?" asked Leo quietly. "Do you remember a certain scene in the Caves of Kôr yonder, when the living looked upon the dead, and dead and living were the same? And do you remember what Ayesha swore, that she would come again—yes, to this world; and how could that be except by re-birth, or, what is the same thing, by the transmigration of the spirit?"

I did not answer this argument. I was struggling with myself.

"No sign has come to me," I said, "and yet I have had a part in the play—humble enough, I admit—and I believe that I have still a part."

"No," he said, "no sign has come to you. I wish that it had. Oh! how I wish you could be convinced as I am, Horace!"

Then we were silent for a long while, silent, with our eyes fixed upon the sky.

*   *   *   *   *

It was a stormy dawn. Clouds in fantastic masses hung upon the ocean. One of them was like a great mountain, and we watched it idly. It changed its shape, the crest of it grew hollow like a crater. From this crater sprang a projecting cloud, a rough

pillar with a knob or lump resting on its top. Suddenly the rays of the risen sun struck upon this mountain and the column, and they turned white like snow. Then as though melted by those fiery arrows, the centre of the excrescence above the pillar thinned out and vanished, leaving an enormous loop of inky cloud.

"Look," said Leo in a low, frightened voice, "that is the shape of the mountain which I saw in my vision. There upon it is the black loop, and there through it shines the fire. *It would seem that the sign is for both of us, Horace.*"

I looked and looked again till presently the vast loop vanished into the blue of heaven. Then I turned and said—

"I will come with you to Central Asia, Leo."

CHAPTER II.

THE LAMASERY.

SIXTEEN years had passed since that night vigil in the old Cumberland house, and, behold! we two, Leo and I, were still travelling, still searching for that mountain peak shaped like the Symbol of Life which never, never could be found.

Our adventures would fill volumes, but of what use is it to record them? Many of a similar nature are already written of in books; those that we endured were more prolonged, that is all. Five years we spent in Thibet, for the most part as guests of various monasteries, where we studied the law and traditions of the Lamas. Here we were once sentenced to death in punishment for having visited a forbidden city, but escaped through the kindness of a Chinese official.

Leaving Thibet, we wandered east and west and north, thousands and thousands of miles, sojourning amongst many tribes in Chinese territory and elsewhere, learning many tongues, enduring much hardship. We would hear a legend of a place, say nine hundred miles away, and spend two years in reaching it, to find, when we came there, nothing.

And so the time went on. Yet never once did we think of giving up the quest and returning, since, before we started, we had sworn an oath that we would achieve or die. Indeed, we ought to have died a score of times, yet always were preserved, most mysteriously preserved.

Now we were in a country where, so far as I could learn, no European had ever set a foot. In a part of the vast land called

"'See there!' he said, pointing to something dim and enormous,"

Turkestan there is a great lake named Balh-kash, of which we visited the shores. Two hundred miles or so to the westward is a range of mighty mountains marked on the maps as Arkarty-Tau, on which we spent a year, and five hundred or so to the eastward are other mountains called Cherga, whither we journeyed at last, having explored the triple ranges of the Tau.

Here it was that at last our true adventures began. On one of the spurs of these awful Cherga mountains—it is unmarked on any map—we well-nigh perished of starvation. The winter was coming on and we could find no game. The last traveller we had met, hundreds of miles south, told us that on that range was a monastery inhabited by Lamas of surpassing holiness. He said that they dwelt in this wild land, over which no Power claimed dominion and where no tribes lived, to acquire "merit," with no other company than that of their own pious contemplations. We did not believe in its existence, still we were searching for that monastery, driven onward by the blind fatalism which was our only guide through all these endless wanderings. As we were starving and could find no "argals"—that is, fuel with which to make a fire—we walked all night by the light of the moon, driving between us a single yak—for now we had no attendant, the last having died a year before.

He was a noble beast, that yak, and had the best constitution of any animal I ever knew, though now, like his masters, he was near his end. Not that he was over-laden, for a few rifle cartridges, about a hundred and fifty, the remnant of a store which we had fortunately been able to buy from a caravan two years before, some money in gold and silver, a little tea, and a bundle of skin rugs and sheepskin garments were his burden. On, on we trudged across a plateau of snow, having the great mountains on our right, till at length the yak gave a sigh and stopped. So we stopped also, because we must, and, wrapping ourselves in the skin rugs, sat down in the snow to wait for daylight.

"We shall have to kill him and eat his flesh raw," I said, patting the poor yak that lay patiently at our side.

"Perhaps we may find game in the morning," answered Leo, still hopeful.

"And perhaps we may not, in which case we must die."

"Very good," he replied, "then let us die. It is the last resource of failure. We shall have done our best."

"Certainly, Leo, we shall have done our best, if sixteen years of tramping over mountains and through eternal snows in pursuit of a dream of the night can be called best."

"You know what I believe," he answered stubbornly, and there was silence between us, for here arguments did not avail. Also even then I could not think that all our toils and sufferings would be in vain.

The dawn came, and by its light we looked at one another anxiously, each of us desiring to see what strength was left to his companion. Wild creatures we should have seemed to the eyes of any civilised person. Leo was now over forty years of age, and certainly his maturity had fulfilled the promise of his youth, for a more magnificent man I never knew. Very tall, although he seemed spare to the eye, his girth matched his height, and those many years of desert life had turned his muscles to steel. His hair had grown long, like my own, for it was a protection from sun and cold, and hung upon his neck, a curling, golden mane, as his great beard hung upon his breast, spreading outwards almost to the massive shoulders. The face, too—what could be seen of it—was beautiful, though burnt brown with weather ; refined and full of thought, sombre almost, and in it, clear as crystal, steady as stars, shone his large grey eyes.

And I—I was what I have always been—ugly and hirsute, iron-grey now also, but, in spite of my sixty odd years, still wonderfully strong, for my strength seemed to increase with time, and my health was perfect. In fact, during all this period of rough travels, although now and again we had met with accidents which laid us up for awhile, neither of us had known a day of sickness. Hardship seemed to have turned our constitutions to iron and made them impervious to every human ailment. Or was this because we alone amongst living men had once inhaled the breath of the Essence of Life ?

Our fears relieved—for, notwithstanding our foodless night, as yet neither of us showed any signs of exhaustion—we turned to contemplate the landscape. At our feet, beyond a little belt of fertile soil, began a great desert of the sort with which we were familiar — sandy, salt - encrusted, treeless, waterless, and here and there streaked with the first snows of winter. Beyond it, eighty or a hundred miles away—in that lucent atmosphere it was impossible to say how far exactly—rose more mountains, a veritable sea of them, of which the white peaks soared upwards by scores.

As the golden rays of the rising sun touched their snows to splendour, I saw Leo's eyes become troubled. Swiftly he turned and looked along the edge of the desert.

"See there!" he said, pointing to something dim and enormous. Presently the light reached it also. It was a mighty mountain, not more than ten miles away, that stood out by itself among the sands. Then he turned once more, and with his back to the desert stared at the slope of the hills, along the base of which we had been travelling. As yet they were in gloom, for the sun was behind them, but presently light began to flow over their crests like a flood. Down it crept, lower, and yet lower, till it reached a little plateau not three hundred yards above us. There, on the edge of the plateau, looking out solemnly across the waste, sat a great ruined idol, a colossal Buddha, while to the rear of the idol, built of yellow stone, appeared the low, crescent-shaped mass of a monastery.

"At last!" cried Leo, "oh, Heaven! at last!" and, flinging himself down, he buried his face in the snow as though to hide it there, lest I should read something written on it which he did not desire that even I should see.

I let him lie a space, understanding what was passing in his heart, and indeed in mine also. Then going to the yak, that, poor brute, had no share in these joyous emotions, but only lowed and looked round with hungry eyes, I piled the sheepskin rugs on to its back. This done, I laid my hand on Leo's shoulder, saying, in the most matter-of-fact voice I could command—

"Come. If that place is not deserted, we may find food and shelter there, and it is beginning to storm again."

He rose without a word, brushed the snow from his beard and garments, and came to help me to lift the yak to its feet, for the worn-out beast was too stiff and weak to rise of itself. Glancing at him covertly, I saw on Leo's face a very strange and happy look; a great peace appeared to possess him.

We plunged upwards through the snow slope, dragging the yak with us, to the terrace whereon the monastery was built. Nobody seemed to be about there, nor could I discern any footprints. Was the place but a ruin? We had found many such; indeed, this ancient land is full of buildings that had once served as the homes of men, learned and pious enough after their own fashion, who lived and died hundreds, or even thousands, of years ago, long before our Western civilisation came into being.

My heart, also my stomach, which was starving, sank at the thought; but while I gazed doubtfully, a little coil of blue smoke sprang from a chimney, and never, I think, did I see a more joyful sight. In the centre of the edifice was a large building, evidently the temple, but nearer to us I saw a small door, almost above which the smoke appeared. To this door I went and knocked, calling aloud—

"Open! open, holy Lamas! Strangers seek your charity." After a while there was a sound of shuffling feet, and the door creaked upon its hinges, revealing an old, old man, clad in tattered, yellow garments.

"Who is it? Who is it?" he exclaimed, blinking at me through a pair of horn spectacles. "Who comes to disturb our solitude, the solitude of the holy Lamas of the Mountains?"

"Travellers, Sacred One, who have had enough of solitude," I answered in his own dialect, with which I was well acquainted, "Travellers who are starving and who ask your charity, which," I added, "by the Rule you cannot refuse."

He stared at us through his horn spectacles, and, able to make nothing of our faces, let his glance fall to our garments, which were as ragged as his own and of much the same pattern. Indeed, they were those of Thibetan monks, including a kind of quilted petticoat and an outer vestment not unlike an Eastern *burnous*. We had adopted them because we had no others. Also they protected us from the rigours of the climate and from remark, had there been any to remark upon them.

"Are you Lamas?" he asked doubtfully, "and if so, of what monastery?"

"Lamas sure enough," I answered, "who belong to a monastery called the World, where, alas! one grows hungry."

The reply seemed to please him, for he chuckled a little, then shook his head, saying—

"It is against our custom to admit strangers unless they be of our own faith, which I am sure you are not."

"And much more is it against your Rule, holy Khubilghan," for so these abbots are entitled, "to suffer strangers to starve"; and I quoted a well-known passage from the sayings of Buddha which fitted the point precisely.

"I perceive that you are instructed in the Books," he exclaimed, with wonder on his yellow, wrinkled face, "and to such we cannot refuse shelter. Come in, brethren of the monastery called the World. But stay, there is the yak, who also has claims upon our charity," and, turning, he struck upon a gong or bell which hung within the door.

At the sound another man appeared, more wrinkled and to all appearance older than the first, who stared at us open-mouthed.

"Brother," said the abbot, "shut that great mouth of yours, lest an evil spirit should fly down it; take this poor yak and give it fodder with the other cattle."

So we unstrapped our belongings from the back of the beast, and the old fellow, whose grandiloquent title was "Master of the Herds," led it away.

When it had gone, not too willingly—for our faithful friend disliked parting from us and distrusted this new guide—the abbot, who was named Kou-en, led us into the living-room, or rather the kitchen, of the monastery, for it served both purposes. Here we found the rest of the monks, about twelve in all, gathered round the fire of which we had seen the smoke, and engaged, one of them in preparing the morning meal, and the rest in warming themselves.

They were all old men; the youngest could not have been less than sixty-five. To these we were solemnly introduced as "Brethren of the Monastery called the World, where folk grow hungry," for the abbot Kou-en could not make up his mind to part from this little joke.

They stared at us, they rubbed their thin hands, they bowed and wished us well, and evidently were delighted at our arrival. This was not strange, however, seeing that ours were the first new faces which they had seen for four long years.

Nor did they stop at words, for while they made water hot for us to wash in, two of them went to prepare a room, and others drew off our rough hide boots and thick outer garments and brought us slippers for our feet. Then they led us to the guest-chamber, which they informed us was a "propitious place," for once it had been slept in by a noted saint. Here a fire was lit, and, wonder of wonders! clean garments, including linen, all of them ancient and faded, but of good quality, were brought for us to put on.

So we washed—yes, actually washed all over—and having arrayed ourselves in the robes, which were somewhat small for Leo, struck the bell that hung in the room, and were conducted by a monk who answered it, back to the kitchen, where the meal was now served. It consisted of a kind of porridge, to which was added new milk brought in by the "Master of the Herds," dried fish from a lake, and buttered tea, the last two luxuries produced in our special honour. Never had food tasted more delicious to us, and, I may add, never did we eat more. Indeed, at last I was obliged to request Leo to stop, for I saw the monks staring at him and heard the old abbot chuckling to himself—

"Oho! The Monastery called the World, where folk grow *hungry*," to which another monk, who was called "The Master of the Provisions," replied uneasily that if we went on like this, their store of food would scarcely last the winter. So we finished at length, feeling—as some book of maxims which I can remember in my youth said all polite people should do—that we could eat more, and much impressed our hosts by chanting a long Buddhist grace.

"Their feet are in the Path! Their feet are in the Path!" they said, astonished.

"Yes," replied Leo, "they have been in it for sixteen years of our present incarnation. But we are only beginners, for you, holy Ones, know how star-high, how ocean-wide, and how desert-long is that path. Indeed, it is to be instructed as to the right way of walking therein that we have been miraculously directed by a dream to seek you out, as the most pious, the most saintly, and the most learned of all the Lamas in these parts."

"Yes, certainly we are that," answered the abbot Kou-en, "seeing that there is no other monastery within five months' journey," and again he chuckled, "though, alas!" he added with a pathetic little sigh, "our numbers grow few."

After this we asked leave to retire to our chamber in order to rest, and there, upon very good imitations of beds, we slept solidly for four-and-twenty hours, rising at last perfectly refreshed and well.

Such was our introduction to the Monastery of the Mountains—for it had no other name —where we were destined to spend the next six months of our lives. Within a few days— for they were not long in giving us their complete confidence—those good-hearted and simple old monks told us all their history.

It seemed that of old time there was a Lamasery here, in which dwelt several hundred brethren. This, indeed, was ob-

"'Who is it? Who is it?' he exclaimed, blinking at me through a pair of horn spectacles."

viously true, for the place was enormous, although for the most part ruined, and, as the weather-worn statue of Buddha showed, very ancient. The story ran, according to the old abbot, that two centuries or so before, the monks had been killed out by some fierce tribe who lived beyond the desert and across the distant mountains, which tribe were heretics and worshippers of fire. Only a few of them escaped to bring the sad news to other communities, and for five generations no attempt was made to reoccupy the place.

At length it was revealed to him, our friend Kou-en, when a young man, that he was a reincarnation of one of the old monks of this monastery, who also was named Kou-en, and that it was his duty during his present life to return thither, as by so doing he would win much merit and receive many wonderful revelations. So he gathered a band of zealots and, with the blessing and consent of his superiors, they started out and, after many hardships and losses, found and took possession of the place, repairing it sufficiently for their needs.

This happened about fifty years before, and here they had dwelt ever since, only communicating occasionally with the outside world. At first their numbers were recruited from time to time by new brethren, but at length these ceased to come, with the result that the community was dying out.

"And what then?" I asked.

"And then," the abbot answered, "nothing. We have acquired much merit; we have been blest with many revelations, and, after the repose we have earned in Devachan, our lots in future existences will be easier. What more can we ask or desire, removed as we are from all the temptations of the world?"

For the rest, in the intervals of their endless prayers, and still more endless contemplations, they were husbandmen, cultivating the soil, which was fertile at the foot of the mountain, and tending their herd of yaks. Thus they wore away their blameless lives until at last they died of old age, and, as they believed—and who shall say that they were wrong?—the eternal round repeated itself elsewhere.

* * * * *

Immediately after—indeed, on the very day of our arrival at the monastery, the winter began in earnest, with bitter cold and snow-storms so heavy and frequent that all the desert was covered deep. Very soon it became obvious to us that here we must stay until the spring, since to attempt to move in

any direction would be to perish. With some misgivings we explained this to the abbot Kou-en, offering to remove to one of the empty rooms in the ruined part of the building, supporting ourselves with fish that we could catch by cutting a hole in the ice of the lake above the monastery, and, if we were able to find any, on game, which we might trap or shoot in the scrublike forest of stunted pines and junipers that grew around its border. But he would listen to no such thing. We had been sent to be their guests, he said, and their guests we should remain for so long as might be convenient to us. Would we lay upon them the burden of the sin of inhospitality? Besides, he remarked with his chuckle—

"We who dwell alone like to hear about that other great monastery called the World, where the monks are not so favoured as we who are set in this blessed situation, and where folk even go hungry in body, and," he added, "in soul."

Indeed, as we soon found out, the dear old man's object was to keep our feet in the Path until we reached the goal of Truth, or, in other words, became excellent Lamas like himself and his flock.

So we walked in the Path, as we had done in many another Lamasery, and assisted at the long prayers in the ruined temple, and studied the *Kandjur*, or "Translation of the Words" of Buddha, which is their Bible, and a very long one, and generally showed that our "minds were open." Also we expounded to them the doctrines of our own faith, and greatly delighted were they to find so many points of similarity between it and theirs. Indeed, I am not certain but that if we could have stopped there long enough, say ten years, we might have persuaded some of them to accept a new revelation of which we were the prophets. Further, in spare hours we told them many tales of "The Monastery called the World," and it was really delightful, and in a sense piteous, to see the joy with which they listened to these stories of wondrous countries and new races of men; they who knew only of Russia and China and some semi-savage tribes, inhabitants of the mountains and the deserts.

"It is right for us to learn all this," they declared, "for, who knows, perhaps in future incarnations we may become inhabitants of these places."

But though the time passed thus in comfort and, indeed, compared to many of our experiences, in luxury, oh! our hearts were hungry, for in them burned the consuming fire of our quest. We felt that we were on the threshold—yes, we knew it, we knew it, and yet our wretched physical limitations made it impossible for us to advance by a single step. On the desert beneath fell the snow, moreover great winds arose suddenly that drove those snows like dust, piling them in heaps as high as trees, beneath which any unfortunate traveller would be buried. Here we must wait, there was nothing else to be done.

One alleviation we found, and only one. In a ruined room of the monastery was a library of many volumes, placed there, doubtless, by the monks who were massacred in times bygone. These had been more or less cared for and rearranged by their successors, who gave us liberty to examine them as often as we pleased. Truly it was a strange collection, and I should imagine of priceless value, for among them were to be found Buddhistic, Sivaistic and Shamanistic writings that we had never before seen or heard of, together with the lives of a multitude of Bodhisatvas, or distinguished saints, written in various tongues, some of which we did not understand.

What proved more interesting to us, however, was a diary in many tomes that for generations had been kept by the Khubilghans or abbots of the old Lamasery, in which every event of importance was recorded in great detail. Turning over the pages of one of the last volumes of this diary, written apparently about two hundred and fifty years earlier, and shortly before the destruction of the monastery, we came upon an entry of which the following—for I can only quote from memory—is the substance :—

"In the summer of this year, after a very great sandstorm, a brother (the name was given, but I forget it) found in the desert a man of the people who dwell beyond the Far Mountains, of whom rumours have reached this Lamasery from time to time. He was living, but beside him were the bodies of two of his companions, who had been overwhelmed by sand and thirst. He was very fierce-looking. He refused to say how he came into the desert, telling us only that he had followed the road known to the ancients before communication between his people and the outer world ceased. We gathered, however, that his brethren with whom he fled had committed some crime for which they had been condemned to die, and that he had accompanied them in their flight. He told us that there was a fine country beyond the mountains, fertile, but plagued with droughts and earthquakes, which latter, indeed, we often feel here.

"The people of that country were, he said, warlike and very numerous, but followed agriculture. They had always lived there, though ruled by monarchs who were descendants of the Greek king called Alexander, who conquered much country to the southwest of us. This may be true, as our records tell us that about two thousand years ago an army sent by that invader penetrated to these parts, though of his being with them nothing is said.

"The stranger-man told us also that his people worship a priestess called Hes or the Hesea, who is said to rule from generation to generation. She lives in a great mountain, apart, and is feared and adored by all, but is not the queen of the country, in the government of which she seldom interferes. To her, however, sacrifices are offered, and he who incurs her vengeance dies, so that even the monarchs of that land are afraid of her. Still their subjects often fight, for they hate each other.

"We answered that he lied when he said that this woman was immortal—for that was what we supposed he meant—since nothing is immortal; also we laughed at his tale of her power. This made the man very angry. Indeed, he declared that our Buddha was not so strong as this priestess, and that she would show it by being avenged upon us.

"After this we gave him food and turned him out of the Lamasery, and he went, saying that when he returned we should learn who spoke the truth. We do not know what became of him, and he refused to reveal to us the road to his country, which lies beyond the desert and the Far Mountains. We think that perhaps he was an evil spirit sent to frighten us, in which he did not succeed."

Such is a *précis* of this strange entry, the discovery of which, vague as it was, thrilled us with hope and excitement. Nothing more appeared about the man or his country, but within a little over a year from that date the diary of the abbot came to a sudden end without any indication that unusual events had occurred or were expected.

Indeed, the last item written in the parchment book mentioned the preparation of certain new lands to be used for the sowing of grain in future seasons, which suggested that the brethren neither feared nor expected disturbance. We wondered whether the man from beyond the mountains was as good as his word and had brought down the vengeance of that priestess called the Hesea upon the community which sheltered him. Also we wondered—ah! how we wondered!—who and what this Hesea might be.

On the day following this discovery we prayed the abbot, Kou-en, to accompany us to the library, and having read him the passage, asked if he knew anything of the matter. He swayed his wise old head, which always reminded me of that of a tortoise, and answered—

"A little. Very little, and that mostly about the army of the Greek king who is mentioned in the writing."

We inquired what he could possibly know of this matter, whereon Kou-en replied calmly—

"In those days when the faith of the Holy One was still young, I dwelt as a humble brother in this very monastery, which was one of the first built, and I saw the army pass, that is all. That," he added meditatively, "was in my fiftieth incarnation of this present Round—no, I am thinking of another army—in my seventy-third." *

Here Leo began a great laugh, but I managed to kick him beneath the table, and he turned it into a sneeze. This was fortunate, as such ribald merriment would have hurt the old man's feelings terribly. After all, also, as Leo himself had once said, surely we were not the people to mock at the theory of reincarnation, which, by the way, is the first article of faith among nearly one quarter of the human race, and this not the most foolish quarter.

"How can that be—I ask for instruction, learned One—seeing that memory perishes with death?"

"Ah!" he answered, "Brother Holly, it may seem to do so, but oftentimes it comes back again, especially to those who are far advanced upon the Path. For instance, until you read this passage I had forgotten all about that army, but now I see it passing, passing, and myself with other monks standing by the statue of the big Buddha in front yonder, and watching it go by. It was not a very large army, for most of the soldiers had died, or been killed, and it was being pursued by the wild people who lived south of us in those days, so that it was in a great hurry to put the desert between it and them. The general of the army was a swarthy man

* As students of their lives and literature will be aware, it is common for Buddhist priests to state positively that they remember events which occurred during their previous incarnations.—ED.

—I wish that I could remember his name, but I cannot.

"Well," he went on, "that general came up to the Lamasery and demanded a sleeping-place for his wife and children, also provisions and medicines, and guides across the desert. The abbot of that day told him it was against our law to admit a woman under our roof, to which he answered that if we did not, we should have no roof left, for he would burn the place and kill every one of us with the sword. Now, as you know, to be killed by violence means that we must pass sundry incarnations in the forms of animals, a horrible thing, so we chose the lesser evil and gave way, and afterwards obtained absolution for our sins from the Great Lama. Myself I did not see this queen, but I saw the priestess of their worship—alas! alas!" and Kou-en beat his breast.

"Why alas?" I asked, as unconcernedly as I could, for this story interested me strangely.

"Why? Oh! because I may have forgotten the army, but I have never forgotten that priestess, and she has been a great hindrance to me through many ages, delaying me upon my journey to the Other Side, to the Shore of Salvation. I, as a humble Lama, was engaged in preparing her apartment when she entered and threw aside her veil; yes, and perceiving a young man, spoke to me, asking many questions, and even if I was not glad to look again upon a woman."

"What—what was she like?" said Leo anxiously.

"What was she like? Oh! she was all loveliness in one shape; she was like the dawn upon the snows; she was like the evening star above the mountains; she was like the first flower of the spring. Brother, ask me not what she was like—nay, I will say no more. Oh! my sin, my sin! I am slipping backward, and you draw my black shame out into the light of day. Nay, I will confess it, that you may know how vile a thing I am—I whom perhaps you have thought holy — like yourselves. That woman, if woman she were, lit a fire in my heart which will not burn out; oh! and more, more," and Kou-en rocked himself to and fro upon his stool, while tears of contrition trickled from beneath his horn spectacles, " *she made me worship her!* For first she asked me of my faith, and listened eagerly as I expounded it, hoping that the light would come into her heart; then, after I had finished she said—

"'So your Path is Renunciation and your

"Such was our introduction to the Monastery."

Nirvana a most excellent Nothingness which some would think it scarce worth while to strive so hard to reach. Now I will show you a more joyous way, and a goddess more worthy of your worship.'

"'What way, and what goddess?' I asked of her.

"'The way of Love and Life,' she answered, 'that makes all the world to be, that made *you*, O seeker of Nirvana, and the goddess called Nature.'

"Again I asked: 'Where is that goddess?' and, behold! she drew herself up, looking most royal, and, touching her ivory breast, she said: 'I am she. Now kneel you down and do me homage.'

"My brethren, I knelt, yes, I kissed her foot, and then I fled away ashamed and broken-hearted; and as I went she laughed, and cried: 'Remember me when you reach Devachan, O servant of the Buddha-saint, for though I change, I do not die, and even there I shall be with you who once have given me worship.'

"And it is so, my brethren, it is so ; for though I obtained absolution for my sin, and have suffered much for it through this, my next incarnation, yet I cannot be rid of her, and for me the Utter Peace is far, far away," and Kou-en placed his withered hands before his face and sobbed outright.

A ridiculous sight, truly, to see a holy Khubilghan, well on the wrong side of eighty, weeping like a child over a dream of a beautiful woman, which he imagined he had once dreamt in his last life more than two thousand years ago. So the reader will say. But I, Holly, for reasons of my own, felt deep sympathy with that poor old man, and Leo was also sympathetic. We patted him on the back ; we assured him that he was the victim of some evil hallucination, which could never be brought up against him in this or any future existence, since, if sin there were, it must have been forgiven long ago, and so forth. When his calm was somewhat restored, we tried also to extract further information from him, but with poor results so far as the priestess was concerned.

He said that he did not know to what religion she belonged, and did not care, but thought that it must be an evil one. She went away the next morning with the army, and he never saw or heard of her any more, though it came into his mind that he was obliged to be locked in his cell for eight days to prevent himself from following her. Yes, he had heard one thing, for the abbot of that day had told the brethren. This priestess was the real general of the army, not the king or the queen, the latter of whom hated her. It was by her will that they pushed on northwards across the desert to some country beyond the mountains, where she desired to establish herself and her worship.

We asked if there really was any country beyond the mountains, and Kou-en answered wearily that he believed so. Either in this or in a previous life he had heard that people lived there who worshipped fire. Certainly, also, it was true that about thirty years ago a brother, who had climbed the great peak yonder to spend some days in solitary meditation, returned and reported that he had seen a marvellous thing—namely, a shaft of fire burning in the heavens beyond those same mountains, though whether this were a vision, or what, he could not say. He recalled, however, that about that time they had felt a great earthquake.

Then the memory of that fancied transgression again began to afflict Kou-en's innocent old heart, and he crept away lamenting and was seen no more for a week. Nor would he ever speak again to us of this matter.

But we spoke of it much with hope and wonder, and made up our minds that we would at once ascend this mountain.

AYESHA

THE RETURN OF "SHE."

By H. RIDER HAGGARD.

SYNOPSIS OF FOREGOING CHAPTERS.—The return of "She-Who-Must-Be-Obeyed" is recorded by Ludwig Horace Holly, the friend of that Leo Vincey whom Ayesha the beautiful loved in the awful tombs of Kôr. When the record begins, the two men are living in an old house remote upon the seashore of Cumberland, where they have been slowly recovering from the horror of the passing of Ayesha in the flames—a doom that seemed one of complete extinction, yet was charged with the strange last words: "I die not. I shall come again and shall once more be beautiful. I swear it—it is true." On a sullen August night, Leo is thrilled by a vision of Ayesha in all her former loveliness. She beckons him, and in a vision his spirit follows her into a realm of snowy peaks far beyond the furthest borders of Thibet. A sign in the clouds at dawn is repeated from this vision to both Leo and Holly, and together they start for Central Asia. Sixteen years of toil, struggle, and strange adventure pass, and they are still searching for "a mountain peak shaped like the Symbol of Life." After many wanderings they find themselves in a country where no European has ever set foot, on one of the spurs of the vast Cherga mountains, far eastward from Turkestan. Sheltered awhile in a Buddhist monastery, they hear of the recent visit of a stranger who has told the Lamas that his countryfolk, "dwelling beyond the Far Mountains," worship a priestess called Hes, or the Hesea, and upon persuasion the abbot of the monastery tells them that in a former incarnation he himself has seen the great priestess, who was "all loveliness."

CHAPTER III.

THE BEACON LIGHT.

A WEEK later came our opportunity of making this ascent of the mountain, for now in midwinter it ceased storming, and hard frost set in, which made it possible to walk upon the surface of the snow. Learning from the monks that at this season *ovis poli*, and other kinds of big-horned sheep and game, descended from the hills to take refuge in certain valleys, where they scraped away the snow to find food, we announced that we were going out to hunt. The excuse we gave was that we were suffering from confinement and needed exercise, having, by the teaching of our religion, no scruples about killing game.

Our hosts replied that the adventure was dangerous, as the weather might change at any moment. They told us, however, that on the slopes of this very mountain, which we desired to climb, there was a large natural cave where, if need be, we could take shelter, and to this cave one of them, somewhat younger and more active than the rest, offered to guide us. So, having manufactured a rough tent from skins, and laden our old yak, now in the best of condition,

with food and garments, on one still morning we started as soon as it was light. Under the guidance of the monk, who, notwithstanding his years, walked very well, we reached the northern slope of the peak before midday. Here, as he had said, we found a great cave, of which the opening was protected by an overhanging ledge of rock. Evidently this cave was a favourite place of shelter for game at certain seasons of the year, since in it were heaped vast accumulations of their droppings, which removed any fear of a lack of fuel.

The rest of that short day we spent in setting up our tent in the cave, in front of which we lit a large fire, and in a survey of the slopes of the mountain, for we told the monk that we were searching for the tracks of wild sheep. Indeed, as it happened, on our way back to the cave we came across a small herd of ewes feeding upon the mosses in a sheltered spot where in summer a streamlet ran. Of these we were so fortunate as to kill two, for no sportsman had ever come here, and they were tame enough, poor things. As meat would keep for ever in that temperature, we had now sufficient food to last us for a fortnight, and dragging the animals down the snow-slopes to the cave, we skinned them by the dying light.

That evening we supped upon fresh mutton, a great luxury, which the monk enjoyed as much as we did, since, whatever might be his views as to taking life, he liked mutton. Then we turned into the tent and huddled ourselves together for warmth, as the temperature must have been some degrees below zero. The old monk rested well enough, but neither Leo nor I slept overmuch, for wonder as to what we might see from the top of that mountain banished sleep.

Next morning at the dawn, the weather being still favourable, our companion returned to the monastery, whither we said we would follow him in a day or two.

Now at last we were alone, and without wasting an instant began our ascent of the peak. It was many thousand feet high, and in certain places steep enough, but the deep, frozen snow made climbing easy, so that by midday we reached the top. Hence the view was magnificent. Beneath us stretched the desert, and beyond it a broad belt of fantastically shaped, snow-clad mountains, hundreds and hundreds of them—in front, to the right, to the left, as far as the eye could reach.

"They are just as I saw them in my dream so many years ago," muttered Leo : "the same, the very same."

"And where was the fiery light ? " I asked.

"Yonder, I think," and he pointed north by east.

"Well, it is not there now," I answered, "and this place is cold."

So, since it was dangerous to linger, lest the darkness should overtake us on our return journey, we descended the peak again, reaching the cave about sunset. The next four days we spent in the same way. Every morning we crawled up those wearisome banks of snow, and every afternoon we slid and tobogganed down them again, till I grew heartily tired of the exercise.

On the fourth night, instead of coming to sleep in the tent, Leo sat himself down at the entrance to the cave. I asked him why he did this, but he answered impatiently, because he wished it, so I left him alone. I could see, indeed, that he was in a strange and irritable mood, for the failure of our search oppressed him. Moreover, we knew, both of us, that it could not be much prolonged, since the weather might break at any moment, when ascents of the mountain would become impossible.

In the middle of the night I was awakened by Leo shaking me and saying—

"Come here, Horace ; I have something to show you."

Reluctantly enough I crept from between the rugs and out of the tent. To dress there was no need, for we slept in all our garments. He led me to the mouth of the cave and pointed northward. I looked. The night was very dark ; but far, far away appeared a faint patch of light upon the sky, such as might be caused by the reflection of a distant fire.

"What do you make of it ? " he asked anxiously.

"Nothing in particular," I answered ; "it may be anything. The moon—no, there is none ; dawn—no, it is too northerly, and it does not break for three hours. Something burning, a house, or a funeral pyre ; but how can there be such things here ? I give it up ! "

"I think it is a reflection, and that if we were on the peak, we should see the light which throws it," said Leo slowly.

"Yes, but we are not, and cannot get there in the dark."

"Then, Horace, we must spend a night there."

"It will be our last in this incarnation," I answered with a laugh, "that is—if it comes on to snow."

"We must risk it—or I will risk it. Look, the light has faded " ; and there at least he was right, for undoubtedly it had. The night was as black as pitch.

"Let's talk it over to-morrow," I said, and went back to the tent, for I was sleepy and incredulous, but Leo sat on by the mouth of the cave.

At dawn I awoke and found breakfast already cooked.

"I must start early," Leo explained.

"Are you mad ? " I asked. "How can we camp on that place ? "

"I don't know, but I am going. I must go, Horace."

"Which means that we both must go. But how about the yak ? "

"Where we can climb, it can follow," he answered.

So we strapped the tent and other baggage, including a good supply of cooked meat, upon the beast's back, and started. The tramp was long, since we were obliged to make some detours to avoid slopes of frozen snow in which, on our previous ascents, we had cut footholds with an axe, for up these the laden animal could not clamber. Reaching the summit at length, we dug a hole, and there pitched the tent, piling the excavated snow about its sides. By this time it began to grow dark, and having descended into the tent, yak and all, we ate our food and waited.

Oh, what cold was that ! The frost was fearful, and at this height a wind blew whose icy breath passed through all our wrappings and seemed to burn our flesh beneath as

"Dragging the animals down the snow-slopes."

though with hot irons. It was fortunate that we had brought the yak, for without the warmth from its shaggy body I believe that we should have perished even in our tent. For some hours we watched, as indeed we must, since to sleep might mean to die, yet saw nothing save the lonely stars, and heard nothing in that awful silence, for here even the wind made no noise as it slid across the snows. Accustomed as I was to such exposure, my faculties began to grow numb and my eyes to shut, when suddenly Leo said—

" Look, below the red star ! "

I looked, and there, high in the sky, was the same curious glow which we had seen upon the previous night. There was more than this indeed, for beneath it, almost on a line with us and just above the crests of the intervening peaks, appeared a faint sheet of fire, and, revealed against it, something black. Whilst we watched, the fire widened, spread upwards, and grew in power and intensity. Now against its flaming background the black object became clearly visible, and lo ! it was the top of a soaring pillar surmounted by a loop. Yes, we could see its every outline. It was the *crux ansata*, the Symbol of Life itself.

The symbol vanished, the fire sank. Again it blazed up, more fiercely than before, and the loop appeared afresh, then once more disappeared. A third time the fire shone, and with such intensity that no lightning could surpass its brilliance. All around the heavens were lit up, and through the black, needle-shaped eye of the symbol, as from the flare of a beacon or the searchlight of a ship, one fierce ray shot across the sea of mountain-tops and the spaces of the desert, straight as an arrow to the lofty peak on which we lay. Yes, it lit upon the snow, staining it red, and upon the wild, white faces of us who watched, though to the right and left of us spread thick darkness. My compass lay before me on the snow, and I could even see its needle ; and beyond us the shape of a white fox that had crept near, scenting food. Then it was gone as swiftly as it came. Gone, too, were the symbol and the veil of flame behind it ; only the glow lingered a little on the distant sky.

For awhile there was silence between us, then Leo said—

" Do you remember, Horace, when we lay upon the Rocking Stone where *her* cloak fell upon me——" as he said the words, the breath caught in his throat—" how the ray of light was sent to us in farewell, and to show us a path of escape from the Place of Death ? Now I think that it has been sent again in greeting to point out the path to the Place of Life where Ayesha dwells, whom we have lost."

" It may be so," I answered shortly, for the matter was beyond speech or argument, beyond wonder even. But I knew then, as I know now, that we were players in some mighty, predestined drama ; that our parts were written and we must speak them, as our path was prepared and we must tread it to the end unknown. Fear and doubt were left behind, hope was lost in certainty ; the fore-shadowing visions of the night had found an actual fulfilment, and the pitiful seed of the promise of her who died, growing unseen through all the cruel, empty years, had come to harvest.

No, we feared no more, not even when with the dawn rose the roaring wind, through which we struggled down the mountain-slopes, as it would seem in peril of our lives at every step ; not even as hour by hour we fought our way onwards through the whirling snow-storm, that made us deaf and blind. For we knew that those lives were charmed. We could not see or hear, yet we were led. Clinging to the yak, we struggled downward and homewards, till at length out of the tur-moil and the gloom its instinct brought us unharmed to the door of the monastery, where the old abbot embraced us in his joy, and the monks put up prayers of thanks. For they were sure that we must be dead. Through such a storm, they said, no man had ever lived before.

*   *   *   *   *

It was still midwinter, and oh ! the awful weariness of those months of waiting. In our hands was the key, yonder amongst those mountains lay the door, but not yet might we set that key within its lock. For between us and these stretched the great desert, where the snow rolled like billows, and until that snow melted we dared not attempt its passage. So we sat in the monastery and schooled our hearts to patience.

Still, even to these frozen wilds of Central Asia spring comes at last. One evening the air felt warm, and that night there were only a few degrees of frost. The next the clouds banked up, and in the morning not snow was falling from them, but rain, and we found the old monks preparing their instru-ments of husbandry, as they said that the season of sowing was at hand. For three days it rained, while the snows melted before our eyes. On the fourth, torrents of water were rushing down the mountain, and the desert was once more brown and bare, though not for long, for within another week it was carpeted with flowers. Then we knew that the time had come to start.

"But whither go you? Whither go you?" asked the old abbot in dismay. "Are you not happy here? Do you not make great strides along the Path, as may be known by your pious conversation? Is not everything that we have your own? Oh! why would you leave us?"

"We are wanderers," we answered, "and when we see mountains in front of us, we must cross them."

Kou-en looked at us shrewdly, then asked—

"What do you seek beyond the mountains? And, my brethren, what merit is gathered by hiding the truth from an old man, for such concealments are separated from falsehoods but by the length of a single barleycorn. Tell me, that at least my prayers may accompany you."

"Holy abbot," I said, "awhile ago yonder in the library you made a certain confession to us."

"Oh! remind me not of it," he said, holding up his hands. "Why do you wish to torment me?"

"Far be the thought from us, most kind friend and virtuous man," I answered. "But, as it chances, your story is very much our own, and we think that we have experience of this same priestess."

"Speak on," he said, much interested.

So I told him the outlines of our tale; for an hour or more I told it, while he sat opposite to us swaying his head like a tortoise and saying nothing. At length it was done.

"Now," I added, "let the lamp of your wisdom shine upon our darkness. Do you not find this story wondrous, or do you perchance think that we are liars?"

"Brethren of the great monastery called the World," Kou-en answered with his customary chuckle, "why should I think you liars, who, from the moment my eyes fell upon you, knew you to be true men? Moreover, why should I hold this tale so very wondrous? You have but stumbled upon the fringe of a truth with which we have been acquainted for many, many ages.

"Because in a vision she showed you this monastery, and led you to a spot beyond the mountains where she vanished, you hope that this woman whom you saw die is reincarnated yonder. Why not? In this there is nothing impossible to those who are instructed in the truth, though the lengthening of her last life was strange and contrary to experience. Doubtless you will find her there as you expect, and doubtless her *khama*, or identity, is the same as that which in some earlier life of hers once brought me to sin.

"Only be not mistaken, she is no immortal; nothing is immortal. She is but a being held back by her own pride, her own greatness if you will, upon the path towards Nirvana. That pride will be humbled, as already it has been humbled; that brow of majesty will be sprinkled with the dust of change and death, that sinful spirit will be purified by sorrows and by separations. Brother Leo, if you win her, it will be but to lose, and then the ladder must be re-climbed. Brother Holly, for you as for me, loss is our only gain, since thereby we are spared much woe. Oh! bide here and pray with me. Why dash yourselves against a rock? Why labour to pour water into a broken jar whence it must sink into the sands of profitless experience, and there be wasted, whilst you remain athirst?"

"Water makes the sand fertile," I answered. "Where water falls, life comes, and sorrow is the seed of joy."

"Love is the law of life," broke in Leo; "without love there is no life. I seek love that I may live. I believe that all these things are ordained to an end which we do not know. Fate draws me on—I fulfil my fate——"

"And do but delay your freedom. Yet I will not argue with you, brother, who must follow your own road. See now, what has this woman—this priestess of a false faith, if she be so still—brought you in the past? Once in another life, or so I understand your story, you were sworn to a certain Nature-goddess who was named Isis, were you not, and to her alone? Then a woman tempted you, and you fled with her afar. And there what found you? The betrayed and avenging goddess who slew you, or if not the goddess, one who had drunk of her wisdom and was the minister of her vengeance. Having that wisdom, this minister—woman or evil spirit—refused to die because she had learned to love you, but waited knowing that in your next life she would find you again, as indeed she would have done more swiftly in Devachan had she died without living on alone in so much misery. And she found you, and she died, or seemed to die, and now she is re-born, as she must be, and doubtless you will meet once more, and again there must be misery. Oh, my friends, go not across the mountains; bide here with me and lament your sins!"

"Nay," answered Leo, "we are sworn to a tryst, and we do not break our word."

"Then, brethren, go keep your tryst; and when you have reaped its harvest, think upon my sayings, for I am sure that the wine you crush from the vintage of your desire will run red like blood, and that in its drinking you will find neither forgetfulness nor peace. Made blind by a passion of which well I know the sting and power, you seek to add a fair-faced evil to your lives, thinking that from this unity there shall be born all knowledge and great joy.

"Rather should you desire to live alone in holiness until at length your separate lives are merged and lost in the Good Unspeakable, the eternal bliss that lies in the last Nothingness. Ah! you do not believe me now; you shake your heads and smile; yet a day will come, it may be after many incarnations, when you will bow them in the dust and weep, saying to me: 'Brother Kou-en, yours were the words of wisdom, ours the deeds of foolishness'"; and with a deep sigh the old man turned and left us.

"A cheerful faith, truly," said Leo, looking after him, "to dwell through æons in monotonous misery in order that consciousness may be swallowed up at last in some void and formless abstraction called the 'Utter Peace.' I would rather take my share of a bad world and keep my hope of a better. Also I do not think that he knows anything of Ayesha and her destiny."

"So would I," I answered, "though perhaps he is right, after all. Who can tell? Moreover, what is the use of reasoning? Leo, we have no choice; we follow our fate. To what that fate may lead us we shall learn in due season."

Then we went to rest, for it was late, though I found little sleep that night. The warnings of the ancient abbot, good and learned man as he was, full also of ripe experience and of the foresighted wisdom that is given to such as he, oppressed me deeply. He promised us sorrow and bloodshed beyond the mountains, ending in death and re-births full of misery. Well, it might be so, but no approaching sufferings could stay our feet. And even if they could, they should not, since to see her face again I was ready to brave them all. And if this was my case, what must be that of Leo?"

A strange theory that of Kou-en's, that Ayesha was the goddess in old Egypt to whom Kallikrates was priest, or at the least her representative. That the princess Amenartas, with whom he fled, seduced him from the goddess to whom he was sworn. That this goddess incarnate in Ayesha—or using the woman Ayesha and her passions as her instruments—was avenged upon them both at Kôr, and that there in an after age the bolt she shot fell back upon her own head.

Well, I had often thought as much myself. Only I was sure that *She* herself could be no actual divinity, though she might be a manifestation of one, a priestess, a messenger, charged to work its will, to avenge or to reward, and yet, herself a human soul, with hopes and passions to be satisfied, and a destiny to fulfil. In truth, writing now when all is past and done with, I find much to confirm me in, and little to turn me from that theory, since life and powers of a quality which are more than human do not alone suffice to make a soul divine. On the other hand, however, it must be borne in mind that on one occasion, at any rate, Ayesha did undoubtedly suggest that in the beginning she was "a daughter of Heaven," and that there were others, notably the old Shaman Simbri, who seemed to take it for granted that her origin was supernatural. But of all these things I hope to speak in their season.

Meanwhile what lay beyond the mountains? Should we find her there who held the sceptre and upon earth wielded the power of the outraged Isis, and with her, that other woman who wrought the wrong? And if so, would the dread, inhuman struggle reach its climax around the person of the sinful priest? In a few months, a few days even, we might begin to know.

Thrilled by this thought, at length I fell asleep.

CHAPTER IV.

THE AVALANCHE.

On the morning of the second day from that night, the sunrise found us already on our path across the desert. There, nearly a mile behind us, we could see the ruined statue of Buddha seated in front of the ancient monastery, and in that clear atmosphere could even distinguish the bent form of our friend, the old abbot, Kou-en, leaning against it until we were quite lost to sight. All the monks had wept when we parted from them, and Kou-en even more bitterly than the rest, for he had learned to love us.

"It was the *crux ansata*, the Symbol of Life itself."

"I am grieved," he said, "much grieved, which, indeed, I should not be, for such emotion partakes of sin. Yet I find comfort, for I know well that although I must soon leave this present life, yet we shall meet again in many future incarnations, and after you have put away these follies, together tread the path to Perfect Peace. Now take with you my blessings and my prayers, and begone, forgetting not that should you live to return "—and he shook his head doubtfully —"here you will be ever welcome."

So we embraced him and went sorrowfully.

It will be remembered that when the mysterious light fell upon us on the peak, I had my compass with me and was able roughly to take its bearings. For lack of any better guide we now followed these bearings, travelling almost due north-east, for in that direction had shone the fire. All day in the most beautiful weather we marched across the flower-strewn desert, seeing nothing except bunches of game and one or two herds of wild asses which had come down from the mountains to feed upon the new grass. As evening approached, we shot an antelope and made our camp—for we had brought the yak and a tent with us—among some tamarisk scrub, of which the dry stems furnished us with fuel. Nor did we lack for water, since by scraping in the sand soaked with melted snow, we found plenty of fair quality. So that night we supped in luxury upon tea and antelope meat, which, indeed, we were glad to have, as it spared our little store of dried provisions.

The next morning we ascertained our position as well as we could, and estimated that we had crossed about a quarter of the desert, a guess which proved very accurate, for on the evening of the fourth day of our journey we reached the bottom slopes of the opposing mountains, without having experienced either accident or fatigue. As Leo said, things were "going like clockwork," but I reminded him that a good start often meant a bad finish. Nor was I wrong, for now came our hardships. To begin with, the mountains proved to be exceeding high : it took us two days to climb their lower slopes. Also the heat of the sun had softened the snow, which made walking through it laborious, whilst, accustomed though we were to such conditions through long years of travelling, its continual glitter affected our eyes.

The morning of the seventh day found us in the mouth of a defile which wound away into the heart of the mountains. As it seemed the only possible path, we followed it, and were much cheered to discover that here must once have run a road. Not that we could see any road, indeed, for everything was buried in snow. But that one lay beneath our feet we were certain, since, although we marched along the edge of precipices, our path, however steep, was always flat ; moreover, the rock upon one side of it had often been scarped by the hand of man. Of this there could be no doubt, for as the snow did not cling here, we saw the tool marks upon its bare surface.

Also we came to several places where galleries had been built out from the mountain-side, by means of beams let into it, as is still a common practice in Thibet. These beams, of course, had long since rotted away, leaving a gulf between us and the continuation of the path. When we met with such gaps, we were forced to go back and make a detour round or over some mountain ; but although much delayed thereby, as it happened, we always managed to regain the road, if not without difficulty and danger.

What tried us more—for here our skill and experience as mountaineers could not help us—was the cold at night, obliged as we were to camp in the severe frost at a great altitude, and to endure through the long hours of darkness penetrating and icy winds, which soughed ceaselessly down the pass.

At length, on the tenth day, we reached the end of the defile, and as night was falling, camped there in the most bitter cold. Those were miserable hours, for now we had no fuel with which to boil water, and must satisfy our thirst by eating frozen snow, while our eyes smarted so sorely that we could not sleep, and notwithstanding all our wraps and the warmth that we gathered from the yak in the little tent, the cold caused our teeth to chatter like castanets.

The dawn came, and, after it, the sunrise. We crept from the tent and, leaving it standing awhile, dragged our stiffened limbs a hundred yards or so to a spot where the defile took a turn, in order that we might thaw in the rays of the sun, which at that hour could not reach us where we had camped.

Leo was round it first, and I heard him utter an exclamation. In a few seconds I reached his side, and lo ! before us lay our Promised Land.

Far beneath us, ten thousand feet at least —for it must be remembered that we viewed it from the top of a mountain—it stretched away and away till its distances met the horizon. In character it was quite flat, an alluvial plain that probably, in some primeval age, had been the bottom of one of the vast lakes of which a number exist in Central Asia, most of them now in process of desiccation. One object only relieved this dreary flatness—a single, snow-clad, and gigantic mountain, of which even at that distance—for it was very far from us—we could clearly see the outline. Indeed, we could see more, for from its rounded crest rose a great plume of smoke, showing that it was an active volcano, and on the hither lip of the crater an enormous pillar of rock, whereof the top was formed to the shape of a loop.

Yes, there it stood before us, that symbol of our vision which we had sought these many years, and at the sight of it our hearts beat fast and our breath came quickly. We noted at once that although we had not seen it during our passage of the mountains, since the peaks ahead and the rocky sides of the defile hid it from view, so great was its height that it overtopped the tallest of them. This made it clear to us how it came to be possible that the ray of light passing through the loop could fall upon the highest snows of that towering pinnacle which we had climbed upon the further side of the desert.

Also now we were certain of the cause of that ray, for the smoke behind the loop explained this mystery. Doubtless, at times when the volcano was awake, that smoke must be replaced by flame, emitting light of fearful intensity, and this light it was that reached us, concentrated and directed by the loop.

For the rest, we thought that about thirty miles away we could make out a white-roofed town set upon a mound, situated among trees upon the banks of a wide river which flowed across the plain. Also it was evident that this country had a large population who cultivated the soil, for by the aid of a pair of field-glasses, one of our few remaining and most cherished possessions, we could see the green of springing crops pierced by irrigation canals and the lines of trees that marked the limits of the fields.

Yes, there before us stretched the Promised Land, and there rose the mystic Mount, so that all we had to do was to march down the snow-slopes and enter it where we would.

Thus we thought in our folly, little guessing what lay before us, what terrors and weary

suffering we must endure before we stood at length beneath the shadow of the Symbol of Life.

Our fatigues forgotten, we returned to the tent, hastily swallowed some of our dried food, which we washed down with lumps of snow that gave us toothache and chilled us inside, but which thirst compelled us to eat, dragged the poor yak to its feet, loaded it up, and started.

All this while, so great was our haste and so occupied was each of us with his own thoughts, that, if my memory serves me, we scarcely interchanged a word. Down the snow-slopes we marched swiftly and without hesitation, for here the road was marked for us by means of pillars of rock set opposite to each other at intervals. These pillars we observed with satisfaction, for they told us that we were still upon a highway which led to the Promised Land.

Yet, as we could not help noting, it was one which seemed to have gone out of use, since with the exception of a few wild-sheep tracks and the spoor of some bears and mountain foxes, not a single sign of beast or man could we discover. This, however, was to be explained, we reflected, by the fact that doubtless the road was only used in the summer season. Or perhaps the inhabitants of the country were now stay-at-home people who never travelled it at all.

Those slopes were longer than we thought; indeed, when darkness closed in we had not reached the foot of them. So we were obliged to spend another night in the snow, pitching our tent in the shelter of an overhanging rock. As we had descended many thousand feet, the temperature proved, fortunately, a little milder; indeed, I do not think that there were more than eighteen or twenty degrees of frost that night. Also here and there the heat of the sun had melted the snow in secluded places, so that we were able to find water to drink, while the yak could fill its poor old stomach with dead-looking mountain mosses, which it seemed to think better than nothing.

Again the still dawn came, throwing its red garment over the lonesome, endless mountains, and we dragged ourselves to our numbed feet, ate some of our remaining food, and started onwards. Now we could no longer see the country beneath, for it and even the towering volcano were hidden from us by an intervening ridge that seemed to be pierced by a single narrow gully, towards which we headed. Indeed, as the pillars showed us, thither ran the buried road. By midday it

"'Why dash yourselves against a rock?'"

appeared quite close to us, and we tramped on in feverish haste. As it chanced, however, there was no need to hurry, for an hour later we learned the truth.

Between us and the mouth of the gully rose—or, rather, sank—a sheer precipice that was apparently three or four hundred feet in depth, and at its foot we could hear the sound of water.

Right to the edge of this precipice ran the path, for one of the stone pillars stood upon its extreme brink; and yet how could a road descend such a place as that? We stared aghast; then a possible solution occurred to us.

"Don't you see," said Leo, with a hollow laugh, "the gulf has opened since this track was used? Volcanic action probably."

"Perhaps, or perhaps there was a wooden bridge or stairway which has rotted. It does not matter. We must find another path, that is all," I answered as cheerfully as I could.

"Yes, and soon," he said, "if we do not wish to stop here for ever."

So we turned to the right and marched along the edge of the precipice till, a mile or so away, we came to a small glacier, of which the surface was sprinkled with large stones frozen into its substance. This glacier hung down the face of the cliff like a petrified waterfall, but whether or no it reached the foot we could not discover. At any rate, to think of attempting its descent seemed out of the question. From this point onwards we could see that the precipice increased in depth, and far as the eye could reach was absolutely sheer.

So we went back again and searched to the left of our road. Here the mountains receded, so that above us was a mighty, dazzling slope of snow, and below us that same pitiless, unclimbable gulf. As the light began to fade, we perceived, half a mile or more in front, a bare-topped hillock of rock, which stood on the verge of the precipice, and hurried to it, thinking that from its crest we might be able to discover a way of descent.

When at length we had struggled to the top, it was about a hundred and fifty feet high; what we did discover was that, here also, as beyond the glacier, the gulf was infinitely deeper than at the spot where the road ended—so deep, indeed, that we could not see its bottom, although from it rose the sound of roaring water. Moreover, it was quite half a mile in width.

Whilst we stared round us, the sinking sun vanished behind a mountain and, the sky being heavy, the light went out like that of a candle. Now the ascent of this hillock had proved so steep, especially at one place, where we were obliged to climb a sort of rock ladder, that we scarcely cared to attempt to struggle down it again in that gloom. Therefore, remembering that there was little to choose between the top of this knoll and the snow plain at its foot in the matter of temperature or other conveniences, and being quite exhausted, we determined to spend the night upon it, thereby, as we were to learn, saving our lives.

Unloading the yak, we pitched our tent under the lee of the topmost knob of rock and ate a couple of handfuls of dried fish and corn-cake. This was the last of the food that we had brought with us from the Lamasery, and we reflected with dismay that unless we could shoot something, our commissariat was now represented by the carcass of our old friend the yak. Then we wrapped ourselves up in our thick rugs and fur garments and forgot our miseries in sleep.

It cannot have been long before daylight when we were awakened by a sudden and terrific sound like the boom of a great cannon, followed by thousands of other sounds which might be compared to the fusillade of musketry.

"Great Heaven! What is that?" I said.

We crawled from the tent, but as yet could see nothing, whilst the yak began to low in a terrified manner. But if we could not see, we could hear and feel. The booming and cracking had ceased, and was followed by a soft, grinding noise, the most sickening sound, I think, to which I ever listened. This was accompanied by a strange, steady, unnatural wind, which seemed to press upon us as water presses. Then the dawn broke and we saw.

The mountain-side was moving down upon us in a vast avalanche of snow!

Oh, what a sight was that! On from the crest of the precipitous slopes above, two miles and more away, it came, a living thing, rolling, sliding, gliding; piling itself in long, leaping waves, hollowing itself into cavernous valleys, like a tempest-driven sea, whilst above its surface hung a powdery cloud of frozen spray.

As we watched, clinging to each other terrified, the first of these waves struck our hill, causing the mighty mass of solid rock to quiver like a yacht beneath the impact of an ocean roller, or an aspen in a sudden rush of wind. It struck and slowly separated, then with a majestic motion flowed like water over the edge of a precipice on either side, and fell with a thudding sound into the unmeasured depths beneath. And this was but a little thing, a mere forerunner, for after it, with a slow, serpentine movement, rolled the body of the avalanche.

It came in combers, it came in level floods. It piled itself against our hill—yes, to within fifty feet of the head of it—till we thought that even that rooted rock must be torn from its foundations and hurled like a pebble to the deeps beneath. And the turmoil of it all! The screaming of the blast caused by the compression of the air, the dull, continuous thudding of the fall of millions of tons of snow as they rushed through space and ended their journey in the gulf!

Nor was this the worst of it, for as the deep snows above thinned, great boulders that had been buried beneath them, perhaps for centuries, were loosened from their resting-places and began to thunder down the hill. At first they moved slowly, throwing up the hard snow around them as the prow of a ship throws foam. Then gathering momentum, they sprang into the air with leaps such as those of shells ricocheting upon water, till in the end, singing and hurtling, many of them rushed past and even over us, to vanish far beyond. Some, indeed, struck our little mountain with the force of shot fired from the great guns of a battleship, and shattered there, or, if they fell upon its side, tore away tons of rock and passed with them into the chasm like a meteor surrounded by its satellites. Indeed, no bombardment devised and directed by man could have been half so terrible or, had there been anything to destroy, half so destructive.

The scene was appalling in its unchained and resistless might evolved suddenly from the completest calm. There in the lap of the quiet mountains, looked down upon by the peaceful, tender sky, the powers hidden in the breast of Nature were suddenly set free, and, companioned by whirlwinds and all the terrifying majesty of sound, loosed upon the heads of us two human atoms.

At the first rush of snow we had leapt back behind our protecting peak and, lying at full length upon the ground, gripped it and clung there, fearing lest the wind should whirl us to the abyss. Long ago our tent had gone like a dead leaf in an autumn gale, and at times it seemed as if we must follow.

The boulders hurtled over and past us; one of them fell full upon the little peak, shattering its crest and bursting into fragments, which fled away, each singing its own wild song. We were not touched, but when we looked behind us, it was to see the yak, which had risen in its terror, lying dead and headless. Then in our fear we lay still, waiting for the end, and wondering dimly whether we should be buried in the surging snow or swept away with the hill, or crushed by the flying rocks, or lifted and lost in the hurricane.

How long did it last? We never knew. It may have been ten minutes or two hours, for in such a scene time loses its proportions. Only we became aware that the wind had fallen, while the noise of grinding snow and hurtling boulders ceased. Very cautiously we gained our feet and looked.

In front of us the sheer mountain-side, for a depth of over two miles, by the width of about a thousand yards, which had been covered with many feet of snow, was now bare rock. Piled up against the face of our hill, almost to its summit, lay a tongue of snow, pressed to the consistency of ice and spotted with boulders that had lodged there. The peak itself was torn and shattered, so that it revealed great gleaming surfaces and pits, in which glittered mica or some other mineral. The vast gulf behind was half filled with the avalanche and its *débris*. But for the rest, it seemed as though nothing had happened, for the sun shone sweetly overhead, and the solemn snows reflected back its rays from the sides of a hundred hills. And we had endured it all and were still alive; yes, and unhurt.

But what a position was ours! We dared not attempt to descend the mount, lest we should sink into the loose snow and be buried there. Moreover, all along the breadth of the path of the avalanche, boulders from time to time still thundered down the rocky slope, and with them came patches of snow that had been left behind by the big slide, small in themselves, it is true, but each of them large enough to kill a hundred men. It was obvious, therefore, that until these conditions changed, or death released us, we must abide where we were upon the crest of the hillock.

So there we sat, foodless and frightened, wondering what our old friend Kou-en would say if he could see us now. By degrees hunger mastered all our other sensations, and we began to turn longing eyes upon the headless body of the yak.

"Let's skin him," said Leo; "it will be something to do, and we shall want his hide to-night."

So with affection, and even reverence, we performed this office for the dead companion of our journeyings, rejoicing the while that it was not we who had brought him to his end. Indeed, long residence among peoples who believed fully that the souls of men could pass into, or were risen from, the bodies of animals, had made us a little superstitious on this matter. It would be scarcely pleasant, we reflected, in some future incarnation to find our faithful friend clad in human form and to hear him bitterly reproach us for his murder.

Being dead, however, these arguments did not apply to eating him, as we were sure he would himself acknowledge. So we cut off little bits of his flesh and, rolling them in snow till they looked as though they were nicely floured, hunger compelling us, swallowed them at a gulp. It was a disgusting meal, and we felt like cannibals; but what could we do?

"On the morning of the second day, the sunrise found us already on our path across the desert."

CHAPTER V.

THE GLACIER.

EVEN that day came to an end at last, and after a few more lumps of yak, our tent being gone, we drew his hide over us and rested as best we could, knowing that at least we had no more avalanches to fear. That night it froze sharply, so that had it not been for the yak's hide and the other rugs and garments, which fortunately we were wearing when the snow-slide began, it would, I think, have gone hard with us. As it was, we suffered a great deal.

"Horace," said Leo at the dawn, "I am going to leave this. If we have to die, I would rather do so moving ; but I don't believe that we shall die."

"Very well," I said, "let us start. If the snow won't bear us now, it never will."

So we tied up our rugs and the yak's hide in two bundles and, having cut off some more of the frozen meat, began our descent. Now, although the mount was under two hundred feet high, its base, fortunately for us—for otherwise it must have been swept away by the mighty pressure of the avalanche —was broad, so that there was a long expanse of piled-up snow between us and the level ground.

Since, owing to the overhanging conformation of the place, it was quite impossible for us to descend in front, where pressure had made the snow hard as stone, we were obliged to risk a march over the looser material upon its flank. As there was nothing to be gained by waiting, off we went, Leo leading and, step by step, trying the snow. To our joy we discovered that the sharp night frost had so hardened its surface that it would bear us. About half way down, however, where the pressure had been less, it became much softer, so that we were forced to lie upon our faces, which enabled us to distribute our weight over a larger surface, and thus slither gently down the hill.

All went well until we were within twenty paces of the bottom, where we must cross a soft mound formed of the powdery dust thrown off by the avalanche in its rush. Leo slipped over safely, but I, following a yard or two to his right, of a sudden felt the hard crust yield beneath me. An ill-judged but quite natural flounder and wriggle, such as a newly landed flat-fish gives upon the sand, completed the mischief, and with one piercing but swiftly stifled yell, I vanished.

Anyone who has ever sunk in deep water will know that the sensation is not pleasant, but I can assure him that to go through the same experience in soft snow is infinitely worse ; mud alone could surpass its terrors. Down I went, and down, till at length I seemed to reach a rock which alone saved me from disappearing for ever. Now I felt the snow closing above me, and with it came darkness and a sense of suffocation. So soft was the drift, however, that before I was overcome I contrived with my arms to thrust away the powdery dust from about my head, thus forming a little hollow into which air filtered slowly. Getting my hands upon the stone, I strove to rise, but could not, the weight upon me was too great.

Then I abandoned hope and prepared to die. The process proved not altogether unpleasant. I did not see visions from my past life, as drowning men are supposed to do, but —and this shows how strong was her empire over me—my mind flew back to Ayesha. I seemed to behold her and a man at her side, standing over me in some dark, rocky gulf. She was wrapped in a long travelling cloak, and her lovely eyes were wild with fear. I rose to salute her and make report, but she cried in a fierce, concentrated voice—

"What evil thing has happened here ? Thou livest ; then where is my lord Leo ? Speak, man, and say where thou hast hid my lord—or die."

The vision was extraordinarily real and vivid, I remember, and, considered in connection with a certain subsequent event, in all ways most remarkable, but it passed as swiftly as it came.

Then my senses left me.

I saw light again. I heard a voice, that of Leo! "Horace!" he cried, " Horace, hold fast to the stock of the rifle!" Something was thrust against my outstretched hand. I gripped it despairingly, and there came a strain. It was useless, I did not move. Then, bethinking me, I drew up my legs and, by chance or the mercy of Heaven, I know not, got my feet against a ridge of the rock on which I was lying. Again I felt the strain and thrust with all my might. Of a sudden the snow gave, and out of that hole I shot like a fox from its earth.

I struck something. It was Leo straining at the gun, and I knocked him backwards. Then down the slope we rolled, landing at length upon the very edge of the precipice. I sat up, drawing in the air with great gasps, and oh ! how sweet it was. My eyes fell upon my hand, and I saw that the veins stood out on the back of it, black as ink and large as cords. Clearly I must have been near my end.

"How long was I in there?" I gasped to Leo, who sat at my side, wiping off the sweat that ran from his face in streams.

"Don't know. Nearly twenty minutes, I should think."

"Twenty minutes! It seemed like twenty centuries. How did you get me out? You could not stand upon the drift dust."

"No. I lay upon the yak skin where the snow was harder, and tunnelled towards you through the powdery stuff with my hands, for I knew where you had sunk, and it was not far off. At last I saw your finger-tips; they were so blue that for a few seconds I took them for rock, and thrust the butt of the rifle against them. Luckily you still had life enough to catch hold of it, and you know the rest. Were we not both very strong, it could never have been done."

"Thank you, old fellow," I said simply.

"Why should you thank me?" he asked, with one of his quick smiles. "Do you suppose that I wish to continue this journey alone? Come, if you have got your breath, let us be getting on. You have been sleeping in a cold bed and want exercise. Look, my rifle is broken, and yours is lost in the snow. Well, it will save us the trouble of carrying the cartridges," and he laughed drearily.

Then we began our march, heading for the spot where the road ended four miles or so away, for to go forward seemed useless. In due course we reached it safely. Once a mass of snow as large as a church swept down just in front of us, and once a great boulder loosened from the mountain rushed at us suddenly like an attacking lion, or the stones thrown by Polyphemus at the ship of Odysseus, and, leaping over our heads, vanished with an angry scream into the depths beneath. But we took little heed of these things: our nerves were deadened, and no danger seemed to affect them.

There was the end of the road, and there were our own footprints and the impress of the yak's hoofs in the snow. The sight of them affected me, for it seemed strange that we should have lived to look upon them again. We stared over the edge of the precipice. Yes, it was sheer and absolutely unclimbable.

"Come to the glacier," said Leo.

So we went on to it and, scrambling a little way down its root, made an examination. Here, so far as we could judge, the cliff was about four hundred feet deep. But whether or no the tongue of ice reached to the foot of it, we were unable to tell, since about two-thirds of the way down it arched inwards, like the end of a bent bow, and the conformation of the overhanging rocks on either side was such that we could not see where it terminated. We climbed back again and sat down, and despair took hold of us—bitter, black despair.

"What are we to do?" I asked. "In front of us death. Behind us death, for how can we recross those mountains without food, or guns to shoot it with? Here death, for we must sit and starve. We have striven and failed. Leo, our end is at hand. Only a miracle can save us."

"A miracle," he answered. "Well, what was it that led us to the top of the mount, so that we were able to escape the avalanche? And what was it which put that rock in your way as you sank into the bed of dust, and gave me wit and strength to dig you out of your grave of snow? And what is it that has preserved us through seventeen years of dangers such as few men have known and lived? Some directing Power. Some Destiny that will accomplish itself in us. Why should the Power cease to guide? Why should the Destiny be baulked at last?"

He paused, then added fiercely: "I tell you, Horace, that even if we had guns, food, and yaks, I would not turn back upon our spoor, since to do so would prove me a coward and unworthy of her. I will go on."

"How?" I asked.

"By that road," and he pointed to the glacier.

"It is a road to death!"

"Well, if so, Horace, it would seem that in this land men find life in death, or so they believe. If we die now, we shall die travelling our path, and in the country where we perish we may be born again. At least I am determined, so you must choose."

"I have chosen long ago. Leo, we began this journey together, and we will end it together. Perhaps Ayesha knows and will help us," and I laughed drearily. "If not—come, we are wasting time."

Then we took counsel, and the end of it was that we cut a skin rug and the yak's tough hide into strips and knotted these together into two serviceable ropes, which we fastened about our middles, leaving one end loose, for we thought that they might help us in our descent.

Next we bound fragments of another skin rug about our legs and knees, to protect them from the chafing of the ice and rocks, and for the same reason put on our thick leather gloves. This done, we took the remainder of our gear and heavy robes and, having placed stones in them, threw them over the brink of the precipice, trusting to find them again should we ever reach its foot. Now our preparations were complete, and it was time for us to start upon perhaps one of the most desperate journeys ever undertaken by men of their own will.

Yet we stayed a little, looking at each other in a piteous fashion, for we could not speak. Only we embraced, and I confess I think I wept a little. It all seemed so sad and hopeless, these longings endured through many years, these perpetual, weary travellings, and now—the end. I could not bear to think of that splendid man, my ward, my most dear friend, the companion of my life, who stood before me so full of beauty and of vigour, but who must within a few short minutes be turned into a heap of quivering, mangled flesh. For myself, it did not matter. I was old, it was time that I should die. I had lived innocently, if it were innocent to follow this lovely image, this Siren of the caves, who lured us on to doom.

No, I don't think that I thought of myself then, but I thought a great deal of Leo, and when I saw his determined face and flashing eyes as he nerved himself to the last endeavour, I was proud of him. So in broken accents I blessed him and wished him well through all the æons, praying that I might be his companion to the end of time. In few words and short he thanked me and gave me back my blessing. Then he muttered—

"Come."

So side by side we began the terrible descent. At first it was easy enough, although a slip would have hurled us to eternity. But we were strong and skilful, accustomed to such places moreover, and made none. About a quarter of the way down we paused, standing upon a great boulder that was embedded in the ice, and, turning round cautiously, leaned our backs against the glacier and looked about us. Truly it was a horrible place, almost sheer, nor did we learn much, for beneath us, a hundred and twenty feet or more, the projecting bend cut off our view of what lay below.

So, feeling that our nerves would not bear a prolonged contemplation of that dizzy gulf, once more we set our faces to the ice and proceeded on the downward climb. Now matters were more difficult, for the stones were fewer, and once or twice we must slide to reach them, not knowing if we should ever stop again. But the ropes which we threw over the angles of the rocks or salient points of ice, letting ourselves down by their help and drawing them after us when we reached the next foothold, saved us from disaster.

Thus at length we came to the bend, which was more than half way down the precipice, being, so far as I could judge, about two hundred and fifty feet from its lip, and say one hundred and fifty from the darksome bottom of the narrow gulf. Here were no stones, but only some rough ice, on which we sat to rest.

"We must look," said Leo presently.

But the question was, how to do this. Indeed, there was only one way—to hang over the bend and discover what lay below. We read each other's thought without the need of words, and I made a motion as though I would start.

"No," said Leo, "I am younger and stronger than you. Come, help me," and he began to fasten the end of his rope to a strong, projecting point of ice. "Now," he said, "hold my ankles."

It seemed an insanity, but there was nothing else to be done, so, fixing my heels in a niche, I grasped them, and slowly he slid forward till his body vanished to the middle. What he saw does not matter, for I saw it all afterwards, but what happened was that suddenly all his great weight came upon my arms with such a jerk that his ankles were torn from my grip!

Or, Heaven knows! perhaps in my terror I loosed them, obeying the natural impulse which prompts a man to save his own life. If so, may I be forgiven; but had I held on, I must have been jerked into the abyss. Then the rope ran out and remained taut.

"Leo!" I screamed, "Leo!" and I heard a muffled voice saying, as I thought: "Come!" What it really said was: "Don't come!" But, indeed—and may it go to my credit—I did not pause to think, but face outwards, just as I was sitting, began to slide and scramble down the ice.

In two seconds I had reached the curve, in three I was over it. Beneath was what I can only describe as a great icicle broken off short, and separated from the cliff by about four yards of space. This icicle was not more than fifteen feet in length, and sloped outwards, so that my descent was not sheer. Moreover, at the end of it the trickling of water, or some such accident, had worn away the ice, leaving a little ledge as broad, perhaps, as a man's hand. There were roughnesses on the surface below the curve, upon which my clothing caught, also I gripped them desperately with my fingers. Thus it

"He was hacking at the cord with it fiercely."

came about that I slid down quite gently and, my heels landing upon the little ledge, remained almost upright, with outstretched arms—like a person crucified to a cross of ice.

Then I saw everything, and the sight curdled the blood within my veins. Hanging to the rope, four or five feet below the broken point, was Leo, out of reach of it, and out of reach of the cliff, as he hung turning slowly round and round, much as—for in a dreadful, inconsequent fashion the absurd similarity struck me even then—a joint turns before the fire. Below yawned the black gulf, and at the bottom of it, far, far beneath, appeared a faint, white sheet of snow. That is what I saw.

Think of it! Think of it! I crucified upon the ice, my heels resting upon a little ledge; my fingers grasping excrescences on which a bird could scarcely have found a foothold; round and below me dizzy space. To climb back whence I came was impossible, to stir even was impossible, since one slip and I must be gone.

And below me, hung like a spider to its cord, Leo turning slowly round and round!

I could see that rope of green hide stretch beneath his weight, and the double knots in it slip and tighten, and I remember wondering which would give first, the hide or the knots, or whether it would hold till he dropped from the noose limb by limb.

Oh! I have been in many a perilous place—I who sprang from the Swaying Stone to the point of the Trembling Spur, and missed my aim—but never, never in such a one as this. Agony took hold of me; a cold sweat burst from every pore. I could feel it running down my face like tears; my hair bristled upon my head. And below, in utter silence, Leo turned round and round; and each time he turned, his upcast eyes met mine with a look that was horrible to see.

The silence was the worst of it, the silence and the helplessness. If he had cried out, if he had struggled, it would have been better. But to know that he was alive there, with every nerve and perception at its utmost stretch!

My limbs began to ache, and yet I dared not stir a muscle. They ached horribly, or so I thought, and beneath this torture, mental and physical, my mind gave. I remembered things: remembered how, as a child, I had climbed a tree and reached a place whence I could move neither up nor down, and what I suffered then. Remembered how once in Egypt a foolhardy friend of mine had ascended the Second Pyramid alone, and become thus crucified upon its shining cap, where he remained for a whole half-hour, with four hundred feet of space beneath him. I could see him now, stretching his stockinged foot downwards in a vain attempt to reach the next crack, and drawing it back again; could see his tortured face, a white blot upon the red granite.

Then that face vanished, and blackness gathered round me, and in the blackness visions: of the living, restless avalanche, of the snow-grave into which I had sunk—oh! years and years ago; of Ayesha demanding Leo's life at my hands. Blackness and silence, through which I could only hear the cracking of my muscles.

*   *   *   *   *

Suddenly in the blackness a flash, and in the silence a sound. The flash was the flash of a knife which Leo had drawn. He was hacking at the cord with it fiercely, fiercely, to make an end. And the sound was that of the noise he made, a ghastly noise, half shout of defiance and half yell of terror, as at the third stroke it parted.

I saw it part. The tough hide was half cut through, and its severed portion curled upwards and downwards like the upper and lower lips of an angry dog, whilst that which was unsevered stretched out slowly, slowly, till it grew quite thin. Then it snapped, so that the rope flew upwards and struck me across the face like the blow of a whip.

Another instant and I heard a crackling, thudding sound. Leo had struck the ground below. Leo was dead, a mangled mass of flesh and bone as I had pictured him. I could not bear it. My nerve and human dignity came back. I would not wait until, my strength exhausted, I slid from my perch as a wounded bird falls from a tree. No, I would follow him at once, of my own act.

I let my arms fall against my sides, and rejoiced in the relief from pain that the movement gave me. Then, balanced upon my heels, I stood upright, took my last look at the sky, muttered my last prayer. For an instant I remained thus poised.

Shouting: "I come!" I raised my hands above my head and dived as a bather dives, dived into the black gulf beneath.

AYESHA

THE RETURN OF "SHE."

By H. RIDER HAGGARD.

SYNOPSIS OF FOREGOING CHAPTERS.—The return of "She-Who-Must-Be-Obeyed" is recorded by Ludwig Horace Holly, the friend of that Leo Vincey whom Ayesha the beautiful loved in the awful tombs of Kôr. When the record begins, the two men are living in an old house remote upon the seashore of Cumberland, where they have been slowly recovering from the horror of the passing of Ayesha in the flames - a doom that seemed one of complete extinction, yet was charged with the strange last words: "I die not. I shall come again and shall once more be beautiful. I swear it—it is true." On a sullen August night, Leo is thrilled by a vision of Ayesha in all her former loveliness. She beckons him, and in a vision his spirit follows her into a realm of snowy peaks far beyond the furthest borders of Thibet. A sign in the clouds at dawn is repeated from this vision to both Leo and Holly, and together they start for Central Asia. Sixteen years of toil, struggle, and strange adventure pass, and they are still searching for "a mountain peak shaped like the Symbol of Life." After many wanderings they find themselves in a country where no European has ever set foot, on one of the spurs of the vast Cherga mountains, far eastward from Turkestan. Sheltered awhile in a Buddhist monastery, they hear of the recent visit of a stranger who has told the Lamas that his countryfolk, "dwelling beyond the Far Mountains," worship a priestess called Hes, or the Hesea, and upon persuasion the abbot of the monastery tells them that in a former incarnation he himself has seen the great priestess, who was "all loveliness." A perilous ascent into the unexplored mountain fastness leads them to the revelation of "the *crux ansata*, the Symbol of Life itself." The symbol vanishes, the fire sinks, but they are sure that as it was sent of old to show them a path of escape from the Place of Death, so now it has been sent again in greeting to point out the path to the Place of Life where Ayesha dwells. A further ascent into the mountains reveals their Promised Land, with the symbol of their vision, an enormous pillar of rock, whereof the top was formed to the shape of a loop. Peril by avalanche and glacier intervenes, but brings them slowly nearer to their hopes.

CHAPTER VI

IN THE GATE.

OH! that rush through space! Folk falling thus are supposed to lose consciousness, but I can assert that this is not true. Never were my wits and perceptions more lively than while I travelled from that broken glacier to the ground, and never did a short journey seem to take a longer time. I saw the white floor, like some living thing, leaping up through empty air to meet me, then—*finis!*

Crash! Why, what was this? I still lived. I was in water, for I could feel its chill, and going down, down, till I thought I should never rise again. But rise I did, though my lungs were nigh to bursting first. As I floated up towards the top I remembered the crash, which told me that I had passed through ice. Therefore I should meet ice at the surface again. Oh! to think that after surviving so much I must be drowned like a kitten and beneath a sheet of ice!

My hands touched it. There it was above me, shining white like glass. Heaven be praised! My head broke through; in this low and sheltered gorge it was but a film no thicker than a penny, formed by the light frost of the previous night. So I rose from the deep and stared about me, treading water with my feet.

Then I saw the gladdest sight that ever my eyes beheld, for on the right, not ten yards away, the water running from his hair and beard, was Leo. Leo alive, for he broke the thin ice with his arms as he struggled towards the shore from the deep river.* He saw me also, and his grey eyes seemed to start out of his head.

"Still living, both of us, and the precipice passed!" he shouted in a ringing, exultant voice. "I told you we were led."

"Aye, but whither?" I answered, as I, too, fought my way through the film of ice.

Then it was I became aware that we were no longer alone, for on the bank of the river, some thirty yards from us, stood two figures, a man leaning upon a long staff, and a woman. He was a very old man,

---

* Usually, as we learned afterwards, the river at this spot was quite shallow—only a foot or two in depth. It was the avalanche that, by damming it with fallen heaps of snow, had raised its level very many feet. Therefore, to this avalanche, which had threatened to destroy us, we in reality owe our lives; for had the stream stood only at its normal height, we must have been dashed to pieces upon its stones.—L. H. H.

for his eyes were horny, his snow-white hair and beard hung upon the bent breast and shoulders, and his sardonic, wrinkled features were yellow as wax. They might have been those of a death-mask cut in marble. There, clad in an ample, monkish robe, and leaning upon the staff, he stood still as a statue and watched us. I noted it all, every detail, although at the time I did not know that I was doing so, as we broke our way through the ice towards them, and afterwards the picture came back to me. Also I saw that the woman, who was very tall, pointed to us.

Nearer the bank, or rather to the rock edge of the river, its surface was free of ice, for here the stream ran very swiftly. Seeing this, we drew close together and swam on side by side, to help each other if need were. There was much need, for in the fringe of the torrent the strength that had served me so long seemed to desert me, and I became helpless ; numbed, too, with the biting coldness of the water. Indeed, had not Leo grasped my clothes, I think that I should have been swept away by the current to perish. Thus aided, I fought on a while, till he said—

" I am going under. Hold to the rope end."

So I gripped the strip of yak's hide that was still fast about him, and, his hand thus freed, Leo made a last splendid effort to keep us both, cumbered as we were with the thick, soaked garments that dragged us down like lead, from being sucked beneath the surface. Moreover, he succeeded where any other swimmer of less strength must have failed. Still, I believe that we should have drowned, since here the water ran like a mill-race, had not the man upon the shore, seeing our plight and urged thereto by the woman, run, with surprising swiftness in one so aged, to a point of rock that jutted some yards into the stream, past which we were being swept, and seating himself, stretched out his long stick towards us.

With a desperate endeavour, Leo grasped it as we went by, rolling over and over each other, and held on. Round we swung into the eddy, found our feet, were knocked down again, rubbed and pounded on the rocks. But still gripping that staff of salvation, to his end of which the old man clung like a limpet to a stone, while the woman clung to him, we recovered ourselves and, sheltered somewhat by the rock, floundered towards the shore. Lying on his face—for we were still in great danger—the man extended his arm. We could not reach it ; and worse,

suddenly the staff was torn from him—we were being swept away.

Then it was that the woman did a noble thing, for springing into the water—yes, up to her armpits—and holding fast to the old man by her left hand, with the right she seized Leo's hair and dragged him shorewards. Now he found his feet for a moment, and throwing one arm about her slender form, steadied himself thus, while with the other he supported me. Next followed a long, confused struggle, but the end of it was that three of us, the old man, Leo, and I, rolled in a heap upon the bank and lay there gasping.

Presently I looked up. The woman stood over us, water streaming from her garments, staring like one in a dream at Leo's face, smothered as it was with blood running from a deep cut in his head. Even then I noticed how stately and beautiful she was. Now she seemed to awake and, glancing at the robes that clung to her splendid shape, said something to her companion, then turned and ran towards the cliff.

As we lay before him, utterly exhausted, the old man, who had risen, contemplated us solemnly with his dim eyes. He spoke, but we did not understand. Again he tried another language, but without success. A third time, and our ears were opened, for the tongue he used was Greek ; yes, there in Central Asia he addressed us in Greek— not very pure, it is true, but still Greek.

" Are you wizards," he said, " that you have lived to reach this land ? "

" Nay," I answered in the same tongue, though in broken words—since of Greek I had thought little for many a year—" for then we should have come otherwise," and I pointed to our hurts and the precipice behind us.

" They know the ancient speech ; it is as we were told from the Mountain," he muttered to himself. Then he asked—

" Strangers, what seek you ? "

Now I grew cunning and did not answer, fearing lest, should he learn the truth, he would thrust us back into the river. But Leo had no such caution—or, rather, all reason had left him · he was light-headed.

" We seek," he stuttered out—his Greek, which had always been feeble, now was simply barbarous and mixed with various Thibetan dialects—" we seek the land of the Fire Mountain that is crowned with the Sign of Life."

The man stared at us. " So you know," he said, then broke off and added : " And *whom* do you seek ? "

"Throwing one arm about her slender form, steadied himself thus, while with the other he supported me."

"Her," answered Leo wildly—"the Queen." I think that he meant to say the priestess, or the goddess, but could only think of the Greek for queen, or rather something resembling it. Or perhaps it was because the woman who had gone looked like a queen.

"Oh!" said the man, "you seek a queen—then you *are* those for whom we were bidden to watch. Nay, how can I be sure?"

"Is this a time to put questions?" I gasped angrily. "Answer me one rather: who are you?"

"I? Strangers, my title is Guardian of the Gate, and the lady who was with me is the Khania of Kaloon."

At this point Leo began to faint.

"That man is sick," said the Guardian, "and now that you have got your breath again, you must have shelter, both of you, and at once. Come, help me."

So, supporting Leo on either side, we dragged ourselves away from that accursed cliff and Styx-like river up a narrow, winding gorge. Presently it opened out, and there, stretching across the glade, we saw the Gate. Of this all I observed then—for my memory of the details of this scene and of the conversation that passed is very weak and blurred—was that it seemed to be a mighty wall of rock in which a pathway had been hollowed where doubtless once passed the road. On one side of this passage was a stair, which we began to ascend with great difficulty, for Leo was now almost senseless and scarcely moved his legs. Indeed, at the head of the first flight he sank down in a heap, nor did our strength suffice to lift him.

While I wondered feebly what was to be done, I heard footsteps, and looking up, saw the woman who had saved him descending the stair, and after her two robed men with a Tartar cast of countenance, very impassive, small eyes and yellowish skin. Even the sight of us did not appear to move them to astonishment. She spoke some words to them, whereon they lifted Leo's heavy frame, apparently with ease, and carried him up the steps.

We followed, and reached a room that seemed to be hewn from the rock above the gateway, where the woman called Khania left us. From it we passed through other rooms, one of them a kind of kitchen, in which a fire burned, till we came to a large chamber, evidently a sleeping-place, for in it were wooden bedsteads, mattresses, and rugs. Here Leo was laid down, and with the assistance of one of his servants, the old Guardian undressed him, at the same time motioning me to take off my own garments. This for the first time during many days I did gladly enough, though with great pain and difficulty, to find that I was a mass of wounds and bruises.

Presently our host blew upon a whistle, and the other servant appeared, bringing hot water in a jar, with which we were washed over. Then the Guardian dressed our hurts with some soothing ointment, and wrapped us round with blankets. After this, broth was brought, into which he mixed medicine, and giving me a portion of it to drink where I lay upon one of the beds, he took Leo's head upon his knee and poured the rest of it down his throat. Instantly a wonderful warmth ran through me, and my aching brain began to swim. Then I remembered no more.

*   *   *   *   *

After this we were very, very ill. What may be the exact medical definition of our sickness, I do not know, but in effect it was such as follows loss of blood, extreme exhaustion of body, paralysing shock to the nerves, and extensive cuts and contusions. These taken together produced a long period of semi-unconsciousness, followed by another period of fever and delirium. All that I can recall of those weeks while we remained the guests of the Guardian of the Gate may be summed up in one word—dreams; that is, until at last I recovered my senses.

The dreams themselves are forgotten, which is perhaps as well, as they were very confused and for the most part awful: a hotch-potch of nightmares, reflected without doubt from vivid memories of our recent and fearsome sufferings. At times I would wake up from them a little—I suppose when food was administered to me—and receive impressions of whatever was passing in the place. Thus I can recollect that yellow-faced old Guardian standing over me like a ghost in the moonlight, stroking his long beard, his eyes fixed upon my face, as though he would search out the secrets of my soul.

"They are the men," he muttered to himself; "without doubt they are the men," then walked to the window and looked up long and earnestly, like one who studies the stars.

After this I remember a disturbance in the room, and dominating it, as it were, the rich sound of a woman's voice and the rustle of a woman's silks sweeping the stone floor. I opened my eyes and saw that it was she who had helped to rescue us—who *had* rescued us, in fact—a tall and noble-looking lady with a beauteous, weary face and liquid eyes which seemed to burn. From the heavy cloak she wore I thought that she must have just returned from a journey.

She stood above me and looked at me, then turned away with a gesture of indifference, if not of disgust, speaking to the Guardian in a low voice. By way of answer he bowed, pointing to the other bed where Leo lay asleep, and thither she passed with slow, imperious movements. I saw her bend down and lift the corner of a wrapping which covered his wounded head, and heard her utter some smothered words before she turned round to the Guardian as though to question him further.

But he had gone, and being alone, for she thought me senseless, she drew a rough stool to the side of the bed and, seating herself, studied Leo, who lay thereon, with an earnestness that was almost terrible, for her soul seemed to be concentrated in her eyes and to find expression through them. Long she gazed thus, then rose and began to walk swiftly up and down the chamber, pressing her hands now to her bosom and now to her brow, a certain passionate perplexity stamped upon her face, as though she struggled to remember something and could not.

"Where and when?" she whispered. "Oh! where and when?"

Of the end of that scene I know nothing, for although I fought hard against it, oblivion mastered me. After this I became aware that the regal-looking woman called Khania was always in the room, and that she seemed to be nursing Leo with great care and tenderness. Sometimes even she nursed me when Leo did not need attention, and she had nothing else to do, or so her manner seemed to suggest. It was as though I excited her curiosity, and she wished me to recover that it might be satisfied.

Again I awoke, how long afterwards I cannot say. It was night, and the room was lighted by the moon only, now shining in a clear sky. Its steady rays, entering at the window-place, fell on Leo's bed, and by them I saw that the dark, imperial woman was watching at his side. Some sense of her presence must have communicated itself to him, for he began to mutter in his sleep, now in English, now in Arabic. She became intensely interested, as her every movement showed. Then, rising suddenly, she glided across the room on tiptoe to look at me. Seeing her coming, I feigned to be asleep, and so well that she was deceived.

For I was also interested. Who was this lady whom the Guardian had called the Khania of Kaloon? Could it be she whom we sought? Why not? And yet if I saw Ayesha, surely I should know her, surely there would be no room for doubt?

Back she went again to the bed, kneeling down beside Leo, and in the intense silence that followed—for he had ceased his mutterings—I thought that I could hear the beating of her heart. Now she began to speak, very low and in that same bastard Greek tongue, mixed here and there with Mongolian words such as are common to the dialects of Central Asia. I could not hear or understand all she said, but some sentences I did understand, and they frightened me not a little.

"Man of my dreams," she murmured, "whence come you? Who are you? Why did the Hesea bid me to meet you?" Then some sentences I could not catch. "You sleep; in sleep the eyes are opened. Answer, I bid you; say what is the bond between you and me? Why have I dreamt of you? Why do I know you? Why——?" and the sweet, rich voice died slowly from a whisper into silence, as though she were ashamed to utter what was on her tongue.

As she bent over him, a lock of her hair broke loose from its jewelled fillet and fell across his face. At its touch Leo seemed to wake, for he lifted his gaunt, white hand and touched the hair, then said in English—

"Where am I? Oh! I remember"; and their eyes met as he strove to lift himself and could not. Then he spoke again in his broken, stumbling Greek: "You are the lady who saved me from the water. Say, are you also that Queen whom I have sought so long and endured so much to find?"

"I know not," she answered in a voice as sweet as honey, a low, trembling voice; "but true it is I am a queen—if a Khania be a queen."

"Say then, Queen, do you remember me?"

"We have met in dreams," she answered. "I think that we have met in a past that is far away. Yes; I knew it when first I saw you there by the river. Stranger with the well-remembered face, tell me, I pray you, how you are named?"

"Leo Vincey."

She shook her head, whispering—

"I know not the name, yet you I know."

"You know me! How do you know me?" he said heavily, and seemed to sink again into slumber or swoon.

She watched him for awhile very intently.

Then, as though some force that she could not resist drew her, I saw her bend down her head over his sleeping face. Yes; and I saw her kiss him swiftly on the lips, then spring back, crimson to the hair, as though overwhelmed with shame at this victory of her mad passion.

Now it was that she discovered me.

Bewildered, fascinated, amazed, I had raised myself upon my bed, not knowing it; I suppose that I might see and hear the better. It was wrong, doubtless, but no common curiosity overmastered me, who had my share in all this story. More, it was foolish, but illness and wonder had killed my reason.

Yes, she saw me watching them, and such fury seemed to take hold of her that I thought my hour had come.

"Man! have you dared—— ?" she said in an intense whisper, and snatching at her girdle. Now in her hand shone a knife, and I knew that it was destined for my heart. Then in this sore danger my wit came back to me, and as she advanced I stretched out my shaking hand, saying—

"Oh! of your pity, give me to drink! The fever burns me, it burns!" and I looked round like one bewildered who sees not, repeating: "Give me drink, you who are called Guardian," and I fell back exhausted.

She stopped like a hawk in its stoop and swiftly sheathed the dagger. Then taking a bowl of milk that stood on a table near her, she held it to my lips, searching my face the while with her flaming eyes, for indeed passion, rage, and fear had lit them till they seemed to flame. I drank the milk in great gulps, though never in my life did I find it more hard to swallow.

"You tremble," she said. "Have dreams haunted you?"

"Aye, friend," I answered—"dreams of that fearful precipice and of the last leap."

"Aught else?" she asked.

"Nay; is it not enough? Oh! what a journey to have taken to befriend a queen!"

"To befriend a queen!" she repeated, puzzled. "What means the man? You swear you have had no other dreams?"

"Aye, I swear by the Symbol of Life and the Mount of the Wavering Flame, and by yourself, O Queen from the ancient days!"

Then I sighed and pretended to swoon, for I could think of nothing else to do. As I closed my eyes I saw her face, that had been red as dawn, turn pale as eve, for my words and all which might lie behind them had gone home. Moreover, she was in

doubt, for I could hear her fingering the handle of the dagger. Then she spoke aloud, words for my ears if they still were open.

"I am glad," she said, "that he dreamed no other dreams; since had he done so and babbled of them, it would have been ill-omened, and I do not wish that one who has travelled far to visit us should be hurled to the death-dogs for burial; one, moreover, who, although old and hideous, still has the air of a wise and silent man."

Now while I shivered at these unpleasant hints—though what the "death-dogs" in which people were buried might be, I could not conceive—to my intense joy I heard the foot of the Guardian on the stair; heard him, too, enter the room, and saw him bow before the lady.

"How go these sick men, niece*?" he said in his cold voice.

"They swoon, both of them," she answered.

"Indeed, is it so? I thought otherwise. I thought they woke."

"What have you heard, Shaman (i.e., wizard)?" she asked angrily.

"I? Oh! I heard the grating of a dagger in its sheath and the distant baying of the death-hounds."

"And what have you seen, Shaman," she asked again, "looking through the Gate you guard?"

"Strange sights, Khania, my niece. But—men awake from swoons."

"Aye," she answered. "So while this one sleeps, bear him to another chamber, for he needs change, and the lord yonder needs more space and untainted air."

The Guardian, whom she called "Shaman," or Magician, held a lamp in his hand, and by its light it was easy to see his face, which I watched out of the corner of my eye. I thought it wore a very strange expression—one, moreover, that alarmed me somewhat. From the beginning I had misdoubted me of this old man, whose cast of countenance was vindictive as it was able; now I was afraid of him.

"To which chamber, Khania?" he said with meaning.

"I think," she answered slowly, "to one that is healthful, where he will recover. The man has wisdom," she added as though in explanation; "moreover, having the word from the Mountain, to harm him would be dangerous. But why do you ask?"

* I found later that the Khania, Atene, was not Simbri's niece, but his great-niece, on the mother's side.—L. H. H.

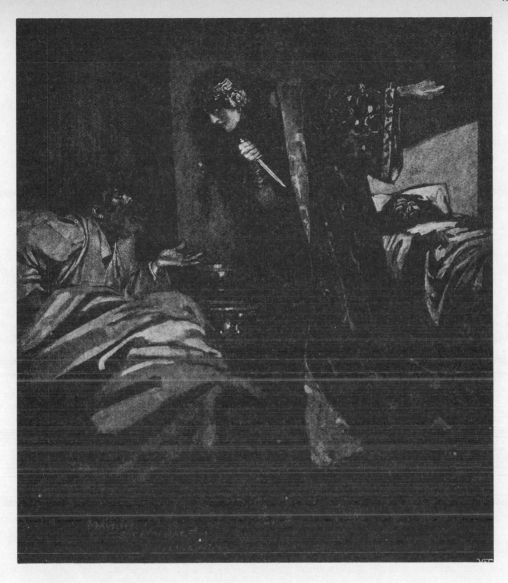

"'Man! have you dared——?'"

He shrugged his shoulders.

"I tell you I heard the death-hounds bay, that is all. Yes, with you I think that he has wisdom, and the bee which seeks honey should suck the flower—before it fades! Also, as you say, there are commands with which it is ill to trifle, even if we cannot guess their meaning."

Then going to the door, he blew upon his whistle, and instantly I heard the feet of his servants upon the stairs. He gave them an order, and gently enough they lifted the mattress on which I lay, and followed him down sundry passages and past some stairs into another chamber shaped like that we had left, but not so large, where they placed me upon a bed.

The Guardian watched me awhile to see that I did not wake. Next he stretched out his hand and felt my heart and pulse; an examination the results of which seemed to puzzle him, for he uttered a little exclamation and shook his head. After this he left the room, and I heard him bolt the door behind him. Then, being still very weak, I fell asleep in earnest.

When I awoke, it was broad daylight. My mind was clear, and I felt better than I had done for many a day, signs by which I knew that the fever had left me and that I was on the high road to recovery. Now I remembered all the events of the previous night and was able to weigh them carefully. This, to be sure, I did for many reasons— among them that I knew I had been, and still was, in great danger.

I had seen and heard too much, and this woman called Khania guessed that I had seen and heard. Indeed, had it not been for my hints about the Symbol of Life and the Mount of Flame, after I had disarmed her first rage by my artifice, I felt sure that she would have ordered the old Guardian or Shaman to do me to death in this way or the other; sure also that he would not have hesitated to obey her. I had been spared partly because for some unknown reason she was afraid to kill me, and partly that she might learn how much I knew, although the "death-hounds had bayed," whatever that might mean. Well, up to the present I was safe, and for the rest I must take my chance. Moreover, it was necessary to be cautious, and, if need were, to feign ignorance. So, dismissing the matter of my own fate from my mind, I fell to considering the scene which I had witnessed and what might be it purport.

Was our quest at an end? Was this woman Ayesha? Leo had so dreamed, but he was still delirious, therefore here was little on which to lean. What seemed more to the point was that she herself evidently appeared to think that there existed some tie between her and this sick man. Why had she embraced him? I was sure that she could be no wanton, nor indeed would any woman in- dulge for its own sake in such folly with a stranger who hung between life and death. What she had done was done because irre- sistible impulse, born of knowledge, or at least of memories, drove her on, though mayhap the knowledge was imperfect and the memories were undefined. Who save Ayesha could have known anything of Leo in the past? None who lived upon the earth to-day.

And yet, why not, if what Kou-en the abbot and tens of millions of his fellow- worshippers believed were true? If the souls of human beings were, in fact, strictly limited in number and became the tenants of an endless succession of physical bodies which they change from time to time as we change our worn-out garments, why should not others have known him? For instance, that daughter of the Pharaohs who "caused

him through love to break the vows that he had vowed" knew a certain Killikrates, a priest of "Isis whom the gods cherish and the demons obey"; even Amenartas, the mistress of magic.

Oh! now a light seemed to break upon me, a terrible light. What if Amenartas and this Khania, this woman with royalty stamped on every feature, should be the same? Would not that "magic of my own people that I have" of which she wrote upon the Sherd, enable her to pierce the darkness of the Past and recognise the man whom she had bewitched to love her, snatching him out of the very hand of the goddess? What if it were not Ayesha, but Amenartas re- incarnate, who ruled this hidden land and once more sought to make the man she loved break through his vows? If so, knowing the evil that must come, I shook even at its shadow. The truth must be learned, but how?

Whilst I wondered, the door opened, and the sardonic, inscrutable-old-faced man, whom this Khania had called Magician, and who called the Khania niece, entered and stood before me.

CHAPTER VII.

THE FIRST ORDEAL.

THE Shaman advanced to my side and asked me courteously how I fared.

I answered: "Better. Far better, O my host—but how are you named?"

"Simbri," he answered, "and, as I told you by the water, my title is Hereditary Guardian of the Gate. By profession I am the royal Physician in this land."

"Did you say physician or magician?" I asked carelessly, as though I had not caught the word. He gave me a curious look.

"I *said* physician, and it is well for you and your companion that I have some skill in my art. Otherwise I think perhaps you would not have been alive to-day, O my guest—but how are *you* named?"

"Holly," I said.

"O my guest Holly."

"Had it not been for the foresight that brought you and the lady Khania to the edge of yonder darksome river, certainly we should *not* have been alive, venerable Simbri, a foresight that seems to me to savour of magic in such a lonely place. That is why I thought you might have described your- self as a magician; though it is true that you may have been but fishing in those waters."

"Certainly I was fishing, stranger Holly—for men, and I caught two."

"Fishing by chance, host Simbri ? "

"Nay, by design, guest Holly. My trade of physician includes the study of future events, for I am the chief of the Shamans or Seers of this land, and having been warned of your coming quite recently, I awaited your arrival."

"Indeed, that is strange, most courteous also. So here physician and magician mean the same."

"You say it," he answered with a grave bow; "but tell me, if you will, how did you find your way to a land whither visitors do not wander ? "

"Oh ! " I answered, "perhaps we are but travellers, or perhaps we also have studied—medicine."

"I think that you must have studied it deeply, since otherwise you would not have lived to cross those mountains in search of—now, what did you seek ? Your companion, I think, spoke of a queen—yonder, on the banks of the torrent."

"Did he ? Did he, indeed ? Well, that is strange, since he seems to have found one; for surely that royal-looking lady, named Khania, who sprang into the stream and saved us, must be a queen."

"A queen she is, and a great one, for in our land Khania means queen; though how, friend Holly, a man who has lain senseless can have learned this I do not know. Nor do I know how you come to speak our language."

"That is simple, for the tongue you talk is very ancient, and as it chances in my own country it has been my lot to study and to teach it. It is Greek, but although it is still spoken in the world, how it reached these mountains I cannot say."

"I will tell you," he answered. "Many generations ago, a great conqueror born of the nation that spoke this tongue fought his way through the country to the south of us. He was driven back, but a general of his of another race advanced and crossed the mountains, and overcame the people of this land, bringing with him his master's language and his own worship. Here he established his dynasty, and here it remains, for being ringed in with deserts and with pathless mountain snows, we hold no converse with the outer world."

"Yes, I know something of that story; the conqueror was named Alexander, was he not ?" I asked.

"He was so named, and the name of the general was Rassen, a native of a country called Egypt, or so our records tell us. His descendants hold the throne to this day, and the Khania is of his blood."

"Was the goddess whom he worshipped called Isis ? "

"Nay," he answered, "she was called Hes."

"Which," I interrupted, "is but another title for Isis. Tell me, is her worship continued here ? I ask because it is now dead in Egypt, which was its home."

"There is a temple on the Mountain yonder," he replied indifferently, "and in it are priests and priestesses who practise some ancient cult. But the real god of this people now, as long before the day of Rassen their conqueror, is the fire that dwells in this same Mountain, which from time to time breaks out and slays them."

"And does the goddess dwell in the fire ?" I asked.

Again he searched my face with his cold eyes, then answered—

"Stranger Holly, I know nothing of any goddess. That Mountain is sacred, and to seek to learn its secrets is to die. Why do you ask such questions ? "

"Only because I am curious in the matter of old religions, and seeing the Symbol of Life upon yonder peak, came hither to study yours, of which indeed a tradition still remains among the learned."

"Then abandon that study, friend Holly, for the road to it runs through the jaws of the death-hounds and the spears of savages. Nor, indeed, is there anything to learn."

"And what, physician, are the death-hounds ? "

"Certain dogs to which, according to our ancient custom, all offenders against the law or the will of the Khan are cast to be torn to pieces."

"The will of the Khan ! Has this Khania of yours a husband, then ? "

"Aye," he answered, "her cousin, who was the ruler of half the land. Now they and the land are one. But you have talked enough; I am here to say that your food is ready," and he turned to leave the room.

"One more question, friend Simbri. How came I to this chamber, and where is my companion ? "

"You were borne hither in your sleep; and see, the change has bettered you. Do you remember nothing ? "

"Nothing, nothing at all," I answered earnestly. "But what of my friend ? "

"He also is better. The Khania Atene nurses him."

"Atene ?" I said. "That is an old Egyptian

name. It means the Disc of the Sun, and a woman who bore it thousands of years ago was famous for her beauty."

"Well, and is not my niece Atene beautiful ?"

"How can I tell, O uncle of the Khania," I answered wearily, "who have scarcely seen her ? "

Then he departed, and presently his yellow-faced, silent servants brought me food.

Later in the morning the door opened again, and through it, unattended, came the Khania Atene, who shut and bolted it behind her. This action did not reassure me ; still, rising in my bed, I saluted her as best I could, although at heart I was afraid. She seemed to read my doubts, for she said—

"Lie down, and have no fear. At present you will come by no harm from me. Now, tell me what is the man called Leo to you ? Your son ? Nay, it cannot be, since—forgive me—light is not born of darkness."

"I have always thought that it was so born, Khania. Yet you are right ; he is but my adopted son, and a man whom I love."

"Say, what seek you here ? " she asked.

"We seek, Khania, whatsoever Fate shall bring us on yonder Mountain, that which is crowned with flame."

Her face paled at the words, but she answered in a steady voice—

"Then there you will find nothing but doom, if, indeed, you do not find it out before you reach its slopes, which are guarded by savage men. Yonder is the College of Hes, and to violate its Sanctuary is death to any man, death in the ever-burning fire."

"And who rules this College, Khania—a priestess ? "

"Yes, a priestess, whose face I have never seen, for she is so old that she veils herself from curious eyes."

"Ah ! she veils herself, does she ? " I answered, as the blood went thrilling through my veins—I who remembered another who also was so old that she veiled herself from curious eyes. "Well, veiled or unveiled, we would visit her, trusting to find that we are welcome."

"That you shall not do," she said, "for it is unlawful, and I will not have your blood upon my hands."

"Which is the stronger," I asked of her, "you, Khania, or this priestess of the Mountain ? "

"I am the stronger, Holly, for so you are named, are you not ? Look you, at my need I can summon sixty thousand men in war, while she has naught but her priests and the fierce, untrained tribes."

"The sword is not the only power in the world," I answered. "Tell me, now, does this priestess ever visit the country of Kaloon ? "

"Never, never ; for by the ancient pact, made after the last great struggle long centuries ago between the College and the people of the Plain, it was decreed and sworn to that should she set her foot across the river, this means war to the end between us, and rule for the victor over both. Like-wise, save when unguarded they bear their dead to burial, or for some such high purpose, no Khan or Khania of Kaloon ascends the Mountain."

"Which, then, is the true master—the Khan of Kaloon or the head of the College of Hes ? " I asked again.

"In matters spiritual, the priestess of Hes, who is our Oracle and the voice of Heaven. In matters temporal, the Khan of Kaloon."

"The Khan. Ah ! you are married, lady, are you not ? "

"Aye," she answered, her face flushing. "And I will tell you what you soon must learn, if you have not learned it already : I am the wife of a madman, and he is—hateful to me."

"I *have* learned the last already, Khania."

She looked at me with her piercing eyes.

"What ! Did my uncle, the Shaman— he who is called Guardian—tell you ? Nay, you saw, as I knew you saw, and it would have been best to slay you for—oh ! what must you think of me ? "

I made no answer, for in truth I did not know what to think, also I feared lest rash admissions should be followed by swift vengeance.

"You must believe," she went on, "that I, who have ever hated men, that I—I swear that it is true—whose lips are purer than those mountain snows, I, the Khania of Kaloon, whom they name Heart-of-Ice, am but a shameless thing." And, covering her face with her hand, she moaned in the bitterness of her distress.

"Nay," I said, "there may be reasons— explanations, if it pleases you to give them."

"Wanderer, there are such reasons ; and since you know so much, you shall learn them also. Like that husband of mine, I have become mad. When first I saw the face of your companion, as I dragged· him from the river, madness entered me, and I—I——"

"Loved him," I suggested. "Well, such

"Opposite to me stood the Khania."

things have happened before to people who were not mad."

"Oh!" she went on, "it was more than love. I was possessed, and that night I knew not what I did. A Power drove me on, a Destiny compelled me; and to the end I am his, and his alone. Yes, I am his, and I swear that he shall be mine"; and with this wild declaration, dangerous enough under the conditions, she turned and fled the room.

She was gone, and after the struggle, for such it was, I sank back exhausted. How came it that this sudden passion had mastered her? Who and what was this Khania, I wondered again, and—this was more to the point—who and what would Leo believe her to be? If only I could be with him before he said words or did deeds impossible to recall!

*   *   *   *   *

Three days went by, during which time I saw no more of the Khania, who—or so I was informed by Simbri, the Shaman—had returned to her city to make ready for us, her guests. I begged him to allow me to rejoin Leo, but he answered politely, though with much firmness, that my foster-son did better without me. Now I grew suspicious, fearing lest some harm had come to Leo, though how to discover the truth I knew not. In my anxiety I tried to convey a note to him, written upon a leaf of a water-stained pocket-book, but the yellow-faced servant refused to touch it, and Simbri said drily that he would have naught to do with writings which he could not read. At length, on the third night I made up my mind that, whatever the risk, with leave or without it, I would try to find him.

By this time I could walk well and, indeed, was almost strong again. So about midnight, when the moon was up, for I had no other light, I crept from my bed, threw on my garments, and taking a knife, which was the only weapon I possessed, opened the door of my room and started.

Now, when I was carried from the rock-chamber where Leo and I had been together, I took note of the way. First, reckoning from my sleeping-place, there was a passage thirty paces long, for I had counted the footfalls of my bearers. Then came a turn to the left and ten more paces of passage, and lastly, near certain steps running to some place unknown, another sharp turn to the right which led to our old chamber.

Down the long passage I walked stealthily and, although it was pitch dark, found the turn to the left, and followed it till I came to the second sharp turn to the right, that of the gallery from which rose the stairs. I crept round it, only to retreat, hastily enough, as well I might, for at the door of Leo's room, which she was in the act of locking on the outside, as I could see by the light of the lamp that she held in her hand, stood the Khania herself.

My first thought was to fly back to my own chamber, but I abandoned it, feeling sure that I should be seen. Therefore I determined, if she discovered me, to face the matter out and say that I was trying to find Leo and to learn how he fared. So I crouched against the wall and waited with a beating heart. I heard her sweep down the passage, and—yes—begin to mount the stair.

Now, what should I do? To try to reach Leo was useless, for she had locked the door with the key she held. Go back to bed? No, I would follow her, and if we met would make the same excuse. Thus I might get some tidings, or perhaps — a dagger-thrust.

So round the corner and up the steps I went, noiselessly as a snake. They were many and winding, like those of a church tower, but at length I came to the head of them, where was a little landing, and opening from it a door. It was a very ancient door; the light streamed through cracks where its panels had rotted, and from the room beyond came the sound of voices, those of the Shaman Simbri and the Khania.

"Have you learned aught, my niece?" I heard him say, and also heard her answer—

"A little. A very little."

Then in my thirst for knowledge I grew bold, and stealing to the door, looked through one of the cracks in its wood. Opposite to me, in the full flood of light thrown by a hanging lamp, her hand resting on a table at which Simbri was seated, stood the Khania. Truly she was a beauteous sight, for she wore robes of royal purple, and on her brow a little coronet of gold, beneath which her curling hair streamed down her shapely neck and bosom. Seeing her, I guessed at once that she had arrayed herself thus for some secret end, enhancing her loveliness by every art and grace that is known to woman. Simbri was looking at her earnestly, with fear and doubt written on even his cold, impassive features.

"What passed between you, then?" he asked, peering at her.

"I questioned him closely as to the reason

of his coming to this land, and wrung from him the answer that it was to seek some beauteous woman—he would say no more. I asked him if she were more beauteous than I am, and he replied with courtesy—nothing else, I think—that it would be hard to say, but that she had been different. Then I said that, though it behoved me not to speak of such a matter, there was no lady in Kaloon whom men held to be so fair as I; moreover, that I was its ruler, and that I and no other had saved him from the water. Aye, and I added that my heart told me I was the woman whom he sought."

"Have done, niece," said Simbri impatiently. "I would not hear of the arts you used—well enough, doubtless. What then?"

"Then he said that it might be so, since he thought that this woman was born again, and studied me awhile, asking me if I had ever 'passed through fire.' To this I replied that the only fires I had passed were those of the spirit, and that I dwelt in them now. He said, 'Show me your hair,' and I placed a lock of it in his hand. Presently he let it fall, and from that satchel which he wears about his neck drew out another tress of hair—oh! Simbri, my uncle, the loveliest hair that ever eyes beheld, for it was soft as silk, and reached from my coronet to the ground! Moreover, no raven's wing in the sunshine ever shone as did that fragrant tress.

"'Yours is beautiful,' he said; 'but see, they are not the same.'

"'Mayhap,' I answered, 'since no woman ever wore such locks.'

"'You are right,' he replied, 'for she whom I seek was more than a woman.'

"And then—and then—though I tried him in many ways, he would say no more, so, feeling hate against this unknown rising in my heart, and fearing lest I should utter words that were best unsaid, I left him. Now I bid you search the books which are open to your wisdom and tell me of this woman whom he seeks, who she is and where she dwells. Oh! search them swiftly, that I may find her and—kill her, if I can."

"Aye, if you can," answered the Shaman, "and if she lives to kill. But say, where shall we begin our quest? Now, this letter from the Mountain that the head-priest Oros sent to your court a while ago?"—and he selected a parchment from a pile which lay upon the table, and looked at her.

"Read," she said. "I would hear it again." So he read—

"From the Hesea of the House of Fire to Atene, Khania of Kaloon.

"MY SISTER,—Warning has reached me that two strangers of a Western race journey to your land, seeking my Oracle, of which they would ask a question. On the first day of the next moon, I command that Simbri, your great-uncle, the wise Shaman, Guardian of the Gate, shall be at his post watching the river in the gulf at the foot of the ancient road, for by that steep path the strangers travel. Let him aid them in all things and bring them safely to the Mountain, knowing that in this matter I shall hold him and you to account. Myself I will not meet them, since to do so would be to break the pact between our powers, which says that the Hesea of the Sanctuary visits not the territory of Kaloon, save in war. Also their coming is otherwise appointed."

"It would seem," said Simbri, laying down the parchment, "that these are no chance wanderers, since Hes awaits them."

"Aye, they are no chance wanderers, since my heart awaited one of them also. Yet the Hesea cannot be that woman, for reasons which are known to you."

"There are many women on the Mountain," suggested the Shaman in a dry voice, "if, indeed, any woman has to do with this matter."

"I at least have to do with it, and he shall not go to the Mountain."

"Hes is powerful, my niece, and beneath these smooth words of hers lies a dreadful threat. I say that she is mighty from of old, and has servants in the earth and air who warned her of the coming of these men, and will warn her of what befalls them. I know it, who hate her, and to your royal house of Rassen it has been known for many a generation. Therefore thwart her not, lest ill befall us all, for she is a spirit and terrible. She says that it is appointed that they shall go——"

"And I say it is appointed that he shall not go. Let the other go if he desires."

"Atene, be plain: what will you with the man called Leo—that he should become your lover?" asked the Shaman.

She stared him straight in the eyes and answered boldly—

"Nay, I will that he should become my husband."

"First he must will it, too, who seems to have no mind that way. Also, how can a woman have two husbands?"

She laid her hand upon his shoulder and said—

"I have no husband. You know it well, Simbri. I charge you, by the close bond of blood between us, brew me another draught—— "

"That we may be bound yet closer in a bond of murder! Nay, Atene, I will not; already your sin lies heavy on my head. You are very fair; take the man in your own net, if you may, or let him be, which is better far."

"I cannot let him be. Would that I were able! I must love him as I must hate the other whom he loves, yet some power hardens his heart against me. Oh! great Shaman, you that peep and mutter, you who can read the future and the past, tell me what you have learned from your stars and divinations."

"Already I have sought through many a secret, toilsome hour and learned this, Atene," he answered. "You are right—the fate of yonder man is intertwined with yours; but between you and him there rises a mighty wall that my vision cannot pierce nor my familiars climb. Yet I am taught that in death you and he—aye, and I also—shall be very near together."

"Then come death!" she exclaimed with sullen pride, "for thence at least I'll pluck out my desire."

"Be not so sure," he answered, "for I think that the Power follows us even down this dark gulf of death. I think also that I feel the sleepless eyes of Hes watching our secret souls."

"Then blind them with the dust of illusions—as you can. To-morrow, also, saying nothing of their sex, send a messenger to the Mountain and tell the Hesea that two old strangers have arrived—mark you, *old*— but that they are very sick, that their limbs were broken in the river, and that when they have healed again, I will send them to ask the question of her Oracle—that is, some three moons hence. Perchance she may believe you and be content to wait; or if she does not, at least no more words. I must sleep, or my brain will burst. Give me that medicine which brings dreamless rest, for never did I need it more, who also feel eyes upon me," and she glanced towards the door.

Then I left, and not too soon, for as I crept down the darksome passage, I heard it open behind me.

CHAPTER VIII.

THE DEATH-HOUNDS.

It may have been ten o'clock on the following morning, or a little past it, when the Shaman Simbri came into my room and asked me how I had slept.

"Like a log," I answered, "like a log. A drugged man could not have rested more soundly."

"Indeed, friend Holly, and yet you look fatigued."

"My dreams troubled me somewhat," I answered. "I suffer from such things. But surely, from your face, friend Simbri, you cannot have slept at all, for never yet have I seen you wear so weary an air."

"I am weary," he said with a sigh. "Last night I spent on my business—watching at the Gates."

"What gates?" I asked. "Those by which we entered this kingdom; for, if so, I would rather watch than travel them."

"The Gates of the Past and of the Future. Yes, those by which you entered, if you will; for did you not travel out of a wondrous Past towards a Future that you cannot guess?"

"But both of which interest you," I suggested.

"Perhaps," he answered, then added: "I come to tell you that within an hour you are to start for the city, whither the Khania has but now gone on to make ready for you."

"Yes; only you told me that she had gone some days ago. Well, I am sound again and prepared to march. But say, how is my foster-son?"

"He mends, he mends. But you shall see him for yourself. It is the Khania's will. Here come the slaves bearing your robes, and with them I leave you."

So with their assistance I dressed myself, first in good, clean under-linen, then in wide woollen trousers and vest, and lastly in a fur-lined camel-hair robe dyed black that was very comfortable to wear, and in appearance not unlike a long overcoat. A flat cap of the same material and a pair of boots made of untanned hide completed my attire.

Scarcely was I ready when the yellow-faced servants, with many bows, took me by the hand and led me down the passages and stairs of the Gatehouse to its door. Here, to my great joy, I found Leo, looking pale and troubled, but otherwise as well as I could expect after his sickness. He was attired like myself, save that his garments were of a finer quality, and the overcoat was white, with a hood to it, added, I suppose, to protect the wound in his head from cold and the sun. This white dress I thought became him very well, also about it there was nothing grotesque or even remarkable. He sprang to me and seized my hand, asking how I

"Slaves took the leading ponies by the bridle."

fared and where I had been hidden away, a greeting of which, as I could see, the warmth was not lost upon Simbri, who stood by.

I answered, well enough now that we were together again, and for the rest I would tell him later.

Then they brought us palanquins, carried, each of them, by two ponies, one of which was harnessed ahead, and the other behind between long, shaft-like poles. In these we seated ourselves, and at a sign from Simbri, slaves took the leading ponies by the bridle, and we started, leaving behind us that grim old Gatehouse through which we were the first strangers to pass for many a generation.

For a mile or more our road ran down a winding, rocky gorge, till suddenly it took a turn, and the country of Kaloon lay stretched before us. At our feet was a river, probably the same with which we had made acquaint-ance in the gulf, where, fed by the mountain snows, it had its source. Here it flowed rapidly, but on the vast, alluvial lands be-neath became a broad and gentle stream that wound its way through the limitless plains till it was lost in the blue of the distance.

To the north, however, this smooth, monotonous expanse was broken by that Mountain which had guided us from afar, the House of Fire. It was a great distance from us, more than a hundred miles, I should say, yet even so a most majestic sight in that clear air. Many leagues from the base of its peak the ground began to rise in brown and rugged hillocks, from which sprang the holy Mountain itself, a white and dazzling point that soared full twenty thousand feet into the heavens.

Yes, and there upon the nether lip of its crater stood the gigantic pillar, surmounted by a yet more gigantic loop of virgin rock, whereof the blackness stood out grimly against the blue of the sky beyond and the blinding snow beneath.

We gazed at it with awe, as well we might, this beacon of our hopes that, for aught we knew, might also prove their monument, feeling even then that yonder our fate would declare itself. I noted further that all those with us did it reverence by bowing their heads as they caught sight of the peak, and by laying the first finger of the right hand across the first finger of the left, a gesture, as we afterwards discovered, designed to avert its evil influence. Yes, even Simbri bowed, a yielding to inherited superstition of which I should scarcely have suspected him.

"Have you ever journeyed to that Moun-tain?" asked Leo of him.

Simbri shook his head and answered evasively.

"The people of the Plain do not set foot upon the Mountain. Among its slopes, be-yond the river which washes them, live hordes of brave and most savage men, with whom we are oftentimes at war; for when they are hungry, they raid our cattle and our crops. Moreover, there, when the Mountain labours, run red streams of molten rock, and now and again hot ashes fall that slay the traveller."

"Do the ashes ever fall in your country?" asked Leo.

"They have been known to do so when the Spirit of the Mountain is angry, and that is why we fear her."

"Who is this Spirit?" said Leo eagerly.

"I do not know, lord," he answered with impatience. "Can men see a spirit?"

"*You* look as though you might, and had, not so long ago," replied Leo, fixing his gaze on the old man's waxen face and uneasy eyes. For now their horny calm was gone from the eyes of Simbri, which seemed as though they had beheld some sight that haunted him.

"You do me too much honour, lord," he replied. "My skill and vision do not reach so far. But see, here is the landing-stage, where boats await us, for the rest of our journey is by water."

These boats proved to be roomy and comfortable, having flat bows and sterns, since, although sometimes a sail was hoisted, they were designed for towing, not to be rowed with oars. Leo and I entered the largest of them, and to our joy were left alone except for the steersman.

Behind us was another boat, in which were attendants and slaves, and some men who looked like soldiers, for they carried bows and swords. Now the ponies were taken from the palanquins, which were packed away, and ropes of green hide, fastened to iron rings in the prows of the boats, were fixed to the towing-tackle with which the animals had been reharnessed. Then we started, the ponies, two arranged tandem fashion to each punt, trotting along a well-made towing-path that was furnished with wooden bridges wherever canals or tributary streams entered the main river.

"Thank Heaven," said Leo, "we are together again at last! Do you remember, Horace, that when we entered the land of Kôr, it was thus, in a boat? The tale repeats itself."

"I can quite believe it," I answered. "I can believe anything. Leo, I say that we are but gnats meshed in a web, and yonder

Khania is the spider, and Simbri the Shaman guards the net. But tell me all you remember of what has happened to you; and be quick, for I do not know how long they may leave us alone."

"Well," he said, "of course I remember our arrival at that Gate after the lady and the old man had pulled us out of the river; and, Horace, talking of spiders reminds me of hanging at the end of that string of yak's hide. Not that I need much reminding, for I am not likely to forget it. Do you know I cut the rope because I felt that I was going mad, and wished to die sane? What happened to you? Did you slip?"

"No; I jumped after you. It seemed best to end together, so that we might begin again together."

"Brave old Horace!" he said affectionately, the tears starting to his grey eyes.

"Well, never mind all that," I broke in. "You see you were right when you said that we should get through, and we have. Now for your tale."

"It is interesting, but not very long," he answered, colouring. "I went to sleep, and when I woke it was to find a beautiful woman leaning over me; and, Horace—at first I thought that it was—you know who, and that she kissed me; but perhaps it was all a dream."

"It was no dream," I answered. "I saw it."

"I am sorry to hear it—very sorry. At any rate, there was the beautiful woman—the Khania—for I saw her plenty of times afterwards, and talked to her in my best modern Greek—by the way, Ayesha knew the old Greek; that's curious."

"She knew several of the ancient tongues, and so did other people. Go on."

"Well, she nursed me very kindly, but, so far as I know, until last night there was nothing more affectionate, and I had sense enough to refuse to talk about our somewhat eventful past. I pretended not to understand, said that we were explorers, etc., and kept asking her where you were, for I forgot to say I found that you had gone. I think that she grew rather angry with me, for she wanted to know something, and, as you can guess, I wanted to know a good deal. But I could get nothing out of her except that she was the Khania—a person in authority. There was no doubt about that, for when one of those slaves or servants came in and interrupted her while she was trying to draw the facts out of me, she called to some of her people to throw him out of the window, and

he only saved himself by going down the stairs very quickly.

"Well, I could make nothing of her, and she could make little of me, though why she should be so tenderly interested in a stranger I don't know—unless, unless—oh! who is she, Horace?"

"If you will go on, I will tell you what I think presently. One tale at a time."

"Very good. I got quite well and strong, comparatively speaking, till the climax last night, which upset me again. After that old prophet, Simbri, had brought me my supper, just as I was thinking of going to sleep, the Khania came in alone, dressed like a queen. I can tell you she looked really royal, like a princess in a fairy book, with a crown on, and her chestnut black hair flowing round her.

"Well, Horace, then she began to make love to me in a refined sort of way, or so I thought, looked at me and sighed, saying that we had known each other in the past—very well indeed, I gathered—and implying that she wished to continue our friendship. I fenced with her as best I could; but a man feels fairly helpless lying on his back with a very handsome and very imperial-looking lady standing over him and paying him compliments.

"The end of it was that, driven to it by her questions, and to stop that sort of thing, I told her that I was looking for my wife, whom I had lost; for, after all, Ayesha is my wife, Horace. She smiled and suggested that I need not look far; in short, that the lost wife was already found in herself, who had come to save me from death in the river. Indeed, she spoke with such conviction that I grew sure that she was not merely amusing herself, and felt very much inclined to believe her; for, after all, Ayesha may be changed now.

"Then while I was at my wits' end I remembered the lock of hair—all that remains to us of *her*," and Leo touched his breast. "I drew it out and compared it with the Khania's, and at the sight of it she became quite different—jealous, I suppose, for it is longer than hers, and not in the least like.

"Horace, I tell you that the touch of that lock of hair—for she did touch it—appeared to act upon her nature like nitric acid upon sham gold. It turned it black; all the bad in her came out. In her anger her voice sounded coarse; yes, she grew almost vulgar—and, as you know, when Ayesha was in a rage, she might be wicked as we understand it, and was certainly terrible, but she was never either coarse or vulgar, any more than lightning is.

"Well, from that moment I was sure that, whoever this Khania may be, she has nothing to do with Ayesha; they are so different that they never could have been the same—like the hair. So I lay quiet and let her talk, and coax, and threaten on, until at length she drew herself up and marched from the room, and I heard her lock the door behind her. That's all I have to tell you; and quite enough, too, for I don't think that the Khania has done with me, and, to say the truth, I am afraid of her."

"Yes," I said, "quite enough. Now sit still, and don't start or talk loud, for that steersman is probably a spy, and I can feel old Simbri's eyes fixed upon our backs. Don't interrupt, either, for our time alone may be short."

Then I set to work and told him everything I knew, while he listened in blank astonishment.

"Great Heavens! what a tale!" he exclaimed as I finished. "Now, who is this Hesea who sent the letter from the Mountain? And who, who is the Khania?"

"Who does your instinct tell you that she is, Leo?"

"Amenartas?" he whispered doubtfully. "The woman who wrote the *Sherd*, whom Ayesha said was the Egyptian princess—my wife two thousand years ago? Amenartas re-born?"

I nodded. "I think so. Why not? As I have told you again and again, I have always been certain of one thing—that if we were allowed to see the next act of the piece, we should find Amenartas—or, rather, the spirit of Amenartas—playing a leading part in it. You will remember I wrote as much in that record.

"If the old Buddhist monk Kou-en could remember *his* past, as many thousands of them swear that they do, and be sure of his identity continued from that past, why should not this woman, with so much at stake, helped as she is by the wizardry of the Shaman, her uncle, faintly remember hers?

"At any rate, Leo, why should she not still be sufficiently under its influence to cause her, without any fault or seeking of her own, to fall madly in love at first sight with a man whom, after all, she has always loved?"

"The argument seems sound enough, Horace; and if so, I am sorry for the Khania, who hasn't much choice in the matter—been forced into it, so to speak."

"Yes, but meanwhile your foot is in a trap again. Guard yourself, Leo, guard yourself. I believe that this is a trial sent to you, and doubtless there will be more to follow. But I believe also that it would be better for you to die than to make any mistake."

"I know it well," he answered; "and you need not be afraid. Whatever this Khania may have been to me in the past—if she was anything at all—that story is done with. I seek Ayesha, and Ayesha alone, and Venus herself shall not tempt me from her."

Then we began to speak with hope and fear of that mysterious Hesea who had sent the letter from the Mountain, commanding the Shaman Simbri to meet us; the priestess or spirit whom he declared was "mighty from of old" and had "servants in the earth and air."

Presently the prow of our barge bumped against the bank of the river; and looking round, I saw that Simbri had left the boat in which he sat and was preparing to enter ours. This he did, and, placing himself gravely on a seat in front of us, explained that nightfall was coming on, and he wished to give us his company and protection through the dark.

"And to see that we do not give him the slip in it," muttered Leo.

Then the drivers whipped up their ponies, and we went on again.

"Look behind you," said Simbri presently, "and you will see the city where you will sleep to-night."

We turned ourselves, and there, about ten miles away, perceived a flat-roofed town of considerable, though not of very great, size. Its position was good, for it was set upon a large island that stood a hundred feet or more above the level of the plain, the river dividing into two branches at the foot of it, and, as we discovered afterwards, uniting again beyond.

The vast mound upon which this city was built had the appearance of being artificial, but very possibly the soil whereof it was formed had been washed up in past ages during times of flood, so that from a mudbank in the centre of the broad river it grew by degrees to its present proportions. With the exception of a columned and towered edifice that crowned the city and seemed to be encircled by gardens, we could see no great buildings in the place.

"How is the city named?" asked Leo of Simbri.

"Kaloon," he answered, "as was all this land even when my forefathers, the conquerors,

"As he passed, he turned his face . . . it was that of a madman."

marched across the mountains and took it, more than two thousand years ago. They kept the ancient title, but the territory of the Mountain they called Hes, because they said that the loop upon yonder peak was the symbol of a goddess of this name whom their general worshipped."

"Priestesses still live there, do they not?" said Leo.

"Yes, and priests also. The College of them was established by the conquerors, who subdued all the land. Or, rather, it took the place of another College of those who fashioned the Sanctuary and the Temple whose God was the fire in the Mountain, as it is that of the people of Kaloon to-day."

"Then who is worshipped there now?"

"The goddess Hes, it is said; but we know little of the matter, for between us and the Mountain folk there has been enmity for ages. They kill us and we kill them, for they are jealous of their shrine, which none may visit save by permission to consult the Oracle and to make prayer or offering in times of calamity, when a Khan dies, or the waters of the river sink and the crops fail, or when ashes fall and earthquakes shake the land, or great sickness comes. Otherwise, unless they attack us, we leave them alone; for though every man is trained to arms, and can fight if need be, we are a peaceful folk, who cultivate the soil from generation to generation, and thus grow rich. Look round you. Is it not a scene of peace?"

We stood up in the boat and gazed about us at the pastoral prospect. Everywhere appeared herds of cattle feeding upon meadow-lands, or troops of mules and horses, or square fields sown with corn and outlined with trees. Village folk also, clad in long, grey gowns, were labouring on the land, or, their day's toil finished, driving their beasts homewards along roads built upon the banks of the irrigation-dykes, towards the hamlets that were placed on rising knolls amidst tall groves of trees.

In its sharp contrast with the arid deserts and fearful mountains amongst which we had wandered for so many years, this country struck us as most charming, and, indeed, seen by the red light of the sinking sun on that spring day, even as beautiful with the same kind of beauty which is to be found in Holland. One could understand, too, that these landowners and peasant-farmers would by choice be men of peace, and what a temptation their wealth must offer to the hungry, half-savage tribes of the mountains.

Also it was easy to guess when the sur-

vivors of Alexander's legions under their Egyptian general burst through the iron band of snow-clad hills and saw this sweet country, with its homes, its herds, and its ripening grain, that they must have cried with one voice: "We will march and fight and toil no more. Here we will sit us down to live and die." Thus doubtless they did, taking them wives from among the women of the people of the land which they had conquered —perhaps after a single battle.

Now, as the light faded, the wreaths of smoke which hung over the distant Fire Mountain began to glow luridly. Redder and more angry did they become while the darkness gathered, till at length they seemed to be charged with pulsing sheets of flame propelled from the womb of the volcano, which threw piercing beams of light through the eye of the giant loop that crowned its brow. Far, far fled those beams, making a bright path across the land, and striking the white crests of the bordering wall of mountains. High in the air ran that path, over the dim roofs of the city of Kaloon, over the mountains, and doubtless—though there we could not follow them—across the desert to that high eminence on its farther side where we had lain bathed in their radiance. It was a wondrous and most impressive sight, one, too, that filled our companions with fear, for the steersmen in our boats and the drivers on the towing-path groaned aloud and began to utter prayers.

"What do they say?" asked Leo of Simbri.

"They say, lord, that the Spirit of the Mountain is angry, and pray her not to destroy them."

"Then does that light not always shine thus?" he asked again.

"Nay, but seldom. Once about three months ago, and now to-night, but before that not for years. Let us pray that it portends no evil to the land and its inhabitants."

For some minutes this fearsome illumination continued, then it ceased as suddenly as it had begun, and there remained of it only the dull glow above the crest of the peak.

Presently the moon rose, a white, shining ball, and by its rays we perceived that we drew near to the city. But there was still something left for us to see before we reached its shelter. While we sat quietly in the boat— for the silence was broken only by the lapping of the still waters against its sides and the occasional splash of the slackened tow-line upon their surface—we heard a distant sound as of a hunt in full cry.

Nearer and nearer it came, its volume swelling every moment, till it was quite close at last. Now echoing from the trodden earth of the towing-path—not that on which our ponies travelled, but the other on the west bank of the river—was heard the beat of the hoofs of a horse galloping furiously. Presently it appeared, a fine, white animal, on the back of which sat a man. It passed us like a flash; but as he went by, the man lifted himself and turned his head, so that we saw his face in the moonlight; saw also the agony of fear that was written on it and in his eyes.

He had come out of the darkness. He was gone into the darkness, but after him swelled that awful music. Look! a dog appeared, a huge red dog, that dropped his foaming muzzle to the ground as it galloped, then lifted it and uttered a deep-throated, bell-like bay. Others followed, and yet others: in all there must have been a hundred of them, every one baying as it took the scent.

"*The death-hounds!*" I muttered, clasping Leo by the arm.

"Yes," he answered, "they are running that poor devil. Here comes the huntsman."

As he spoke there appeared a second figure, splendidly mounted, a cloak streaming from his shoulders, and in his hand a long whip, which he waved. He was big but loosely jointed; and as he passed, he turned his face also, and we saw that it was that of a madman. There could be no doubt of it; insanity blazed in those hollow eyes and rang in that savage, screeching laugh.

"The Khan! The Khan!" said Simbri, bowing, and I could see that he was afraid.

Now he, too, was gone, and after him came his guards. I counted eight of them, all carrying whips, with which they flogged their horses.

"What does this mean, friend Simbri?" I asked, as the sounds grew faint in the distance.

"It means, friend Holly," he answered, "that the Khan does justice in his own fashion—hunting to death one that has angered him."

"What, then, is his crime? And who is that poor man?"

"He is a great lord of this land, one of the royal kinsmen, and the crime for which he has been condemned is that he told the Khania he loved her, and offered to make war upon her husband and kill him, if she would promise herself to him in marriage. But she hated the man, as she hates all men, and brought the matter before the Khan. That is all the story."

"Happy is that prince who has so virtuous a wife!" I could not help saying unctuously, but with meaning, and the old wretch of a Shaman turned his head at my words and began to stroke his white beard.

It was but a little while afterwards that once more we heard the baying of the death-hounds. Yes, they were heading straight for us, this time across country. Again the white horse and its rider appeared, utterly exhausted, both of them, for the poor beast could scarcely struggle on to the towing-path. As it gained it, a great red hound with a black ear gripped its flank, and at the touch of the fangs it screamed aloud in terror as only a horse can. The rider sprang from its back, and, to our horror, ran to the river's edge, thinking evidently to take refuge in our boat. But before ever he reached the water the devilish brutes were upon him.

What followed I will not describe, but never shall I forget the scene of those two heaps of worrying wolves, and of the maniac Khan, who yelled in his fiendish joy and cheered on his death-hounds to finish their red work.

AYESHA

THE RETURN OF "SHE."

By H. RIDER HAGGARD.

SYNOPSIS OF FOREGOING CHAPTERS.—The return of "She-Who-Must-Be-Obeyed" is recorded by Ludwig Horace Holly, the friend of that Leo Vincey whom Ayesha the beautiful loved in the awful tombs of Kôr. When the record begins, the two men are living in an old house remote upon the seashore of Cumberland, where they have been slowly recovering from the horror of the passing of Ayesha in the flames—a doom that seemed one of complete extinction, yet was charged with the strange last words: "I die not. I shall come again and shall once more be beautiful. I swear it—it is true." On a sullen August night, Leo is thrilled by a vision of Ayesha in all her former loveliness. She beckons him, and in a vision his spirit follows her into a realm of snowy peaks far beyond the furthest borders of Thibet. A sign in the clouds at dawn is repeated from this vision to both Leo and Holly, and together they start for Central Asia. Sixteen years of toil, struggle, and strange adventure pass, and they are still searching for "a mountain peak shaped like the Symbol of Life." After many wanderings they find themselves in a country where no European has ever set foot, on one of the spurs of the vast Cherga mountains, far eastward from Turkestan. Sheltered awhile in a Buddhist monastery, they hear of the recent visit of a stranger who has told the Lamas that his countryfolk, "dwelling beyond the Far Mountains," worship a priestess called Hes, or the Hesea, and upon persuasion the abbot of the monastery tells them that in a former incarnation he himself has seen the great priestess, who was "all loveliness." A perilous ascent into the unexplored mountain fastness leads them to the revelation of "the *crux ansata*, the Symbol of Life itself." The symbol vanishes, the fire sinks, but they are sure that as it was sent of old to show them a path of escape from the Place of Death, so now it has been sent again in greeting to point out the path to the Place of Life where Ayesha dwells. A further ascent into the mountains reveals their Promised Land, with the symbol of their vision, an enormous pillar of rock, whereof the top was formed to the shape of a loop. Peril by avalanche and glacier intervenes, but brings them slowly nearer to their hopes. Rescued from drowning by a beautiful woman and an aged man, they are conducted through "The Gate" into the kingdom and city of Kaloon. Their saviours, they learn, are the Khania or Queen of Kaloon, and a venerable physician of magical powers. Is this woman Ayesha? No; they conjecture her rather to be Amenartas, who wrote the "sherd" of the former chronicle. She falls in love with Leo, and he and Holly learn that her husband, the Khan, is a madman, and see him chase to a hideous death at the fangs of his hounds a great lord of the land who has dared to make love to her. Simbri, the magician, and Atene, the Khania, have already received a solemn charge from the Hesea of the "College" in the Mountain of Fire to receive two strangers at the Gate, the message concluding: "Bring them safely to the Mountain, knowing that in this matter I shall hold him and you to account. Myself I will not meet them, since to do so would be to break the pact between our powers, which says that the Hesea of the Sanctuary visits not the territory of Kaloon, save in war. Also their coming is otherwise appointed."

CHAPTER IX.

THE COURT OF KALOON.

ORRIFIED, sick at heart, we continued our journey. No wonder that the Khania hated this mad despot. And this woman was in love with Leo ; and this lunatic Khan, her husband, was a victim to jealousy, which he avenged after the very unpleasant fashion that we had witnessed! Truly an agreeable prospect for all of us! Yet, I could not help reflecting, as an object lesson that horrid scene had its advantages.

Now we reached the place where the river forked at the end of the island, and disembarked upon a quay. Here a guard of men, commanded by some household officer,

was waiting to receive us. They led us through a gate in the high wall—for the town was fortified—up a narrow, stone-paved street which ran between houses apparently of the usual Central Asian type, and, so far as I could judge by moonlight, with no pretensions to architectural beauty, and not large in size.

Clearly our arrival was expected and excited interest, for people were gathered in knots about the street to watch us pass ; also at the windows of the houses, and even on their flat roofs. At the top of the long street came a sort of market-place, crossing which, accompanied by a curious crowd who made remarks about us that we could not understand, we reached a gate in an inner wall. Here we were challenged, but at a word from Simbri it opened, and we passed through to find ourselves in gardens. Following a road or drive, we came to a large, rambling house or palace, surmounted by high towers and very solidly built of stone in a heavy bastard Egyptian style.

Beyond its doorway we found ourselves in a courtyard surrounded by a kind of verandah from which short passages led to different rooms. Down one of these passages we were conducted by the officer to an apartment—or, rather, a suite—consisting of a sitting- and two bed-chambers, which were panelled, richly furnished in rather barbaric fashion, and well lighted with primitive oil-lamps.

Here Simbri left us, saying that the officer would wait in the outer room to conduct us to the dining-hall as soon as we were ready. Then we entered the bed-chambers, where we found servants, or slaves, quiet-mannered, obsequious men. These valets changed our footgear, and taking off our heavy travelling robes, replaced them with others fashioned like civilised frock-coats, but made of some white material and trimmed with a beautiful ermine fur.

Having dressed us in these, they bowed to show that our toilet was finished, and led us to the large outer room where the officer awaited us. He conducted us through several other rooms, all of them spacious and apparently unoccupied, to a great hall lit with many lamps, and warmed—for the nights were still cold—with large peat fires. The roof of this hall was flat, and supported by thick, stone columns with carved capitals, and its walls were hung with worked tapestries that gave it an air of considerable comfort.

At the head of the hall on a *daïs* stood a long, narrow table, spread with a cloth and set with platters and cups of silver. Here we waited till butlers with wands appeared through some curtains, which they drew. Then came a man beating a silver gong, and after him a dozen or more courtiers, all dressed in white robes like ourselves, followed by perhaps as many ladies, some of them young and good-looking, and for the most part of a fair type, with well cut features, though others were rather yellow-skinned. They bowed to us, and we to them.

Then there was a pause while we studied one another, till a trumpet blew, and, heralded by footmen in a kind of yellow livery, two figures were seen advancing down the passage beyond the curtains, preceded by the Shaman Simbri and followed by other officers. They were the Khan and the Khania of Kaloon.

No one looking at this Khan as he entered his dining-hall clad in festal white attire would have imagined him to be the same raving human brute whom we had just seen urging on his devilish hounds to tear a fellow-creature and a helpless horse to fragments and devour them. Now he seemed a heavy, loutish man, very strongly built, and not ill-looking, but with shifty eyes, evidently a person of dulled intellect, whom one would have thought incapable of keen emotions of any kind. The Khania need not be described. She was as she had been in the chambers of the Gate, only more weary-looking; indeed, her eyes had a haunted air, and it was easy to see that the events of the previous night had left their mark upon her mind. At the sight of us she flushed a little, then beckoned to us to advance, and said to her husband—

"My lord, these are the strangers of whom I have told you."

His dull eyes fell upon me first, and my appearance seemed to amuse him vaguely; at any rate, he laughed rudely, saying in barbarous Greek mixed with words from the local *patois*—

"What a curious old animal! I have never seen you before, have I?"

"No, great Khan," I answered; "but I have seen you out hunting this night. Did you have good sport?"

Instantly he became wide awake and answered, rubbing his hands—

"Excellent! He gave us a fine run; but my little dogs caught him at last, and then——" and he snapped his powerful jaws together.

"Cease your brutal talk!" broke in his wife fiercely, and he slunk away from her, and in so doing stumbled against Leo, who was waiting to be presented to him.

The sight of this great, golden-bearded man seemed to astonish him, for he stared at him, then asked—

"Are you the Khania's other friend whom she went to see in the mountains of the Gate? Then I could not understand why she took so much trouble, but now I do. Well, be careful, or I shall have to hunt you also."

Now Leo grew angry and was about to reply, but I laid my hand upon his arm and said in English—

"Don't answer; the man is mad."

"Bad, you mean," grumbled Leo; "and if he tries to set his cursed dogs on me, I will break his neck!"

Then the Khania motioned to Leo to take a seat beside her, placing me upon her other hand, between herself and her uncle, the Guardian, while the Khan shuffled to a chair a little way down the table, where he called two of the prettiest ladies to keep him company.

Such was our introduction to the Court of Kaloon. As for the meal that followed, it

"We disembarked upon a quay."

was very plentiful, but coarse, consisting for the most part of fish, mutton, and sweetmeats, all of them presented upon huge silver platters. Also much strong drink was served, a kind of spirit distilled from grain, of which nearly all present drank more than was good for them. After a few words to me about our journey, the Khania turned to Leo and talked to him for the rest of the evening, while I devoted myself to the old Shaman Simbri.

Put briefly, the substance of what I learned from him then and afterwards was as follows—

Trade was unknown to the people of Kaloon, for the reason that all communication with the south had been cut off for ages, the bridges that once existed over the chasm having been allowed to rot away. Their land, which was very large and densely inhabited, was ringed round with unclimbable mountains, except to the north, where stood the great Fire Peak. The slopes of this Peak, and an unvisited expanse of country behind that ran up to the confines of a desert, were the home of ferocious mountain tribes, untamable highlanders, who killed every stranger they caught. Consequently, although the precious and other metals were mined to a certain extent and manufactured into articles of use and ornament, money did not exist among the peoples either of the Plain or of the Mountain, all business being transacted on the principle of barter, and even the revenue collected in kind.

Amongst the tens of thousands of the aborigines of Kaloon dwelt a mere handful of a ruling class, who were said to be—and probably were—descended from the conquerors that appeared in the time of Alexander. Their blood, however, was now much mixed with that of the first inhabitants, who, to judge from their appearance and the yellow hue of their descendants, must have belonged to some branch of the great Tartar race. The government, if so it could be called, was, on the whole, of a mild though of a very despotic nature, and vested in an hereditary Khan or Khania, according as a man or a woman might be in the most direct descent.

Of religions there were two—that of the people, who worshipped the Spirit of the Fire Mountain, and that of the rulers, who believed in magic, ghosts, and divinations. Even this shadow of a religion, if so it can be called, was dying out, like its followers; for, generation by generation, the white lords grew less in number or became absorbed in the bulk of the people.

Still their rule was tolerated. I asked Simbri why, seeing that they were so few. He shrugged his shoulders and answered, because it suited the country of which the natives had no ambition. Moreover, the present Khania, our hostess, was the last of the direct line of rulers, her husband and cousin having less of the blood royal in his veins, and as such the people were attached to her.

Also, as is commonly the case with bold and beautiful women, she was popular among them, especially as she was just and very liberal to the poor. These were many, as the country was over-populated, which accounted for its wonderful state of cultivation. Lastly, they trusted to her skill and courage to defend them from the continual attacks of the Mountain tribes who raided their crops and herds. Their one grievance against her was that she had no child to whom the khanship could descend; which meant that after her death, as had happened after that of her father, there would be struggles for the succession.

"Indeed," added Simbri with meaning, and glancing at Leo out of the corners of his eyes, "the folk say openly that it would be a good thing if the Khan, who oppresses them and whom they hate, should die, so that the Khania might take another husband while she is still young. Although he is mad, he knows this, and that is why he is so jealous of any lord who looks at her, as, friend Holly, you saw to-night. For should such a one gain her favour, Rassen thinks that it would mean his death."

"Also he may be attached to his wife," I suggested, speaking in a whisper.

"Perhaps so," answered Simbri; "but if so, she loves not him, nor any of these men," and he glanced round the hall.

Certainly they did not look lovable, for by this time most of them were half drunk, while even the women seemed to have taken as much as was good for them. The Khan himself presented a sorry spectacle; for he was leaning back in his chair, shouting something about his hunting, in a thick voice. The arm of one of his pretty companions was round his neck, while the other gave him to drink from a gold cup, some of the contents of which had been spilt down his white robe.

Just then Atene looked round and saw him, and an expression of hatred and contempt gathered on her beautiful face.

"See," I heard her say to Leo, "see the companion of my days, and learn what it is to be Khania of Kaloon."

"Then why do you not cleanse your Court?" he asked.

"Because, lord, if I did so, there would be no Court left. Swine will to their mire, and these men and women, who live in idleness upon the toil of the humble folk, will to their liquor and vile luxury. Well, the end is near, for it is killing them, and their children are but few; weakly also, for the ancient blood grows thin and stale. But you are weary and would rest. To-morrow we will ride together," and calling to an officer, she bade him conduct us to our rooms.

So we rose and, accompanied by Simbri, bowed to her and went, she standing and gazing after us, a royal and pathetic figure in the midst of all that dissolute revelry. The Khan rose also, and in his cunning fashion understood something of the meaning of it all.

"You think us gay!" he shouted. "And why should we not be who do not know how long we have to live? But you yellow-haired fellow, you must not let Atene look at you like that. I tell you she is my wife; and if you do, I shall certainly have to hunt you."

At this drunken sally the courtiers roared with laughter; but taking Leo by the arm, Simbri hurried him from the hall.

"Friend," said Leo, when we were outside, "it seems to me that this Khan of yours threatens my life."

"Have no fear, lord," answered the Guardian; "so long as the Khania does not threaten it, you are safe. She is the real ruler of this land, and I stand next to her."

"Then, I pray you, keep me out of the way of that drunken man; for, look you, if I am attacked, I defend myself."

"And who can blame you?" Simbri replied, with one of his slow, mysterious smiles.

Then we parted, and having placed both our beds in one chamber, slept soundly enough, for we were very tired, till we were awakened in the morning by the baying of those horrible death-hounds, being fed, I suppose, in a place near by.

* * * *

Now in this city of Kaloon it was our weary destiny to dwell for three long months, one of the most hateful times, perhaps, that we ever passed in all our lives. Indeed, compared to it, our endless wanderings amid the Central Asian snows and deserts were but pleasure pilgrimages, and our stay at the monastery beyond the mountains a sojourn in Paradise. To set out its record in full would be both tedious and useless, so I will only tell briefly of our principal adventures.

On the morrow of our arrival, the Khania Atene sent us two beautiful white horses of pure and ancient blood, and at noon we mounted them and went out to ride with her, accompanied by a guard of soldiers. First she led us to the kennels where the death-hounds were kept, great flagged courts surrounded by iron bars, in which were narrow, locked gates. Never have I seen brutes so large and fierce; the mastiffs of Thibet were but as lapdogs compared to them. They were red and black, smooth-coated, and with a bloodhound head, and the moment they saw us they came ravening and leaping at the bars as an angry wave leaps against a rock.

These hounds were in the charge of men of certain families, who had tended them for generations. They obeyed their keepers and the Khan readily enough, but no stranger might venture near them. Also these brutes were the executioners of the land, for to them all murderers and other criminals were thrown, and with them, as we had seen, the Khan hunted any who had incurred his displeasure. Moreover, they were used for a more innocent purpose, the chasing of certain great bucks which were preserved in woods and swamps of reeds. Thus it came about that they were a terror to the country, since no man knew but what in the end he might be devoured by them. "Going to the dogs" is a term full of meaning in any land, but in Kaloon it had a significance that was terrible.

After we had looked at the hounds, not without a prophetic shudder, we rode round the walls of the town, which were laid out as a kind of *boulevard*, where the inhabitants walked and took their pleasure in the evenings. On these, however, there was not much to see except the river beneath and the plain beyond; moreover, though they were thick and high, there were places in them that must be passed carefully, for, like everything else with which the effete ruling class had to do, they had been allowed to fall into disrepair.

The town itself was an uninteresting place also, for the most part peopled by hangers-on of the Court. So we were not sorry when we crossed the river by a high-pitched bridge—where in days to come I was destined to behold one of the strangest sights ever seen by mortal man—and rode out into the country. Here all was different, for we found ourselves among the husbandmen, who were the descendants of the original owners of the land and lived upon its produce. Every available inch of soil seemed to be cultivated by the aid of a wonderful system of irrigation. Indeed, water was lifted to levels where it would not flow naturally, by means of wheels turned by mules, or even in some places carried up by the women, who bore poles on their shoulders to which were balanced buckets.

Leo asked the Khania what happened if there was a bad season. She replied grimly that famine happened, in which thousands of people perished, and that after the famine came pestilence. These famines were periodical, and were it not for them, she added, the people would long ago have been driven to kill each other like hungry rats, since having no outlet and increasing so rapidly, the land, large as it was, could not hold them all.

"Will this be a good year?" I asked.

"It is feared not," she answered; "for the river has not risen well, and but few rains have fallen. Also the light that shone last night on the Fire Mountain is thought to be a bad omen, which means, they say, that the Spirit of the Mountain is angry, and that drought will follow. Let us hope they will not say also that this is because strangers have visited the land, bringing with them bad luck."

"If so," said Leo, with a laugh, "we shall have to fly to the Mountain to take refuge there."

"Do you, then, wish to take refuge in death?" she asked darkly. "Of this be sure, my guest, that never while I live shall you be allowed to cross the river which borders the slopes of yonder peak."

"Why not, Khania?"

"Because, my lord Leo—that is your name, is it not?—such is my will; and while I rule here, my will is law. Come, let us turn homewards."

*   *   *   *   *

That night we did not eat in the great hall, but in the room which adjoined our bedchambers. We were not left alone, however, for the Khania and her uncle, the Shaman, who always attended her, joined our meal. When we greeted them wondering, she said briefly that it was arranged thus because she refused to expose us to more insults. She added that a festival had begun which would last for a week, and that she did not wish us to see how vile were the ways of her people.

That evening, and many others which followed it—we never dined in the central hall again—passed pleasantly enough, for the Khania made Leo tell her of England, where he was born, and of the lands that he had visited, their peoples and customs. I spoke also of the history of Alexander, whose general Rassen, her far-off forefather, conquered the country of Kaloon, and of the land of Egypt, whence the latter came; and so it went on till midnight, while Atene listened to us greedily, her eyes fixed always on Leo's face.

Many such nights did we spend thus in the Palace of the city of Kaloon, where, in fact, we were close prisoners. But oh! the days hung heavy on our hands. If we went into the courtyard or reception-rooms of the palace, the lords and their followers gathered round us and pestered us with questions, for, being very idle, they were also very curious.

Also the women, some of whom were fair enough, began to talk to us on this pretext or on that, and did their best to make love to Leo; for, in contrast with their slim, delicate-looking men, they found this deep-chested, yellow-haired stranger to their taste. Indeed, they troubled him much with gifts of flowers and messages sent by servants or soldiers, making assignations with him, which, of course, he did not keep.

If we went out into the streets, matters were as bad, for then the people ceased from their business, such as it was, and followed us about, staring at us till we took refuge again in the Palace gardens.

There remained, therefore, only our rides in the country with the Khania; but after three or four of them, these came to an end, owing to the jealousy of the Khan, who vowed that if we went out together any more, he would follow with the death-hounds. So we must ride alone, if at all, in the centre of a large guard of soldiers sent to see that we did not attempt to escape, and accompanied very often by a mob of peasants, who with threats and entreaties demanded that we should give back the rain which they said we had taken from them. For now the great drought had begun in earnest.

Thus it came about that at length our only resource was making pretence to fish in the river, where the water was so clear and low that we could catch nothing, watching the while the Fire Mountain, that loomed in the distance mysterious and unreachable, and vainly racking our brains for plans to escape thither, or at least to communicate with its priestess, of whom we could learn no more.

For two great burdens lay upon our souls—

"'Are you the Khania's other friend?'"

the burden of desire to continue our search and to meet with its reward, which we were sure that we should pluck amid the snows of yonder peak, if we could but come there ; and the burden of approaching catastrophe at the hands of the Khania Atene. She had made no love to Leo since that night in the Gateway, and, indeed, even if she had wished to, this would have been difficult, since I took care that he was never left for one hour alone. No *duenna* could have clung to a Spanish princess more closely than I did to Leo.

Yet I could see well that her passion was no whit abated ; that it grew day by day, indeed, as the fire swells in the heart of a volcano, and that soon it must break loose and spread its ruin round. The omen of it was to be read in her words, her gestures, and her tragic eyes.

CHAPTER X.

IN THE SHAMAN'S CHAMBER.

ONE night Simbri asked us to dine with him in his own apartments in the highest tower of the Palace—had we but known it, for us a fateful place indeed, for here the last act of the mighty drama was destined to be fulfilled. So we went, glad enough of any change. When we had eaten, Leo grew very thoughtful, then said suddenly—

"Friend Simbri, I wish to ask a favour of you—that you will beg the Khania to let us go our ways."

Instantly the Shaman's cunning old face became like a mask of ivory.

"Surely you had better ask your favours of the lady herself, lord. I do not think that any in reason will be refused to you," he replied.

"Let us stop fencing," said Leo, "and consider the facts. It has seemed to me that the Khania Atene is not happy with her husband."

"Your eyes are very keen, lord, and who shall say that they have deceived you ? "

"It has seemed, further," went on Leo, reddening, " that she has been so good as to look on me with—some undeserved regard."

"Ah ! perhaps you guessed that in the Gatehouse yonder, if you have not forgotten what most men would remember."

"I remember certain things, Simbri, that have to do with her and you."

The Shaman only stroked his beard and said "Proceed !"

"There is little to add, Simbri, except that I am not minded to bring scandal on the name of the first lady in your land."

"Nobly said, lord, nobly said, though here they do not trouble much about such things. But how if the matter could be managed without scandal ? If, for instance, the Khania chose to take another husband, the whole land would rejoice, for she is the last of her royal race."

"How can she take another husband when she has one living ? "

"True ; indeed, that is a question which I have considered, but the answer to it is that men die. It is the common lot, and the Khan has been drinking very heavily of late."

"You mean that men can be murdered," said Leo angrily. "Well, I will have nothing to do with such a crime. Do you understand me ? "

As the words passed his lips I heard a rustle and turned my head. Behind us were curtains beyond which the Shaman slept, kept his instruments of divination, and worked out his horoscopes. Now they had been drawn, and between them, in her royal array, stood the Khania, still as a statue.

"Who was it that spoke of crime ? " she asked in a cold voice. "Was it you, my lord Leo ? "

Rising from his chair, he faced her and said—

"Lady, I am glad that you have heard my words, even if they should vex you."

"Why should it vex me to learn that there is one honest man in this Court who will have naught to do with murder ? Nay, I honour you for those words. Know also that no such foul thoughts have come near to me. Yet, Leo Vincey, that which is written—is written."

"Doubtless, Khania ; but what is written ? "

"Tell him, Shaman."

Now Simbri passed behind the curtain and returned thence with a roll from which he read : "The heavens have declared by their signs infallible that before the next new moon the Khan Rassen will lie dead at the hands of the stranger lord who came to this country from across the mountains."

"Then the heavens have declared a lie," said Leo contemptuously.

"That is as you will," answered Atene ; "but so it must befall—not by my hand or those of my servants, but by yours. And then ? "

"Why by mine ? Why not by Holly's ? Yet, if so, then doubtless I shall suffer the punishment of my crime at the hands of his mourning widow," he replied, exasperated.

"You are pleased to mock me, Leo Vincey, well knowing what a husband this man is to me."

Now I felt that the crisis had come, and so did Leo, for he looked her in the face and said—

"Speak on, lady—say all you wish; perhaps it will be better for us both."

"I obey you, lord. Of the beginning of this fate I know nothing, but I read from the first page that is open to me. It has to do with this present life of mine. Learn, Leo Vincey, that from my childhood onwards you have haunted me. Oh! when first I saw you yonder by the river, your face was not strange to me, for I knew it—I knew it well in dreams. When I was a little maid, and slept one day amidst the flowers by the river's brim, it came first to me—ask my uncle here if this be not so, though it is true that your face was younger then. Afterwards again and again I saw it in my sleep, and learned to know that you were mine, for the magic of my heart taught me this.

"Then passed the long years while I felt that you were drawing near to me—slowly, very slowly, but ever drawing nearer, wending onward and outward through the peoples of the world; across the hills, across the plains, across the sands, across the snows, on to my side. At length came the end, for one night not three moons ago, whilst this wise man, my uncle, and I sat together here studying the lore that he has taught me, and striving to wring its secrets from the past, a vision came to me.

"Look you, I was lost in a charmed sleep which looses the spirit from the body and gives it strength to stray afar and to see those things that have been and that are yet to be. Then I saw you and your companion clinging to a point of broken ice, over the river of the gulf. I do not lie; it is written here upon the scroll. Yes, it was you, the man of my dreams, and no other; and we knew the place and hurried thither and waited by the water, thinking that perhaps beneath it you lay dead.

"Then, while we waited, lo! two tiny figures appeared far above the icy tongue that no man may climb, and oh! you know the rest. Spellbound we stood and saw you slip and hang, saw you sever the thin cord and rush downwards—yes, and saw that brave man, Holly, leap headlong after you.

"But mine was the hand that drew you from the torrent, where otherwise you must have drowned—you, the love of the long past and of to-day—aye, and of all time. Yes,

you and no other, Leo Vincey. It was this spirit that foresaw your danger, and this hand which delivered you from death; and —and would you refuse them now, when I, the Khania of Kaloon, proffer them to you?"

So she spoke, and leaned upon the table, looking up into his face with lips that trembled and with appealing eyes.

"Lady," said Leo, "you saved me, and again I thank you, though perhaps it would have been better if you had let me drown. But—forgive me the question—if all this tale be true, why did you marry another man?"

Now she shrank back as though a knife had pricked her.

"Oh! blame me not," she moaned. "It was but policy which bound me to this madman, whom I ever loathed. They urged me to it; yes, even you, Simbri, my uncle—and for that deed accursed be your head!—urged me, saying that it was necessary to end the war between Rassen's faction and my own. That I was the last of the true race, more-over, which must be carried on; saying also that my dreams and my rememberings were but sick phantasies. So, alas! alas! I yielded, thinking to make my people great."

"And yourself the greatest of them, if all I hear is true," commented Leo bluntly, for he was determined to end this thing. "Well, I do not blame you, Khania, although now you tell me that I must cut a knot you tied, by taking the life of this husband of your own choice; for so, forsooth, it is decreed by Fate, that Fate which *you* have shaped. Yes, I must do what you will not do, and kill him. Also your tale of the decree of the heavens, and of that vision which led you to the precipice to save us, is false. Lady, you met me by the river because the 'mighty' Hesea, the Spirit of the Mountain, so commanded you."

"How know you that?" Atene said, springing up and facing him, while the jaw of old Simbri dropped, and the eyelids blinked over his glazed eyes.

"In the same way that I know much else. Lady, it would have been better if you had spoken all the truth."

Now Atene's face went ashen and her cheeks sank in.

"Who told you?" she whispered. "Was it you, magician?" and she turned upon her uncle like a snake about to strike. "Oh! if so, be sure that I shall learn it; and though we are of one blood and have loved each other, I will pay you back in agony."

"Atene, Atene!" Simbri broke in, holding

up his clawlike hands, " you know well it was not I ! "

" Then it was you, you ape-faced wanderer, you messenger of the evil gods ! Oh ! why did I not kill you at the first ? Well, that fault can be remedied."

" Lady," I said blandly, " am I also a magician ? "

" Aye," she answered, " I think that you are, and that you have a mistress who dwells in fire."

" Then, Khania," I said, " such servants and such mistresses are ill to meddle with. Say, what answer has the Hesea sent to your report of our coming to this land ? "

" Listen," broke in Leo before she could reply. " I go to ask a certain question of the Oracle on yonder mountain peak. With your will or without it, I tell you that I go, and afterwards you can settle which is the stronger—the Khania of Kaloon or the Hesea of the House of Fire."

Atene listened and for a while stood silent, perhaps because she had no answer. Then she said with a little laugh—

" Is that your will ? Well, I think that yonder are none whom you would wish to wed. There is fire and to spare, but no lovely, shameless spirit haunts it to drive men mad with evil longings " ; and as though at some secret thought, a spasm of pain crossed her face and caught her breath. Then she went on in the same cold voice—

" Wanderers, this land has its secrets, into which no foreigner must pry. I say to you yet again that while I live, you set no foot upon that Mountain. Know also, Leo Vincey, I have bared my heart to you, and I have been told in answer that this long quest of yours is not for me, as I was sure in my folly, but, as I think, for some demon wearing the shape of woman, whom you will never find. Now I make no prayer to you ; it is not fitting—but you have learned too much.

" Therefore, consider well to-night, and before next sundown answer. Having offered, I do not go back, and to-morrow you shall tell me whether you will take me when the time comes—as come it must—and rule this land and be great and happy in my love, or whether, you and your familiar together, you will—die. Choose, then, between the vengeance of Atene and her love, since I am not minded to be mocked in my own land as a wanton who sought a stranger and was—refused."

Slowly, slowly, in an intense whisper she spoke the words, that fell, one by one, from her lips like drops of blood from a death-wound, and there followed silence. Never shall I forget the scene. There the old wizard watched us through his horny eyes, that blinked like those of some night-bird. There stood the imperial woman in her royal robes, with icy rage written on her face and vengeance in her glance. There, facing her, was the great form of Leo, quiet, alert, determined, holding back his doubts and fears with the iron hand of will. And there to the right was I, noting all things and wondering how long I, " the familiar," who had earned Atene's hate, would be left alive upon the earth.

Thus we stood, watching each other, till suddenly I noted that the flame of the lamp above us flickered, and felt a draught strike upon my face. Then I looked round and became aware of another presence. For yonder in the shadow was the tall form of a man. See ! it shambled forward silently, and I saw that its feet were naked. Now it reached the ring of the lamplight and burst into a savage laugh.

It was the Khan.

Atene, his wife, looked up and saw him, and never did I admire that passionate woman's boldness more, who admired little else about her save her beauty, for her face showed neither anger nor fear, but contempt only. And yet she had some cause to be afraid, as she well knew.

" What do you here, Rassen ? " she asked, " creeping on me with your naked feet ? Get you back to your drink and the ladies of your Court."

But he still laughed on, a hyæna laugh.

" What have you heard," she said, " that makes you so merry ? "

" What have I heard ? " Rassen gurgled out between his screams of hideous glee. " Oho ! I have heard the Khania, the last of the true blood, the first in the land, the proud princess who will not let her robes be soiled by those of the ' ladies of the Court,' and my wife, my wife, who asked me to marry her— mark that, you strangers—because I was her cousin and a rival ruler, and the richest lord in all the land, and thereby she thought she would increase her power—I have heard her offer herself to a nameless wanderer with a great yellow beard, and I have heard him, who hates and would escape from her "— here he screamed with laughter—" refuse her in such a fashion as I would not refuse the lowest woman in the palace !

" I have heard also—but that I always knew—that I am mad ; for, strangers, I was

"'I saw you born, the son of an evil woman.'"

made mad by a hate-philtre which that old Rat," and he pointed to Simbri, " gave me in my drink—yes, at my marriage-feast. It worked well, for truly there is no one whom I hate more than the Khania Atene. Why, I cannot bear her touch, it makes me sick. I loathe to be in the same room with her ; she taints the air ; there is a smell of sorceries about her.

" It seems that it takes you thus also, Yellow-beard ? Well, if so, ask the old Rat for a love-drink ; he can mix it, and then you will think her sweet and sound and fair, and spend some few months jollily enough. Man, don't be a fool ! the cup that is thrust into your hands looks goodly. Drink, drink deep. You'll never guess the liquor's bad— till to-morrow—though it be mixed with a husband's poisoned blood ! " and again Rassen screamed in his unholy mirth.

To all these bitter insults, venomed with the sting of truth, Atene listened without a word. Then she turned to us and bowed.

" My guests," she said, " I pray you pardon me for all I cannot help. You have strayed to a corrupt and evil land, and there stands its crown and flower. Khan Rassen, your doom is written, and I do not hasten it, because once for a little while we were near to each other, though you have been naught to me for this many a year save a snake that haunts my house. Were it otherwise, the next cup you drank should still your madness and that vile tongue of yours which gives its venom voice. My uncle, come with me. Your hand, for I grow weak with shame and woe."

The old Shaman hobbled forward ; but when he came face to face with the Khan, he stopped and looked him up and down with his dim eyes. Then he said—

" Rassen, I saw you born, the son of an evil woman, and your father none knew but I. The flame flared that night upon the Fire Mountain, and the stars hid their faces, for none of them would own you—no, not even those of the most evil influence. I saw you wed and rise drunken from your marriage-feast, your arm round a wanton's neck. I have seen you rule, wasting the land for your cruel pleasure, turning the fertile fields into great parks for your game, leaving those who tilled them to starve upon the road or drown themselves in ditches for very misery. And soon, soon I shall see you die in pain and blood, and then the chain will fall from the neck of this noble lady whom you revile, and another more worthy shall take your place and rear up children to fill your throne, and the land shall have rest again."

Now I listened to these words—and none who did not hear them can guess the fearful bitterness with which they were spoken— expecting every moment that the Khan would draw the short sword at his side and cut the old man down. But he did not ; he cowered before him like a dog before some savage master the weight of whose whip he knows. Yes, answering nothing, he shrank into the corner and cowered there, while Simbri, taking Atene by the hand, went from the room. At its massive, iron-bound door he turned and, pointing to the crouching figure with his staff, said—

" Khan Rassen, I raised you up, and now I cast you down. Remember me when you lay dying—in blood and pain ! "

Their footsteps died away, and the Khan crept from his corner, looking about him furtively.

" Have that Rat and the other gone ? " he asked of us, wiping his damp brow with his sleeve ; and I saw that fear had sobered him and that for awhile the madness had left his eyes.

I answered that they had gone.

" You think me a coward," he went on passionately, " and it is true I am afraid of him and her—as you, Yellow-beard, will be afraid when your turn comes. I tell you that they sapped my strength and crazed me with their drugged drink, making me the thing I am ; for who can war against their wizardries ? Look you now. Once I was a prince, the lord of half this land, noble of form and upright of heart, and I loved her cursed beauty as all must love it on whom she turns her eyes. And she turned them on me, she sought *me* in marriage ; it was that old Rat who bore her message.

" So I stayed the great war and married the Khania and became the Khan ; but better had it been for me if I had crept into her kitchen as a scullion, than into her chamber as a husband. For from the first she hated me ; and the more I loved, the more she hated, till at our wedding-feast she doctored me with that poison which made me loathe her, and thus divorced us ; which made me mad also, eating into my brain like fire."

" If she hated you so sorely, Khan," I asked, " why did she not mix a stronger draught and have done with you ? "

" Why ? Because of policy, for I ruled half the land. Because it suited her also that I should live on, a thing to mock at, since while I was alive no other husband could be forced upon her by the people. For she is not a woman, she is a witch, who desires to live alone, or so I thought until to-night "—and he glowered at Leo.

"She knew also that although I must shrink from her, I still love her in my heart, and can still be jealous, and therefore that I should protect her from all men. It was she who set me on that lord whom my dogs tore awhile ago, because he was powerful and sought her favour and would not be denied. But now," and again he glowered at Leo, "now I know why she has always seemed so cold. It is because there lived a man to melt whose ice she husbanded her fire."

Then Leo, who all this while had stood silent, stepped forward.

"Listen, Khan," he said. "Did the ice seem like melting a little while ago?"

"No—unless you lied. But that was only because the fire is not yet hot enough. Wait awhile until it burns up, and melt you must, for who can match his will against Atene?"

"And what if the ice desires to flee the fire? Khan, they said that I should kill you, but I do not seek your blood. You think that I would rob you of your wife, yet I have no such thought towards her. We desire to escape this town of yours, but cannot, because its gates are locked, and we are prisoners, guarded night and day. Hear me, then. You have the power to set us free and to be rid of us."

The Khan looked at him cunningly.

"And if I set you free, whither would you go? You could tumble down yonder gorge, but only the birds can climb its heights."

"To the Fire Mountain, where we have business."

Rassen stared at him.

"Is it I who am mad, or are you, who wish to visit the Fire Mountain? Yet that is nothing to me, save that I do not believe you. But if so, you might return again and bring others with you. Perchance, having its lady, you wish this land also by right of conquest. It has foes up yonder."

"It is not so," answered Leo earnestly. "As one man to another, I tell you it is not so. I ask no smile of your wife and no acre of your soil. Be wise and help us to be gone, and live on undisturbed in such fashion as may please you."

The Khan stood still awhile, swinging his long arms vacantly, till something seemed to come into his mind that moved him to merriment, for he burst into one of his hideous laughs.

"I am thinking," he said, "what Atene would say if she woke up to find her sweet bird flown. She would search for you and be angry with me."

"It seems that she cannot be angrier than she is," I answered. "Give us a night's start, and let her search never so closely, she shall not find us."

"You forget, wanderer, that she and her old Rat have arts. Those who knew where to meet you might know where to seek you. And yet—and yet—it would be rare to see her rage. 'Oh, Yellow-beard, where are you, Yellow-beard?'" he went on, mimicking his wife's voice. "'Come back and let me melt your ice, Yellow-beard.'"

Again he laughed; then said suddenly—

"When can you be ready?"

"In half an hour," I answered.

"Good. Go to your chambers and prepare. I will join you there presently."

So we went.

AYESHA

THE RETURN OF "SHE."

By H. RIDER HAGGARD.

SYNOPSIS OF FOREGOING CHAPTERS.—The return of "She-Who-Must-Be-Obeyed" is recorded by Ludwig Horace Holly, the friend of that Leo Vincey whom Ayesha the beautiful loved in the awful tombs of Kôr. When the record begins, the two men are living in an old house remote upon the seashore of Cumberland, where they have been slowly recovering from the horror of the passing of Ayesha in the flames—a doom that seemed one of complete extinction, yet was charged with the strange last words: "I die not. I shall come again and shall once more be beautiful. I swear it—it is true." On a sullen August night, Leo is thrilled by a vision of Ayesha in all her former loveliness. She beckons him, and in a vision his spirit follows her into a realm of snowy peaks far beyond the furthest borders of Thibet. A sign in the clouds at dawn is repeated from this vision to both Leo and Holly, and together they start for Central Asia. Sixteen years of toil, struggle, and strange adventure pass, and they are still searching for "a mountain peak shaped like the Symbol of Life." After many wanderings they find themselves in a country where no European has ever set foot, on one of the spurs of the vast Cherga mountains, far eastward from Turkestan. Sheltered awhile in a Buddhist monastery, they hear of the recent visit of a stranger who has told the Lamas that his countryfolk, "dwelling beyond the Far Mountains," worship a priestess called Hes, or the Hesea, and upon persuasion the abbot of the monastery tells them that in a former incarnation he himself has seen the great priestess, who was "all loveliness." A perilous ascent into the unexplored mountain fastness leads them to the revelation of "the *crux ansata*, the Symbol of Life itself." The symbol vanishes, the fire sinks, but they are sure that as it was sent of old to show them a path of escape from the Place of Death, so now it has been sent again in greeting to point out the path to the Place of Life where Ayesha dwells. A further ascent into the mountains reveals their Promised Land, with the symbol of their vision, an enormous pillar of rock, whereof the top was formed to the shape of a loop. Peril by avalanche and glacier intervenes, but brings them slowly nearer to their hopes. Rescued from drowning by a beautiful woman and an aged man, they are conducted through "The Gate" into the kingdom and city of Kaloon. Their saviours, they learn, are the Khania or Queen of Kaloon, and a venerable physician of magical powers. Is this woman Ayesha? No; they conjecture her rather to be Amenartas, who wrote the "sherd" of the former chronicle. She falls in love with Leo, and he and Holly learn that her husband, the Khan, is a madman, and see him chase to a hideous death at the fangs of his hounds a great lord of the land who has dared to make love to her. Simbri, the magician, and Atene, the Khania, have already received a solemn charge from the Hesea of the "College" in the Mountain of Fire to receive two strangers at the Gate, the message concluding: "Bring them safely to the Mountain, knowing that in this matter I shall hold him and you to account. Myself I will not meet them, since to do so would be to break the pact between our powers, which says that the Hesea of the Sanctuary visits not the territory of Kaloon, save in war. Also their coming is otherwise appointed." But Atene's love for Leo makes her detain the travellers awhile in Kaloon, and she even proposes that the Khan shall be murdered so that she can wed Leo. To this the Englishman replies: "I go to ask a certain question of the Oracle on yonder mountain peak. With your will or without it, I tell you that I go, and afterwards you can settle which is the stronger—the Khania of Kaloon or the Hesea of the House of Fire." The jealous Khan himself assists the escape of the travellers for their further journey.

CHAPTER XI.

THE HUNT AND THE KILL.

WE reached our rooms, meeting no one in the passages, and there made our preparations. First we changed our festal robes for those warmer garments in which we had travelled to the city of Kaloon. Then we ate and drank what we could of the victuals which stood in the ante-chamber, not knowing when we should find more food, and filled two satchels such as these people sling about their shoulders, with the remains of the meat and liquor and a few necessaries. Also we strapped our big hunting-knives about our middles, and armed ourselves with short spears that were made for the stabbing of game.

"Perhaps he has laid a plot to murder us, and we may as well defend ourselves while we can," suggested Leo.

I nodded, for the echoes of the Khan's last laugh still rang in my ears. It was a very evil laugh.

"Likely enough," I said. "I do not trust that insane brute. Still, he wishes to be rid of us."

"Yes; but, as he said, live men may return, whereas the dead do not."

"Atene thinks otherwise," I commented.

"And yet she threatened us with death," answered Leo.

"Because her shame and passion make her mad," I replied, after which we were silent.

Presently the door opened, and through it came the Khan, muffled in a great cloak, as though to disguise himself.

"Come," he said, "if you are ready."

Then catching sight of the spears we held, he added : "You will not need those things. You do not go a-hunting."

"No," I answered ; "but who can say—we might be hunted."

"If you believe that, perhaps you had best stay where you are till the Khania wearies of Yellow-beard and opens the gates for you," he replied, eyeing me with his cunning glance.

"I think not," I said, and we started, the Khan leading the way and motioning us to be silent.

We passed through the empty rooms on to the verandah, and from the verandah down into the courtyard, where he whispered to us to keep in the shadow. For the moon shone very clearly that night—so clearly, I remember, that I could see the grass which grew between the joints of the pavement, and the little shadows thrown by each separate blade upon the worn surface of its stones. Now I wondered how we should pass the gate, for there a guard was stationed, which had of late been doubled by order of the Khania. But this gate we left upon our right, taking a path that led into the great walled garden, where Rassen brought us to a door hidden behind a clump of shrubs, which he unlocked with a key he carried.

Now we were outside the Palace wall, and our road ran past the kennels. As we went by these, the great, sleepless death-hounds, that wandered to and fro like prowling lions, caught our wind and burst into a sudden chorus of terrific bays. I shivered at the sound, for it was fearful in that silence, also I thought that it would arouse the keepers. But the Khan went to the bars and showed himself, whereon the brutes, which knew him, ceased their noise.

"Fear not," he said as he returned ; "the huntsmen know that they are starved to-night, for to-morrow certain criminals will be thrown to them."

Now we had reached the Palace gates. Here the Khan bade us hide in an archway, and departed. We looked at each other, for the same thought was in both our minds— that he had gone to fetch the murderers who were to make an end of us. But in this we did him wrong, for presently we heard the sound of horses' hoofs upon the stones, and he returned, leading the two white steeds that Atene had given us.

"I saddled them with my own hands," he whispered. "Who can do more to speed the parting guest ? Now mount, hide your faces in your cloaks as I do, and follow me."

So we mounted, and he trotted before us like a running footman, such as the great lords of Kaloon employed when they went about their business or their pleasure. Leaving the main street, he led us through a quarter of the town that had an evil reputation, and down its tortuous byways. Here we met a few revellers, while from time to time night-birds flitted from the doorways and, throwing aside their veils, looked at us ; but as we made no sign, drew back again, thinking that we passed to some assignation. We reached the deserted docks upon the river's edge and came to a little quay, alongside of which a broad ferry-boat was fastened.

"You must put your horses into it and row across," Rassen said, "for the bridges are guarded, and without discovering myself I cannot bid the soldiers to let you pass."

So with some little trouble we urged the horses into the boat, where I held them by their bridles, while Leo took the oars.

"Now go your ways, accursed wanderers !" cried the Khan, as he thrust us from the quay, " and pray the Spirit of the Mountain that the old Rat and his pupil—your love, Yellow-beard, your love—are not watching you in their magic-glass. For if so, we may meet again."

Then as the stream caught us, sweeping the boat out towards the centre of the river, he began to laugh that horrible laugh of his, calling after us—

"Ride fast, ride fast for safety, strangers ; there is death behind ! "

Leo put out his strength and backed water, so that the punt hung upon the edge of the stream.

"I think that we should do well to land again and kill that man, for he means mischief," he said.

He spoke in English, but Rassen must have caught the ring of his voice and guessed its meaning with the cunning of the mad. At least, he shouted—

"Too late, fools ! " and with a last laugh turned, ran so swiftly up the quay that his cloak flew out upon the air behind him, and vanished into the shadows at its head.

"Row on," I said, and Leo bent himself to the oars.

But the ferry-boat was cumbersome, and the current swift, so that we were swept down a long way before we could cross it. At length we reached still water near the further shore, and seeing a landing-place, managed to beach the punt and to drag our horses to the bank. Then leaving the craft to drift, for we had no time to scuttle her,

"'Ride fast, ride fast for safety, strangers!'"

we looked to our girths and bridles, and mounted, heading towards the far column of glowing smoke which showed like a beacon above the summit of the House of Fire.

At first our progress was very slow, for here there seemed to be no path, and we were obliged to pick our way across the fields, and to search for bridges that spanned such of the water-ditches as were too wide for us to jump. More than an hour was spent in this work, till we came to a village wherein none was stirring, and here struck a road which seemed to run towards the Mountain, though, as we learned afterwards, it took us very many miles out of our true path. Now for the first time we were able to canter, and pushed on at some speed, though not too fast, for we wished to spare our horses, and feared lest they might fall in the uncertain light.

A while before dawn the moon sank behind the Mountain, and the gloom grew so dense that we were forced to stop, which we did, holding the horses by their bridles and letting them graze a little on some young corn. Then the sky turned grey, the light faded from the column of smoke that was our guide, the dawn came, blushing red upon the vast snows of the distant Peak, and shooting its arrows through the loop above the pillar. We let the horses drink from a channel that watered the corn, and, mounting them, rode onward slowly.

Now, with the shadows of the night, a weight of fear seemed to be lifted off our hearts, and we grew hopeful—aye, almost joyous. That hated city was behind us. Behind us were the Khania, with her surging, doom-driven passions and her stormy loveliness, the wizardries of her horny-eyed mentor, so old in years and secret sin, and the madness of that strange being, half-devil, half-martyr, at once cruel and a coward—the Khan, her husband, and his polluted Court. In front lay the fire, the snow, and the mystery they hid, sought for so many empty years. Now we could solve it, or we would die. So we pressed forward joyfully to meet our fate, whatever it might he.

For many hours our road ran deviously through cultivated land, where the peasants at their labour laid down their tools and gathered into knots to watch us pass, and quaint, flat-roofed villages, whence the women snatched up their children and fled at the sight of us. They believed us to be lords from the Court who came to work them some harm in person or in property, and their terror told us how the country smarted beneath the rod of the oppressor. By midday, although the Peak seemed to be but little nearer, the character of the land had changed. Now it sloped gently upwards, and therefore could not be irrigated.

Evidently all this great district was dependent on the fall of timely rains, which had not come that spring. Therefore, although the population was still dense, and every rod of the land was under the plough or spade, the crops were failing. It was pitiful to see the green, uneared corn already turning yellow because of the lack of moisture, the beasts searching the starved pastures for food, and the poor husbandmen wandering about their fields or striving to hoe the iron soil.

Here the people seemed to know us as the two foreigners whose coming had been noised abroad, and, the fear of famine having made them bold, they shouted at us as we went by to give them back the rain which we had stolen, or so we understood their words. Even the women and the children in the villages prostrated themselves before us, pointing first to the Mountain and then to the hard, blue sky, and crying to us to send them rain. Once, indeed, we were threatened by a mob of peasants armed with spades and reaping-hooks, who seemed inclined to bar our path, so that we were obliged to put our horses to a gallop and pass through them with a rush. As we went forward, the country grew ever more arid, and its inhabitants more scarce, till we saw no man save a few wandering herds who drove their cattle from place to place in search of provender.

By evening we guessed that we had reached that border tract which was harried by the Mountain tribes, for here strong towers built of stone were dotted about the heaths, doubtless to serve as watch-houses or places of refuge. Whether they were garrisoned by soldiers, I do not know, but I doubt it, for we saw none. It seems probable, indeed, that these forts were relics of days when the land of Kaloon was guarded from attack by rulers of a very different character from that of the present Khan and his immediate predecessors.

At length even the watch-towers were left behind, and by sundown we found ourselves upon a vast uninhabited plain, where we could see no living thing. Now we made up our minds to rest our horses awhile, proposing to push forward again with the moon; for, having the wrath of the Khania behind us, we did not dare to linger. By this evening doubtless she would have discovered our escape, since before sundown, as she had decreed, Leo must make his choice and give his answer. Then, as we were sure, she would strike swiftly. Perhaps her messengers were already at their work rousing the country to capture us, and her soldiers following on our path.

We unsaddled the horses and let them refresh themselves by rolling on the sandy soil, and graze after a fashion upon the coarse tufts of withering herbage which grew around. There was no water here; but this did not so much matter, for both they and we had drunk at a little muddy pool we found not more than an hour before. We were finishing our meal of the food that

"'I felt my bones crack in its mighty jaws.'"

we had brought with us—which, indeed, we needed sorely after our sleepless night and long day's journey—when my horse, which was knee-haltered close at hand, lay down to roll again. This it could not do with ease, because of the rope about its fore-leg, and I watched its efforts idly, till at length, at the fourth attempt, after hanging for a few seconds upon its back, its legs sticking straight into the air, it fell over slowly towards me, as horses do.

"Why are its hoofs so red? Has it cut itself?" asked Leo in an indifferent voice.

As it chanced, I also had just noticed this red tinge, and for the first time, since it was most distinct about the animal's frogs, which until it rolled thus I had not seen. So I rose to look at them, thinking that probably the evening light had deceived us, or that we might have passed through some ruddy-coloured mud. Sure enough, they *were* red, as though a dye had soaked into the horn and the substance of the frogs. What was more, they gave out a pungent, aromatic smell that was unpleasant, such a smell as might arise from blood mixed with musk and spices.

"It is very strange," I said. "Let us look at your beast, Leo."

So we did, and found that its hoofs had been similarly treated.

"Perhaps it is a native mixture to preserve the horn," suggested Leo.

I thought awhile, then a terrible idea struck me.

"I don't want to frighten you," I said, "but I think that we had better saddle up and get on."

"Why?" he asked.

"Because I believe that villain of a Khan has doctored our horses."

"What for? To make them go lame?"

"No, Leo, to make them leave a strong scent upon dry ground."

He turned pale. "Do you mean—those hounds?"

I nodded. Then, wasting no more time in words, we saddled up in frantic haste. Just as I fastened the last strap of my saddle, I thought that a faint sound reached my ear.

"Listen," I said. Again it came, and now there was no doubt about it. It was the sound of baying dogs.

"By Heaven! the death-hounds!" said Leo.

"Yes," I answered quietly enough, for at this crisis my nerves hardened and all fear left me, "our friend the Khan is out a-hunting. That is why he laughed."

"What shall we do?" asked Leo. "Leave the horses?"

I looked at the Peak. Its nearest flanks were miles and miles away.

"Time enough to do that when we are forced. We can never reach that mountain on foot; and after they had run down the horses, they would hunt us by spoor or gaze. No, man; ride as you never rode before."

We sprang to our saddles, but before we gave rein I turned and looked behind me. It will be remembered that we had ridden up a long slope which terminated in a ridge, about three miles away, the border of the great plain whereon we stood. Now the sun had sunk behind that ridge, so that, although it was still light, the plain had fallen into shadow. Therefore, while no distant object could be seen upon the plain, anything crossing the ridge remained visible enough in that clear air—at least, to persons of keen sight.

This is what we saw. Over the ridge poured a multitude of little objects, and amongst the last of these galloped a man mounted on a great horse, who led another horse by the bridle.

"All the pack are out," said Leo grimly, "and Rassen has brought a second mount with him. Now I see why he wanted us to leave the spears; and I think," he shouted as we began to gallop, "that before all is done, the Shaman may prove himself a true prophet."

Away we sped through the gathering darkness, heading straight for the Peak. While we went, I calculated our chances. Our horses, as good as any in the land, were strong and fresh, for although we had ridden far, we had not over-pressed them, and their condition was excellent. But doubtless the death-hounds were fresh also, for meaning to run us down at night when he thought that he might catch us sleeping, Rassen would have brought them along easily, following us by inquiry among the peasants, and only laying them on our spoor after the last village had been left behind.

Also he had two mounts, and for aught we knew—though afterwards this proved not to be the case, for he wished to work his wickedness alone and unseen—he might be followed by attendants with relays. Therefore, it would appear that unless we reached some place whither he did not dare to follow, before him—that is, the slopes of the Peak many miles away—he must run us down. There remained the chance also that the dogs would tire and refuse to pursue the chase.

This, however, seemed scarcely probable, for they were extraordinarily swift and strong, and so savage that when once they had scented blood, in which doubtless our horse's hoofs were steeped, they would fall dead from exhaustion sooner than abandon the trail. Indeed, both the Khania and Simbri had often told us as much. Another chance—they might lose the scent; but, seeing its nature, again, this was not probable. Even an English pack will carry the trail of a red herring breast high without a fault for hours, and here was something stronger—a cunning compound of which the tell-tale odour would hold for days. A last chance. If we were forced to abandon our horses, we, their riders, might possibly escape, could we find any place to hide in on that great plain. If not, we should be seen as well as scented, and then——

No, the odds were all against us, but so they had often been before; meanwhile we had three miles start, and perhaps help would come to us from the Mountain, some help unforeseen. So we set our teeth and sped away like arrows while the light lasted.

Very soon it failed, and whilst the moon was hidden behind the mountains, the night grew dark.

Now the hounds gained on us, for in the gloom, which to them was nothing, we did not dare to ride full speed, fearing lest our horses should stumble and lame themselves, or fall. Then it was for the second time since we had dwelt in this land of Kaloon that of a sudden the fire flamed upon the Peak. When we had seen it before, it had appeared to flash across the heavens in one great lighthouse ray concentrated through the loop above the pillar, and there this night also the ray ran far above us like a lance of fire. But now that we were nearer to its fount, we found ourselves bathed in a soft, mysterious radiance like that of the phosphorescence on a summer sea, reflected downwards, perhaps, from the clouds and massy rock roof of the column loop and diffused by the snows beneath.

This unearthly glimmer, faint as it was, helped us much—indeed, but for it, we must have been overtaken, for here the ground was very rough, full of holes, also, made by burrowing marmots. Thus in our extremity help did come to us from the Mountain, until at length the moon rose, when, as quickly as they had appeared, the volcanic fires vanished, leaving behind them nothing but the accustomed pillar of dull, red smoke.

It is a commonplace to speak of the music of hounds at chase, but often I have wondered how that music sounds in the ears of the deer or the fox fleeing for its life. Now, when we filled the place of the quarry, it was my destiny to solve this problem, and I assert with confidence that the progeny of earth can produce no more hideous noise. It had come near to us, and in the desolate silence of the night the hellish harmonies of its volume seemed terrific, yet I could discern the separate notes of which it was composed, especially one deep, bell-like bay.

I remembered that I had heard this bay when we sat in the boat upon the river and saw that poor noble done to death for the crime of loving the Khania. As the hunt passed us then, I observed that it burst from the throat of the leading hound, a huge brute, red in colour, with a coal-black ear, fangs that gleamed like ivory, and a mouth which looked like a hot oven. I even knew the name of the beast, for afterwards the Khan, whose peculiar joy it was, had pointed it out to me. He called it Master, because no dog in the pack dared fight it, and told me that it could kill an armed man alone.

Now, as its baying warned us, Master was not half a mile away!

The coming of the moonlight enabled us to gallop faster, especially as here the ground was smooth, being covered with a short, dry turf, and for the next two hours we gained upon the pack. Yes, it was only two hours, or perhaps less, but it seemed a score of centuries. The slopes of the Peak were now not more than ten miles ahead, but our horses were giving out at last. They had borne us nobly, poor beasts, though we were no light weights, yet their strength had its limits. The sweat ran from them, their sides panted like bellows, they breathed in gasps, they stumbled and would scarcely answer to the flogging of our spear-shafts. Their gallop sank to a jolting canter, and I thought that soon they must come to a dead stop.

We crossed the brow of a gentle rise, from which the ground, that was sprinkled with bush and rocks, sloped downwards to where, some miles below us, the river ran, bounding the enormous flanks of the Mountain. When we had travelled a little way down this slope, we were obliged to turn, in order to pass between two heaps of rock, which brought us side on to its brow. And there, crossing it not more than three hundred yards away, we saw the pack. There were fewer of them now; doubtless many had fallen out of the hunt, but many still remained. Moreover, not far behind them rode the Khan, though his second mount was gone, or, more probably, he was riding it, having galloped the first to a standstill.

Our poor horses saw them also, and the sight lent them wings, for all the while they knew that they were running for their lives. This we could tell from the way they quivered whenever the baying came near to them—not as horses tremble with the pleasurable excitement of the hunt, but in an extremity of terror, as I have often seen them do when a prowling tiger roars close to their camp. On they went as though they were fresh from the stable, nor did they fail again until another four miles or so were covered and the river was but a little way ahead, for we could hear the rush of its waters.

Then slowly but surely the pack overtook us. We passed a clump of bush, but when we had gone a couple of hundred yards or so across the open plain beyond, feeling that the horses were utterly spent, I shouted to Leo—

"Ride round back to the bush and hide there."

So we did, and scarcely had we reached it and dismounted when the hounds came past. Yes, they went within fifty yards of us, lolloping along upon our spoor and running all but mute, for now they were too weary to waste their breath in vain. "Run for it," I said to Leo as soon as they had gone by, "for they will be back on the scent presently," and we set off to the right across the line that the hounds had taken, so as not to cut our own spoor.

About a hundred yards away was a rock, which fortunately we were able to reach before the pack swung round upon the horses' tracks, and therefore they did not view us. Here we stayed until, following the loop, they came to the patch of bush and passed behind it. Then we ran forward again as far as we could go. Glancing backwards as we went, I saw our two poor, foundered beasts plunging away across the plain, happily almost in the same line along which we had ridden from the rise. They were utterly done, but, freed from our weights and urged on by fear, could still gallop and keep ahead of the dogs, though we knew that this would not be for very long. I saw also that the Khan, guessing what we had done in our despair, was trying to call his hounds off the horses, but as yet without avail, for they would not leave the quarry which they had viewed.

All this came to my sight in a flash, but I remember the picture well. The mighty, snow-clad Peak surmounted by its column of glowing smoke, and casting its shadow for mile upon mile across the desert flats; the plain with its isolated rocks and grey bushes; the doomed horses struggling across it with convulsive bounds; the trailing line of great dogs that loped after them, and amongst these, looking small and lonely in that vast place, the figure of the Khan and his horse, of which the black hide was beflecked with foam. Then, above, the blue and tender sky, where the round moon shone so clearly that in her quiet, level light no detail, even the smallest, could escape the eye.

Now, youth and even middle age were far behind me, and although a very strong man for my years, I could not run as I used to do. Also I was most weary, and my limbs were stiff and chafed with long riding, so I made but slow progress; and, to make matters worse, I struck my left foot against a stone and hurt it much. I implored Leo to go on and leave me, for we thought that if we could once reach the river, our scent would be lost in the water; at any rate, that it would give us a chance of life. Just then I heard the belling bay of the hound Master, and waited for the next. Yes, it was nearer to us. The Khan had made a cast and found our line. Presently we must face the end.

"Go, go!" I said. "I can keep them back for a few minutes, and you may escape. It is your quest, not mine. Ayesha awaits you, not me, and I am weary of life. I wish to die and have done with it."

Thus I gasped—not all at once, but in broken words—as I hobbled along, clinging to Leo's arm. But he only answered in a low voice—

"Be quiet, or they will hear you," and on he went, dragging me with him.

We were quite near the water now, for we could see it gleaming below us, and oh! how I longed for one deep drink. I remember that this was the uppermost desire in my mind—to drink and drink. But the hounds were nearer still to us, so near that we could hear the pattering of their feet on the dry ground, mingled with the thud of the hoofs of the Khan's galloping horse. We had reached some rocks upon a little rise, just where the bank began, when Leo said suddenly—

"No use; we can't make it. Stop and let's see the thing through."

So we wheeled round, resting our backs against the rock. There, about a hundred yards off, were the death-hounds; but, Heaven be praised! *only three of them!* The

"'We go to accomplish our fate.'"

rest had followed the flying horses, and doubtless when they caught them at last, which may have been far distant, had stopped to gorge themselves upon them. So they were out of the fight. Only three, and the Khan, a wild figure, who galloped with them; but those three, the black and red brute, Master, and two others almost as fierce and big.

"It might be worse," said Leo. "If you will try to tackle the dogs, I'll do my best with the Khan," and stooping down, he rubbed his palms in the grit, for they were wet as water—an example which I followed. Then we gripped the spears in our right hands and the knives in our left, and waited.

The dogs had seen us now and came on, growling and baying fearfully. With a rush they came, and I am not ashamed to own that I felt terribly afraid, for the brutes seemed the size of lions and more fierce. One—it was the smallest of them, outstripped the others and, leaping up the little rise, sprang straight at my throat.

Why or how, I do not know, but on the impulse of the moment I, too, sprang to meet it, so that its whole weight came upon the point of my spear, which was backed by my weight. The spear entered between its fore-legs, and such was the shock that I was knocked backwards. But when I regained my feet, I saw the dog rolling on the ground before me and gnashing at the spear-shaft, which had been twisted from my hand.

The other two had jumped at Leo, but failed to get hold, though one of them tore away a large fragment from his tunic. Foolishly enough, he hurled his spear at it, but missed, for the steel passed just under its belly and buried itself deep in the ground. The pair of them did not come on again at once. Perhaps the sight of their dying companion made them pause. At any rate, they stood at a little distance snarling, where, as our spears were gone, they were safe from us.

Now the Khan had ridden up and sat upon his horse glowering at us, and his face was like the face of a devil. I had hoped that he might fear to attack, but the moment I saw his eyes, I knew that this would not be. He was quite mad with hate, jealousy, and the long-drawn excitement of the hunt, and had come to kill or be killed. Sliding from the saddle, he drew his short sword—for either he had lost his spear or had brought none—and made a hissing noise to the two dogs, pointing at me with the sword. I saw them spring, and I saw him rush at Leo, and after that who can tell exactly what happened?

My knife went home to the hilt in the body of one dog, and it came to the ground and lay there—for its hind-quarters were paralysed—howling, snarling, and biting at me. But the other, the fiend called Master, got me by the right arm beneath the elbow, and I felt my bones crack in its mighty jaws; and the agony of it—or so I suppose—caused me to drop the knife, so that I was weaponless. The brute dragged me from the rock and began to shake and worry me, although I kicked it in the stomach with all my strength. I fell to my knees and, as it chanced, my left hand came upon a stone of about the size of a large orange, which I gripped. I gained my feet again and pounded at its skull with the stone, but still

it did not leave go ; and this was well for me, for its next hold would have been on my throat.

We twisted and tumbled to and fro, man and dog together. At one turn I thought that I saw Leo and the Khan rolling over and over each other upon the ground ; at another, that he, the Khan, was sitting against a stone looking at me, and it came into my mind that he must have killed Leo and was watching while the dog worried me to death.

Then, just as things began to grow black, something sprang forward, and I saw the huge hound lifted from the earth. Its jaws opened, my arm came free and fell against my side. Yes ! the brute was whirling round in the air. Leo held it by its hind-legs, and with all his great strength whirled it round and round.

Thud ! He had dashed its head against a rock, and it fell and lay still, a huddled heap of black and red.

Oddly enough, I did not faint ; I suppose that the pain and the shock to my nerves kept me awake, for I heard Leo say in a matter-of-fact voice between his gasps for breath—

"Well, that's over, and I think that I have fulfilled the Shaman's prophecy. Let's look and make sure."

Then he led me with him to one of the rocks, and there, resting, supinely against it, sat the Khan, still living, but unable to move hand or foot. The madness had quite left his face, and he looked at us with melancholy eyes, like the eyes of a sick child.

"You are brave men," he said slowly ; "strong also, to have killed those hounds and broken my back. So it has come about as was foretold by the old Rat. After all, I should have hunted Atene, not you ; though now she lives to avenge me, for her own sake, not mine. Yellow-beard, she hunts you too, and with deadlier hounds than these—those of her thwarted passions. Forgive me and fly to the Mountain, Yellow-beard, whither I go before you, for there one dwells who is stronger than Atene."

Then his jaw dropped and he was dead.

CHAPTER XII.

THE MESSENGER.

"He is gone," I panted, "and the world hasn't lost much."

"Well, it didn't give him much, did it, poor devil ? so don't let's speak ill of him," answered Leo, who had thrown himself exhausted to the ground. "Perhaps he was all right before they made him mad. At any rate, he had pluck, for I don't want to tackle such another."

"How did you manage it?" I asked.

"Dodged in beneath his sword, closed with him, threw him, and smashed him over that lump of stone. Sheer strength, that's all. A cruel business, but it was his life or mine, and there you are. It's lucky I finished it in time to help you, before that oven-mouthed brute tore your throat out. Did you ever see such a dog? It looks as large as a young donkey. Are you much hurt, Horace?"

"Oh, my forearm is chewed to a pulp, but nothing else, I think. Let us get down to the water; if I can't drink soon, I shall faint. Also the rest of the pack is somewhere about —fifty or more of them."

"I don't think they will trouble us; they have got the horses, poor beasts. Wait a minute, and I will come."

Then he rose, found the Khan's sword, a beautiful and ancient weapon, and with a single cut of its keen edge killed the second dog that I had wounded, which was still yowling and snarling at us. After this he collected the two spears and my knife, saying that they might be useful, and without trouble caught the Khan's horse, which stood with hanging head close by, so tired that even this desperate fight had not frightened it away.

"Now," he said, "up you go, old fellow— you are not fit to walk any farther"; and with his help I climbed into the saddle.

Then slipping the rein over his arm, he led the horse, which walked stiffly, on to the river, that ran within a quarter of a mile of us, though to me, tortured as I was by pain, and half delirious with exhaustion, the journey seemed long enough.

Still, we came there somehow, and forgetting my wounds, I tumbled from the horse, threw myself flat, and drank and drank, more, I think, than ever I did before. Not in all my life have I tasted anything so delicious as was that long draught of water. When I had satisfied my thirst, I dipped my head and made shift to jerk my wounded arm into it, for its coolness seemed to still the pain. Presently Leo rose, the water running from his face and beard, and said—

"What shall we do now? The river seems to be wide, over a hundred yards, and it is low, but there may be deep water in the middle. Shall we try to cross—in which case we might drown; or stop where we are till daylight and take our chance of the death-hounds?"

"I can't go another foot," I murmured faintly, "much less try to ford an unknown river."

Now, about thirty yards from the shore was an island covered with reeds and grasses.

"Perhaps we could reach that," he said. "Come, get on to my back, and we will try."

I obeyed with difficulty, and we set out, he feeling his way with the handle of the spear. The water proved to be quite shallow; indeed, it never came much above his knees, so that we reached the island without trouble. Here Leo laid me down on the soft rushes, and, returning to the mainland, brought over the black horse and the remaining weapons, and having unsaddled the beast, knee-haltered and turned it loose, whereon it immediately lay down, for it was too spent to feed.

Then he set to work to doctor my wounds. Well it proved for me that the sleeve of my garment was so thick, for even through it the flesh of my forearm was torn to ribbons; moreover, a bone seemed to be broken. Leo collected a double handful of some soft, wet moss and, having washed the arm, wrapped it round with a handkerchief, over which he laid the moss. Then with a second handkerchief and some strips of linen torn from our undergarments, he fastened a couple of split reeds to serve as rough splints to the wounded limb. While he was doing this I suppose that I slept or swooned. At any rate, I remember no more.

*   *   *   *   *

Sometime during that night Leo had a strange dream, of which he told me the next morning. I suppose that it must have been a dream, as certainly I saw or was aware of nothing. Well, he dreamed—I use his own words as nearly as possible—that again he heard those accursed death-hounds in full cry. Nearer and nearer they came, following our spoor to the edge of the river—all the pack that had run down the horses. At the water's brink they halted and were mute. Then suddenly a puff of wind brought the scent of us upon the island to one of them, which lifted up its head and uttered a single bay. The rest clustered about it, and all at once they made a dash at the water.

Leo could see and hear everything. He felt that, after all, our doom was now at hand, and yet, held in the grip of nightmare, if nightmare it were, he was quite unable to stir or even to cry out to wake and warn me.

Now followed the marvel of this vision. Giving tongue as they came, half swimming and half plunging, the hounds drew near to the island where we slept. Then suddenly Leo saw that we were no longer alone. In front of us, on the brink of the water, stood the figure of a woman clad in some dark garment. He could not describe her face or appearance, for her back was towards him. All he knew was that she stood there, like a guard, holding some object in her raised hand, and that suddenly the advancing hounds caught sight of her. In an instant it was as though they were paralysed by fear—for their bays turned to fearful howlings. One or two of those that were nearest to the island seemed to lose their footing and be swept away by the stream. The rest struggled back to the bank and fled wildly like whipped curs.

Then the dark, commanding figure, which in his dream Leo took to be the guardian Spirit of the Mountain, vanished. That it left no footprints behind it I can vouch, for in the morning we looked to see.

* * * * *

When, awakened by the sharp pangs in my arm, I opened my eyes again, the dawn was breaking. A thin mist hung over the river and the island, and through it I could see Leo sleeping heavily at my side, and the shape of the black horse, which had risen and was grazing close at hand. I lay still for awhile, remembering all that we had undergone and wondering that I should live to wake, till presently above the murmuring of the water I heard a sound which terrified me, the sound of voices. I sat up and peered through the reeds, and there upon the bank, looking enormous in the mist, I saw two figures mounted upon horses, those of a woman and a man.

They were pointing to the ground, as though they examined spoor in the sand. I heard the man say something about the dogs not daring to enter the territory of the Mountain, a remark which came back to my mind again after Leo had told me his dream. Then I remembered how we were placed.

"Wake!" I whispered to Leo. "Wake! we are pursued!"

He sprang to his feet, rubbing his eyes and snatching at a spear. Now those upon the bank saw him, and a sweet voice spoke through the mist, saying—

"Lay down that weapon, my guest, for we are not come to harm you."

It was the voice of the Khania Atene, and the man with her was the old Shaman Simbri.

"What shall we do now, Horace?" asked Leo with something like a groan, for in the whole world there were no two people whom he less wished to see.

"Nothing," I answered; "it is for them to play."

"Come to us!" called the Khania across the water. "I swear that we mean no harm. Are we not alone?"

"I do not know," answered Leo, "but it seems unlikely. Where we are, we stop until we are ready to march again."

Atene spoke to Simbri. What she said we could not hear, for she whispered, but she appeared to be arguing with him and persuading him to some course of which he strongly disapproved. Then suddenly both of them put their horses at the water and rode to us through the shallows. Reaching the island, they dismounted, and we stood staring at each other. The old man seemed very weary in body and oppressed in mind, but the Khania was strong and beautiful as ever, nor had passion and fatigue left any trace upon her inscrutable face. It was she who broke the silence, saying—

"You have ridden fast and far since last we met, my guests, and left an evil token to mark the path you took. Yonder among the rocks one lies dead. Say, how came he to his end, who has no wound upon him?"

"By these," answered Leo, stretching out his hands.

"I knew it," she answered; "and I blame you not, for Fate decreed that death for him, and now it is fulfilled. Still, there are those to whom you must answer for his blood, and I only can protect you from them."

"Or betray me to them," said Leo. "Khania, what do you seek?"

"That answer which you should have given me this twelve hours gone. Remember, before you speak, that I alone can save your life—aye, and will do it and clothe you with that dead madman's crown and mantle."

"You shall have your answer on yonder Mountain," said Leo, pointing to the Peak above us, "where I seek mine."

She paled a little and replied: "To find that it is death; for, as I have told you, the place is guarded by savage folk who know no pity."

"So be it. Then Death is the answer that we seek. Come, Horace, let us go to meet him."

"I swear to you," she broke in, "that there dwells not the woman of your dreams.

"It stood up, a human figure."

I am that woman—yes, even I, as you are the man of mine."

"Then, lady, prove it yonder upon the Mountain," Leo answered.

"There dwells there no woman," Atene went on hurriedly—"nothing dwells there. It is the home of fire and—a Voice."

"What voice?"

"The Voice of the Oracle that speaks from the fire. The Voice of a spirit whom no man has ever seen or shall see."

"Come, Horace," said Leo, and he moved towards the horse.

"Men," broke in the old Shaman, "would you rush upon your doom? Listen; I have visited yonder haunted place, for it was I who according to custom brought thither the body of the Khan Atene's father for burial, and I warn you to set no foot within its temples."

"Which your mistress said that we should never reach," I commented, but Leo only answered—

"We thank you for your warning," and added: "Horace, watch them while I saddle the horse, lest they do us a mischief."

So I took the spear in my uninjured hand and stood ready. But they made no attempt to hurt us, only fell back a little and began to talk in hurried whispers. It was evident to me that they were much perturbed. In a few minutes the horse was saddled and Leo assisted me to mount it. Then he said—

"We go to accomplish our fate, whatever it may be; but before we part, Khania, I thank you for the kindness you have shown us, and pray you to be wise and forget that we have ever been. Through no will of mine your husband's blood is on my hands, and that alone must separate us for ever. We are divided by the doors of death and destiny. Go back to your people, and pardon me if most unwillingly I have brought you doubt and trouble. Farewell."

She listened with bowed head, then replied, very sadly—

"I thank you for your gentle words; but, Leo Vincey, we do not part thus easily. You have summoned me to the Mountain, and even to the Mountain I will follow you. Aye, and there I will meet its Spirit, as I have always known I must, and as the Shaman here has always known I must. Yes, I will match my strength and magic against hers, as it is decreed that I shall do. To the victor be that crown for which we have warred for ages!"

Then suddenly Atene sprang to her saddle, and turning her horse's head, rode it back through the water to the shore, followed by old Simbri, who lifted up his cruel hands as though in woe and fear, muttering as he went—

"You have entered the forbidden river, and now, Atene, the day of decision is upon us all—upon us and her—that predestined day of ruin and of war."

"What do they mean?" asked Leo of me.

"I don't know," I answered; "but I have no doubt we shall find out soon enough, and that it will be something unpleasant. Now for this river."

Before we had struggled through it I thought more than once that the day of drowning was upon us also, for in places there were deep rapids which nearly swept us away. But Leo, who waded, leading the Khan's horse by the bridle, felt his path and supported himself with the spear-shaft, so that in the end we reached the other bank safely.

Beyond it lay a breadth of marshy lands, that doubtless were overflowed when the torrent was in flood. Through these we pushed our way as fast as we could, for we feared lest the Khania had gone to fetch her escort, which we thought she might have left behind the rise, and would return with it presently to hunt us down. At that time we did not know what we learned afterwards —that with its bordering river the soil of the Mountain was absolutely sacred and, in practice, inviolable. True, it had been invaded by the people of Kaloon in several wars, but on each occasion their army was destroyed or met with terrible disaster. Little wonder, then, that they had come to believe that the House of Fire was under the protection of some unconquerable spirit.

Leaving the marsh, we reached a bare, rising plain, which led to the first slope of the Mountain three or four miles away. Here we expected every moment to be attacked by the savages of whom we had heard so much; but no living creature did we see. The place was a desert streaked with veins of rock that once had been molten lava. I do not remember much else about it; indeed, the pain in my arm was so sharp that I had no eyes for physical features. At length the rise ended in a bare, broad *donga*, quite destitute of vegetation, of which the bottom was buried in lava and a *débris* of rocks washed down by the rain or melting snows from slopes above. This *donga* was bordered on the farther side by a cliff, perhaps fifty feet in height, in which we could see no opening.

Still we descended the place, that was dark and rugged ; pervaded, moreover, by an extraordinary gloom ; and as we went, perceived that its lava floor was sprinkled over with a multitude of white objects. Soon we came to the first of these, and found that it was the skeleton of a human being. Here was a veritable Valley of Dry Bones, thousands upon thousands of them, a gigantic graveyard. It seemed as though some great army had perished here.

Indeed, we found afterwards that this was the case, for on one of those occasions in the far past, when the people of Kaloon had attacked the Mountain tribes, they were trapped and slaughtered in this gully, leaving their bones as a warning and a token. Among these sad skeletons we wandered disconsolately, seeking a path up the opposing cliff, and finding none, until at length we came to a halt, not knowing which way to turn. Then it was that we met with our first strange experience on the Mountain.

The gulf and its mouldering relics depressed us, so that for a while we were silent, and, to tell the truth, somewhat afraid. Yes, even the horse seemed afraid, for it snorted a little, hung its head, and shivered. Close by us lay a pile of bones, the remains evidently of a number of wretched creatures that, dead or living, had been hurled down from the cliff above, and on the top of the pile was a little huddled heap, which we took for more bones.

"Unless we can find a way out of this accursed charnel-house before long, I think that we shall add to its company," I said, staring round me.

As the words left my lips it seemed to me that from the corner of my eye I saw the heap on the top of the bones stir. I looked round. Yes, it was stirring. It rose—it stood up, a human figure, apparently that of a woman, but of this I could not be sure—wrapped from head to foot in white, and wearing a hanging veil over its face, or, rather, a mask with cut eyeholes. It advanced towards us while we stared at it, till the horse, catching sight of the thing, shied violently and nearly threw me. When at a distance of about ten paces, it paused and beckoned with its hand, that was also swathed in white like the arm of a mummy.

"What the devil are you ?" shouted Leo, and his voice echoed drearily among those naked rocks. But the creature did not answer, it only continued to beckon.

Leo walked up to it to assure himself that we were not the victims of some hallucination. As he came, it glided back to its heap of bones and stood there like a ghost of one dead arisen from amidst these grinning evidences of death—or, rather, a swathed corpse, for that is what it resembled. Leo followed with the intention of touching it to assure himself of its reality, whereon it lifted its white-wrapped arm and struck him lightly on the breast. Then, as he recoiled, it pointed with its hand, first upwards, as though to the Peak or the sky, and next at the wall of rock which faced us.

He returned to me, saying : " What shall we do ? "

"Follow, I suppose. It may be a messenger from above " ; and I nodded towards the mountain crest.

"From below, more likely," Leo muttered ; "for I don't like the look of this guide."

Still he motioned with his hand to the creature to proceed. Apparently it understood, for it turned to the left and began to pick its way amongst the stones and skeletons swiftly and without noise. We followed for several hundred yards till it reached a shallow cleft in the rock. This cleft we had seen already, but as it appeared to end at a depth of about thirty feet, we passed on. The figure entered here and vanished.

"It must be a shadow," said Leo doubtfully.

"Nonsense !" I answered ; "shadows don't strike one. Go on."

So he led the horse up the cleft, to find that at the end it turned sharply to the right, and that the form was standing there awaiting us. Forward it went again, and we after it, down a little gorge that grew ever gloomier till it terminated in what might have been a cave or a gallery cut in the rock.

Here our guide came back to us, apparently with the intention of taking the horse by the bridle ; but at this nearer sight of it the brute snorted and reared up, so that it almost fell backwards upon me. As it found its feet again, the figure struck it on the head in the same passionless, inhuman way that it had struck Leo, whereon the horse trembled and burst into a sweat as though with fear, making no further attempt to escape or to disobey. Then it took one side of the bridle in its swathed hand, and, Leo clinging to the other, we plunged into the tunnel.

Our position was not pleasant, for we knew not whither we were being led by this horrible conductor, and suspected that it might be to meet our deaths in the darkness. Moreover, I guessed that the path was narrow and bordered by some gulf, for as we went I heard stones fall, apparently to a considerable depth, while the poor horse lifted its feet gingerly and snorted in abject fear. At length we saw daylight, and never was I more glad of its advent, although it showed us that there *was* a gulf on our right, and that the path we travelled could not measure more than ten feet in width.

Now we were out of the tunnel, that evidently had saved us a wide detour, and standing for the first time upon the actual slope of the Mountain, which stretched upwards for a great number of miles till it reached the snow-line above. Here also we saw evidences of human life, for the ground was cultivated in patches, and herds of mountain sheep and cattle were visible in the distance.

Presently we entered a gully, following a rough path that led along the edge of a raging torrent. It was a desolate place, half a mile wide or more, having hundreds of fantastic lava boulders strewn about its slopes. Before we had gone a mile I heard a shrill whistle, and suddenly from behind these boulders sprang a number of men, quite fifty of them. All we could note at the time was that they were brawny, savage-looking fellows, for the most part red haired and bearded, although their complexions were rather dark, who wore cloaks of white goatskins and carried spears and shields. I should imagine they were not unlike the ancient Picts and Scots as they appeared to the invading Romans. At us they came, uttering their shrill, whistling cries, evidently with the intention of spearing us on the spot.

"Now for it," said Leo, drawing his sword, for escape was impossible; they were all round us. "Good-bye, Horace."

"Good-bye," I answered rather faintly, understanding what the Khania and the old Shaman had meant when they said that we should be killed before we ascended the first slope of the Mountain.

Meanwhile, our ghastly looking guide had slipped behind a great boulder, and even then it occurred to me that her part in the tragedy being played, she, if it were a woman at all, was withdrawing herself while we met our miserable fate. But here I did her injustice, for she had, I suppose, come to save us from this very fate which without her presence we must most certainly have suffered. When the savages were within a few yards, suddenly she appeared on the top of the boulder, looking like a second Witch of Endor, and stretched out her arm. Not a word did she speak, only stretched out her draped arm, but the effect was remarkable and instantaneous.

At the sight of her, down on to their faces went those wild men, every one of them, as though a lightning stroke had in an instant swept them out of existence. Then she let her arm fall and beckoned, whereon a great fellow, who, I suppose, was the leader of the band, rose and crept towards her with bowed head, submissive as a beaten dog. To him she made signs, pointing to us, pointing to the far-off Peak, crossing and uncrossing her white-wrapped arms, but, so far as I could hear, speaking no word. It was evident that the chief understood her, however, for he said something in a guttural language. Then he uttered his shrill whistle, whereon the band arose and departed thence at full speed, this way and that, so that in another minute they had vanished as quickly as they came.

Now our guide motioned to us to proceed, and led the way upward as calmly as though nothing had happened.

For over two hours we went on thus, till our path brought us from the ravine on to a grassy declivity, across which it wound its way. Here, to our astonishment, we found a fire burning, and hanging above the fire an earthenware pot, which was on the boil, although we could see no man tending it. The figure signalled to me to dismount, pointing to the pot in token that we were to eat the food which doubtless she had ordered the wild men to prepare for us; and very glad was I to obey her. Provision had been made for the horse also, for near the fire lay a great bundle of green forage.

While Leo off-saddled the beast and spread the provender for it, taking with me a spare earthern vessel that lay ready, I went to the edge of the torrent to drink and steep my wounded arm in its ice-bound stream. This relieved it greatly, though by now I was sure from various symptoms that the brute Master's fangs had fortunately only broken or injured the small bone, a discovery for which I was thankful enough. Having finished attending to it as well as I was able, I filled the jar with water.

On my way back a thought struck me, and going to where our mysterious guide stood still as Lot's wife after she had been turned into

MAURICE GREIFFENHAGEN
1905

" At length it seemed to lift its paw and strike the girl upon the face."

a pillar of salt, I offered it to her, hoping that she would unveil her face and drink. Then for the first time she showed some sign of being human, or so I thought, for it seemed to me that she bowed ever so little in acknowledgment of the courtesy. If so—and I may have been mistaken—this was all, for the next instant she turned her back upon me to show that it was declined. So she would not —or, for aught I knew, could not—drink. Neither would she eat, for when Leo tried her afterwards with food, she refused it in like fashion.

Meanwhile he had taken the pot off the fire, and as soon as its contents grew cool enough we fell on them eagerly, for we were starving. After we had eaten and drunk, Leo re-dressed my arm as best he could, and we rested awhile. Indeed, I think that, being very tired, we began to doze, for I was awakened by a shadow falling on us, and looked up to see our corpselike guide standing close by and pointing first to the sun, then at the horse, as though to show us that we had far to travel. So we saddled up and went on again somewhat refreshed, for at least we were no longer ravenous.

All the rest of that day we journeyed on up the grassy slopes, seeing no man, although occasionally we heard the wild whistle which told us that we were being watched by the Mountain savages. By sundown the character of the country had changed, for the grass was replaced with rocks, amongst which grew stunted firs. We had left the lower slopes and were beginning to climb the Mountain itself.

The sun sank, and we went on through the twilight. The twilight died, and we went on through the dark, our path lit only by the stars and the faint radiance of the glowing pillar of smoke above the Peak, which was reflected on to us from the mighty mantle of its snows. Forward we toiled, whilst a few paces ahead of us walked our unwearying guide. If she had seemed weird and inhuman before, now she appeared a very ghost, as, clad in her graveyard white, upon which the faint light shimmered, never speaking, never looking back, she glided on noiselessly between the black rocks and the twisted, dark-green firs and junipers.

Soon we lost all count of the road. We turned this way and turned that way, we passed an open patch and through the shadows of a grove, till at length as the moon rose we entered a ravine, and following a path that ran down it, came to a place which is best described as a large amphitheatre cut by the

hand of Nature out of the rock of the Mountain. Evidently it was chosen as a place of defence, for its entrance was narrow and tortuous, built up at the end also, so that only one person could pass its gateway at a time. Within an open space and at its farther side stood low, stone houses built against the rock. In front of these houses, the moonlight shining full upon then, were gathered several hundred men and women arranged in a semicircle and in alternate companies, who appeared to be engaged in the celebration of some rite.

. It was wild enough. In front of them, and in the exact centre of the semicircle, stood a gigantic, red-bearded man, who was naked except for a skin girdle about his loins. He was swinging himself backwards and forwards, his hands resting upon his hips, and as he swung, shouting something like " *Ho, haha, ho!* " When he bent towards the audience, it bent towards him ; and every time he straightened himself, it echoed his final shout of " *Ho!* " in a volume of sound that made the precipices ring. Nor was this all, for perched upon his hairy head, with arched back and waving tail, stood a great white cat.

Anything stranger, and, indeed, more fantastic, than the general effect of this scene, lit by the bright moonlight and set in that wild arena, it was never my lot to witness. The red-haired, half-naked men and women, the gigantic priest, the mystical white cat, that, gripping his scalp with its claws, waved its tail and seemed to take a part in the performance ; the unholy chant and its volleying chorus, all helped to make it extraordinarily impressive. This struck us the more, perhaps, because at the time we could not in the least guess its significance, though we imagined that it must be preliminary to some sacrifice or offering. It was like the fragment of a nightmare preserved by the awakened senses in all its mad, meaningless reality.

Now, round the open space where these savages were celebrating their worship, or whatever it might be, ran a rough stone wall about six feet in height, in which wall was a gateway. Towards this we advanced quite unseen, for upon our side of the wall grew many stunted pines. Through these pines our guide led us, till in the thickest of them, some few yards from the open gateway and a little to the right of it, she motioned to us to stop.

Then she went to a low place in the wall and stood there, as though she were considering the scene beyond. It seemed to us, indeed, that she saw what she had not expected, and was thereby perplexed or angered. Presently she appeared to make up her mind, for again she motioned to us to remain where we were, enjoining silence upon us by placing her swathed hand upon the mask that hid her face. Next moment she was gone. How she went, or whither, I cannot say ; all we knew was that she was no longer there.

"What shall we do now?" whispered Leo to me.

"Stay where we are till she comes back again or something happens," I answered.

So, there being nothing else to be done, we stayed, hoping that the horse would not betray us by neighing, or that we might not be otherwise discovered, since we were certain that, if so, we should be in danger of our lives. Very soon, however, we forgot the anxieties of our own position in the study of the wild scene before us, which now began to develop a fearful interest.

It would seem that what has been described was but preliminary to the drama itself, and that this drama was the trial of certain people for their lives. This we could guess, for after awhile the incantation ceased, and the crowd in front of the big man with the cat upon his head opened out, while behind him a column of smoke rose into the air, as though light had been set to some sunk furnace.

Into the space that had thus been cleared were now led seven persons, whose hands were tied behind them. They were of both sexes and included an old man and a woman with a tall and handsome figure, who appeared to be quite young—scarcely more than a girl, indeed. These seven were ranged in a line where they stood, clearly in great fear, for the old man fell upon his knees, and one of the women began to sob. Thus they were left awhile, perhaps to allow the fire behind them to burn up, which it soon did with great fierceness, throwing a vivid light upon every detail of the spectacle.

Now all was ready, and a man brought a wooden tray to the red-bearded priest, who was seated on a stool, the white cat upon his knees, whither we had seen it leap from his head a little while before. He took the tray by its handles, and at a word from him the cat jumped on to it and sat there. Then amidst the most intense silence he rose and uttered some prayer, apparently to the cat, which sat facing him. This done, he turned the tray round so that the creature's back was now towards him, and, advancing to the

line of prisoners, began to walk up and down in front of them, which he did several times, at each turn drawing a little nearer.

Holding out the tray, he presented it at the face of the prisoner on the left, whereon the cat rose, arched its back, and began to lift its paws up and down. Presently he moved to the next prisoner and held it before him awhile, and so on till he came to the fifth, that young woman of whom I have spoken. Now the cat grew very angry, for in the deathlike stillness we could hear it spitting and growling. At length it seemed to lift its paw and strike the girl upon the face, whereon she screamed aloud, a terrible scream. Then all the audience broke out into a shout, a single word, which we understood, for we had heard one very like it used by the people of the Plain. It was "Witch ! Witch ! *Witch !*"

Executioners, who were waiting for the victim to be chosen in this ordeal by cat, rushed forward and seizing the girl began to drag her towards the fire. The prisoner who was standing by her, and whom we rightly guessed to be her husband, tried to protect her, but his arms being bound, poor fellow, he could do nothing. One of the executioners knocked him down with a stick. For a moment his wife escaped and threw herself upon him, but the brutes lifted her up again, haling her towards the fire, whilst all the audience shouted wildly.

"I can't stand this," said Leo ; "it's murder—cold-blooded murder," and he drew his sword.

"Best leave the beasts alone," I answered doubtfully, though my own blood was boiling in my veins.

Whether he heard or not, I do not know, for the next thing I saw was Leo rushing through the gate waving the Khan's sword and shouting at the top of his voice. Then I struck my heels into the ribs of the horse and followed after him. In ten seconds we were among them. As we came, the savages fell back this way and that, staring at us amazed, for at first I think they took us for apparitions. Thus, Leo on foot and I galloping after him, we came to the place.

The executioners and their victim were near the fire now—a very great fire of resinous pine logs built in a pit that measured about eight feet across. Close to it sat the priest upon his stool, watching the scene with a cruel smile, and rewarding the cat with little gobbets of raw meat that he took from a leathern pouch at his side, occupations in which he was so deeply engaged that he never saw us until we were right on to him.

Shouting : "Leave her alone, you black-guards!" Leo rushed at the executioners, and with a single blow of his sword severed the arm of one of them who gripped the woman by the nape of the neck.

With a yell of pain and rage the man sprang back and stood waving the stump towards the people and staring at it wildly. In the confusion that followed I saw the victim slip from the hands of her astonished would-be murderers and run into the darkness, where she vanished. Also I saw the witch-doctor spring up, still holding the tray on which the cat was sitting, and heard him begin to shout a perfect torrent of furious abuse at Leo, who in reply waved his sword and cursed them roundly in English and many other languages.

Then of a sudden the cat upon the tray, infuriated, I suppose, by the noise and the interruption of its meal, sprang straight at Leo's face. He appeared to catch it in mid-air with his left-hand, and with all his strength dashed it to the ground, where it lay writhing and screeching. Then, as though by an afterthought, he stooped, picked the devilish creature up again, and hurled it into the heart of the fire, for he was mad with rage and knew not what he did.

At the sight of that awful sacrilege—for such it was to them who worshipped this beast—a gasp of horror rose from the spectators, followed by a howl of execration. Then like a wave of the sea they rushed at us. I saw Leo cut one man down, and next instant I was off the horse and being dragged towards the furnace. At the edge of it I met Leo in like plight, but fighting furiously, for his strength was great and they were half afraid of him.

"Why couldn't you leave the cat alone?" I shouted at him in idiotic remonstrance, for my brain had gone, and all I knew was that we were about to be thrown into the fiery pit. Already I was over it; I felt the flames singe my hair and saw its red caverns awaiting me, when of a sudden the brutal hands that held me were unloosened and I fell backwards to the ground, where I lay staring upwards.

This was what I saw. Standing in front of the fire, her draped form quivering as though with rage, was our ghostly looking guide, who pointed with her hand at the gigantic, red-headed witch-doctor. But she was no longer alone, for with her were a score or more of men clad in white robes and armed with swords; black-eyed, ascetic-looking men, with clean-shaved heads and faces, for their scalps shone in the firelight.

At the sight of them terror had seized that multitude, which, mad as goaded bulls but a few seconds before, now fled in every direction like sheep frightened by a wolf. The leader of the white-robed priests, a man with a gentle face, which when at rest was clothed in a perpetual smile, was addressing the medicine-man, and I understood something of his talk.

"Dog!" he said in effect, speaking in a smooth, measured voice that yet was terrible, "accursed dog! beast-worshipper! what were you about to do to the guests of the mighty Mother of the Mountain? Is it for this that you and your idolatries have been spared so long? Answer, if you have anything to say. Answer quickly, for your time is short!"

With a groan of fear the great fellow flung himself upon his knees, not to the head-priest who questioned him, but before the quivering shape of our guide, and to her put up half-articulate prayers for mercy.

"Cease!" said the high-priest; "she is the Minister who judges and the Sword that strikes. I am the Ears and the Voice. Speak and tell me—were you about to cast those men, whom you were commanded to receive hospitably, into yonder fire because they saved the victim of your devilries and killed the imp you cherished? Nay, I saw it all. Know that it was but a trap to catch you, who have been allowed to live too long."

But still the wretch writhed before the draped form and howled for mercy.

"Messenger," said the high priest, "with thee the power goes. Declare thy decree."

Then our guide lifted her hand slowly and pointed to the fire. At once the man turned ghastly white, groaned and fell back—as I think, quite dead, slain by his own terror.

Now many of the people had fled, but some remained, and to these the priest called in cold tones, bidding them approach. They obeyed, creeping towards him.

"Look!" he said, pointing to the man, "look and tremble at the justice of Hes the Mother! Aye, and be sure as it is with him, so shall it be with every one of you who dares to defy her and to practise sorcery and murder. Lift up that dead dog who was your chief."

Some of them crept forward and did his bidding.

"Now cast him into the bed which he had made ready for his victims."

Staggering forward to the edge of the flaming pit, they obeyed, and the great body fell with a crash amongst the burning boughs and vanished there.

"Listen, you people," said the priest, "and learn that this man deserved his dreadful doom. Know you why he purposed to kill that woman whom the strangers saved? Because his familiar marked her as a witch, you think. I tell you it was not so. It was because, she being fair, he would have taken her from her husband, as he had taken many another, and she refused him. But the Eye saw, the Voice spoke, and the Messenger did judgment. He is caught in his own snare; and so shall you be, every one of you who dares to think evil in his heart or to do it with his hands.

"Such is the just decree of the Hesea, spoken by her from her throne amidst the fires of the Mountain."

AYESHA

THE RETURN OF "SHE."

By H. RIDER HAGGARD.

SYNOPSIS OF FOREGOING CHAPTERS.—The return of "She-Who-Must-Be-Obeyed" is recorded by Ludwig Horace Holly, the friend of that Leo Vincey whom Ayesha the beautiful loved in the awful tombs of Kôr. When the record begins, the two men are living in an old house remote upon the seashore of Cumberland, where they have been slowly recovering from the horror of the passing of Ayesha in the flames—a doom that seemed one of complete extinction, yet was charged with the strange last words: "I die not. I shall come again and shall once more be beautiful. I swear it—it is true." On a sullen August night, Leo is thrilled by a vision of Ayesha in all her former loveliness. She beckons him, and in a vision his spirit follows her into a realm of snowy peaks far beyond the furthest borders of Thibet. A sign in the clouds at dawn is repeated from this vision to both Leo and Holly, and together they start for Central Asia. Sixteen years of toil, struggle, and strange adventure pass, and they are still searching for "a mountain peak shaped like the Symbol of Life." After many wanderings they find themselves in a country where no European has ever set foot, on one of the spurs of the vast Cherga mountains, far eastward from Turkestan. Sheltered awhile in a Buddhist monastery, they hear of the recent visit of a stranger who has told the Lamas that his countryfolk, "dwelling beyond the Far Mountains," worship a priestess called Hes, or the Hesea, and upon persuasion the abbot of the monastery tells them that in a former incarnation he himself has seen the great priestess, who was "all loveliness." A perilous ascent into the unexplored mountain fastness leads them to the revelation of "the *crux ansata*, the Symbol of Life itself." The symbol vanishes, the fire sinks, but they are sure that as it was sent of old to show them a path of escape from the Place of Death, so now it has been sent again in greeting to point out the path to the Place of Life where Ayesha dwells. A further ascent into the mountains reveals their Promised Land, with the symbol of their vision, an enormous pillar of rock, whereof the top was formed to the shape of a loop. Rescued from drowning by a beautiful woman and an aged man, they are conducted through "The Gate" into the kingdom and city of Kaloon. Their saviours, they learn, are the Khania or Queen of Kaloon, and a venerable physician of magical powers. Is this woman Ayesha? No; they conjecture her rather to be Amenartas, who wrote the "sherd" of the former chronicle. She falls in love with Leo, and he and Holly learn that her husband, the Khan, is a madman. Simbri, the magician, and Atene, the Khania, have already received a solemn charge from the Hesea of the "College" in the Mountain of Fire to receive two strangers and bring them safely to the Mountain. But Atene's love for Leo makes her detain the travellers awhile in Kaloon, and she even proposes that the Khan shall be murdered so that she can wed Leo. To this the Englishman replies: "I go to ask a certain question of the Oracle on yonder mountain peak. With your will or without it, I tell you that I go, and afterwards you can settle which is the stronger—the Khania of Kaloon or the Hesea of the House of Fire." The Khan himself assists the escape of the travellers for their further journey, but his jealousy has been aroused, and after they have set out on their journey to the fire-crowned Mountain he pursues them with his death-hounds. After a long chase, a few of the brutes, and the Khan, overtake them, and a terrible struggle ensues, in which Leo and Holly eventually prove the victors. The Khan is slain, but ere he dies he warns them to beware of Atene, adding that their only hope of safety lies in reaching the fire-crowned Mountain. Not long afterwards the Khania and Simbri overtake them and seek to persuade them to return, but they refuse. The Khania leaves them, saying: "We do not part thus easily. You have summoned me to the Mountain, and even to the Mountain I will follow you. Aye, and there I will meet its spirit. . . . I will match my strength and magic against hers, as it is decreed that I shall do." Preserved by priestly intervention from death at the hands of a strange people, they realise that they are nearing the sphere of influence of the mysterious Hesea.

CHAPTER XIII.

BENEATH THE SHADOWING WINGS.

ONE by one the terrified tribesmen crept away. When the last of them were gone, the priest advanced to Leo and saluted him by placing his hand upon his forehead.

"Lord," he said, in the same corrupt Grecian dialect which was used by the courtiers of Kaloon, "I will not ask if you are hurt, since from the moment that you entered the sacred river and set foot within this land you and your companion were protected by a power invisible, and could not be harmed by man or spirit, however great may have seemed your danger. Yet vile hands have been laid upon you, and this is the command of the Mother whom I serve, that, if you desire it, every one of these men who touched you shall die before your eyes. Say, is that your will?"

"Nay," answered Leo; "they were mad and blind—let no blood be shed for us. All we ask of you, friend—but how are you called?"

"Name me Oros," he answered.

"Friend Oros—a good title for one who dwells upon the Mountain—all we ask is food and shelter, and to be led swiftly into the presence of her whom you name Mother, that Oracle whose wisdom we have travelled far to seek."

He bowed and answered: "The food and shelter are prepared, and to-morrow, when you have rested, I am commanded to conduct you whither you desire to be. Follow me, I pray you"; and he preceded us past the fiery pit to a building that stood about fifty yards away against the rock wall of the amphitheatre.

It would seem that it was a guest-house, or at least had been made ready to serve that purpose, as in it lamps were lit and a fire burned, for here the air was cold. The house was divided into two rooms, the second of them a sleeping-place, to which he led us through the first.

"Enter," he said, "for you will need to cleanse yourselves, and you"—here he addressed himself to me—"to be treated for that hurt to your arm which you had from the jaws of the great hound."

"How know you that?" I asked.

"It matters not, if I do know and have made ready," Oros answered gravely.

This second room was lighted and warmed like the first; moreover, heated water stood in basins of metal, and on the beds were laid clean linen garments and dark-coloured, hooded robes, lined with rich fur. Also upon a little table were ointments, bandages, and splints, a marvellous thing to see, for it told me that the very nature of my hurt had been divined. But I asked no more questions; I was too weary; moreover, I knew that it would be useless.

Now the priest Oros helped me to remove my tattered robe, and undoing the rough bandages upon my arm, washed it gently with warm water, in which he mixed some spirit, and examined it with the skill of a trained doctor.

"The fangs rent deep," he said, "and the small bone is broken, but you will take no harm, save for the scars which must remain." Then, having treated the wounds with ointment, he wrapped the limb with such a delicate touch that it scarcely pained me, saying that by the morrow the swelling would have gone down, and he would set the bone. This indeed happened.

After it was done, he helped me to wash and to clothe myself in the clean garments, and put a sling about my neck to serve as a rest for my arm. Meanwhile Leo had also dressed himself, so that we left the chamber together very different men from the foul, blood-stained wanderers who had entered there. In the outer room we found food prepared for us, of which we ate with a thankful heart and without speaking. Then,

blind with weariness, we returned to the other chamber and, having removed our outer garments, flung ourselves upon the beds and were soon plunged in sleep.

At some time in the night I awoke suddenly, at what hour I do not know, as certain people wake, I among them, when their room is entered, even without the slightest noise. Before I opened my eyes, I felt that someone was with us in the place. Nor was I mistaken. A little lamp still burned in the chamber, a mere wick floating in oil, and by its light I saw a dim, ghost-like form standing near the door. Indeed, I thought almost that it was a ghost, till presently I remembered, and knew it for our corpselike guide, who appeared to be looking intently at the bed on which Leo lay—or so I thought, for the head was bent in that direction.

At first she was quite still, then she moaned aloud, a low and terrible moan, which seemed to well from the very heart.

So the thing was not dumb, as I had believed. Evidently it could suffer, and express its suffering in a human fashion. Look! it was wringing its padded hands as in an excess of woe. Now it would seem that Leo began to feel its influence also, for he stirred and spoke in his sleep, so low at first that I could only distinguish the tongue he used, which was Arabic. Presently I caught a few words.

"Ayesha," he said, "*Ayesha!*"

The figure glided towards him and stopped. He sat up in the bed, still fast asleep, for his eyes were shut. He stretched out his arms as though seeking one whom he would embrace, and spoke again in a low and passionate voice—

"Ayesha, through life and death I have sought thee long. Come to me, my goddess, my desired!"

The figure glided yet nearer, and I could see that it was trembling, and now its arms were extended also.

At the bedside it halted, and Leo laid himself down again. Now the coverings had fallen back, exposing his breast, where lay the leather satchel he always wore, that which contained the lock of Ayesha's hair. He was fast asleep, and the figure seemed to fix its eyes upon this satchel. Presently it did more, for, with surprising deftness, those white-wrapped fingers opened its clasp—yes, and drew out the long tress of shining hair. Long and earnestly she gazed at it, then gently replaced the relic, closed the satchel, and for a little while seemed to weep. While she stood thus, the dreaming Leo once more stretched out his arms and spoke, saying, in the same passion-laden voice—

"Come to me, my darling, my beautiful, my beautiful!"

At those words, with a little muffled scream, like that of a scared night-bird, the figure turned and flitted through the doorway.

*   *   *   *   *

When I was quite certain that she had gone, I gasped aloud.

What might this mean? I wondered, in a very agony of bewilderment. This could certainly be no dream: it was real, for I was wide awake. Indeed, what did it all mean? Who was the ghastly, mummylike thing which had guided us unharmed through such terrible dangers—the Messenger that all men feared, who could strike down a brawny savage with a motion of its hand? Why did it creep into the place thus at dead of night, like a spirit revisiting one beloved? Why did its presence cause me to awake and Leo to dream? Why did it draw out the tress—indeed, how knew it that this tress was hidden there? And why—oh! why, at those tender and passionate words did it flee away at last like some scared bat?

The priest Oros had called our guide Minister, and Sword—that is, one who carries out decrees. But what if they were its own decrees? What if the thing should be she whom we sought, *Ayesha herself?* Why should I tremble at the thought, seeing that, if so, our quest was ended, we had achieved? Oh! it must be because about this being there was something terrible, something unhuman and appalling. If Ayesha lived within those mummy-cloths, then it was a different Ayesha whom we had known and worshipped. Well could I remember the white-draped form of *She-Who-Must-Be-Obeyed,* and how, long before she revealed her glorious face to us, we guessed the beauty and the majesty hidden beneath that veil by which her radiant life and loveliness incarnate could not be disguised.

But what of this creature? I would not pursue the thought. I was mistaken. Doubtless she was what the priest Oros had said—some half-supernatural being to whom certain powers were given, and, doubtless, she had come to spy on us in our rest, that she might make report to the giver of those powers.

Comforting myself thus, I fell asleep again, for fatigue overcame even such doubts and fears. In the morning, when they were naturally less vivid, I made up my mind that, for various reasons, it would be wisest to say nothing of what I had seen to Leo. Nor, indeed, did I say so until some days had gone by.

When I awoke, the full light was pouring into the chamber, and by it I saw the priest Oros standing at my bedside. I sat up and asked him what time it was, to which he answered with a smile, but in a low voice, that it lacked but two hours of midday, adding that he had come to set my arm. Now I saw why he spoke low, for Leo was still fast asleep.

"Let him rest on," he said, as he undid the wrappings on my arm, "for he has suffered much, and," he continued significantly, "may still have more to suffer."

"What do you mean, friend Oros?" I asked sharply. "I thought you told us that we were safe upon this Mountain."

"I told you, friend——" and he looked at me.

"Holly is my name——"

"——friend Holly, that your bodies are safe. I said nothing of all the rest of you. Man is more than flesh and blood. He is mind and spirit as well, and these can be injured also."

"Who is there that would injure them?" I asked.

"Friend," he answered gravely, "you and your companion have come to a haunted land, not as mere wanderers, for then you would be dead ere now, but of set purpose, seeking to lift the veil from mysteries which have been hid for ages. Well, your aim is known, and it may chance that it will be achieved. But if this veil is lifted, it may chance also that you will find what shall send your souls shivering to despair and madness. Say, are you not afraid?"

"Somewhat," I answered. "Yet my foster-son and I have seen strange things and lived. We have seen the very Light of Life roll by in majesty; we have been the guests of an Immortal, and watched Death seem to conquer her and leave us untouched. Think you then that we will turn cowards now? Nay, we march on to fulfil our destinies."

At these words Oros showed neither curiosity nor surprise; it was as though I told him only what he knew.

"Good," he replied, smiling, and with a courteous bow of his shaven head. "Within an hour you shall march on—to fulfil your destinies. If I have warned you, forgive me, for I was bidden so to do, perhaps to try your mettle. Is it needful that I should repeat this warning to the lord——?" and again he looked at me.

"Leo Vincey," I said.

"Leo Vincey—yes, Leo Vincey," he repeated, as though the name were familiar to him but had slipped his mind. "But you have not answered my question. Is it needful that I should repeat the warning?"

"Not in the least; but you can do so if you wish when he awakes."

"Nay, I think with you, that it would be but waste of words, for—forgive the comparison—what the wolf dares"—and he looked at me—"the tiger does not flee from," and he nodded towards Leo. "There, see how much better are the wounds upon your arm, which is no longer swollen. Now I will bandage it, and within some few weeks the bone will be as sound again as it was before you met the Khan Rassen hunting in the plains. By the way, you will see him again soon, and his fair wife with him."

"See him again? Do the dead, then, come to life upon this Mountain?"

"Nay, but certain of them are brought hither for burial. It is the privilege of the rulers of Kaloon; also, I think that the Khania has questions to ask of its Oracle."

"Who is its Oracle?" I asked with eagerness.

"The Oracle," he replied darkly, "is a Voice. It was ever so, was it not?"

"Yes; I have heard it from Atene; but a voice implies a speaker. Is this speaker she whom you name Mother?"

"Perhaps, friend Holly."

"And is this Mother a spirit?"

"It is a point that has been much debated. They told you so in the Plains, did they not? Also the Tribes think it on the Mountain. Indeed, the thing seems reasonable, seeing that all of us who live are flesh and spirit. But you will form your own judgment and then we can discuss the matter. There, your arm is finished. Be careful now not to strike it or to fall; and look, your companion awakes."

*   *   *   *   *

Something over an hour later we started upon our upward journey. I was again mounted on the Khan's horse, which, having been groomed and fed, was somewhat rested, while to Leo a litter had been offered. This he declined, however, saying that he had now recovered, and would not be carried like a woman. So he walked by the side of my horse, using his spear as a staff. We passed the fire-pit—now full of dead, white ashes, among which were mixed those of the witch-finder and his horrible cat—preceded by our dumb guide, at the sight of whom, in her pale wrappings, the people of the tribe, who had returned to their village, prostrated themselves, and so remained until she was gone by.

One of them, however, rose again and, breaking through our escort of priests, ran to Leo, knelt before him, and kissed his hand. It was that young woman whose life he had saved, a noble-looking girl, with masses of red hair; and by her was her husband, the marks of his bonds still showing on his arms. Our guide seemed to see this incident, though how she did so I do not know. At any rate, she turned and made some sign which the priest interpreted.

Calling the woman to him, he asked her sternly how she dared to touch the person of this stranger with her vile lips. She answered that it was because her heart was grateful. Oros said that for this reason she was forgiven; moreover, that in reward for what they had suffered he was commanded to lift up her husband to be the ruler of that tribe during the pleasure of the Mother. He gave notice, moreover, that all should obey the new chief in his place, according to their customs; and if he did any evil, make report, that he might suffer punishment. Then waving the pair aside, without listening to their thanks or the acclamations of the crowd, he passed on.

As we went down the ravine by which we had approached the village on the previous night, a sound of chanting struck our ears. Presently the path turned, and we saw a solemn procession advancing up that dismal, sunless gorge. At the head of it rode none other than the beautiful Khania, followed by her great-uncle, the old Shaman, and after these came a company of shaven priests in their white robes, bearing between them a bier, upon which, its face uncovered, lay the body of the Khan, draped in a black garment. Yet he looked better thus than he had ever done, for now death had touched this insane and dissolute man with something of the dignity which he lacked in life.

Thus, then, we met. At the sight of our guide's white form, the horse which the Khania rode reared up so violently that I thought it would have thrown her. But she mastered the animal with her whip and voice and called out—

"Who is this draped hag of the Mountain that stops the path of the Khania Atene and her dead lord? My guests, I find you in ill company, for it seems that you are conducted

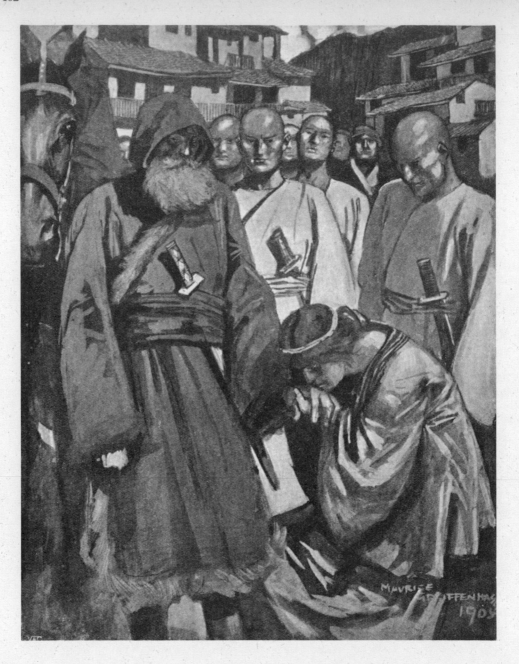

"Ran to Leo, knelt before him, and kissed his hand."

by an evil spirit to meet an evil fate. That guide of yours must surely be something hateful and hideous; for were she a wholesome woman, she would not fear to show her face."

Now the Shaman plucked his mistress by the sleeve, and the priest Oros, bowing to her, prayed her to be silent and cease to speak such ill-omened words into the air,

which might carry them she knew not whither. But some instinctive hate seemed to bubble up in Atene, and she would not be silent, for she addressed our guide, using the direct "thou," a manner of speech that we found was very usual on the Mountain, though rare upon the Plains.

"Let the air carry them whither it will!" she cried. "Sorceress, strip off thy rags, fit only for a corpse too vile to view! Show us what thou art, thou flitting night-owl, who thinkest to frighten me with that livery of death, which only serves to hide the death within!"

"Cease, I pray, lady, cease," said Oros, stirred for once out of his imperturbable calm. "She is the Minister, none other, and with her goes the Power."

"Then it goes not against Atene, Khania of Kaloon," she answered; "or so I think. Power, forsooth! Let her show her power. If she has any, it is not her own, but that of the Witch of the Mountain, who feigns to be a spirit, and by her sorceries has drawn away my guests"—and she pointed to us—"thus bringing my husband to his death."

"Niece, be silent!" said the old Shaman, whose wrinkled face was white with terror, whilst Oros held up his hands as though in supplication to some unseen Strength, saying—

"O thou that hearest and seest, be merciful, I beseech thee, and forgive this woman her madness, lest the blood of a guest should stain the hands of thy servants, and the ancient honour of our worship be brought low in the eyes of men."

Thus he prayed; but although his hands were uplifted, it seemed to me that his eyes were fixed upon our guide, as ours were. While he spoke, I saw her hand raised, as she had raised it when she slew—or, rather, sentenced—the witch-doctor. Then she seemed to reflect, and stayed it in mid-air, so that it pointed at the Khania. She did not move, she made no sound, only she pointed, and the angry words died upon Atene's lips, the fury left her eyes, and the colour her face. Yes, she grew white and silent as the corpse upon the bier behind her. Then, cowed by that invisible power, she struck her horse so fiercely that it bounded by us onward towards the village, at which the funeral company were to rest awhile.

As the Shaman Simbri followed the Khania, the priest Oros caught his horse's bridle and said to him—

"Magician, we have met before—for instance, when your lady's father was brought to his funeral. Warn her, then, you that know something of the truth and of her power, to speak more gently of the ruler of this land. Say to her, from me, that had she not been the ambassadress of Death, and therefore inviolate, surely ere now she would have shared her husband's bier. Farewell; to-morrow we will speak again," and, loosing the Shaman's bridle, Oros passed on.

Soon we had left the melancholy procession behind us, and, issuing from the gorge, turned up the Mountain slope towards the edge of the bright snows that lay not far above. It was as we came out of this darksome valley, where the overhanging pine trees almost eclipsed the light, that suddenly we missed our guide.

"Has she gone back to—to reason with the Khania?" I asked of Oros.

"Nay!" he answered, with a slight smile, "I think that she has gone forward to give warning that the Hesea's guests draw near."

"Indeed," I answered, staring hard at the bare slope of mountain, up which not a mouse could have passed without being seen. "I understand—she has gone forward," and the matter dropped. But what I did *not* understand was—how she had gone. As the Mountain was honeycombed with caves and galleries, I suppose, however, that she entered one of them.

All the rest of that day we marched upwards, gradually drawing nearer to the snowline, as we went gathering what information we could from the priest Oros. This was the sum of it—

From the beginning of the world, as he expressed it—that is, from thousands and thousands of years ago—this Mountain had been the home of a peculiar fire-worship, of which the head heirophant was a woman. About twenty centuries before, however, the invading general, named Rassen, had made himself Khan of Kaloon. Rassen established a new priestess on the Mountain, a worshipper of the Egyptian goddess, Hes, or Isis. This priestess had introduced certain modifications in the ancient doctrines, superseding the cult of fire, pure and simple, by a new faith, which, while holding to some of the old ceremonies, revered as its head the Spirit of Life or Nature, of whom they looked upon their priestess as the earthly representative.

Of this priestess Oros would only tell us that she was "ever present," although we gathered that when one priestess died, or was "taken to the fire," as he put it, her child, whether in fact or by adoption, succeeded her and was known by the same names—those of "Hes" or the "Hesea," and "Mother." We asked if we should see this Mother, to which he answered that she manifested herself very rarely. As to her appearance and attributes he would say nothing, except that the former changed from time to time, and that when she chose to use it she had "all power."

The priests of her College, he informed us, numbered three hundred, never more nor less, and there were also three hundred priestesses. Certain of those who desired it were allowed to marry, and from among their children were reared up the new generation of priests and priestesses. Thus they were a people apart from all others, with distinct racial characteristics. This, indeed, was evident, for our escort were all exceedingly like to each other, very handsome and refined in appearance, with dark eyes, clean-cut features, and olive-hued skins; such a people as might well have descended from Easterns of high blood, with a dash of that of the Egyptians and Greeks thrown in.

We asked him whether the mighty looped pillar that towered from the topmost cup of the Mountain was the work of men. He answered; No; the hand of Nature had fashioned it, and that the light shining came from the fires which burned in the crater of the volcano. The first priestess, having recognised in this gigantic column the familiar Symbol of Life of the Egyptian worship, established her altars beneath its shadow.

For the rest, the Mountain, with its mighty slopes and borderlands, was peopled by a multitude of half-savage folk, who accepted the rule of the Hesea, bringing her tribute of all things necessary, such as food and metals. Much of the meat and grain, however, the priests raised themselves on sheltered farms, and the metals they worked with their own hands. This rule, however, was of a moral nature, since for centuries the College had sought no conquests, and the Mother contented herself with punishing crime in some such fashion as we had seen. For the petty wars between the Tribes and the people of the Plain they were not responsible, and those chiefs who carried them on were deposed, unless they had themselves been attacked. All the Tribes, however, were sworn to the defence of the Hesea and the College, and, however much they might quarrel amongst themselves, if need arose, were ready to die for her to the last man. That war must one day break out again between the priests of the Mountain and the people of Kaloon was recognised; therefore they endeavoured to be prepared for that great and final struggle.

Such was the gist of his history, which, as we learned afterwards, proved to be true in every particular.

*　　*　　*　　*　　*

Towards sundown we came to a vast cup extending over many thousand acres, situated beneath the snowline of the peak, and filled with rich soil, washed down, I suppose, from above. So sheltered was the place by its configuration and the overhanging mountain that, facing south-west as it did, notwithstanding its altitude it produced corn and other temperate crops in abundance. Here the College had its farms, and very well cultivated these seemed to be. This great cup, which could not be seen from below; we entered through a kind of natural gateway, that might be easily defended against a host.

There were other peculiarities, but it is not necessary to describe them further than to say that I think the soil benefited by the natural heat of the volcano, and that when this erupted, as happened occasionally, the lava streams always passed to the north and south of the cup of land. Indeed, it was these lava streams that had built up the protecting cliffs.

Crossing the gardenlike lands, we came to a small town beautifully built of lava rock. Here dwelt the priests, except those who were on duty, no man of the Tribes or other stranger being allowed to set foot within the place.

Following the main street of this town, we arrived at the face of the precipice beyond, and found ourselves in front of a vast archway, closed with massive iron gates fantastically wrought. Here, taking my horse with them, our escort left us alone with Oros. As we drew near, the great gates swung back upon their hinges. We passed them—with what sensations I cannot describe—and groped our way down a short corridor which ended in tall, iron-covered doors. These also rolled open at our approach, and next instant we staggered back amazed and half-blinded by the intense blaze of light within.

Imagine, you who read, the nave of the vastest cathedral with which you are acquainted. Then double or treble its size, and you will have some conception of that temple in which we found ourselves. Perhaps in the beginning it had been a cave—who can say?—but now its sheer walls, its multitudinous columns springing to the arched roof far above us, had all been worked on and fashioned by the labour of men long dead; doubtless the old fire-worshippers of thousands of years ago.

You will wonder how so great a place was lighted, but I think that never would you guess. Thus—by twisted columns of living flame! I counted eighteen of them, but there may have been others. They sprang from the floor at regular intervals along the lines of what in a cathedral would be the aisles. Right to the roof they sprang, of even height and girth, so fierce was the force that drove them, and there were lost, I suppose, through chimneys bored in the thickness of the rock. Nor did they give off smell or smoke, or in that great, cold place, any heat which could be noticed, only an intense, white light like that of molten iron, and a sharp, hissing noise as of a million angry snakes.

The huge temple was utterly deserted, and, save for this sibilant, pervading sound, utterly silent; an awsome, an overpowering place.

"Do these candles of yours ever go out?" asked Leo of Oros, placing his hand before his dazzled eyes.

"How can they," replied the priest in his smooth, matter-of-fact voice, "seeing that they rise from the eternal fire which the builders of this hall worshipped? Thus they have burned from the beginning, and thus they will burn for ever, though, if we wish it, we can shut off their light.* Be pleased to follow me : you will see greater things."

So in awed silence we followed, and, oh! how small and miserable we three human beings looked, alone in that vast temple illuminated by this lightning radiance! We reached the end of it at length, only to find that to right and left ran transepts on a like gigantic scale, and lit in the same amazing fashion. Here Oros bade us halt, and we waited a little while, till presently, from either transept, arose a sound of chanting, and we perceived two white-robed processions advancing towards us from their depths.

On they came, very slowly, and we saw that the procession to the right was a company of priests, and that to the left a company of priestesses, a hundred or so of them in all.

Now the men ranged themselves in front of us, while the women ranged themselves behind, and at a signal from Oros, all of them still chanting some wild and thrilling hymn, once more we started forward, this time along a narrow gallery closed at the end with double wooden doors. As our procession reached these, they opened, and

before us lay the crowning wonder of this marvellous fane—a vast, ellipse-shaped apse. Now we understood. The plan of the temple was the plan of the looped pillar which stood upon the brow of the Peak, and, as we rightly guessed, its dimensions were the same.

At intervals around this ellipse the fiery columns flared, but otherwise the place was empty.

No, not quite, for at the head of the apse, almost between two of the flame columns, stood a plain, square altar of the size of a small room, in front of which, as we saw when we drew nearer, were hung curtains of woven silver thread. On this altar was placed a large statue of silver, that, backed as it was by the black rock, seemed to concentrate and reflect from its burnished surface the intense light of the two blazing pillars.

It was a lovely thing, but to describe it is hard indeed. The figure, which was winged, represented a draped woman of mature years, and pure but gracious form, half hidden by the forward-bending wings. Sheltered by these, yet shown between them, appeared the image of a male child, clasped to its bearer's breast with her left arm, while the right was raised towards the sky. A study of motherhood, evidently; but how shall I write of all that was conveyed by those graven faces?

To begin with the child. It was that of a sturdy boy, full of health and the joy of life. Yet he had been sleeping, and in his sleep some terror had overshadowed him with the dark shades of death and evil. There was fear in the lines of his sweet mouth and on the lips and cheeks, that seemed to quiver. He had thrown his little arm about his mother's neck, and, pressing close against her breast, looked up to her for safety, his right hand and outstretched finger pointing downwards and behind him, as though to indicate whence the danger came. Yet it was passing, already half-forgotten, for the upturned eyes expressed confidence renewed, peace of soul attained.

And the mother. She did not seem to mock or chide his fears, for her lovely face was anxious and alert. Yet upon it breathed a very atmosphere of unchanging tenderness and power invincible; care for the helpless, strength to shelter it from every harm. The great, calm eyes told their story, the parted lips were whispering some tale of hope, sure and immortal; the raised hand revealed whence that hope arose. All love seemed to

---

* This, as I ascertained afterwards, was done by thrusting a broad stone of great thickness over the apertures through which the fire rushed, and thus cutting off the air. These were worked to and fro by means of pulleys connected with iron rods.—L. H. H.

be concentrated in the brooding figure, so human, yet so celestial ; all heaven seemed to lie an open path before those quivering wings. And see, the arching instep, the upward-springing foot, suggested that thither those wings were bound, bearing their God-given burden far from the horror of the earth, deep into the bosom of a changeless rest above.

The statue was only that of an affrighted child in its mother's arms : its interpretation made clear even to the dullest by the simple symbolism of some genius—Humanity rescued by the Divine.

While we gazed at its enchanting beauty, the priests and priestesses, filing away to right and left, arranged themselves alternately, first a man and then a woman, within the ring of the columns of fire that burned around the loop-shaped shrine. So great was its circumference that the whole hundred of them must stand wide apart one from another, and, to our sight, resembled little lonely children clad in gleaming garments, while their chant of worship reached us only like echoes thrown from a far precipice. In short, the effect of this holy shrine and its occupants was superb yet overwhelming—at least, I know that it filled me with a feeling akin to fear.

Oros waited till the last priest had reached his appointed place. Then he turned and said, in his gentle, reverent tones—

"Draw nigh, now, O Wanderers well-beloved, and give greeting to the Mother," and he pointed towards the statue.

"Where is she ? " asked Leo, in a whisper, for here we scarcely dared to speak aloud. "I see no one."

"The Hesea dwells yonder," he answered ; and taking each of us by the hand, he led us forward across the great emptiness of the apse to the altar at its head.

As we drew near, the distant chant of the priests gathered in volume, assuming a glad, triumphant note, and it seemed to me—though this, perhaps, was fancy—that the light from the twisted columns of flame grew even brighter.

At length we were there, and, Oros, loosing our hands, prostrated himself thrice before the altar. Then he rose again, and, falling behind us, stood in silence with bent head and folded fingers. We stood silent also, our hearts filled with mingled hope and fear like a cup with wine.

Were our labours ended ? Had we found her whom we sought, or were we, perchance, but enmeshed in the web of some marvellous mummery, and about to make acquaintance with the secret of another new and mystical worship ? For years and years we had searched, enduring every hardness of flesh and spirit that man can suffer, and now we were to learn whether we had endured in vain. Yes, and Leo would learn if the promise was to be fulfilled to him, or whether she whom he adored had become but a departed dream, to be sought for only beyond the gate of Death. Little wonder that he trembled and turned white in the agony of that great suspense.

Long, long was the time. Hours, years, ages, æons seemed to flow over us as we stood there before glittering silver curtains that hid the front of the black altar beneath the mystery of the sphinxlike face of the glorious image which was its guardian, clothed with that frozen smile of eternal love and pity. All the past went before us as we struggled in those dark waters of our doubt. Item by item, event by event, we rehearsed the story which began in the Caves of Kôr, for our thoughts, so long attuned, were open to each other and flashed from soul to soul.

Oh ! now we knew they were open also to *another* soul. We could see nothing save the altar and the effigy, we could only hear the slow chant of the priests and priestesses, and the snakelike hiss of the rushing fires. Yet we knew that our hearts were as an open book to One who watched beneath the Mother's shadowing wings.

CHAPTER XIV.

THE COURT OF DEATH.

Now the curtains were open. Before us appeared a chamber hollowed from the thickness of the altar, and in its centre a throne, and on the throne a figure clad in waves of billowy white flowing from the head over the arms of the throne down to its marble steps. We could see no more in the comparative darkness of that place, save that beneath the folds of the drapery the Oracle held in its hand a loop-shaped, jewelled sceptre.

Moved by some impulse, we did as Oros had done, prostrating ourselves, and there remained upon our knees. At length we heard a tinkling as of little bells, and, looking up, saw that the sistrum-shaped sceptre was stretched towards us by the draped arm which held it. Then a thin, clear voice spoke, and I thought that it trembled just a little. It spoke in Greek, but in a much purer Greek than all those people used.

"She grew white and silent as the corpse upon the bier behind her."

"I greet you, Wanderers, who have journeyed so far to visit this most ancient shrine, and although doubtless of some other faith, are not ashamed to do reverence to that unworthy one who is for this time its Oracle and the guardian of its mysteries. Rise now and have no fear of me; for have I not sent my Messenger and servants to conduct you to this Sanctuary?"

Slowly we rose, and stood silent, not knowing what to say.

"I greet you, Wanderers," the voice repeated. "Tell me thou"—and the sceptre pointed towards Leo — "how art thou named?"

"I am named Leo Vincey," he answered.

"Leo Vincey! I like the name, which to me well befits a man so goodly. And thou, the companion of—Leo Vincey?"

"I am named Horace Holly."

"So. Then tell me, Leo Vincey and Horace Holly, what came ye so far to seek?"

We looked at each other, and I said—

"The tale is long and strange, O—but by what title must we address thee?"

"By the name which I bear here—Hes."

"O Hes," I said, wondering what name she bore elsewhere.

"Yet I desire to hear that tale," she went on, and to me her voice sounded eager. "Nay, not all to-night, for I know that you both are weary; a little of it only. In sooth, Strangers, there is a sameness in this home of contemplations, and no heart can feed only on the past, if such a thing there be. Therefore I welcome a new history from the world without. Tell it me, thou, Leo, as briefly as thou wilt, so that thou tell the truth, for in the Presence of which I am a Minister may nothing else be uttered."

"Priestess," he said, in his curt fashion, "I obey. Many years ago, when I was young, my friend and foster-father and I, led by records of the past, travelled to a wild land, and there found a certain divine woman who had conquered Time."

"Then that woman must have been both aged and hideous."

"I said, Priestess, that she had conquered Time, not suffered it, for the gift of immortal youth was hers. Also, she was not hideous—she was beauty itself."

"Therefore, stranger, thou didst worship her for her beauty's sake, as a man does."

"I did not worship her; I loved her, which is another thing. The priest Oros here worships thee, whom he calls Mother. I loved that immortal woman."

"Then thou shouldst love her still. Yet, not so, since love is very mortal."

"I love her still," he answered, "although she died."

"Why, how is that? Thou saidst she was immortal."

"Perchance she only seemed to die; perchance she changed. At least, I lost her; and what I lost I seek, and have sought this many a year."

"Why dost thou seek her in my Mountain, Leo Vincey?"

"Because a vision led me to ask counsel of its Oracle. I am come hither to learn tidings of my lost love, since here alone these may be found."

"And thou, Holly, didst thou also love an immortal woman, whose immortality, it seems, must bow to Death?"

"Priestess," I answered, "I am sworn to this quest, and where my foster-son goes, I follow. He follows beauty that is dead——"

"And thou dost follow him. Therefore, both of you follow beauty, as men have ever done, being blind and mad."

"Nay," I answered, "if they were blind, beauty would be naught to them who could not see it; and if they were mad, they could not know it when it was seen. Knowledge and vision belong to the wise, O Hes."

"Thou art quick of wit and tongue, Holly, as——" and she checked herself, then of a sudden said: "Tell me, did my servant the Khania of Kaloon entertain both of you hospitably in her city, and speed you on your journey hither, as I commanded her?"

"We knew not that she was thy servant," I replied. "Hospitality we had and to spare, but we were sped from her Court hitherward by the death-hounds of the Khan, her husband. Tell us, Priestess, what thou knowest of this journey of ours."

"A little," she answered carelessly. "More than three moons ago my spies saw you upon the far mountains, and, creeping very close to you at night, heard you speak together of the object of your wanderings, then, returning thence swiftly, made report to me. Thereon I bade the Khania Atene, and that old magician her great-uncle, who is Guardian of the Gate, go down to the ancient gates of Kaloon to receive you and bring you hither with all speed. Yet for men who burned to learn the answer to a riddle, you have been long in coming."

"We came as fast as we might, O Hes," said Leo; "and if thy spies could visit those mountains, where no man was, and find a path down that hideous precipice, they must have been able also to tell thee the reason of our delay. Therefore, I pray, ask it not of us."

"Nay, I will ask it of Atene herself, and she shall surely answer me, for she stands without," replied the Hesea in a cold voice. "Oros, lead the Khania hither, and be swift."

The priest turned and walking quickly to the wooden doors by which we had entered the shrine, vanished there.

"Now," said Leo to me nervously in the silence that followed, and speaking in English, "now I wish we were somewhere else, for I think that there will be trouble."

"I don't think—I am sure," I answered; "but the more, the better; for out of trouble may come the truth, which we need sorely." Then I stopped, reflecting that the strange woman before us said that her spies had overheard our talk upon the mountains, where we had spoken nothing but English.

As it proved, I was wise, for quite quietly the Hesea repeated after me—

"Thou hast experience, Holly, for out of trouble comes the truth, as out of wine."

Then she was silent, and, needless to say, I did not pursue the conversation.

* * * * *

The doors swung open, and through them came a procession clad in black, followed by the Shaman Simbri, who walked in front of a bier, upon which lay the body of the Khan, carried by eight priests. Behind it was Atene, draped in a black veil from head to foot, and after her marched another company of priests. In front of the altar the bier was set down, and the priests fell back, leaving Atene and her uncle standing alone before the corpse.

"What seeks my vassal, the Khania of Kaloon?" asked the Hesea in a cold voice.

Now Atene advanced and bent the knee, but with little graciousness.

"Ancient Mother, Mother from of old, I do reverence to thy holy Office, as my fore-fathers have done for many a generation," and again she curtsied. "Mother, this dead man asks of thee that right of sepulchre in the fires of the holy Mountain which from the beginning has been accorded to the royal departed who went before him."

"It has been accorded as thou sayest," answered the Hesea, "by those priestesses who filled my place before me, nor shall it be refused to thy dead lord—nor to thee, Atene—when thy time comes."

"I thank thee, O Hes, and I pray that this decree may be written down, for the snows of age have gathered on thy venerable head, and soon thou must leave us for awhile. Therefore bid thy scribes that it be written down, so that the Hesea who rules after thee may fulfil it in its season."

"Cease," said the Hesea, "cease to pour out thy bitterness at that which should command thy reverence, oh! thou foolish child, who dost not know but that to-morrow the fire shall claim the frail youth and beauty which are thy boast. I bid thee cease, and tell me how did death find this lord of thine?"

"Ask those wanderers yonder, that were his guests, for his blood is on their heads and cries for vengeance at thy hands."

"I killed him," said Leo, "to save my own life. He tried to hunt us down with his dogs, and there are the marks of them," and he pointed to my arm. "The priest Oros knows, for he dressed the hurts."

"How did this chance?" asked the Hesea of Atene.

"My lord was mad," she answered boldly, "and such was his cruel sport."

"So. And was thy lord jealous also? Nay, keep back the falsehood I see rising to thy lips. Leo Vincey, answer thou me. Yet —I will not ask thee to lay bare the secrets of a woman who has offered thee her love. Thou, Holly, speak, and let it be the truth."

"It is this, O Hes," I answered. "Yonder lady and her uncle, the Shaman Simbri, saved us from death in the waters of the river that bounds the precipices of Kaloon. Afterwards we were ill, and they treated us kindly, but the Khania became enamoured of my foster-son."

Here the figure of the Priestess stirred beneath its gauzy wrappings, and the Voice asked—

"And did thy foster-son become enamoured of the Khania, as, being a man, he may well have done, for without doubt she is fair?"

"He can answer that question for himself, O Hes. All I know is that he strove to escape from her, and that in the end she gave him a day to choose between death and marriage with her, when her lord should be dead. So, helped by the Khan, her husband, who was jealous of him, we fled towards this Mountain, which we desired to reach. Then the Khan set his hounds upon us, for he was mad and false-hearted. We killed him and came on in spite of this lady, his wife, and her uncle, who would have prevented us, and were met in a Place of Bones by a certain veiled guide, who led us up the Mountain and twice saved us from death. That is all the story."

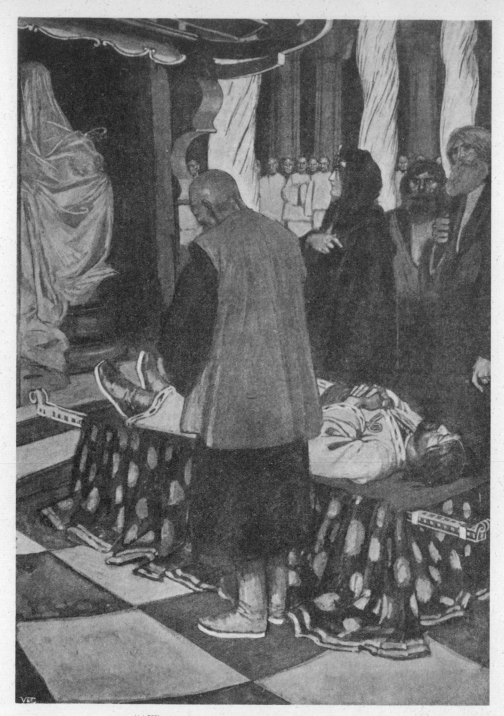

" ' What seeks my vassal, the Khania of Kaloon?' "

"Woman, what hast thou to say?" asked the Hesea in a menacing voice.

"But little," Atene answered without flinching. "For years I have been bound to a madman and a brute, and if my fancy wandered towards this man, and his fancy wandered towards me—well, Nature spoke to us, and that is all. Afterwards it seems that he grew afraid of the vengeance of Rassen; or this Holly, whom I would that the hounds had torn bone from bone, grew afraid. So they strove to escape the land, and perchance wandered to thy Mountain. But I weary of this talk, and ask thy leave to rest before to-morrow's rite."

"Thou sayest, Atene," said the Hesea, "that Nature spoke to this man and to thee, and that his heart is thine; but that, fearing thy lord's vengeance, he fled from thee, he who seems no coward. Tell me, then, is that tress he hides in the satchel on his breast thy gage of love to him?"

"I know nothing of what he hides in the satchel," answered the Khania sullenly.

"And yet, yonder in the Gatehouse, when he lay so sick, he set the lock against thine own—ah! dost remember now?"

"So, O Hes, already he has told thee all our secrets, though they be such as most men hide within their breasts"; and she looked contemptuously at Leo.

"I told her nothing of the matter, Khania," Leo said in an angry voice.

"Nay, *thou* toldest me nothing; Wanderer, my watching spirit told me. Oh, didst thou think, Atene, that thou couldst hide the truth from the all-seeing Hesea of the Mountain? If so, spare thy breath, for I know all, and have known it from the first. I passed thy disobedience by; of thy false messages I took no heed. For my own purposes I, to whom time is naught, suffered even that thou shouldst hold these, my guests, thy prisoners, whilst thou didst strive by threats and force to win a love denied."

She paused, then went on coldly: "Woman, I tell thee that, to complete thy sin, thou hast even dared to lie to me here, in my very Sanctuary."

"If so, what of it?" was the bold answer. "Dost thou love the man thyself? Nay, it is monstrous! Nature would cry aloud at such a shame. Oh! tremble not with rage. Hes, I know thy evil powers, but I know also that I am thy guest, and that in this hallowed place, beneath yonder symbol of eternal Love, thou mayst shed no blood. More, thou canst not harm me, Hes, who am thy equal."

"Atene," replied the measured Voice, "did I desire it, I could destroy thee where thou art. Yet thou art right, I shall not harm thee, thou faithless servant. Did not my writ bid thee through yonder searcher of the stars, thy uncle, to meet these guests of mine and bring them straight to my shrine? Tell me, for I seek to know, how comes it that thou didst disobey me?"

"Have, then, thy desire," answered Atene in a new and earnest voice, devoid now of bitterness and falsehood. "I disobeyed because that man is not thine, but mine, and no other woman's; because I love him and have loved him from of old. Aye, since first our souls sprang into life I have loved him, as he has loved me. My own heart tells me so; the magic of my uncle here tells me so, though how and where and when these things have been I know not. Therefore, I come to thee, Mother of Mysteries, Guardian of the secrets of the past, to learn the truth. At least, thou canst not lie at thine own altar, and I charge thee by the dread name of that Power to which thou also must render thy account, that thou answer now and here.

"Who is this man to whom my being yearns? What has he been to me? What has he to do with thee? Speak, O Oracle, and make the secret clear. Speak, I command, even if afterwards thou dost slay me —if thou canst."

"Aye, speak! speak!" said Leo, "for know I am in sore suspense. I also am bewildered by memories and rent with hopes and fears."

And I, too, echoed: "Speak!"

"Leo Vincey," asked the Hesea, after she had thought awhile, "whom dost thou believe me to be?"

"I believe," he answered solemnly, "that thou art that Ayesha at whose hands I died of old in the Caves of Kôr in Africa. I believe thou art that Ayesha whom not twenty years ago I found and loved in those same Caves of Kôr, and there saw perish miserably, swearing that thou wouldst return again."

"See, now, how madness can mislead a man!" broke in Atene triumphantly. "'Not twenty years ago,' he said, whereas I know well that more than eighty summers have gone by since my grandsire in his youth saw this same priestess sitting on the Mother's throne."

"And whom dost thou believe me to be, O Holly?" the Priestess asked, taking no note of the Khania's words.

"What he believes, I believe," I answered.

"'Let the books be opened!'"

"The dead come back to life—sometimes. Yet alone thou knowest the truth, and by thee only it can be revealed."

"Aye," she said, as though musing, "the dead come back to life—sometimes—and in strange shape, and mayhap I know the truth. To-morrow, when yonder body is borne on high for burial, we will speak of it again. Till then rest you all, and prepare to face that fearful thing—the Truth."

While the Hesea still spoke, the silvery

curtains swung to their place as mysteriously as they had opened. Then, as though at some signal, the black-robed priests advanced. Surrounding Atene, they led her from the Sanctuary, accompanied by her uncle the Shaman, who, as it seemed to me, either through fatigue or fear, could scarcely stand upon his feet, but stood blinking his dim eyes as though the light dazed him. When these were gone, the priests and priestesses, who all this time had been ranged round the walls, far out of hearing of our talk, gathered themselves into their separate companies, and, still chanting, departed also, leaving us alone with Oros and the corpse of the Khan, which remained where it had been set down.

Now the head priest Oros beckoned to us to follow him, and we went also. Nor was I sorry to leave the place, for its deathlike loneliness—enhanced, strangely enough, as it was, by the flood of light that filled it; a loneliness which was concentrated and expressed in the awful figure stretched upon the bier—oppressed and overcame us, whose nerves were broken by all that we had undergone. Thankful enough was I when, having passed the transepts and down the length of the vast nave, we came to the iron doors, the rock passage, and the outer gates, which, as before, opened to let us through, and so at last into the sweet, cold air of the night at that hour which precedes the dawn.

Oros led us to a house well-built and furnished, where at his bidding, like men in a dream, we drank of some liquor which he gave us. I think that drink was drugged; at least, after swallowing it, I remembered no more till I awoke to find myself lying on a bed and feeling wonderfully strong and well. This I thought strange, for a lamp burning in the room showed me that it was still dark and, therefore, that I could have rested but a little time.

I tried to sleep again, but was not able, so fell to thinking till I grew weary of the task. For here thoughts would not help me; nothing could help, except the truth, "that fearful thing," as the veiled Priestess had called it.

Oh! what if she proved not the Ayesha whom we desired, but some "fearful thing"? What was the meaning of the Khania's hints and of her boldness, that surely had been inspired by the strength of a hidden knowledge? What if—nay, it could not be —I would rise and dress my arm. Or I would wake Leo and make him dress it— anything to occupy my mind until the appointed hour, when we must learn—the best—or the worst.

I sat up in bed and saw a figure advancing towards me. It was Oros, who bore a lamp in his hand.

"You have slept long, friend Holly," he said, "and now it is time to be up and doing."

"Long?" I answered testily. "How can that be, when it is still dark?"

"Because, friend, the dark is that of a new night. Many hours have gone by since you lay down upon this bed. Well, you were wise to rest you while you may, for who knows when you will sleep again? Come, let me bathe your arm."

"Tell me——" I broke in.

"Nay, friend," he interrupted firmly, "I will tell you nothing, except that soon you must start to be present at the funeral of the Khan and, perchance, to learn the answer to your questions."

Ten minutes later he led me to the eating-chamber of the house, where I found Leo already dressed, for Oros had awakened him before he came to me and bidden him to prepare himself. Oros told us here that the Hesea had not suffered us to be disturbed until the night came again, since we had much to undergo that day. So presently we started.

Once more we were led through the flame-lit hall till we came to the loop-shaped apse. The place was empty now, even the corpse of the Khan had gone, and no draped Oracle sat in the altar shrine, for its silver curtains were drawn, and we saw that it was untenanted.

"The Mother has departed to do honour to the dead, according to the ancient custom," Oros explained to us.

Then we passed the altar, and behind the statue found a door in the rock wall of the apse, and beyond the door a passage, and a hall as of a house, for out of it opened other doors leading to chambers. These, our guide told us, were the dwelling-places of the Hesea and her maidens. He added that they ran to the side of the Mountain and had windows that opened on to gardens and let in the light and air. In this hall six priests were waiting, each of whom carried a bundle of torches beneath his arm and held in his hand a lighted lamp.

"Now our road runs through the dark," said Oros; "though were it day, we might climb the outer snows, but this at night it is dangerous to do."

Then taking torches, he lit them at a lamp and gave one to each of us.

Now our climb began. Up endless sloping galleries we went, hewn with inconceivable labour by the primeval fire-worshippers from the living rock of the Mountain. It seemed to me that they stretched for miles, and indeed this was so, since, although the slope was always gentle, it took us more than an hour to climb them. At length we came to the foot of a great stair.

"Rest awhile here, my lord," Oros said, bowing to Leo with the reverence that he had shown him from the first, "for this stair is steep and long. Now we stand upon the Mountain's topmost lip, and are about to climb that tall, looped column which soars above."

So we sat down in the vaultlike place and let the sharp draught of air rushing to and from the passages play upon us, for we were heated with journeying up those close galleries. As we sat thus, I heard a roaring sound, and asked Oros what it might be. He answered that we were very near to the crater of the volcano, and that what we heard through the thickness of the rock was the rushing of its everlasting fires. Then the ascent commenced.

It was not dangerous, though very wearisome, for there were nearly six hundred of those steps. The climb of the passages had reminded me of that of the gallery of the Great Pyramid drawn out for whole furlongs; that of the pillar was like the ascent of a cathedral spire—or, rather, of several spires piled one upon another.

Resting from time to time, we dragged ourselves up the steep steps, each of them quite a foot in height, till the pillar was climbed and only the loop remained. Up it we went also, Oros leading us, and glad was I that the stairway still ran within the substance of the rock, for I could feel the needle's mighty eye quiver in the rush of the winds which swept about its sides.

At length we saw light before us, and in another twenty steps emerged upon a platform. As Leo, who went in front of me, walked from the stairway, I saw Oros and another priest seize him by the arms, and called to him to ask what they were doing.

"Nothing," he cried back, "except that this is a dizzy place, and they feared lest I should fall. Mind how you come, Horace!" and he stretched out his hand to me.

Now I was clear of the tunnel, and I believe that had it not been for that hand I should have sunk to the rocky floor, for the sight before me seemed to paralyse my brain. Nor was this to be wondered at, for I doubt whether the world can show such another.

We stood upon the very apex of the loop, a flat space of rock about eighty yards in length by some thirty in breadth, with the star-strewn sky above us. To the south, twenty thousand feet or more below, stretched the dim Plain of Kaloon, and to the east and west the snow-clad shoulders of the Peak and the broad, brown slopes beneath. To the north was a different sight, and one more awsome. There, right under us, as it seemed—for the pillar bent inwards—lay the vast crater of the volcano, and in the centre of it a wide lake of fire that broke into bubbles and flowers of sudden flame, or spouted, writhed, and twisted like an angry sea.

From the surface of this lake rose smoke and gases that took fire as they floated upwards and, mingling together, formed a gigantic sheet of living light. Right opposite to us burned this sheet, and the flare of it, passing through the needle-eye of the pillar under us, sped away in one dazzling beam across the country of Kaloon, across the mountains beyond, till it was lost on the horizon.

The wind blew from south to north, being sucked in towards the hot crater of the volcano; and its fierce breath, that screamed through the eye of the pillar and against its rugged surface, bent the long crest of the sheet of flame as an ocean roller is bent over by the gale, and tore from it fragments of fire, that floated away to leeward like the blown-out sails of a burning ship.

Had it not been for this strong and steady wind, indeed, no creature could have lived upon the pillar, for the vapours would have poisoned him; but its unceasing blast drove these all away towards the north. For the same reason, in the thin air of that icy place the heat was not too great to be endured.

Appalled by that terrific spectacle, which seemed more appropriate to the terrors of the Pit than to this earth of ours, and fearful lest the blast should whirl me like a dead leaf into the glowing gulf beneath, I fell on to my sound hand and my knees, shouting to Leo to do likewise, and looked about me. Now I observed lines of priests wrapped in great capes, kneeling upon the face of the rock and engaged apparently in prayer; but of Hes the Mother, or of Atene, or of the corpse of the dead Khan, I could see nothing.

Whilst I wondered where they might be, Oros, upon whose nerves this dread scene appeared to have no effect, and some of our attendant priests surrounded us and led us onwards by a path that ran perilously near to the rounded edge of the rock. A few downward steps and we found that we were under shelter, for the gale was roaring over us. Twenty more paces and we came to a recess cut, I suppose, by man in the face of the loop, in such fashion that a lava roof was left projecting half across its width.

This recess, or rock chamber, which was large enough to shelter a great number of people, we reached safely, to discover that it was already tenanted. Seated in a chair hewn from the rock was the Hesea, wearing a broidered, purple mantle above her gauzy wrappings that enveloped her from head to foot. There, too, standing near to her, were the Khania Atene and her uncle, the old Shaman, who looked but ill at ease; and lastly, stretched upon his funeral couch, the fiery light beating upon his stark form and face, lay the dead Khan Rassen.

We advanced to the throne and bowed to her who sat thereon. The Hesea lifted her hooded head, which seemed to have been sunk upon her breast as though she were overcome by thought or care, and addressed Oros the priest. For in the shelter of those massive walls by comparison there was silence, and folk could hear each other speak.

"So thou hast brought them safely, my servant," she said; "and I am glad, for to those that know it not this road is fearful. My guests, what say you of the burying-pit of the Children of Hes?"

"Our faith tells us of a hell, lady," answered Leo, "and I think that yonder cauldron looks like its mouth."

"Nay," she answered, "there is no hell, save that which from life to life we fashion for ourselves within the circle of this little star. Leo Vincey, I tell thee that hell is here—aye, here!" and she struck her hand upon her breast, while once more her head drooped forward as though bowed down beneath some load of secret misery.

Thus she stayed awhile, then lifted it and spoke again, saying—

"Midnight is past, and much must be done and suffered before the dawn. Aye, the darkness must be turned to light, or perchance the light to eternal darkness.

"Royal woman," she went on, addressing Atene, "as is his right, thou hast brought thy dead lord hither for burial in this consecrated place, where the ashes of all who went before him have become fuel for the holy fires. Oros, my priest, summon thou the Accuser and him who makes defence, and let the books be opened, that I may pass my judgment on the dead,

and call his soul to live again, or pray that from it the breath of life may be withheld.

"Priest, I say the Court of Death is open!"

CHAPTER XV.
THE SECOND ORDEAL.

OROS bowed and left the place, whereon the Hesea signed to us to stand upon her right, and to Atene to stand upon her left. Presently from either side the hooded priests and priestesses stole into the chamber, and to the number of fifty or more ranged themselves along its walls. Then came two figures draped in black and masked, who bore parchment books in their hands, and placed themselves on either side of the corpse, while Oros stood at its feet, facing the Hesea.

Now she lifted the sistrum that she held, and, in obedience to the signal, Oros said—

"Let the books be opened!"

Thereon the masked Accuser to the right broke the seal of his book and began to read its pages. It was a tale of the sins of this dead man, entered as fully as though that officer were his own conscience given life and voice. In cold and horrible detail it told of the evil doings of his childhood, of his youth, and of his riper years; and thus massed together, the record was black indeed.

I listened amazed, wondering what spy had been set upon the deeds of yonder man throughout his days; thinking also with a shudder of how heavy would be the tale against any one of us, if such a spy should companion him from the cradle to the grave; remembering, too, that full surely this count is kept by scribes even more watchful than the ministers of Hes.

At length the story drew to its close. Lastly it told of the murder of that noble upon the banks of the river; it told of the plot against our lives for no just cause; it told of our cruel hunting with the death-hounds, and of its end. Then the Accuser shut his book and cast it on the ground, saying—

"Such is the record, O Mother. Sum it up as thou hast been given wisdom."

Without speaking, the Hesea pointed with her sistrum to the Defender, who thereon broke the seal of his book and began to read.

Its tale spoke of all the good that the dead man had done; of every noble word that he had said, of every kind action; of plans which he had made for the welfare of his vassals; of temptations to ill that he had resisted; of the true love that he had borne to the

"Hurled it feet foremost into the fiery lake below."

woman who became his wife ; of the prayers which he had made and of the offerings which he had sent to the temple of Hes.

Making no mention of her name, it told of how that wife of his had hated him, of how she and the magician, who had fostered and educated her, and was her relative and guide, had set other women to lead him astray, that she might be free of him. Of how also they had driven him mad with a poisonous drink which took away his judgment, unchained all the evil in his heart, and caused him by its baneful influence to shrink unnaturally from her whose love he still desired.

Also it set out that the heaviest of his crimes were inspired by this wife of his, who sought to befoul his name in the ears of the people whom she led him to oppress, and how bitter jealousy drove him to cruel acts, the last and worst of which caused him foully to violate the law of hospitality, and in attempting to bring about the death of blameless guests, at their hands to find his own.

Thus the Defender read, and having read, closed the book and threw it on the ground, saying—

"Such is the record, O Mother. Sum it up as thou hast been given wisdom."

Then the Khania, who all this time had stood cold and impassive, stepped forward to speak, and with her, her uncle, the Shaman Simbri. But before a word passed Atene's lips, the Hesea raised her sceptre and forbade, saying—

"Thy day of trial is not yet, nor have we aught to do with thee. When thou liest where he lies, and the books of thy deeds are read aloud to her who sits in judgment, then let thine advocate make answer for these things."

"So be it," answered Atene haughtily, and fell back.

Now it was the turn of the high-priest Oros. "Mother," he said, "thou hast heard. Balance the writings, assess the truth, and according to thy wisdom issue thy commands. Shall we hurl him who was Rassen feet first into the fiery gulf, that he may walk again in the paths of life, or head first, in token that he is dead indeed ?"

Then, while all waited in hushed expectancy, the great Priestess delivered her verdict.

"I hear, I balance, I assess, but judge I do not, who claim no such power. Let the Spirit who sent him forth, to whom he is returned again, pass judgment on his spirit.

This dead one has sinned deeply, yet has he been more deeply sinned against. Nor against that man can be reckoned the account of his deeds of madness. Cast him then to his grave feet first, that his name may be whitened in the ears of those unborn, and that thence he may return again at the time appointed. It is spoken."

Now the Accuser lifted the book of his accusations from the ground and, advancing, hurled it into the gulf, in token that it was blotted out. Then he turned and vanished from the chamber ; while the Advocate, taking his book, gave it into the keeping of the priest Oros, that it might be preserved in the archives of the temple for ever. This done, the priests set up a funeral chant and a solemn invocation to the great Lord of the Under-world that he would receive this spirit and acquit it there as here it had been acquitted by the Hesea, his minister.

Ere their dirge ended, certain of the priests, advancing with slow steps, lifted the bier and carried it to the edge of the gulf ; then, at a sign from the Mother, hurled it feet foremost into the fiery lake below, whilst all watched to see how it struck the flame. For this they held to be an omen, since should the body turn over in its descent, it was taken as a sign that the judgment of mortal men had been refused in the Place of the Immortals.

It did not turn ; it rushed downwards straight as a plummet and plunged into the fire hundreds of feet below, and there for ever vanished. This, indeed, was not strange, since, as we discovered afterwards, the feet were weighted.

In fact, this solemn rite was but a formula that, down to the exact words of judgment and committal, had been practised here from unknown antiquity over the bodies of the priests and priestesses of the Mountain, and of certain of the great ones of the Plain. So it was in ancient Egypt, whence without doubt this ceremony of the trial of the dead was derived, and so it continued to be in the land of Hes, for no priestess ever ventured to condemn the soul of one departed.

*   *   *   *   *

The service, if I may call it so, was finished ; the dead man had followed the record of his sins into that lurid sea of fire, and by now was but a handful of charred dust. But if his book had closed, ours remained open and at its strangest chapter. We knew it, all of us, and waited, our nerves thrilled with expectancy.

AYESHA

THE RETURN OF "SHE."

By H. RIDER HAGGARD.

SYNOPSIS OF FOREGOING CHAPTERS.—The return of "She-Who-Must-Be-Obeyed" is recorded by Ludwig Horace Holly, the friend of that Leo Vincey whom Ayesha the beautiful loved in the awful tombs of Kôr. When the record begins, the two men are living in an old house remote upon the seashore of Cumberland, where they have been slowly recovering from the horror of the passing of Ayesha in the flames—a doom that seemed one of complete extinction, yet was charged with the strange last words: "I die not. I shall come again and shall once more be beautiful. I swear it—it is true." On a sullen August night, Leo is thrilled by a vision of Ayesha in all her former loveliness. She beckons him, and in a vision his spirit follows her into a realm of snowy peaks far beyond the furthest borders of Thibet. A sign in the clouds at dawn is repeated from this vision to both Leo and Holly, and together they start for Central Asia. Sixteen years of toil, struggle, and strange adventure pass, and they are still searching for "a mountain peak shaped like the Symbol of Life." After many wanderings they find themselves in a country where no European has ever set foot, on one of the spurs of the vast Cherga mountains, far eastward from Turkestan. Sheltered awhile in a Buddhist monastery, they hear of the recent visit of a stranger who has told the Lamas that his countryfolk, "dwelling beyond the Far Mountains," worship a priestess called Hes, or the Hesea, and upon persuasion the abbot of the monastery tells them that in a former incarnation he himself has seen the great priestess, who was "all loveliness." A perilous ascent into the unexplored mountain fastness leads them to the revelation of "the *crux ansata*, the Symbol of Life itself." Rescued from drowning by a beautiful woman and an aged man, they are conducted through "The Gate" into the kingdom and city of Kaloon. Their saviours, they learn, are the Khania or Queen of Kaloon, and a venerable physician of magical powers. Is this woman Ayesha? No; they conjecture her rather to be Ameuartas, who wrote the "sherd" of the former chronicle. She falls in love with Leo, and he and Holly learn that her husband, the Khan, is a madman. Simbri, the magician, and Atene, the Khania, have already received a solemn charge from the Hesea of the "College" in the Mountain of Fire to receive two strangers and bring them safely to the Mountain. But Atene's love for Leo makes her detain the travellers awhile in Kaloon, and she even proposes that the Khan shall be murdered so that she can wed Leo. To this the Englishman replies: "I go to ask a certain question of the Oracle on yonder mountain peak. With your will or without it, I tell you that I go, and afterwards you can settle which is the stronger—the Khania of Kaloon or the Hesea of the House of Fire." The Khan himself assists the escape of the travellers for their further journey, but his jealousy has been aroused, and after they have set out on their journey to the fire-crowned Mountain he pursues them with his death-hounds. After a long chase, a few of the brutes, and the Khan, overtake them, and a terrible struggle ensues, in which Leo and Holly eventually prove the victors, and the Khan is slain. Not long afterwards the Khania and Simbri overtake them and seek to persuade them to return, but they refuse. The Khania leaves them, saying: "We do not part thus easily. You have summoned me to the Mountain, and even to the Mountain I will follow you. Aye, and there I will meet its spirit. . . . I will match my strength and magic against hers, as it is decreed that I shall do." Preserved by priestly intervention from death at the hands of a strange people, they realise that they are nearing the sphere of influence of the mysterious Hesea. And on the Mountain itself, conducted by the veiled form of a strange woman, they meet again with Atene, who brings thither her dead husband to the burying-place of the rulers of Kaloon. From a priest, Oros, who goes with them, they learn that for thousands of years this Mountain has been the home of a peculiar fire-worship, of which the head hierophant is a woman. To the veiled figure of Hes, on her throne, the two Englishmen tell of their wandering search; but before they can learn whether she is really the Ayesha of their former knowledge, they are witnesses of the solemn judgment of the dead Khan and the consignment of his corpse to "the Fiery Gulf."

CHAPTER XV.

THE SECOND ORDEAL.

(*Continued*.)

THE Hesea sat brooding on her rocky throne. She also knew that the hour had come. Presently she sighed, then motioned with her sceptre and spoke a word or two, dismissing the priests and priestesses, who departed and were seen no more. Two of them remained, however—Oros and the head priestess, who was called Papave, a young woman of a noble countenance.

"Listen, my servants," she said. "Great things are about to happen, which have to do with the coming of yonder strangers, for

whom I have waited these many years, as is well known to you. Nor can I tell the issue, since to me, to whom power is given so freely, foresight of the future is denied. It well may happen, therefore, that this seat will soon be empty and this frame but food for the eternal fires. Nay, grieve not, grieve not, for I do not die; and if so, the spirit shall return again.

"Hearken, Papave. Thou art of the blood, and to thee alone have I opened all the doors of wisdom. If I pass now or at any time, take thou the ancient power, fill thou my place, and in all things do as I have instructed thee, that from this Mountain light may shine upon the world. Further, I command thee, and thee also, Oros my priest, that if I be summoned hence, you entertain these strangers hospitably, until it is possible to escort them from the land, whether by the road they came or across the northern hills and deserts. Should the Khania Atene attempt to detain them against their will, then raise the Tribes upon her in the name of the Hesea; depose her from her seat, conquer her land and hold it. Hear and obey."

"Mother, we hear and we will obey," answered Oros and Papave as with a single voice.

She waved her hand to show that this matter was finished; then after long thought spoke again, addressing herself to the Khania.

"Atene, last night thou didst ask me a question—why thou dost love this man," and she pointed to Leo. "To that the answer would be easy, for is he not one who might well stir passion in the breast of a woman such as thou art? But thou didst say also that thine own heart and the wisdom of yonder magician, thy uncle, told thee that since thy soul first sprang to life thou hadst loved him, and didst adjure me, by the Power to whom I must give my account, to draw the curtain from the past and let the truth be known.

"Woman, the hour has come, and I obey thy summons—not because thou dost command, but because it is my will. Of the beginning I can tell thee nothing, who am still human and no goddess. I know not why we three are wrapped in this coil of fate; I know not the destinies to which we journey up the ladder of a thousand lives, with grief and pain climbing the endless stair of circumstance; or, if I know, I may not say. Therefore I take up the tale where my own memory gives me light."

The Hesea paused, and we saw her frame shake as though beneath some fearful inward effort of the will. "Look now behind you!" she cried, throwing her arms wide.

We turned, and at first saw nothing save the great curtain of fire that rose from the abyss of the volcano, whereof, as I have told, the crest was bent over by the wind like the crest of a breaking billow. But presently, as we watched, in the depths of this red veil, Nature's awful lamp-flame, a picture began to form as it forms in the seer's magic crystal.

Behold! a temple set amid sands and washed by a wide palm-bordered river, and across its pyloned court processions of priests, who pass to and fro with flaunting banners. The court empties; I could see the shadow of a falcon's wings that fled across its sunlit floor. A man clad in a priest's white robe, shaven-headed, and barefooted, enters through the southern pylon gate and walks slowly towards a painted granite shrine, in which sits the image of a woman crowned with the double crown of Egypt, surmounted by a lotus bloom, and holding in her hand the sacred sistrum. Now, as though he heard some sound, he halts and looks towards us, and by the heaven above me, his face is the face of Leo Vincey in his youth, the face, too, of that Kallikrates whose corpse we had seen in the Caves of Kôr!

"Look, look!" gasped Leo, catching me by the arm; but I only nodded my head in answer.

The man walks on again, and kneeling before the goddess in the shrine, embraces her feet and makes his prayer to her. Now the gates roll open, and a procession enters, headed by a veiled, noble-looking woman, who bears offerings which she sets on the table before the shrine, bending her knee to the effigy of the goddess. Her oblations made, she turns to depart, and as she goes brushes her hand against the hand of the watching priest, who hesitates, then follows her.

When all her company have passed the gate, she lingers alone in the shadow of the pylon, whispering to the priest and pointing to the river and the southern land beyond. He is disturbed; he reasons with her, till after one swift glance round, she lets drop her veil, bending towards him and—their lips meet.

As she flies, her face is turned towards us, and lo! it is the very face of Atene, and amid her dusky hair the uræus rears itself in jewelled gold, the symbol of her royal rank. She looks at the shaven priest; she laughs as though in triumph; she points to the western sun and to the river, and is gone.

Aye, and that laugh of long ago is echoed by Atene at our side, for she also laughs in triumph and cries aloud to the old Shaman—

"True diviners were my heart and thou! Behold how I won him in the past!"

Then like ice on fire fell the cold voice of the Hesea.

"Be silent, woman, and see how thou didst lose him in the past."

Lo! the scene changes, and on a couch a lovely shape lies sleeping. She dreams; she is afraid; and over her bends and whispers in her ear a shadowy form clad with the emblems of the goddess in the shrine, but now wearing upon her head the vulture cap. The woman wakes from her dream and looks

"Alone in the shadow of the pylon."

round, and oh ! the face is the face of Ayesha as it was seen of us when first she loosed her veil in the Caves of Kôr.

A sigh went up from us ; we could not speak who thus fearfully once more beheld her loveliness.

Again she sleeps, again the awful form bends over her and whispers. It points, the distance opens. Lo ! on a stormy sea a boat, and in the boat two wrapped in each other's arms, the priest and the royal woman, while over them like a Vengeance, raw-necked and ragged-pinioned, hovers a following vulture, such a vulture as the goddess wore for head-dress.

That picture fades from its burning frame, leaving the vast sheet of fire empty as the noonday sky. Then another forms. First a great, smooth-walled cave carpeted with sand, a cave that we remembered well. Then, lying on the sand, now no longer shaven, but golden-haired, the corpse of the priest staring upwards with his glazed eyes, his white skin streaked with blood, and standing over him two women. One holds a javelin in her hand and is naked except for her flowing hair, and beautiful, beautiful beyond imagining. The other, wrapped in a dark cloak, beats the air with her hands, casting up her eyes as though to call the curse of Heaven upon her rival's head. And those women were she into whose sleeping ear the shadow had whispered, and the royal Egyptian who had kissed her lover beneath the pylon gate.

Slowly all the figures faded ; it was as though the fire ate them up, for first they became thin and white as ashes, then vanished. The Hesea, who had been leaning forward, sank backwards in her chair, as if weary with the toil of her own magic.

For a while confused pictures flitted rapidly to and fro across the vast mirror of the flame, such as might be reflected from an intelligence crowded with the memories of over two thousand years which it was too exhausted to separate and define.

Wild scenes, multitudes of people, great caves, and in them faces, amongst others our own, starting up distorted and enormous, to grow tiny in an instant and depart ; stark imaginations of Forms towering and divine ; of Things monstrous and inhuman ; armies marching, illimitable battlefields, and corpses rolled in blood, and hovering over them the spirits of the slain.

These pictures died as the others had died, and the fire was blank again.

* * * * *

Then the Hesea spoke in a voice very faint at first, that by slow degrees grew stronger.

"Is thy question answered, O Atene ? "

"I have seen strange sights, Mother, mighty limnings worthy of thy magic, but how know I that they are more than vapours of thine own brain cast upon yonder fire to deceive and mock us ? "*

"Listen, then," said the Hesea in her weary voice, "to the interpretation of the writing, and cease to trouble me with thy doubts. Many an age ago, but shortly after I began to live this last, long life of mine, Isis, the great goddess of Egypt, had her Holy House at Behbit, near the Nile. It is a ruin now, and Isis has departed from Egypt, though still under the Power that fashioned it and her : she rules the world, for she is Nature's self. Of that shrine a certain man, a Greek, Kallikrates by name, was chief priest, chosen for her service by the favour of the goddess, vowed to her eternally and to her alone, by the dreadful oath that might not be broken without punishment as eternal.

"In the flame thou sawest that priest, and here at thy side he stands, re-born to fulfil his destiny and ours.

"There lived also a daughter of Pharaoh's house, one Amenartas, who cast eyes of love upon this Kallikrates, and, wrapping him in her spells—for then as now she practised witcheries—caused him to break his oaths and fly with her, as thou sawest written in the flame. Thou, Atene, was that Amenartas.

"Lastly, there lived a certain Arabian, named Ayesha, a wise and lovely woman, who, in the emptiness of her heart and the sorrow of much knowledge, had sought refuge in the service of the universal Mother, thinking there to win the true wisdom which ever fled from her. That Ayesha, as thou sawest also, the goddess visited in a dream, bidding her to follow those faithless ones, and work Heaven's vengeance on them, and promising her in reward victory over death upon the earth, and beauty such as had not been known in woman.

"She followed far ; she awaited them where they wandered. Guided by a sage named Noot, one who from the beginning had been appointed to her service, and that of another —thou, O Holly, wast that man—she found

---

* Considered in the light of subsequent revelations, vouchsafed to us by Ayesha herself, I am inclined to believe that Atene's shrewd surmise was accurate, and that these fearful pictures, although founded on events that had happened in the past, were in the main "vapours" cast upon the crater fire—visions raised in our minds to "deceive and mock us."—L. H. H.

122

the essence in which to bathe is to outlive Generations, Faiths, and Empires, saying—

"'I will slay these guilty ones. I will slay them presently, as I am commanded.'

"Yet Ayesha slew not, for now their sin was her sin, since she, who had never loved, came to desire this man. She led them to the Place of Life, purposing there to clothe him and herself with immortality, and let the woman die. But it was not so fated, for then the goddess smote. The life was Ayesha's, as had been promised, but in its first hour, blinded with jealous rage because he shrank from her unveiled glory to the mortal woman at his side, this Ayesha brought him to his death, and alas! alas! left herself undying.

"Thus did the angry goddess work woe upon her faithless ministers, giving to the priest swift doom, to the priestess Ayesha long remorse and misery, and to the royal Amenartas jealousy more bitter than life or death, and the fate of unending effort to win back that love which, defying Heaven, she had dared to steal, but to be bereft thereof again.

*　　*　　*　　*　　*

"Lo! now the ages pass, and at the time appointed, to that undying Ayesha who, whilst awaiting his re-birth, from century to century mourned his loss, and did bitter penance for her sins, came back the man, her heart's desire. Then, whilst all went well for her and him, again the goddess smote and robbed her of her reward. Before her lover's living eyes, sunk in utter shame and misery, the beautiful became hideous, the undying seemed to die.

"Yet, O Kallikrates, I tell thee that she died not. Did not Ayesha swear to thee yonder in the Caves of Kôr that she would come again? for even in that awful hour this comfort kissed her soul. Thereafter, Leo Vincey, who art Kallikrates, did not her spirit lead thee in thy sleep and stand with thee upon this very pinnacle which should be thy beacon light to guide thee back to her? And didst thou not search these many years, not knowing that she companioned thy every step and strove to guard thee in every danger till at length in the permitted hour thou camest back to her?"

She paused, and looked towards Leo, as though awaiting his reply.

"Of the first part of the tale, except from the writing on the sherd, I know nothing, Lady," he said; "of the rest, I—or, rather, we—know that it is true. Yet I would ask a question, and I pray thee of thy charity let

thy answer be swift and short. Thou sayest that in the permitted hour I came back to Ayesha? Where, then, is Ayesha? Art thou Ayesha? And if so, why is thy voice changed? Why art thou less in stature? Oh! in the name of whatever god thou dost worship, tell me art thou Ayesha?"

"*I am Ayesha,*" she answered solemnly, "that very Ayesha to whom thou didst pledge thyself eternally."

"She lies, she lies!" broke in Atene. "I tell thee, husband—for such with her own lips she declares thou art to me—that yonder woman who says that she parted from thee young and beautiful, less than twenty years ago, is none other than the aged priestess who, for a century, at least, has borne rule in these halls of Hes. Let her deny it if she can."

"Oros," said the Mother, "tell thou the tale of the death of that priestess of whom the Khania speaks."

The priest bowed, and in his usual, calm voice, as though he were narrating some event of every day, said mechanically, in a fashion that carried no conviction to my mind—

"Eighteen years ago, on the fourth night of the first month of winter in the year 2333 of the founding of the worship of Hes on this Mountain, the priestess of whom the Khania Atene speaks died of old age in my presence, in the hundred and eighth year of her rule. Three hours later, we went to lift her from the throne on which she died, to prepare her corpse for burial in this fire, according to the ancient custom. Lo! a miracle, for she lived again, the same, yet very changed.

"Thinking this a work of evil magic, the Priests and Priestesses of the College rejected her and would have driven her from the throne. Thereon the Mountain blazed and thundered, the light from the fiery pillars died, and great terror fell upon the souls of men. Then from the deep darkness above the altar where stands the statue of the Mother of Men, the voice of the living goddess spoke, saying—

"'Accept ye her whom I have set to rule over you, that my judgments and my purposes may be fulfilled.'

"The voice ceased, the fiery torches burnt again, and we bowed the knee to the new Hesea, and named her Mother in the ears of all. That is the tale to which hundreds can bear witness."

"Thou hearest, Atene," said the Hesea. "Dost thou still doubt?"

MAURICE
GREIFFENHAGEN
1905

"Leo knelt down and kissed her on the brow."

"Aye," answered the Khania, "for I hold that Oros also lies ; or if he lies not, then he dreams, or perchance that voice he heard was thine own. Now, if thou art this undying woman, this Ayesha, let proof be made of it to these two men who knew thee in the past. Tear away those wrappings that guard thy loveliness thus jealously. Let thy shape divine, thy beauty incomparable, shine out upon our dazzled sight. Surely thy lover will not forget such charms ; surely he will know thee, and bow the knee, saying : 'This is my Immortal, and no other woman.'

"Then, and not till then, will I believe that thou art even what thou declarest thyself to be, an evil spirit, who bought undying life with murder, and used thy demon loveliness to bewitch the souls of men."

Now the Hesea on the throne seemed to be much troubled, for she rocked herself to and fro, and wrung her white-draped hands.

"Kallikrates," she said in a voice that sounded like a moan, "is this thy will ? For if it be, know that I must obey. Yet I pray thee command it not, for the time is not yet come ; the promise unbreakable is not yet fulfilled. *I am somewhat changed*, Kallikrates, since I kissed thee on the brow and named thee mine, yonder in the Caves of Kôr."

Leo looked about him desperately, till his eyes fell upon the mocking face of Atene, who cried—

"Bid her unveil, my lord. I swear to thee I'll not be jealous."

At that taunt he took fire.

"Aye," he said, "I bid her unveil, that I may learn the best or worst, who otherwise must die of this suspense. Howsoever changed, if she be Ayesha, I shall know her ; and if she be Ayesha, I shall love her."

"Bold words, Kallikrates," answered the Hesea ; "yet from my very heart I thank thee for them : those sweet words of trust and faithfulness to thou knowest not what. Learn now the truth, for I may keep naught back from thee. When I unveil, it is decreed that thou must make thy choice for the last time on this earth between yonder woman, my rival from the beginning, and that Ayesha to whom thou art sworn. Thou canst reject me if thou wilt, and no ill shall come to thee, but many a blessing, as men reckon them—power and wealth and love. Only then thou must tear my memory from thy heart, for then I leave thee to follow thy fate alone, till at the last the purpose of these deeds and sufferings is made clear.

"Be warned. No light ordeal lies before thee. Be warned. I can promise thee naught save such love as woman never gave to man, love that perchance—I know not— must yet remain unsatisfied upon the earth."

Then she turned to me and said : "Oh ! thou, Holly, thou true friend, thou guardian from of old, thou, next to him most beloved by me, to thy clear and innocent spirit perchance wisdom may be given that is denied to us, the little children whom thine arms protect. Counsel thou him, my Holly, with the counsel that is given thee, and I will obey thy words and his, and, whatever befalls, will bless thee from my soul. Aye, and should he cast me off, then in the Land beyond the lands, in the Star appointed, where all earthly passions fade, together will we dwell eternally in a friendship glorious, thou and I alone.

"For *thou* wilt not reject ; thy steel, forged in the furnace of pure truth and power, shall not lose its temper in these small fires of temptation, and become a rusted chain to bind thee to another woman's breast —until it canker to her heart and thine."

"Ayesha, I thank thee for thy words," I answered simply, "and by them and that promise of thine, I, thy poor friend—for more I never thought to be—am a thousand-fold repaid for many sufferings. This I will add—that for my part I know that thou art She whom we have lost, since, whate'er the lips that speak them, those thoughts and words are Ayesha's, and hers alone."

Thus I spoke, not knowing what else to say, for I was filled with a great joy, a calm and ineffable satisfaction, which broke thus feebly from my heart. For now I knew that I was dear to Ayesha as I had always been dear to Leo ; the closest of friends, from whom she never would be parted. What more could I desire ?

*　　*　　*　　*　　*

We fell back ; we spoke together, whilst they watched us silently. What we said I do not quite remember, but the end of it was that, as the Hesea had done, Leo bade me judge and choose. Then into my mind there came a clear command, from my own conscience or otherwhere, who can say ? This was the command, that I should bid her to unveil, and let Fate declare its purposes.

"Decide," said Leo. "I cannot bear much more. Like that woman, whoever she may be, whatever happens, I will not blame you, Horace."

"Good," I answered. "I have decided ¿" ; and stepping forward, I said : "We have taken counsel, Hes, and it is our will, who would learn the truth and be at rest, that thou shouldst unveil before us, here and now."

"I hear and obey," the Priestess answered in a voice like to that of a dying woman; "only, I beseech you both, be pitiful to me, spare me your mockeries; add not the coals of your hate and scorn to the fires of a soul in hell, for whate'er I am, I became it for thy sake, Kallikrates. Yet, yet I also am athirst for knowledge; for though I know all wisdom, although I wield much power, one thing remains to me to learn—what is the worth of the love of man, and if, indeed, it can live beyond the horrors of the grave?"

Then, rising slowly, the Hesea walked—or, rather, tottered—to the unroofed open space in front of the rock chamber, and stood there quite near to the brink of the flaming gulf beneath.

"Come hither, Papave, and loose these veils," she cried in a shrill, thin voice.

Papave advanced, and with a look of awe upon her handsome face began the task. She was not a tall woman, yet as she bent over her I noted that she seemed to tower above her mistress, the Hesea.

The outer veils fell, revealing more within. These fell also, and now before us stood the mummylike shape, although it seemed to be of less stature, of that strange being who had met us in the Place of Bones. So it would seem that our mysterious guide and the high priestess Hes were the same.

Look! Length by length the wrappings sank from her. Would they never end? How small grew the frame within? She was very short now, unnaturally short for a full-grown woman, and oh! I grew sick at heart. The last bandages uncoiled themselves like shavings from a stick; two wrinkled hands appeared, if hands they could be called. Then the feet—once I had seen such on the mummy of a princess of Egypt, and even now, by some fantastic play of the mind, I remembered that on her coffin this princess was named "The Beautiful."

Everything was gone now, except a shift and a last inner veil about the head. Hes waved back the priestess Papave, who fell half fainting to the ground and lay there covering her eyes with her hand. Then uttering something like a scream, she gripped this veil in her thin talons, tore it away, and with a gesture of uttermost despair, turned and faced us.

Oh! she was—nay, I will not describe her. I knew her at once, for thus had I seen her last before the Fire of Life, and, strangely enough, through the mask of unutterable age, through that cloak of humanity's last decay, still shone some resemblance to the glorious and superhuman Ayesha: the shape of the face, the air of defiant pride that for an instant bore her up—I know not what.

Yes, there she stood, and the fierce light of the heartless fires beat upon her, revealing every shame.

*　　*　　*　　*　　*

There was a dreadful silence. I saw Leo's lips turn white and his knees begin to give; but by some effort he recovered himself, and stayed still and upright like a dead man held by a wire. Also I saw Atene—and this is to her credit—turn her head away. She had desired to see her rival humiliated, but that horrible sight shocked her; some sense of their common womanhood for the moment touched her pity. Only Simbri—who, I think, knew what to expect—and Oros remained quite unmoved; indeed, in that ghastly silence the latter spoke, and ever afterwards I loved him for his words.

"What of the vile vessel, rotted in the grave of time? What of the flesh that perishes?" he said. "Look through the ruined lamp to the eternal light which burns within. Look through its covering carrion to the inextinguishable soul."

My heart applauded these noble sentiments. I was of one mind with Oros; but oh, Heaven! I felt that my brain was going, and I wished that it would go, so that I might hear and see no more.

That look which gathered on Ayesha's mummy face! At first there had been a little hope, but the hope died, and anguish, anguish, *anguish* took its place.

Something must be done—this could not endure. My lips clave together, no word would come; my feet refused to move.

I began to contemplate the scenery. How wonderful were that sheet of flame and the ripples which ran up and down its height! How awsome its billowy crest! It would be warm lying in yonder red gulf below with the dead Rassen, but, oh! I wished that I shared his bed and had finished with these agonies.

Thank Heaven! Atene was speaking. She had stepped to the side of the naked-headed Thing, and stood by it in all the pride of her rich beauty and perfect womanhood.

"Leo Vincey, or Kallikrates," said Atene— "take which name thou wilt—thou thinkest ill of me, perhaps, but know that at least I scorn to mock a rival in her mortal shame.

"From the east a single ray of upward-springing light."

She told us a wild tale, but now, a tale true or false, but more false than true, I think, of how I robbed a goddess of a votary, and of how that goddess—Ayesha's self, perchance—was avenged upon me for the crime of yielding to the man I loved. Well, let goddesses—if such indeed there be—take their way and work their will upon the helpless, and I, a mortal, will take mine until the clutch of doom closes round my throat and chokes out life and memory, and I, too, am a goddess—or a clod.

"Meanwhile, thou man, I shame not to say it before all these witnesses, I love thee, and it seems that this—this woman or goddess—loves thee also, and she has told us that now, *now* thou must choose between us once and for ever. She has told us, too, that if I sinned against Isis—whose minister, be it remembered, she declares herself—herself she sinned yet more. For she would have taken thee both from a heavenly mistress and from an earthly bride, and yet snatch that guerdon of immortality which is hers to-day. Therefore, if I am evil, she is worse, nor does the flame that burns within the casket whereof Oros spoke shine so very pure and bright.

"Choose thou, then, Leo Vincey, and let there be an end. I vaunt not myself; thou knowest what I have been and seest what I am. Yet I can give thee love and happiness and, mayhap, children to follow after thee, and with them some place and power. What yonder witch can give thee thou canst guess. Tales of the past, pictures on the flame, wise maxims and honeyed words, and after thou art dead once more, promises, perhaps, of joy to come when that terrible goddess whom she serves so closely shall be appeased. I have spoken. Yet I will add a word:

"O thou for whom, if the Hesea's tale be true, I did once lay down my royal rank and dare the dangers of an unsailed sea; O thou whom in ages gone I would have sheltered with my frail body from the sorceries of this cold, self-seeking witch; O thou whom but a little while ago at my own life's risk I drew from death in yonder river, choose, choose!"

*   *   *   *   *

To all this speech, so moderate yet so cruel, so well-reasoned and yet so false, because of its glosses and omissions, the huddled Ayesha seemed to listen with a fierce intentness. Yet she made no answer, not a single word, not a sign even; she who had said her say and scorned to plead her part.

I looked at Leo's ashen face. He leaned towards Atene, drawn perhaps by the passion shining in her beauteous eyes, then of a sudden straightened himself, shook his head, and sighed. The colour flamed to his brow, and his eyes grew almost happy.

"After all," he said, thinking aloud rather than speaking, "I have to do not with unknowable pasts or with mystic futures, but with the things of my own life. Ayesha waited for me through two thousand years; Atene could marry a man she hated for power's sake, and then could poison him, as perhaps she would poison me when I wearied her. I know not what oaths I swore to Amenartas, if such a woman lived. I remember the oaths I swore to Ayesha. If I shrink from her now, why, then my life is a lie and my belief a fraud; then love will not endure the touch of age and never can survive the grave.

"Nay, remembering what Ayesha was, I take her as she is, in faith and hope of what she shall be. At least love is immortal; and if it must, why, let it feed on memory alone till death sets free the soul."

Then stepping to where stood the dreadful, shrivelled form, Leo knelt down and kissed her on the brow.

Yes, he kissed the trembling horror of that wrinkled head, and I think it was one of the greatest, bravest acts ever done by man.

"Thou hast chosen," said Atene in a cold voice, "and I tell thee, Leo Vincey, that the manner of thy choice makes me mourn my loss the more. Take now thy—thy bride and let me hence."

But Ayesha still said no word and made no sign, till presently she sank upon her bony knees and began to pray aloud. These were the words of her prayer, as I heard them, though the exact Power to which it was addressed is not very easy to determine, as I never discovered who or what it was that she worshipped in her heart—

*   *   *   *   *

"O Thou Minister of the Almighty Will, Thou sharp Sword in the hand of Doom, Thou inevitable Law that art named Nature; Thou who wast crowned as Isis of the Egyptians, but art the goddess of all climes and ages; Thou that leadest the man to the maid, and layest the infant on its mother's breast, that bringest our dust to its kindred dust, that givest life to death, and into the dark of death breathest the light of life again; Thou who causest the abundant earth to bear, whose smile is Spring, whose laugh is the ripple of the sea, whose noontide rest is drowsy Summer, and whose sleep is Winter's night, hear Thou the supplication of thy chosen child and minister:

"Of old Thou gavest me Thine own strength with deathless days, and beauty above every daughter of this Star. But I sinned against Thee sore, and for my sin I paid in endless centuries of solitude, in the vileness that makes me loathsome to my lover's eyes, and for its diadem of perfect power sets upon my brow this crown of naked mockery. Yet in Thy breath, the swift essence that brought me light, that brought me gloom, Thou didst vow to me that I who cannot die should once more pluck the lost flower of my immortal loveliness from this foul slime of shame.

"Therefore, merciful Mother that bore me, to Thee I make my prayer. Oh, let his true love atone my sin; or, if it may not be, then give me death, the last and most blessed of Thy boons!"

CHAPTER XVI.

THE CHANGE.

SHE ceased, and there was a long, long silence. Leo and I looked at each other in dismay. We had hoped against hope that this beautiful and piteous prayer, addressed apparently to the great, dumb spirit of Nature, would be answered. That meant a miracle, but what of it? The prolongation of the life of Ayesha was a miracle, though it is true that some humble reptiles are said to live as long as she had done.

The transference of her spirit from the Caves of Kôr to this temple was a miracle—that is, to our Western minds, though the dwellers in these parts of Central Asia would not hold it so. That she should reappear with the same hideous body was a miracle. But was it the same body? Was it not the body of the last Hesea? One very ancient woman is much like another, and eighteen years of the working of the soul or identity within might well wear away their trivial differences and give to the borrowed form some resemblance to that which it had left.

At least the figures on that mirror of the flame were a miracle. Nay, why so? A hundred clairvoyants in a hundred cities can produce or see their like in water and in crystal, the difference being only one of size. They were but reflections of scenes familiar to the mind of Ayesha, or perhaps not so much as that. Perhaps they were only phantasms called up in *our* minds by her mesmeric force.

Nay, none of these things were true miracles, since all, however strange, might be capable of explanation. What right, then, had we to expect a marvel now?

Such thoughts as these rose in our minds as the endless minutes were born and died and—nothing happened.

* * * * *

Yes, at last one thing did happen. The light from the sheet of flame died gradually away, as the flame itself sank downwards into the abysses of the pit. But about this in itself there was nothing wonderful, for, as we had seen with our own eyes from afar, this fire varied much, and, indeed, it was customary for it to die down at the approach of dawn, which now drew very near.

Still, that onward-creeping darkness added to the terrors of the scene. By the last rays of the lurid light we saw Ayesha rise and advance some few paces to that little tongue of rock at the edge of the pit off which the body of Rassen had been hurled; saw her standing on it also, looking like some black, misshapen imp against the smoky glow which still rose from the depths beneath.

Leo would have gone forward to her, for he believed that she was about to hurl herself to doom, which, indeed, I thought was her design. But the priest Oros and the priestess Papave, obeying, I suppose, some secret command that reached them I know not how, sprang to him and, seizing his arms, held him back. Then it became quite dark, and through the darkness we could hear Ayesha chanting a dirgelike hymn in some secret holy tongue which was unknown to us.

A great flake of fire floated through the gloom, rocking to and fro like some vast bird upon its pinions. We had seen many such that night, torn by the gale from the crest of the blazing curtain as I have described. But—but——

"Horace," whispered Leo through his chattering teeth, "that flame is coming up *against the wind!*"

"Perhaps the wind has changed," I answered, though I knew well that it had not, that it blew stronger than ever from the south.

Nearer and nearer sailed the rocking flame, two enormous wings was the shape of it, with something dark between them. It reached the little promontory. The wings appeared to fold themselves about the dwarfed figure that stood thereon—illuminating it for a moment. Then the light went out of them and they vanished—everything vanished.

* * * * *

A while passed, it may have been a minute or an hour, when suddenly the priestess Papave, in obedience to some summons which we could not hear, crept by me. I knew that it was she, because her woman's garments touched me as she went. Another space of silence and of deep darkness, during which I heard Papave return, breathing in short, sobbing gasps like one who is very frightened.

Ah! I thought, she has cast herself into the pit! The tragedy is finished!

Then it was that the wondrous music came. Of course, it *may* only have been the sound of the priests chanting beyond us, but I do not think so, since its quality was quite different from any that I heard in the temple before or afterwards—to any, indeed, that ever I heard upon the earth.

I cannot describe it, but it was awful to listen to, yet most entrancing. From the black, smoke-veiled pit where the fire had burned, it welled and echoed—now a single, heavenly voice, now a sweet chorus, and now an air-shaking thunder as of a hundred organs played to time.

That diverse and majestic harmony seemed to include, to express every human emotion, and I have often thought since then that in its all-embracing scope and range, this, the song or pæan of her re-birth, was symbolical of the infinite variety of Ayesha's spirit. Yet, like that spirit, it had its master notes—power, passion, suffering, mystery, and loveliness. Also there could be no doubt as to the general significance of the chant, by whomsoever it was sung. It was the changeful story of a mighty soul; it was worship, worship, worship of a queen divine!

Like slow clouds of incense fading to the bannered roof of some high choir, the bursts of unearthly melodies grew faint; in the far distance of the hollow pit they wailed themselves away.

* * * * *

Look! from the east a single ray of upward-springing light.

"Behold the dawn!" said the quiet voice of Oros.

That ray pierced the heavens above our heads, a very sword of flame. It sank downwards, swiftly. Suddenly it fell—not upon us, for as yet the rocky walls of our chamber warded it away, but on to the little promontory at its edge.

Oh! and there—a Glory covered with a single garment—stood a shape celestial. It seemed to be asleep, since the eyes were shut. Or was it dead, for at first that face was a face of death? Look, the sunlight played upon her, shining through the thin veil, the dark eyes opened like the eyes of a wondering child; the blood of life flowed up the ivory bosom into the pallid cheeks; the raiment of black and curling tresses wavered in the wind; the head of the jewelled snake that held them sparkled beneath her breast.

Was it an illusion, or was this Ayesha as she had been when she entered the rolling flame in the caverns of Kôr? Our knees gave way beneath us, and down, our arms about each other's necks, Leo and I sank till we lay upon the ground. Then a voice, sweeter than honey, softer than the whisper of a twilight breeze among the reeds, spoke near to us, and these were the words it said—

"*Come hither to me, Kallikrates, that I may pay thee back that redeeming kiss of faith and love thou gavest me but now!*"

* * * * *

Leo struggled to his feet. Like a drunken man he staggered to where Ayesha stood; then overcome, sank before her on his knees.

"Arise!" she said. "It is I who should kneel to thee," and she stretched out her hand to raise him, whispering in his ear the while.

Still he would not, or could not rise; so very slowly she bent over him and touched him with her lips upon the brow. Next she beckoned to me. I came, and would have knelt also, but she suffered it not.

"Nay," she said, in her rich, remembered voice, "thou art no suitor; it shall not be. Of lovers and worshippers henceforth as before I can find a plenty if I will, or even if I will it not. But where shall I find another friend like to thee, O Holly, whom thus I greet?" and leaning towards me, with her lips she touched me also on the brow—just touched me, and no more.

Fragrant was Ayesha's breath as roses, the odour of roses clung to her lovely hair; her sweet body gleamed like some white sea-pearl; a faint but palpable radiance crowned her head; no sculptor ever fashioned such a marvel as the arm with which she held her veil about her; no stars in heaven ever shone more purely bright than did her calm, entranced eyes.

Yet it is true, even with her lips upon me, all I felt for her was a love divine into which no human passion entered. Once, I

"She bent over him and touched him with her lips upon the brow."

acknowledge to my shame, it was otherwise; but I am an old man now, and have done with such frailties. Moreover, had not Ayesha named me Guardian, Protector, Friend, and sworn to me that with her and Leo I should ever dwell where all earthly passions fail? I repeat: What more could I desire?

Taking Leo by the hand, Ayesha returned with him into the shelter of the rock-hewn chamber, and when she entered its shadows, shivered a little as though with cold. I rejoiced at this, I remember, for it seemed to show me that she still was human, divine as she might appear. Here her priest and priestess prostrated themselves before her, but she motioned to them to rise, laying a hand upon the head of each as though in blessing.

"I am a' cold," she said; "give me my mantle," and Papave threw the purple-broidered garment upon her shoulders, whence now it hung royally, like a coronation robe.

"Nay," she went on, "it is not this long-lost shape of mine, which in his kiss my lord gave back to me, that shivers in the icy wind; it is my spirit's self bared to the bitter breath of Destiny. O my love, my love, offended powers are not easily appeased, even when they appear to pardon; and though I shall no more be made a mockery in thy sight, how long is given us together upon the world I know not—but a little hour perchance. Well, ere we pass otherwhere, we will make it glorious, drinking as deeply of the cup of joy as we have drunk of those of sorrows and of shame. This place is hateful to me, for in it I have suffered more than ever woman did on earth or phantom in the deepest hell. It is hateful—it is ill-omened. I pray that never again may I behold it.

"Say, what is it passes in thy mind, magician?" and of a sudden she turned fiercely upon the Shaman Simbri, who stood near, his arms crossed upon his breast.

"Only, thou Beautiful," he answered, "a dim shadow of things to come. I have what thou dost lack, with all thy wisdom—the gift of foresight; and here I see a dead man lying——"

"Another word," she broke in, with fury born of some dark fear, "and thou shalt be that man! Fool! put me not in mind that now I have strength again to rid me of the ancient foes I hate, lest I should use a sword thou thrustest to my hand," and her eyes, that had been so calm and happy, blazed upon him like fire.

The old wizard felt their fearsome might, and shrank from it till the wall stayed him.

"Great One! now as ever I salute thee. Yes, now as at the first beginning whereof we know alone," he stammered. "I had no more to say; the face of that dead man was not revealed to me. I saw only that some crowned Khan of Kaloon to be shall lie here, as he whom the flame has taken lay an hour ago."

"Doubtless many a Khan of Kaloon will lie here," she answered coldly. "Fear not, Shaman, my wrath is past; yet be wise, mine enemy, and prophesy no more evil to the great. Come, let us hence."

So, still led by Leo, she passed from that chamber and stood presently upon the apex of the soaring pillar. The sun was up now, flooding the Mountain flanks, the plains of Kaloon far beneath, and the distant, misty peaks with a sheen of gold. Ayesha stood considering the mighty prospect, then addressing Leo, she said—

"The world is very fair; I give it all to thee."

Now Atene spoke for the first time.

"Dost thou mean, Hes—if thou art still the Hesea, and not a demon from the Pit—that thou offerest my territories to this man as a love-gift? If so, I tell thee that first thou must conquer them."

"Ungentle are thy words and mien," answered Ayesha, "yet I forgive them both, for I also can scorn to mock a rival in my hour of victory. When thou wast the fairer, thou didst proffer him these very lands; but say, who is the fairer now? Look at us, all of you, and judge," and she stood by Atene and smiled.

The Khania was a lovely woman. Never to my knowledge have I seen one lovelier, but oh! how coarse and poor she showed beside the wild, ethereal beauty of Ayesha born again! For that beauty was not altogether human—far less so, indeed, than it had been in the Caves of Kôr; now it was the beauty of a spirit.

The little light that always shone upon Ayesha's brow; the wide-set, maddening eyes which were filled sometimes with the fire of the stars and sometimes with the blue darkness of the heavens wherein they float; the curved lips, so wistful yet so proud; the tresses fine as glossy silk that still spread and rippled as though with a separate life; the general air, not so much of majesty as of some secret power hard to be restrained, that strove in that delicate body and proclaimed its presence to the most careless; that flame of the soul within whereof Oros had spoken, shining now through no "vile vessel,"

" In a second the attempt had been made and failed."

but in a vase of alabaster and of pearl—none of these things and qualities were altogether human. I felt it and was afraid, and Atene felt it also, for she answered—

"I am but a woman. What thou art, thou knowest best. Still, a taper cannot shine midst yonder fires, nor a glow-worm against a fallen star; nor can my mortal flesh compare with the glory thou hast earned from hell in payment for thy gifts and homage to the Lord of Ill. Yet as woman I am thy equal, and as spirit I shall be thy mistress, when, robbed of these borrowed beauties, thou, Ayesha, standest naked and ashamed before the Judge of all whom thou hast deserted and defied; yes, as thou stoodest but now upon yonder brink above the burning pit where thou yet shalt wander, wailing thy lost love. For this I know, mine enemy, that *man and spirit cannot mate*," and Atene ceased, choking in her bitter rage and jealousy.

Now, watching Ayesha, I saw her wince a little beneath these evil-omened words, saw also a tinge of grey touch the carmine of her lips, and her deep eyes grow dark and troubled. In an instant it had gone, and she was asking in a voice that rang clear as silver bells—

"Why ravest thou, Atene, like some short-lived summer torrent against the barrier of a seamless cliff? Dost think, poor creature of an hour, to sweep away the rock of my eternal strength with foam and bursting bubbles? Have done and listen. I do not seek thy petty rule, who, if I will it, can take the empire of the world. Yet learn, thou holdest it of my hand. More—I purpose soon to visit thee in thy city—choose thou if it shall be in peace or war!

"Therefore, Khania, purge thy Court and amend thy laws, that when I come I may find contentment in the land which now it lacks, and confirm thee in thy government. My counsel to thee also is that thou choose some worthy man to husband; let him be whom thou wilt, if only he is just and upright, and one upon whom thou mayest rest, needing wise guidance as thou dost, Atene.

"Come, now, my guests, let us hence." and she walked past the Khania, stepping fearlessly upon the very edge of the wind-swept, rounded peak.

* * * * *

In a second the attempt had been made and failed; so quickly, indeed, that it was not until Leo and I compared our impressions afterwards that we could be sure of what had happened. As Ayesha passed her, the maddened Khania drew a hidden dagger and struck with all her force at her rival's back. I saw the knife vanish to the hilt in her body, as I thought; but this cannot have been so, since it fell to the ground, and she who should have been dead took no hurt at all.

Feeling that she had failed, with a movement like the sudden lurch of a ship, Atene thrust at Ayesha, proposing to hurl her to destruction in the depths beneath. Lo! her outstretched arms went past her, although Ayesha never seemed to stir. Yes, it was Atene who would have fallen, Atene who already fell, had not Ayesha put out her hand and caught her by the wrist, bearing all her backward-swaying weight as easily as though she were but an infant, and without effort drawing her to safety.

"Foolish woman!" she said in pitying tones. "Wast thou so vexed that thou wouldst strip thyself of the pleasant shape which Heaven has given thee? Surely this is madness, Atene; for how knowest thou in what likeness thou mightest be sent to tread the earth again? As no queen, perhaps, but as a peasant's child, deformed, unsightly; for such reward, it is said, is given to those that achieve self-murder. Or even, as many think, shaped like a beast—a snake, a cat, a tigress! Why, see," and she picked up the dagger from the ground and cast it into the air, "that point was poisoned. Had it but pricked thee, now!" and she smiled at her and shook her head.

But Atene could bear no more of this mockery, more venomed than her own steel.

"Thou art not mortal!" she wailed. "How can I prevail against thee? To Heaven I leave thy punishment," and there upon the rocky peak Atene sank down and wept.

Leo stood nearest to her, and the sight of this royal woman in her misery proved too much for him to bear. Stepping to her side, he stooped and lifted her to her feet, muttering some kind words. For a moment she rested on his arm, then shook herself free of him and took the proffered hand of her old uncle Simbri.

"I see," said Ayesha, "that, as ever, thou art courteous, my lord Leo; but it is best that her own servant should take charge of her, for—she may hide more daggers. Come, the day grows, and surely we need rest."

AYESHA

THE RETURN OF "SHE."

By H. RIDER HAGGARD.

SYNOPSIS OF FOREGOING CHAPTERS.—The return of "She-Who-Must-Be-Obeyed" is recorded by Ludwig Horace Holly, the friend of that Leo Vincey whom Ayesha the beautiful loved in the awful tombs of Kôr. When the record begins, the two men are living in an old house remote upon the seashore of Cumberland, where they have been slowly recovering from the horror of the passing of Ayesha in the flames—a doom that seemed one of complete extinction, yet was charged with the strange last words: "I die not. I shall come again and shall once more be beautiful. I swear it—it is true." On a sullen August night, Leo is thrilled by a vision of Ayesha in all her former loveliness. She beckons him, and in a vision his spirit follows her into a realm of snowy peaks far beyond the furthest borders of Thibet. A sign in the clouds at dawn is repeated from this vision to both Leo and Holly, and together they start for Central Asia. Sixteen years of toil, struggle, and strange adventure pass, and they are still searching for "a mountain peak shaped like the Symbol of Life." After many wanderings they find themselves in a country where no European has ever set foot, on one of the spurs of the vast Cherga mountains, far eastward from Turkestan. A perilous ascent into the unexplored mountain fastness leads them to the revelation of "the *crux ansata*, the Symbol of Life itself." Rescued from drowning by a beautiful woman and an aged man, they are conducted through "The Gate" into the kingdom and city of Kaloon. Their saviours, they learn, are the Khania or Queen of Kaloon, and a venerable physician of magical powers. Is this woman Ayesha? No; they conjecture her rather to be Amenartas, who wrote the "sherd" of the former chronicle. She falls in love with Leo, and he and Holly learn that her husband, the Khan, is a madman. Simbri, the magician, and Atene, the Khania, have already received a solemn charge from the "Hesea" of a "College" in the Mountain of Fire to receive two strangers and bring them safely to the Mountain. But Atene's love for Leo makes her detain the travellers awhile in Kaloon, and she even proposes that the Khan shall be murdered so that she can wed Leo. To this the Englishman replies: "I go to ask a certain question of the Oracle on yonder mountain peak. With your will or without it, I tell you that I go, and afterwards you can settle which is the stronger—the Khania of Kaloon or the Hesea of the House of Fire." The Khan himself assists the escape of the travellers for their further journey, but his jealousy has been aroused, and after they have set out on their journey to the fire-crowned Mountain he pursues them with his death-hounds. After a long chase, a few of the brutes, and the Khan, overtake them, and a terrible struggle ensues, in which Leo and Holly eventually prove the victors, and the Khan is slain. The Khania and Simbri overtake them and seek to persuade them to return, but they refuse. The Khania leaves them, saying: "We do not part thus easily. You have summoned me to the Mountain, and even to the Mountain I will follow you. Aye, and there I will meet its spirit. . . . I will match my strength and magic against hers, as it is decreed that I shall do." On the Mountain itself they meet again with Atene, who brings thither her dead husband to the burying-place of the rulers of Kaloon. From a priest, Oros, who goes with them, they learn that for thousands of years this Mountain has been the home of a peculiar fire-worship, of which the head hierophant is a woman. To the veiled figure of Hes, on her throne, the two Englishmen tell of their wandering search. In answer to the challenge of Atene, the Hesea shows them a vision of events which happened long ago in the Caves of Kôr. Picture succeeds picture until all is blank, and then she tells how Ayesha first met Kallikrates in the early ages. Suddenly she reveals herself as Ayesha; but to remove all doubt she unveils before them, revealing herself in all her withered age. Ayesha bids Leo choose between her and Ayesha. Leo then kneels down and kisses the wrinkled head. At which Atene says: "Thou hast chosen. Take now thy bride and let me hence." Ayesha then begins to pray aloud, to some unseen Power, for the return of her former loveliness, and suddenly she is transfigured into radiant beauty once again, and claims Leo for the man whom she loved of old. Atene is baffled in a sudden attack upon the mysterious creature's life.

CHAPTER XVII.

THE BETROTHAL.

TOGETHER we descended the multi-tudinous steps and passed the endless, rock-hewn passages till we came to the door of the dwelling of the high-priestess and were led through it into a hall beyond. Here Ayesha parted from us, saying that she was outworn, as, indeed, she seemed to be with an utter weariness, not of the body, but of the spirit. For her delicate form drooped like a rain-laden lily, her eyes grew dim as those of a person in a trance, and her voice came in a soft, sweet whisper, the voice of one speaking in her sleep.

"Good-bye," she said to us. "Oros will guard you both, and lead you to me at the appointed time. Rest you well."

So she went, and the priest led us into a beautiful apartment that opened on to a sheltered garden. So overcome were we also by all that we had endured and seen, that we could scarcely speak, much less discuss these marvellous events.

"My brain swims," said Leo to Oros. "I desire to sleep."

He bowed and conducted us to a chamber where were beds, and on these we flung ourselves down and slept, dreamlessly, like little children.

When we awoke, it was afternoon. We rose and bathed, then saying we wished to be alone, went together into the garden, where even at this altitude, now, at the end of August, the air was still mild and pleasant   Behind a rock by a bed of campanulas and other mountain flowers and ferns, was a bench near to the banks of a little stream, on which we seated ourselves.

"What have you to say, Horace?" asked Leo, laying his hand upon my arm.

"Say?" I answered. "That things have come about most marvellously! that we have dreamed aright and laboured not in vain; that you are the most fortunate of men, and should be the most happy."

He looked at me somewhat strangely and answered—

"Yes, of course; she is lovely, is she not? But," and his voice dropped to its lowest whisper, "I wish, Horace, that Ayesha were a little more human, even as human as she was in the Caves of Kôr. I don't think she is quite flesh and blood; I felt it when she kissed me—if you can call it a kiss—for she barely touched my hair. Indeed, how can she be who changed thus in an hour? Flesh and blood are not born of flame, Horace."

"Are you sure that she was so born?" I asked. "Like the visions on the fire, may not that hideous shape have been but an illusion of our minds? May she not be still the same Ayesha whom we knew in Kôr, not re-born, but wafted hither by some mysterious agency?"

"Perhaps. Horace, we do not know—I think that we shall never know. But I admit that to me the thing is terrifying. I am drawn to her by an infinite attraction; her eyes set my blood on fire, the touch of her hand is as that of a wand of madness laid upon my brain. And yet between us there is some wall, invisible, still present. Or perhaps it is only fancy. But, Horace, I think that she is afraid of Atene. Why, in the old days the Khania would have been dead and forgotten in an hour—you remember Ustane?"

"Perhaps she may have grown more gentle, Leo, who, like ourselves, has learned hard lessons."

"Yes," he answered, "I hope that is so. At any rate, she has grown more divine—only, Horace, what kind of a husband shall I be for that bright being, if ever I get so far?"

"Why should you not get so far?" I asked angrily, for his words jarred upon my tense nerves.

"I don't know," he answered; "but on general principles, do you think that such

fortune will be allowed to a man? Also, what did Atene mean when she said that man and spirit cannot mate—and—other things?"

"She meant that she *hoped* they could not, I imagine; and, Leo, it is useless to trouble yourself with forebodings that are more fitted to my years than yours, and probably are based on nothing. Be a philosopher, Leo. You have striven by wonderful ways such as are unknown in the history of the world; you have attained. Take the goods the gods provide you—the glory, the love and the power—and let the future look to itself."

Before he could answer, Oros appeared from round the rock, and, bowing with more than his usual humility to Leo, said that the Hesea desired our presence at a service in the Sanctuary. Rejoiced at the prospect of seeing her again before he had hoped to do so, Leo sprang up, and we accompanied him back to our apartment.

Here priests were waiting, who, somewhat against his will, trimmed his hair and beard, and would have done the same for me had I not refused their offices. Then they placed gold-embroidered sandals on our feet, and wrapped Leo in a magnificent, white robe, also richly worked with gold and purple; a somewhat similar robe, but of less ornate design, being given to me. Lastly, a silver sceptre was thrust into his hand, and into mine a plain wand. This sceptre was shaped like a crook, and the sight of it gave me some clue to the nature of the forthcoming ceremony.

"The crook of Osiris!" I whispered to Leo.

"Look here," he answered, "I don't want to impersonate any Egyptian god, nor to be mixed up in their heathen idolatries; in fact, I won't."

"Better go through with it," I suggested; "probably it is only something symbolical."

But Leo, who, notwithstanding the strange circumstances connected with his life, retained the religious principles in which I had educated him, very strongly indeed, refused to move an inch until the nature of this service was made clear to him. Indeed, he expressed himself upon the subject with vigour to Oros. At first the priest seemed puzzled what to do, then explained that the forthcoming ceremony was one of betrothal.

On learning this, Leo raised no further objections, asking only, with some nervousness, whether the Khania would be present. Oros answered "No," as she had already

"'What have you to say, Horace?'"

departed to Kaloon, vowing war and vengeance.

Then we were led through long passages, till finally we emerged into the gallery immediately in front of the great wooden doors of the apse. At our approach these swung open, and we entered it, Oros going first, then Leo, then myself, and following us, the procession of attendant priests.

As soon as our eyes became accustomed to the dazzling glare of the flaming pillars, we saw that some great rite was in progress in the temple, for in front of the divine statue of Motherhood, white-robed, and arranged in serried ranks, stood the company of the priests to the number of over two hundred, and behind these the company of the priestesses. Facing this congregation, and a little in advance of the two pillars of fire that flared on either side of the shrine, Ayesha herself was seated in a raised chair so that she could be seen of all, while to her right stood a similar chair, of which I could guess the purpose.

She was unveiled and gorgeously apparelled, though, save for the white beneath, her robes were those of a queen rather than of a priestess. About her radiant brow ran a narrow band of gold, whence rose the head of a hooded asp cut out of a single, crimson jewel, beneath which, in endless profusion, the glorious, waving hair flowed down and around, hiding even the folds of her purple cloak.

This cloak, opening in front, revealed an under-tunic of white silk cut low upon her bosom, and kept in place by a golden girdle, a double-headed snake, so like to that which "She" had worn in Kôr that it might have been the same. Her naked arms were bare of ornament, and in her right hand she held the jewelled sistrum set with its gems and bells.

No empress could have looked more royal, and no woman was ever half so lovely, for to Ayesha's human beauty was added a spiritual glory, her heritage alone. Seeing her, we could see naught else. The rhythmic movement of the bodies of the worshippers, the rolling grandeur of their chant of welcome echoed from the mighty roof, the fearful torches of living flame—all these things were lost on us. For there, new-born, enthroned, her arms stretched out in gracious welcome, sat that perfect and immortal woman, the appointed bride of one of us, the friend and lady of the other, her divine presence breathing power, mystery, and love.

On we marched between the ranks of hierophants, till Oros and the priests left us, and we stood alone face to face with Ayesha. Now she lifted her sceptre, and the chant ceased. In the midst of the following silence, she rose from her seat and, gliding down its steps, came to where Leo stood, and touched him on the forehead with her sistrum, crying in a loud, sweet voice—

"Behold the Chosen of the Hesea!" whereon all that audience echoed in a shout of thunder—

"Welcome to the Chosen of the Hesea!"

Then while the echoes of that glad cry yet rang round the rocky walls, Ayesha motioned to me to stand at her side, and taking Leo by the hand, drew him towards her, so that now he faced the white-robed company. Holding him thus, she began to speak in clear and silvery tones.

"Priests and priestesses of Hes, servants with her of the Mother of the world, hear me. Now for the first time I appear among you as I am, you who heretofore have looked but on a hooded shape, not knowing its form or fashion. Learn now the reason that I draw my veil. Ye see this man, whom ye believed a stranger that with his companion had wandered to our shrine. I tell you that he is no stranger; that of old, in lives forgotten, he was my lord who now comes to seek his love again. Say, is it not so, Kallikrates?"

"It is so," answered Leo.

"Priests and priestesses of Hes, as ye know, from the beginning it has been the right and custom of her who holds my place to choose one to be her lord. Is it not so?"

"It is so, O Hes," they answered.

She paused awhile; then, with a gesture of infinite sweetness, turned to Leo, bent towards him thrice, and slowly sank upon her knee.

"Say, thou," Ayesha said, looking up at him with her wondrous eyes, "say before these here gathered, and all those witnesses whom thou canst not see, dost thou again accept me as thy affianced bride?"

"Aye, Lady," he answered, in a deep but shaken voice, "now and for ever."

Then while all watched, in the midst of a great silence, Ayesha rose, cast down her sistrum sceptre that rang upon the rocky floor, and stretched out her arms towards him.

Leo also bent towards her and would have kissed her upon the lips. But I who watched saw his face grow white as it drew near to hers. While the radiance crept from her brow to his, turning his bright hair to gold, I saw also that this strong man trembled like a reed and seemed as though he were about to fall.

I think that Ayesha noted it too, for ere ever their lips met, she thrust him from her, and again that grey mist of fear gathered on her face.

In an instant it was gone. She had slipped from him, and with her hand held his hand as though to support him. Thus they stood till his feet grew firm and his strength returned.

Oros restored the sceptre to her, and lifting it, she said—

"O love and lord, take thou the place prepared for thee, where thou shalt sit for ever at my side, for with myself I give thee more than thou canst know or than I will tell thee now. Mount thy throne, O Affianced of Hes, and receive the worship of thy priests."

"Nay," he answered with a start, as that word fell upon his ears. "Here and now I say it once and for all. I am but a man who knows nothing of strange gods, their attributes and ceremonials. None shall bow the knee to me; and on earth, Ayesha, I bow mine to thee alone."

Now at this bold speech some of those who heard it looked astonished and whispered to each other, while a voice called—

"Beware, thou Chosen, of the anger of the Mother!"

Again for a moment Ayesha looked afraid; then, with a little laugh, swept the thing aside, saying—

"Surely with that I should be content. For me, O Love, thy adoration; for thee the betrothal song, no more."

So, having no choice, Leo mounted the throne, where notwithstanding his splendid presence, enhanced as it was by those glittering robes, he looked ill enough at ease—as, indeed, must any man of his faith and race. Happily, however, if some act of semi-idolatrous worship had been proposed, Ayesha found a means to prevent its celebration, and soon all such matters were forgotten both by the singers who sang, and we who listened to the majestic chant that followed.

Of its words, unfortunately, we were able to understand but little, both because of the volume of sound and of the secret, priestly language in which it was given, though its general purport could not be mistaken.

The female voices began it, singing very low, and conveying a strange impression of time and distance. Now followed bursts of gladness alternating with melancholy chords suggesting sighs and tears and sorrows long endured, and at the end a joyous, triumphant pæan thrown to and fro between the men and women singers, terminating in one united chorus repeated again and again, louder and yet louder, till it culminated in a veritable crash of melody, then of a sudden ceased.

Ayesha rose and waved her sceptre, whereon all the company bowed thrice; then turned and, breaking into some sweet, low chant that sounded like a lullaby, marched, rank after rank, across the width of the Sanctuary and through the carven doors, which closed behind the last of them.

When all had gone, leaving us alone, save for the priest Oros and the priestess Papave, who remained in attendance on their mistress, Ayesha, who sat gazing before her with dreaming, empty eyes, seemed to awake, for she rose and said—

"A noble chant, is it not, and an ancient? It was the wedding song of the feast of Isis and Osiris at Behbit in Egypt, and there I heard it before ever I saw the darksome Caves of Kôr. Often have I observed, my Holly, that music lingers longer than aught else in this changeful world, though it is rare that the very words should remain unvaried. Come, beloved—tell me, by what name shall I call thee? Thou art Kallikrates, and yet——"

"Call me Leo, Ayesha," he answered, "as I was christened in the only life of which I have any knowledge. This Kallikrates seems to have been an unlucky man, and the deeds he did, if in truth he was aught other than a tool in the hand of Destiny, have bred no good to the inheritors of his body—or his spirit, whichever it may be—or to those women with whom his life was intertwined. Call me Leo, then, for of Kallikrates I have had enough since that night when I looked upon the last of him in Kôr."

"Ah! I remember," she answered—"when thou sawest thyself lying in that narrow bed, and I sang thee a song, did I not, of the past and of the future? I can recall two lines of it; the rest I have forgotten—

"Onward, never weary, clad with splendour for a robe! Till accomplished be our fate, and the night is rushing down.

"Yes, my Leo, now indeed we are 'clad with splendour for a robe,' and now our fate draws near to its accomplishment. Then perchance will come the downrushing of the night"; and she sighed, looked up tenderly, and said: "See, I am talking to thee in Arabic. Hast thou forgotten it?"

"No."

"Then let it be our tongue, for I love it best of all, who lisped it at my mother's knee. Now leave me here alone awhile; I would think. Also," she added thoughtfully, and speaking with a strange and impressive inflexion of the voice, "there are some to whom I must give audience."

* * * * *

So we went, all of us supposing that Ayesha was about to receive a deputation of the Chiefs of the Mountain Tribes who came to felicitate her upon her betrothal.

CHAPTER XVIII.

THE THIRD ORDEAL.

AN hour, two hours passed, while we two strove to rest in our sleeping-place, but could not, for some influence disturbed us.

"Why does not Ayesha come?" asked Leo at length, pausing in his walk up and down the room. "I want to see her again; I cannot bear to be apart from her. I feel as though she were drawing me to her."

"How can I tell you? Ask Oros; he is outside the door."

So he went and asked him; but Oros only smiled and answered that the Hesea had not entered her chamber, so doubtless she must still remain in the Sanctuary.

"Then I am going to look for her. Come, Oros, and you too, Horace."

Oros bowed, but declined, saying that he was bidden to bide at our door, adding that we, "to whom all the paths were open," could return to the Sanctuary if we thought well.

"I do think well," replied Leo sharply. "Will you come, Horace, or shall I go alone?"

I hesitated. The Sanctuary was a public place, it is true, but Ayesha had said that she desired to be alone there for a while. Without more words, however, Leo shrugged his shoulders and started.

"You will never find your way," I said, and followed him.

We went down the long passages, that were dimly lighted with lamps, and came to the gallery. Here we found no lamps; still we groped our way to the great wooden doors. They were shut, but Leo pushed upon them impatiently, and one of them swung open a little, so that we could squeeze ourselves between them. As we passed, it closed noiselessly behind us.

Now we should have been in the Sanctuary, and in the full blaze of those awful columns of living fire. But they were out, or we had strayed elsewhere; at least, the darkness was intense. We tried to work our way back to

the doors again, but could not. We were lost.

More, something oppressed us; we did not dare to speak. We went on a few paces and stopped, for we became aware that we were not alone. Indeed, it seemed to me that we stood in the midst of a thronging multitude, but not of men and women. Beings pressed about us; we could feel their robes, yet could not touch them; we could feel their breath, but it was *cold*. The air stirred all round us as they passed to and fro, passed in endless numbers. It was as though we had entered a cathedral filled with the vast congregation of all the dead who once had worshipped there. We grew afraid—my face was damp with fear, the hair stood up upon my head. We seemed to have wandered into a hall of the Shades.

At length light appeared far away, and we saw that it emanated from the two pillars of fire which burned on either side of the Shrine, that of a sudden had become luminous. So we were in the Sanctuary, and still near to the doors. Now those pillars were not bright; they were low and lurid; the rays from them scarcely reached us standing in the dense shadow.

But if we could not be seen in them, we still could see. Look! Yonder sat Ayesha on a throne, and oh! she was awful in her deathlike majesty. The blue light of the sunken columns played upon her, and in it she sat erect, with such a face and mien of pride as no human creature ever wore. Power seemed to flow from her; yes, it flowed from those wide-set, glittering eyes like light from jewels.

She seemed a Queen of Death receiving homage from the dead. More, she *was* receiving homage from dead or living—I know not which—for, as I thought it, a shadowy Shape arose before the throne and bent the knee to her, then another, and another, and another.

As each vague Being appeared and bowed its starry head, she raised her sceptre in answering salutation. We could hear the distant tinkle of the sistrum bells, the only sound in all that place; yes, and see her lips move, though no whisper reached us from them. Surely spirits were worshipping her!

We gripped each other. We shrank back and found the door. It gave to our push. Now we were in the passages again, and now we had reached our room.

At its entrance Oros was standing as we had left him. He greeted us with his fixed smile, taking no note of the terror written on

The betrothal.

our faces. We passed him, and entering the room, stared at each other.

"What is she?" gasped Leo. "An angel?"

"Yes," I answered, "something of that sort." But to myself I thought that there are doubtless many kinds of angels.

"And what were those—those *shadows*—doing?" he asked again.

"Welcoming her after her transformation, I suppose. But perhaps they were not shadows—only priests disguised and conducting some secret ceremonial!"

Leo shrugged his shoulders, but made no other answer.

At length the door opened, and Oros, entering, said that the Hesea commanded our presence in her chamber.

So, still oppressed with fear and wonder—for what we had seen was perhaps more dreadful than anything that had gone before—we went, to find Ayesha seated and looking somewhat weary, but otherwise unchanged. With her was the priestess Papave, who had just unrobed her of the royal mantle which she wore in the Sanctuary.

Ayesha beckoned Leo to her, taking his hand and searching his face with her eyes, not without anxiety, as I thought.

Now I turned, purposing to leave them alone; but she saw, and said to me, smiling—

"Why wouldst thou forsake us, Holly? To go back to the Sanctuary once more?" and she looked at me with meaning in her glance. "Hast thou questions to ask of the statue of the Mother yonder, that thou lovest the place so much? They say it speaks, telling of the future to those who dare to kneel beside it uncompanioned from night till dawn. Yet I have often done so, but to me it has never spoken, though none long to learn the future more."

I made no answer, nor did she seem to expect any, for she went on at once—

"Nay, bide here, and let us have done with all sad and solemn thoughts. We three will sup together as of old, and for a while forget our fears and cares, and be happy as children who know not sin and death, nor that change which is death indeed. Oros, await my lord without. Papave, I will call thee later to disrobe me. Till then let none disturb us."

The room that Ayesha inhabited was not very large, as we saw by the hanging lamps with which it was lighted. It was plainly though richly furnished, the rock walls being covered with tapestries, and the tables and chairs inlaid with silver; but the only token that here a woman had her home was that

about it stood several bowls of flowers. One of these, I remember, was filled with the delicate harebells I had admired, dug up roots and all, and set in moss.

"A poor place," said Ayesha, "yet better than that in which I dwelt those two thousand years awaiting thy coming, Leo; for see, beyond it is a garden, wherein I sit," and she sank down upon a couch by the table, motioning to us to take our places opposite to her.

The meal was simple; for us, eggs boiled hard and cold venison; for her, milk, some little cakes of flour, and mountain berries.

Presently Leo threw off his gorgeous, purple-broidered robe, which he still wore, and cast upon a chair the crook-headed sceptre that Oros had again thrust into his hand. Ayesha smiled as he did so, saying—

"It would seem that thou holdest these sacred emblems in but small respect."

"Very small," he answered. "Thou heardest my words in the Sanctuary, Ayesha; so let us make a pact. Thy religion I do not understand, but I understand my own, and not even for thy sake will I take part in what I hold to be idolatry."

Now I thought that she would be angered by this plain speaking, but she only bowed her head and answered meekly—

"Thy will is mine, Leo, though it will not be easy always to explain thy absence from the ceremonies in the Temple. Yet thou hast a right to thine own faith, which doubtless is mine also."

"How can that be?" he asked, looking up.

"Because all great Faiths are the same, changed a little to suit the needs of passing times and peoples. What taught that of Egypt, which, in a fashion, we still follow here? That hidden in a multitude of manifestations, one Power, great and good, rules all the universes: that the holy shall inherit a life eternal, and the vile, eternal death: that men shall be shaped and judged by their own deeds, and here and hereafter drink of the cup which they have brewed: that their real home is not on earth, but beyond the earth, where all riddles shall be answered and all sorrow cease. Say, dost thou believe these things, as I do?"

"Aye, Ayesha; but Hes or Isis is thy goddess, for hast thou not told us tales of thy dealings with her in the past, and did we not hear thee make thy prayer to her? Who, then, is this goddess Hes?"

"Know, Leo, that she is what I named her—Nature's soul; no divinity, but the secret Spirit of the World; that universal Motherhood whose symbol thou hast seen yonder, and in whose mysteries lie hid all earthly life and knowledge."

"Does, then, this merciful Motherhood follow her votaries with death and evil, as thou sayest she has followed thee for thy disobedience, and me—and another—because of some unnatural vows broken long ago?" Leo asked quietly.

Resting her arm upon the table, Ayesha looked at him with sombre eyes and answered—

"In that Faith of thine of which thou speakest are there perchance two gods, each having many ministers: a god of good and a god of evil, an Osiris and a Set?"

He nodded.

"I thought it. And the god of ill is strong, is he not, and can put on the shape of good? Tell me, then, Leo, in the world that is to-day, whereof I know so little, hast thou ever heard of frail souls who for some earthly bribe have sold themselves to that evil one, or to his minister, and been paid their price in bitterness and anguish?"

"All wicked folk do as much in this form or in that," he answered.

"And if once there lived a woman who was mad with the thirst for beauty, for life, for wisdom, and for love, might she not—oh! might she not perchance——"

"Sell herself to the god called Set, or one of his angels? Ayesha, dost thou mean"—and Leo rose, speaking in a voice that was full of fear—"that thou art such a woman?"

"And if so?" she asked, also rising and drawing slowly near to him.

"If so," he answered hoarsely, "if so, I think that perhaps we had best fulfil our fates apart——"

"Ah!" she said, with a little scream of pain as though a knife had stabbed her, "wouldst thou away to Atene? I tell thee that thou canst not leave me. I have power —above all men thou shouldst know it, whom once I slew. Nay, thou hast no memory, poor creature of a breath, and I—I remember too well. I will not hold thee dead again—I'll hold thee living. Look now on my beauty, Leo"—and she bent her swaying form towards him, compelling him with her glorious, alluring eyes—" and begone if thou canst. Why, thou drawest nearer to me. Man, that is not the path of flight.

"Nay, I will not tempt thee with these common lures. Go, Leo, if thou wilt. Go, my love, and leave me to my loneliness and my sin. Now—at once. Atene will shelter thee till spring, when thou canst cross the mountains and return to thine own world again, and to those things of common life which are thy joy. See, Leo, I veil myself, that thou mayst not be tempted," and she flung the corner of her cloak about her head, then asked a sudden question through it—

"Didst thou not but now return to the Sanctuary with Holly after I bade thee leave me there alone? Methought I saw the two of you standing by its doors."

"Yes, we came to seek thee," he answered.

"And found more than ye sought, as often chances to the bold—is it not so? Well, I willed that ye should come and see, and protected you where others might have died."

"What didst thou there upon the throne, and whose were those forms which we saw bending before thee?" he asked coldly.

"I have ruled in many shapes and lands, Leo. Perchance they were ancient companions and servitors of mine come to greet me once again and to hear my tidings. Or perchance they were but shadows of thy brain, pictures like those upon the fire, that it pleased me to summon to thy sight, to try thy strength and constancy.

"Leo Vincey, know now the truth: that all things are illusions, even that there exists no future and no past, that what has been and what shall be already *is* eternally. Know that I, Ayesha, am but a magic wraith, foul when thou seest me foul, fair when thou seest me fair; a spirit-bubble reflecting a thousand lights in the sunshine of thy smile, grey as dust and gone in the shadow of thy frown. Think of the throned Queen before whom the shadowy Powers bowed, and worship, for that is I. Think of the hideous, withered Thing thou sawest naked on the rock, and flee away, for that is I. Or keep me lovely, and adore, knowing all evil centred in my spirit, for that is I. Now, Leo, thou hast the truth. Put me from thee for ever and for ever if thou wilt, and be safe; or clasp me, clasp me to thy heart, and in payment for my lips and love take my sin upon thy head! Nay, Holly, be thou silent, for now he must judge alone."

Leo turned, as I thought, at first, to find the door. But it was not so, for he did but walk up and down the room awhile. Then he came back to where Ayesha stood, and spoke quite simply and in a very quiet voice, such as men of his nature often assume in moments of great emotion.

"Ayesha," he said, "when I saw thee as

thou wast, aged and—thou knowest how—I clung to thee. Now, when thou hast told me the secret of this unholy pact of thine, when with my eyes, at least, I have seen thee reigning a mistress of spirits good or ill, yet I cling to thee. Let thy sin, great or little—whate'er it is—be my sin also. In truth, I feel its weight sink to my soul and become a part of me ; and although I have no vision or power of prophecy, I am sure that I shall not escape its punishment. Well, though I be innocent, let me bear it for thy sake. I am content."

Ayesha heard, the cloak slipped from her head, and for a moment she stood silent like one amazed, then burst into a passion of sudden tears. Down she went before him, and clinging to his garments, she bowed her stately shape until her forehead touched the ground. Yes, that proud being, who was more than mortal, whose nostrils but now had drunk the incense of the homage of ghosts or spirits, humbled herself at this man's feet.

With an exclamation of horror, half-maddened at the piteous sight, Leo sprang to one side, then stooping, lifted and led her still weeping to the couch.

"Thou knowest not what thou hast done," Ayesha said at last. "Let all thou sawest on the Mountain's crest or in the Sanctuary be but visions of the night ; let that tale of an offended goddess be a parable, a fable, if thou wilt. This at least is true, that ages since, I sinned for thee and against thee and another ; that ages since, I bought beauty and life indefinite wherewith I might win thee and endow thee at a cost which few would dare ; that I have paid interest on the debt, in mockery, utter loneliness, and daily pain which scarce could be endured, until the bond fell due at last and must be satisfied.

"Yes, how I may not tell thee, thou and thou alone stoodst between me and the full discharge of this most dreadful debt—for know that in mercy it is given to us to redeem one another."

Now he would have spoken, but with a motion of her hand she bade him be silent, and continued—

"See now, Leo ; three great dangers has thy body passed of late upon its journey to my side : the Death-hounds, the Mountains, and the Precipice. Know that these were but types and ordained foreshadowings of the last threefold trial of thy soul. From the pursuing passions of Atene, which must have undone us both, thou hast fled vic-torious. Thou hast endured the desert loneliness of the sands and snows, starving for a comfort that never came. Even when the avalanche thundered round thee, thy faith stood fast, as it stood above the Pit of flame, while after bitter years of doubt a rushing flood of horror swallowed up thy hopes. As thou didst descend the glacier's steep, not knowing what lay beneath that fearful path, so but now of thine own choice, for very love of me, thou hast plunged head-long into an abyss that is deeper far, to share its terrors with my spirit. Dost thou understand at last ? "

"Something ; not all, I think," he answered slowly.

"Surely thou art wrapped in a double veil of blindness," she cried impatiently. "Listen again :

"Hadst thou yielded to Nature's crying and rejected me but yesterday, in that foul shape I must perchance have lingered for uncounted time, playing the poor part of priestess of a forgotten faith. This was the first temptation, the ordeal of thy flesh—nay, not the first—the second, for Atene and her lurings were the first. But thou wast loyal, and in the magic of thy con-quering love my beauty and my womanhood were re-born.

"Hadst thou rejected me to-night, when, as I was bidden to do, I showed thee that vision in the Sanctuary and confessed to thee my soul's black crime, then hopeless and helpless, unshielded by my earthly power, I must have wandered on into the deep and endless night of solitude. This was the third appointed test, the trial of thy spirit ; and by thy steadfastness, Leo, thou hast loosed the hand of Destiny from about my throat. Now I am regenerate in thee—through thee may hope again for some true life beyond, which thou shalt share. And yet, and yet, if thou shouldst suffer, as well may chance——"

"Then I suffer, and there's an end," broke in Leo serenely. "Save for a few things, my mind is clear, and there must be justice for us all at last. If I have broken the bond that bound thee, if I have freed thee from some threatening, spiritual ill by taking a risk upon my head, well, I have not lived and, if need be, shall not die in vain. So let us have done with all these problems ; or, rather, first answer thou me one. Ayesha, how wast thou changed upon that peak ? "

"In flame I left thee, Leo, and in flame I did return, as in flame, mayhap, we shall

"A shadowy Shape arose before the throne and bent the knee to her."

both depart. Or perhaps the change was in the eyes of all of you who watched, and not in this shape of mine. I have answered. Seek to learn no more."

"One thing I do still seek to learn. Ayesha, we were betrothed to-night. When wilt thou marry me?"

"Not yet, not yet," she answered hurriedly, her voice quivering as she spoke. "Leo, thou must put that hope from thy thoughts awhile, and for some few months, a year perchance, be content to play the part of friend and lover."

"Why so?" he asked with bitter disappointment. "Ayesha, those parts have been mine for many a day; more, I grow no younger, and, unlike thee, shall soon be old. Also, life is fleeting, and sometimes I think that I near its end."

"Speak no such evil-omened words!" she said, springing from the couch and stamping her sandalled foot upon the ground in anger born of fear. "Yet thou sayest truth: thou art unfortified against the accidents of time and chance. Oh! horrible, horrible! thou mightest die again, and leave me living!"

"Then give me of thy life, Ayesha."

"That would I gladly, all of it, couldst thou but repay me with the boon of death to come.

"Oh, ye poor mortals!" she went on with a sudden burst of passion; "ye beseech your gods for the gift of many years, being ignorant that ye would sow a seed within your breasts whence ye must garner ten thousand miseries. Know ye not that this world is indeed the wide house of hell, in whose chambers from time to time the spirit tarries a little while, then, weary and aghast, speeds wailing to the peace that it has won.

"Think, then, what it is to live on here eternally and yet be human; to age in soul and see our beloved die and pass to lands whither we cannot hope to follow; to wait while drop by drop the curse of the long centuries falls upon our imperishable being, like water slow dripping on a diamond that it cannot wear, till they be born anew, forgetful of us, and again sink from our helpless arms into the void unknowable.

"Think what it is to see the sins we sin, the tempting look, the word idle or unkind — aye, even the selfish thought or struggle — multiplied ten thousandfold and more eternal than ourselves, spring up upon the universal bosom of the earth to be the bane of a million destinies, whilst the everlasting Finger writes its endless count, and a cold voice of Justice cries in our conscience-haunted solitude : 'Oh, soul unshriven! behold the ripening harvest thy wanton hand did scatter, and long in vain for the waters of forgetfulness!'

"Think what it is to have every earthly wisdom, yet to burn unsatisfied for the deeper and forbidden draught; to gather up all wealth and power and let them slip again, like children weary of a painted toy; to sweep the lyre of fame, and, maddened by its jangling music, to stamp it small beneath our feet; to snatch at pleasure's goblet and find its wine is sand; and at length, outworn, to cast us down and pray the pitiless gods with whose stolen garment we have wrapped ourselves, to take it back again, and suffer us to slink naked to the grave!

"Such is the life thou askest, Leo. Say, wilt thou have it now?"

"If it may be shared with thee," he answered. "These woes are born of loneliness, but then our perfect fellowship would turn them into joy."

"Aye," she said, "while it was permitted to endure. So be it, Leo. In the spring, when the snows melt, we will journey together to Libya, and there thou shalt be bathed in the Fount of Life, that forbidden Essence of which once thou didst fear to drink. Afterwards I will wed thee."

"That place is closed for ever, Ayesha."

"Not to my feet and thine," she answered. "Fear not, my love. Were this mountain heaped thereon, I would blast a path through it with mine eyes and lay its secret bare. Oh! would that thou wast as I am, for then before to-morrow's sun we'd watch the rolling pillar thunder by, and thou shouldst taste its glory.

"But it may not be. Hunger or cold can starve thee, and waters drown; swords can slay thee, or sickness sap away thy strength. Had it not been for the false Atene, who disobeyed my words, as it was foredoomed that she should do, by this day we were across the mountains, or had travelled northward through the frozen desert and the rivers. Now we must await the melting of the snows, for winter is at hand, and in it, as thou knowest, no man can live upon their heights."

"Eight months till April before we can start, and how long to cross the mountains, and all the vast distances beyond, and the seas and the swamps of Kôr? Why, at the best, Ayesha, two years must go by before we can even find the place"; and he fell

"'Ayesha, dost thou mean that thou art such a woman?'"

to entreating her to let them be wed at once and journey afterwards.

But she said, Nay, and nay, and nay, it should not be ; till at length, as though fearing his pleading, or that of her own heart, she rose and dismissed us.

"Ah, my Holly !" she said to me, as we three parted, "I promised thee and myself some few hours of rest and of the happiness of quiet, and thou seest how my desire has been fulfilled. Those old Egyptians were wont to share their feasts with one grizzly skeleton, but here I counted four to-night that you both could see, and they are named Fear, Suspense, Foreboding, and Love-denied. Doubtless also, when these are buried, others will come to haunt us and snatch the poor morsel from our lips.

"So hath it ever been with me, whose feet misfortune dogs. Yet I hope on, and now many a barrier lies behind us ; and Leo, thou hast been tried in the appointed triple fires, and yet proved true. Sweet be thy slumbers, O my love, and sweeter still thy dreams, for know, my soul shall share them ! I vow to thee that to-morrow we'll be happy—aye, to-morrow without fail."

* * * * *

"Why will she not marry me at once ?" asked Leo, when we were alone in our chamber.

"Because she is afraid," I answered.

AYESHA

THE RETURN OF "SHE."

By H. RIDER HAGGARD.

SYNOPSIS OF FOREGOING CHAPTERS.—The return of "She-Who-Must-Be-Obeyed" is recorded by Ludwig Horace Holly, the friend of that Leo Vincey whom Ayesha the beautiful loved in the awful tombs of Kôr. When the record begins, the two men are living in an old house remote upon the seashore of Cumberland, where they have been slowly recovering from the horror of the passing of Ayesha in the flames—a doom that seemed one of complete extinction, yet was charged with the strange last words: "I die not. I shall come again and shall once more be beautiful. I swear it—it is true." On a sullen August night, Leo is thrilled by a vision of Ayesha in all her former loveliness. She beckons him, and in a vision his spirit follows her into a realm of snowy peaks far beyond the furthest borders of Thibet. A sign in the clouds at dawn is repeated from this vision to both Leo and Holly, and together they start for Central Asia. Sixteen years of toil, struggle, and strange adventure pass, and they are still searching for "a mountain peak shaped like the Symbol of Life." After many wanderings they find themselves in a country where no European has ever set foot, on one of the spurs of the vast Cherga mountains, far eastward from Turkestan. A perilous ascent into the unexplored mountain fastness leads them to the revelation of "the *crux ansata*, the Symbol of Life itself." Rescued from drowning by a beautiful woman and an aged man, they are conducted through "The Gate" into the kingdom and city of Kaloon. Their saviours, they learn, are the Khania or Queen of Kaloon, and a venerable physician of magical powers. Is this woman Ayesha? No; they conjecture her rather to be Amenartas, who wrote the "sherd" of the former chronicle. She falls in love with Leo, and he and Holly learn that her husband, the Khan, is a madman. Simbri, the magician, and Atene, the Khania, have already received a solemn charge from the "Hesea" of a "College" in the Mountain of Fire to receive two strangers and bring them safely to the Mountain. But Atene's love for Leo makes her detain the travellers awhile in Kaloon, and she even proposes that the Khan shall be murdered so that she can wed Leo. To this the Englishman replies: "I go to ask a certain question of the Oracle on yonder mountain peak. With your will or without it, I tell you that I go, and afterwards you can settle which is the stronger—the Khania of Kaloon or the Hesea of the House of Fire." The Khan himself assists the escape of the travellers for their further journey, but his jealousy has been aroused, and after they have set out on their journey to the fire-crowned Mountain he pursues them with his death-hounds. After a long chase, a few of the brutes, and the Khan, overtake them, and a terrible struggle ensues, in which Leo and Holly eventually prove the victors, and the Khan is slain. The Khania and Simbri overtake them and seek to persuade them to return, but they refuse. The Khania leaves them, saying: "We do not part thus easily. You have summoned me to the Mountain, and even to the Mountain I will follow you. Aye, and there I will meet its spirit. . . . I will match my strength and magic against hers, as it is decreed that I shall do." On the Mountain itself they meet again with Atene, who brings thither her dead husband to the burying-place of the rulers of Kaloon. From a priest, Oros, who goes with them, they learn that for thousands of years this Mountain has been the home of a peculiar fire-worship, of which the head hierophant is a woman. To the veiled figure of Hes, on her throne, the two Englishmen tell of their wandering search. In answer to the challenge of Atene, the Hesea shows them a vision of events which happened long ago in the Caves of Kôr. Picture succeeds picture until all is blank, and then she tells how Ayesha first met Kallikrates in the early ages. Suddenly she reveals herself as Ayesha; but to remove all doubt she unveils before them, revealing herself in all her withered age. Atene bids Leo choose between her and Ayesha. Leo then kneels down and kisses the wrinkled head. At which Atene says: "Thou hast chosen. Take now thy bride and let me hence." Ayesha then begins to pray aloud, to some unseen Power, for the return of her former loveliness, and suddenly she is transfigured into radiant beauty once again, and claims Leo for the man whom she loved of old. Atene is baffled in a sudden attack upon the mysterious creature's life. Then leading Leo and Holly through rock-hewn passages into a hall beyond, Ayesha bids them "Good-bye," saying: "Oros will guard you both, and lead you to me at the appointed time." After a long sleep they are led by Oros to the Sanctuary, where, before a white-robed company of priests and priestesses, Ayesha is seated as a queen on a throne. A ceremony of betrothal takes place, after which Ayesha bids them leave her alone awhile. Many hours pass before they are brought once more into the presence of Ayesha. Then, after recalling many incidents of the days gone by, Ayesha bids them "Seek to learn no more." But Leo takes leave to ask: "One thing I do still seek to learn. Ayesha, we were betrothed to-night. When wilt thou marry me?" "Not yet, not yet," she answers hurriedly. "I vow to thee that to-morrow we'll be happy—aye, to-morrow without fail."

CHAPTER XIX.

LEO AND THE LEOPARD.

DURING the weeks that followed these momentous days, often and often I wondered to myself whether a more truly wretched being had ever lived than the woman, or the spirit, whom we knew as She, Hes, and Ayesha. Whether in fact also, or in our imagination only, she had arisen from the ashes of her hideous age into the full bloom of perpetual life and beauty inconceivable.

These things at least were certain: Ayesha had achieved the secret of an existence so enduring that for all human purposes it might be called unending. Within certain limitations—such as her utter inability to foresee the future—undoubtedly also, she was endued with powers that can only be described as supernatural.

Her rule over the strange community amongst whom she lived was absolute; indeed, its members regarded her as a goddess, and as such she was worshipped. After marvellous adventures, the man who was her very life, I might almost say her soul, whose being was so mysteriously intertwined with hers, whom she loved also with the intensest human passion of which woman can be capable, had sought her out in this hidden corner of the world.

More, thrice he had proved his unalterable fidelity to her. First, by his rejection of the royal and beautiful, if undisciplined, Atene. Secondly, by clinging to Ayesha when she seemed to be repulsive to every natural sense. Thirdly, after that homage scene in the Sanctuary — though with her unutterable perfections before his eyes this did not appear to be so wonderful — by steadfastness in the face of her terrible avowal, true or false, that she had won her gifts and him through some dim, unholy pact with the Powers of Evil, in the fruits and consequences of which he must be involved as the price of her possession.

Yet Ayesha was miserable. Even in her lightest moods it was clear to me that those skeletons at the feast of which she had spoken were her continual companions. Indeed, when we were alone, she would acknowledge it in dark hints and veiled allegories or allusions. Crushed though her rival the Khania Atene might be, also she was still jealous of her.

Perhaps "afraid" would be a better word, for some instinct seemed to warn Ayesha that soon or late her hour would come to Atene again, and that then it would be her own turn to drink of the bitter waters of despair.

What troubled her more a thousandfold, however, were her fears for Leo. As may well be understood, to stand in his intimate relationship to this half-divine and marvellous being, and yet not to be allowed so much as to touch her lips, did not conduce to his physical or mental well-being, especially as he knew that the wall of separation must not be climbed for at least two years. Little wonder that Leo lost appetite, grew thin and pale, and could not sleep, or that he implored her continually to rescind her decree and marry him.

But on this point Ayesha was immovable. Instigated thereto by Leo, and I may add my own curiosity, when we were alone I questioned her again as to the reasons of this self-denying ordinance. All she would tell me, however, was that between them rose the barrier of Leo's mortality, and that until his physical being had been impregnated with the mysterious virtue of the Vapour of Life, it was not wise that she should take him as a husband.

I asked her why, seeing that though a long-lived one, she was still a woman, whereon her face assumed a calm but terrifying smile, and she answered—

"Art so sure, my Holly? Tell me, do your women wear such jewels as that set upon my brow?" and she pointed to the faint but lambent light which glowed about her forehead.

More, she began slowly to stroke her abundant hair, then her breast and body. Wherever her fingers passed, the mystic light was born, until in that darkened room—for the dusk was gathering—she shimmered from head to foot like the water of a phosphorescent sea—a being glorious yet fearful to behold. Then she waved her hand, and, save for the gentle radiance on her brow, became as she had been.

"Art so sure, my Holly?" Ayesha repeated. "Nay, shrink not; that flame will not burn thee. Mayhap thou didst but imagine it, as I have noted thou dost imagine many things; for surely no woman could clothe herself in light and live; nor has so much as the smell of fire passed upon my garments."

Then at length my patience was outworn, and I grew angry.

"I am sure of nothing, Ayesha," I answered, "except that thou wilt make us mad with all these tricks and changes. Say, art thou a spirit, then?"

"We are all spirits," she said reflectively, "and I, perhaps, more than some. Who can be certain?"

"Not I," I answered. "Yet I implore, woman or spirit, tell me one thing—tell me the truth. In the beginning, what wast thou to Leo, and what was he to thee?"

She looked at me very solemnly and answered—

"Does my memory deceive me, Holly, or is it written in the first book of the Law of the Hebrews, which once I used to study, that the sons of Heaven came down to the daughters of men, and found that they were fair?"

"It is so written," I answered.

"Then, Holly, might it not have chanced that once a daughter of Heaven came down to a man of earth and loved him well? Might it not chance that for this great sin she, who had befouled her immortal state for him, was doomed to suffer, till at length his love, purified by pain and faithful even to a memory, was permitted to redeem her?"

"In that darkened room she shimmered from head to foot like the water of a phosphorescent sea."

Now at length I saw light, and sprang up eagerly, but in a cold voice she added—

"Nay, Holly, cease to question me, for there are things of which I can but speak to thee in figures and in parables, not to mock and bewilder thee, but because I must. Interpret them as thou wilt. Still, Atene thought me no mortal, since she told us that man and spirit may not mate; and there are matters in which I let her judgment weigh with me, as without doubt now, as in other lives, she and that old Shaman, her uncle, have wisdom—aye, and foresight. So bid my lord press me no more to wed him, for it gives me pain to say him nay—ah! thou knowest not how much.

"Moreover, I will declare myself to thee, old friend; whatever else I be, at least I am too womanly to listen to the pleadings of my best beloved and not myself be moved. See, I have set a curb upon desire, and drawn it until my heart bleeds; but if he pursues me with continual words and looks of burning love, who knoweth but that I shall kindle in his flame and throw the reins of reason to the winds?

"Oh, then together we might race adown our passions' steep; together dare the torrent that rages at its foot, and there, perchance, be whelmed or torn asunder! Nay, nay, another space of journeying, but a little space, and we reach the bridge my wisdom found, and cross it safely, and beyond for ever ride on at ease through the happy meadows of our love."

Then she was silent, nor would she speak more upon the matter. Also—and this was the worst of it—even now I was not sure that she told me the truth, or, at any rate, all of it, for to Ayesha's mind truth was many coloured as are the rays of light thrown from the different faces of a cut jewel. We never could be certain which shade of it she was pleased to present, who, whether by preference or of necessity, as she herself had said, spoke of such secrets in figures of speech and parables.

It is a fact that to this hour I do not know whether Ayesha was spirit or woman, or, as I suspect, a blend of both. I do not know the limits of her powers, or if that elaborate story of the beginning of her love for Leo was true—which personally I doubt —or but a fable, invented by her mind, and through it, as she had hinted, pictured on the flame for her own hidden purposes.

I do not know whether, when first we saw her on the Mountain, she was really old and hideous, or did but put on that shape in our eyes in order to test her lover. I do not know whether, as the priest Oros bore witness —which he may well have been bidden to do—her spirit passed into the body of the dead priestess of Hes, or whether, when she seemed to perish there so miserably, her body and her soul were wafted straightway from the caves of Kôr to this Central Asian peak.

I do not know why, as she was so powerful, she did not come to seek us, instead of leaving us to seek her through so many weary years, though I suggest that some superior force forbade her to do more than companion us unseen, watching our every act, reading our every thought, until at length we reached the predestined place and hour. Also, as will appear, there were other things of which this is not the time to speak, whereby I am still more tortured and perplexed.

In short, I know nothing, except that my existence has been intertangled with one of the great mysteries of the world; that the glorious being called Ayesha won the secret of life from whatever power holds it in its keeping; that she alleged—although of this, remember, we have no actual proof—such life was to be attained by bathing in a certain emanation, vapour, or essence; that she was possessed by a passion not easy to understand, but terrific in its force and immortal in its nature, concentrated upon one other being and one alone. That through this passion also some angry fate smote her again, again, and yet again, making of her countless days a burden, and leading the power and the wisdom which knew all, but could foreknow nothing, into abysses of anguish, suspense, and disappointment such as—Heaven be thanked!—we common men and women are not called upon to plumb.

For the rest, should human eyes ever fall upon it, each reader must form his own opinion of this history, its true interpretation and significance. These and the exact parts played by Atene and myself in its development, I hope to solve shortly, though not here.

* * * * *

Well, as I have said, the upshot of it all was that Ayesha was devoured with anxiety about Leo. Except in this matter of marriage, his every wish was satisfied, and, indeed, forestalled. Thus he was never again asked to share in any of the ceremonies of the Sanctuary, though, indeed, stripped of its rites and spiritual symbols, the religion of the College of Hes proved pure and harmless enough. It was but a diluted version of the Osiris and Isis worship of old Egypt, from which it had been inherited, mixed with the Central Asian belief in the transmigration or reincarnation of souls and the possibility of drawing near to the ultimate Godhead by holiness of thought and life.

In fact, the Head Priestess and Oracle was only worshipped as a representative of the Divinity, while the temporal aims of the College in practice were confined to good works, although it is true that they still sighed for their lost authority over the country of Kaloon. Thus they had hospitals, and during the long and severe winters, when the Tribes of the Mountain slopes were often driven to the verge of starvation, gave liberally to the destitute from their stores of food.

Leo liked to be with Ayesha continually, so we spent each evening in her company, and much of the day also, until she found that this inactivity told upon him who for years had been accustomed to endure every rigour of climate in the open air. After this came home to her—although she was always haunted by terror lest any accident should befall him—Ayesha insisted upon his going out to kill the wild sheep and the ibex, which lived in numbers on the Mountain ridges, placing him in the charge of the chiefs and huntsmen of the Tribes, with whom thus he became well acquainted. In this exercise, however, I accompanied him but rarely, as, if used too much, my arm still gave me pain.

Once, indeed, such an accident did happen. I was seated in the garden with Ayesha and watching her. Her head rested on her hand, and she was looking with her wide eyes, across which the swift thoughts passed like clouds over a windy sky, or dreams through the mind of a sleeper—looking out vacantly towards the Mountain snows. Seen thus, her loveliness was inexpressible, amazing ; merely to gaze upon it was an intoxication. Contemplating it, I understood indeed that, like to that of the fabled Helen, this gift of hers alone—and it was but one of many—must have caused infinite sorrows had she ever been permitted to display it to the world. It would have driven humanity to madness : the men with longings and the women with jealousy and hate.

And yet in what did her surpassing beauty lie ? Ayesha's face and form were perfect, it is true ; but so are those of some other women. Not in these, then, did it live alone,

but rather, I think, especially while what I may call her human moods were on her, in the soft mystery that dwelt upon her features and gathered and changed in her splendid eyes. Some such mystery may be seen, however faintly, on the faces of certain of the masterpieces of the Greek sculptors ; but Ayesha it clothed like an ever-present atmosphere, suggesting a glory that was not of earth, making her divine.

As I gazed at her and wondered thus, of a sudden she became terribly agitated, and, pointing to a shoulder of the Mountain miles and miles away, said—

"Look !"

I looked, but saw nothing except a sheet of distant snow.

"Blind fool ! canst thou not see that my lord is in danger of his life ? " she cried. "Nay, I forgot, thou hast no vision. Take it now from me and look again " ; and laying her hand, from which a strange, numbing current seemed to flow, upon my head, she muttered some swift words.

Instantly my eyes were opened, and, not upon the distant Mountain, but in the air before me as it were, I saw Leo rolling over and over at grips with a great snow-leopard, whilst the chief and huntsmen with him ran round and round, seeking an opportunity to pierce the savage brute with their spears and yet leave him unharmed.

Ayesha, rigid with terror, swayed to and fro at my side, till presently the end came, for I could see Leo drive his long knife into the bowels of the leopard, which at once grew limp, separated from him, and after a struggle or two in the bloodstained snow, lay still. Then he rose, laughing and pointing to his rent garments, whilst one of the huntsmen came forward and began to bandage some wounds in his hands and thigh with strips of linen torn from his under-robe.

The vision vanished suddenly as it had come, and I felt Ayesha leaning heavily upon my shoulder like any other frightened woman, and heard her gasp—

"That danger also has passed by, but how many are there to follow ? Oh, tormented heart ! how long canst thou endure ? "

Then her wrath flamed up against the chief and his huntsmen, and she summoned messengers and sent them out at speed with a litter and ointments, bidding them to bear back the lord Leo and to bring his companions to her very presence.

"Thou seest what days are mine, my Holly —aye, and have been these many years," she

" I saw Leo rolling over and over at grips with a great snow-leopard."

said ; " but those hounds shall pay me for this agony ! "

Nor would she suffer me to reason with her.

*   *   *   *   *

Four hours later, Leo returned, limping after the litter in which, instead of himself, for whom it was sent, lay a Mountain sheep and the skin of the snow-leopard, that he had placed there to save the huntsmen the labour of carrying them. Ayesha was waiting for him in the hall of her dwelling, and gliding to him—I cannot say she walked—overwhelmed him with mingled solicitude and reproaches. He listened awhile, then asked—

" How dost thou know anything of this matter ? The leopard skin has not yet been brought to thee."

" I know because I saw," she answered. " The worst hurt was above thy knee ; hast thou dressed it with the salve I sent ? "

" Not I," he said. " But thou hast not left this Sanctuary ; how didst thou see ? By thy magic ? "

" If thou wilt. At least I saw ; and Holly also saw thee rolling in the snow with that fierce brute, while those curs ran round like scared children."

" I am weary of this magic," interrupted Leo crossly. " Cannot a man be left alone for an hour even with a leopard of the Mountain ? As for those brave men——"

At this moment Oros entered and whispered something, bowing low.

" As for those ' brave men,' I will deal with them," said Ayesha with bitter emphasis, and covering herself—for she never appeared unveiled to the people of the Mountain—she swept from the place.

" Where has she gone, Horace ? " asked Leo. " To one of her services in the Sanctuary ? "

" I don't know," I answered ; " but if so, I think it will be that chief's burial service."

" Will it ? " he exclaimed, and instantly limped after her.

A minute or two later, I thought it wise to follow. In the Sanctuary a curious scene was in progress. Ayesha was seated in front of the statue. Before her, very much frightened, knelt a brawny, red-haired chieftain and five of his followers, who still carried their hunting-spears, while with folded arms and an exceedingly grim look upon his face, Leo, who, as I learned afterwards, had already interfered and been silenced, stood upon one side listening to what passed. At a little distance behind were a dozen or more of the Temple guards,

men armed with swords and picked for their strength and stature.

Ayesha, in her sweetest voice, was questioning the men as to how the leopard, of which the skin lay before her, had come to attack Leo. The chief answered that they had tracked the brute to its lair between two rocks ; that one of them had gone in and wounded it, whereon it sprang upon him and struck him down ; that then the lord Leo had engaged it while the man escaped, and was also struck down, after which, rolling with it on the ground, he stabbed and slew the animal. That was all.

" No, not all," said Ayesha ; " for you forget, cowards that you are, that, keeping yourselves in safety, you left my lord to the fury of this beast. Good. Drive them out on to the Mountain, there to perish also at the fangs of beasts, and make it known that he who gives them food or shelter dies ! "

Offering no prayer for pity or excuse, the chief and his followers rose, bowed, and turned to go.

" Stay a moment, comrades," said Leo ; " and, chief, give me your arm ; my scratch grows stiff ; I cannot walk fast. We will finish this hunt together."

" What doest thou ? Art mad ? " asked Ayesha.

" I know not whether I am mad," he answered, " but I know that thou art wicked and unjust. Look, now, than these hunters none braver ever breathed. That man "—and he pointed to the one whom the leopard had struck down—" took my place and went in before me because I ordered that we should attack the creature, and thus was felled. As thou seest all, thou mightest have seen this also. Then it sprang on me, and the rest of these, my friends, ran round waiting a chance to strike, which at first they could not do, unless they would have killed me with it, since I and the brute rolled over and over in the snow. As it was, one of them seized it with his bare hands : look at the teeth-marks on his arm. So if they are to perish on the Mountain, I, who am the man to blame, perish with them."

Now, while the hunters looked at him with fervent gratitude in their eyes, Ayesha thought a little, then said, cleverly enough—

" In truth, my lord Leo, had I known all the tale, well mightest thou have named me wicked and unjust ; but I knew only what I saw, and out of their own mouths did I condemn them. My servants, my lord here has pleaded for you, and you are forgiven ; more, he who rushed in upon the leopard, and he who seized it with his hands, shall be rewarded and advanced. Go; but I warn you, if you suffer my lord to come into more danger, you shall not escape so easily again."

So they bowed and went, still blessing Leo with their eyes, since death by exposure on the Mountain snows was the most terrible form of punishment known to these people, and one only inflicted by the direct order of Hes upon murderers or other great criminals.

*　　*　　*　　*　　*

When we had left the Sanctuary, and were alone again in the hall, the storm that I had seen gathering upon Leo's face broke in earnest. Ayesha renewed her inquiries about his wounds, and wished to call Oros, the physician, to dress them, and as he refused this, offered to do so herself. He begged that she would leave his wounds alone, and then, his great beard bristling with wrath, asked her solemnly if he were a child in arms, a query so absurd that I could not help laughing.

Then he scolded her — yes, he scolded Ayesha! Wishing to know what she meant (1) by spying upon him with her magic, an evil gift that he had always disliked and mistrusted; (2) by condemning brave and excellent men, his good friends, to a death of fiendish cruelty upon such evidence or, rather, out of temper, on no evidence at all; and (3) by giving him into charge of them, as though he were a little boy, and telling them that they would have to answer for it if he were hurt: he who, in his time, had killed every sort of big game known, and passed through some perils and encounters?

Thus he beat her with his words, and, wonderful to say, Ayesha, in this being more than woman, submitted to the chastisement meekly. Yet, had any other man dared to address her with roughness even, I doubt not that his speech and his life would have come to a swift and simultaneous end, for I knew that now, as of old, she could slay by the mere effort of her will. But she did not slay; she did not even threaten, only, as any other loving woman might have done, she began to cry. Yes, great tears gathered in those lovely eyes of hers, and, rolling one by one down her face, fell—for her head was bent humbly forward—like heavy raindrops on the marble floor.

At the sight of this touching evidence of her human, loving heart, all Leo's anger melted. Now it was he who grew penitent and prayed her pardon humbly. She gave him her hand in token of forgiveness, saying—

"Let others speak to me as they will" (sorry should I have been to try it!), "but from thee, Leo, I cannot bear harsh words. Oh, thou art cruel, cruel! In what have I offended? Can I help it if my spirit keeps its watch upon thee, as, indeed, though thou knewest it not, it has done ever since we parted yonder in the Place of Life? Can I help it if, like some mother who sees her little child at play upon a mountain's edge, my soul is torn with agony when I know thee to be in dangers that I am powerless to prevent or share? What are the lives of a few half-wild huntsmen, that I should let them weigh for a single breath against thy safety, seeing that if I slew these, others would be more careful of thee? Whereas if I slay them not, they or their fellows may even lead thee into perils that would bring about—thy *death!*" and she gasped with horror at the word.

"Listen, beloved," said Leo. "The life of the humblest of those men is of as much value to him as mine is to me, and thou hast no more right to kill him than thou hast to kill me. It is evil that, because thou carest for me, thou shouldst suffer thy love to draw thee into cruelty and crime. If thou art afraid for me, then clothe me with that immortality of thine, which, although I dread it somewhat, holding it a thing unholy, and, on this earth, not permitted by my Faith, I should still rejoice to inherit for thy dear sake, knowing that then we could never more be parted. Or if, as thou sayest, this as yet thou canst not do, then let us be wed, and take what fortune gives us. All men must die; but at least, before I die I shall have been happy with thee for a while —yes, if only for a single hour."

"Would that I dared!" Ayesha answered, with a little piteous motion of her hand. "Oh! urge me no more, Leo, lest that, at last, I should take the risk and lead thee down a dreadful road. Leo, hast thou never heard of the love which slays, or of the poison that may lurk in the cup of joy too perfect?"

Then, as though she feared herself, Ayesha turned from him and fled.

*　　*　　*　　*　　*

Thus this matter ended. In itself it was not a great one, for Leo's hurts were mere scratches, and the hunters, instead of being killed, were promoted to be members of his bodyguard. Yet it told us many things. For instance, that whenever she chose to do so, Ayesha had the power of perceiving all Leo's movements from afar, and even of

" ' Drive them out on to the Mountain ! ' "

communicating her strength of mental vision to others, although to help him in any predicament she appeared to have no power, which, of course, accounted for the hideous and ever-present might of her anxiety.

Think what it would be to any one of us were we mysteriously acquainted with every open danger, every risk of sickness, every secret peril through which our best-beloved must pass ! To see the rock trembling to its fall, and they loitering beneath it ; to see them drink of water, and know it full of foulest poison ; to see them embark upon a ship, and be aware that it was doomed to sink, but not to be able to warn them or to prevent them ! Surely no mortal brain could endure such constant terrors, since hour by hour the arrows of death flit unseen and unheard past the breasts of each of us, till at length one finds its home there.

What, then, must Ayesha have suffered, watching with her spirit's eyes all the hair-breadth escapes of our journeyings? When, for instance, in the beginning she saw Leo at my house in Cumberland about to kill himself in his madness and despair, and by some mighty effort of her superhuman will, wrung from whatever Power it was that held her in its fearful thraldrom, the strength to hurl her soul across the world, and thereby in his sleep reveal to him the secret of the hiding-place where he would find her? Or—to take one more example out of many — when she saw him hanging by that slender thread of yak's-hide from the face of the waterfall of ice, and herself remained unable to save him, or even to look forward for a single moment and learn whether or no he was about to meet a hideous death, in which event she must live on alone until in some dim age he was born again?

Nor can her sorrows have ended with these more material fears, since others as piercing must have haunted her. Imagine, for instance, the agonies of her jealous heart when she knew her lover to be exposed to the temptations incident to his solitary existence, and more especially to those of her ancient rival Atene, who, by Ayesha's own account, had once been his wife. Imagine also her fears lest time and human change should do their natural work on him, so that, by degrees, the memory of her wisdom and her strength and the image of her loveliness faded from his thought, and with them his desire for her company; thus leaving her, who had endured so long, forgotten and alone at last!

Truly, the Power that limited our perceptions did so in purest mercy, for were it otherwise with us, our race would go mad and perish raving in its terrors.

Thus it would seem that Ayesha, great, tormented soul, thinking to win life and love eternal and most glorious, was in truth but another blind Pandora. From her stolen casket of beauty and superhuman power had leapt into her bosom, there to dwell unceasingly, a hundred torturing demons, of whose wings mere mortal kind do but feel the far-off, icy shadowing.

Yes; and that the parallel might be complete, Hope alone still lingered in that rifled chest.

CHAPTER XX.

AYESHA'S ALCHEMY.

IT was shortly after this incident of the snow-leopard that one of these demon familiars of Ayesha's, her infinite ambition, made its formidable appearance. When we had dined with her in the evening, Ayesha's habit was to discuss plans for our mighty and unending future, that awful inheritance which she had promised to us.

Here I must explain, if I have not done so already, that she had graciously informed me that, notwithstanding my refusal in past years of such a priceless opportunity, I also was to be allowed to bathe my superannuated self in the vital fires, though in what guise I should emerge from them, like Herodotus when he treats of the mysteries of old Egypt, if she knew, she did not think it lawful to reveal.

Secretly I hoped that my outward man might change for the better, as the prospect of being fixed for ever in the shape of my present and somewhat unpleasing personality did not appeal to me as attractive. In truth, so far as I was concerned, the matter had an academic rather than an actual interest, such as we take in a fairy tale, since I did not believe that I should ever put on this kind of immortality. Nor, I may add, now as before, was I at all certain that I wished to do so.

These plans of Ayesha's were far-reaching and, indeed, terrific. Her acquaintance with the modern world, its political and social developments, was still strictly limited; for if she had the power to follow its growth and activities, certainly it was one of which she made no use. In practice her knowledge seemed to be confined to what she had gathered during the few brief talks which took place between us upon this subject in past time at Kôr. Now her thirst for information was insatiable, although it is true that ours was scarcely up to date, seeing that ever since we lost touch with the civilised peoples—namely, for the last fifteen years or so—we had been as much buried as she was herself.

Still, we were able to describe to her the condition of the nations and their affairs as they were at the period when we bade them farewell, and, more or less incorrectly, to draw maps of the various countries and their boundaries, over which she pondered long.

The Chinese were the people in whom she proved to be most interested, perhaps because she was acquainted with the Mongolian type and, like ourselves, understood a good many of their dialects. Also she had a motive for her studies, which one night she revealed to us in the most matter-of-fact fashion.

Those who have read the first part of her history, which I left in England to be published, may remember that when we found her at Kôr, *She* horrified us by expressing a determination to possess herself of Great Britain, for the simple reason that we belonged to that country. Now, however, like her powers, her ideas had grown, for she purposed to make Leo the absolute monarch of the world. In vain did he assure her most earnestly that he desired no such empire. She merely laughed at him and said—

"If I arise amidst the Peoples, I must rule the Peoples, for how can I take a second place among mortal men? And thou, my Leo, rulest me; yes, mark the truth, thou art my master! Therefore it is plain that thou wilt be the master of this earth—aye, and perchance of others which do not yet appear, for of these also I know something, and, I think, can reach them if I will, though hitherto I have had no mind that way. My true life has not yet begun. Its little space within this world has been filled with thought and care for thee—in waiting till thou wast born again, and during these last years of separation, until thou didst return.

"But now a few more months, and the days of preparation past, endowed with energy eternal, with all the wisdom of the ages, and with a strength that can bend the mountains or turn the ocean from its bed, and we begin to be. Oh, how I sicken for that hour when first, like twin stars new to the firmament of heaven, we break in our immortal splendour upon the astonished sight of men! It will please me, I tell thee, Leo, it will please me to see Powers, Principalities, and Dominions, marshalled by their kings and governors, bow themselves before our thrones and humbly crave the liberty to do our will. At least," she added, "it will please me for a little time, until we seek higher things."

So she spoke, while the radiance upon her brow increased and spread itself, gleaming above her like a golden fan, and her slumbrous eyes took fire from it till, to my thought, they became glowing mirrors in which I saw pomp enthroned and suppliant peoples pass.

"And how," asked Leo, with something like a groan—for this vision of universal rule viewed from afar did not seem to charm him —"how, Ayesha, wilt thou bring these things about?"

"How, my Leo? Why, easily enough. For many nights I have listened to the wise discourses of our Holly here—at least, he thinks them wise, who still has so much to learn; and pored over his crooked maps, comparing them with those that are written in my memory, who of late have had no time for the study of such little matters. Also I have weighed and pondered your reports of the races of this world—their various follies, their futile struggling for wealth and small supremacies; and I have determined that it would be wise and kind to weld them to one whole, setting ourselves at the head of them to direct their destinies, and cause wars, sickness, and poverty to cease, so that these creatures of a little day" ("*ephemeridæ*" was the word she used) "may live happy from the cradle to the grave.

"Now, were it not because of thy strange shrinking from bloodshed, however politic and needful—for my Leo, as yet thou art no true philosopher—this were quickly done, since I can command a weapon which would crush their armouries and whelm their navies in the deed; yes, I, whom even the lightnings and Nature's elemental powers must obey. But thou shrinkest from the sight of death, and thou believest that Heaven would be displeased because I make myself—or am chosen —the instrument of Heaven. Well, so let it be, for thy will is mine, and therefore we will tread a gentler path."

"And how wilt thou persuade the kings of the earth to place their crowns upon thy head?" I asked, astonished.

"By causing their peoples to offer them to us," she answered suavely. "Oh! Holly, Holly, how narrow is thy mind, how strained the quality of thine imagination! Set its poor gates ajar, I pray, and bethink thee. When we appear among men, scattering gold to satisfy their want, clad in terrifying power, in dazzling beauty, and in immortality of days, will they not cry: 'Be ye our monarchs and rule over us'?"

"Perhaps," I answered dubiously; "but where wilt thou appear?"

She took a map of the Eastern Hemisphere which I had drawn, and, placing her finger upon Pekin, said—

"There is the place that shall be our home for some few centuries—say three, or five, or seven, should it take so long to shape this people to my liking and our purposes. I have chosen these Chinese because thou tellest me that their numbers are uncountable, that they are brave, subtle, and patient, and though now powerless because ill-ruled and untaught, able with their multitudes to flood the little Western nations. Therefore, among them we will begin our reign, and for some few ages be at rest while they learn wisdom from us, and thou, my Holly, makest their armies unconquerable and givest their land good government, wealth, peace, and a new religion."

What the new religion was to be I did not ask. It seemed unnecessary, since I was convinced that in practice it would prove a form of Ayesha-worship. Indeed, my mind was so occupied with conjectures, some of them quaint and absurd enough, as to what would happen at the first meeting between Ayesha and the Empress-Dowager of China —a lady of whose character and ambitions I had heard much in Thibet—that I forgot this subsidiary development of our future rule.

"And if the 'little Western nations' will not wait to be flooded?" suggested Leo. "If they combine with Russia, for instance —in whose territory we may be at this moment, for aught I know—and attack thee first?"

"Ah!" she said, with a flash of her eyes. "I have thought of it, and for my part hope that it will chance, since then thou canst not blame me if I put out my strength. Oh! then the East, that has slept so long, shall awake—shall awake, and upon battlefield after battlefield such as history cannot tell of, thou shalt see my flaming standards sweep on to victory. One by one thou shalt see the nations fall and perish, until at length I build thee a throne upon the hecatombs of their countless dead and crown thee emperor of a world regenerate in blood and fire!"

Leo, whom this new gospel of regeneration seemed to appal—who was, in fact, a hater of absolute monarchies, and somewhat republican in his views and sympathies—continued the argument, but I took no further heed. The thing was grotesque in its tremendous and fantastic absurdity; Ayesha's ambitions were such as no imperial-minded madman could conceive.

Yet—here came the rub—I had not the slightest doubt but that she was well able to put them into practice and carry them to some marvellous and awful conclusion. Why not? Death could not touch her; she had triumphed over death. Her beauty and her reckless will would compel the hosts of men to follow her. Her piercing intelligence would enable her to invent new weapons with which the most highly trained army could not possibly compete. Indeed, it might be as she said, and as I for one believed—with good reason, as it proved—that she held at her command the elemental forces of Nature, such as those that lie hid in electricity, which

would give all living beings to her for a prey.

Ayesha was still woman enough to have worldly ambitions, and the most dread circumstance about her superhuman powers was that they appeared to be unrestrained by any responsibility to God or man. She was, as we might well imagine a fallen angel to be—if, indeed, as she herself once hinted and as Atene and the old Shaman believed, this were not her true place in creation. By only two things that I was able to discover could she be moved—her love for Leo, and, in a very small degree, her friendship for myself.

Yet her devouring passion for this one man, inexplicable in its endurance and intensity, would, I felt sure, even then, in the future as in the past, prove to be her heel of Achilles. When Ayesha was dipped in the waters of Dominion and Deathlessness, this human love left her heart mortal, that through it she might be rendered harmless as a child, who otherwise would have devastated the universe.

I was right.

* * * * *

Whilst I was still indulging myself in these reflections, and hoping that Ayesha would not take the trouble to read them in my mind, I became aware that Oros was bowing to the earth before her.

"Thy business, priest?" she asked sharply; for when she was with Leo, Ayesha did not like to be disturbed.

"Hes, the spies are returned."

"Why didst thou send them out?" she asked indifferently. "What need have I of thy spies?"

"Hes, thou didst command me."

"Well, their report?"

"Hes, it is most grave. The people of Kaloon are desperate because of the drought which has caused their crops to fail, so that starvation stares them in the eyes, and this they lay to the charge of the strangers who came into their land and fled to thee. The Khania Atene also is mad with rage against thee and our holy College. Labouring night and day, she has gathered two great armies, one of forty, and one of twenty thousand men, and the latter of these she sends against the Mountain under the command of her uncle, Simbri the Shaman. In case it should be defeated, she purposes to remain with the second and greater army on the plains about Kaloon."

"Tidings indeed!" said Ayesha, with a scornful laugh. "Has her hate made this

" She took a map, and, placing her finger upon Pekin, said : 'There is the place that shall be our home.' "

woman mad, that she dares thus to match herself against me? My Holly, it crossed thy mind but now that it was I who am mad, boasting of what I have no power to perform. Well, within six days thou shalt learn—oh! verily thou shalt learn, and, though the issue be so very small, in such a fashion that thou wilt doubt no more for ever. Stay, I will look, though the effort of it wearies me, for those spies may be but victims to their own fears or to the falsehoods of Atene."

Then suddenly, as was common with her when thus Ayesha threw her sight afar, which, either from indolence, or because, as she said, it exhausted her, she did but rarely, her lovely face grew rigid like that of a person in a trance; the light faded from her brow, and the great pupils of her eyes contracted themselves and lost their colour.

In a little while, five minutes perhaps, she sighed like one awakening from a deep sleep, passed her hand across her forehead, and was as she had been, though somewhat languid, as though strength had left her.

"It is true enough," she said, "and soon I must be stirring, lest many of my people should be killed. My lord, wouldst thou see war? Nay, thou shalt bide here in safety whilst I go forward—to visit Atene as I promised."

"Where thou goest, I go," said Leo angrily, his face flushing to the roots of his hair with shame.

"I pray thee not, I pray thee not," she answered, yet without venturing to forbid him. "We will talk of it hereafter. Oros, away! Send round the Fire of Hes to every chief. Three nights hence at the moonrise bid the Tribes gather—nay, not all, twenty thousand of their best will be enough; the rest shall stay to guard the Mountain and this Sanctuary. Let them bring food with them for fifteen days. I join them at the following dawn. Go!"

He bowed and went, whereon, dismissing the matter from her mind, Ayesha began to question me again about the Chinese and their customs.

* * * * *

It was in course of a somewhat similar conversation on the following night, of which, however, I forget the exact details, that a remark of Leo's led to another exhibition of Ayesha's marvellous powers.

Leo—who had been considering her plans for conquest, and again combating them as best he could, for they were entirely repugnant to his religious, social, and political views—said suddenly that, after all, they must break down, since they would involve the expenditure of sums of money so vast that even Ayesha herself would be unable to provide them by any known methods of taxation. She looked at him and laughed a little.

"Verily, Leo," she said, "to thee, yes; and to Holly here I must seem as some madcap girl blown to and fro by every wind of fancy, and building me a palace wherein to dwell out of dew and vapours, or from the substance of the sunset fires. Thinkest thou then that I would enter on this war—one woman against all the world"—and as she spoke her shape grew royal, and in her awful eyes there came a look that chilled my blood—"and make no preparation for its necessities? Why, since last we spoke upon this matter, foreseeing all, I have considered in my mind, and now thou shalt learn how, without cost to those we rule—and for that reason alone shall they love us dearly—I will glut the treasuries of the Empress of the Earth.

"Dost remember, Leo, how in Kôr I found but a single pleasure during all those weary ages—that of forcing my mother Nature one by one to yield me up her choicest secrets; I, who am a student of all things which are and of the forces that cause them to be born. Now follow me, both of you, and ye shall look on what mortal eyes have not yet beheld."

"What are we to see?" I asked doubtfully, having a lively recollection of Ayesha's powers as a chemist.

"That thou shalt learn, or shalt not learn if it pleases thee to stay behind. Come, Leo, my love, my love, and leave this wise philosopher first to find his riddle and next to guess it."

Then turning her back to me, she smiled on him so sweetly that, although really he was more loth to go than I, Leo would have followed her through a furnace door—as indeed, had he but known it, he was about to do.

So they started, and I accompanied them, since with Ayesha it was useless to indulge in any foolish pride or to make oneself a victim to consistency. Also I was anxious to see her new marvel, and did not care to rely for an account of it upon Leo's descriptive skill, which at its best was never more than moderate.

She took us down passages that we had not passed before, to a door which she signed to Leo to open. He obeyed, and from the cave within issued a flood of light.

As we guessed at once, the place was her laboratory, for about it stood metal flasks and various strange-shaped instruments. Moreover, there was a furnace in it, one of the best conceivable, for it needed neither fuel nor stoking, whose fires, like those of the twisted columns in the Sanctuary, sprang from the womb of the volcano beneath our feet.

When we entered, two priests were at work there: one of them stirring a cauldron with an iron rod, and the other receiving its molten contents into a mould of clay. They stopped to salute Ayesha, but she bade them to continue their task, asking them if all went well.

"Very well, O Hes," they answered; and we passed through that cave and sundry doors and passages to a little chamber cut in the rock. There was no lamp or flame of fire in it, and yet the place was filled with a gentle light which seemed to flow from the opposing wall.

"What were those priests doing?" I said, more to break the silence than for any other reason.

"Why waste breath upon foolish questions?" she replied. "Are no metals smelted in thy country, O Holly? Now, hadst thou sought to know what I am doing—— But that, without seeing, thou wouldst not believe; so, Doubter, thou shalt see."

Then she pointed to and bade us don two strange garments that hung upon the wall, made of a material which seemed to be half-cloth and half-wood, and having head-pieces not unlike a diver's helmet.

So under her directions Leo helped me into mine, lacing it up behind, after which—or so I gathered from the sounds, for no light came through the helmet—she did the same service for him.

"I seem very much in the dark," I said presently; for now there was silence again, and beneath this extinguisher I felt alarmed and wished to be sure that I was not left alone.

"Aye, Holly," I heard Ayesha's mocking voice make answer, "in the dark, as thou wast ever—the thick dark of ignorance and unbelief. Well, now, as ever also, I will give thee light." As she spoke I heard something roll back; I suppose that it must have been a stone door.

Then, indeed, there was light; yes, even through the thicknesses of that prepared garment, such light as seemed to blind me. By it I saw that the wall opposite to us had opened and that we were, all three of us, on the threshold of another chamber. At the end of it stood something like a little altar of hard, black stone, and on this altar lay a mass of substance of the size of a child's head, but fashioned, I suppose from fantasy, to the oblong shape of a human eye.

Out of this eye there poured that blistering and intolerable light. It was shut round by thick, funnel-shaped screens of a material that looked like fire-brick, yet it pierced them as though they were but muslin. More, the rays thus directed upwards struck full upon a lump of metal held in place above them by a massive framework.

And what rays they were! If all the cut diamonds of the world were brought together and set beneath a mighty burning-glass, the light flashed from them would not have been a thousandth part so brilliant. They scorched my eyes and caused the skin of my face and limbs to smart, yet Ayesha stood there unshielded from them. Aye, she even went down the length of the room and, throwing back her veil, bent over them, as it seemed a woman of molten steel in whose body the bones were visible, and examined the mass that was supported by the hanging cradle.

"It is ready, and somewhat sooner than I thought," she said. Then, as though it were but a feather-weight, she lifted the lump in her bare hands and glided back with it to where we stood, laughing and saying—

"Tell me now, O thou well-read Holly, if thou hast ever heard of a better alchemist than this poor priestess of a forgotten faith?" And she thrust the glowing substance up almost to the mask that hid my face.

Then I turned and ran—or, rather, waddled, for in that gear I could not run—out of the chamber, until the rock wall beyond stayed me, and there, with my back towards her, thrust my helmeted head against it, for I felt as though red-hot bradawls had been plunged into my eyes. So I stood, while she laughed and mocked behind me, until at length I heard the door close, and the blessed darkness came like a gift from Heaven.

Then Ayesha began to loose Leo from his ray-proof armour—if so it can be called—and he in turn loosed me; and there in that gentle radiance we stood blinking at each other like owls in the sunlight, while the tears streamed down our faces.

"Well, art satisfied, my Holly?" she asked.

"Satisfied with what?" I answered angrily, for the smarting of my eyes was unbearable. "Yes, with burnings and bedevilments I am well satisfied."

"And I also," grumbled Leo, who was swearing softly but continuously to himself in the other corner of the place.

But Ayesha only laughed—oh! she laughed until she seemed the goddess of all merriment

"When we entered, two priests were at work there."

come to earth; laughed till she also wept, then said—

"Why, what ingratitude is this? Thou, my Leo, didst wish to see the wonders that I work, and thou, O Holly, didst come unbidden after I bade thee stay behind, and now both of you are rude and angry—aye, and weeping like a child with a burnt finger. Here, take this," and she gave us some salve that stood upon a shelf, "and rub it on your eyes, and the smart will pass away."

So we did, and the pain went from them, though for hours afterwards mine remained red as blood.

"And what are these wonders?" I asked her presently. "If thou meanest that unbearable flame——"

"Nay, I mean what is born of the flame, as, in thine ignorance, thou dost call that mighty agent. Look, now"; and she pointed to the metallic lump she had brought with her, which, still gleaming faintly, lay upon the floor. "Nay, it has no heat. Thinkest thou that I would wish to burn my tender hands, and so make them unsightly? Touch it, Holly."

But I would not, who thought to myself that Ayesha might be well accustomed to the hottest fires, and feared her impish mischief. I looked, however, long and earnestly.

"Well, what is it, Holly?"

"Gold," I said; then corrected myself and added: "Copper," for the dull, red glow might have been that of either metal.

"Nay, nay," she answered; "it is gold, pure gold."

"The ore in this place must be rich," said Leo incredulously, for I would not speak any more.

"Yes, my Leo, the iron ore is rich."

"Iron ore?" And he looked at her.

"Surely," she answered, "for from what mine do men dig out gold in such great masses? Iron ore, beloved, that by my alchemy I change to gold, which soon shall serve us in our need."

Now Leo stared and I groaned, for I did not believe that it was gold, and still less that she could make that metal. Then, reading my thought, she grew very angry.

"By Nature's self!" she cried, "wert thou not my friend, Holly, the fool whom it pleases me to cherish, I would bind that right hand of thine in those secret rays till the very bones within it were turned to gold. Nay, why should I be vexed with thee, who art both blind and deaf? Yet thou *shalt* be persuaded"; and leaving us, she passed down the passages, called something to the priests who were labouring in the workshop, then returned to us.

Presently they followed her, carrying on a kind of stretcher between them an ingot of iron ore that seemed to be as much as they could lift.

"Now," she said, "how wilt thou that I mark this mass which, as thou must admit, is only iron? With the Sign of Life? Good"; and at her bidding the priests took cold-chisels and hammers and roughly cut upon its surface the symbol of the looped cross—the *Crux Ansata*.

"It is not enough," she said, when they had finished. "Holly, lend me that knife of thine; to-morrow I will return it to thee, and of more value."

So I drew my hunting-knife, an Indian-made thing, that had a handle of steel, and gave it her.

"Thou knowest the marks on it," and she pointed to various dents and to the maker's name upon the blade; for though the hilt was Indian work, the steel was of Sheffield manufacture.

I nodded. Then she bade the priests put on the ray-proof armour that we had discarded, and told us to go without the chamber and lie in the darkness of the passage with our faces against the floor.

This we did, and remained so until, a few minutes later, she called us again. We rose and returned into the chamber to find the priests, who had removed the protecting garments, gasping and rubbing the salve upon their eyes; to find also that the lump of iron ore and my knife were gone. Next she commanded them to place the block of gold-coloured metal upon their stretcher, and to bring it with them. They obeyed, and we noted that, although those priests were both of them strong men, they groaned beneath its weight.

"How came it," said Leo, "that thou, a woman, couldst carry what these men find so heavy?"

"It is one of the properties of that force which thou callest fire," she answered sweetly, "to make what has been exposed to it, if for a little while only, as light as thistledown. Else how could I, who am so frail, have borne yonder block of gold?"

"Quite so! I understand now," answered Leo.

* * * * *

Well, that was the end of it. The lump of metal was hid away in a kind of rock pit, with an iron cover, and we returned to Ayesha's apartments.

"So all wealth is thine, as well as all power," said Leo presently; for, remembering Ayesha's awful threat, I scarcely dared to open my mouth.

"It seems so," she answered wearily, "since centuries ago I discovered that great secret, though until ye came I had put it to no use. Holly here, after his common fashion, believes that this is magic; but I tell thee again that there is no magic, only knowledge which I have chanced to win."

"Of course," said Leo, "looked at in the right way—that is, in thy way—the thing is simple." I think he would have liked to add, "as lying," but as the phrase would have involved explanations, did not. "Yet, Ayesha," he went on, "hast thou thought that this discovery of thine will wreck the world?"

"Leo," she answered, "is there, then, nothing that I can do which will not wreck this world, for which thou hast such tender care, who shouldst keep all thy care—for me?"

I smiled, but, remembering in time, turned the smile into a frown at Leo; then, fearing lest that also might anger her, made my countenance as blank as possible.

"If so," she continued, "well, let the world be wrecked. But what meanest thou? Oh, my lord Leo, forgive me if I am so dull that I cannot always follow thy quick thought—I who have lived these many years alone, without converse with nobler minds, or even those to which mine own is equal."

"It pleases thee to mock me," said Leo in a vexed voice, "and that is not too brave."

Now Ayesha turned on him fiercely, and I looked towards the door. But he did not shrink, only folded his arms and stared her straight in the face. She contemplated him a little, then said—

"After that great ordained reason which thou dost not know, I think, Leo, that why I love thee so madly is that thou alone art not afraid of me. Not like Holly there, who, ever since I threatened to turn his bones to gold—which, indeed, I was minded to do," and she laughed—"trembles at my footsteps and cowers beneath my softest glance.

"Oh, my lord, how good thou art to me! how patient with my moods and woman's weaknesses!" and she made as though she were about to embrace him. Then suddenly remembering herself, with a little start that somehow conveyed more than the most tragic gesture, she pointed to the couch in token that he should seat himself. When he had done so, she drew a footstool to his feet and sank upon it, looking up into his face with attentive eyes, like a child who listens for a story.

"Thy reasons, Leo—give me thy reasons. Doubtless they are good, and, oh! be sure I'll weigh them well."

"Here they are in brief," he answered. "The world—as thou knewest in thy——" And he stopped.

"Thy earlier wanderings there," she suggested.

"Yes, thy earlier wanderings there—has set up gold as the standard of its wealth. On it all civilisations are founded. Make it as common as it seems thou canst, and these must fall to pieces. Credit will fail and, like their savage forefathers, men must once more take to barter to supply their needs, as they do in Kaloon to-day."

"Why not?" she asked. "It would be more simple and bring them closer to the time when they were good and knew not luxury and greed."

"And smashed in each other's heads with stone axes," added Leo.

"Who now pierce each other's hearts with steel, or those leaden missiles of which thou hast told me. Oh, Leo! when the nations are beggared and their golden god is down; when the usurer and the fat merchant tremble and turn white as chalk because their hoards are but useless dross; when I have made the bankrupt Exchanges of the world my mock, and laugh across the ruin of its richest markets, why, then, will not true worth come to its heritage again?

"What of it if I do discomfort those who think more of pelf than of courage and of virtue; those who, as that Hebrew prophet wrote, lay field to field and house to house, until the wretched whom they have robbed find no place left whereon to dwell? What if I prove your sagest chapmen fools, and gorge your greedy money-changers with the gold that they desire until they loathe its very sight and touch? What if I uphold the cause of the poor and the oppressed against the ravening lusts of Mammon? Why, will not this world of yours be happier then?"

"I do not know," answered Leo. "All that I know is that it would be a different world, one shaped upon a new plan, governed by untried laws, and seeking other ends. In so strange a place, who can say what might or might not chance?"

"That we shall learn in its season, Leo. Or, rather, if it be against thy wish, we will not turn this hidden page. Since thou dost desire it, that old evil, the love of lucre, shall still hold its mastery upon the earth. Let the peoples keep their yellow king; I'll not crown another in his place, as I was minded

"She thrust the glowing substance up almost to the mask that hid my face."

—such as that living Strength thou sawest burning eternally but now; that Power whereof I am the mistress, which can give health to men, or even change the character of metals, and in truth, if I so desire, obedient to my word, destroy a city or rend this Mountain from its roots.

"But see, Holly is wearied with much wondering and needs his rest. Oh, Holly! thou wast born a critic of things done, not a doer of them. I know thy tribe, for even in my day the colleges of Alexandria echoed with their wranglings, and already the winds blew thick with the dust of their forgotten bones. Holly, I tell thee that at times those who create and act are impatient of such petty doubts and cavillings. Yet fear not, old friend, nor take my anger ill. Already thy heart is gold without alloy, so what need have I to gild thy bones?"

I thanked Ayesha for her compliment, and went to my bed wondering which was real, her kindness or her wrath, or if both were but assumed. Also I wondered in what way she had fallen foul of the critics of Alexandria. Perhaps once she had published a poem or a system of philosophy and been roughly handled by them! It is quite possible, only if Ayesha had ever written poetry, I think that it would have endured, like Sappho's.

In the morning I discovered that whatever else about her might be false, Ayesha was a true chemist—the very greatest, I suppose, who ever lived. For as I dressed myself, those priests whom we had seen in the laboratory staggered into the room, carrying between them a heavy burden, that was covered with a cloth, and, directed by Oros, placed it upon the floor.

"What is that?" I asked of Oros.

"A peace-offering sent by the Hesea," he said, "with whom, as I am told, you dared to quarrel yesterday."

Then he withdrew the cloth, and there beneath it shone that great lump of metal which, in the presence of myself and Leo, had been marked with the Symbol of Life, that still appeared upon its surface. Only now it was gold, not iron—gold so good and soft that I could write my name upon it with a nail. My knife lay with it also, and of that, too, the handle, though not the blade, had been changed from steel to gold.

Ayesha asked to see this afterwards, and was but ill-pleased with the result of her experiment. She pointed out to me that lines and blotches of gold ran for an inch or more down the substance of the steel, which she feared that they might weaken or distemper, whereas it had been her purpose that the hilt only should be altered.*

Often since that time I have marvelled how Ayesha performed this miracle, and from what substances she gathered or compounded the lightning-like material which was her servant in the work; also, whether or no it had been impregnated with the immortalising fire of Life that burned in the caves of Kôr.† Yet to this hour I have found no answer to the problem, for it is beyond my guessing.

I suppose that, in preparation for her conquest of the inhabitants of this globe—to which, indeed, it would have sufficed unaided by any other power—the manufacture of gold from iron went on in the cave unceasingly.

However this may be, during the few days that we remained together, Ayesha never so much as spoke of it again. It seemed to have served her purpose for the while, or, in the press of other and more urgent matters, to have been forgotten or thrust from her mind. Still, amongst others, whereof I have said nothing, since it is necessary to select, I record this strange incident, and our conversations concerning it at length, for the reason that it made a great impression upon me, and furnishes a striking example of Ayesha's dominion over the hidden forces of Nature.

---

* I proved in after days how real were Ayesha's alchemy and the knowledge which enabled her to solve the secret that chemists have hunted for in vain, and, like Nature's self, to transmute the commonest into the most precious of the metals. At the first town that I reached on the frontiers of India, I took this knife to a jeweller, a native, who was as clever as he proved dishonest, and asked him to test the handle. He did so with acids and by other means, and told me that it was of very pure gold—twenty-four carats, I think he said. Also he pointed out that this gold became gradually merged into the steel of the blade in a way which was quite inexplicable to him, and asked me to clear up the matter. Of course I could not, but at his request I left the knife in his shop, to give him an opportunity of examining it further. The next day I was taken ill with one of the heart attacks to which I have been liable of late, and when I became able to move about again a while afterwards, I found that this jeweller had gone, none knew whither. So had my knife.—L. H. H.

† Recent discoveries would apppear to suggest that this mysterious "Fire of Life," which, whatever else it may have been, was evidently a force and no true fire, since it did not burn, owed its origin to the emanations from radium, or some kindred substance. Although in the year 1885, Mr. Holly would have known nothing of the properties of these marvellous rays or emanations, doubtless Ayesha was familiar with them and their enormous possibilities, of which our chemists and scientific men have, at present, but explored the fringe.—H. R. H.

AYESHA

THE RETURN OF "SHE."

By H. RIDER HAGGARD.

SYNOPSIS OF FOREGOING CHAPTERS.—The return of "She-Who-Must-Be-Obeyed" is recorded by Ludwig Horace Holly, the friend of that Leo Vincey whom Ayesha the beautiful loved in the awful tombs of Kôr. When the record begins, the two men are living in an old house remote upon the seashore of Cumberland, where they have been slowly recovering from the horror of the passing of Ayesha in the flames—a doom that seemed one of complete extinction, yet was charged with the strange last words: "I die not. I shall come again and shall once more be beautiful. I swear it—it is true." On a sullen August night, Leo is thrilled by a vision of Ayesha in all her former loveliness. She beckons him, and in a vision his spirit follows her into a realm of snowy peaks far beyond the furthest borders of Thibet. A sign in the clouds at dawn is repeated from this vision to both Leo and Holly, and together they start for Central Asia. Sixteen years of toil, struggle, and strange adventure pass, and they are still searching for "a mountain peak shaped like the Symbol of Life." After many wanderings they find themselves in a country where no European has ever set foot, on one of the spurs of the vast Cherga mountains, far eastward from Turkestan. Rescued from drowning by a beautiful woman and an aged man, they are conducted through "The Gate" into the kingdom and city of Kaloon. Their saviours, they learn, are the Khania or Queen of Kaloon, and a venerable physician of magical powers. Is this woman Ayesha? No; they conjecture her rather to be Amenartas, who wrote the "sherd" of the former chronicle. She falls in love with Leo, and he and Holly learn that her husband, the Khan, is a madman. Simbri, the magician, and Atene, the Khania, have already received a solemn charge from the "Hesea" of a "College" in the Mountain of Fire to receive two strangers and bring them safely to the Mountain. But Atene's love for Leo makes her detain the travellers awhile in Kaloon, and she even proposes that the Khan shall be murdered so that she can wed Leo. To this the Englishman replies: "I go to ask a certain question of the Oracle on yonder mountain peak. With your will or without it, I tell you that I go, and afterwards you can settle which is the stronger—the Khania of Kaloon or the Hesea of the House of Fire." The Khan himself assists the escape of the travellers for their further journey, but his jealousy has been aroused, and after they have set out on their journey to the fire-crowned Mountain he pursues them with his death-hounds. After a terrible struggle the Khan is slain. The Khania and Simbri overtake them and seek to persuade them to return, but they refuse. The Khania leaves them, saying: "We do not part thus easily. You have summoned me to the Mountain, and even to the Mountain I will follow you. Aye, and there I will meet its spirit. . . . I will match my strength and magic against hers, as it is decreed that I shall do." On the Mountain itself they meet again with Atene, who brings thither her dead husband to the burying-place of the rulers of Kaloon. From a priest, Oros, who goes with them, they learn that for thousands of years this Mountain has been the home of a peculiar fire-worship, of which the head hierophant is a woman. To the veiled figure of Hes, on her throne, the two Englishmen tell of their wandering search. In answer to the challenge of Atene, the Hesea shows them a vision of events which happened long ago in the Caves of Kôr. Picture succeeds picture until all is blank, and then she tells how Ayesha first met Kallikrates in the early ages. Suddenly she reveals herself as Ayesha; but to remove all doubt she unveils before them, revealing herself in all her withered age. Atene bids Leo choose between her and Ayesha. Leo then kneels down and kisses the wrinkled head. At which Atene says: "Thou hast chosen. Take now thy bride and let me hence." Ayesha then begins to pray aloud, to some unseen Power, for the return of her former loveliness, and suddenly she is transfigured into radiant beauty once again, and claims Leo for the man whom she loved of old. Atene is baffled in a sudden attack upon the mysterious creature's life. Led by Oros to the Sanctuary, where, before a white-robed company of priests and priestesses, Ayesha is seated as a queen on a throne, they take part in a ceremony of betrothal, after which Ayesha bids them leave her alone awhile. During the weeks that follow, Ayesha is very miserable, and though Leo continually implores her to rescind her decree and marry him, she only says that it is not wise that she shall take him as a husband until his physical being has been impregnated with the mysterious virtue of the Vapour of Life. Presently Oros, the priest, comes with the news that the people of Kaloon have two great armies rising against Ayesha, gathered by the Khania Atene. Ayesha commands Oros to send round the Fire of Hes to every chief and bid the tribes assemble. On Leo questioning her as to the expenditure of sums of money for the preparation for war, should they be involved, Ayesha conducts the two Englishmen down passages to her laboratory, where they see two priests smelting metal, and by marvellous preparation manufacturing gold that will supply all their needs.

CHAPTER XXI.

THE PROPHECY OF ATENE.

ON the day following this strange experience of the iron that was turned to gold, some great service was held in the Sanctuary—as we understood, "to consecrate the war." We did not attend it, but that night we ate together as usual. Ayesha was moody at the meal; that is, she varied from sullenness to laughter.

"Know you," she said, "that to-day I was an Oracle, and those fools of the Mountain sent their medicine-men to ask of the Hesea how the battle would go, and which of them would be slain, and which gain honour. And I—I could not tell them, but juggled with my words, so that they might take them as they would. How the battle will go I know well, for I shall direct it; but the future—ah! that I cannot read better than thou canst, my Holly, and that is ill indeed. For me, the past and all the present lie bathed in light reflected from that black wall—the future."

Then she fell to brooding, and looking up at length with an air of entreaty, said to Leo—

"Wilt thou not hear my prayer, and bide where thou art for some few days, or even go a-hunting? Do so, and I will stay with thee, and send Holly and Oros to command the Tribes in this petty fray."

"I will not," answered Leo, trembling with indignation, for this plan of hers that I should be sent out to war, while he bided in safety in a temple, moved him, a man brave to rashness, who, although he disapproved of it in theory, loved fighting for its own sake also, to absolute rage.

"I say, Ayesha, that I will not," he repeated; "moreover, that if thou leavest me here, I will find my way down the Mountain alone and join the battle."

"Then come," she answered, "and on thine own head be it! Nay, not on thine, beloved; on mine, on mine."

After this, by some strange reaction, she became like a merry girl, laughing more than I have ever seen her do, and telling us many tales of the far, far past, but none that were sad or tragic. It was very strange to sit and listen to her while she spoke of people, one or two of them known as names in history, and many others who never have been heard of, that had trod this earth, and with whom she was familiar over two thousand years ago. Yet she told us anecdotes of their loves and hates, their strength or weaknesses, all of them touched with some tinge of humorous satire, or illustrating the comic vanity of human aims and aspirations.

At length her talk took a deeper and more personal note. She spoke of her searchings after truth; of how, aching for wisdom, she had explored the religions of her day and refused them one by one; of how she had preached in Jerusalem and been stoned by the Doctors of the Law. Of how also she had wandered back to Arabia and, being rejected by her own people as a reformer, had travelled on to Egypt, and at the court of the Pharaoh of that time met a famous magician, half-charlatan and half-seer, who, because she was far-seeing—"clairvoyant," we should call it—instructed her in his art so well that soon she became his master and forced him to obey her.

Then, as though she were unwilling to reveal too much, suddenly Ayesha's history passed from Egypt to Kôr. She spoke to Leo of his arrival there, a wanderer who was named Kallikrates, hunted by savages and accompanied by the Egyptian Amenartas, whom she appeared to have known and hated in her own country, and of how she entertained them. Yes, she even told of a supper that the three of them had eaten together on the evening before they started to discover the Place of Life, and of an evil prophecy that this royal Amenartas had made as to the issue of their journey.

"Aye," Ayesha said, "it was such a silent night as this, and such a meal as this we ate, and Leo, not so greatly changed, save that he was beardless then and younger, was at my side. Where thou sittest, Holly, sat the royal Amenartas, a very fair woman; yes, even more beautiful than I before I dipped me in the Essence; foresighted also, though not so learned as I had grown. From the first we hated each other, and more than ever now, when she guessed how I had learned to look upon thee, her lover, Leo; for her husband thou never wast, who didst flee too fast for marriage. She knew also that the struggle between us which had begun of old and afar was for centuries and generations, and that until the end should declare itself neither of us could harm the other, who both had sinned to win thee, that wast appointed by Fate to be the lodestone of our souls. Then Amenartas spoke and said—

"'Lo! to my sight, Kallikrates, the wine in thy cup is turned to blood, and that knife in thy hand, O daughter of Yarâb'—for so she named me—'drips red blood. Aye, and this place is a sepulchre, and thou, O Kallikrates, sleepest here; nor can she, thy murderess, kiss back the breath of life into those cold lips of thine.'

"So indeed it came about as was ordained," added Ayesha reflectively, "for I slew thee in yonder Place of Life—yes, in my madness I slew thee, because thou wouldst not or couldst not understand the change that had come over me, and shrankest from my loveliness like a blind bat from the splendour of flame, hiding thy face in the tresses of her dusky hair—— Why, what is it now, thou Oros? Can I never be rid of thee for an hour?"

"O Hes, a writing from the Khania Atene," the priest said, with his deprecating bow.

"Break the seal and read," she answered carelessly. "Perchance she has repented of her folly and makes submission."

So he read—

"To the Hesea of the College on the Mountain, known as Ayesha upon earth, and in the household of the Over-world whence she has been permitted to wander, as 'Star-that-hath-fallen——'"

" 'Look, yonder is the mouth of that gorge where lived the cat-worshipping sorcerer.' "

"A pretty-sounding name, forsooth!" broke in Ayesha. "Ah! but, Atene, set stars rise again—even from the Under-world. Read on, thou Oros."

"Greetings, O Ayesha. Thou who art very old, hast gathered much wisdom in the passing of the centuries, and with other powers, that of making thyself seem fair in the eyes of men blinded by thine arts. Yet one thing thou lackest that I have—vision of those happenings which are not yet. Know, O Ayesha, that I and my uncle, the great seer, have searched the heavenly books to learn what is written there of the issue of this war.

"This is written: For me, death, whereat I rejoice. For thee, a spear cast by thine own hand. For the land of Kaloon, blood and ruin bred of thee!

"ATENE,

"Khania of Kaloon."

Ayesha listened in silence, but her lips did not tremble, nor her cheek pale. To Oros she said proudly—

"Say to the messenger of Atene that I have received her message, and ere long will answer it, face to face with her in her palace of Kaloon. Go, priest, and disturb me no more."

When Oros had departed, she turned to us and said—

"That tale of mine of long ago was well fitted to this hour, for as Amenartas prophesied of ill, so does Atene prophesy of ill, and Amenartas and Atene are one. Well, let the spear fall, if fall it must, and I will not flinch from it who know that I shall surely triumph at the last. Perhaps the Khania does but think to frighten me with a cunning lie; but if she has read aright, then be sure, beloved, that it is still well with us, since none can escape their destiny, nor can our bond of union, which was fashioned with the universe that bears us, ever be undone.

"I tell thee, Leo, that out of the confusions of our lives and deaths order shall yet be born. Behind the mask of cruelty shine Mercy's tender eyes; and the wrongs of this rough and twisted world are but hot, blinding sparks which stream from the all-righting sword of pure, eternal Justice. The heavy lives we see and know are only links in a golden chain that shall draw us safe to the haven of our rest; steep and painful steps are they whereby we climb to the allotted palace of our joy. Henceforth I fear no more, and fight no more against that which

must befall. For I say we are but winged seeds blown down the gales of fate and change to the appointed garden where we shall grow, filling its blest air with the immortal fragrance of our bloom.

"Leave me now, Leo, and sleep awhile for we ride at dawn."

*   *   *   *   *

It was midday on the morrow when we moved down the Mountain-side with the army of the Tribes, fierce and savage-looking men. The scouts were out before us, then came the great body of their cavalry mounted on wiry horses, while to right and left and behind, the foot-soldiers marched in regiments, each under the command of its own chief.

Ayesha, veiled now—for she would not show her beauty to these wild folk—rode in the midst of the horsemen on a white mare of matchless speed and shape. With her went Leo and myself, Leo on the Khan's black horse, and I on another not unlike it, though thicker built. About us were a bodyguard of armed priests and a regiment of chosen soldiers, among them those hunters that Leo had saved from Ayesha's wrath, and who were now attached to his person.

We were merry, all of us, for in the crisp air of late autumn flooded with sunlight, the fears and forebodings that had haunted us in those gloomy, firelit caves were forgotten. Moreover, the tramp of thousands of armed men and the excitement of coming battle thrilled our nerves.

Not for many a day had I seen Leo look so vigorous and happy. Of late he had grown somewhat thin and pale, probably from causes that I have suggested; but now his cheeks were red and his eyes shone bright again. Ayesha also seemed joyous, for the moods of this strange woman were as fickle as those of Nature's self, and varied as a landscape varies under the sunshine or the shadow. Now she was noon and now dark night; now dawn, now evening; and now thoughts came and went in the blue depths of her eyes like vapours wafted across the summer sky, and in the press of them her sweet face changed and shimmered as broken water shimmers beneath the beaming stars.

"Too long," she said, with a little, thrilling laugh, "have I been shut in the bowels of sombre mountains, companied only by mutes and savages, or by melancholy, chanting priests, and now I am glad to look upon the world again. How beautiful are the snows above, and the brown slopes below, and the broad plains beyond that roll away to those bordering hills! How glorious is the sun, eternal as myself! how sweet the keen air of heaven!

"Believe me, Leo, more than twenty centuries have gone by since I was seated on a steed, and yet thou seest I have not forgot my horsemanship, though this beast cannot match those Arabs that I rode in the wide deserts of Arabia. Oh! I remember how at my father's side I galloped down to war against the marauding Bedouins, and how with my own hand I speared their chieftain and made him cry for mercy. One day I will tell thee of that father of mine; for I was his darling, and though we have been long apart, I hold his memory dear and look forward to our meeting.

"Look, yonder is the mouth of that gorge where lived the cat-worshipping sorcerer who would have murdered both of you because thou, Leo, didst throw his familiar to the fire. It is strange, but several of the Tribes of this Mountain and of the lands behind it make cats their gods, or divine by means of them. I think that the first Rassen, the general of Alexander, must have brought the practice here from Egypt. Of this Macedonian Alexander I could tell thee much, for he was almost a contemporary of mine, and when I last was born, the world still rang with the fame of his great deeds.

"It was Rassen who on the Mountain supplanted the primeval fire-worship whereof the flaming pillars which light its Sanctuary remain as monuments, by that of Hes, or Isis—or, rather, blended the two in one. Doubtless among the priests in his army were some of Pasht or Sekket the Cat-headed, and these brought with them their secret cult, that to-day has dwindled down to the vulgar divinations of savage sorcerers. Indeed, I remember dimly that it was so, for I was the first Hesea of this Temple, and journeyed hither with that same general Rassen, a relative of mine."

Now both Leo and I looked at her wonderingly, and I could see that she was watching us through her veil. As usual, however, it was I whom she reproved, since Leo might think and do what he willed, and still escape her anger.

"Thou, Holly," she said quickly, "who art ever of a cavilling and suspicious mind, remembering what I said but now, believest that I lie to thee."

I protested that I was only reflecting upon an apparent variation between two statements.

"Play not with words," she answered; "in thy heart thou didst write me down a liar, and I take that ill. Know, foolish man, that when I said that the Macedonian Alexander lived before me, I meant before this present life of mine. In the existence that preceded it, though I outlasted him by thirty years, we were born in the same summer, and I knew him well, for I was the Oracle whom he consulted most upon his wars, and to my wisdom he owed his victories. Afterwards we quarrelled, and I left him and pushed forward with Rassen. From that day the bright star of Alexander began to wane."

At this Leo made a sound that resembled a whistle. In a very agony of apprehension, beating back the criticisms and certain recollections of the strange tale of the old abbot, Kou-en, which would rise within me, I asked quickly—

"And dost thou, Ayesha, remember well all that befell thee in this former life?"

"Nay, not well," she answered meditatively; "only the greater facts, and those I have for the most part recovered by that study of secret things which thou callest vision or magic. For instance, my Holly, I recall that thou wast living in that life. Indeed, I seem to see an ugly philosopher clad in a dirty robe and filled both with wine and the learning of others, who disputed with Alexander till he grew wroth with him and caused him to be banished, or drowned: I forget which."

"I suppose that I was not called Diogenes?" I asked tartly, suspecting, perhaps not without cause, that Ayesha was amusing herself by fooling me.

"No," she replied gravely, "I do not think that was thy name. The Diogenes thou speakest of was a much more famous man, one of real if crabbed wisdom; moreover, he did not indulge in wine. I am mindful of very little of that life, however; not of more, indeed, than are many of the followers of the prophet Buddha, whose doctrines I have studied, and of whom thou, Holly, hast spoken to me so much. Maybe we did not meet while it endured. Still, I recollect that the Valley of Bones, where I found thee, my Leo, was the place where a great battle was fought between the Fire-priests with their vassals, the Tribes of the Mountain, and the army of Rassen aided by the people of Kaloon. For between these and the Mountain, in old days as now, there was enmity, since in this present war history does but rewrite itself."

"So thou thyself wast our guide?" said Leo, looking at her sharply.

"Aye, Leo, who else? though it is not wonderful that thou didst not know me beneath those deathly wrappings. I was minded to wait and receive thee in the Sanctuary, yet when I learned that at length both of you had escaped Atene and drew near, I could restrain myself no more, but came forth thus hideously disguised. Yes, I was with you even at the river's bank, and though you saw me not, there sheltered you from harm.

"Leo, I yearned to look upon thee and to be certain that thy heart had not changed, although until the allotted time thou mightest not hear my voice nor see my face who wert doomed to undergo that sore trial of thy faith. Of Holly also I desired to learn whether his wisdom could pierce through my disguise, and how near he stood to truth. It was for this reason that I suffered him to see me draw the lock from the satchel on thy breast and to hear me wail over thee yonder in the Rest-house. Well, he did not guess so ill; but thou, thou knewest me—in thy sleep—knewest me as I am, and not as I seemed to be; yes," she added softly, "and didst say certain sweet words which I remember well."

"Then beneath that shroud was thine own face?" asked Leo again, for he was very curious on this point—"the same lovely face I see to-day?"

"Mayhap—as thou wilt," she answered coldly; "also it is the spirit that matters, not the outward seeming, though men in their blindness think otherwise. Perchance my face is but as thy heart fashions it, or as my will presents it to the sight and fancy of its beholders. But hark! The scouts have touched."

As Ayesha spoke, a sound of distant shouting was borne upon the wind, and presently we saw a fringe of horsemen falling back slowly upon our foremost line. It was only to report, however, that the skirmishers of Atene were in full retreat. Indeed, a prisoner whom they brought with them, on being questioned by the priests, confessed at once that the Khania had no mind to meet us upon the holy Mountain. She proposed to give battle on the river's farther bank, having for a defence its waters which we must ford, a decision that showed good military judgment.

So it happened that on this day there was no fighting.

All that afternoon we descended the slopes of the Mountain, more swiftly by far than we had climbed them after our long flight from the city of Kaloon. Before sunset we came to our prepared camping-ground, a wide and sloping plain that ended at the crest of the Valley of Dry Bones, where in past days we had met our mysterious guide. This, however, we did not reach through the secret mountain tunnel along which she had led us, the shortest way by miles, as Ayesha told us now, since it was unsuited to the passage of an army.

Bending to the left, we circled round a number of unclimbable kopjes, beneath which that tunnel passed, and so at length arrived upon the brow of the dark ravine where we could sleep safe from attack by night.

Here a tent was pitched for Ayesha, but as it was the only one, Leo and I with our guard bivouacked among some rocks at a distance of a few hundred yards. When she found that this must be so, Ayesha was very angry and spoke bitter words to the chief who had charge of the food and baggage, although he, poor man, knew nothing of tents.

Also she blamed Oros, who replied meekly that he had thought us captains accustomed to war and its hardships. But most of all she was angry with herself, who had forgotten this detail, and until Leo stopped her with a laugh of vexation, went on to suggest that we should sleep in the tent, since she had no fear of the rigours of the Mountain cold.

The end of it was that we supped together outside—or, rather, Leo and I supped, for as there were guards around us, Ayesha did not even lift her veil.

That evening Ayesha was disturbed and ill at ease, as though new fears which she could not overcome assailed her. At·length she seemed to conquer them by some effort of her will, and announced that she was minded to sleep and thus refresh her soul—the only part of her, I think, which ever needed rest. Her last words to us were—

"Sleep you also, sleep sound, but be not astonished, my Leo, if I send to summon both of you during the night, since in my slumbers I may find new counsels, and need to speak of them to thee ere we break camp at dawn."

Thus we parted; but ah! little did we guess how and where the three of us would meet again.

*   *   *   *   *

We were weary and soon fell fast asleep beside our camp-fire, for, knowing that the

"He poured some strong fluid down my throat."

whole army guarded us, we had no fear. I remember watching the bright stars which shone in the immense vault above me, until they paled in the pure light of the risen moon, now somewhat past her full, and hearing Leo mutter drowsily from beneath his fur rug that Ayesha was quite right, and that it was pleasant to be in the open air again, as he was tired of caves.

After that I knew no more until I was awakened by the challenge of a sentry in the distance; then after a pause, a second challenge from the officer of our own guard. Another pause, and a priest stood bowing before us, the flickering light from the fire playing upon his shaven head and face, which I seemed to recognise.

"I"—and he gave a name that was familiar to me, but which I forget—"am sent, my lords, by Oros, who commands me to say that the Hesea would speak with you both and at once."

Now Leo sat up yawning and asked what was the matter. I told him, whereon he said he wished that Ayesha could have waited till daylight, then added—

"Well, there is no help for it. Come on, Horace," and he rose to follow the messenger.

The priest bowed again and said—

"The commands of the Hesea are that my lords should bring their weapons and their guard."

"What!" grumbled Leo, "to protect us for a walk of a hundred yards through the heart of an army?"

"The Hesea," explained the man, "has left her tent; she is in the gorge yonder, studying the line of advance."

"How do you know that?" I asked.

"I do not know it," he replied. "Oros told me so, that is all; and therefore the Hesea bade my lords bring their guard, for she is alone."

"Is she mad," ejaculated Leo, "to wander about in such a place at midnight? Well, it is like her."

I, too, thought it was like her, who did nothing that others would have done; and yet I hesitated. Then I remembered that Ayesha had said she might send for us; also I was sure that if any trick had been intended, we should not have been warned to bring an escort. So we called the guard—there were twelve of them—took our spears and swords, and started.

We were challenged by both the first and second lines of sentries, and I noticed that as we gave them the password, the last picket, who of course recognised us, looked astonished.

Still, if they had doubts, they did not dare to express them. So we went on.

Now we began to descend the sides of the ravine by a very steep path, with which the priest, our guide, seemed to be curiously familiar, for he went down it as though it were the stairway of his own house.

"A strange place to take us to at night," said Leo doubtfully, when we were near the bottom, and the chief of the bodyguard, that great, red-bearded hunter who had been mixed up in the matter of the snow-leopard, also muttered some words of remonstrance. Whilst I was trying to catch what he said, of a sudden something white walked into the patch of moonlight at the foot of the ravine, and we saw that it was the veiled figure of Ayesha herself. The chief saw her also and said contentedly—

"Hes! Hes!"

"Look at her," grumbled Leo, "strolling about in that haunted hole as though it were Hyde Park"; and on he went at a run.

The figure turned and beckoned to us to follow her as she glided forward, picking her way through the skeletons which were scattered about upon the lava bed of the cleft. Thus she went on into the shadow of the opposing cliff that the moonlight did not reach. Here in the wet season a stream trickled down a path which it had cut through the rock in the course of centuries, and the grit that it had brought with it was spread about the lava floor of the ravine, so that many of the bones were almost completely buried in the sand.

These, I noticed, as we stepped into the shadow, were more numerous than usual just here, for on all sides I saw the white crowns of skulls, or the projecting ends of ribs and thigh bones. Doubtless, I thought to myself, that streamway made a road to the plain above, and in some past battle, the fighting around it was very fierce and the slaughter great.

Here Ayesha had halted and was engaged in the contemplation of this boulder-strewn path, as though she meditated making use of it that day. Now we drew near to her, and the priest who guided us fell back with our guard, leaving us to go forward alone, since they dared not approach the Hesea unbidden. Leo was somewhat in advance of me, seven or eight yards perhaps, and I heard him say—

"Why dost thou venture into such places at night, Ayesha, unless, indeed, it is not possible for any harm to come to thee?"

She made no answer, only turned and

opened her arms wide, then let them fall to her side again. Whilst I wondered what this signal of hers might mean, from the shadows about us came a strange, rustling sound.

I looked, and lo ! everywhere the skeletons were rising from their sandy beds. I saw their white skulls, their gleaming arm and leg bones, their hollow ribs. The long-slain army had come to life again, and look ! in their hands were the ghosts of spears !

Of course I knew at once that this was but another manifestation of Ayesha's magic powers, which some whim of hers had drawn us from our beds to witness. Yet I confess that I felt frightened. Even the boldest of men, however free from superstition, might be excused should their nerve fail them if, when standing in a churchyard at midnight, suddenly on every side they saw the dead arising from their graves. Also our surroundings were wilder and more eerie than those of any civilised burying-place.

"What new devilment of thine is this ? " cried Leo in a scared and angry voice. But Ayesha made no answer.

I heard a noise behind me and looked round. The skeletons were springing upon our bodyguard, who for their part, poor men, paralysed with terror, had thrown down their weapons and fallen, some of them, to their knees. Now the ghosts began to stab at them with their phantom spears, and I saw that beneath the blows they rolled over. The veiled figure above me pointed with her hand at Leo and said—

"Seize him, but I charge you, harm him not."

I knew the voice ; *it was that of Atene !*

Then too late I understood the trap into which we had fallen.

"Treachery ! " I began to cry, and before the word was out of my lips, a particularly able-bodied skeleton silenced me with a violent blow upon the head. But though I could not speak, my senses still stayed with me for a little. I saw Leo fighting furiously with a number of men who strove to pull him down—so furiously, indeed, that his frightful efforts caused the blood to gush out of his mouth from some burst vessel in the lungs.

Then sight and hearing failed me, and thinking that this was death, I fell and remembered no more.

Why I was not killed outright I do not know, unless in their hurry the disguised soldiers thought me already dead, or perhaps that my life was to be spared also. At least, beyond the knock upon the head I received no injury.

CHAPTER XXII.

THE LOOSING OF THE POWERS.

WHEN I came to myself again, it was daylight. I saw the calm, gentle face of Oros bending over me as he poured some strong fluid down my throat that seemed to shoot through all my body and melt a curtain in my mind. I saw also that beside him stood Ayesha.

"Speak, man, speak ! " she said in a terrible voice. "What has chanced here ? Thou livest ; then where is my lord ? Where hast thou hid my lord ? Tell me—or die ! "

It was the vision that I saw when my senses left me in the snow of the avalanche, fulfilled to the last detail !

"Atene has taken him," I answered.

"Atene has taken him, and thou art left alive ? "

"Do not be wroth with me," I answered, "it is no fault of mine. Little wonder we were deceived after thou hadst said that thou mightest summon us ere dawn."

Then as briefly as I could I told the story.

She listened, went to where our murdered guards lay with unstained spears, and looked at them.

"Well for these that they are dead ! " she exclaimed. "Now, Holly, thou seest what is the fruit of mercy. The men whose lives I gave my lord have failed him at his need."

Then she passed forward to the spot where Leo was captured. Here lay a broken sword —Leo's—that had been the Khan Rassen's, and two dead men. Both of these were clothed in some tight-fitting black garments, having their heads and faces whitened with chalk, and upon their vests a rude imitation of a human skeleton, also daubed in chalk.

"A trick fit to frighten fools with," she said contemptuously. "But oh ! that Atene should have dared to play the part of Ayesha —that she should have dared ! " and she clenched her little hand. "See, surprised and overwhelmed, yet he fought well. Say ! was he hurt, Holly ? It comes upon me— no, tell me that I see amiss."

"Not much, I think," I answered doubtfully ; "a little blood was running from his mouth, no more. Look, there go the stains of it upon that rock."

"For every drop I'll take a hundred lives. By myself I swear it ! " Ayesha muttered, with a groan. Then she cried in a ringing voice—

"Back and to horse, for I have deeds to do this day ! Nay, bide thou here, Holly ;

we go a shorter path, while the army skirts the gorge. Oros, give him food and drink, and bathe that hurt upon his head. It is but a bruise, for his hood and hair are thick."

So while Oros rubbed some stinging lotion on my scalp, I ate and drank as best I could till my brain ceased to swim, for the blow, though heavy, had not fractured the bone. When I was ready, they brought the horses to us, and mounting them, slowly we scrambled up the steep bed of the water-course.

"See," Ayesha said, pointing to tracks and hoof-prints on the plain at its head, "there was a chariot awaiting him, and harnessed to it were four swift horses. Atene's scheme was clever and well laid, and I, grown oversure and careless, slept through it all!"

On this plain the army of the Tribes that had broken camp before the dawn was already gathering fast; indeed, the cavalry, if I may call them so, were assembled there to the number of about five thousand men, each of whom had a led horse. Ayesha summoned the chiefs and captains, and addressed them.

"Servants of Hes," she said, "the stranger lord, my betrothed and guest, has been tricked by a false priest, and, falling into a cunning snare, captured as a hostage. It is necessary that I follow him fast, before harm comes to him. We move down to attack the army of the Khania beyond the river. When its passage is forced, I pass on with the horsemen, for I must sleep in the city of Kaloon to-night. What sayest thou, Oros? That a second and greater army defends its walls? Man, I know it, and if there is need, that army I will destroy. Nay, stare not at me. Already they are as dead. Horsemen, you accompany me.

"Captains of the Tribes, you follow; and woe be to that man who hangs back in the hour of battle! for death and eternal shame shall be his portion, but wealth and honour to those who bear them bravely. Yes, I tell you, theirs shall be the fair land of Kaloon. You have your orders for the passing of yonder river. I, with the horsemen, take the central ford. Let the wings advance."

The chiefs answered with a cheer, for they were fierce men, whose ancestors had loved war for generations. Moreover, mad as seemed the enterprise, they trusted in their Oracle, the Hesea, and, like all hill peoples, were easily fired by the promise of rich plunder.

An hour's steady march down the slopes brought the army to the edge of the marsh-lands. These, as it chanced, proved no obstacle to our progress, for in that season of great drought they were quite dry, and for the same reason the shrunken river was not so impassable a defence as I feared that it would be. Still, because of its rocky bottom and steep, opposing banks, it looked formidable enough, while on the crests of those banks, in squadrons and companies of horse and foot, were gathered the regiments of Atene.

While the wings of footmen deployed to right and left, the cavalry halted in the marshes and let their horses fill themselves with the long grass, now a little browned by frost, that grew on this boggy soil, and afterwards drink some water.

All this time Ayesha stood silent, for she also had dismounted, that the mare she rode and her two led horses might graze with the others. Indeed, she spoke but once, saying—

"Thou thinkest this adventure mad, my Holly? Say, art afraid?"

"Not with thee for captain," I answered. "Still, that second army——"

"Shall melt before me like mist before the gale," she replied in a low and thrilling voice. "Holly, I tell thee thou shalt see things such as no man upon the earth has ever seen. Remember my words when I *loose the Powers* and thou followest the rent veil of Ayesha through the smitten squadrons of Kaloon. Only—what if Atene should dare to murder him? Oh, if she should dare!"

"Be comforted," I replied, wondering what she might mean by this loosing of the Powers. "I think that she loves him too well."

"I bless thee for the words, Holly, yet— I know he will refuse her, and then her hate for me and her jealous rage may overcome her love for him. Should this be so, what will avail my vengeance? Eat and drink again, Holly—nay, I touch no food until I sit in the palace of Kaloon—and look well to girth and bridle, for thou ridest far and on a wild errand. Mount thee on Leo's horse, which is swift and sure; if it dies, the guards will bring thee others."

I obeyed her as best I could, and once more bathed my head in a pool, and with the help of Oros tied a rag soaked in the lini-ment on the bruise, after which I felt sound enough. Indeed, the mad excitement of those minutes of waiting, and some fore-shadowing of the terrible wonders that were about to befall, made me forget my hurts.

Now, Ayesha was standing staring upwards, so that although I could not see her veiled face, I guessed that her eyes must be fixed on the sky above the Mountain-top. I was certain, also, that she was concentrating her fearful will upon an unknown object, for her whole frame quivered like a reed shaken in the wind.

It was a very strange morning—cold and clear, yet curiously still, and with a heaviness in the air such as precedes a great fall of snow, although for much snow the season was yet too early. Once or twice, too, in that utter calm, I thought that I felt everything shudder; not the ordinary trembling of earthquake, however, for the shuddering seemed to be of the atmosphere quite as much as of the land. It was as though all Nature around us were a living creature which is very much afraid.

Following Ayesha's earnest gaze, I perceived that thick, smoky clouds were gathering one by one in the clear sky above the Peak, and that they were edged, each of them, with a fiery rim. Watching these fantastic and ominous clouds, I ventured to say to her that it looked as though the weather would change—not a very original remark, but one which the circumstances suggested.

"Aye," she answered, "ere night the weather will be wilder even than my heart. No longer shall they cry for water in Kaloon! Mount, Holly, mount! The advance begins!" and unaided she sprang to the saddle of the mare that Oros brought her.

* * * * *

Then, in the midst of the five thousand horsemen, we moved down upon the ford. As we reached its brink I noted that the two divisions of Tribesmen were already entering the stream half a mile to the right and left of us. Of what befell them I can tell nothing from observation, although I learned later that they forced it after great slaughter on both sides.

In front of us was gathered the main body of the Khania's army, massed by regiments upon the further bank, while hundreds of picked men stood up to their middles in the water, waiting to spear or hamstring our horses as we advanced.

Now, uttering their wild, whistling cry, our leading companies dashed into the river, leaving us upon the bank, and soon were engaged hotly with the footmen in midstream. While this fray went on, Oros came to Ayesha and told her a spy had reported that Leo, bound in a two-wheeled carriage and accompanied by Atene, Simbri, and a guard, had passed through the enemy's camp at night, galloping furiously towards Kaloon.

"Spare thy words—I know it," she answered, and he fell back behind her.

Our squadrons gained the bank, having destroyed most of the men in the water, but as they set foot upon it the enemy charged them and drove them back with loss. Thrice they returned to the attack, and thrice were repulsed in this fashion. At length Ayesha grew impatient.

"They need a leader, and I will give them one," she said. "Come with me, my Holly," and, followed by the main body of the horsemen, she rode a little way into the river, and there waited until the shattered troops had fallen back upon us. Oros whispered to me—

"It is madness! the Hesea will be slain!"

"Thinkest thou so?" I answered. "More like that we shall be slain"—a saying at which he smiled a little more than usual and shrugged his shoulders, since, for all his soft ways, Oros was a brave man. Also I believe that he spoke to try me, knowing that his mistress would take no harm.

Ayesha held up her hand, in which there was no weapon, and waved it forwards. A great cheer answered that signal to advance, and in the midst of it this frail, white-robed woman spoke to her horse so that it plunged deep into the water.

Two minutes later, and spears and arrows were flying about us so thickly that they seemed to darken the sky. I saw men and horses fall to right and left, but nothing touched me or the white robes that floated a yard or two ahead. Five minutes, and we were gaining the further bank, and there the worst fight began.

It was fierce indeed, yet never an inch did the white robes give back; and where they went, men would follow them or fall. We were up the bank, and the enemy was packed about us, but through them we passed slowly, like a boat through an adverse sea that buffets but cannot stay it. Yes, further and further, till at last the lines ahead grew thin as the living wedge of horsemen forced its path between them—grew thin, broke, and vanished.

We had passed through the heart of the host, and leaving the Tribesmen who followed to deal with its flying fragments, rode on half a mile or so and mustered. Many were dead and more were hurt, but the command was

"Ayesha tore off her veil and held it on high."

issued that all sore-wounded men should fall out and give their horses to replace those that had been killed.

This was done, and presently we moved on, three thousand of us now—not more—heading for Kaloon. The trot grew to a canter, and the canter to a gallop, as we rushed forward across that endless plain, till at midday, or a little after—for this route was far shorter than that taken by Leo and myself in our devious flight from Rassen and his death-hounds—we dimly saw the city of Kaloon set upon its hill.

Now a halt was ordered, for here was a reservoir in which was still some water, whereof the horses drank, while the men ate of the food they carried with them—dried meat and barley-meal. Here, too, more spies met us, who said that the great army of Atene was posted guarding the city bridges, and that to attack it with our little force would mean destruction. But Ayesha took no heed of their words; indeed, she scarcely seemed to hear them. Only she ordered that all wearied horses should be abandoned and fresh ones mounted.

Forward again for hour after hour, in perfect silence save for the thunder of our horses' hoofs. No word spoke Ayesha, nor did her wild escort speak, only from time to time they looked over their shoulders and pointed with their red spears at the red sky behind.

I looked also, nor shall I forget its aspect. The dreadful, fire-edged clouds had grown and gathered so that beneath their shadows the plain lay almost black. They marched above us like an army in the heavens, while from time to time vaporous points shot forward, thin like swords, or massed like charging horse.

Under them a vast stillness reigned. It was as though the earth lay dead beneath their pall.

Kaloon, lit in a lurid light, grew nearer. The pickets of the foe flew homeward before us, shaking their javelins, and their mocking laughter reached us in hollow echoes. Now we saw the vast array, posted rank on rank with silken banners drooping in that stirless air, flanked and screened by glittering regiments of horse.

An embassy approached us, and at the signal of Ayesha's uplifted arm we halted. It was headed by a lord of the Court whose face I knew. He pulled rein and spoke boldly—

"Listen, Hes, to the words of Atene. Ere now the stranger lord, thy darling, is prisoner in her palace. Advance, and we destroy thee and thy little band; but if by any miracle thou shouldst conquer, then he dies. Get thee gone to thy Mountain fastness, and the Khania gives thee peace, and thy people their lives. What answer to the words of the Khania?"

Ayesha whispered to Oros, who called aloud—

"There is no answer. Go, if ye love life, for death draws near to you!"

So they went fast as their swift steeds would carry them, but for a little while Ayesha still sat lost in thought.

Presently she turned, and through her thin veil I saw that her face was white and terrible, and that the eyes in it glowed like those of a lioness at night. She said to me—hissing the words between her clenched teeth—

"Holly, prepare thyself to look into the mouth of hell. I desired to spare them if I could, I swear it; but my heart bids me be bold, to put off human pity, and use all my secret might if I would see Leo living. Holly, I tell thee they are about *to murder him!*"

Then she cried aloud: "Fear nothing, captains. Ye are but few, yet with you goes the strength of ten thousand thousand. Now follow the Hesea, and, whate'er ye meet, be not dismayed. Repeat it to the soldiers, that, fearing nothing, they follow the Hesea through yonder host and across the bridge and into the city of Kaloon."

So the chiefs rode hither and thither, crying out her words, and the savage Tribesmen answered—

"Aye, we who followed through the water will follow across the plain. Onward, Hes, for darkness swallows us!"

Now some orders were given, and the companies fell into a formation that resembled a great wedge, Ayesha herself being its very point and apex; for though Oros and I rode on either side of her, spur as we would, our horses' heads never passed her saddle-bow. In front of that dark mass she shone, a single spot of white—one snowy feather on a black torrent's breast.

A screaming bugle-note—and, like giant arms, from the shelter of some groves of trees, curved horns of cavalry shot out to surround us, while the broad bosom of the opposing army, shimmering with spears, rolled forward as a wave rolls crowned with sunlit foam; and behind it, line upon line, uncountable, lay a surging sea of men.

Our end was near. We were lost, or so it seemed.

Ayesha tore off her veil and held it on high, flowing from her like a pennon, and lo! upon her brow blazed that wide and mystic diadem of light which once only I had seen before.

Denser and denser grew the rushing clouds above; brighter and brighter gleamed the unearthly star of light beneath. Louder and louder beat the sound of the falling hoofs of ten thousand horses. From the Mountain-peak behind us went up sudden sheets of flame; it spouted fire as a whale spouts foam.

The scene was dreadful. In front, the towers of Kaloon lurid in a monstrous sunset. Above, a gloom as of an eclipse. Around, the darkling, sunburnt plain. On it Atene's advancing army, and our rushing wedge of horsemen, destined, it would appear, to inevitable doom.

*　　*　　*　　*　　*

Ayesha let fall her rein. She tossed her arms, waving the torn, white veil as though it were a signal cast to heaven.

Instantly from the churning jaws of the unholy night above belched a blaze of answering flame, that also wavered like a rent and shaken veil in the grasp of a black hand of cloud.

Then did Ayesha roll the thunder of her might upon the Children of Kaloon. Then she called, and the Terror came, such as men had never seen and, perchance, never more will see. Awful bursts of wind tore past us, lifting the very stones and soil before them, and with the wind went hail and level, hissing rain made visible by the arrows of perpetual lightnings that leapt downwards from the sky and upwards from the earth.

It was as she had warned me. It was as though hell had broken loose upon the world, yet through that hell we rushed on unharmed. For always these furies passed before us. No arrow flew, no javelin was stained. The jagged hail was a herald of our coming; the levens that smote and stabbed were our sword and spear, while ever the hurricane roared and screamed with a million separate voices which blended to one yell of sound, hideous and indescribable.

As for the hosts about us, they melted and were gone.

Now the darkness was dense, like to that of thickest night; yet in the fierce flares of the lightnings I saw them run this way and that, and amidst the volleying, elemental voices I heard their shouts of horror and of agony. I saw horses and riders roll confused upon the ground; like storm-drifted leaves I saw their footmen piled in high and whirling heaps, while the brands of heaven struck and struck them till they sank together and grew still.

I saw the groves of trees bend, shrivel up, and vanish. I saw the high walls of Kaloon blown in and flee away, while the houses within the walls took fire, to go out beneath the torrents of the driving rain, and again take fire. I saw blackness sweep over us with great wings; and when I looked, lo! those wide wings were flame, floods of pulsing flame that flew upon the tormented air.

Blackness, utter blackness; turmoil, doom, dismay! Beneath me the labouring horse; at my side the steady crest of light which sat on Ayesha's brow, and through the tumult a clear, exultant voice that sang—

"I promised thee wild weather! Now, Holly, dost thou believe that I can loose the prisoned Powers of the world?"

*　　*　　*　　*　　*

Lo! all was past and gone, and above us shone the quiet evening sky, and before us lay the empty bridge, and beyond it the flaming city of Kaloon. But the armies of Atene, where were they? Go, ask of those great cairns that hide their bones. Go, ask it of her widowed land.

Yet of our wild company of horsemen not one was lost. After us they galloped trembling, white-lipped, like men who face to face had fought and conquered Death, but triumphant—ah, triumphant!

On the high head of the bridge Ayesha wheeled her horse, and so for one proud moment stood to welcome them. At the sight of her glorious, star-crowned countenance, which now her Tribes beheld for the first time and the last, there went up such a shout as men have seldom heard.

"*The Goddess!*" that shout thundered. "Worship the Goddess!"

Then she turned her horse's head again, and they followed on through the long, strait street of the burning city, up to the Palace on its crest.

As the sun set, we sped beneath its gateway. Silence in the courtyard, silence everywhere, save for the distant roar of fire and the scared howlings of the death-hounds in their kennel.

Ayesha sprang from her horse, and waving back all save Oros and myself, swept through the open doors into the halls beyond.

They were empty, every one—all were fled or dead. Yet she never paused or doubted, but, so swiftly that we scarce could follow

182

"Ayesha waved her arm, and the knife fell from Simbri's hand."

her, flitted up the wide stair that led to the topmost tower. Up, still up, until we reached the chamber where had dwelt Simbri the Shaman, that same chamber whence he was wont to watch his stars, in which Atene had threatened us with death.

Its door was shut and barred; still, at

Ayesha's coming—yes, before the mere breath of her presence—the iron bolts snapped like twigs, the locks flew back, and inward burst that massive portal.

Now we were within the lamp-lit chamber, and this is what we saw. Seated in a chair, pale-faced, bound, yet proud and defiant-looking, was Leo. Over him, a dagger in his withered hand—yes, about to strike, in the very act—stood the old Shaman, and on the floor, hard by, gazing upward with wide-set eyes, dead, and still majestic in her death, lay Atene, Khania of Kaloon.

Ayesha waved her arm, and the knife fell from Simbri's hand, clattering on the marble, while in an instant he who had held it was smitten to stillness and became like a man turned to stone.

She stooped, lifted the dagger, and with a swift stroke severed Leo's bonds; then, as though overcome at last, sank on to a bench in silence. Leo rose, looking about him bewildered, and said in the strained voice of one who is weak with much suffering—

"But just in time, Ayesha. Another second, and that murderous dog"—and he pointed to the Shaman—"well, it was in time. But how went the battle, and how camest thou here through that awful hurricane? And, oh, Horace, thank Heaven they did not kill you, after all!"

"The battle went ill for some," Ayesha answered; "and I came not through the hurricane, but on its wings. Tell me now, what has befallen thee since we parted?"

"Trapped, overpowered, bound, brought here, told that I must write to thee and stop thy advance, or die—refused, of course, and then——" And he glanced at the dead body on the floor.

"And then?" repeated Ayesha.

"Then that fearful tempest, which seemed to drive me mad. Oh! if thou couldst have heard the wind howling round these battlements, tearing off their stones as though they were dry leaves; if thou hadst seen the lightnings falling thick and fast as rain——"

"They were my messengers. I sent them to save thee," said Ayesha simply.

"Atene said as much, but I did not believe her. I thought the end of the world had come, that was all. Well, she returned just now more mad even than I was, and told me that her people were destroyed, and that she could not fight against the strength of hell, but that she could send me thither, and took a knife to kill me.

"I said, 'Kill on,' for I knew that wherever I went, thou wouldst follow, and I was sick with the loss of blood from some hurt I had in that struggle, and weary of it all. So I shut my eyes, waiting for the stroke, but instead I felt her lips pressed upon my forehead, and heard her say—

"'Nay, I will not do it. Fare thee well; fulfil thou thine own destiny, as I fulfil mine. For this cast the dice have fallen against me; elsewhere it may be otherwise. I go to load them if I may.'

"I opened my eyes and looked. There Atene stood, a glass in her hand—see, it lies beside her.

"'Defeated, yet I win!' she cried, 'for I do but pass before thee to prepare the path that thou shalt tread, and to make ready thy place in the Under-world. Till we meet again, I pledge thee, for I am destroyed. Ayesha's horsemen are in my streets, and, clothed in lightnings at their head, rides Ayesha's avenging self.'

"So she drank, and fell dead—but now. Look, her breast still quivers. Afterwards, that old man would have murdered me, for, being roped, I could not resist him; but the door burst in, and thou camest. Spare him—he is of her blood, and he loved her."

Then Leo sank back into the chair where we had discovered him bound, and seemed to fall into a kind of torpor, for of a sudden he grew to look like an old man.

"Thou art sick," said Ayesha anxiously. "Oros, thy medicine—the draught I bade thee bring! Be swift, I say."

The priest bowed, and from some pocket in his ample robe produced a phial which he opened and gave to Leo, saying—

"Drink, my lord; this stuff will give thee back thy health, for it is strong."

"The stronger the better," answered Leo. Then he took the draught and emptied it.

There must have been virtue in that potion; at least, the change which it produced in him was wonderful. Within a minute his eyes grew bright again, and the colour returned into his cheeks.

"Thy medicines are very good, as I have learned of old," he said to Ayesha; "but the best of all of them is to see thee safe and victorious before me, and to know that I, who looked for death, yet live to greet thee, my beloved. There is food," and he pointed to a board upon which were meats. "Say, may I eat of them, for I starve?"

"Aye," she answered softly, "eat."

So we fell to—yes, we fell to and ate even in the presence of that dead woman who looked so royal in her death; of the old magician who stood there powerless, like a man petrified; and of Ayesha, the wondrous being that could destroy an army with the fearful weapons which were servant to her will.

AYESHA

THE RETURN OF "SHE."

By H. RIDER HAGGARD.

CHAPTER XXIII.

THE YIELDING OF AYESHA.

WHEN I had satisfied myself, Leo was still at his meal, for loss of blood, or the effects of the tremendous nerve tonic which Ayesha ordered to be administered to him, had made him ravenous.

I watched his face and became aware of a curious change in it—no immediate change, indeed, but one, I think, that had come upon him gradually, although I only fully appreciated it now, after our short separation. In addition to the thinness of which I have spoken, his handsome countenance had grown more ethereal; his eyes were full of the shadows of things that were to come.

His aspect pained me, I knew not why. It was no longer that of the Leo with whom I was familiar—the deep-chested, mighty-limbed, jovial, upright traveller, hunter, and fighting-man, who had chanced to love and be loved of a spiritual power incarnated in a mould of perfect womanhood and armed with all the might of Nature's self. These things were still present indeed, but the man was changed, and I felt sure that this change came from Ayesha, since the look upon his face had become exceeding like to that which often hovered upon hers at rest.

She also was watching him, with speculative, dreamy eyes, till presently, as some thought swept through her, I saw those eyes blaze up, and the red blood pour to cheek and brow. Yes, the mighty Ayesha whose dead, slain for him, lay strewn by the thousand on yonder plain, blushed and trembled like a maiden at her first lover's kiss.

Leo rose from the table. "I would that I had been with thee in the fray," he said.

"At the drift there was fighting," she answered; "afterwards none. My ministers of Fire, Earth and Air smote, no more; I waked them from their sleep, and at my command they smote for thee and saved thee."

"Many lives to take for one man's safety," Leo said solemnly, as though the thought pained him.

"Had they been millions and not thousands, I would have spent them every one. On my head be their deaths, not on thine. Or, rather, on hers," and she pointed to the dead Atene. "Yes, on hers who made this war. At least she should thank me, who have sent so royal a host to guard her through the darkness."

"Yet it is terrible," said Leo, "to think of thee, beloved, red to the hair with slaughter."

"What reck I?" she answered with a splendid pride. "Let their blood suffice to wash the stain of thy blood from off these cruel hands that once did murder thee."

"Who am I, that I should blame thee?" Leo went on, as though arguing with himself—"I who but yesterday killed two men — to save myself from treachery."

"Speak not of it!" she exclaimed in cold rage. "I saw the place; and thou knowest how I swore that a hundred lives should pay for every drop of that dear blood of thine; and I, who lie not, have kept the oath. Look now on that man who stands yonder struck by my will to stone, dead yet living, and say again what was he about to do to thee when I entered here?"

"To take vengeance on me for the doom of his queen and of her armies," answered Leo; "and, Ayesha, how knowest thou that a Power higher than thine own will not demand it yet?"

As he spoke, a pale shadow flickered on Leo's face, such a shadow as might fall from Death's advancing wing, and in the fixed eyes of the Shaman there shone a stony smile.

For a moment terror seemed to take Ayesha, then it was gone as quickly as it came.

"Nay," she said. "I ordain that it shall not be, and, save One who listeth not, what power reigns in this wide earth that dare defy my will?"

So she spoke, and as her words of awful pride—for they were very awful—rang round that stone-built chamber, a vision came to me—Holly.

I saw illimitable space peopled with shining suns, and sunk in the infinite void above them one vast Countenance clad in a calm so terrific that at its aspect my spirit sank to nothingness. Yes, and I knew that this was Destiny enthroned above the spheres. Those lips moved, and obedient worlds rushed up on their course. They moved again, and these rolling chariots of the heavens were turned or stayed, appeared or disappeared. I knew also that against this calm Majesty the being, woman or spirit, at my side had dared to hurl her passion and her strength. My soul reeled. I was afraid.

The dread phantasm passed, and when my mind cleared again, Ayesha was speaking in new, triumphant tones.

"Nay, nay!" she cried. "Past is the night of dread; dawns the day of victory! Look!" and she pointed through the window-places shattered by the hurricane, to the flaming town beneath, whence rose one continual wail of misery, the wail of women mourning their countless slain while the fire roared through their homes like some unchained and rejoicing demon. "Look, Leo, on the smoke of the first sacrifice that I offer to thy royal state, and listen to its music. Perchance thou deemst it naught. Why, then, I'll give thee others. Thou lovest war. Good! we will go down to war, and the rebellious cities of the earth shall be the torches of our march."

She paused a moment, her delicate nostrils quivering, and her face alight with the pre-science of ungarnered splendours; then like a swooping swallow flitted to where, by dead Atene, the gold circlet fallen from the Khania's hair lay upon the floor.

She stooped, lifted it, and coming to Leo, held it high above his head. Slowly she let her hand fall until the glittering coronet rested for an instant on his brow. Then she spoke, in her glorious voice that rolled out rich and low, a very pæan of triumph and of power.

"By this poor, earthly symbol I create thee King of Earth; yea, in its round for thee is gathered all her rule! Be thou its king, and mine!"

Again the coronet was held aloft, again it sank, and again she said, or rather chanted—

"With this unbroken ring, token of eternity, I swear to thee the boon of endless days! Endure thou while the world endures, and be its lord, and mine!"

A third time the coronet touched his brow.

"By this golden round I do endow thee with Wisdom's perfect gold uncountable, that is the talisman whereat all Nature's secret paths shall open to thy feet! Victorious, victorious, tread thou her wondrous ways with me, till from her topmost peak at last she wafts us to our immortal throne whereof the columns twain are Life and Death!"

Then Ayesha cast away the crown, and lo! it fell upon the breast of the lost Atene and rested there.

"Art content with these gifts of mine, my lord?" she cried.

Leo looked at her sadly and shook his head.

"What more wilt thou, then? Ask it, and I swear it shall be thine."

"Thou swearest; but wilt thou keep the oath?"

"Aye, by myself I swear; by myself and by the Strength that bred me. If it be aught that I can grant—then if I refuse it to thee, may such destruction fall upon me as will satisfy even Atene's watching soul!"

I heard, and I think that another heard also—at least, once more the stony smile shone in the eyes of the Shaman.

"I ask of thee nothing that thou canst not give. Ayesha, I ask of thee thyself—not at some distant time when I have been bathed in a mysterious fire, but now, this night."

She shrank back from him a little, as though dismayed.

"Surely," she said slowly, "I am like that foolish philosopher who, walking abroad to read the destinies of nations in the stars, fell down a pitfall dug by idle children, and broke his bones and perished there. Never did I guess that with all these glories stretched before thee like mountain-top on glittering mountain-top, making a stairway for thy mortal feet to the very dome of heaven, thou wouldst still clutch at thy native earth and ask of it—but the common boon of woman's love.

"Oh, Leo! I thought that thy soul was set upon nobler aims, that thou wouldst pray me for wider powers, for a more vast dominion; that as though they were but yonder fallen door of wood and iron, I should break for thee the bars of Hades, and, like the Eurydice of old fable, draw thee living down the steeps of Death, or throne thee midst the fires of the furthest sun to watch its subject worlds at play.

"Or I thought that thou wouldst bid me reveal what no woman ever told, the bitter, naked truth—all my sins and sorrows, all the wandering fancies of my fickle thought;

" ' By this poor, earthly symbol I create thee King of Earth.' "

even what thou knowest not and perchance ne'er shalt know—*who I am and whence I came*, and how to thy charmed eyes I seemed to change from foul to fair, and what is the purpose of my love for thee, and what the meaning of that tale of an angry goddess— who never was except in dreams.

"I thought — nay, no matter what I thought, save that thou wert far otherwise than thou art, my Leo, and in so high a moment that thou wouldst seek to pass the mystic gates my glory can throw wide and with me tread an air supernal to the hidden heart of things. Yet thy prayer is but the same that the whole world whispers beneath the silent moon, in the palace and the cottage, among the snows and on the burning desert's waste : ' Oh ! my love, thy lips, thy lips ! Oh ! my love, be mine, now, now, beneath the moon, beneath the moon ! '

"Leo, I thought better, higher, of thee."

"Mayhap, Ayesha, thou wouldst have thought worse of me had I been content with thy suns and constellations and spiritual gifts and dominations, that I neither desire nor understand.

"If I had said to thee : ' Be thou my angel, not my wife ; divide the ocean, that I may walk its bed ; pierce the firmament and show me how grow the stars ; tell me the origins of being and of death, and instruct me in their issues ; give up the races of mankind to my sword, and the wealth of all the earth to fill my treasuries. Teach me also how to drive the hurricane as thou canst do, and to bend the laws of Nature to my purpose : on earth make me half a god, as thou art.'

"But, Ayesha, I am no god ; I am a man, and as a man I seek the woman whom I love. Oh ! divest thyself of all these wrappings of thy power—that power which strews thy path with dead and keeps me apart from thee. If only for one little hour, forget the ambition that gnaws unceasingly at thy soul ; I say forget thy greatness and be a woman and—my wife."

She made no answer, only looked at him and shook her head, causing her glorious hair to ripple like water beneath a gentle breeze.

"Thou deniest me," he went on with gathering strength ; "and that thou canst not do, that thou mayest not do, for Ayesha, thou hast sworn, and I demand the fulfilment of thine oath.

"Hark thou. I refuse thy gifts ; I will have none of thy rule, who ask no Pharaoh's throne, and wish to do good to men, and not to kill them—that the world may profit. I will not go to Kôr, nor be bathed in the breath of Life. I will leave thee and cross the mountains, or perish on them ; nor with all thy strength canst thou hold me to thy side, who, indeed, needest me not. No longer will I endure this daily torment, the torment of thy presence and thy sweet words ; thy loving looks, thy promises for next year, next year, next year. So keep thine oath or let me begone."

Still Ayesha stood silent, only now her head drooped and her breast began to heave. Then Leo stepped forward ; he seized her in his arms and kissed her. She broke from his embrace, I know not how, for though unreturned it was close enough, and again stood before him, but at a little distance.

"Did I not warn Holly," she whispered with a sigh, "to bid thee beware lest I should catch thy human fire ? Man, I say to thee, it begins to smoulder in my heart, and should it grow to flame——"

"Why, then," he answered laughing, "we will be happy for a little while."

"Aye, Leo, but how long ? Why, wert thou sole lord of this loveliness of mine and not set above their harming, night and day a hundred jealous daggers would seek thy heart and—find it."

"How long, Ayesha ? A lifetime, a year, a month, a minute—I neither know nor care, and while thou art true to me I fear no stabs of envy."

"Is it so ? Wilt take the risk ? I can promise thee nothing. Thou mightest—yes, in this way or in that, thou mightest—die."

"And if I die, what then ? Shall we be separated ? "

"Nay, nay, Leo, that is not possible. We never can be severed, of this I am sure ; it is sworn to me. But then through other lives and other spheres, higher lives and higher spheres mayhap, our fates must force a painful path to their last goal of union."

"Why, then, I take the hazard, Ayesha. Shall the life that I can risk to slay a leopard or a lion, in the sport of an idle day, be too great a price to offer for the splendours of thy breast ? Thine oath ! Ayesha, I claim thine oath."

*　　　*　　　*　　　*　　　*

Then it was that in Ayesha there began the most mysterious and thrilling of her many changes. Yet how to describe it I know not, unless it be by simile.

Once in Thibet we were imprisoned for months by snows that stretched down from the mountain slopes into the valleys, and oh, how weary did we grow of those arid, aching fields of purest white! At length rain set in, and blinding mists in which it was not safe to wander, that made the dark nights darker yet.

So it was until there came a morning, when, seeing the sun shine, we went to our door and looked out. Behold a miracle! Gone were the snows that choked the valley, and in the place of them appeared vivid, springing grass, starred everywhere with flowers, and murmuring brooks, and birds that sang and nested in the willows. Gone was the frowning sky, and all the blue firmament seemed one tender smile. Gone were the austerities of winter, with its harsh winds, and in their place Spring, companioned by her zephyrs, glided down the vale singing her song of love and life.

* * * * *

There in this high chamber, in the presence of the living and the dead, while the last act of the great tragedy unrolled itself before me, looking on Ayesha, that forgotten scene sprang into my mind. For on her face just such a change had come. Hitherto, with all her loveliness, the heart of Ayesha had seemed like that winter mountain wrapped in its unapproachable snow, and before her pure brow and icy self-command, aspirations sank abashed and desire died.

She swore she loved, and her love fulfilled itself in death and many a mysterious way. Yet it was hard to believe that this passion of hers was more than a spoken part, for how can the star seek the moth, although the moth may seek the star? Though the man may worship the goddess, for all her smiles divine, how can the goddess love the man?

But now everything was altered! Look! Ayesha grew human; I could see her heart beat beneath her robes, and hear her breath come in soft, sweet sobs, while o'er her upturned face and in her alluring eyes there spread itself that look which is born of love alone. Radiant and more radiant did she seem to grow, sweeter and more sweet, no longer the veiled hermit of the Caves, no longer the Oracle of the Sanctuary, no longer the Valkyrie of the battleplain, but only the loveliest and most happy bride that ever gladdened a husband's eyes.

She spoke, and it was of little things, for thus she proclaimed the conquest of herself.

"Fie!" she said, showing her white robes torn with spears and stained by the dust and due of war; "Fie, my lord, what marriage garments are these in which at last I come to thee, who would have been adorned in regal gems and raiment befitting to my state and thine?"

"I seek the woman, not her garment," said Leo, his burning eyes fixed upon her face.

"Thou seekest the woman. Ah! there it lies. Tell me, Leo, am I woman or spirit? Say that I am woman, for now the prophecy of this dead Atene lies heavy on my soul—Atene, who said that mortal and immortal may not mate."

"Thou must be woman, or thou wouldst not have tormented me as thou hast done these many weeks."

"I thank thee for the comfort of thy words. Yet, was it *woman* whose breath wrought destruction upon yonder plain? Was it to a *woman* that Blast and Lightning bowed and said: ' We are here: Command us, we obey '? Did that dead thing " (and she pointed to the shattered door) " break inward at a *woman's* will? Or could a *woman* charm this man to stone?

"Oh, Leo! would that I were woman! I tell thee that I'd lay all my grandeur down, a wedding offering at thy feet, could I be sure that for one short year I should be naught but *woman* and—thy happy wife.

"Thou sayest that I did torment thee, but it is I who have known torment, I who desired to yield and dared not. Aye, I tell thee, Leo, were I not sure that thy little stream of life is draining dry into the great ocean of my life, drawn thither as the sea draws its rivers, or as the sun draws mists, e'en now I would not yield. But I know, for my wisdom tells it me, ere ever we could reach the shores of Libya, the ill work would be done, and thou dead of thine own longing—thou dead and I widowed who never was a wife.

"Therefore see! like lost Atene I take the dice and cast them, not knowing how they shall fall. Not knowing how they shall fall, for good or ill I cast," and she made a wild motion as of some desperate gamester throwing his last throw.

"So," Ayesha went on, "the thing is done and the number summed for aye, though it be hidden from my sight. I have made an end of doubts and fears, and come death, come life, I'll meet it bravely.

"Say, how shall we be wed? I have it. Holly here must join our hands; who else? He that ever was our guide shall give me unto thee, and thee to me. This burning city is our altar, the dead and living are our witnesses on earth and heaven. In place of rites and ceremonials, for this first time I lay my lips on thine, and when 'tis done, for music I'll sing thee a nuptial chant of love such as mortal poet has not written nor have mortal lovers heard.

"Come, Holly, do now thy part, and give this maiden to this man."

*   *   *   *   *

Like one in a dream I obeyed her, and took Ayesha's outstretched hand and Leo's. As I held them thus—I tell the truth—it was as though some fire rushed through my veins from her to him, shaking and shattering me with swift waves of burning and unearthly bliss. With the fire, too, came glorious visions and sounds of mighty music, and a sense as though my brain, filled with overflowing life, must burst asunder beneath its weight.

I joined their hands—I know not how; I blessed them—I know not in what words. Then I reeled back against the wall and watched.

This is what I saw.

With an abandonment and a passion so splendid and intense that it seemed more than human, with a murmured cry of "Husband!" Ayesha cast her arms about her lover's neck, and drawing down his head to hers, so that the gold hair was mingled with her raven locks, she kissed him on the lips.

Thus they clung a little while; and as they clung, the gentle diadem of light from her brow spread to his brow also, and through the white wrappings of her robe became visible her perfect shape shining with faint fire. With a little happy laugh she left him, saying—

"Thus, Leo Vincey, oh! thus for the second time do I give myself to thee, and with this flesh and spirit all I swore to thee, there in the dim Caves of Kôr, and here in the Palace of Kaloon. Know thou this—come what may, never, never more shall we be separate who are ordained one. Whilst thou livest, I live at thy side; and when thou diest, if die thou must, I'll follow thee through worlds and firmaments, nor shall all the doors of heaven or hell avail against my love. Where thou goest, thither I will go. When thou sleepest, with thee will I sleep, and it is my voice that thou shalt hear murmuring through the dreams of life and death; my voice that shall summon thee to awaken in the last hour of everlasting

dawn, when all this night of misery hath furled her wings for aye.

"Listen now while I sing to thee, and hear that song aright, for in its melody at length thou shalt learn the truth, which unwed I might not tell to thee. Thou shalt learn who and what *I* am, and who and what *thou* art, and of the high purposes of our love, and this dead woman's hate, and of all that I have hid from thee in veiled, bewildering words and visions.

"Listen, then, my love and lord, to the burden of the Song of Fate."

She ceased speaking and gazed heavenwards with a rapt look, as though she waited for some inspiration to fall upon her, and never, never—not even in the fires of Kôr—had Ayesha seemed so divine as she did now in this moment of the ripe harvest of her love.

My eyes wandered from her to Leo, who stood before her pale and still—still as the deathlike figure of the Shaman—still as the Khania's icy shape which stared upwards from the ground. What was passing in his mind, I wondered, that he could remain thus insensible while in all her might and awful beauty this proud being worshipped him?

Hark! she began to sing in a voice so rich and perfect that its honeyed notes seemed to cloy my blood and stop my breath.

The world was not, was not, and in the womb of Silence
           Slept the souls of men.
Yet I was, and thou—

Suddenly Ayesha stopped, and I felt rather than saw the horror on her face.

Look! Leo swayed to and fro as though the stones beneath him were but a rocking boat. To and fro he swayed, stretched out his blind arms to clasp her—then suddenly fell backwards and lay still.

Oh! what a shriek was that she gave! Surely it must have wakened the very corpses upon the plain. Surely it must have echoed in the stars. One shriek only—then throbbing silence.

*   *   *   *   *

I sprang to him, and there, withered in Ayesha's kiss, slain by the fire of her love, Leo lay dead—lay dead upon the breast of dead Atene!

CHAPTER XXIV.

THE PASSING OF AYESHA.

I HEARD Ayesha say presently—and the words struck me as dreadful in their hopeless

"With a murmured cry of 'Husband!' Ayesha cast her arms about her lover's neck."

acceptance of a doom against which even she had no strength to struggle—

"It seems that my lord has left me for awhile; I must hasten to my lord afar."

After that I do not quite know what happened. I had lost the man who was all in all to me—friend and child in one—and I was crushed as I had never been before. It seemed so sad that I, old and outworn, should still live on, whilst he, in the flower of his age, snatched from joy and greatness such as no man hath known, lay thus asleep.

I think that, by an afterthought, Ayesha and Oros tried to restore him—tried without result, for here her powers were of no avail. Indeed, my conviction is that although some lingering life still kept him on his feet, Leo had really died at the moment of her embrace, since when I looked at him before he fell, his face was that of a dead man.

Yes, I believe that last speech of hers, although she knew it not, was addressed to his spirit, for in her burning kiss his flesh had perished.

*   *   *   *   *

When at length I recovered myself a little, it was to hear Ayesha in a cold, calm voice—her face I could not see, for she had veiled herself—commanding certain priests who had been summoned to "bear away the body of that accursed woman, and bury her as befits her rank." Even then I bethought me, I remember, of the tale of Jehu and Jezebel.

Leo, looking strangely calm and happy, lay now upon a couch, the arms folded on his breast. When the priests had tramped away, bearing their royal burden, Ayesha, who sat by his body brooding, seemed to awake, for she rose and said—

"I need a messenger, and for no common journey, since he must search out the habitations of the Shades"; and she turned herself towards Oros and appeared to look at him.

Now for the first time I saw that priest change countenance a little, for the eternal smile, of which even this scene had not quite rid it, left his face, and he grew pale and trembled.

"Thou art afraid," she said contemptuously. "Be at rest, Oros; I will not send one who is afraid. Holly, wilt thou go for me—and him?"

"Aye," I answered. "I am weary of life, and desire no other end. Only let it be swift and painless."

She mused awhile, then said—

"Nay, thy time is not yet; thou still hast work to do. Endure, my Holly—'tis only for a breath."

Then she looked at the Shaman, the man turned to stone, who all this while had stood there as a statue stands, and cried—

"Awake!"

Instantly he seemed to thaw into life, his limbs relaxed, his breast heaved; he was as he had always been—ancient, gnarled, malevolent.

"I hear thee, mistress," he said, bowing as a man bows to the power that he hates.

"Thou seest, Simbri," and she waved her hand.

"I see. Things have befallen as Atene and I foretold, have they not? 'Ere long the corpse of a new-crowned Khan of Kaloon,'" and he pointed to the gold circlet that Ayesha had set on Leo's brow, "'will lie upon the brink of the Pit of Flame'—as I foretold." An evil smile crept into his eyes, and he went on—

"Hadst thou not smote me dumb, I who watched could have warned thee that they would so befall; but, great mistress, it pleased thee to smite me dumb. And so it seems, O Hes, that thou hast overshot thyself and liest broken at the foot of that pinnacle which step by step thou hast climbed for more than two thousand weary years. See what thou hast bought at the price of countless lives, that now, before the Throne of Judgment, bring accusations against thy powers misused, and cry out for justice on thy head," and he looked at the dead form of Leo.

"I sorrow for them; yet, Simbri, they were well spent," Ayesha answered reflectively, "who, by their forewritten doom—as it was decreed—held thy knife from falling, and thus won me my husband. Aye, and I am happy—happier than such blind bats as thou can see or guess. For know that now with him I have re-wed my wandering soul divorced by sin from me, and that of our marriage kiss which burned his life away there shall still be born to us children of Forgiveness and eternal Grace, and all things that are pure and fair.

"Look thou, Simbri, I will honour thee. Thou shalt be my messenger, and beware! beware, I say, how thou dost fulfil thine office, since of every syllable thou must render an account.

"Go thou down the dark paths of Death, and, since even my thought may not reach to where he sleeps to-night, search out my lord, and say to him that the feet of his spouse Ayesha are following fast. Bid him

"And there Leo lay dead, upon the breast of dead Atene!"

have no fear for me who, by this last sorrow, have atoned my crimes and am in his embrace regenerate. Tell him that thus it was appointed, and thus is best, since now for him also mortality is left behind and true life begins. Command him that he await me in the Gate of Death. Thou hearest!"

"I hear, O Queen, Mighty-from-of-Old."

"One thing more. Say to Atene that I forgive her. Her heart was high, and greatly did she play her part. There in the Gates we will balance our account. Thou hearest?"

"I hear, O Eternal Star that hath conquered Night."

"Then, man, *begone!*"

As the word left Ayesha's lips, Simbri leapt from the floor, grasping at the air as though he would clutch his own departing soul, staggered back against the board where Leo and I had eaten, overthrowing it, and amid a ruin of gold and silver vessels, fell down and died.

She looked at him, then said to me—

"See, though he ever hated me, this magician, who has known Ayesha from the first, did homage to my ancient majesty at last, when lies and defiance would serve his end no more. No longer now do I hear the name that his dead mistress gave to me. The 'Star-that-hath-fallen' in his lips and in very truth is become the 'Star-which-hath-burst-the-bonds-of-Night,' and, re-arisen, shines for ever—shines with its twin immortal, to set no more—my Holly. Well, he is gone, and ere now those that serve me in the Under-world—dost remember? thou sawest their captains in the Sanctuary—bend the head at great Ayesha's word and make her place ready near her spouse.

"But, oh, what folly has been mine! When even here my wrath can show such power, how could I hope that my lord would outlive the fires of my love? Still it was better so, for he sought not the pomp I would have given him, nor desired the death of men. Yet such pomp must have been his portion in this poor shadow of a world, and the steps that encircle a usurper's throne are ever slippery with blood.

"Thou art weary, my Holly; go rest thee. To-morrow night we journey to the Mountain, there to celebrate these obsequies."

* * * * *

I crept into the room adjoining—it had been Simbri's—and laid me down upon his bed, but to sleep I was not able. Its door was open, and in the light of the burning city that shone through the casements I could see Ayesha watching by her dead. Hour after hour she watched, her head resting on her hand—silent, stirless. She wept not—no sigh escaped her; only watched as a tender woman watches a slumbering babe that she knows will awake at dawn.

Her face was unveiled, and I perceived that it had greatly changed. All pride and anger were departed from it; it was grown soft, wistful, yet full of confidence and quietness. For a while I could not think of what it reminded me, till suddenly I remembered. Now it was like—indeed, the counterpart almost—of the holy and majestic semblance of the statue of the Mother in the Sanctuary. Yes, with just such a look of love and power as that Mother cast upon her frightened child new-risen from its dream of death, did Ayesha gaze upon her dead, while her parted lips also seemed to whisper "some tale of hope, sure and immortal."

At length she rose and came into my chamber.

"Thou thinkest me fallen, and dost grieve for me, my Holly," she said in a gentle voice, "knowing my fears lest some such fate should overtake my lord."

"Aye, Ayesha, I grieve for thee as for myself."

"Spare, then, thy pity, Holly, since although the human part of me would have kept him on the earth, now my spirit doth rejoice that for a while he has burst his mortal bonds. For many an age, although I knew it not, in my proud defiance of the Universal Law, I have fought against his true weal and mine. Thrice have I and the angel wrestled, matching strength with strength, and thrice has he conquered me. Yet as he bore away his prize this night he whispered wisdom in my ear. This was his message: That in death is love's home, in death its strength; that from the charnel-house of life this love springs again glorified and pure, to reign a conqueror for ever. Therefore I wipe away my tears and go to join him whom we have lost, there where he awaits me, as it is granted to me that I may do.

"But I am selfish, and forgot. Thou needest rest. Sleep, friend; I bid thee sleep."

And I slept.

When I awoke, it was day, and through the window-place I saw the rain that the people of Kaloon had so long desired, falling in one straight sheet. I saw also that

"'Then, man, *begone!*'"

Ayesha, seated by the shrouded form of Leo, was giving orders to her priests and captains and to some nobles, who had survived the slaughter of Kaloon, as to the new government of the land. Then I slept again.

*   *   *   *   *

It was evening, and Ayesha stood at my bedside.

"All is prepared," she said. "Arise and ride with me."

So we went, escorted by a thousand cavalry, for the rest stayed to occupy, or perchance to plunder, the land of Kaloon. In front the body of Leo was borne by relays of priests, and behind it rode the veiled Ayesha, I at her side.

Strange was the contrast between this departure and our arrival.

Then the rushing squadrons, the elements that raved, the perpetual sheen of lightnings seen through the swinging curtains of the hail; the voices of despair from an army rolled in blood beneath the chariot wheels of thunder.

Now the white-draped corpse, the slow-pacing horses, the riders with their spears reversed, and on either side, seen in that melancholy moonlight, the women of Kaloon burying their innumerable dead.

And Ayesha herself, yesterday a Valkyrie crested with the star of flame, to-day but a bereaved woman humbly following her husband to the tomb.

Yet how they feared her! Some widow standing on the grave mould she had dug, pointed, as we passed, to the body of Leo, uttering bitter words which I could not catch. Thereon her companions flung themselves upon her, and, felling her with fist and spade, prostrated themselves upon the ground, throwing dust on their hair in token of their submission to the Queen of Death.

Ayesha saw them, and said to me, with something of her ancient fire and pride—

"I tread the plain of Kaloon no more, yet, as a parting gift, have I read this high-stomached people a lesson that they needed long. Not for many a generation, O Holly, will they dare to lift spear against the College of Hes and its subject Tribes."

   *   *   *   *   *

Again it was night, and where once lay that of the Khan, the man whom he had killed, flanked by the burning pillars the bier of Leo stood in the inmost Sanctuary before the statue of the Mother, whose gentle, unchanging eye seemed to search his quiet face.

On her throne sat the veiled Hesea, giving commands to her priests and priestesses.

   *   *   *   *   *

"I am weary," she said, "and it may be that I leave you for a while to rest—beyond the mountains. A year, or a thousand years—I cannot say. If so, let Papave, with Oros as her counsellor and husband, and their seed, hold my place till I return again.

"Priests and priestesses of the College of Hes, over new territories have I held my hand; take them as an heritage from me, and rule them well and gently. Henceforth let the Hesea of the Mountain be also the Khania of Kaloon.

"Priests and priestesses of our ancient faith, learn to look through its rites and tokens, outward and visible, to the in-forming Spirit. If Hes the goddess never ruled on earth, still pitying Nature rules. If the name of Isis never rang through the courts of heaven, still in heaven, with all love fulfilled, nursing her human children on her breast, dwells the mighty Motherhood whereof this statue is the symbol, that Motherhood which bore us, and, unforgetting, faithful, will receive us at the end.

"For of the bread of bitterness we shall not always eat, of the water of tears we shall not always drink. Beyond the night the royal suns ride on; ever the rainbow shines around the rain. Though they slip from our clutching hands like melted snow, the lives we lose shall yet be found immortal, and from the burnt-out fires of our human hopes will spring a heavenly star."

She paused and waved her hand as though to dismiss them, then added, by an after-thought, pointing to myself—

"This man is my beloved friend and guest. Let him be yours also. It is my will that you tend and guard him here, and when the snows have melted and summer is at hand, that you fashion a way for him through the gulf and bring him across the mountains by which he came, till you leave him in safety. Hear and forget not, for be sure that to me you will give account of him."

   *   *   *   *   *

The night drew towards the dawn, and we stood upon the peak above the gulf of fire, four of us only—Ayesha and I, and Oros and Papave. For the bearers had laid down the body of Leo upon its edge and gone their way. The curtain of flame flared in front of us, its crest bent over like a billow in the gale, and to leeward, one by one, floated the torn-off clouds and pinnacles of fire. By the dead Leo knelt Ayesha, gazing at that icy, smiling face, but speaking no single word. At length she rose and said—

"Darkness draws near, my Holly, that deep darkness which foreruns the glory of the dawn. Now fare thee well for one little hour. When thou art about to die, but not before, call me, and I will come to thee. Stir not and speak not till all be done, lest when I am no longer here to be thy guard some Presence should pass on and slay thee.

"Think not that I am conquered, for now my name is Victory! Think not that Ayesha's strength is spent or her tale is done, for of it thou readest but a single page. Think not even that I am to-day that thing of sin and pride, the Ayesha thou didst adore and fear, I who in my lord's love and sacrifice have again conceived my soul. For know that now once more, as at the beginning, his soul and mine are *one*."

"Two glorious shapes sweeping upward."

She thought awhile and added—

"Friend, take this sceptre in memory of me; but beware how thou usest it, save at the last to summon me, for it has virtues," and she gave me the jewelled sistrum that she bore; then said—

"So kiss his brow, stand back, and be still."

*   *   *   *   *

Now, as once before, the darkness gathered on the pit, and presently, although I heard no prayer, though now no mighty music broke upon the silence, through that darkness, beating up the gale, came the two-winged flame, and hovered where Ayesha stood.

It appeared, it vanished, and one by one the long minutes crept away until the first spear of dawn lit upon the point of rock.

Lo! it was empty, utterly empty and lonesome. Gone was the corse of Leo, and gone, too, was Ayesha the imperial, the divine.

Whither had she gone? I know not. But this I know, that as the light returned and the broad sheet of flame flared out to meet it, I seemed to see two glorious shapes sweeping upward on its bosom, and the faces that they wore were those of Leo and of Ayesha.

Often and often during the weary months that followed, whilst I wandered through the temple or amid the winter snows upon the Mountain-side, did I seek to solve this question: Whither had She gone? I asked it of my heart; I asked it of the skies; I asked it of the spirit of Leo which often was so near to me.

But no sure answer ever came, nor will I hazard one. As mystery wrapped Ayesha's origin and lives—for the truth of these things I never learned—so did mystery wrap her deaths—or, rather, her departings, for I cannot think her dead. Surely she still is, if not on earth, then in some other sphere?

So I believe; and when my own hour comes—and it draws near swiftly—I shall know whether I believe in vain, or whether she will appear to be my guide as, with her last words, she swore that she would do. Then, too, I shall learn what she was about to reveal to Leo when he died, the purposes of their being and of their love.

So I can wait in patience, who must not wait for long, though my heart is broken and I am desolate.

*   *   *   *   *

Oros and all the priests were very good to me. Indeed, even had it been their wish, they would have feared to be otherwise, who remembered and were sure that in some time to come they must render an account of this matter to their dread Queen. By way of return, I helped them as I was best able to draw up a scheme for the government of the conquered country of Kaloon, and with my advice upon many other questions.

And so at length the long months wore away, till at the approach of summer the snows melted. Then I said that I must be gone. They gave me of their treasures in precious stones, lest I should need money for my faring, since the gold of which I had such plenty was, of course, too heavy to be carried by one man alone. They led me across the plains of Kaloon, where now the husbandmen, those that were left of them, ploughed the land and scattered seed, and so on to its city. But amidst those blackened ruins, over which Atene's palace still frowned unharmed, I would not enter, for to me it was, and always must remain, a home of death. So I camped outside the walls by the river, just where Leo and I had landed after that poor, mad Khan set us free—or, rather, loosed us, to be hunted by his death-hounds.

Next day we took boat and rowed up the river, past the place where we had seen Atene's cousin murdered, till we came to the Gate-house. Here once again I slept—or, rather, did not sleep.

On the following morning I went down into the ravine and found, to my surprise, that the rapid torrent—shallow enough now —had been roughly bridged, and that, in preparation for my coming, rude but sufficient ladders were built on the face of the opposing precipice. At the foot of these I bade farewell to Oros, who at our parting smiled benignantly as on the day we met.

"We have seen strange things together," I said to him, not knowing what else to say.

"Very strange," he answered.

"At least, friend Oros," I went on awkwardly enough, "events have shaped themselves to your advantage, for you inherit a royal mantle."

"I wrap myself in a mantle of borrowed royalty," he answered with precision, "of which doubtless one day I shall be stripped."

"You mean that the great Hesea is not dead?"

"I mean that Hes never dies. She changes; that is all. As the wind blows now hence, now hither, so she comes and goes; and who can tell at what spot upon the earth, or beyond it, for a while that wind lies sleeping ? But at sunset or at dawn, at noon or at midnight, it will begin to blow again, and then woe to those who stand across its path !

"Remember the dead heaped upon the plains of Kaloon. Remember the departing of the Shaman Simbri with his message, and the words that she spoke then. Remember the passing of the Hesea from the Mountain-point. Stranger from the West, surely as to-morrow's sun must rise, as she went, so she will return again, and in my borrowed garment I await her advent."

"I also await her advent," I answered, and thus we parted.

*   *   *   *   *

Accompanied by fifty picked men bearing provisions and arms, I climbed the ladders easily enough, and now that I had food and shelter, crossed the mountains without mishap. They even escorted me through the desert beyond, till one night we camped within sight of the gigantic Buddha that sits before the monastery, gazing eternally across the sands and snows.

When I awoke next morning, the priests were gone. So I took up my pack and pursued my journey alone, and walking slowly came at sunset to the distant lamasery. At its door an ancient figure, wrapped in a tattered cloak, was sitting, engaged apparently in contemplation of the skies. It was our old friend Kou-en. Adjusting his horn spectacles on his nose, he looked at me.

"I was awaiting you, brother of the Monastery called the World," he said in a voice measured, very ineffectually, to conceal his evident delight. "Have you grown hungry there, that you return to this poor place ? "

"Aye, most excellent Kou-en," I answered, "hungry for rest."

"It shall be yours for all the days of this incarnation. But say, where is the other brother ? "

"Dead," I answered.

"And therefore re-born elsewhere. Well, doubtless we shall meet him later on. Come, eat, and afterwards tell me your story."

So I ate, and that night I told him all. Kou-en listened with respectful attention, but the tale, strange as it might seem to most people, excited no particular wonder in his mind. Indeed, he explained it to me at such length, by aid of some marvellous theory of reincarnations, that at last I began to doze.

"At least," I said sleepily, "it would seem that we are all winning merit on the Everlasting Plane," for I thought that favourite catchword would please him.

"Yes, brother of the Monastery called the World," Kou-en answered in a severe voice, "doubtless you are all winning merit ; but, if I may venture to say so, you are winning it very slowly, especially the woman—or the sorceress—or the mighty evil spirit—whose names I understand you to tell me are She, Hes, and Ayesha upon earth, and in *Avitchi*, Star-that-hath-Fallen——"

(*Here Mr. Holly's manuscript ends, its outer sheets having been burnt when he threw it on to the fire at his house in Cumberland.*)

THE END.

BENITA
AN AFRICAN ROMANCE
BY
H. RIDER HAGGARD.

NOTE.

IT may interest readers of this story to know that its author believes it to have a certain foundation in fact.

It was said about five-and-twenty or thirty years ago that an adventurous trader, hearing from some natives in the territory that lies at the back of Quilimane, the legend of a great treasure buried in or about the sixteenth century by a party of Portuguese who were afterwards massacred, as a last resource attempted its discovery by the help of a mesmerist. According to this history the child who was used as a subject in the experiment, when in a state of trance, detailed the adventures and death of the unhappy Portuguese men and women, two of whom leapt from the point of a high rock into the Zambesi. Although he knew no tongue but English, this clairvoyant child is declared to have repeated in Portuguese the prayers these unfortunates offered up, and even to have sung the very hymns they sang. Moreover, with much other detail, he described the burial of the great treasure and its exact situation so accurately that the white man and the mesmerist were able to dig for and find the place where it had been —for the bags were gone, swept out by the floods of the river.

Some gold coins remained, however, one of them a ducat of Aloysius Mocenigo, Doge of Venice. Afterwards the boy was again thrown into a trance (in all he was mesmerised eight times), and revealed where the sacks still lay; but before the white trader could renew his search for them, the party was hunted out of the country by natives, whose superstitious fears were aroused, barely escaping with their lives.

It should be added that, as in the following tale, the chief who was ruling there when the tragedy happened, declared the place to be sacred, and that if it were entered evil would befall his tribe. Thus it came about that for generations it was never violated, until at length his descendants were driven farther from the river by war, and from some of them the white man heard the legend.

CHAPTER I.
CONFIDENCES.

BEAUTIFUL, beautiful was that night! No air stirred; the black smoke from the funnels of the mail steamer *Zanzibar* lay low over the surface of the sea like vast, floating ostrich plumes that vanished one by one in the starlight. Benita Beatrix Clifford, for that was her full name, who had been christened Benita after her mother and Beatrix after her father's only sister, leaning idly over the bulwark rail, thought to herself that a child might have sailed that sea in a boat of bark and come safely into port.

Then a tall man of about thirty years of age, who was smoking a cigar, strolled up to her. At his coming she moved a little as though to make room for him beside her, and there was something in the motion which, had any-one been there to observe it, might have suggested that these two were upon terms of friendship, or still greater intimacy. For a moment he hesitated, and while he did so an expression of doubt, of distress even, gathered on his face. It was as though he understood that a great deal depended upon whether he accepted or declined that gentle invitation, and knew not which to do.

Indeed much did depend upon it, no less than the destinies of both of them. If Robert Seymour had gone by to finish his cigar in solitude, why then this story would have had a very different ending; or, rather, who can say how it might have ended? The dread, foredoomed event with which that night was big would have come to its awful birth leaving certain words unspoken. Violent separation must have ensued, and even if both of them had survived the terror, what prospect was there that their lives would again have crossed each other in that wide Africa?

But it was not so fated, for just as he put his foot forward to continue his march, Benita spoke in her low and pleasant voice.

"Are you going to the smoking-room or to the saloon to dance, Mr. Seymour? One of the officers just told me that there is to be a dance," she added, in explanation, "because it is so calm that we might fancy ourselves ashore."

"Neither," he answered. "The smoking-room is stuffy, and my dancing days are over. No; I proposed to take exercise after that big dinner, and then to sit in a chair and fall asleep. But," he added, and his voice grew interested, "how did you know that it was I? You never turned your head."

"I have ears in my head as well as eyes," she answered with a little laugh, "and after we have been nearly a month together on this ship, I ought to know your step."

"I never remember that anyone ever recognised it before," he said, more to himself than to her, then came and leaned over the rail at her side. His doubts were gone. Fate had spoken.

For a while there was silence between them, then he asked her if she was not going to the dance.

Benita shook her head.

"Why not? You are fond of dancing, and you dance very well. Also there are plenty of officers for partners, especially Captain——" and he checked himself.

"I know," she said; "it would be pleasant but—Mr. Seymour, will you think me foolish if I tell you something?"

"I have never thought you foolish yet, Miss Clifford, so I don't know why I should begin now. What is it?"

"I am not going to the dance because I am afraid, yes, horribly afraid."

"Afraid! Afraid of what?"

"I don't quite know, but, Mr. Seymour, I feel as though we were all of us upon the edge of some dreadful catastrophe—as though there were about to be a mighty change, and beyond it another life, something new and unfamiliar. It came over me at dinner—that was why I left the table. Quite suddenly I looked, and all the people were different, yes, all except a few."

"Was I different?" he asked curiously.

"No, you were not," and he thought he heard her add "Thank God!" beneath her breath.

"And were you different?"

"I don't know. I never looked at myself; I was the seer, not the seen. I have always been like that."

"Indigestion," he said reflectively. "We eat too much on board ship, and the dinner was very long and heavy. I told you so, that's why I'm taking—I mean why I wanted to take exercise."

"And to go to sleep afterwards."

"Yes, first the exercise, then the sleep. Miss Clifford, that is the rule of life—and death. With sleep thought ends, therefore for some of us your catastrophe is much to be desired, for it would mean long sleep and no thought."

"I said that they were changed, not that they had ceased to think. Perhaps they thought the more."

"Then let us pray that your catastrophe may be averted. I prescribe for you bismuth and carbonate of soda. Also in this weather it seems difficult to imagine such a thing. Look now, Miss Clifford," he added, with a note of enthusiasm in his voice, pointing towards the east, "look."

Her eyes followed his outstretched hand, and there, above the level ocean, rose the

"'I CAN SHOOT AS WELL AS YOU, FRIEND'"

great orb of the African moon. Lo! of a sudden all that ocean turned to silver, a wide path of rippling silver stretched from it to them. It might have been the road of angels. The sweet soft light beat upon their ship, showing its tapering masts and every detail of the rigging. It passed on beyond them, and revealed the low, foam-fringed coast-line rising here and there, dotted with kloofs and their clinging bush. Even the round huts of Kaffir kraals became faintly visible in that radiance. Other things became visible also—for instance, the features of this pair.

The man was light in his colouring, fair-skinned, with fair hair which already showed a tendency towards greyness, especially in the moustache, for he wore no beard. His face was clean cut, not particularly handsome, since, their fineness notwithstanding, his features lacked regularity; the cheekbones were too high and the chin was too small, faults redeemed to some extent by the steady and cheerful grey eyes. For the rest, he was broad-shouldered and well set-up, sealed with the indescribable stamp of the English gentleman. Such was the appearance of Robert Seymour.

In that light the girl at his side looked lovely, though, in fact, she had no real claims to loveliness, except perhaps as regards her figure, which was agile, rounded, and peculiarly graceful. Her foreign-looking face was unusual, dark-eyed, a somewhat large and very mobile mouth, fair and waving hair, a broad forehead, a sweet and at times wistful face, thoughtful for the most part, but apt to be irradiated by sudden smiles. Not a beautiful woman at all, but exceedingly attractive, one possessing magnetism.

She gazed, first at the moon and the silver road beneath it, then, turning, at the land beyond.

"We are very near to Africa, at last," she said.

"Too near, I think," he answered. "If I were the captain I should stand out a point or two. It is a strange country, full of surprises. Miss Clifford, will you think me rude if I ask you why you are going there? You have never told me—quite."

"No, because the story is rather a sad one; but you shall hear it if you wish. Do you?"

He nodded, and drew up two deck chairs, in which they settled themselves in a corner made by one of the inboard boats, their faces still towards the sea.

"You know I was born in Africa," she said, "and lived there till I was thirteen years old—why, I find I can still speak Zulu; I did so this afternoon. My father was one of the early settlers in Natal. His father was a clergyman, a younger son of the Lincolnshire Cliffords. They are great people there still, though I don't suppose that they are aware of my existence."

"I know them," answered Robert Seymour. "Indeed, I was shooting at their place last November — when the smash came," and he sighed; "but go on."

"Well, my father quarrelled with his father, I don't know what about, and emigrated. In Natal he married my mother, a Miss Ferreira, whose name—like mine and her mother's—was Benita. She was one of two sisters, and her father, Andreas Ferreira, who married an English lady, was half Dutch and half Portuguese. I remember him well, a fine old man with dark eyes and an iron-grey beard. He was wealthy as things went in those days—that is to say, he had lots of land in Natal and the Transvaal, and great herds of stock. So you see I am half English, some Dutch, and more than a quarter Portuguese—quite a mixture of races. My father and mother did not get on well together. Mr. Seymour, I may as well tell you all the truth: he drank, and although he was passionately fond of her, she was jealous of him. Also he gambled away most of her patrimony, and after old Andreas Ferreira's death they grew poor. One night there was a dreadful scene between them, and in his madness he struck her.

"Well, she was a very proud woman, determined too, and she turned on him and said—for I heard her—'I will never forgive you; we have done with each other.' Next morning, when my father was sober, he begged her pardon, but she made no answer, although he was starting somewhere on a fortnight's trek. When he had gone my mother ordered the Cape cart, packed up her clothes, took some money that she had put away, drove to

Durban, and after making arrangements at the bank about a small private income of her own, sailed with me for England, leaving a letter for my father in which she said that she would never see him again, and if he tried to interfere with me she would put me under the protection of the English court, which would not allow me to be taken to the home of a drunkard.

" In England we went to live in London with my aunt, who had married a Major King, but was a widow with five children. My father often wrote to persuade my mother to go back to him, but she never would, which I think was wrong of her. So things went on for twelve years or more, till one day my mother died suddenly, and I came into her little fortune of between £200 and £300 a year, which she had tied up so that nobody can touch it. That was about a year ago. I wrote to tell my father of her death, and received back a pitiful letter; indeed, I have had several of them. He implored me to come out to him and not to leave him to die in his loneliness, as he soon would do of a broken heart, if I did not. He said that he had long ago given up drinking, which was the cause of the ruin of his life, and sent a certificate signed by a magistrate and a doctor to that effect. Well, in the end, although all my cousins and their mother advised me against it, I consented, and here I am. He is to meet me at Durban, but how we shall get on together is more than I can say, though I long to see him, for after all he is my father."

" It was good of you to come, under all the circumstances. You must have a brave heart," said Robert reflectively.

" It is my duty," she answered. " And for the rest, I am not afraid who was born to Africa. Indeed, often and often have I wished to be back there again, out on the veld, far away from the London streets and fog. I am young and strong, and I want to see things, natural things—not those made by man, you know—the things I remember as a child. One can always go back to London."

" Yes, or at least some people can. It is a curious thing, Miss Clifford, but as it happens I have met your father. You always reminded me of the man, but I had forgotten his name. Now it comes back to me; it *was* Clifford."

" Where on earth ? " she asked, astonished.

" In a queer place. As I told you, I have visited South Africa before, under different circumstances. Four years ago I was out here big-game shooting. Going in from the East coast my brother and I —he is dead now, poor fellow—got up somewhere in the Matabele country, on the banks of the Zambesi. As we didn't find much game there we were going to strike south, when some natives told us of a wonderful ruin that stood on a hill overhanging the river a few miles farther on. So, leaving the waggon on the hither side of the steep nek, over which it would have been difficult to drag it, my brother and I took our rifles and a bag of food and started. The place was farther off than we thought, although from the top of the nek we could see it clearly enough, and before we reached it dark had fallen.

" Now we had observed a waggon and a tent outside the wall which we thought must belong to white men, and headed for them. There was a light in the tent, and the flap was open, the night being very hot. Inside two men were seated, one old, with a grey beard, and the other, a good-looking fellow—under forty, I should say—with a Jewish face, dark, piercing eyes, and a black, pointed beard. They were engaged in examining a heap of gold beads and bangles, which lay on the table between them. As I was about to speak the black-bearded man heard or caught sight of us, and seizing a rifle that leaned against the table, swung round and covered me.

" ' For God's sake don't shoot, Jacob,' said the old man; ' they are English.'

" ' Best dead, any way,' answered the other, in a soft voice, with a slight foreign accent, ' we don't want spies or thieves here.'

" ' We are neither, but I can shoot as well as you, friend,' I remarked, for by this time my rifle was on him.

" Then he thought better of it, and dropped his gun, and we explained that we were merely on an archæological expedition. The end of it was that we became capital friends, though neither of us could cotton much to Mr. Jacob—I forget his other name. He struck us as too handy with his rifle, and was, I gathered, an individual with a mysterious and rather lurid past. To cut a long story short, when he found out that we had no intention of poaching, your father, for it was he, told us frankly that they were treasure-hunting, having got hold of some story about a vast store of gold which had been hidden away there by Portuguese two or three centuries before. Their trouble was, however, that the Makalanga, who lived in the fortress, which was called Bambatse, would not allow them in to dig, because they said the place was haunted and if they did so it would bring bad luck to the tribe.''

"And did they ever get in ? " asked Benita.

"I am sure I don't know, for we went away next day, though before we left we called on the Makalanga, who admitted us all readily enough so long as we brought no spades with us. By the way, the gold we saw your father and his friend examining was found in some ancient graves outside the walls, but had nothing to do with the big and mythical treasure.''

"What was the place like ? I love old ruins,'' broke in Benita again.

"Oh ! wonderful. A gigantic, circular wall built by heaven knows who, then half-way up the hill another wall, and near the top a third wall which, I understood, surrounded a sort of holy of holies, and above everything, on the brink of the precipice, a great cone of granite.''

"Artificial or natural ? "

"I don't know. They would not let us up there, but we were introduced to their chief and high priest, Church and State in one, and a wonderful old man he was, very wise and very gentle. I remember he told me he believed we should meet again, which seemed an odd thing for him to say. I asked him about the treasure and why he would not let the other white men look for it. He answered that it would never be found by any man, white or black, that only a woman would find it at the appointed time, when it pleased the Spirit of Bambatse, under whose guardianship it was.''

"Who was the Spirit of Bambatse, Mr. Seymour ? "

"I can't tell you, couldn't make out anything definite about her, except that she was said to be white, and to appear

sometimes at sunrise, or in the moonlight, standing upon the tall point of rock of which I told you. I remember that I got up before the dawn to look for her —like an idiot, for of course I saw nothing—and that's all I know about the matter.''

"Did you have any talk with my father, Mr. Seymour—alone, I mean ? "

"Yes, a little. The next day he walked back to our waggon with us, being glad, I fancy, of a change from the perpetual society of his partner Jacob. That wasn't wonderful in a man who had been brought up at Eton and Oxford, as I found out he had, like myself, and whatever his failings may have been—although we saw no sign of them, for he would not touch a drop of spirits—was a gentleman, which Jacob wasn't. Still, he—Jacob—had read a lot, especially on out-of-the-way subjects, and could talk every language under the sun—a clever and agreeable scoundrel, in short.''

"Did my father say anything about himself ? "

"Yes ; he told me that he had been an unsuccessful man all his life, and had much to reproach himself with, for we got quite confidential at last. He added that he had a family in England—what family he didn't say—whom he was anxious to make wealthy by way of reparation for past misdeeds, and that was why he was treasure-hunting. However, from what you tell me, I fear he never found anything.''

"No, Mr. Seymour, he never found it and never will, but all the same I am glad to hear that he was thinking of us. Also I should like to explore that place, Bambatse.''

"So should I, Miss Clifford, in your company and your father's, but not in that of Jacob. If ever you should go there with him, I say :—Beware of Jacob.''

"Oh ! I am not afraid of Jacob,'' she answered with a laugh, "although I believe that my father still has something to do with him—at least in one of his letters he mentioned his partner, who was a German.''

"A German ! I think that he must have meant a German Jew.''

After this there was silence between them for a time, then he said suddenly,

"HE LET HIMSELF DOWN THE FALLS"

"You have told me your story, would you like to hear mine?"

"Yes," she answered.

"Well, it won't take you long to listen to it, for, Miss Clifford, like Calverley's needy knife-grinder, I have really none to tell. You see before you one of the most useless persons in the world, an undistinguished member of what is called in England the 'leisured class,' who can do absolutely nothing that is worth doing, except shoot straight."

"Indeed," said Benita.

"You do not seem impressed with that accomplishment," he went on, "yet it is an honest fact that for the last fifteen years—I was thirty-two this month—practically my whole time has been given up to it, with a little fishing thrown in in the spring. As I want to make the most of myself, I will add that I am supposed to be amongst the six best shots in England, and that my ambition—yes, great Heavens! my ambition—was to become better than the other five. By that sin fell the poor man who speaks to you. I was supposed to have abilities, but I neglected them all to pursue this form of idleness. I entered no profession, I did no work, with the result that at thirty-two I am ruined and almost hopeless."

"Why ruined and hopeless?" she asked anxiously, for the way in which they were spoken grieved her more than the words themselves.

"Ruined because my old uncle, the Honourable John Seymour Seymour, whose heir I was, committed the indiscretion of marrying a young lady who has presented him with thriving twins. With the appearance of those twins my prospects disappeared, as did the allowance of £1,500 a year that he was good enough to make me on which to keep up a position as his next-of-kin. I had something of my own, but also I had debts, and at the present moment a draft in my pocket for £2,163 14s. 5d., and a little loose cash, represents the total of my worldly goods, just about the sum I have been accustomed to spend per annum."

"I don't call that ruin, I call that riches," said Benita, relieved. "With £2,000 to begin on you may make a fortune in Africa. But how about the hopelessness?"

"I am hopeless because I have absolutely nothing to which to look forward. Really, when that £2,000 is gone I do not know how to earn a sixpence. In this dilemma it occurred to me that the only thing I could do was to turn my shooting to practical account, and become a hunter of big game. Therefore I propose to kill elephants until an elephant kills me. At least," he added in a changed voice, "I did so propose until half an hour ago."

CHAPTER II.

THE END OF THE "ZANZIBAR."

"UNTIL half an hour ago? Then why——" and Benita stopped.

"Have I changed my very modest scheme of life? Miss Clifford, as you are so good as to be sufficiently interested, I will tell you. It is because a temptation which hitherto I have been able to resist, has during the last thirty minutes become too strong for me. You know everything has its breaking strain." He puffed nervously at his cigar, threw it into the sea, paused, then went on: "Miss Clifford, I have dared to fall in love with you. No; hear me out. When I have done it will be quite time enough to give me the answer that I expect. Meanwhile, for the first time in my life, allow me the luxury of being in earnest. To me it is a new sensation, and therefore very priceless. May I go on?"

Benita made no answer. He rose with a certain deliberateness which characterised all his movements, for Robert Seymour never seemed to be in a hurry, and stood in front of her so that the moonlight shone upon her face, while his own remained in shadow.

"Beyond that £2,000 of which I have spoken, and incidentally its owner, I have nothing whatsoever to offer to you. I am an indigent and a worthless person. Even in my prosperous days, when I could look forward to a large estate, although it was often suggested to me, I never considered myself justified in asking any lady to share—the prospective estate. I think now that the real reason was that I never cared sufficiently for any lady, since otherwise my selfishness would probably have overcome my scruples, as it does to-night. Benita, for I will call you so, if for the first and last time, I—I—love you.

"Listen now," he went on, dropping his measured manner, and speaking hurriedly, like a man with an earnest message and little time in which to deliver it, "it is an odd thing, an incomprehensible thing, but true, true—I fell in love with you the first time I saw your face. You remember, you stood there leaning over the bulwark when I came on board at Southampton, and as I walked up the gangway, I looked and my eyes met yours. Then I stopped, and that stout old lady who got off at Madeira bumped into me, and asked me to be good enough to make up my mind if I were going backward or forward. Do you remember?"

"Yes," she answered in a low voice.

"Which things are an allegory," he continued. "I felt it so at the time. Yes, I had half a mind to answer 'Backward' and give up my berth in this ship. Then I looked at you again, and something inside of me said 'Forward.' So I came up the rest of the gangway and took off my hat to you, a salutation I had no right to make, but which, I recall, you acknowledged."

He paused, then continued: "As it began, so it has gone on. It is always like that, is it not? The beginning is everything, the end must follow. And now it has come out, as I was fully determined that it should not do half an hour ago, when suddenly you developed eyes in the back of your head, and—oh! dearest, I love you. No, please be quiet; I have not done. I have told you what I am, and really there isn't much more to say about me, for I have no particular vices except the worst of them all, idleness, and not the slightest trace of any virtue that I can discover. But I have a certain knowledge of the world acquired in a long course of shooting parties, and as a man of the world I will venture to give you a bit of advice. It is possible that to you my life and death affair is a mere matter of board-ship amusement. Yet it is possible also that you might take another view of the matter. In that case, as a friend and a man of the world, I entreat you—don't. Have nothing to do with me. Send me about my business; you will never regret it."

"Are you making fun, or is all this meant, Mr. Seymour?" asked Benita, still speaking beneath her breath, and looking straight before her.

"Meant? Of course it is meant. How can you ask?"

"Because I have always understood that on such occasions people wish to make the best of themselves."

"Quite so, but I never do what I ought, a fact for which I am grateful now that I come to think of it, since otherwise I should not be here to-night. I wish to make the worst of myself, the very worst, for whatever I am not, at least I am honest. Now having told you that I am, or was half an hour ago, an idler, a good-for-nothing, prospectless failure, I ask you—if you care to hear any more?"

She half rose, and, glancing at him for the first time, saw his face contract itself and turn pale in the moonlight. It may be that the sight of it affected her, even to the extent of removing some adverse impression left by the bitter mocking of his self-blame. At any rate, Benita seemed to change her mind, and sat down again, saying:

"Go on, if you wish."

He bowed slightly and said:

"I thank you. I have told you what I *was* half an hour ago; now, hoping that you will believe me, I will tell you what I *am*. I am a truly repentant man, one upon whom a new light has risen. I am not very old, and I think that underneath it all I have some ability. Opportunity may still come my way; if it does not, for your sake I will make the opportunity. I do not believe that you can ever find anyone who would love you better or care for you more tenderly. I desire to live for you in the future, more completely even than in the past I have lived for myself. I do not wish to influence you by personal appeals, but in fact I stand at the parting of the ways. If you will give yourself to me I feel as though I might still become a husband of whom you could be proud—if not, I write 'Finis' upon the tombstone of the possibilities of Robert Seymour. I adore you. You are the one woman with whom I desire to pass my days; it is you who have always been lacking to my life. I ask you to be brave, to take the risk of marrying me, although I can see nothing but poverty ahead of us, for I am an adventurer."

"Don't speak like that," she said quickly. "We are all of us adventurers in this world, and I more than you. We have just to consider ourselves, not what we have or have not."

"So be it, Miss Clifford. Then I have nothing more to say; now it is for you to answer."

Just then the sound of the piano and the fiddle in the saloon ceased. One of the waltzes was over, and some of the dancers came upon deck to flirt or to cool themselves. One pair, engaged very obviously in the former occupation, stationed themselves so near to Robert and Benita that further conversation between them was impossible, and there proceeded to interchange the remarks common to such occasions.

For a good ten minutes did they stand thus, carrying on a mock quarrel as to a dance of which one of them was supposed to have been defrauded, until Robert Seymour, generally a very philosophical person, could have slain those innocent lovers. He felt, he knew not why, that his chances were slipping away from him; that sensation of something bad about to happen, of which Benita had spoken, spread from her to him. The suspense grew exasperating, terrible even, nor could it be ended. To ask her to come elsewhere was under the circumstances not feasible, especially as he would also have been obliged to request the other pair to make way for them. And all this time, with a sinking of the heart, he felt that probably Benita was beating down any tenderness which she might feel towards him; that when her long-delayed answer did come the chances were it would be "No."

The piano began to play again in the saloon, and the young people, still squabbling archly, at length prepared to depart. Suddenly there was a stir upon the bridge, and against the tender sky Robert saw a man dash forward. Next instant the engine-room bell rang fiercely. He knew the signal—it was "Stop," followed at once by other ringings that meant "Full speed astern."

"I wonder what is up?" said the young man to the young woman.

Before the words had left his lips they knew. There was a sensation as though all the hull of the great ship had come to a complete standstill, while the top part of her continued to travel forward; followed by another sensation still more terrible and sickening in its nature—that of slipping over something, helplessly, heavily, as a man slips upon ice or a polished floor. Spars cracked, ropes flew in two with a noise as of pistol shots. Heavy objects rushed about the deck, travelling forwards all of them. Benita was hurled from her chair against Robert so that the two of them rolled into the scuppers. He was unhurt and picked himself up, but she lay still, and he saw that something had struck her upon the head, for blood was running down her cheek. He lifted her and, filled with black horror and despair—for he thought her gone—pressed his hand upon her heart. Thank God! it began to beat again—she still lived.

The music in the saloon had stopped, and for a little while there was silence. Then of an instant there arose the horrible clamour of shipwreck; wild-eyed people rushed to and fro aimlessly; here and there women and children shrieked; a clergyman fell upon his knees and began to pray.

This went on for a space, till presently the second officer appeared and, affecting an unconcerned air, called out that it was all right, the captain said no one was to be afraid. He added that they were not more than six miles from the shore, and that the ship would be beached in half an hour. Indeed, as he spoke the engines, which had been stopped, commenced to work again, and her head swung round in a wide circle, pointing to the land. Evidently they had passed over the rock and were once more in deep water, through which they travelled at a good speed but with a heavy list to starboard. The pumps got to work also with a monotonous, clanging beat, throwing out great columns of foaming water on to the oily sea. Men began to cut the covers off the boats, and to swing some of them outboard. Such were the things that went on about them.

With the senseless Benita clasped to his breast, the blood from her cut head running down his shoulder, Robert stood still awhile, thinking. Then he made up his mind. As it chanced, she had a deck cabin and thither he forced his way, carrying her tenderly and with patience through the distracted throng of passengers, for there were five hundred souls on board that ship. He reached the place to find that it was quite empty, her cabin-mate having fled. Laying Benita upon the lower bunk, he lit the swinging candle. As soon as it burned up he searched for the lifebelts and by good fortune found two of them, one of which, not without great difficulty, he succeeded in fastening round her. Then he took a sponge and bathed her head with water. There was a great bruise upon her temple where the block or whatever it was had struck her, and the blood still flowed, but the wound was not very deep or extensive, nor, so far as he could discover, did the bone appear to be broken or driven in. He had good hope that she was only stunned, and would revive presently. Unable to do more for her, a thought struck him. On the floor of the cabin, thrown by the shock from the rack, lay her writing case. He opened it, and taking a piece of paper wrote these words hurriedly in pencil :

"You gave me no answer, and it is more than probable that I shall receive none in this world which one or both of us may be upon the verge of leaving. In the latter case we can settle the matter elsewhere—perhaps. In the former, should it be my lot to go and yours to stay, I hope that you will think kindly of me at times as of one who loved you truly. Should it be yours to go, then you will never read these words. Yet if to the dead is given knowledge, be assured that as you left me so you shall find me, yours and yours alone. Or perhaps we both may live ; I pray so.—S. R. S."

Folding up the paper, he undid a button of Benita's blouse and thrust it away there, knowing that thus she would certainly find it should she survive. Then he stepped out on to the deck to see what was happening. The vessel still steamed, but made slow progress ; moreover, the list to starboard was now so pronounced that it was difficult to stand upright. On account of it nearly all the passengers were huddled together upon the port side, having instinctively taken refuge as far as possible above the water. A man with a white, distraught face staggered towards him, supporting himself by the bulwarks. It was the captain. For a moment he paused as though to think, holding to a stanchion. Robert Seymour saw his opportunity and addressed him.

"Forgive me," he said, " I do not like interfering with other people's business, but for reasons unconnected with myself I suggest to you that it would be wise to stop this ship and get out the boats. The sea is calm; if it is not left till too late there should be no difficulty in launching them."

The man stared at him absently, then said :

"They won't hold everybody, Mr. Seymour. I hope to beach her."

"At least they will hold some," he answered, " whereas—" and he pointed to the water, which by now was almost level with the deck.

"Perhaps you are right, Mr. Seymour. It doesn't matter to me, any way. I am a ruined man ; but the poor passengers ! the poor passengers !" and he scrambled away fiercely towards the bridge like a wounded cat along the bough of a tree, whence in a few seconds Robert heard him shouting orders.

A minute or so afterwards the steamer stopped. Too late the captain had decided to sacrifice his ship and save those she carried. They were beginning to get out the boats. Now Robert returned to the cabin where Benita was still lying senseless, and wrapped her up in a cloak and some blankets. Then, seeing the second lifebelt on the floor, by an afterthought he put it on, knowing that there was time to spare. Next he lifted Benita, and feeling sure that the rush would be for the starboard side, on which the boats were quite near the water, carried her, with difficulty, for the slope was steep, to the port-cutter, which he knew would be in the charge of a good man, the second officer, whom he had seen in command there at Sunday boat-drills.

Here, as he had anticipated, the crowd was small, since most people thought that it would not be possible to get this boat down safely to the water; or if their powers of reflection were gone, instinct told them so. That skilful seaman, the second officer, and his appointed crew, however, were already at work lowering the cutter from the davits.

"Now," he said, "women and children first."

A number rushed in, and Robert saw that the boat would soon be full.

"I am afraid," he said, "that I must count myself a woman as I carry one," and by a great effort, holding Benita with one arm, with the other he let himself down the falls and, assisted by a quartermaster, gained the boat in safety.

One or two other men scrambled after him.

"Push her off," said the officer; "she can hold no more," and the ropes were let go.

When they were about twelve feet from the ship's side, from which they thrust themselves clear with oars, there came a rush of people, disappointed of places in the starboard boats. A few of the boldest of these swarmed down the falls, others jumped and fell among them, or missed and dropped into the sea, or struck upon the sides of the boat and were killed. Still she reached the water upon an even keel, though now much overladen. The oars were got out, and they rowed round the bow of the great ship wallowing in her death-throes, their first idea being to make for the shore, which was not three miles away.

This brought them to the starboard side, where they saw a hideous scene. Hundreds of people seemed to be fighting for room, with the result that some of the boats were overturned, precipitating their occupants into the water. Others hung by the prow or the stern, the ropes having jammed in the davits in the frantic haste and confusion, while from them human beings dropped one by one. Round others not yet launched a hellish struggle was in progress, the struggle of men, women, and children battling for their lives, in which the strong, mad with terror, showed no mercy to the weak.

From that mass of humanity, most of them about to perish, went up a babel of sounds which in its sum shaped itself to one prolonged scream, such as might proceed from a Titan in his agony. All this beneath a brooding, moonlit sky, and on a sea as smooth as glass. Upon the ship itself, which now lay upon her side, the siren still sent up its yells for succour, and some brave man continued to fire rockets, which rushed heavenwards and burst in showers of stars.

Robert remembered that the last rocket he had seen was fired at an evening *fête* for the amusement of the audience. The contrast struck him as dreadful. He wondered whether there were any power or infernal population that could be amused by a tragedy such as enacted itself before his eyes; how it came about also that such a tragedy was permitted by the merciful Strength in which mankind put their faith.

The vessel was turning over, compressed air or steam burst up the decks with loud reports; fragments of wreckage flew into the air. There the poor captain still clung to the rail of the bridge. Seymour could see his white face—the moonlight seemed to paint it with a ghastly smile. The officer in command of their boat shouted to the crew to give way lest they should be sucked down with the steamer.

Look! now she wallowed like a dying whale, the moonrays shone white upon her bottom, showing the jagged rent made in it by the rock on which she struck, and now she was gone. Only a little cloud of smoke and steam remained to mark where the *Zanzibar* had been.

CHAPTER III.

HOW ROBERT CAME ASHORE.

IN place of the *Zanzibar* a great pit on the face of the ocean, in which the waters boiled and black objects appeared and disappeared.

"Sit still, for your lives' sake," said the officer in a quiet voice; "the suck is coming."

In another minute it came, dragging them downward till the water trickled over the sides of the boat, and backward towards the pit. But before ever they reached it the deep had digested its prey and, save for the great air-bubbles which burst about them and a mixed, unnatural swell, was calm again. For the moment they were safe.

"Passengers," said the officer, "I am going to put out to sea, at any rate, till daylight. We may meet a vessel there, and if we try to row ashore we shall certainly be swamped in the breakers."

No one objected; they seemed too stunned to speak, but Robert thought to himself that the man was wise. They began to move, but before they had gone a dozen yards something dark rose beside them. It was a piece of wreckage, and clinging to it a woman, who clasped a bundle to her breast. More, she was alive, for she began to cry to them to take her in.

"Save me and my child!" she cried. "For God's sake save me!"

Robert recognised the choking voice; it was that of a young married lady with whom he had been very friendly, who was going out with her baby to join her husband in Natal. He stretched out his hand and caught hold of her, whereon the officer said heavily:

"The boat is already overladen. I must warn you that to take more aboard is not safe."

Thereon the passengers awoke from their stupor.

"Push her off," said a voice; "she must take her chance," and there was a murmur of approval at the dreadful words.

"For Christ's sake, for Christ's sake!" wailed the drowning woman, who clung desperately to Robert's hand.

"If you try to pull her in, we will throw you overboard," said the voice again, and a knife was lifted as though to hack at his arm. Then the officer spoke once more.

"This lady cannot come into the boat unless someone goes out of it. I would myself, but it is my duty to stay. Is there any man here who will make place for her?"

But all the men there—seven of them, besides the crew—hung their heads and were silent.

"Give way," said the officer in the same heavy voice; "she will drop off presently."

While the words passed his lips Robert seemed to live a year. Here was an opportunity of atonement for his idle and luxurious life. An hour ago he would have taken it gladly, but now—now, with Benita senseless on his breast, and that answer still locked in her sleeping heart? Yet Benita would approve of such a death as this, and even if she loved him not in life, would learn to love his memory. In an instant his mind was made up, and he was speaking rapidly.

"Thompson," he said to the officer, "if I go, will you swear to take her in and her child?"

"Certainly, Mr. Seymour."

"Then lay to; I am going. If any of you live, tell this lady how I died," and he pointed to Benita, "and say I thought that she would wish it."

"She shall be told," said the officer again, "and saved, too, if I can do it."

"Hold Mrs. Jeffreys, then, till I am out of this. I'll leave my coat to cover her."

A sailor obeyed, and with difficulty Robert wrenched free his hand.

Very deliberately he pressed Benita to his breast and kissed her on the forehead, then let her gently slide on to the bottom of the boat. Next he slipped off his overcoat and slowly rolled himself over the gunwale into the sea.

"Now," he said, "pull Mrs. Jeffreys in."

With some difficulty it was done, and he saw her and her child sink swooning into the place that he had left.

"God bless you; you are a brave man," said Thompson. "I shall remember you if I live a hundred years."

But no one else said anything; perhaps they were all too much ashamed, even then.

"I have only done my duty," Seymour answered from the water. "How far is it to the shore?"

"About three miles," shouted Thompson; "but keep on that plank or you will never live through the rollers. Good-bye."

"Good-bye," answered Robert.

Then the boat passed away from him and soon vanished on the misty face of the deep.

Resting on the plank which had saved the life of Mrs. Jeffreys, Robert Seymour

"'I SHALL REMEMBER YOU IF I LIVE A HUNDRED YEARS'"

looked about him and listened. Now and again he heard a faint, choking scream uttered by some drowning wretch, and a few hundred yards away caught sight of a black object which he thought might be a boat. If so, he reflected that it must be full. Moreover, he could not overtake it. No; his only chance was to make for the shore. He was a strong swimmer, and happily the water was almost as warm as milk. There seemed to be no reason why he should not reach it, supported as he was by a lifebelt, if the sharks would leave him alone, which they might as there was plenty for them to feed on. The direction he knew well enough, for now in the great silence of the sea he could hear the boom of the mighty rollers breaking on the beach.

Ah, those rollers! He remembered how that very afternoon Benita and he had watched them through his field glass spouting up against the cruel walls of rock, and wondered that when the ocean was so calm they had still such power. Now, should he live to reach them, he was doomed to match himself against that power. Well, the sooner he did so the sooner it would be over, one way or the other. This was in his favour: The tide had turned and was flowing shorewards. Indeed, he had little to do but to rest upon his plank, which he placed crosswise beneath his breast, and steer himself with his feet. Even thus he made good progress, nearly a mile an hour perhaps. He could have gone faster had he swum, but he was saving his strength.

It was a strange journey upon that silent sea beneath those silent stars, and strange thoughts came into Robert's soul. He wondered whether Benita would live and what she would say. Perhaps, however, she was already dead and he would meet her presently. He wondered if he were doomed to die, and whether this sacrifice of his would be allowed to atone for his past errors. He hoped so, and put up a petition to that effect, for himself and for Benita, and for all the poor people who had gone before, hurled from their pleasure into the halls of Death.

So he floated on while the boom of the breakers grew ever nearer, companioned by his wild, fitful thoughts, till at length what he took to be a shark appeared quite close to him, and in the urgency of the moment he gave up wondering. It proved to be only a piece of wood, but later on a real shark did come, for he saw its back fin. However, this cruel creature was either gorged or timid, for when he splashed upon the water and shouted, it went away, to return no more.

Now, at length, Robert entered upon the deep hill and valley swell which preceded the field of the rollers. Suddenly he shot down a smooth slope, and without effort of his own found himself borne up an opposing steep, from the crest of which he had a view of white lines of foam, and beyond them of a dim and rocky shore. At one spot, a little to his right, the foam seemed thinner and the line of cliff to be broken, as though here there was a cleft. For this cleft, then, he steered his plank, taking the swell obliquely, which by good fortune the set of the tide enabled him to do without any great exertion.

The valleys grew deeper, and the tops of the opposing ridges were crested with foam. He had entered the rollers, and the struggle for life began. Before him they rushed solemn and mighty. Viewed from some safe place even the sight of these combers is terrible, as any who have watched them from this coast, or from that of the Island of Ascension, can bear witness. What their aspect was to this shipwrecked man, supported by a single plank, may therefore be imagined, seen, as he saw them, in the mysterious moonlight and in utter loneliness. Yet his spirit rose to meet the dread emergency; if he were to die, he would die fighting. He had grown cold and tired, but now the chill and weariness left him; he felt warm and strong. From the crest of one of the high rollers he thought he saw that about half a mile away from him a little river ran down the centre of the gorge, and for the mouth of this river he laid his course.

At first all went well. He was borne up the seas; he slid down the seas in a lather of white foam. Presently the rise and fall grew steeper, and the foam began to break over his head. Robert could no longer guide himself; he must go as he was carried. Then in an instant he entered into a hell of waters where, had it not been for his lifebelt and the plank, he must have been beaten down and have perished. As it was, now he was driven into the depths, and now he emerged upon their surface to hear their seething hiss around him, and above it all a continuous boom as of great guns—the boom of the breaking seas.

The plank was almost twisted from his grasp, but he clung to it desperately, although its edges tore his arms. When the rollers broke over him he held his breath, and when he was tossed skywards on their curves, drew it again in quick, sweet gasps. Now he sat upon the very brow of one of them as a merman might; now he dived like a dolphin, and now, just as his senses were leaving him, his feet touched bottom. Another moment and Robert was being rolled along that bottom with a weight on him like the weight of mountains. The plank was rent from him, but his cork jacket brought him up. The backwash drew him with it into deeper water, where he lay helpless and despairing, for he no longer had any strength to struggle against his doom.

Then it was that there came a mighty roller, bigger than any that he had seen —such a one as on that coast the Kaffirs call "a father of waves." It caught him in the embrace of its vast green curve. It bore him forward as though he were but a straw, far forward over the stretch of cruel rocks. It broke in thunder, dashing him again upon the stones and sand of the little river bar, rolling him along with its resistless might, till even that might was exhausted and its foam began to return seawards, sucking him with it.

Robert's mind was almost gone, but enough of it remained to tell him that if once more he was dragged into the deep water he must be lost. As the current haled him along he gripped at the bottom with his hands, and by the mercy of Heaven they closed on something. It may have been a tree-stump embedded there, or a rock—he never knew. At least, it was firm, and to it he hung despairingly. Would that rush never go by? His lungs were bursting; he must let go! Oh! the foam was thinning; his head was above it; now it had departed, leaving him like a stranded fish upon the shingle. For half a minute or more he lay there gasping, then looked behind him to see another comber approaching through the gloom. He struggled to his feet, fell, rose again, and ran, or rather staggered forward with that tigerish water hissing at his heels. Forward, still forward, till he was beyond its reach—yes, on dry sand. Then his vital forces failed him; one of his legs gave way, and, bleeding from a hundred hurts, he fell heavily on to his face and there was still.

The boat in which Benita lay, being so deep in the water, proved very hard to row against the tide, for the number of its passengers encumbered the oarsmen. After a while a light off-land breeze sprang up, as here it often does towards morning; and the officer, Thompson, determined to risk hoisting the sail. Accordingly this was done—with some difficulty, for the mast had to be drawn out and shipped— although the women screamed as the weight of the air bent their frail craft over till the gunwale was almost level with the water.

"Anyone who moves shall be thrown overboard!" said the officer, who steered, after which they were quiet.

Now they made good progress seawards, but the anxieties of those who knew were very great, since the wind showed signs of rising, and if any swell should spring up that crowded cutter could scarcely hope to live. In fact, two hours later they were forced to lower the sail again and drift, waiting for the dawn. Mr. Thompson strove to cheer them, saying that now they were in the track of vessels, and if they could see none when the light came, he would run along the shore in the hope of finding a place free of breakers where they might land. If they did not inspire hope, at least his words calmed them, and they sat in heavy silence, watching the sky.

At length it grew grey, and then, with a sudden glory peculiar to South Africa, the great red sun arose and began to dispel the mist from the surface of the sea. Half an hour more and this was gone, and now the bright rays brought life back into their chilled frames as they stared at each other to see which of their company were still left alive. They even asked for food, and biscuit was given to them with water.

All this while Benita remained unconscious. Indeed, one callous fellow, who had been using her body as a footstool, said that she must be dead, and had better be thrown overboard, as it would lighten the boat.

" If you throw that lady into the sea, living or dead," said Mr. Thompson, with an ominous lift of his eye, " you go with her, Mr. Batten. Remember who brought her here and how he died."

Then Mr. Batten held his peace, while Thompson stood up and scanned the wide expanse of sea. Presently he whispered to a sailor near him, who also stood up, looked, and nodded.

" That will be the other Line's intermediate boat," he said, and the passengers, craning their heads round, saw far away to the right a streak of smoke upon the horizon. Orders were given, a little corner of sail was hoisted, with a white cloth of some sort tied above it, and the oars were got out. Once more the cutter moved forward, bearing to the left in the hope of intercepting the steamer.

She came on with terrible swiftness, and they who had miles of water to cover, dared hoist no more sail in that breeze. In half an hour she was nearly opposite to them, and they were still far away. A little more sail was let out, driving them through the water at as quick a rate as they could venture to go. The steamer was passing three miles or so away, and black despair took hold of them. Now the resourceful Thompson, without apologies, undressed, and removing the white shirt that he had worn at the dance, bade a sailor tie it to an oar and wave it to and fro.

Still the steamer went on, until presently they heard her siren going, and saw that she was putting about.

" She has seen us," said Thompson. " Thank God, all of you, for there is wind coming up. Pull down that sail ; we shan't need it any more."

Half an hour later, with many precautions, for the wind he prophesied was already troubling the sea and sending little splashes of water over the stern of their deeply laden boat, they were fast to a line thrown from the deck of the three thousand ton steamer Castle, bound for Natal. Then, with a rattle, down came the accommodation ladder, and strong-armed men, standing on its grating, dragged them one by one from the death to which they had been so near. The last to be lifted up, except Thompson, was Benita, round whom it was necessary to reeve a rope.

" Any use ? " asked the officer on the grating as he glanced at her quiet form.

" Can't say ; I hope so," answered Thompson. " Call your doctor " ; and gently enough she was borne up the ship's side.

They wanted to cast off the boat, but Thompson remonstrated, and in the end that also was dragged to deck. Meanwhile the news had spread, and the awakened passengers of the Castle, clad in pyjamas, dressing-gowns, and even blankets, were crowding round the poor castaways or helping them to their cabins.

" I am a teetotaller," said second officer Thompson when he had made a brief report to the captain of the Castle, " but if anyone will stand me a whiskey and soda I shall be obliged to him."

CHAPTER IV.

MR. CLIFFORD.

ALTHOUGH the shock of the blow she had received upon her head was sufficient to make her insensible for so many hours, Benita's injuries were not of a really serious nature, for as it happened the falling block, or whatever it may have been, had hit her forehead slantwise, and not full, to which accident she owed it that, although the skin was torn and the scalp bruised, her skull had escaped fracture. Under proper medical care her senses soon came back to her, but as she was quite dazed and thought herself still on board the Zanzibar, the doctor considered it wise to preserve her in that illusion for a while. So after she had swallowed some broth he gave her a sleeping draught, the effects of which she did not shake off till the following morning.

Then she came to herself completely, and was astonished to feel the pain in her head, which had been bandaged, and to see a strange stewardess sitting by her with a cup of beef-tea in her hand.

" Where am I ? Is it a dream ? " she asked.

" Drink this and I will tell you," answered the stewardess.

Benita obeyed, for she felt hungry, then repeated her question.

" Your steamer was shipwrecked," said the stewardess, " and a great many poor people were drowned, but you were saved in a boat. Look, there are your clothes ; they were never in the water."

" Who carried me into the boat ? " asked Benita in a low voice.

" A gentleman, they say, Miss, who had wrapped you in a blanket and put a lifebelt on you."

Now Benita remembered everything that happened before the darkness fell—the question to which she had given no answer, the young couple who stood flirting by her—all came back to her.

" Was Mr. Seymour saved ? " she whispered, her face grey with dread.

" I dare say, Miss," answered the stewardess evasively. " But there is no gentleman of that name aboard this ship."

At that moment the doctor came in, and him, too, she plied with questions. But having learned the story of Robert's self-sacrifice from Mr. Thompson and others, he would give her no answer, for he guessed how matters had stood between them, and feared the effects of the shock. All he could say was that he hoped Mr. Seymour had escaped in some other boat.

It was not until the third morning that Benita was allowed to learn the truth, which indeed it was impossible to conceal any longer. Mr. Thompson came to her cabin and told her everything, while she listened silently, horrified, amazed.

" Miss Clifford," he said, " I think it was one of the bravest things that a man ever did. On the ship I always thought him rather a head-in-air kind of swell, but he was a splendid fellow, and I pray God that he has lived, as the lady and child for whom he offered himself up have done, for they are both well again."

" Yes," she repeated after him mechanically, " splendid fellow indeed, and," she added with a strange flash of conviction, " I believe that he *is* still alive. If he were dead I should know it."

" I am glad to hear you say so," said Mr. Thompson, who believed the exact contrary.

" Listen," she went on, " I will tell you something. When that dreadful accident occurred Mr. Seymour had just asked me to marry him, and I was going to answer that I would—because I love him. I believe that I shall still give him that answer."

Mr. Thompson replied again that he hoped so, which, being as honest and tender-hearted as he was brave and capable, he did most earnestly ; but in his heart he reflected that her answer would not be given this side of the grave. Then, as he had been deputed to do, he handed her the note which had been found in the bosom of her dress and, able to bear no more of this painful scene, hurried from the cabin. She read it greedily twice, and pressed it to her lips, murmuring :

" Yes, I will think kindly of you, Robert Seymour, kindly as woman can of man, and now or afterwards you shall have your answer, if you still wish for it. Whenever you come or wherever I go, it shall be ready for you."

That afternoon, when she was more composed, Mrs. Jeffreys came to see Benita, bringing her baby with her. The poor woman was still pale and shaken, but the child had taken no hurt at all from its immersion in that warm water.

" What can you think of me ? " she said, falling on her knees by Benita. " But oh ! I did not know what I was doing. It was terror and my child," and she kissed the sleeping infant passionately. " Also I did not understand at the time—I was too dazed. And—that hero—he gave his life for me when the others wished to beat me off with oars. Yes, his blood is upon my hands, he who died that I and my child might live."

Benita looked at her and answered very gently :

" Perhaps he did not die after all. Do not grieve, for if he did it was a very glorious death, and I am prouder of him than I could have been had he lived on like the others—who wished to beat you off with oars. Whatever is, is by God's Will, and doubtless for the best. At the least you and your child will be restored to your husband, though it cost me one who would have been—my husband."

"ITS FOAM BEGAN TO RETURN SEAWARDS, SUCKING HIM WITH IT"

That evening Benita came upon the deck and spoke with the other ladies who were saved, learning every detail that she could gather. But to none of the men, except to Mr. Thompson, would she say a single word, and soon, seeing how the matter stood, they hid themselves away from her as they had already done from Mrs. Jeffreys.

The *Castle* had hung about the scene of the shipwreck for thirty hours, and rescued one other boatload of survivors, also a stoker clinging to a piece of wreckage. But with the shore she had been unable to communicate, for the dreaded wind had risen, and the breakers were quite impassable to any boat. To a passing steamer bound for Port Elizabeth, however, she had reported the terrible disaster, which by now was known all over the world, together with the names of those whom she had picked up in the boats.

On the night of the day of Benita's interview with Mrs. Jeffreys, the *Castle* arrived off Durban and anchored, since she was too big a vessel to cross the bar as it was in those days. At dawn the stewardess awoke Benita from the uneasy sleep in which she lay, to tell her that an old gentleman had come off in the tug and wished to see her; for fear of exciting false hopes she was very careful to add that word "old." With her help Benita dressed herself, and as the sun rose, flooding the Berea, the Point, the white town and fair Natal beyond with light, she went on to the deck and there, leaning over the bulwark, saw a thin, grey-bearded man of whom after all these years the aspect was still familiar.

A curious thrill went through her as she looked at him leaning there lost in thought. After all, he was her father, the man to whom she owed her presence upon this bitter earth, this place of terrors and delights, of devastation and hope supernal. Perhaps, too, he had been as much sinned against as sinning. She stepped up to him and touched him on the shoulder.

"Father," she said.

He turned round with all the quickness of a young man, for about him there was a peculiar agility which his daughter had inherited. Like his mind, his body was still nimble.

"My darling," he said, "I should have known your voice anywhere. It has haunted my sleep for years. My darling, thank you for coming back to me, and thank God for preserving you when so many were lost"; then he threw his arms about her and kissed her.

She shrank from him a little, for by inadvertence he had pressed upon the wound in her forehead.

"Forgive me," she said, "it is my head. It was injured, you know."

Then he saw the bandage about her brow, and was very penitent.

"They did not tell me that you had been hurt, Benita," he exclaimed in his light, refined voice, one of the stamps of that gentility of blood and breeding whereof all his rough years and errors had been unable to deprive him. "They only told me that you were saved. It is part of my ill-fortune that at our first moment of meeting I should give you pain, who have caused you so much already."

Benita felt that the words were an apology for the past, and her heart was touched.

"It is nothing," she answered. "You did not know or mean it."

"No, dear, I never knew or meant it. Believe me, I was not a willing sinner, only a weak one. You are a beautiful woman, Benita, far more so than I expected."

"What," she answered smiling, "with this bandage round my head? Well, in your eyes, perhaps." But inwardly she thought to herself that the description would be more applicable to her father, who in truth, notwithstanding his years, was wonderfully handsome, with his quick blue eyes, mobile face, gentle mouth with the wistful droop at the corners so like her own, and grey beard. How, she wondered, could this be the man who had struck her mother. Then she remembered him as he had been years before when he was a slave to liquor, and knew that the answer was simple.

"Tell me about your escape, love," he said, patting her hand with his thin fingers. "You don't know what I have suffered. I was waiting at the Royal Hotel here, when the cable came announcing the loss of the *Zanzibar* and all on board. For the first time for many a year I drank spirits to drown my grief—don't be afraid, dear, for the first time and the last. Then afterwards came another cable giving the names of those who were known to be saved, and—thank God, oh! thank God—yours among them," and he gasped at the recollection of that relief.

"Yes," she said, "I suppose I should thank—Him—and another. Have you heard the story about—how Mr. Seymour saved me, I mean?"

"Some of it. While you were dressing yourself, I have been talking to the officer who was in command of your boat. He was a brave man, Benita, and I am sorry I must tell you he is gone."

She grasped a stanchion and clung there, staring at him with a wild, white face.

"How do you know that, father?"

Mr. Clifford drew a copy of the *Natal Mercury* of the previous day from the pocket of his ulster, and while she waited in an agony he hunted through the long columns descriptive of the loss of the *Zanzibar*. Presently he came to the paragraph he sought, and read it aloud to her. It ran:

"The searchers on the coast opposite the scene of the shipwreck report that they met a Kaffir who was travelling along the seashore, who produced a gold watch which he said he had taken from the body of a white man that he found lying on the sand at the mouth of the Umvoli River. Inside the watch is engraved 'To Seymour Robert Seymour, from his uncle, on his twenty-first birthday.' The name of Mr. Seymour appears as a first-class passenger to Durban by the *Zanzibar*. He was a member of an old English family in Lincolnshire. This was his second journey to South Africa, which he visited some years ago with his brother upon a big-game shooting expedition. All who knew him then will join with us in deploring his loss. Mr. Seymour was a noted shot and an English gentleman of the best stamp. He was last seen by one of the survivors of the catastrophe, carrying Miss Clifford, the daughter of the well-known Natal pioneer of that name, into a boat, but as this young lady is reported to have been saved, and as he entered the boat with her, no explanation is yet forthcoming as to how he came to his sad end."

"I fear that is clear enough," said Mr. Clifford, as he folded up his paper.

"Yes, clear enough," she repeated in a strained voice. "And yet—yet—oh! father, he had just asked me to marry him, and I can't believe that he is dead before I had time to answer."

"Good Heavens!" said the old man, "they never told me that. It is dreadfully sad. God help you, my poor child. There is nothing more to say except that he was only one among three hundred who have gone with him. Be brave now, before all these people. Look, here comes the tug."

The following week was very much of a blank to Benita. When they reached shore some old friends of her father's took her and him to their house, a quiet place upon the Berea. Here, now that the first excitement of rescue and grief was over, the inevitable reaction set in, bringing with it weakness so distressing that the doctor insisted upon her going to bed, where she remained for the next five days. With the healing up of the wound in her head her strength came back to her at last, but it was a very sad Benita who crept from her room one afternoon on to the verandah and looked out at the cruel sea, peaceful now as the sky above.

Her father, who had nursed her tenderly during these dark days, came and sat by her, taking her hand in his.

"This is capital," he said, glancing at her anxiously. "You are getting quite yourself again."

"I shall never be myself again," she answered. "My old self is dead, although the outside of me has recovered. Father, I suppose that it is wrong, but I wish that I were dead too. I wish that he had taken me with him when he jumped into the sea to lighten the boat."

"Don't speak like that," he broke in hastily. "Of course I know that I am not much to you—how can I be after all that is past? But I love you, dear, and if I were left quite alone again——" and he broke off.

"You shall not be left alone if I can help it," she replied, looking at the old man with her dark and tender eyes. "We have only each other in the world now, have we? The rest have gone, never to return."

He threw his arms about her, and, drawing her to him, kissed her passionately.

"If only you could learn to love me," he said.

"I do love you," she answered, "who now shall never love any other man upon the earth."

This was the beginning of a deep affection which sprang up between Mr. Clifford and his daughter, and continued to the end.

"Is there any news?" she asked a little later.

"None, none about him. The tide took his body away, no doubt, after the Kaffir had gone. I remember him well now. He was a fine young man, and it comes into my mind that when I said good-bye to him up above those old ruins, I wished that I had a son like that. And to think that he went so near to becoming a son to me! Well, the grass must bend when the wind blows, as the natives say."

"I am glad that you knew him," she answered simply.

Then they began talking about other matters. He told her that all the story had become known, and that people spoke of Robert Seymour as "the hero"; also that there was a great deal of curiosity about her.

"Then let us get away as soon as we can," she said nervously. "But, father, where are we going?"

"That will be for you to decide, love. Listen now, this is my position. I have been quite steady for years, and worked hard, with the result that I and my partner have a fine farm in the Transvaal, on the high land near Lake Chrissie, out Wakkerstroom way. We breed horses there, and have done very well with them. I have £1,500 saved, and the farm brings us in quite £600 a year beyond the expenses. But it is a lonely place, with only a few Boers about, although they are good fellows enough. You might not care to live there with no company."

"I don't think that I should mind," she answered, smiling.

"Not now, but by-and-by you would when you know what it is like. Now I might sell my share in the farm to my partner, who, I think, would buy it, or I might trust to him to send me a part of the profits, which perhaps he would not. Then, if you wish it, we could live in or near one of the towns, or even, as you have an income of your own, go home to England, if that is your will."

"Is it your will?" she asked.

He shook his head. "No; all my life is here. Also, I have something to find before I die—for your sake, dear."

"Do you mean up among those ruins?" she asked, looking at him curiously.

"Yes. So you know about it," he answered, with a flash of his blue eyes. "Oh! of course, Seymour told you. Yes, I mean among the ruins—but I will tell you that story another time, not here, not here. What do you wish to do, Benita? Remember, I am in your hands; I will obey you in all things."

"Not to stop in a town and not to go to England," she replied, while he hung eagerly upon her words, "for this has become my holy land. Father, I will go with you to your farm; there I can be quiet, you and I together."

"Yes," he answered rather uneasily, "but you see, Benita, we shall not be quite alone there. My partner, Jacob Meyer, lives with me."

"Jacob Meyer? Ah! I remember," and she winced. "He is a German, is he not, and odd?"

"German Jew, I imagine, and very odd. Should have made his fortune a dozen times over, and yet has never done anything. Too unpractical, too visionary, with all his brains and scheming. Not a good man, Benita, although he suits me, and, for the matter of that, under our agreement I cannot get rid of him."

"How did he become your partner?" she asked.

"Oh! a good many years ago he turned up at the place with a doleful story. Said that he had been trading among the Zulus; he was what we call a 'smouse' out here, and got into a row with them, I don't know how. The end of it was that they burned his waggon, looted his trade-goods and oxen, and killed his servants. They would have

"AFTER ALL, HE WAS HER FATHER"

killed him too, only, according to his own account, he escaped in a very queer fashion."

" How ? "

" Well, he says by mesmerising the chief and making the man lead him through his followers. An odd story enough, but I can quite believe it of Jacob. He worked for me for six months, and showed himself very clever. Then one night, I remember it was a few days after I had told him the story of the Portuguese treasure in Matabeleland, he produced £500 in Bank of England notes out of the lining of his waistcoat, and offered to buy a half interest in the farm. Yes, £500! although for all those months I had believed him to be a beggar. Well, as he was so *slim*, and better than no company in that lonely place, in the end I accepted. We have done well since, except for the expedition after the treasure which we did not get, although we more than paid our expenses out of the ivory we bought. But next time we shall succeed, I am

sure," he added with enthusiasm, " that is, if we can persuade those Makalanga to let us search on the mountains."

Benita smiled.

" I think you had better stick to the horse-breeding," she said.

" You shall judge when you hear the story. But you have been brought up in England; will you not be afraid to go to Lake Chrissie ? "

" Afraid of what ? " she asked.

" Oh ! of the loneliness, and of Jacob Meyer."

" I was born on the veld, father, and I have always hated London. As for your odd friend, Mr. Meyer, I am not afraid of any man on earth. I have done with men. At the least I will try the place and see how I get on."

" Very well," answered her father with a sigh of relief. " You can always come back, can't you ? "

" Yes," she said indifferently. " I suppose that I can always come back."

"HE OFFERED TO BUY A HALF INTEREST IN THE FARM."

BENITA.

An African Romance by . . .
H. RIDER HAGGARD.

SYNOPSIS OF CHAPTERS I.—IV.

BENITA CLIFFORD, bound for Africa on board the steamer *Zanzibar* to join her father at Durban, meets Robert Seymour, who falls in love with her. Seymour tells how he met her father and Jacob Meyer at Bambatse, a place where it was supposed there was a big treasure hoard. He declares his love for Benita, but they are interrupted as she is about to answer. Soon afterwards the steamer strikes a rock, and all leave her. Seymour with great difficulty gets Benita into a boat, she being unconscious owing to a blow. He gives his place up to a woman who would otherwise perish, for the boat could hold no more. Before leaving the boat he leaves a letter, which he had written beforehand on the ship, asking for her answer in the event of their meeting again. He eventually reaches the shore in an exhausted condition. The boat is picked up by another steamer, and Benita joins her father eventually at Durban, where she hears from a newspaper report that a Kaffir took a watch inscribed with Seymour's name from a body on the shore some miles away.

CHAPTER V.

JACOB MEYER.

MORE than three weeks had gone by when one morning Benita, who slept upon the cartel or hide-strung bed in the waggon, having dressed herself as best she could in that confined place, thrust aside the curtain and seated herself upon the voorkisse, or driving-box. The sun was not yet up, and the air was cold with frost, for they were on the Transvaal high-veld at the end of winter. Even through her thick cloak Benita shivered and called to the driver of the waggon, who also acted as cook, and whose blanket-draped form she could see bending over a fire into which he was blowing life, to make haste with the coffee.

"By and by, Missie, by and by," he answered, coughing the rank smoke from his lungs. "Kettle no sing yet, and fire black as hell."

Benita reflected that popular report painted this locality red, but without entering into argument sat still upon the chest waiting till the water boiled, and her father appeared.

Presently he emerged from under the side flap of the waggon where he slept, and remarking that it was really too cold to think of washing, climbed to her side by help of the dissel-boom, and kissed her.

"How far are we now from Rooi Krantz, Father?" she asked, for that was the name of Mr. Clifford's farm.

"About forty miles, dear. The waggon cannot make it to-night with these two sick oxen, but after the midday outspan we will ride on, and be there by sundown. I am afraid you are tired of this trekking."

"No," she answered. "I like it very much, it is so restful, and I sleep sound upon that cartel. I feel as though I should like to trek on for the rest of my life."

"So you shall if you wish, dear, for whole months. South Africa is big, and when the grass grows, if you still wish it, we will take a long journey."

She smiled but made no answer, knowing that he was thinking of the place so far away where he believed that once the Portuguese had buried gold.

The kettle was singing now merrily enough, and Hans, the cook, lifting it from the fire in triumph, for his blowing exertions had been severe, poured into it a quantity of ground coffee from an old mustard tin. Then, having stirred the mixture with a stick, he took a red ember from the fire and dropped it into the kettle, a process which, as travellers in the veld know well, has a clearing effect upon the coffee. Next he produced pannikins, and handed them up with a pickle-jar full of sugar to Mr. Clifford, upon the waggon chest. Milk they had none, yet that coffee tasted a great deal better than it looked ; indeed Benita drank two cups of it to warm herself and wash down the hard biscuit. Before the day was over glad enough was she that she had done so.

The sun was rising ; huge and red it looked seen through the clinging mist, and, their breakfast finished, Mr. Clifford gave orders that the oxen which were filling themselves with the dry grass near at hand, should be got up and inspanned. The voorlooper, a Zulu boy, who had left them for a little while to share the rest of the coffee with Hans, rose from his haunches with a grunt, and departed to fetch them. A minute or two later Hans ceased from his occupation of packing up the things, and said in a low voice :

"*Kek!* Baas"—that is, "Look !"

Following the line of his outstretched hand Benita and her father perceived not more than a hundred yards away from them a great troop of wilderbeeste or gnu, travelling along a ridge, and pausing now and again to indulge in those extraordinary gambols which cause the Boers to declare that these brutes have a worm in their brains.

"Give me my rifle, Hans," said Mr. Clifford. "We want meat."

By the time that the Westley-Richards was drawn from its case and loaded, only one buck remained, for having caught sight of the waggon, it turned to stare at it suspiciously. Mr. Clifford aimed and fired. Down went the buck, then springing to its feet again vanished behind the ridge. Mr. Clifford shook his head sadly.

"I don't often do that sort of thing, my dear, but the light is still very bad. Still, he's hit. What do you say ? Shall we get on the horses and catch him ? A canter would warm you."

Benita, who was tender-hearted, reflected that it would be kinder to put the poor creature out of its pain, and nodded her head. Five minutes later, they were cantering together up the rise, Mr. Clifford having first ordered the waggon to trek on till they rejoined it, and slipped a packet of cartridges into his pocket. Beyond the rise lay a wide stretch of marshy ground, bordered by another rise half a mile or more away, from the crest of which—for now the air was clear enough —they saw the wounded bull standing. On they went after him, but before they could come within shot, he had moved forward once more, for he was only lightly hurt in the flank, and guessed whence his trouble came.

Again and again did he retreat as they drew near, until at length, just as Mr. Clifford was about to dismount to risk a long shot, the beast took to its heels in earnest.

"Come on," he said, "don't let's be beat," for by this time the hunter was alive in him.

So off they went at a gallop, up slopes and down slopes that reminded Benita of the Bay of Biscay in a storm, across half-dried vleis that in the wet season were ponds, through stony ground and patches of ant-bear holes in which they nearly came to grief. For five miles at least that chase went on, since at the end of winter the wilderbeeste was thin and could gallop well, notwithstanding its injury, faster even than their good horses. At last, rising a ridge, they found whither it was going, for suddenly they were in the midst of vast herds of game, thousands and tens of thousands of them stretching as far as the eye could reach.

It was a wondrous sight that now alas ! will be seen no more, at any rate upon the Transvaal veld ; wilderbeeste, blesbok, springbok, in countless multitudes, and amongst them a few quagga and hartebeeste. With a sound like that of thunder, their flashing myriad hoofs casting up clouds of dust from the fire-blackened veld, the great herds separated at the appearance of their enemy, man. This way and that they went in groups and long brown lines, leaving the wounded and exhausted wilderbeeste behind them, so that presently he was the sole tenant of that great cup of land.

At him they rode until Mr. Clifford, who was a little ahead of his daughter, drew almost alongside. Then the poor maddened brute tried its last shift. Stopping suddenly, it wheeled round and charged

" BENITA SAW JACOB MEYER FOR THE FIRST TIME "

head down. Mr. Clifford, as it came, held out his rifle in his right hand and fired at a hazard. The bullet passed through the bull, but could not stop its charge. Its horns held low, struck the forelegs of the horse, and next instant horse, man and wilderbeeste rolled on the veld together.

Benita, who was fifty yards behind, uttered a little cry of fear, but before ever she reached him, her father had risen laughing, for he was quite unhurt. The horse, too, was getting up, but the bull could rise no more. It struggled to its forefeet, uttered a kind of sobbing groan, stared round wildly, and rolled over, dead.

"I never knew a wilderbeeste charge like that before," said Mr. Clifford. "Confound it! I believe my horse is lamed."

Lamed it was, indeed, where the bull had struck the foreleg, though as it chanced, not badly. Having tied a handkerchief to the horn of the buck in order to scare away the vultures, and thrown some tufts of dry grass upon its body, which he proposed if possible to fetch or send for, Mr. Clifford mounted his lame horse and headed for the waggon. But they had galloped farther than they thought, and it was midday before they came to what they took to be the road. As there was no spoor upon it, they followed this track backwards, expecting to find the waggon outspanned, but although they rode for mile upon mile, no waggon could they see. Then realising their mistake, they retraced their steps, and leaving this path at the spot where they had found it, struck off again to the right.

Meanwhile, the sky was darkening, and at about three o'clock in the afternoon a thunderstorm broke over them accompanied by torrents of icy rain, the first fall of the spring, and a bitter wind which chilled them through. More, after the heavy rain came drizzle and a thick mist that deepened as evening approached.

Now their plight was very wretched. Lost, starved, soaked to the skin, with tired horses one of which was lame, they wandered about in the lonely veld. Only one stroke of fortune came to them. As the sun set for a few moments its rays pierced the mist, telling them in which direction they should go. Turning their horses they headed for it, and so rode on until the darkness fell. Then they halted a while, but feeling that if they stood still in that horrible cold, they would certainly perish before morning, once more pushed on again. By now Mr. Clifford's horse was almost too lame to ride, so he led it, walking at his daughter's side, and reproaching himself bitterly for his foolishness in having brought her into this trouble.

"It doesn't matter, Father," she answered wearily, for she was very tired; "nothing matters; one may as well die upon the veld as in the sea or anywhere else."

On they plodded, they knew not whither. Benita fell asleep upon her saddle, and was awakened once by a hyena howling quite close to them, and once by her horse falling to its knees.

"What is the time?" she said at last.

Her father struck a match and looked at his watch. It was ten o'clock; they had been fifteen hours away from the waggon and without food. At intervals Mr. Clifford, who had re-mounted, fired his rifle. Now there was but one cartridge left, and having caught sight of his daughter's exhausted face by the light of the match, he fired this also, though in that desperate wilderness there was little hope of its bringing succour.

"Shall we stop or go on?" he asked.

"I do not care," she answered. "Only if I stop I think it will be for ever. Let us go on."

Now the rain had ceased, but the mist was as dense as before. Also they seemed to have got among bush, for wet leaves brushed their faces. Utterly exhausted they stumbled forward, till suddenly Benita felt her horse stop as though a hand had seized its bridle, and heard a man's voice speaking with a foreign accent, say:

"Mein Gott! Where are you going?"

"I wish I knew," she answered like one in a dream.

At this instant the moon rose above the mists, and Benita saw Jacob Meyer for the first time.

In that light his appearance was not unpleasing. A man of about forty years of age, not over tall, slight and active in build with a pointed black beard, regular, Semitic features, a complexion of an ivory pallor which even the African sun did not seem to tan, and dark, lustrous eyes that appeared, now to sleep, and now to catch the fire of the thoughts within. Yet weary though she was, there was something in the man's personality which repelled and alarmed Benita, something wild and cruel. She felt that he was filled with unsatisfied ambitions and desires, and that to attain to them he would shrink at nothing. In a moment he was speaking again in tones that compelled her attention.

"It was a good thought that brought me here to look for you—no, not a thought—what do you call it?—an instinct. I think your mind must have spoken to my mind, and called me to save you. See now, Clifford, my friend, where you have led your daughter; see, see!" and he pointed downwards.

They leant forward and stared. There immediately beneath them was a mighty gulf whereof the moonlight did not reveal the bottom.

"You are no good veld traveller, Clifford, my friend; one more step of those silly beasts and down below there would have been two red heaps with bits of bones sticking out of them; yes, there on the rocks five hundred feet beneath. Ah! you would have slept soundly to-night, both of you."

"What is the place?" asked Mr. Clifford in a dazed fashion. "Leopard's Kloof?"

"Yes, Leopard's Kloof, no other. You have travelled along the top of the hill, not at the bottom. Certainly that was a good thought which came to me from the lady your daughter, for she is one of the thought-senders, I am sure. Ah! it came to me suddenly, it hit me like a stick whilst I was searching for you, having found that you had lost the waggon. It said to me—'Ride to the top of Leopard's Kloof. Ride hard.' I rode hard through the rocks and the darkness, through the mist and the rain, and not one minute had I been here when you came and I caught the lady's bridle."

"I am sure we are very grateful to you," murmured Benita.

"Then I am paid back ten thousand times. No, it is I who am grateful, I who have saved your life through the thought you sent me."

"Thought or no thought, all's well that ends well," broke in Mr. Clifford impatiently, "and thank heaven we are not more than three miles from home. Will you lead the way, Jacob? You always could see in the dark."

"Yes, yes," and he took hold of Benita's bridle with his firm, white hand. "Oh! my horse will follow, or put your arm through his rein, so. Now come on, Miss Clifford, and be afraid no more. With Jacob Meyer you are safe."

So they began their descent of the hill. Meyer did not speak again; all his attention seemed to be concentrated upon finding a safe path on which the horses would not stumble. Nor did Benita speak; she was too utterly exhausted—so exhausted, indeed, that she could no longer control her mind and imagination. These seemed to loose themselves from her and to acquire new powers, notably that of entering into the secret thoughts of the man at her side. She saw them pass before her like living things, and yet she could not read them. Still, something she did understand—that she had suddenly grown important to this man, not in the way in which women are generally important to men, but otherwise. She felt as though she had become interwoven with the objects of his life, and was henceforth necessary to their fulfilment, as though she were someone whom he had been seeking for years on years, the one person who could give him light in his darkness.

These imaginings troubled her so that she was very thankful when they passed away as swiftly as they had arisen, and she knew only that she was half dead with weariness and cold; that her limbs ached and that the steep path seemed endless.

At length they reached level ground, and after travelling along it for a while and crossing the bed of a stream, passed through a gate and stopped suddenly at the door of a house with lighted windows.

"Here is your home at last, Miss Clifford," said the musical voice of Jacob Meyer, "and I thank the Fate which rules us that it has taught me to bring you to it safely."

Making no answer she slid from the saddle, only to find that she could not stand, for she sank into a heap upon the ground. With a gentle exclamation he lifted her, and calling to two Kaffirs who had appeared to take the horses, led her into the house.

"You must go to bed at once," he said, conducting her to a door which opened out of the sitting-room. "I have had a fire lit in your chamber in case you should come, and old Tante Sally will bring you soup with brandy in it, and hot water for your feet. Ah! there you are, old vrouw; come now, help the lady, your mistress. Is all ready?"

"All, Baas," answered the woman, a stout half-breed with a kindly face. "Come now, my little one, and I will undress you."

Half an hour later Benita, having drunk more brandy than ever she had done in her life before, was wrapped up and fast asleep.

When she awoke the sun was streaming through the curtained window of her room, and by the light of it she saw that the clock which stood upon the mantel-piece pointed to half-past eleven. She had slept for nearly twelve hours, and felt that notwithstanding the cold and exposure, save for stiffness and a certain numb feeling in her head, the result, perhaps, of the unaccustomed brandy, she was well and what was more, quite hungry.

" THEN SUDDENLY HURLED HERSELF INTO THE RIVER "

Outside on the verandah she heard the voice of Jacob Meyer, with which she seemed already to have become familiar, telling some natives to stop singing as they would awake the chieftainess inside. He used the Zulu word Inkosi-kaas, which she remembered meant head-lady or chieftainess. He was very thoughtful for her, she reflected, and was grateful, till suddenly she remembered the dislike she had taken to the man.

Then she looked round her room and saw that it was very pretty, well-furnished and papered, with water-colour pictures on the walls of no mean merit, things that she had not expected in this far-off place. Also on a table stood a great bowl of arum lilies. She wondered who had put them there; whether it were the old half-breed, Sally, or Jacob Meyer. Also she wondered who had painted the pictures, which were all of African scenery, and something told her that both the flowers and the pictures came from Jacob Meyer.

On the little table by her bed was a handbell which presently she rang. Instantly she heard the voice of Sally calling for the coffee "quick," and next minute the woman entered bringing a tray with it, and bread and butter, yes, and toast and eggs, that had evidently been made ready for her. Speaking in

English mixed with Dutch words, she told Benita that her father was still in bed, but sent her his love and wished to know how she did. Then, while she ate her breakfast with appetite, Sally set her a bath, and subsequently appeared carrying the contents of the box she had used upon the waggon, which had now arrived safely at the farm. Benita asked who had ordered the box to be unpacked, and Sally answered that the Heer Meyer had ordered it so that she might not be disturbed in her sleep, and that her things should be ready for her when she woke.

" The Heer Meyer thinks a great deal about other people," said Benita.

" Ja, ja," answered the old half-breed, " he tink much about people when he want to tink about them, but he tink most about himself. Baas Meyer, he a very clever man, oh ! a very clever man who want to be a great man, too. And one day, Missee, he be a great man, great and rich—if the Heer God Almighty let him."

CHAPTER VI.

THE GOLD COIN.

SIX weeks had gone by since the eventful night of Benita's arrival at Rooi Krantz. Now the spring had fully come, the veld was emerald with grass and bright with flowers. In the kloof behind the house trees had put out their leaves, and the mimosas were in bloom, making the air heavy with their scent. Amongst them the ringdoves nested in hundreds, and on the steep rocks of the precipice the red-necked vultures fed their young. Along the banks of the stream and round the borders of the lake the pig-lilies bloomed, a sheet of white. All the place was beautiful and full of life and hope. Nothing seemed dead and hopeless except Benita's heart.

Her health had quite come back to her ; indeed, never before had she felt so strong and well; but the very soul had withered in her breast. All day she thought, and all night she dreamed, of the man who, in cold blood, had offered up his life to save those of a helpless woman and her child. She wondered whether he would have done this if he had heard the answer that was upon her lips. Perhaps that was why she had not been given time to speak that answer, which might have made a coward of him. For nothing more had been heard of Robert Seymour ; indeed already the tragedy of the ship *Zanzibar* was forgotten. The dead had buried their dead, and since then worse disasters had happened in the world.

But Benita could not bury her dead. She rode about the veld, she sat by the lake and watched the wild fowl, or at night heard them flighting over her in flocks. She listened to the cooing of the doves, the booming of the bitterns in the reeds, and the drumming of the snipe high in air. She counted the game trekking along the ridge till her mind grew weary. She sought consolation from the breast of Nature and found none, she sought it in the starlit skies, and oh ! they were very far away. Death reigned within her who outwardly was so fair to see.

In the society of her father, indeed, she took pleasure, for he loved her, and love comforted her wounded heart. In that of Jacob Meyer also she found interest, for now her first fear of the man had died away, and undoubtedly he was very interesting ; well-bred also after a fashion, although a Jew who had lost his own faith and rejected that of the Christians.

He told her that he was a German by birth, that he had been sent to England as a boy, to avoid the conscription, which Jews dislike, since in soldiering there is little profit. Here he had become a clerk in a house of South African merchants, and, as a consequence—having shown all the ability of his race—was despatched to take charge of a branch business in Cape Colony. What happened to him there Benita never discovered, but probably he had shown too much ability of an oblique nature. At any rate, his connection with the firm terminated, and for years he became a wandering " smouse" or trader, until at length he drifted into partnership with her father.

Whatever might have been his past, however, soon she found that he was an extremely able and agreeable man. It was he and no other who had painted the water-colours that adorned her room, and he could play and sing as well as he painted. Also, as Robert had told her, Mr. Meyer was very well-read in subjects that are not usually studied on the veld of South Africa; indeed, he had quite a library of books, most of them histories or philosophical and scientific works, of which he would lend her volumes. Fiction, however, he never read, for the reason, he told her, that he found life itself and the mysteries and problems which surround it so much more interesting.

One evening, when they were walking together by the lake, watching the long lights of sunset break and quiver upon its surface, Benita's curiosity overcame her, and she asked him boldly how it happened that such a man as he was content to live the life he did.

"In order that I may reach a better," he answered. "Oh! no, not in the skies, Miss Clifford, for of them I know nothing, nor, as I believe, is there anything to know. But here, here."

"What do you mean by a better life, Mr. Meyer?"

"I mean," he answered, with a flash of his dark eyes, "great wealth, and the power that wealth brings. Ah! I see you think me very sordid and materialistic, but money is God in this world, Miss Clifford, money is God."

She smiled and answered: "I fear, then, that he is likely to prove an invisible god on the high veld, Mr. Meyer. You will scarcely make a great fortune out of horse-breeding, and here there is no one to rule."

"Do you suppose, then, that is why I stop at Rooi Krantz, just to breed horses? Has not your father told you about the great treasure hidden away up there among the Makalanga?"

"I have heard something of it," she answered with a sigh. "Also that both of you went to look for it and were disappointed!"

"Ah! the Englishman who was drowned, Mr. Seymour, he spoke of it, did he not? He found us there."

"Yes, and you wished to shoot him, do you remember?"

"God in Heaven! yes, because I thought he had come to rob us. Well, I did not shoot, and afterwards we were

hunted out of the place, which does not much matter, as those fools of natives refused to let us dig in the fortress."

"Then why do you still think about this treasure which probably does not exist?"

"Why, Miss Clifford, do you think about various things that probably do not exist? Perhaps because you feel that here or elsewhere they *do* exist. Well, that is what I feel about the treasure and what I have always felt. It exists, and I shall find it—now. I shall live to see more gold than you can even imagine, and that is why I still continue to breed horses on the Transvaal veld. Ah! you laugh; you think it is a nightmare that I breed——"

Then suddenly he became aware of Sally, who had appeared over the fold of the rise behind them, and asked irritably:

"What is it now, old vrouw?"

"The Baas Clifford wants to speak with you, Baas Jacob. Messengers have come to you both from far away."

"What messengers?" he asked.

"I know not," answered Sally, fanning her fat face with a yellow pocket-handkerchief, "they are strange people to me, and thin with travelling, but they talk a kind of Zulu. The Baas wishes you to come."

"Will you come also, Miss Clifford? No? Then forgive me if I leave you," and lifting his hat he went.

"A strange man, Missee," said old Sally, when he had vanished, walking very fast.

"Yes," answered Benita, in an indifferent voice.

"A very strange man," went on the old woman, "too much in his kop," and she tapped her forehead. "I tink it will burst one day, but if it does not burst, then he will be great. I tell you that before, now I tell it you again, for I tink his time come. Now I go cook dinner."

Benita sat by the lake till the twilight fell, and the wild geese began to flight over her. Then she walked back to the house thinking no more of Heer Meyer, thinking only that she was weary of this place in which there was nothing to occupy her mind, and distract it from its ever present sorrow.

At dinner, or rather supper, that night, she noticed that both her father and his partner seemed to be suffering from suppressed excitement, of which she thought she could guess the cause.

"Did you find your messengers, Mr. Meyer?" she asked, when the men had lit their pipes, and the square-face, as Hollands was called in those days from the shape of the bottle, was set upon the rough table of speckled buchenhout wood.

"Yes, I found them," he answered; "they are in the kitchen now," and he looked at Mr. Clifford.

"Benita, my dear," said her father, "rather a curious thing has happened." Her face lit up, but he shook his head. "No, nothing to do with the shipwreck; that is all finished; still, something that may interest you, if you care to hear a story."

Benita nodded; she was in a mood to hear anything that would occupy her thoughts.

"You know something about this treasure business," went on her father. "Well, this is the tale of it. Years ago, after you and your mother had gone to England, I went on a big game shooting expedition into the interior. My companion was an old fellow called Tom Jackson, a rolling stone, and one of the best elephant hunters in Africa. We did pretty well, but the end of it was that we separated north of the Transvaal, I bringing down the ivory that we had shot, and traded, and Tom stopping to put in another season, the arrangement being that he was to join me afterwards, and take his share of the money. I came here and bought this farm from a Boer who was tired of it, cheap enough, too, for I only gave him £100 for the 6,000 acres. The kitchens behind were his old house, for I built the new one.

"A year had gone by before I saw any more of Tom Jackson, and then he turned up more dead than alive. He had been injured by an elephant, and lay for some months among the Makalanga to the north of Matabeleland, where he got fever badly at a place called Bambatse, on the Zambesi. These Makalanga are a strange folk. I believe their name means the People of the Sun; at any rate, they are the last of some ancient race. Well, while he was there he cured the old Molimo, or hereditary high-priest of this tribe, of a bad fever by giving him quinine, and naturally they grew friendly. The Molimo lived among ruins of which there are many over all that part of South Africa. No one knows who built them now, probably it was people who lived thousands of years ago. However, this Molimo told Tom Jackson a more recent legend connected with the place.

"He said that six generations before, when his great-great-great grandfather was chief (Mambo, he called it), the natives of all that part of South Africa rose against the white men, Portuguese, I suppose, who still worked the gold there. They massacred them and their slaves by thousands, driving them up from the southward where Lobengula rules now, to the Zambesi by which the Portuguese hoped to escape to the coast. At length a remnant of them, not more than about two hundred men and women, arrived at the stronghold called Bambatse, where the Molimo now lives in a great ruin built by the ancients upon an impregnable mountain which overhangs the river. With them they brought an enormous quantity of gold, all the stored-up treasure of the land which they were trying to carry off. But although they reached the river they could not escape by it, since the natives, who pursued them in thousands, watched day and night in canoes, and the poor fugitives had no boats. Therefore it came about that they were shut up in this fortress which it was impossible to storm, and there slowly perished of starvation.

"When it was known that they were all dead, the natives who had followed them from the south, and who wanted blood and revenge, not gold, which was of no use to them, went away, but the old priest's forefather who knew the secret entrance to the place, and who had been friendly to the Portuguese, forced his way in and there amidst the dead found one woman living but mad with grief, a young and beautiful girl, the daughter of the Portuguese lord or captain. He gave her food, but in the night when some strength had returned to her, she left him, and at daybreak he found her standing on the peak that overhangs the river, dressed all in white.

"He called some of his councillors, and they tried to persuade her to come down from the rock, but she answered 'No, her betrothed and all her family and friends were dead, and it was her will to follow them.' Then they asked where was the gold, for having watched day and night they knew it had not been thrown into the river. She answered that it was where it was, and that, seek as he might, no black man would ever find it. She added that she gave it into his keeping, and that of his descendants, to safeguard until she came again. Also she said that if they were faithless to that trust, then it had been revealed to her from heaven above that those same savages who had killed her father and her people, would kill his people also. When she had spoken thus she stood a while praying on the peak, then suddenly hurled herself into the river, and was seen no more.

"From that day to this the ruin has been held to be haunted, and save the Molimo himself who retires there to meditate and receive revelations from the spirits, no one is allowed to set a foot in its upper part; indeed the natives would rather die than do so. Consequently the gold still remains where it was hidden. This place itself Tom Jackson did not see, since, notwithstanding his friendship for him, the Molimo refused to allow him to enter there.

"Well, Tom never recovered; he died here, and is buried in the little graveyard behind the house which the Boers made for some of their people. It was shortly after his death that Mr. Meyer became my partner, for I forgot to say that I had told him the story, and we determined to have a try for that great wealth. You know the rest. We trekked to Bambatse, pretending to be traders, and found the old Molimo who knew of me as having been Tom Jackson's friend. We asked him if the story he had told to Jackson were true, and he answered that, surely as the sun shone in the heavens, it was true, every word of it, for it, and much more than he had spoken of, had been handed down from father to son, and that they even knew the name of the white lady who had killed herself. It was Ferreira—your mother's name, Benita, though a common one enough in South Africa.

"We asked him to allow us to enter the topmost stronghold, which stands upon the hill, but he refused, saying that the curse still lay upon him and his, and that no man should enter until the lady Ferreira came again. For the rest the place was free to us; we might dig where we would. So we did dig and found some gold buried with the ancients, beads and bangles and wire, about £100 worth. Also—that was on the day when the young Seymours came upon us, and accounts for Meyer's excitement, for he thought that we were on the track of the treasure—we found a single gold coin, no doubt one that had been dropped by the Portuguese. Here it is—" and he threw a thin piece of gold on the table before her. "I have shown it to a man learned in those matters, and he says that it is a ducat struck by one of the doges of Venice.

"Well, we never found any more. The end of it was that the Makalanga caught us trying to get in to the secret stronghold by stealth, and gave us the choice of clearing out or being killed. So we cleared out, for treasure is not of much use to dead men."

Mr. Clifford ceased speaking, and filled his pipe, while Meyer helped himself to square-face in an absent manner. As for Benita she stared at the quaint old coin which had a hole in it, wondering with what scenes of terror and of bloodshed it had been connected.

"Keep it," said her father. "It will go on that bracelet of yours."

"Thank you, dear," she answered. "Though I don't know why I should take all the Portuguese treasure since we shall never see any more of it."

"Why not, Miss Clifford?" asked Meyer quickly.

"The story tells you why—because the natives won't even let you look for it; also, looking and finding are different things."

"Natives change their minds sometimes, Miss Clifford. That story is not done, it is only begun, and now you shall hear its second chapter. Clifford, may

"THERE THEY STOOD, ALL FOUR OF THEM . . . . . STARING AT THE WHITE BENITA"

I call in the messengers?" and without waiting for an answer he rose and left the room.

Neither Mr. Clifford nor his daughter said anything after he had gone. Benita appeared to occupy herself in fixing the broad gold coin to a little swivel on her bracelet, but while she did so once more that strange sixth sense of hers awoke within her. As she had been afraid at the dinner on the doomed steamer, so again she was afraid. Again death and great fear cast their advancing shadows on to her soul. That piece of gold seemed to speak to her, yet, alas! she could not understand its story. Only she knew that her father and Jacob Meyer and—yes, yes, yes—Robert Seymour, had all a part in that tragedy. Oh! how could that be when he was dead? How could this gold link him to her? She knew not, she cared not, all she knew was that she would follow this treasure to the edge of the world, and if need be, over it, if only it brought her back to him again.

CHAPTER VII.

THE MESSENGERS.

THE door opened, and through it came Jacob Meyer, followed by three natives. Benita did not see or hear them, her soul was far away. There at the head of the room, clad all in white, for she wore no mourning save in her heart, illuminated by the rays of the lamp that hung above her, she stood still and upright, for she had risen; on the face and in her wide, dark eyes, a look that was very strange to see. Jacob Meyer perceived it and stopped, the three natives perceived it also and stopped. There they stood, all four of them, at the end of the long sitting-room, staring at the white Benita and at her haunted eyes.

One of the natives pointed with his thin finger to her face, and whispered to the others. Meyer, who understood their tongue, caught the whisper. It was:

"Behold the Spirit of the Rock!"

"What spirit, and what rock?" he asked in a low voice.

"She who haunts Bambatse; she whom our eyes have seen," answered the man, still staring at Benita.

Benita heard the whispering, and knew that it was about herself, though not one word of it did she catch. With a sigh she shook herself free from her visions and sat down in a chair close by. Then one by one the messengers drew near to her, and each, as he came, made a profound obeisance, touching the floor with his finger-tips, and staring at her face. But her father they only saluted with an uplifted hand. She looked at them with interest, and indeed they were interesting in their way; tall, spare men, light-coloured, with refined, mobile faces. Here was no negro-blood, but rather that of some ancient people such as Egyptians or Phœnicians; men whose forefathers had been wise and civilised thousands of years ago, and perchance had stood in the courts of Pharaoh or of Solomon.

Their salutations finished, the three men squatted in a line upon the floor, drawing their fur karosses, or robes, about them, and waited in silence. Jacob Meyer thought a while, then said:

"Clifford, will you translate to your daughter so that she may be sure she is told exactly what passes?"

Next he turned and addressed the natives.

"Your names are Tamas, Tamala, and Hoba, and you, Tamas, are the son of the Molimo of Bambatse, who is called Mambo, and you, Tamala and Hoba, are his initiated councillors. Is it so?"

They bowed their heads.

"Good. You, Tamas, tell the story and give again your message that this lady, the lady Benita, may hear it, for she has a part in the matter."

"We understand that she has a part," answered Tamas; "we read in her face that she has the greatest part. Doubtless it is of her that the Spirit spoke to my father. These, spoken by my mouth, are the words of the Molimo, my father, which we have travelled so far to deliver.

"'When you two white men visited Bambatse four years ago, you asked of me, Mambo, to be admitted to the holy place, that you might look for the treasure there which the Portuguese hid in the time of my ancestor in the sixth generation. I refused to allow you to look, or even to enter the holy place, because I am by birth the guardian of that treasure, although I know not where it lies. But now I am in a great strait. I have news that Lobengula the usurper, who is king of the Matabele, has taken offence against me for certain reasons, among them that I did not send him a sufficient tribute. It is reported to me that he purposes next summer to despatch an impi to wipe me and my people out, and to make my kraal black as the burnt veld. I have little strength to resist him who is mighty, and my people are not warlike. From generation to generation they have been traders, cultivators of the land, workers in metals, and men of peace, who desire not to kill or be killed. Also they are few. Therefore I have no power to stand against Lobengula.

" 'I remember the guns that you and your companion brought with you, which can kill things from far away. If I had a supply of those guns from behind my walls I might defy the impi of Lobengula, whose warriors use the assegai. If you will bring me a hundred good guns and plenty of powder and bullets for them, it is revealed to me that it will be lawful for me to admit you to the secret, holy place, where you may look for the buried gold for as long as you wish, and if you can find it, take it all away without hindrance from me or my people. But I will be honest with you. That gold will never be found save by the one appointed. The white lady said so in the time of my forefather ; he heard it with his ears, and I have heard it from his descendants with my ears, and so it shall be. Still, if you bring the guns you can come and see if either of you is that one appointed. But I do not think that any man is so appointed, for the secret is hid in woman. But of this you can learn for yourselves. I do but speak as I am bidden.

" 'This is my message spoken by my mouth, Tamas, son of my body, and my councillors who go with him will bear witness that he speaks the truth. I, Mambo, the Molimo of Bambatse, send you greeting, and will give you good welcome and fulfil my promise, if you come with the far-shooting guns, ten times ten of them, and the powder, and the bullets wherewith I may drive off the Matabele, but not otherwise. My son,

Tamas, and my councillors will drive your waggon into my country, but you must bring no strange servants. The Spirit of the white woman who killed herself before the eyes of my forefather has been seen of late standing upon the point of rock ; also she has visited me at night in my secret place where her companions died. I do not know all that this portends, but I think that amongst other things she wished to tell me that the Matabele are about to attack us. I await the decree of the Heavens. I send you two karosses as a gift, and a little ancient gold, since ivory is too heavy for my messengers to carry, and I have no waggon. Farewell.' "

"We have heard you," said Meyer, when Mr. Clifford had finished translating, "and we wish to ask you a question. What do you mean when you say that the Spirit of the white woman has been seen ? "

"I mean what I say, white man," answered Tamas. "She was seen by all three of us, standing upon the pinnacle at the dawn ; also my father saw and spoke with her alone in his sleep at night. This is the third time in my father's day that she has appeared thus, and always before some great event."

"What was she like ? " asked Meyer.

"Like ? Oh ! like the lady who sits yonder. Yes, quite the same, or so it seemed to us. But who knows ? We have seen no other white women, and we were not very near. Let the lady come and stand side by side with the Spirit, so that we can examine them both, and we shall be able to answer better. Do you accept the offer of the Molimo ? "

"We will tell you to-morrow morning," replied Meyer. "A hundred rifles are many to find, and will cost much money. Meanwhile, for you there is food and a sleeping-place."

The three men seemed disappointed at his answer, which they evidently believed to be preliminary to a refusal. For a moment or two they consulted together, then Tamas put his hand into a pouch and drew from it something wrapped in dry leaves, which he undid, revealing a quaint and beautiful necklace, fashioned of twisted gold links, wherein were set white stones, that they had no difficulty in recognising as uncut diamonds of considerable value. From this necklace also hung a crucifix moulded in gold.

"We offer this gift," he said, "on behalf of Mambo, my father, to the lady yonder, to whom the karosses and the rough gold are of no use. The chain has a story. When the Portuguese lady hurled herself into the river she wore it about her neck. As she fell into the river she struck against a little point of rock which tore the chain away from her—see where it is broken and mended with gold wire. It remained upon the point of rock, and my forefather took it thence. It is a gift to the lady if she will promise to wear it."

"Accept it," muttered Mr. Clifford, when he had finished translating this, "or you will give offence."

So Benita said : "I thank the Molimo, and accept his gift."

Then Tamas rose, and, advancing, cast the ancient, tragic thing over her head. As it fell upon her shoulders, Benita knew that it was a chain of destiny drawing her she knew not where, this ornament that had last been worn by that woman, bereaved and unhappy as herself, who could find no refuge from her sorrow except in death. Had she felt it torn from her breast, she wondered, as she, the living Benita of to-day, felt it fall upon her own?

The three envoys rose, bowed and went, leaving them alone. Jacob Meyer lifted his head as though to address her, then changed his mind and was silent. Both the men waited for her to speak, but she would not, and in the end it was her father who spoke first.

"What do you say, Benita?" he asked anxiously.

"I? I have nothing to say, except that I have heard a very curious story. This priest's message is to you and Mr. Meyer, father, and must be answered by you. What have I to do with it?"

"A great deal, I think, my dear, or so those men seemed to believe. At any rate, I cannot go up there without you, and I will not take you there against your wish, for it is a long way off, and a queer business. The question is, will you go?"

She thought a space, while the two men watched her anxiously.

"Yes," she answered at length, in a quiet voice. "I will go if you wish to go, not because I want to find treasure, but because the story and the country where it happened interest me. Indeed, I don't believe much in the treasure. Even if they are superstitious and afraid to look for it themselves, I doubt whether they would allow you to look if they thought it could be found. To me the journey does not seem a good business speculation, also there are risks."

"We think it good enough," broke in Meyer decidedly. "And one does not expect to get millions without trouble."

"Yes, yes," said her father, "but she is right—there are risks, great risks, fever, wild beasts, savages, and others that one cannot foresee. Have I a right to expose her to them? Ought we not to go alone?"

"It would be useless," answered Meyer, "those messengers have seen your daughter, and mixed her up with their superstitious story of a ghost of which I, who know that there are no such things, believe nothing. Without her now we shall certainly fail."

"As for the risks, father," said Benita, "personally I take no account of them, for I am sure that what is to happen will happen, and if I knew that I was to die upon the Zambesi, it would make no difference to me who do not care. But as it chances, I think—I cannot tell you why—that you and Mr. Meyer are in more danger than I am. It is for you to consider whether you will take the risks."

Mr. Clifford smiled. "I am old," he said, "that is my answer."

"And I am accustomed to such things," said Meyer, with a shrug of his shoulders. "Who would not run a little danger for the sake of such a glorious chance? Wealth, wealth, more wealth than we can dream of, and with it, power ; power to avenge, to reward, to buy position, and pleasure, and all beautiful things which are the heritage of the very rich alone," and he spread out his hands and looked upwards, as though in adoration of this golden god.

"Except such trifles as health and happiness," commented Benita, not without sarcasm, for this man and his material desires disgusted her somewhat, especially when she contrasted him with another man who was lost to her, though it was true that *his* past had been idle and unproductive enough. Yet they interested her also, for Benita had never met anyone like Mr. Meyer, so talented, so eager, and so soulless.

"Then I understand it is settled," she said.

Mr. Clifford hesitated, but Meyer answered at once:

"My daughter thinks it will bring us ill-fortune," said Mr. Clifford, when the door had closed behind her. "That is her way of saying so."

"Yes," answered Meyer gloomily, "she thinks that, and she is one of those who have vision. Well, she may be wrong; also the question is, shall we seize our opportunity and its dangers, or remain here and breed bad horses all our lives, while she who is

"'BEHOLD THE CITY OF MY PEOPLE'"

"Yes, settled, as far as anything can be."

She waited a moment for her father to speak, but he said nothing; his chance had gone by.

"Very well. Now we shall not need to trouble ourselves with further doubts or argument. We are going to Bambatse on the Zambesi, a distant place, to look for buried gold, and I hope, Mr. Meyer, that if you find it, the results will come up to your expectations, and bring you all sorts of good luck. Good-night, father dear, good-night."

not afraid laughs at us? I am going to Bambatse."

Again Mr. Clifford made no direct answer, only asked a question:

"How long will it take to get the guns and ammunition, and what will they cost?"

"About a week from Wakkerstroom," replied Meyer. "Old Potgieter, the trader there, has just imported a hundred Martinis and a hundred Westley-Richards falling-blocks. Fifty of each, with ten thousand rounds of cartridges will cost about £600, and we have as much as that in the bank; also we have the new waggon, and plenty of good oxen and horses. We can take a dozen of the horses with us, and sell them in the north of the Transvaal for a fine price, before we get into the tetse-fly belt. The oxen will probably carry us through, as they are most of them salted."

"You have thought it all out, Jacob, I see, but it means a lot of money one way and another, to say nothing of other things."

"Yes, a lot of money, and those rifles are too good for Kaffirs. Birmingham gas-pipes would have done for them, but there are none to be had. But what is the money, and what are the guns compared to all they will bring us?"

"I think you had better ask my daughter, Jacob. She seems to have her own ideas upon the subject."

"Miss Clifford has made up her mind, and it will not change; I shall ask her no more," replied Meyer.

Then he, too, left the room, to give orders about the journey to Wakkerstroom that he must take upon the morrow. But Mr. Clifford sat there till past midnight, wondering whether he had done right, and if they would find the treasure of which he had dreamed for years, and what the future had in store for them.

If only he could have seen!

When Benita came to breakfast the next morning, she asked where Mr. Meyer was, and learned that he had already departed for Wakkerstroom.

"Certainly he is in earnest," she said with a laugh.

"Yes," answered her father, "Jacob is always in earnest, though, somehow, his earnestness has not brought him much good so far. If we fail, it will not be want of thought and preparation on his part."

Nearly a week went by before Meyer returned again, and meanwhile Benita made ready for her journey. In the intervals of her simple preparations also she talked a good deal, with the help of her father, to the three stately-looking Makalanga, who were resting thankfully after their long journey. Their conversation was general, since by tacit consent no further mention was made of the

treasure or of anything to do with it, but it enabled her to form a fair opinion of them and their people. She gathered that although they spoke a dialect of Zulu, they had none of the bravery of the Zulus, and indeed lived in deadly terror of the Matabele, who are bastard Zulus—such terror, in fact, that she greatly doubted whether the hundred rifles would be of much use to them, should they ever be attacked by that tribe.

They were what their fathers had been before them, agriculturists and workers in metals, not fighting men. Also she set herself to learn what she could of their tongue, which she did not find difficult, for Benita had a natural aptitude for languages, and had never forgotten the Dutch and Zulu she used to prattle as a child, which now came back to her very fast. Indeed, she could already talk fairly in either of those languages, especially as she spent her spare hours in studying their grammar, and reading them.

So the days went on, till one evening Jacob Meyer appeared with two Scotch carts laden with ten long boxes that looked like coffins, and other smaller boxes which were very heavy, to say nothing of a multitude of stores. As Mr. Clifford prophesied, he had forgotten nothing, for he even brought Benita various articles of clothing, and a revolver for which she had not asked.

Three days later they trekked away from Rooi Krantz upon a peculiarly beautiful Sunday morning in the early spring, giving it out that they were going upon a trading and shooting expedition in the north of the Transvaal. Benita looked back at the pretty little stead and the wooded kloof behind it over which she had nearly fallen, and the placid lake in front of it where the nesting wildfowl wheeled, and sighed. For to her, now that she was leaving it, the place seemed like home, and it came into her mind that she would never see it any more.

CHAPTER VIII.

BAMBATSE.

NEARLY four months had gone by when at length the waggon with which were Mr. Clifford, Benita and Jacob Meyer, camped one night within the country of the Molimo of Bambatse, whose name was Mambo. Or perhaps that was his title, since (according to Tamas his son) every chief in succession was called Mambo, though not all of them were Molimos, or representatives and prophets of God, or the Great Spirit whom they knew as Munwali. Thus sometimes the Molimo, or priest of Munwali, and the Mambo or chief were different persons. For instance, he said that he, Tamas, would be Mambo on his father's death, but no visions were given to him; therefore as yet, at any rate, he was not called to be Molimo.

In the course of this long journey they had met with many adventures, such as were common to African travellers before the days of railroads; adventures with wild beasts and native tribes, adventures with swollen rivers also, and one that was worse, with thirst, since for three days (owing to the failure of a pit or pan, where they expected to find water) they were obliged to go without drink. Still, none of these were very serious, nor had any of the three of them ever been in better health than they were at this moment, for by good luck they had escaped all fever. Indeed, their rough, wild life had agreed with Benita extraordinarily well, so well that any who had known her in the streets of London would scarcely have recognised her as the sunburnt, active and well-formed young woman who sat that night by the camp fire.

All the horses they had brought with them had been sold, except some which had died, and three that were "salted," or proof against the deadly horse sickness, which they took on with them. Their own servants also had been sent back to Rooi Krantz in charge of a Scotch cart laden with ivory, purchased from Boer hunters who had brought it down from the north of the Transvaal. Therefore, for this was part of the bargain, the three Makalanga were now their only attendants who drove and herded the cattle, while Benita cooked the food which the two white men shot, or sometimes bought from natives.

For days they had been passing through a country that was practically deserted, and now, having crossed a high nek, the same on which Robert Seymour had left his waggon, they were camped in low land which, as they could see by the remains of walls that appeared everywhere, had once been extensively enclosed and cultivated. To their right was a rising mountainous ground, beyond which, said the Makalanga, ran the Zambesi, and in front of them, not more than ten miles away, a great isolated hill, none other than the place that they had journeyed so far to reach, Bambatse, round which flowed the great river. Indeed, thither one of the three Makalanga, he who was named Hoba, had gone on to announce their approach.

They had outspanned amongst ruins, most of them circular in shape, and Benita, studying them in the bright moonlight, guessed that once these had been houses. That place now so solitary, hundreds or thousands of years ago was undoubtedly the home of a great population. Thousands, rather than hundreds, she thought, since close at hand in the middle of one of these round houses, grew a mighty baobab tree, that could not have seen less than ten or fifteen centuries since the seed whence it sprang pierced the cement floor which was still visible about its giant bole.

Tamas, the Molimo's son, saw her studying these evidences of antiquity, and, approaching, saluted her.

"Lady," he said in his own language, which by now she spoke very well; "lady"—and he waved his hand with a fine gesture—"behold the city of my people."

"How do you know that it was their city?" she asked.

"I do not know, lady. Stones cannot speak, the spirits are silent, and we have forgotten. Still I think so, and our fathers have told us that but six or eight generations ago many folk lived here, though it was not they who built these walls. Even fifty years ago there were many, but now the Matabele have killed them, and we are few; to-morrow you will see how few. Come here and look," and he led her through the entrance of a square cattle kraal which stood close by. Within were tufts of rank grass, and a few bushes and among these scores of skulls and other bones.

"The Matabele killed these in the time of Moselikatse," he said. "Now do you wonder that we who remain fear the Matabele, and desire guns to defend ourselves from them, even if we must sell our secrets, in order to buy those guns, who have no money to pay for them?"

"No," she answered, looking at the tall, dignified man, into whose soul the irons of fear and slavery had burnt so deep. "No, I do not wonder."

Next morning at daybreak they trekked on, always through these evidences of dead, forgotten peoples. They had not more than ten miles to cover to reach their long journey's end, but the road, if so it could be called, ran up-hill, and the oxen, whereof only fourteen were now left to drag the heavy-laden waggon, were thin and footsore, so that their progress was very slow. Indeed, it was past midday when at length they began to enter what by apology might be called the town of Bambatse.

"When we go away from this, it will have to be by water, I think, unless we can buy trek-cattle," said Meyer, looking at the labouring oxen with a doubtful eye.

"Why?" asked Mr. Clifford anxiously.

"Because several of those beasts have been bitten by tetse-fly, like my horse, and the poison is beginning to work. I thought so last night, but now I am sure. Look at their eyes. It was down in that bit of bush veld eight days ago. I said that we ought not to camp there."

At this moment they came to the crest of the ridge, and on its further side saw the wonderful ruins of Bambatse close at hand. In front of them stood a hill jutting out as it were into the broad waters of the Zambesi river, which, to a great extent, protected it upon three sides. The fourth, that opposite to them, except at one place where a kind of natural causeway led into the town, was also defended by Nature, since here for more than fifty feet in height the granite rock of the base of the hill rose sheer and unclimbable. On the mount itself, that in all may have covered eight or ten acres of ground, and surrounded by a deep donga or ditch, were three rings of fortifications, set one above the other, mighty walls which, it was evident, had been built by no modern hand. Looking

at them Benita could well understand how it came about that the poor fugitive Portuguese had chosen this as their last place of refuge, and were overcome at length, not by the thousands of savages who followed and surrounded them, but by hunger. Indeed, the place seemed impregnable to any force that was not armed with siege guns.

On the hither side of this natural fosse, which, doubtless, in ancient times had been filled with water led from the Zambesi, stood the village of the Bambatse Makalanga, a collection of seventy or eighty wretched huts, round, like those of their forefathers, but built of mud and thatch. About them lay the gardens, or square fields, that were well cultivated, and at this season rich with ripening corn. Benita, however, could see no cattle, and concluded, therefore, that these must be kept on the hill for safety, and within its walls.

Down the rough road they lumbered, and through the village where the few women and children stared at them in a frightened way. Then they came to the causeway, which, on its further side, was blocked with thorns and rough stones taken from the ruins. While they waited for these to be removed by some men who now appeared, Benita looked at the massive, circular wall still thirty or forty feet in height, by perhaps twenty through its base, built of granite blocks without mortar, and ornamented with quaint patterns of other coloured stones. In its thickness she could see grooves, where evidently had once been portcullises, but these had disappeared long ago.

"It is a wonderful place," she said to her father. "I am glad that I came. Have you been all over it?"

"No, only between the first and second walls, and once between the second and third. The old temple, or whatever it is, is on the top, and into that they would never admit us. It is there that the treasure lies."

"That the treasure is supposed to lie," she answered with a smile. "But, father, what guarantee have you that they will do so now? Perhaps they will take the guns and show us the door, or rather the gate."

"'WHITE MAIDEN,' HE SAID, . . . 'FOR YOU AT LEAST I HAVE GOOD TIDINGS'"

" Your daughter is right, there is none, and before a box is taken off the waggon we must get one," said Meyer. " Oh ! I know it is risky, and it would have been better to make sure first, but it is too late to talk of that now. Look, the stones are cleared ; trek on, trek ! "

The long waggon-whip cracked, the poor, tired-out oxen strained at the yokes and on they went through the entrance of that fateful fortress that was but just wide enough to admit them. Inside lay a great open space which, as they could see from the numerous ruins, had once been filled with buildings that now were half hidden by grass, trees and creepers. This was the outer ring of the temple where, in ancient days, the priests and captains had their home. Travelling across it for perhaps a hundred and fifty yards, they came near the second wall which was like the first, only not quite so solid, and saw that on a stretch of beaten ground, and seated in the shadow, for the day was hot, the people of Bambatse were gathered to greet them.

When within fifty yards they dismounted from the horses, which were left with the waggon in the charge of the Makalanga, Tamala. Then Benita taking her position between her father and Jacob Meyer, they advanced towards the ring of natives, of whom there may have been two hundred—all of them adult men.

As they came except one figure who remained seated with his back against the wall, the human circle stood up as a token of respect, and Benita saw that they were of the same stamp as the messengers, tall and good-looking, with melancholy eyes and a cowed expression, wearing the appearance of people who from day to day live in dread of slavery and death. Opposite to them was a break in the circle, through which Tamas led them, and as they crossed it Benita felt that all those people were staring at her with their sad eyes. A few paces from where the man crouched against the wall, his head hidden by a beautifully-worked blanket, that was thrown over it, were placed three well-carved stools. Upon these, at a motion from Tamas, they sat themselves down, and, as it was not dignified for them to speak first, remained silent.

" Be patient and forgive," said Tamas at length ; " my father, Mambo, prays to the Munwali and the spirits of his fathers that this coming of yours may be fortunate, and that a vision of those things that are to be may descend upon him."

Benita, feeling nearly two hundred pairs of eyes concentrated upon her, wished that the vision might come quickly, but after a minute or two, fell into tune with the thing, and almost enjoyed this strange experience. Those mighty ancient walls built by hands unknown, which had seen so much history and so much death ; the silent, triple ring of patient, solemn men, the last descendants of a cultured race, the crouching figure hidden beneath the blanket, who imagined himself to be communing with his god— it was all very strange, very well worth the seeing to one who had wearied of the monotony of civilisation.

Look, the man stirred, and threw back his blanket, revealing a head white with age, a spiritual, ascetic face, so thin that every bone showed in it, and dark eyes which stared upwards unseeingly, like those of a person in a trance. Thrice he sighed, while his tribesmen watched him. Then he let his eyes fall upon the three white people seated in front of him. First he looked at Mr. Clifford, and his face grew troubled, then at Jacob Meyer, and it was anxious and alarmed. Lastly, he stared at Benita, and while he did so the dark eyes became calm and happy.

" White maiden," he said in a soft, low voice, " for you at least I have good tidings. Though Death come near to you, though you see him on your right hand and your left, and in front of you and behind you, I say, fear not. Here you, who have known deep sorrow, shall find happiness and rest, O maiden with whom goes the spirit of one pure and fair as you, who died so long ago."

Then while Benita wondered at his words, spoken with such sweet earnestness, that although she believed nothing of them, they brought a kind of comfort to her, he looked once more at her father and Jacob Meyer, and, as it were with an effort, was silent.

" Have you no pleasant prophecy for me, old friend ? " said Jacob, " who have come so far to hear it ? "

At once the aged face grew inscrutable, all expression vanished behind a hundred wrinkles, and he answered :

"None, white man, none that I am charged to deliver. Search the skies for yourself, you who are so wise, and read them if you can. Lords," he went on in another voice, "I greet you in the name and presence of my children. Son Tamas, I greet you also; you have done your mission well. Listen now—you are weary and would rest and eat; still, bear with me—for I have a word to say. Look around you. You see all my tribe, not twenty times ten above the age of boys, we who once were countless as the leaves on yonder trees in spring. Why are we dead ? Because of the Amandabele, those fierce dogs whom, two generations ago, Moselikatse, the general of Chaka, brought up to the south of us, who ravish us and kill us year by year.

"We are not warlike, we who have outlived war and the lust of slaying. We are men of peace who desire to cultivate the land, and to follow our arts which have descended to us from our ancestors, and to worship the Heavens above us, whither we depart to join the spirits of our forefathers. But they are fierce and strong and savage, and they come up and murder our children and old people, and take away the young women and the maidens to be slaves, and with them all our cattle. Where are our cattle ? Lobengula, chief of the Amandabele, has them ; scarce a cow is left to give milk to the sick or to the motherless babe. And yet he sends for cattle. Tribute, say his messengers, deliver tribute, or my impi will come and take it with your lives. But we have no cattle, all are gone. We have nothing left to us but this ancient mountain and the works built thereon, and a little corn on which we live. Yes I say it, I, the Molimo, I whose ancestors were great kings, I who have still more wisdom in me than all the hosts of the Amandabele," and as he spoke the old man's grey head sank upon his breast and the tears ran down his withered cheeks, while his people answered :

"Mambo, it is true."

"Now listen again," he went on. "Lobengula threatens us, therefore I sent to these white men who were here before, saying that if they would bring me a hundred guns, and powder and ball, to enable us to beat off the Amandabele from behind these strong walls of ours, I would take them into the secret holy place where for six generations no white man has set a foot, and there suffer them to search for the treasure which is hid therein, no man knows where, that treasure which they asked leave to find four winters gone. We refused it then, and drove them hence, because of the curse laid upon us by the white maid who died, the last of the Portuguese, who foretold her people's fate for us if we gave up the buried gold save to one appointed. My children, the Spirit of Bambatse has visited me; I have seen her and others have seen her, and in my sleep she said to me : 'Suffer the men to come and search, for with them is one of the blood to whom my people's wealth is given; and great is your danger, for many spears draw nigh.' My children, I sent my son and other messengers on a far journey to where I knew the men dwelt, and they have returned after many months bringing those men with them, bringing with them also another of whom I knew nothing, yes, her who is appointed, her of whom the Spirit spoke."

Then he lifted his withered hand and held it towards Benita, saying : "I tell you that yonder she sits for whom the generations have waited."

"It is so," answered the Makalanga. "It is the White Lady come again to take her own."

"Friends," asked the Molimo, while they wondered at his strange speech, "tell me, have you brought the guns ?"

"Surely," answered Mr. Clifford, "they are there in the waggon, every one of them, the best that can be made, and with them ten thousand cartridges, bought at a great cost. We have fulfilled our share of the bargain; now will you fulfil yours, or shall we go away again with the guns and leave you to meet the Matabele with your assegais ?"

"Say you the agreement while we listen," answered the Molimo.

"Good," said Mr. Clifford, "it is this : That you shall find us food and shelter while we are with you. That you shall lead us into the secret place at the head of the hill, where the Portuguese died, and the gold is hidden. That you shall allow us to search for that gold when and where we will. That if we discover the gold or anything else of value to us, you shall suffer us to take it away, and assist us upon our journey, either by giving us boats and manning them to travel down the Zambesi, or in whatever fashion may be most easy. That you shall permit none to hurt, molest or annoy us during our sojourn among you. Is that our contract?"

"Not quite all of it," said the Molimo. "There is this to add: first that you shall teach us how to use the guns; secondly, that you shall search for and find the treasure, if so it is appointed, without our help, since in this matter it is not lawful for us to meddle; thirdly, that if the Amandabele should chance to attack us while you are here, you shall do your best to assist us against their power."

"Do you then expect attack?" asked Meyer suspiciously.

"White man, we always expect attack. Is it a bargain?"

"Yes," answered Mr. Clifford and Jacob Meyer in one voice, the latter adding: "the guns and the cartridges are yours. Lead us now to the hidden place. We have fulfilled our part, we trust to the honour of you and all your people to fulfil yours."

"White Maiden," asked the Molimo, addressing Benita. "Do you also say that it is a bargain?"

"What my father says, I say."

"Good," said the Molimo, "then in the presence of my people, and in the name of the Munwali, I, Mambo, who am his prophet, declare that it is so agreed between us, and may the vengeance of the heavens fall upon those who break our pact! Let the oxen of the white men be outspanned, their horses fed, their waggon unloaded, that we may count the guns. Let food be brought into the guesthouse also, and after they have eaten I, who alone of all of you have ever entered it, will lead them to the holy place, that there they may begin to search for that which the white men desire from age to age—to find it if they can; if not, to depart satisfied and at peace."

BENITA.

An African Romance by . . .
H. RIDER HAGGARD.

CHAPTER IX.

THE OATH OF MADUNA.

M R. CLIFFORD and Meyer rose to return to the waggon in order to superintend the unyoking of the oxen and to give directions as to their herding, and the off-saddling of the horses. Benita rose also, wondering when the food that had been promised would be ready, for she was hungry. Meanwhile, the Molimo was greeting his son Tamas, patting his hand affectionately and talking to him, when suddenly Benita, who watched this domestic scene with interest, heard a commotion behind her. Turning to discover its cause, she perceived three great men clad in full war panoply, shields on their left arms, spears in their right hands, black ostrich plumes rising from the polished rings woven in their hair, black moochas about their middles, and black ox-tails tied beneath their knees, who marched through the throng of Makalanga as though they saw them not.

"The Matabele! The Matabele are on us!" cried a voice; while other voices shouted, "Fly to your walls!" and yet others—"Kill them! They are few."

But the three men marched on unheeding till they stood before Mambo.

"Who are you, and what do you seek?" the old man asked boldly, though the fear that had taken hold of him at the sight of these strangers was evident enough, for his whole body shook.

"Surely you should know, chief of Bambatse," answered their spokesman with a laugh, "for you have seen the like of us before. We are the children of Lobengula, the Great Elephant, the King, the Black Bull, the Father of the Amandabele, and we have a message for your ear, little Old Man, which, finding that you leave your gate open, we have walked in to deliver."

"Speak your message then, envoys of Lobengula, in my ear and in those of my people," said the Molimo.

"Your people! Are these all your people?" the spokesman replied con-

245

246

temptuously. "Why then, what need was there for the indunas of the King to send so large an impi under a great general against you, when a company of lads armed with sticks would have served the turn ? We thought that these were but the sons of your house, the men of your own family, whom you had called together to eat with the white strangers."

"Close the entrance in the wall," cried the Molimo, stung to fury by the insult, and a voice answered :

"Father, it is already done."

But the Matabele, who should have been frightened, only laughed again, and their spokesman said :

"See, my brothers, he thinks to trap us who are but three. Well, kill on, Old Wizard, if you will, but know that if a hand is lifted, this spear of mine goes through your heart, and that the children of Lobengula die hard. Know also that then the impi which waits not far away will destroy you every one, man and woman, youth and maiden, little ones who hold the hand and infants at the breast; none shall be left—none at all, to say, 'Here once lived the cowardly Makalanga of Bambatse.' Nay, be not foolish, but talk softly with us, so that perhaps we may spare your lives."

Then the three men placed themselves back to back, in such fashion that they faced every way, and could not be smitten down from behind, and waited.

"I do not kill envoys," said the Molimo, "but if they are foul-mouthed, I throw them out of my walls. Your message, men of the Amandabele ?"

"I hear you. Hearken now to the word of Lobengula."

Then the envoy began to speak, using the pronoun I as though it were the Matabele king himself who spoke to his vassal, the Makalanga chief : "I sent to you last year, you slave, who dare to call yourself Mambo of the Makalanga, demanding a tribute of cattle and women, and warning you that if they did not come, I would take them. They did not come, but that time I spared you. Now I send again. Hand over to my messengers fifty cows and fifty oxen, with herds to drive them, and twelve maidens to be approved by them, or I wipe you out, who have troubled the earth too

long, and that before another moon has waned.

"Those are the words of Lobengula," he concluded, and taking the horn snuff-box from the slit in his ear, helped himself, then insolently passed it to the Molimo.

So great was the old chief's rage that, forgetting his self-control, he struck the box from the hand of his tormentor to the ground, where the snuff lay spilled.

"Just so shall the blood of your people be spilled through your rash foolishness," said the messenger calmly, as he picked up the box, and as much of the snuff as he could save.

"Hearken," said the Molimo, in a thin, trembling voice. "Your king demands cattle, knowing that all the cattle are gone, that scarce a cow is left to give drink to a motherless babe. He asks for maidens also, but if he took those he seeks we should have none left for our young men to marry. And why is this so ? It is because the vulture, Lobengula, has picked us to the bone ; yes, while we are yet alive he has torn the flesh from us. Year by year his soldiers have stolen and killed, till at last nothing is left of us. And now he seeks what we have not got to give, in order that he may force a quarrel upon us and murder us. There is nought left for us to give Lobengula. You have your answer."

"Indeed !" replied the envoy with a sneer. "How comes it, then, that yonder I see a waggon laden with goods, and oxen in the yokes ? Yes," he repeated with meaning, "with goods whereof we have known the like at Buluwayo ; for Lobengula also sometimes buys guns from white men, O ! little Makalanga. Come now, give us the waggon with its load and the oxen and the horses, and though it be but a small gift, we will take it away and ask nothing more this year."

"How can I give you the property of my guests, the white men ?" asked the Molimo. "Get you gone, and do your worst, or you shall be thrown from the walls of the fortress."

"Good, but know that very soon we shall return and make an end of you, who are tired of these long and troublesome journeys to gather so little. Go, tend your corn, dwellers in Bambatse,

"'WE HAVE A MESSAGE FOR YOUR EAR, LITTLE OLD MAN'".

for this I swear in the name of Lobengula, never shall you see it ripen more.''

Now the crowd of listening Makalanga trembled at his words, but in the old Molimo they seemed only to rouse a storm of prophetic fury. For a moment he stood staring up at the blue sky, his arms outstretched as though in prayer. Then he spoke in a new voice, a clear, quiet voice that did not seem to be his own.

"Who am I?" he said. "I am the Molimo of the Bambatse Makalanga; I am the ladder between them and Heaven; I sit on the topmost bough of the tree under which they shelter, and there in the crest of the tree Munwali speaks with me. What to you are winds, to me are voices whispering in my spirit's ears. Once my forefathers were great kings, they were Mambos of all this land, and that is still my name and dignity. We lived in peace; we laboured, we did wrong to no man. Then you Zulu savages came upon us from the south-east and your path was red with blood. Year after year you robbed and you destroyed; you raided our cattle, you murdered our men, you took our maidens and our children to be your women and your slaves, until at length, of all this pit filled with the corn of life, there is left but a little handful. And this you say you will eat up also, lest it should fall into good ground and grow again. I tell you that I think it will not be so; but whether or no that happens, I have words for the ear of your king, a message for a message. Say to him that thus speaks the wise old Molimo of Bambatse.

" I see him hunted like a wounded hyena through the rivers, in the deep bush, and over the mountain. I see him die in pain and misery; but his grave I see not, for no man shall know it. I see the white men take his land and all his wealth; yea, to them and to no son of his shall his people give the Bayéte, the royal salute. Of his greatness and his power, this alone shall remain to him—a name accursed from generation to generation. And last of all I see peace upon the land and upon my children's children." He paused, then added: " For you, cruel dog that you are, this message also from the Munwali, by the lips of his Molimo. I lift no hand against you, but you shall not live to look again upon your king's face. Begone now, and do your worst.''

For a moment the three Matabele seemed to be frightened, and Benita heard one of them say to his companions:

" The Wizard has bewitched us! He has bewitched the Great Elephant and all his people! Shall we kill him?''

But quickly shaking off his fears their spokesman laughed, and answered:

" So that is what you have brought the white people here for, old traitor, to plot against the throne of Lobengula.''

He wheeled round and stared at Mr. Clifford and Jacob Meyer; then added:

" Good, Grey-beard and Black-beard: I myself will put you both to such a death as you have never heard of, and as for the girl, since she is well-favoured, she shall brew the king's beer, and be numbered among the king's wives, unless, indeed, he is pleased to give her to me.''

In an instant the thing was done! At the man's words about Benita, Meyer, who had been listening to his threats and bombast unconcerned, suddenly seemed to awake. His dark eyes flashed, his pale face turned cruel. Snatching the revolver from his belt he seemed to point and fire it with one movement, and down—dead or dying—went the Matabele.

Men did not stir, they only stared. Accustomed as they were to death in that wild land, the suddenness of this deed surprised them. The contrast between the splendid, brutal savage who had stood before them a moment ago, and the limp, black thing going to sleep upon the ground, was strange enough to move their imaginations. There he lay, and there over him, the smoking pistol in his hand, Meyer stood and laughed.

Benita felt that the act was just, and the awful punishment deserved. Yet that laugh of Jacob's jarred upon her, for in it she thought she heard the man's heart speaking; and oh, its voice was merciless! Surely Justice should not laugh when her sword falls!

"Behold, now," said the Molimo in his still voice, pointing at the dead Matabele with his finger; " do I speak lies, or is it true that this man shall not look more upon his king's face? Well, as it was with the servant, so it shall be with the lord, only more slowly. It is the decree of the Munwali spoken by the voice of his Mouth, the Molimo of Bambatse. Go, children of Lobengula, and bear with you as an offering this first-fruit of the harvest that the white men shall reap among the warriors of his people."

The thin voice died away, and there was silence so intense that Benita thought she heard the scraping of the feet of a green lizard which crept across a stone a yard or two away.

Then of a sudden it ended. Of a sudden the two remaining Matabele turned and fled for their lives, and as, when dogs run, a flock of sheep will wheel about and pursue them, so did the Makalanga. They grabbed at the messengers with their hands, tearing their finery from them; they struck them with sticks, they pounded them with stones, till at length two bruised and bleeding men, finding all escape cut off, and led perhaps by some instinct, staggered back to where Benita stood horrified at this dreadful scene, and throwing themselves upon the ground, clutched her dress and prayed for mercy.

"Move a little, Miss Clifford," said Meyer. "Three of those brutes will not weigh heavier than one upon my conscience."

"No, no, you shall not," she answered. "Mambo, these men are messengers; spare them."

"Hearken to the voice of pity," said the old prophet, "spoken in a place where pity never was, and not in vain. Let them go. Give mercy to the merciless, for she buys their lives with prayer."

"They will bring the others on us," muttered Tamas, and even old Mr. Clifford shook his head sadly. But the Molimo only said:

"I have spoken. Let them go. That which will befall must befall, and from this deed no ill shall come that would not have come otherwise."

"You hear. Depart swiftly," said Benita, in Zulu.

With difficulty the two men dragged themselves to their feet, and supporting each other, stood before her. One of them, a clever, powerful-faced man, whose black hair was tinged with grey, addressing himself to Benita, gasped:

"Hear me. That fool there," and he pointed to his dead companion, "whose boasting brought his death upon him, was but a low fellow. I, who kept silence and let him talk, am Maduna, a prince of the royal house, who justly deserve to die because I turned my back upon these dogs. Yet I and my brother here take life at your hands, Lady, who, now that I have had time to think, would refuse it at theirs. For, whether I stay or go does not matter. The impi waits, the slayers are beneath the walls. Those things which are decreed will happen; there, yonder old Wizard speaks true. Listen, Lady: should it chance that you have cause to demand two lives at the hands of Maduna, in his own name and the name of his king he promises them to you. In safety shall they pass, they and all that is theirs without toll taken. Remember the oath of Maduna, Lady, in the hour of your need, and do you, my brother, bear witness to it among our people."

Then, straightening themselves as well as they were able, these two sorely hurt men lifted their right arms and gave to Benita the salute due to a chieftainess. This done, taking no note of any other creature there, they limped away to the gate that had been opened for them, and vanished beyond the wall.

All this while Meyer had stood silent, now he spoke with a bitter smile.

"Charity, Miss Clifford, said a certain Paul, as reported in your New Testament, covers a multitude of sins. I hope very much that it will serve to cover our remains from the aasvogels, after we have met our deaths in some such fashion as that brute promised us," and he pointed to the dead man.

Benita looked at her father in question.

"Mr. Meyer means, my dear, that you have done a foolish thing in begging the lives of those Matabele. It would have been safer for us all if they were dead, who as it is have gone off burning for revenge. Of course, I understand it was natural enough, but," and he hesitated and stopped.

"The chief did not say so," broke in Benita with agitation; "besides, if he had, I should not have cared. It was bad enough to see one man killed like that," and she shivered; "I could not bear any more."

"You should not be angry at the fellow's death, seeing that it was what he said of you which brought it upon him," Meyer replied with meaning. "Otherwise he might have gone unharmed so far as I was concerned. For the rest, I did not interfere because I saw it was useless; also I am a fatalist like our friend, the Molimo, and believe in what is decreed. The truth is," he added sharply, "among savages ladies are not in place."

"Why did you not say that down at Rooi Krantz, Jacob?" asked Mr. Clifford. "You know I thought so all the while, but somehow I was over-ruled. Now what I suggest is, that we had better get out of this place as fast as we can—instantly, as soon as we have eaten, before our retreat is cut off."

Meyer looked at the oxen which had been outspanned: nine were wandering about picking up what food they could, but the five which were supposed to have been bitten by tetse fly had lain down.

"Nine worn out and footsore oxen will not draw the waggon," he said; "also in all probability the place is already surrounded by Matabele, who merely let us in to be sure of the guns which their spies must have told them we were carrying. Lastly, having spent so much and come so far, I do not mean to go without what we seek. Still, if you think that your daughter's danger is greater within these walls than outside of them, you might try, if we can hire servants, which I doubt. Or possibly, if any rowers are to be had, you could go down the Zambesi in a canoe, risking the fever. You and she must settle it, Clifford."

"Difficulties and dangers every way one looks. Benita, what do you say?" asked her father distractedly.

Benita thought a moment. She wished to escape from Mr. Meyer, of whom she was weary and afraid, and would have endured much to do so. On the other hand, her father was tired out, and needed rest; also to turn his back upon this venture now would have been a bitter blow to him. Moreover, lacking cattle and men, how was it to be done? Lastly, something within her, that same voice which had bidden her to come, seemed to bid her to stay. Very soon she had made up her mind.

"Father, dear," she said, "thank you for thinking of me, but as far as I can see, we should run more risks trying to get away than we do in stopping here. I wanted to come, though you warned me against it, and now I must take my chance and trust to God to bring us safe through all dangers. Surely with all those rifles the Makalanga ought to be able to hold such a place as this against the Matabele."

"I hope so," answered her father; "but they are a timid folk. Still, though it would have been far better never to have come, I think with you that it is best to stay where we are, and trust to God."

CHAPTER X.

THE MOUNTAIN TOP.

IF our adventurers, or any of them, hoped that they were going to be led to the secret places of the fortress that day, they were destined to disappointment. Indeed, the remainder of it was employed arduously enough in unpacking rifles, and a supply of ammunition; also in giving to a few of the leading Makalanga preliminary lessons in the method of their use, a matter as to which their ideas were of the vaguest. The rest of the tribe, having brought their women and children into the outer enclosure of the ancient stronghold, and with them their sheep and goats and the few cattle which remained to them, were employed in building up the entrance permanently with stones, a zig-zag secret path upon the river side, that could be stopped in a few minutes, being now their only method of ingress and egress through the thickness of the walls. A certain number of men also were sent out as spies to discover, if possible, the whereabouts of the Matabele impi.

That there was some impi they were almost sure, for a woman who had followed them reported that the injured captain, Maduna, and his companion had been met at a distance of about three miles from Bambatse by a small party of Matabele who were hiding in some bushes, and that these men had made litters for them, and carried them away; whither she did not know, for she had not dared to pursue them further.

That night Benita passed in the guest-

"DOWN—DEAD OR DYING—WENT THE MATABELE"

house which was only a hut rather larger than the others, while the two men slept in the waggon just outside. She was so tired that for a long while she could not rest. Her mind kept flying back to all the events of the day: the strange words of that mystic old Molimo, concerning herself; the arrival of the brutal messengers and the indaba that followed; then the sudden and awful destruction of their spokesman at the hand of Jacob Meyer. The scene would not leave her eyes: she saw it again and yet again; the quick transformation of Meyer's indifferent face when the soldier began to insult and threaten her, the lightning-like movement of his hand, the flash, the report, the change from life to death, and the slayer's cruel laugh. He could be very terrible, Jacob Meyer, when his passions were roused!

And what had aroused them then? She could not doubt that it was herself—not mere chivalry towards a woman. Even if he were capable of chivalry, merely for that he would never have taken such risk of future trouble and revenge. No: it was something deeper. He had never said anything or done anything, yet long ago instinct or insight had caused Benita to suspect the workings of his mind, and now she was sure of them. The thought was terrible—worse than all her other dangers put together. True, she had her father to rely on, but he had been somewhat ailing of late; age and these arduous journeys and anxieties had told upon him. Supposing that anything were to happen to him—if he died, for instance, how dreadful her position might become, left alone far from the reach of help, with savages—and Jacob Meyer.

Oh! if it had not been for that dreadful shipwreck, how different might be her lot to-day! Well, it was the thought of the shipwreck and of him whom she had lost therein, which had driven her on to this adventure, that in it perhaps her suffering mind might be numbed to rest; and now she must face its issues. God still remained above her, and she would put her trust in Him. After all, if she died, what did it matter?

But that old Molimo had promised her that she was safe from death, that she should find here happiness and rest, though not that of the grave. He promised this, speaking as one who knew of all her grief, and a very little while afterwards, in the case of the Matabele soldier, he had proved himself a prophet of awful power. Also—she knew not how, she knew not why—now as before, her inmost heart seemed to bear witness that this old dreamer's words were true, and that for her, in some strange manner unforeseen, there still remained a rest.

Comforted a little by this intuition, at length Benita fell asleep.

Next morning, when she came out of the hut, Benita was met by her father, who with a cheerful countenance informed her that at any rate as yet there was no sign of the Matabele. A few hours later, too, some spies came in who said that for miles round nothing could be seen or heard of them. Still the preparations for defence went on, and the hundred best men having been furnished with the rifles, were being drilled in the use of them by Tamas and his two companions, Tamala and Hoba, who had learned how to handle a gun very well in the course of their long journey. The shooting of these raw recruits, however, proved to be execrable; indeed, so dangerous were they that when one of them fired at a mark set upon the wall, it was found necessary to order all the rest to lie down. As it was, a poor trek-ox—luckily it was sick—and two sheep were killed.

Foreseeing a scarcity of provisions in the event of a siege, Meyer, provident as ever, had already decreed the death of the tetse-bitten cattle. These were accordingly despatched, and having been skinned and cut up, their flesh was severed into long strips to be dried in the burning sun as biltong, which secretly Benita hoped she might never be called upon to eat. Yet the time was to come when she would swallow that hard, tetse-poisoned flesh with thankfulness.

At midday, after they had eaten, Mr. Clifford and Meyer went to the Molimo, where he sat against the second wall, and pointing to the men with the guns, said:

"We have fulfilled our bargain. Now fulfil yours. Lead us to the holy place that we may begin our search."

"So be it," he answered. "Follow me, white people."

Then, quite unattended, he guided them round the inner wall till they came to a path of rock not more than a yard wide, beneath which was a precipice fifty feet or so in depth that almost overhung the river. This giddy path they followed for about twenty paces, to find that it ended in a cleft in the wall so narrow that only one person could walk through it at a time. That it must have been the approach to the second stronghold was evident, however, since it was faced on either side with dressed stones, and even the foundation granite had been worn by the human feet which had passed here for ages upon ages. This path zig-zagged to and fro in the thickness of the wall till it brought them finally within its circle, a broad belt of steeply-rising ground, covered like that below with the tumbled ruins of buildings amidst which grew bush and trees.

"Heaven send that the gold is not buried here," said Mr. Clifford, surveying the scene; "for if it is, we shall never find it."

The Molimo seemed to guess the meaning of his words from his face, for he answered:

"I think not here. The besiegers won this place and camped in it for many weeks. I could show you where they built their fires and tried to undermine the last wall within which the Portuguese sat about until hunger killed them, for they could not eat their gold. Follow me again."

So on they went up the slope till they came to the base of the third wall, and as before, passed round it, and reached a point above the river. But now there was no passage, only some shallow and almost precipitous steps cut from single stones leading from the foot of the wall to its summit, more than thirty feet above.

"Really," said Benita, contemplating this perilous ascent with dismay; "the ways of treasure-seekers are hard. I don't think I can;" while her father also looked at them and shook his head.

"We must get a rope," said Meyer to the Molimo angrily. "How can we climb that place without one, with such a gulf below?"

"I am old, but I climb it," answered the aged man in mild surprise, since to him, who had trodden it all his life, it seemed not difficult. "Still," he added, "I have a rope above which I use upon dark nights. I will ascend and let it down."

Ascend he did accordingly; indeed, it was a wondrous sight to see his withered legs scrambling from step to step as unconcernedly as though he were going upstairs. No monkey could have been more agile, or more absolutely impervious to the effects of height. Soon he vanished in or rather through the crest of the wall, and presently appeared again on the top step, whence he let down a stout hide rope, remarking that it was securely tied. So anxious was Meyer to enter the hidden place of which he had dreamed so long that he scarcely waited for it to reach his hand before he began the climb, which he accomplished safely. Then, sitting on the top of the wall, he directed Mr. Clifford to fasten the end of the rope round Benita's waist, and her turn came.

It was not so bad as she expected, for she was agile, and the knowledge that the rope would prevent disaster gave her confidence. In a very little while she had grasped Meyer's outstretched hand, and been drawn into safety through a kind of aperture above the top step. Then the rope was let down again for her father, who tied it about his middle. Well was it that he did so, since when he was about half way up, awkwardness or, perhaps, loss of nerve—neither of them wonderful in an old man—caused his foot to slip, and had it not been for the rope which Meyer and the Molimo held, he would certainly have fallen into the river some hundreds of feet below. As it was, he recovered himself, and presently arrived panting and very pale. In her relief Benita kissed him, and even as she did so thought again that she had been very near to being left alone with Jacob Meyer.

"All's well that ends well, my dear," he said. "But upon my word I am beginning to wish that I had been content with the humble profits of horse-breeding."

Benita made no answer; it seemed too late for any useful consideration of the point.

"Clever men, those ancients," said Meyer. "See," and he pointed out to

"LOSS OF NERVE . . . CAUSED HIS FOOT TO SLIP"

her how, by drawing a heavy stone which still lay close by over the aperture through which they had crept, the ascent of the wall could be made absolutely impossible to any enemy, since at its crest it was battened outwards, not inwards, as is usual in these ancient ruins.

"Yes," she answered, "we ought to be safe enough inside here, and that's as well, since I do not feel inclined to go out again at present."

Then they paused to look about them, and this was what they saw :

The wall, built like those below, of unmortared blocks of stone, remained in a wonderfully good state of preservation, for its only enemies had been time, the tropical rains, and the growth of shrubs and trees which here and there had cracked and displaced the stones. It enclosed all the top of the hill, perhaps three acres of ground, and on it at intervals were planted soap-stone pillars, each of them about twelve feet in height, and fashioned at the top to a rude resemblance of a vulture. Many of these columns, however, had been blown down, or perhaps struck by lightning, and lay broken upon the wall, or if they had fallen inward, at its foot; but some, six or eight perhaps, were still standing.

Benita learned afterwards that they must have been placed there by the ancient Phœnicians, or whatever people constructed this gigantic fortification, and had something to do with the exact recording of the different seasons of the year, and their sub-divisions, by means of the shadows which they cast. As yet, however, she did not pay much attention to them, for she was engaged in considering a more remarkable relic of antiquity which stood upon the very verge of the precipice, the wall, indeed, being built up to its base on either side.

It was the great cone of which Robert Seymour had told her, fifty feet high or more, such as is to be found in most Phœnician temples. But in this case it was not built of masonry, but shaped by the hand of man out of a single gigantic granite monolith of the sort that are sometimes to be met with in Africa, that thousands or millions of years ago had been left standing thus when the softer rock around it was worn away by time and weather. On the inner side of this cone were easy steps whereby it could be ascended, and its top, which might have been six feet in diameter, was fashioned to the shape of a cup, probably for the purposes of acts of worship and of sacrifice. This extraordinary monument, which except on the river side could not be seen from below on account of the slope of the hill, leaned slightly outwards, so that a stone dropped from its crest would fall into the waters of the stream.

"Thence it was," said the Molimo, "that my forefathers saw the last of the Portuguese, the fair daughter of the great Captain Ferreira, hurl herself to death after she had given the gold into our keeping, and laid the curse upon it, until she came again. So in my dreams have I seen and heard her also, ay, and others have seen her, but these only from the river far below."

He paused awhile, looking at Benita with his queer, dreamy eyes; then said suddenly :

"Say, Lady, do you remember nothing of that matter ? "

Now Benita grew vexed, for the whole thing was uncanny and jarred upon her.

"How can I remember ? " she asked, "who was born not five and twenty years ago ? "

"I do not know," he answered. "How should I know who am but an ignorant old black man, who was born not much more than eighty years ago ? Yet, Lady, tell me, for I seek your wisdom, where were you born from ? Out of the earth or out of the heavens ? What ? You shake your head; you who do not remember. Well, neither do I remember; yet it is true that all circles meet somewhere, and it is true that the Portuguese maiden said she would come again, and lastly it is true that she was such an one as you are, for she haunts this place, and I, who have seen her sitting yonder in the moonlight, know her beauty well. Yet mayhap she comes no more in flesh, but still her spirit comes; for Lady, out of those eyes of yours I see it gaze at me. Come," he added abruptly, "let us descend the wall, for as you cannot remember, there is more to show you. Have no fear, the steps are easy."

So they went down without much

difficulty, since, from the accumulation of rubbish and other causes, the wall was a great deal lower on this side, and found themselves in the usual dense growth of vegetation and brushwood through which ran a little path. It led them past the ruins of buildings whereof the use and purpose were long since forgotten, for their roofs had fallen in hundreds or thousands of years ago, to the entrance of a cave which was placed almost at the foot of the monolithic cone, but thirty or forty yards further from the circle of the wall. Here the Molimo bade them stay while he lit the lamps within. Five minutes passed and he returned, saying that all was ready.

"Be not afraid of what you may see," he added, "for know, white people, that save my forefathers and myself, none have entered this place since the Portuguese perished here, nor have we who do but come hither to pray and receive the word of the Munwali, ever ventured to disturb it. As it was, so it is. Come, Lady, come; she whose spirit goes with you was the last of your white race to pass this door. It is therefore fitting that your feet and her spirit should be the first to enter it again."

Benita hung back a little, for the adventure was eërie; then, determined that she would show no fear in the presence of this old priest, took the thin hand he stretched out to her and walked forward with head erect. The two men began to follow her, but the Molimo stopped them, saying:

"Not so, the maiden enters first alone with me; it is her house and should it please her to ask you to dwell therein, so be it. But first she must visit her house alone."

"Nonsense," said Mr. Clifford angrily. "I will not have it. It will frighten her."

"Lady, do you trust me?" asked the Molimo.

"Yes," she answered, adding: "Father, I think that you had better let me go alone. I am not afraid now, and it may be wisest not to thwart him. This is a very strange business—not like anything else—and really I think that I had better go alone. If I do not come back presently, you can follow."

"Those who break in upon the sleep of the dead should walk gently, gently," piped the old Molimo in a sing-song voice; "the maiden's breath is pure, the maiden's foot is light, her breath will not offend the dead, her step will not disturb the dead. White men, white men, anger not the dead, for the dead are mighty and will be revenged upon you when you are dead; soon, very soon, when you are dead—dead in your sorrows, dead in your sins, dead, gathered to that company of the dead who await us here."

And still chanting his mystic song, he led Benita by the hand out of the light, onward into darkness, away from life, onward into the place of death.

CHAPTER XI.

THE SLEEPERS IN THE CAVE.

LIKE every other passage in this old fortress, the approach to the cave was narrow and winding; presumably the ancients had arranged them thus to facilitate their defence. After the third bend, however, Benita saw a light ahead which flowed from a native lamp lit in the arched entrance. At the side of this arch was a shell-shaped hollow, cut in the rock about three feet above the floor. Its appearance seemed familiar to her; why, she was soon to learn, although at the moment she did not connect it with anything in particular. The cave beyond was large, lofty, and not altogether natural, for its walls had evidently been shaped, or at any rate trimmed by man. Probably here the Phœnicians had established their oracle, or place of offering.

At first Benita could not see much, since in that great cavern two lamps of hippopotamus oil gave but little light. Presently, however, her eyes became accustomed to the gloom, and as they advanced up its length she perceived that save for a skin rug upon which she guessed the Molimo sat at his solitary devotions, and some gourds and platters for water and food, all the front part of the place appeared to be empty. Beyond, in its centre, stood an object of some gleaming metal, that from its double handles and roller borne upon supports of rock, she took to be some kind of winch, and rightly, for beneath it was the mouth of a great well, the water supply of this topmost fortification.

Beyond the well was a stone altar, shaped like a truncated cone or pyramid, and at some distance away against the far wall, as she dimly discovered by the lamp that stood upon the altar, cut in relief upon that wall indeed, a colossal cross to which, vigorously if rudely executed in white stone, hung the image of Christ crucified, the crown of thorns upon His drooping head. Now she understood. Whatever may have been the first worship to which this place was dedicated Christians had usurped it, and set up here the sacred symbol of their faith, awful enough to look upon in such surroundings. Doubtless, also, the shell-shaped basin at the entrance had served the worshippers in this underground chapel as a stoup for holy water.

The Molimo lifted the lamp from the altar, and having adjusted its wick, held it up in front of the rood before which, although she was no Catholic, Benita bowed her head and crossed herself, while he watched her curiously. Then he lowered it, and she perceived that on the cemented floor lay great numbers of shrouded forms that at first looked to her like folk asleep. He stepped to one of them and touched it with his foot, whereon the cloth with which it was covered crumbled into dust, revealing beneath a white skeleton.

All those sleepers rested well indeed, for they had been dead at least two hundred years. There they lay, men, women, and children, though of the last but few. Some of them had ornaments on their bones, some were clad in armour, and by all the men were swords, or spears, or knives, and here and there what she took to be primitive fire-arms. Certain of them also had turned into mummies in that dry air—grotesque and dreadful objects from which she gladly averted her eyes.

The Molimo led her forward to the foot of the crucifix, where, upon its lowest step and upon the cemented floor immediately beneath it respectively, lay two shapes decorously covered with shawls of some heavy material interwoven with gold wire, for the manufacture of which the Makalanga were famous when first the Portuguese came into contact with them. The Molimo took hold of the cloths that seemed almost as good now as on the day when they were woven, and lifted them, revealing beneath the figures of a man and woman. The features were unrecognisable, although the hair, white in the man's case and raven black in that of the woman, remained perfect. They had been great people, for orders glittered upon the man's breast, and his sword was gold hilted, whilst the woman's bones were adorned with costly necklaces and jewels, and in her hand was still a book bound in sheets of silver. Benita took it up and looked at it; it was a missal beautifully illuminated, which doubtless the poor lady had been reading when at length she sank exhausted into the sleep of death.

"See the Lord Ferreira and his wife," said the Molimo, "whom their daughter laid thus before she went to join them." Then, at a motion from Benita, he covered them up again with the golden cloths.

"Here they sleep," he went on in his chanting voice, "a hundred and fifty and three of them, a hundred and fifty and three, and when I dream in this place at night I have seen the ghosts of everyone of them arise from beside their forms and come gliding down the cave, the husband with the wife, the child with the mother, to look at me and ask when the maiden returns again to take her heritage and give them burial."

Benita shuddered; the solemn awfulness of the place and scene oppressed her. She began to think that she, too, saw those ghosts.

"It is enough," she said; "let us be going."

So they went, and the pitiful, agonised Christ upon the cross, at which she glanced from time to time over her shoulder, faded to a white blot, then vanished away in the darkness, through which, from generation to generation, it kept its watch above the dead, those dead that in their despair once had cried to it for mercy, and bedewed its feet with tears.

Glad, oh! glad, was she when she had left that haunted place behind her, and saw the wholesome light again.

"What have you seen?" asked her father and Meyer, in one breath, as they noted her white and frightened face.

She sank upon a stone seat at the

entrance of the cave, and before she could open her lips the Molimo answered for her:

"The maiden has seen the dead. The Spirit who goes with her has given greeting to its dead that it left so long ago. The maiden has done reverence to the White One who hangs upon the cross, and asked a blessing and a pardon of Him, as she whose Spirit goes with her did reverence before the eyes of my forefathers, and asked a blessing and a pardon ere she cast herself away;" and he pointed to the little golden crucifix which hung upon Benita's bosom, attached to the necklace which Tamas, the messenger, had given her at Rooi Krantz.

"Now," he went on, "now the spell is broken, and the sleepers must depart to sleep elsewhere. Enter, white men, enter if you dare, and ask for pardon and for blessing if it may be found, and gather up the dry bones and take the treasure that was theirs, if it may be found, and conquer the curse that goes with the treasure for all save one, if you can, if you can, if you can! Rest you here, maiden, in the sweet sunshine, and follow me, white men, follow me into the dark of the dead to seek for that which the white men love;" and once more he vanished down the passage, turning now and again to beckon to them, while they went after him as though drawn against their wish. For now, at the last moment, some superstitious fear spread from him to them, and showed itself in their eyes.

To Benita, half fainting upon the stone seat, for this experience had shaken her to the heart, it seemed but a few minutes, though really the best part of an hour had gone by, when her father reappeared as white-faced as she had been.

"Where is Mr. Meyer?" she asked.

"Oh," he answered, "he is collecting all the golden ornaments off those poor bodies, and tumbling their bones together in a corner of the cave."

Benita uttered an exclamation of horror.

"I know what you mean," said her father; "but, curse the fellow! he has no reverence, although at first he seemed almost as scared as I was myself. He said that as we could not begin our search with all those corpses about, they had best be got out of the way as soon as possible. Or, perhaps it was because he is really afraid of them and wanted to prove to himself that they are nothing more than dust. Benita," went on the old man, "to tell you the truth, I wish heartily that we had left this business alone. I don't believe that any good will come of it, and certainly it has brought enough trouble already. That old prophet of a Molimo has the second sight, or something like it, and he does not hide his opinion, but keeps chuckling away in that dreadful place, and piping out his promises of ill to be."

"He promised me nothing but good," said Benita with a little smile, "though I don't see how it can happen. But if you dislike the thing, father, why not give it up and try to escape?"

"It is too late, dear," he replied passionately. "Meyer would never come, and I can't in honour leave him. Also, I should laugh at myself for the rest of my life; and after all, why should we not have the gold if it can be found? It belongs to nobody; we do not get it by robbery or murder; nuggets are of no use to Portuguese who have been dead two hundred years, and whose heirs, if they have any, it is impossible to discover. Nor can it matter to them whether they lie about singly as they died or were placed after death, or piled together in a corner. Our fears are mere churchyard superstitions, which we have caught from that ghoul of a Molimo. Don't you agree with me?"

"Yes, I suppose so," answered Benita, "though a fate may cling to certain things or places, perhaps. At any rate, I think that it is of no use turning back now, even if we had anywhere to turn, so we may as well go through with the venture and await its end. Give me the water-bottle, please. I am thirsty."

A while later and Jacob Meyer appeared also, carrying a great bundle of precious objects wrapped in one of the gold cerecloths, which bundle he hid away behind a stone.

"The cave is much tidier, now," he said, as he flicked the thick dust which had collected on them during his unhallowed task from his hands, and hair, and garments. Then he drank greedily, and asked,

"ON THE CEMENTED FLOOR LAY GREAT NUMBERS OF SHROUDED FORMS"

"Have you two made any plans for our future researches?"

They shook their heads.

"Well then, I have. I thought them out while I was bone-carting, and here they are. It is no use our going down below again; for one thing, the journey is too dangerous, and takes too long; and for another, we are safer up above, where we have plenty to do."

"But," said Benita, "how about things to eat and sleep on, and the rest?"

"Simple enough, Miss Clifford: we must get them up. The Kaffirs will bring them to the foot of the third wall, and we will haul them to its top with a rope. Of water it seems there is plenty in that well, which is fed by a spring a hundred and fifty feet down, and the old chain is still on the roller, so we only need a couple of buckets from the waggon. Of wood for cooking there is plenty also, growing on the spot, and we can camp in the cave or outside of it, as we like, according to the state of the weather. Now, do you rest here while I go down. I will be back in an hour with some of the gear, and then you must help me."

So he went, and the end of it was that before nightfall they had enough things for their immediate needs, and by the second night, working very hard, were more or less comfortably established in their strange habitation. The canvas flap from the waggon was arranged as a tent for Benita, the men sleeping beneath a thick-leaved tree near by. Close at hand under another tree was their cooking place. The provisions of all sorts, including a couple of cases of square-face and a large supply of biltong from the slaughtered cattle, they stored with a quantity of ammunition in the mouth of the cave. Fresh meat also was brought to them daily, and hauled up in baskets—that is until there was none to bring—and with it grain for bread, and green mealies to serve as vegetables. Therefore, as the water from the well proved to be excellent and quite accessible, they were soon set up in all things necessary, and to these they added from time to time as opportunity offered.

In all these preparations the old Molimo took a part, nor, when they were completed, did he show any inclination to leave them. In the morning he would descend to his people below, but before nightfall he always returned to the cave, where for many years it had been his custom to sleep, at any rate several times a week, in the gruesome company of the dead Portuguese. Jacob Meyer persuaded Mr. Clifford that his object was to spy upon them, and talked of turning him out, but Benita, between whom and the old man had sprung up a curious friendship and sympathy, prevented it, pointing out that they were much safer with the Molimo, as a kind of hostage, than they could be without him; also, that his knowledge of the place, and of other things, might prove of great help to them. So in the end he was allowed to remain, as indeed he had a perfect right to do.

All this while there was no sign of any attack by the Matabele. Indeed, the fear of such a thing was to some extent dying away, and Benita, watching from the top of the wall, could see that their nine remaining oxen, together with the two horses—for that belonging to Jacob Meyer had died—and the Makalanga goats and sheep, were daily driven out to graze; also, that the women were working in the crops upon the fertile soil around the lowest wall. Still a strict watch was kept, and at night everyone slept within the fortifications; moreover, the drilling of the men and their instruction in the use of fire-arms went on continually under Tamas, who now, in his father's old age, was the virtual chief of the people.

It was on the fourth morning that at length, all their preparations being completed, the actual search for the treasure began. First, the Molimo was closely interrogated as to its whereabouts, since they thought that even if he did not know this exactly, some traditions of the fact might have descended to him from his ancestors. But he declared with earnestness that he knew nothing, save that the Portuguese maiden had said that it was hidden; nor, he added, had any dream or vision ever come to him concerning this matter, in which he took no interest. If it was there, it was there; if it was not there, it was not there—it remained for the white men to search and see.

For no very good reason Meyer had

concluded that the gold must have been concealed in or about the cave, so here it was that they began their investigations.

First, they bethought them of the well into which it might possibly have been thrown, but the fact of this matter proved very difficult to ascertain. Tying a piece of metal—it was an old Portuguese sword-hilt, to a string, they let it down and found that it touched water at a depth of a hundred and twenty feet, and bottom at a depth of one hundred and forty-seven feet. Therefore there were twenty-seven feet of water. Weighting a bucket they sank it until it rested upon this bottom, then wound it up again several times. On the third occasion it brought up a human bone and a wire anklet of pure gold. But this proved nothing, except that some ancient, perhaps thousands of years ago, had been thrown, or had fallen into the well.

Still unsatisfied, Jacob Meyer, who was a most intrepid person, determined to investigate the place himself, a task of no little difficulty and danger, since proper ladders were wanting, nor, had they existed, was there anything to stand them on. Therefore it came to this: a seat must be rigged on to the end of the old copper chain, and be lowered into the pit after the fashion of the bucket. But, as Benita pointed out, although they might let him down, it was possible that they would not be able to draw him up again, in which case his plight must prove unfortunate. So, when the seat had been prepared, an experiment was made with a stone weighing approximately as much as a man. This Benita and her father let down easily enough, but, as they anticipated, when it came to winding it up again, their strength was barely sufficient to the task. Three people could do it well, but with two the thing was risky. Now Meyer asked, or rather commanded the Molimo to order some of his men to help them, but this the old chief refused point blank to do.

First, he made a number of excuses. They were all employed in drilling and in watching for the Matabele; they were afraid to venture here, and so forth. At last Meyer grew furious, his eyes flashed, he ground his teeth, and began to threaten.

"White man," said the Molimo, when he had done, "it cannot be. I have fulfilled my bargain with you. Search for the gold; find it and take it away if you can. But this place is holy. None of my tribe, save he who holds the office of Molimo for the time, may set a foot therein. Kill me if you will, I care not; but so it is, and if you kill me, afterwards they will kill you."

Now Meyer, seeing that nothing was to be gained by violence, changed his tone, and asked if he himself would help them.

"I am old, my strength is small," he replied; "yet I will put my hand to the chain and do my best. But, if I were you, I would not descend that pit."

"Still I will descend it, and to-morrow," said Meyer.

CHAPTER XII.

THE BEGINNING OF THE SEARCH.

ACCORDINGLY, on the next day the great experiment was made. The chain and ancient winding gear had been tested and proved to be amply sufficient to the strain. Therefore, nothing remained save for Meyer to place himself in the wooden seat with an oil-lamp, and in case this should be extinguished, matches and candles, of both of which they had a large supply.

He did so boldly enough, and swung out over the mouth of the pit, while the three of them clutched the handles of the winch. Then they began to lower, and slowly his white face disappeared into the black depth. At every few turns his descent was stopped that he might examine the walls of the well, and when he was about fifty feet down he called to them to hold on, which they did, listening while he struck at the rock with a hammer, for here it sounded very hollow.

At length he shouted to them to lower away again, and they obeyed, until nearly all the chain was out, and they knew he must be near the water. Now Benita, peeping over the edge, saw that the star of light had vanished. His lamp was out, nor did he appear to attempt to re-light it. They shouted down the well to him, but no answer coming, began to wind up as fast as they were able. It was all that their united strength could manage, and very exhausted were they when at length

Jacob reappeared at the top. At first, from the look of him they thought that he was dead, and had he not tied himself to the chain, dead he certainly would have been, for evidently his senses had left him long ago. Indeed, he had fallen almost out of the seat, over which his legs hung limply, his weight being supported by the hide rope beneath his arms which was made fast to the chain.

They swung him in and dashed water over his face, till, to their relief, at last he began to gasp for breath, and revived sufficiently to enable them to half-lead and half-carry him out into the fresh air.

"What happened to you?" asked Clifford.

"Poisoned with gases, I suppose," Meyer answered with a groan, for his head was aching sadly; "the air is often bad at the bottom of deep wells, but I could smell or feel nothing until suddenly my senses left me, It was a near thing—a very near thing."

Afterwards, when he had recovered a little, he told them that at one spot deep down in the well, on the river side of it, he found a place where it looked as though the rock had been cut away for a space of about six feet by four, and afterwards built up again with another sort of stone set in hard mortar or cement. Immediately beneath, too, were socket holes in which the ends of beams still remained, suggesting that here had been a floor or platform. It was while he was examining these rotted beams that insensibility overcame him. He added that he thought that this might be the entrance to the place where the gold was hidden.

"If so," said Mr. Clifford, "hidden it must remain, since it can have no better guardian than bad air. Also, floors like that are common in all wells to prevent rubbish from falling into the water, and the stonework you saw probably was only put there by the ancients to mend a fault in the rock and prevent the wall from caving in."

"I hope so," said Meyer, "since unless that atmosphere purifies a good deal, I don't think that even I dare go down again, and until one gets there, of that it is difficult to be sure, though of course a lantern on a string will tell one something."

This was the end of their first attempt. The search was not renewed until the following afternoon, when Meyer had recovered a little from the effects of the poisoning and the chafing of the hide ropes beneath his arms. Indeed, from the former he never did quite recover, since thenceforward Benita, who for her own reasons watched the man closely, discovered a marked and progressive change in his demeanour. Hitherto he had appeared to be a reserved man, one who kept tight hand upon himself, and if she knew certain things about him, it was rather because she guessed, or deduced them, than because he allowed them to be seen. On two occasions only had he shown his heart before her—when they had spoken together by the shores of Lake Chrissie on the day of the arrival of the messengers, and he declared his ardent desire for wealth and power; and quite recently, when he killed the Matabele envoy. Yet she felt certain that this heart of his was very passionate and insurgent; that his calm was like the ice that hides the stream, beneath which its currents run fiercely, none can see whither. The fashion in which his dark eyes would flash, even when his pale countenance remained unmoved, told her so, as did other things.

For instance, when he was recovering from his swoon, the first words that passed his lips were in German, of which she understood a little, and she thought that they shaped themselves to her name, coupled with endearing epithets. From that time forward he became less guarded, or rather it seemed as though he were gradually losing power to control himself. He would grow excited without apparent cause, and begin to declaim as to what he would do when he had found the gold; how he would pay the world back all it had caused him to suffer, how he would become a "king."

"I am afraid you will find that exalted position rather lonely," said Benita with a careless laugh, and next minute was sorry that she had spoken, for he answered—looking at her in a way that she did not like:

"Oh, no! there will be a queen, a beautiful queen, whom I shall endow with wealth, and deck with jewels, and surround with love and worship."

"AT LAST MEYER GREW FURIOUS . . . AND BEGAN TO THREATEN"

"What a fortunate lady!" she said, still laughing, but taking the opportunity to go away upon some errand.

At other times, especially after dark, he would walk up and down in front of the cave, muttering to himself, or singing wild old German songs in his rich voice. Also, he made a habit of ascending the granite pillar and seating himself there, and more than once called down to her to come up and share his "throne." Still these outbreaks were so occasional that her father, whose perceptions appeared to Benita to be less keen than formerly, scarcely noticed them, and for the rest his demeanour was what it had always been.

Further researches in the well being out of the question, their next step was to make a thorough inspection of the chapel-cave itself. They examined the walls inch by inch, tapping them with a hammer to hear if they sounded hollow, but without result. They examined the altar, but it proved to be a solid mass of rock. By the help of a little ladder they had made, they examined the crucifix and discovered that the white figure on the cross had evidently been fashioned out of some heathen statue of soft limestone, for at its back were the remains of draperies, and long hair which the artist had not thought it necessary to cut away. Also, they found that the arms had been added and were of a slightly different stone, and that the weight of the figure was taken partly by an iron staple which supported the body, and partly by strong copper wire twisted to resemble cord, and painted white, which was passed round the wrists and supported the arms. This wire ran through loops of rock cut in the traverse of the cross, that itself was only raised in relief by chiselling away the solid stone behind.

Curiously enough, this part of the search was left to Mr. Clifford and Benita, since it was one that Jacob Meyer seemed reluctant to undertake. A Jew by birth, and a man who openly professed his want of belief in that or any other religion, he yet seemed to fear this symbol of the Christian faith, speaking of it as horrible and unlucky; yes, he who without qualm or remorse had robbed and desecrated the dead that lay about its feet. Well, the crucifix told them nothing; but as Mr. Clifford, lantern in hand, descended the ladder which Benita held, Jacob Meyer, who was in front of the altar, called to them excitedly that he had found something.

"Then it is more than we have," said Mr. Clifford, as he laid down the ladder and hurried to him.

Meyer was sounding the floor with a staff of wood, an operation which he had only just begun after the walls proved barren.

"Listen now," he said, letting the heavy staff drop a few paces to the right of the altar, where it produced the hard metallic clang that comes from solid stone when struck. Then he moved to the front of the altar and dropped it again, but now the note was hollow and reverberant. Again and again he repeated the experiment, till they had exactly mapped out where the solid rock ended and that which seemed to be hollow began, a space of about eight feet square.

"We've got it," he said triumphantly; "that's the entrance to the place where the gold is," and the others were inclined to agree with him.

Now it remained to put their theory to the proof, a task of no small difficulty. Indeed, it took them three days of hard, continual work. It will be remembered that the floor of the cave was cemented over, and first of all this cement, which proved to be of excellent quality, being largely composed of powdered granite, must be broken up. By help of a steel crowbar, which they had brought with them in the waggon, at length that part of their task was completed, revealing the rock beneath. By this time Benita was confident that, whatever might lie below, it was not the treasure, since it was evident that the poor, dying Portuguese would not have had the time or the strength to cement it over. When she told the others so, however, Meyer, convinced that he was on the right tack, answered that doubtless it was done by the Makalanga after the Portuguese days, as it was well known that they retained a knowledge of the building arts of their forefathers until quite a recent period, when the Matabele began to kill them out.

When at length the cement was cleared

away and the area swept, they discovered —for there ran the line of it—that here a great stone was let into the floor; it must have weighed several tons. As it was set in cement, however, to lift it, even if they had the strength to work the necessary levers, proved quite impossible. There remained only one thing to be done —to cut a way through. When they had worked at this task for several hours, and only succeeded in making a hole six inches deep, Mr. Clifford, whose old bones ached and whose hands were very sore, suggested that perhaps they might break it up with gunpowder. Accordingly a pound flask of that explosive was poured into the hole, which they closed over with wet clay and a heavy rock, leaving a quill through which ran an extemporised fuse of cotton wick. All being prepared, their fuse was lit, and they left the cave and waited.

Five minutes afterwards the dull sound of an explosion reached their ears, but more than an hour went by before the smoke and fumes would allow them to enter the place, and then it was to find that the results did not equal their expectations. To begin with, the slab was only cracked, not shattered, since the strength of the powder had been expended upwards, not downwards, as would have happened in the case of dynamite, of which they had none. Moreover, either the heavy stone which they had placed upon it, striking the roof of the cave, or the concussion of the air, had brought down many tons of rock and caused wide and dangerous looking cracks. Also, though she said nothing of it, it seemed to Benita that the great white statue on the cross was leaning a little further forward than it used to do. So the nett result of the experiment was that they were obliged to drag away great fragments of the fallen roof that lay upon the stone, which remained almost as solid and obdurate as before.

So there was nothing for it but to go on working with the crowbar. At length, towards the evening of the third day of their labour, when the two men were utterly tired out, a hole was broken through, demonstrating the fact that beneath this cover lay a hollow of some sort. Mr. Clifford, to say nothing of

Benita, who was heartily weary of the business, wished to postpone further proceedings till the morrow, but Jacob Meyer would not. So they toiled on until about eleven o'clock at night, when at length the aperture was of sufficient size to admit a man. Now, as in the case of the well, they let down a stone tied to a string, to find that the place beneath was not more than eight feet deep. Then, to ascertain the condition of the air, a candle was lowered, which at first went out, but presently burnt well enough. This point settled, they brought their ladder, whereby Jacob descended with a lantern.

In another minute they heard the sound of guttural German oaths rising through the hole. Mr. Clifford asked what was the matter, and received the reply that the place was a tomb, with nothing in it but an accursed dead monk, information at which Benita could not help bursting into laughter.

The end of it was that both she and her father went down also, and there, sure enough, lay the remains of the old missionary in his cowl, with an ivory crucifix about his neck, and on his breast a scroll stating that he, Marco, born at Lisbon in 1438, had died at Bambatse in the year 1503, having laboured in the Empire of Monomotapa for seventeen years, and suffered great hardships and brought many souls to Christ. The scroll added that it was he, who before he entered into religion was a sculptor by trade, that had fashioned the figure on the cross in this chapel out of that of the heathen goddess which had stood in the same place from unknown antiquity. It ended with a request, addressed to all good Christians in Latin, that they who soon must be as he was would pray for his soul and not disturb his bones, which rested here in the hope of a blessed resurrection.

When this pious wish was translated to Jacob Meyer by Mr. Clifford, who still retained some recollection of the classics which he had painfully acquired at Eton and Oxford, the Jew could scarcely contain his wrath. Indeed, looking at his bleeding hands, instead of praying for the soul of that excellent missionary, to reach whose remains he had laboured with such arduous, incessant toil, he cursed it wherever it might be, and unceremoniously swept the bones, which the document asked him not to disturb, into a corner of the tomb, in order to ascertain whether there was not, perhaps, some stair beneath them.

"Really, Mr. Meyer," said Benita, who, in spite of the solemnity of the surroundings, could not control her sense of humour, "if you are not careful the ghosts of all these people will haunt you."

"Let them haunt me if they can," he answered furiously. "I don't believe in ghosts, and defy them all."

At this moment, looking up, Benita saw a figure gliding out of the darkness into the ring of light, so silently that she started, for it might well have been one of those ghosts in whom Jacob Meyer did not believe. In fact, however, it was the old Molimo, who had a habit of coming upon them thus.

"What says the white man?" he asked of Benita, while his dreamy eyes wandered over the three of them, and the hole in the violated tomb.

"He says that he does not believe in spirits, and that he defies them," she answered.

"The white gold-seeker does not believe in spirits, and he defies them," Mambo repeated in his sing-song voice. "He does not believe in the spirits that I see all around me now, the angry spirits of the dead, who speak together of where he shall lie and of what shall happen to him when he is dead, and of how they will welcome one who disturbs their rest and defies and curses them in his search for the riches which he loves. There is one standing by him now, dressed in a brown robe with a dead man cut in ivory like to that," and he pointed to the crucifix in Jacob's hand, "and he holds the ivory man above him and threatens him with sleepless centuries of sorrow, when he is also one of those spirits in which he does not believe."

Then Meyer's rage blazed out. He turned upon the Molimo and reviled him in his own tongue, saying that he knew well where the treasure was hidden, and that if he did not point it out he would kill him and send him to his friends, the spirits. So savage and evil did he look that Benita retreated a little way, while Mr. Clifford strove in vain to calm him. But although Meyer laid his hand upon the knife in his belt and advanced upon him, the old Molimo neither budged an inch nor showed the slightest fear.

"Let him rave on," he said, when at length Meyer paused exhausted. "Just so in a time of storm the lightnings flash and the thunder peals, and the water foams down the face of rock; but then comes the sun again, and the hill is as it has ever been, only the storm is spent and lost. I am the rock, he is but the wind, the fire, and the rain. It is not permitted that he should hurt me, and those spirits in whom he does not believe treasure up his curses, to let them fall again like stones upon his head."

Then, with a contemptuous glance at Jacob, the old man turned and glided back into the darkness out of which he had appeared.

BENITA.

An African Romance by . . .
H. RIDER HAGGARD.

SYNOPSIS OF CHAPTERS I.—XII.

BENITA CLIFFORD, bound for Africa on board the steamer *Zanzibar*, to join her father at Durban, meets Robert Seymour, who falls in love with her. Seymour tells how he met her father and his partner, Jacob Meyer, at Bambatse, a place where it was supposed there was a big treasure hoard. He declares his love for Benita, but they are interrupted as she is about to answer. Soon afterwards the steamer strikes a rock, and all leave her. Seymour with great difficulty gets Benita into a boat, she being unconscious owing to a blow. He gives his place up to a woman who would otherwise perish, for the boat could hold no more. Before leaving the boat he leaves a letter, which he had written beforehand on the ship, asking for her answer, in the event of their meeting again. He reaches the shore in an exhausted condition. The boat is picked up by another steamer, and Benita joins her father eventually at Durban, where she hears from a newspaper report that a Kaffir took a watch inscribed with Seymour's name from a body on the shore some miles away. Benita and her father set out for Mr. Clifford's farm, Rooi Krantz, and when nearly there they leave their waggon to give chase to a wounded wilderbeeste, lose their way, and when night came on would have gone over a precipice, had not Jacob Meyer come to their rescue and led them safely to the farm. There a deputation from the Makalanga tribe, natives of Bambatse, comes to Clifford and Meyer, and promises them all the gold they can find if they will bring five hundred guns with their cartridges, in order to resist the Matabele. They agree, buy the rifles and ammunition, and go on to Bambatse. Arrived there, a deputation of three men from the Matabele comes, demanding tribute of the Makalanga, and threatening extermination if it be not forthcoming. The chief of the Makalanga, Mambo, replies that he cannot do what they want, whereupon the spokesman of the deputation repeats his threats, insulting Benita at the same time. Meyer shoots the man in a rage, and would have killed the other two had not Benita interceded with the Molimo, Mambo, for them, and they are allowed to depart. Before going, one of them, Maduna, a prince of the royal house of Lobengula, promises Benita two lives if by chance she ever has to demand them from Lobengula. Next day, Benita, Mr. Clifford, and Jacob Meyer are shown over the cave where the treasure is supposed to be, and find in it several skeletons, and a huge carved figure of Christ on the Cross. Afterwards they begin the search for the treasure, but find nothing.

CHAPTER XIII.

BENITA PLANS ESCAPE.

THE next morning, while she was cooking the breakfast, Benita saw Jacob Meyer seated upon a rock at a little distance, sullen and disconsolate. His chin was resting on his hand, and he watched her intently, never taking his eyes from her face. She felt that he was concentrating his will upon her; that some new idea concerning her had come into his mind; for it was one of her miseries that she possessed the power of interpreting the drift of this man's thoughts. Much as she detested him, there existed that curious link between them.

It may be remembered that, on the night when they first met at the crest of Leopard's Kloof, Jacob had called her a "thought-sender," and the knowledge of their mental intimacy had come home to Benita. From that day forward her chief desire had been to shut a door between their natures, to isolate herself from him and him from her. Yet the attempt was never entirely successful.

Fear and disgust took hold of her, bending there above the fire, all the while aware of the Jew's dark eyes that searched her through and through. Benita formed a sudden determination. She would implore her father to come away with her.

Of course, such an attempt would be terribly dangerous. Of the Matabele nothing had been seen; but they might be about, and even if enough cattle could be collected to draw the waggon, it belonged to Meyer as much as to her father, and must therefore be left for him. Still, there remained the two horses, which the Molimo had told her were well and getting fat.

At this moment Meyer rose and began to speak to her.

"What are you thinking of, Miss Clifford?" he asked in his soft, foreign voice.

She started, but answered readily enough:

"Of the wood which is green, and the kid cutlets which are getting smoked. Are you not tired of kid, Mr. Meyer?" she went on.

He waved the question aside. "You are so good—oh! I mean it—so really good that you should not tell stories even about small things. The wood is not green; I cut it myself from a dead tree; and the meat is not smoked; nor were you thinking of either. You were thinking of me, as I was thinking of you; but what exactly was in your mind, this time I do not know, and that is why I ask you to tell me."

"Really, Mr. Meyer," she answered flushing; "my mind is my own property."

"Ah! do you say so? Now I hold otherwise—that it is my property, as mine is yours, a gift that Nature has given to each of us."

"I seek no such gift," she answered; but even then, much as she would have wished to do so, she could not utter a falsehood, and deny this horrible and secret intimacy.

"I am sorry for that, as I think it very precious; more precious even than the gold which we cannot find; for, Miss Clifford, it brings me nearer you."

She turned upon him, but he held up his hand, and went on:

"Oh! do not be angry with me, and do not fear that I am going to trouble you with soft speeches, for I shall not, unless a time should come, as I think that perhaps it will, when you may wish to listen to them. But I want to point out something to you, Miss Clifford. Is it not a wonderful thing that our minds should be so in tune, and is there not an object in all this? Did I believe as you do, I should say that it was Heaven working

in us—no: do not answer that the working comes from lower down. I take no credit for reading that upon your lips; the retort is too easy and obvious. I am content to say, however, that the work is that of instinct and nature, or, if you will, of fate, pointing out a road by which together we might travel to great ends."

"I travel my road alone, Mr. Meyer."

"I know, I know, and that is the pity of it. The trouble between man and woman is that not in one case out of a million, even if they be lovers, do they understand each other. Their eyes may seek one another, their hands and lips may meet, and yet they remain distinct, apart, and often antagonistic. There is no communion of the soul. But when it chances to be otherwise, when they chance to complete each other, to be hewn from the same rock as it were—oh! then what happiness may be theirs, and what opportunities!"

"Possibly, Mr. Meyer; but, to be frank, the question does not interest me."

"Not yet; but I am sure that one day it will. Meanwhile, I owe you an apology. I lost my temper before you last night. Well, do not judge me hardly, for I was utterly worn out, and that old idiot vexed me with his talk about ghosts in which I do not believe."

"Then why did it make you so angry? Surely you could have afforded to treat it with contempt, instead of doing—as you did."

"Upon my word! I don't know, but I suppose most of us are afraid lest we should be forced to accept that which we refuse. This ancient place gets upon the nerves, Miss Clifford; yours as well as mine. I can afford to be open about it, because I know that you know. Think of its associations: all the crime that has been committed here for ages and ages, all the suffering that has been endured here. Doubtless human sacrifices were offered in this cave or outside of it; that great burnt ring in the rock there may have been where they built the fires. And then those Portuguese starving to death, slowly starving to death while thousands of savages watched them die. Have you ever thought what it means? But of course you have, for like myself you are cursed with imagination. God

"SHE HAD COME HERE WITH A PURPOSE"

in heaven! is it wonderful that it gets upon the nerves? especially when one cannot find what one is looking for, that vast treasure"—and his face became ecstatic—"that shall yet be yours and mine, and make us great and happy."

"But which at present only makes me a scullery-maid and most unhappy," replied Benita cheerfully, for she heard her father's footstep. "Don't talk any more of the treasure, Mr. Meyer, or we shall quarrel. We have enough of that during business hours, when we are hunting for it, you know. Give me the dish, will you? This meat is cooked at last."

Still Benita could not be rid of that treasure, since after breakfast the endless, unprofitable search began again. Once more the cave was sounded, and other hollow places were discovered upon which the two men got to work. With infinite labour three of them were broken into in as many days, and like the first, found to be graves, only this time of ancients who, perhaps, had died before Christ was born. There they lay upon their sides, their bones burnt by the hot cement that had been poured over them, their gold-headed and gold-feruled rods of office in their hands, their gold-covered pillows of wood, such as the Egyptians used, beneath their skulls, gold bracelets upon their arms and ankles, cakes of gold beneath them which had fallen from the rotted pouches that once hung about their waists, vases of fine glazed pottery that had been filled with offerings, or in some cases with gold dust to pay the expenses of their journey in the other world, standing round them, and so forth.

In their way these discoveries were rich enough; from one tomb alone they took over a hundred and thirty ounces of gold, to say nothing of their surpassing archæ-ological interest. Still they were not what they sought: all that gathered wealth of Monomotapa which the fleeing Portuguese had brought with them and buried in this, their last stronghold.

Benita ceased to take the slightest interest in the matter; she would not even be at the pains to go to look at the third skeleton, although it was that of a man who had been almost a giant, and, to judge from the amount of bullion which he took to the tomb with him, a person of great importance in his day. She felt as though she wished never to see another human bone or ancient bead or bangle; the sight of a street in Bayswater in a London fog—yes, of a toy-shop window in Westbourne Grove—would have pleased her a hundred times better than these unique remains that, had they known of them in those days, would have sent half the learned societies of Europe crazy with delight. She wished to escape from Bambatse, its wondrous fortifications, its mysterious cone, its cave, its dead, and—from Jacob Meyer.

Benita stood upon the top of her prison wall and looked with longing at the wide, open lands below. She even dared to climb the stair which ran up the mighty cone of granite, and seated herself in the cup-like depression on its crest, whence Jacob Meyer had called to her to come and share his throne. It was a dizzy place, for the pillar leaning outwards, its point stood almost clear of the water-scarped rock, so that beneath her was a sheer drop of about four hundred feet to the Zambesi bed. At first the great height made her feel faint. Her eyes swam, and unpleasant tremors crept along her spine, so that she was glad to sink to the floor, whence she knew she could not fall. By degrees, however, she recovered her nerve, and was able to study the glorious view of stream and marshes and hills beyond.

For she had come here with a purpose, to see whether it would not be possible to escape down the river in a canoe, or in native boats such as the Makalanga owned and used for fishing, or to cross from bank to bank. Apparently it was impossible, for although the river beneath and above them was still enough, about a mile below began a cataract that stretched as far as she could see, and was bordered on either side by rocky hills covered with forest, over which, even if they could obtain porters, a canoe could not be carried. This, indeed, she had already heard from the Molimo, but knowing his timid nature, she wished to judge of the matter for herself. It came to this then: if they were to go, it must be on the horses.

Descending the cone Benita went to find her father, to whom as yet she had said nothing of her plans. The opportunity was good, for she knew that he would be alone. As it chanced, on that afternoon Meyer had gone down the hill in order to try to persuade the Makalanga to give them ten or twenty men to help in their excavations. In this, it will be remembered, he had already failed so far as the Molimo was concerned, but he was not a man easily turned from his purpose, and he thought that if he could see Tamas and some of the other captains he might be able by bribery, threats, or otherwise, to induce them to forget their superstitious fears, and help in the search. As a matter of fact, he was utterly unsuccessful, since one and all they declared that for them to enter that sacred place would mean their deaths, and that the vengeance of Heaven would fall upon their tribe and destroy it root and branch.

Mr. Clifford, on whom all this heavy labour had begun to tell, was taking advantage of the absence of his taskmaster, Jacob, to sleep awhile in the hut which they had now built for themselves beneath the shadow of the baobab-tree. As she reached it he came out yawning, and asked her where she had been. Benita told him.

"A giddy place," he said. "I have never ventured to try it myself. What did you go up there for, dear?"

"To look at the river while Mr. Meyer was away, father; for if he had seen me do so he would have guessed my reason; indeed, I dare say that he will guess it now."

"What reason, Benita?"

"To see whether it would not be possible to escape down it in a boat. But there is no chance. It is all rapids below, with hills and rocks and trees on either bank."

"What need have you to escape at present?" he asked, eyeing her curiously

"Every need," she answered with passion, "I hate this place; it is a prison, and I loathe the very name of treasure. Also," and she paused.

"Also what, dear?"

"Also," and her voice sank to a whisper, as though she feared that he should overhear her even at the bottom of the hill; "also, I am afraid of Mr. Meyer."

This confession did not seem to surprise her father, who merely nodded his head and said:

"Go on."

"Father, I think that he is going mad, and it is not pleasant for us to be cooped up here alone with a madman, especially when he has begun to speak to me as he does now."

"You don't mean that he has been impertinent to you," said the old man, flushing up, "for if so——"

"No, not impertinent—as yet," and she told him what had passed between Meyer and herself, adding, "You see, father, I detest this man; indeed, I want to have nothing to do with any man; for me all that is over and done with," and she gave a dry little sob which appeared to come from her very heart. "And yet, he seems to be getting some kind of power over me. He follows me about with his eyes, prying into my mind, and I feel that he is beginning to be able to read it. I can bear no more. Father, father, for God's sake, take me away from this hateful hill and its gold and its dead, and let us get out into the veld again together."

"I should be glad enough, dearest," he answered. "I have had plenty of this wild goose chase, which I was so mad as to be led into by the love of wealth. Indeed, I am beginning to believe that if it goes on much longer I shall leave my bones here."

"And if such a dreadful thing as that were to happen, what would become of me, alone with Jacob Meyer?" she asked quietly. "I might even be driven to the same fate as that poor girl two hundred years ago," and she pointed to the cone of rock behind her.

"For Heaven's sake, don't talk like that," he broke in.

"Why not? One must face things, and it would be better than Jacob Meyer, for who would protect me here?"

Mr. Clifford walked up and down for a few minutes, while his daughter watched him anxiously.

"I can see no plan," he said, stopping opposite her. "We cannot take the waggon even if there are enough oxen left to draw it, for it is his as much as mine, and I am sure that he will never leave this treasure unless he is driven away."

"BENITA HEARD THE BULLET CLAP UPON THE HIDE SHIELD"

" And I am sure I hope that he will not. But, father, the horses are our own; it was his that died, you remember. We can ride away on them."

He stared at her and answered:

" Yes, we could ride away to our deaths. Suppose they got sick or lame; suppose we met the Matabele, or could find no game to shoot; suppose one of us fell ill—oh! and a hundred things. What then ? "

" Why, then it is just as well to perish in the wilderness as here, where our risks are almost as great. We must take our chance, and trust to God. Perhaps He will be merciful and help us. Listen now, father. To-morrow is Sunday, when you and I do no work that we can help. But Mr. Meyer is a Jew, and he won't waste Sunday. Well now, I will say that I want to go down to the outer wall to fetch some clothes which I left in the waggon, and to take others for the native women to wash, and of course you will come with me. Perhaps he will be deceived and stay behind, especially as he has been there to-day. Then we can get the horses and guns and ammunition, and anything else that we can carry in the way of food, and persuade the old Molimo to open the gate for us. You know, the little side gate that cannot be seen from up here, and before Mr. Meyer misses us and comes to look, we shall be twenty miles away, and—horses can't be overtaken by a man on foot."

" He will say that we have deserted him, and that will be true."

" You can leave a letter with the Molimo explaining that it was my fault, that I was getting ill and thought that I should die, and that you knew it would not be fair to ask him to come, and so to lose the treasure, to every halfpenny of which he is welcome when it is found. Oh! father, don't hesitate any longer; say that you will take me away from Mr. Meyer."

" So be it then," answered Mr. Clifford, and as he spoke, hearing a sound, they looked up and saw Jacob approaching them.

Luckily he was so occupied with his own thoughts that he never noted the guilty air upon their faces, and they had time to compose themselves a little.

But even thus his suspicions were aroused.

" What are you talking of so earnestly?" he asked.

" We were wondering how you were getting on with the Makalanga," answered Benita, fibbing boldly, " and whether you would persuade them to face the ghosts. Did you ? "

" Not I," he answered with a scowl. " Those ghosts are our worst enemies in this place; the cowards swore that they would rather die. I should have liked to take some of them at their word and make ghosts of them; but I remembered the situation and didn't. Don't be afraid, Miss Clifford, I never even lost my temper, outwardly at any rate. Well, there it is; if they won't help us, we must work the harder. I've got a new plan, and we'll begin on it to-morrow."

" Not to-morrow, Mr. Meyer," replied Benita with a smile. " It is Sunday, and we rest on Sunday, you know."

" Oh! I forgot. The Makalanga with their ghosts and you with your Sunday—really I do not know which is the worse. Well, then, I must do my own share and yours too, I suppose," and he turned away with a shrug of his shoulders.

CHAPTER XIV.

THE FLIGHT.

THE next morning, Sunday, Meyer went to work on his new plan. What it was Benita did not trouble to inquire, but she gathered that it had something to do with the measuring out of the chapel cave into squares for the more systematic investigation of each area. At twelve o'clock he emerged for his midday meal, in the course of which he remarked that it was very dreary working in that place alone, and that he would be glad when it was Monday, and they could accompany him. His words evidently disturbed Mr. Clifford not a little, and even excited some compunction in the breast of Benita.

What would his feelings be, she wondered, when he found that they had run away, leaving him to deal with their joint undertaking single-handed! Almost was she minded to tell him the whole truth; yet—and this was a curious evidence of the man's ascendancy over her—she did not. Perhaps she felt that to do so would be to put an end to their scheme, since then by argument, blandishments, threats, force, or appeal to their sense of loyalty, it mattered not which, he would bring about its abandonment. But she panted to fulfil that scheme, to be free of Bambatse, its immemorial ruins, its graveyard cave, and the ghoul, Jacob Meyer, who could delve among dead bones and in living hearts with equal skill and insight, and yet was unable to find the treasure that lay beneath either of them.

So they hid the truth, and talked with feverish activity about other things, such as the drilling of the Makalanga, and the chances of an attack by the Matabele, which happily now seemed to be growing small; also of the condition of their cattle, and the prospect of obtaining more to replace those that had died. Indeed, Benita went farther; in her new-found zeal of deception she proceeded to act a lie, yes, even with her father's reproachful eyes fixed upon her. Incidentally she mentioned that they were going to have an outing, to climb down the ladder and visit the Makalanga camp between the first and second walls and mix with the great world for a few hours; also to carry their washing to be done there, and bring up some clean clothes and certain books which she had left below.

Jacob came out of his thoughts and calculations, and listened gloomily.

"I have half a mind to come with you," he said, words at which Benita shivered. "It certainly is most cursed lonesome in that cave, and I seem to hear things in it, as though those old bones were rattling, sounds like sighs and whispers too, which are made by the draught."

"Well, why don't you?" asked Benita.

It was a bold stroke, but it succeeded. If he had any doubts they vanished, and he answered at once:

"Because I have not the time. We have to get this business finished one way or another before the wet season comes on, and we are drowned out of the place with rain, or rotted by fever. Take your afternoon out, Miss Clifford; every maid of all work is entitled to as much, and I

am afraid that is your billet here. Only," he added, with that care for her safety which he always showed in his more temperate moods, "pray be careful, Clifford, to get back before sundown. That wall is too risky for your daughter to climb in the dusk. Call me from the foot of it; you have the whistle, and I will come down to help her up. I think I'll go with you after all. No, I won't. I made myself so unpleasant to them yesterday that those Makalanga can't wish to see any more of me at present. I hope you will have a more agreeable afternoon than I shall. Why don't you take a ride outside the wall? Your horses are fat and want exercise, and I do not think that you need be afraid of the Matabele." Then without waiting for an answer, he rose and left them.

Mr. Clifford looked after him doubtfully.

"Oh, I know," said Benita, "it seems horribly mean, but one must do shabby things sometimes. Here are the bundles all ready, so let us be off."

Accordingly they went, and from the top of the wall Benita glanced back to bid good-bye to that place which she hoped never to see again. Yet she could not feel as though she looked her last upon it; to her it wore no air of farewell, and even as she descended the perilous stairs, she found herself making mental notes as to how they might best be climbed again. Also, she could not believe that she had done with Mr. Meyer. It seemed to her as though for a long while yet her future would be full of him.

They reached the outer fortification in safety, and there were greeted with some surprise but with no displeasure by the Makalanga, whom they found still drilling with the rifles, in the use of which a certain number of them appeared to have become fairly proficient. Going to the hut in which the spare goods from the waggon had been stored, they quickly made their preparations. Here also, Mr. Clifford wrote a letter, one of the most unpleasant that he had ever been called upon to compose. It ran thus:

Dear Meyer,

I don't know what you will think of us, but we are escaping from this place. The truth is that I am not well, and my daughter can bear it no longer. She says that if she stops here, she will die, and that hunting for treasure in that ghastly grave-yard is shattering her nerves. I should have liked to tell you, but she begged me not, being convinced that if I did, you would overpersuade us or stop us in some way. As for the gold, if you can find it, take it all. I renounce my share. We are leaving you the waggon and the oxen, and starting down country on our horses. It is a perilous business, but less so than staying here under the circumstances. If we never meet again we hope that you will forgive us, and wish you all good fortune.—Yours sincerely and with much regret,

T. CLIFFORD.

The letter written, they saddled the horses which had been brought up for their inspection, and were found to be in good case, and fastened their scanty belongings, and as many cartridges as they could carry in packs behind their saddles. Then, each of them armed with a rifle—for during their long journeyings Benita had learned to shoot—they mounted and made for the little side-entrance, as the main gate through which they had passed on their arrival was now built up. This side-entrance, a mere slit in the great wall, with a precipitous approach, was open, for now that their fear of the Matabele had to some extent passed off, the Makalanga used it to drive their sheep and goats in and out, since it was so constructed with several twists and turns in the thickness of the wall, that in a few minutes it could be effectually blocked by stones that lay at hand. Also, the ancient architect had arranged it in such a fashion that it was entirely commanded from the crest of the wall on either side.

The Makalanga, who had been watching their proceedings curiously, made no attempt to stop them, although they guessed that they might have a little trouble with the sentries who guarded the entrance all day, and even when it was closed at night, with whom also Mr. Clifford proposed to leave the letter.

When they reached the place, however, and had dismounted to lead the horses down the winding passage and the steep ascent upon its further side, it was to find that the only guard visible proved to be the old Molimo himself, who sat there, apparently half asleep.

But as they came he showed himself to be very much awake, for without moving he asked them at once whither they were going.

" To take a ride," answered Mr. Clifford. " The lady, my daughter, is weary of being cooped up in this fortress, and wishes to breathe the air without. Let us pass, friend, or we shall not be back by sunset."

" If you are coming back at sunset, white man, why do you carry so many things upon your packs, and why are your saddle-bags filled with cartridges ? " he asked. " Surely you do not speak the truth to me, and you hope that never more will you see the sun set upon Bambatse."

Now understanding that it was hopeless to deceive him, Benita exclaimed boldly :

" It is so ; but oh ! my Father, stay us not, for fear is behind us, and therefore we fly hence."

" And is there no fear before you, maiden ? Fear of the wilderness, where none wander save perchance the Amandabele with their bloody spears ; fear of wild beasts and of sickness that may overtake you so that, first one and then the other, you perish there ? "

" There is plenty, my Father, but none of them are so bad as the fear behind. Yonder place is haunted, and we give up our search and would dwell there no more."

" It is haunted truly, maiden, but its spirits will not harm you whom they welcome as one appointed, and we are ever ready to protect you because of their command that has come to me in dreams. Nor, indeed, is it the spirits whom you fear, but rather the white man, your companion, who would bend you to his will. Deny it not, for I have seen all."

" Then knowing the truth, surely you will let us go," she pleaded, " for I swear to you that I dare not stay."

" Who am I that I should forbid you ? "

he asked. " Yet I tell you that you would do well to stay and save yourselves much terror. Maiden, have I not said it days and days ago, that here and here only you must accomplish your fate? Go now if you will, but you shall return again," and once more he seemed to begin to doze in the sun.

The two of them consulted hastily together.

" It is no use turning back now," said Benita, who was almost weeping with doubt and vexation. " I will not be frightened by his vague talk. What can he know of the future more than any of the rest of us? Besides, all he says is that we shall come back again, and if that does happen, at least we shall have been free for a little while. Come, father."

" As you wish," answered Mr. Clifford, who seemed too miserable and depressed to argue. Only he threw down the letter upon the Molimo's lap, and begged him to give it to Meyer when he came to look for them.

The old man took no notice; no, not even when Benita bade him farewell and thanked him for his kindness, praying that all good fortune might attend him and his tribe, did he answer a single word or even look up. So they led their horses down the narrow passage where there was scarcely room for them to pass, and up the steep path beyond. On the further side of the ancient ditch they remounted them while the Makalanga watched them from the walls, and cantered away along the same road by which they had come.

Now this road, or rather track, ran first through the gardens and then among the countless ruined houses that in bygone ages formed the great city whereof the mount Bambatse had been the citadel and sanctuary. These relics of a lost civilisation extended for several miles, and were bounded by a steep and narrow neck or pass in the encircling hills, the same that Robert Seymour and his brother had found too difficult for their waggon at the season in which they visited the place some years before. This pass, or poort as it is called in South Africa, had been strongly fortified, for on either side of it were the ruins of towers. Moreover, at its crest it was so

narrow and steep-sided that a few men posted there, even if they were armed only with bows and arrows, could hold an attacking force in check for a considerable time. Beyond it, after the hill was descended, a bush-clad plain dotted with kopjes and isolated granite pillars formed of boulders piled one upon another, rolled away for many miles.

Mr. Clifford and Benita had started upon their mad journey about three o'clock in the afternoon, and when the sun began to set they found themselves upon this plain fifteen or sixteen miles from Bambatse, of which they had long lost sight, for it lay beyond the intervening hills. Near to them was a kopje, where they had outspanned by a spring of water when on their recent journey, and since they did not dare to travel in the dark, here they determined to off-saddle, for round this spring was good grass for the horses.

As it chanced, they came upon some hartebeeste here which were trekking down to drink, but although they would have been glad of meat, were afraid to shoot, fearing lest they should attract attention; nor for the same reason did they like to light a fire. So having knee-haltered the horses in such fashion that they could not wander far, and turned them loose to feed, they sat down under a tree, and made some sort of a meal off the biltong and cooked corn which they had brought with them. By the time this was finished darkness fell, for there was little moon, so that nothing remained to do except to sleep within a circle of a few dead thorn-boughs which they had drawn about their camp. This, then, they did, and so weary were they both, that notwithstanding all the emotions through which they had passed, and their fears lest lions should attack them—for of these brutes there were many in this veld—rested soundly and undisturbed till within half an hour of dawn.

Rising somewhat chilled, for though the air was warm a heavy dew had soaked their blankets, once more they ate and drank by starlight, while the horses, which they had tied up close to them during the night, filled themselves with grass. At the first break of day they saddled them, and before the sun rose were on their road

"BY WAY OF ANSWER BENITA PULLED UP THE HORSE"

again. At length up it came, and the sight and warmth of it put new heart into Benita. Her fears seemed to depart with the night, and she said to her father that this successful start was of good augury, to which he only answered that he hoped so.

All that day they rode forward in beautiful weather, not pressing their horses, for now they were sure that Jacob Meyer, who if he followed at all must do so on foot, would never be able to overtake them. At noon they halted, and having shot a small buck, Benita cooked some of it in the one pot that they had brought with them, and they ate a good meal of fresh meat.

Riding on again, towards sundown they came to another of their old camping-places, also a bush-covered kopje. Here the spring of water was more than halfway up the hill, so there they off-saddled in a green bower of a place that because of its ferns and mosses looked like a rock garden. Now, although they had enough cold meat for food, they thought themselves quite safe in lighting a fire. Indeed, this it seemed necessary to do, since they had struck the fresh spoor of lions, and even caught sight of one galloping away in the tall reeds on the marshy land at the foot of the hill.

That evening they fared sumptuously upon venison, and as on the previous day lay down to rest in a little " boma " or fence made of boughs. But they were not allowed to sleep well this night, for scarcely had they shut their eyes when a hyena began to howl about them. They shouted and the brute went away, but an hour or two later, they heard ominous grunting sounds, followed presently by a loud roar, which was answered by another roar, whereat the horses began to whinny in a frightened fashion.

" Lions ! " said Mr. Clifford, jumping up and throwing dead wood on to the fire till it burnt to a bright blaze.

After that all sleep became impossible, for although the lions did not attack them, having once winded the horses they would not go away, but continued wandering round the kopje, grunting and growling. This went on till about three o'clock in the morning, when at last the beasts took their departure, for they heard them roaring in the distance. Now that they seemed safe, having first made up the fire, they tried to get some rest.

When, as it appeared to her, Benita had been asleep but a little while, she was awakened by a new noise. It was still dark, but the starlight showed her that the horses were quite quiet; indeed one of them was lying down, and the other eating some green leaves from the branches of the tree to which it was tethered. Therefore that noise had not come from any wild animal of which they were afraid. She listened intently, and presently heard it again; it was a murmur like to that of people talking somewhere at the bottom of the hill. Then she woke her father and told him, but although once or twice they thought they heard the sound of footsteps, nothing else could be distinguished. Still they rose, and having saddled and bridled the horses as noiselessly as might be, waited for the dawn.

At last it came. Up on the side of the kopje they were in clear air above which shone the red lights of morning, but under them lay billows of dense, pearl-hued mist. By degrees this thinned beneath the rays of the risen sun, and through it, looking gigantic in that light, Benita saw a savage wrapped in a kaross, who was walking up and down and yawning, a great spear in his hand.

" Look," she whispered, " look ! " and Mr. Clifford stared down the line of her outstretched finger.

" The Matabele," he said. " My God ! the Matabele ! "

CHAPTER XV.

THE CHASE.

THE Matabele it was, sure enough; there could be no doubt of it, for soon three other men joined the sentry and began to talk with him, pointing with their great spears at the side of the hill. Evidently they were arranging a surprise when there was sufficient light to carry it out.

" They have seen our fire," whispered her father to Benita ; " now, if we wish to save our lives there is only one thing to do—ride for it before they muster. The impi will be camped upon the other side of the hill, so we must take the road we came by."

"That runs back to Bambatse," faltered Benita.

"Bambatse is better than the grave," said her father. "Pray Heaven that we may get there."

To this argument there was no answer, so having drunk a sup of water, and swallowing a few mouthfuls of food as they went, they crept to the horses, mounted them, and as silently as possible began to ride down the hill.

The sentry was alone again, the other three men having departed. He stood with his back towards them. Presently, when they were quite close on to him, he heard their horses' hoofs upon the grass, wheeled round at the sound, and saw them. Then with a great shout he lifted his spear and charged.

Mr. Clifford, who was leading, held out his rifle at arm's length—to raise it to his shoulder he had no time—and pulled the trigger. Benita heard the bullet clap upon the hide shield, and next instant saw the Matabele warrior lying on his back, beating the air with his hands and feet. Also, she saw beyond the shoulder of the kopje which they were rounding, hundreds of men marching, and behind them a herd of cattle, the dim light gleaming upon the stabbing spears and on the horns of the oxen. She glanced to the right, and there were more men. The two wings of the impi were closing upon them. Only a little lane was left in the middle. They must get through before it shut.

"Come," she gasped, striking the horse with her heel and the butt of her gun, and jerking at its mouth.

Her father saw also, and did likewise, so that the beasts broke into a gallop. Now from the point of each wing sprang out thin lines of men looking like great horns or nippers, whose business it was to meet and cut them off. Could they pass between before they did meet? That was the question, and upon its answer it depended whether or no they had another three minutes to live. To think of mercy at the hands of these bloodthirsty brutes, after they had just killed one of their number before their eyes, was absurd. It was true he had been shot in self-defence, but what count would savages take of that, or of the fact that they were but harmless travellers? White people were not very popular with the Matabele just then, as they knew well; also their murder in this remote place with not another of their race within a couple of hundred miles, would never even be reported, and much less avenged. It was as safe as any crime could possibly be.

All this passed through their minds as they galloped towards those closing points. Oh! the horror of it! But two hundred yards to cover, and their fate would be decided. Either they would have escaped at least for a while, or time would be done with for them; or, a third alternative, they might be taken prisoners, in all probability a yet more dreadful doom. Even then Benita determined that if she could help it this should not befall her. She had the rifle and the revolver that Jacob Meyer had given her. Surely she would be able to find a moment to use one or the other of them upon herself. She clenched her teeth, and struck the horse again and again, so that now they flew along. The Matabele soldiers were running their best to catch them, and if these had been given but five seconds of start, caught they must have been. But that short five seconds saved their lives.

When they rushed through them the foremost men of the nippers were not more than twenty yards apart. Seeing that they had passed these halted and hurled a shower of spears after them. One flashed by Benita's cheek, a line of light; she felt the wind of it. Another cut her dress, and a third struck her father's horse in the near hind leg just above the knee joint, remaining fast there for a stride or two, and then falling to the ground. At first the beast did not seem to be incommoded by this wound; indeed, it only caused it to gallop quicker, and Benita rejoiced, thinking that it was but a scratch. Then she forgot about it, for some of the Matabele, who had guns, began to shoot at them, and although their marksmanship was vile, one or two of the bullets went nearer than was pleasant. Lastly a man, the swiftest runner of them all, shouted after them in Zulu:

"HE . . . ; AIMED AND FIRED AT THE SOLDIER WHO WAS COMING ON CARELESSLY
IN THE OPEN"

"The horse is wounded. We will catch you both before the sun sets."

Then they passed over the crest of a rise and lost sight of them for a while.

"Thank God!" gasped Benita when they were alone again in the silent veld; but Mr. Clifford shook his head.

"Do you think they will follow us?" she asked.

"You heard what the fellow said," he answered evasively. "Doubtless they are on their way to attack Bambatse, and have been round to destroy some other wretched tribe, and steal the cattle which we saw. Yes, I fear that they will follow. The question is, which of us can get to Bambatse first."

"Surely we ought to on the horses, father."

"Yes, if nothing happens to them," and as he spoke the words the mare which he was riding dropped sharply upon her hind leg, the same that had been struck with the spear; then recovered herself and galloped on.

"Did you see that?" he asked.

She nodded; then said:

"Shall we get off and look at the cut?"

"Certainly not," he answered. "Our only chance is to keep her moving; if once the wound stiffens, there's an end. The sinew cannot have been severed, or it would have come before now."

So they pushed on.

All that morning did they canter forward wherever the ground was smooth enough to allow them to do so, and notwithstanding the increasing lameness of Mr. Clifford's mare, made such good progress that by midday they reached the place where they had passed the first night after leaving Bambatse. Here sheer fatigue and want of water forced them to stop a little while. They dismounted and drank greedily from the spring, after which they allowed the horses to drink also; indeed it was impossible to keep them away from the water. Then they ate a little, not because they desired food but to keep up their strength, and while they did so examined the mare. By now her hind leg was much swollen, and blood still ran from the gash made by the assegai. Moreover, the limb was drawn up so that the point of the hoof only rested on the ground.

"We must get on before it sets fast," said Mr. Clifford, and they mounted again.

Great heavens! what was this? The mare would not stir. In his despair Mr. Clifford beat it cruelly, whereupon the poor brute hobbled forward a few paces on three legs, and again came to a standstill. Either an injured sinew had given or the inflammation was now so intense that it could not bend its knee. Understanding what this meant to them, Benita's nerve gave out at last, and she burst into weeping.

"Don't cry, love," he said. "God's will be done. Perhaps they have given up the hunt by now; at any rate my legs are left, and Bambatse is not more than sixteen miles away. Forward now," and holding to her saddle-strap they went up the long, long slope which led to the poort in the hills around Bambatse.

They would have liked to shoot the mare, but being afraid to fire a rifle, could not do so. So they left the unhappy beast to its fate, and with it everything it carried, except a few of the cartridges. Before they went, however, at Benita's prayer, her father devoted a few seconds to unbuckling the girths and pulling off the bridle, so that it might have a chance of life. For a little way it hobbled after them on three legs, then, the saddle still upon its back, stood whinnying piteously till at last, to Benita's intense relief, a turn in their path hid it from their sight.

Half a mile further on she looked round in the faint hope that it might have recovered itself and followed. But no mare was to be seen. Something else was to be seen, however, for there, three or four miles away upon the plain behind them, easy to be distinguished in that dazzling air, were a number of black spots that occasionally seemed to sparkle.

"What are they?" she asked faintly, who feared the answer.

"The Matabele who follow us," answered her father, "or rather a company of their swiftest runners. It is their spears that glitter so. Now, my love, this is the position," he went on, as they struggled forward; "those men will catch us before ever we can get to Bambatse; they are trained to run like that, for fifty miles, if need be. But with this start they cannot catch your horse, you must go on and leave me to look after myself."

"Never, never!" she exclaimed.

"But you shall and you must. I am your father and I order you. As for me, what does it matter? I may hide from them and escape, or—at least I am old, my life is done, whereas yours is before you. Now, good-bye, and go on," and he let go of the saddle-strap.

By way of answer Benita pulled up the horse.

"Not one yard," she said, setting her mouth.

Then he began to storm at her, calling her disobedient and undutiful, and when this means failed to move her, to implore her almost with tears.

"Father, dear," she said, leaning down towards him as he walked, for now they were going on again, "I told you why I wanted to run away from Bambatse, didn't I?—because I would rather risk my life than stay. Well, do you think that I wish to return there and live in that place alone with Jacob Meyer? Also I will tell you another thing. You remember about Mr. Seymour? Well, I can't get over that; I can't get over it at all, and therefore, although of course I am afraid, it is all one to me. No, we will escape together, or die together; the first if we can."

Then with a groan he gave up the argument, and as he found breath they discussed their chances. Their first idea was to hide, but save for a few trees all the country was open; there was no place to cover them. They thought of the banks of the Zambesi, but between them and the river rose a bare, rock-strewn hill with several miles of slope. Long before they could reach its crest, even if a horse were able to travel there, they must be overtaken. In short, there was nothing to do except to push for the nek, and if they were fortunate enough to reach it before the Matabele, to abandon the horse there and try to conceal themselves among the ruins of the houses beyond. This, perhaps, they might do when once the sun was down.

But they did not deceive themselves; the chances were at least fifty to one against them, unless indeed their pursuers grew weary and let them go.

At present, however, they were by no means weary, for having perceived them from far away, the long-legged runners put on the pace, and the distance between them and their quarry was lessening.

"Father," said Benita, "please understand one thing. I do not mean to be taken alive by those savages."

"Oh! how can I——" he faltered.

"I don't ask you," she answered. "I will see to that myself. Only, if I should make any mistake——" and she looked at him.

The old man was getting very tired. He panted up the steep hillside, and stumbled against the stones. Benita noted it, and slipping from the horse, made him mount while she ran alongside. Then when he was a little rested they changed places again, and so covered several miles of country. Subsequently, when both of them were nearly exhausted, they tried riding together—she in front and he behind, for their baggage had long since been thrown away. But the weary beast could not carry this double burden, and after a few hundred yards of it, stumbled, fell, struggled to its feet again and stopped.

So once more they were obliged to ride and walk alternately.

Now there was not much more than an hour of daylight left, and the narrow pass lay about three miles ahead of them. That dreadful three miles; ever thereafter it was Benita's favourite nightmare! At the beginning of it the leading Matabele were about two thousand yards behind them; halfway, about a thousand; and at the commencement of the last mile, say five hundred.

Nature is a wonderful thing, and great are its resources in extremity. As the actual crisis approached, the weariness of these two seemed to depart, or at any rate it was forgotten. They no longer felt exhausted, nor, had they been fresh from their beds, could they have climbed or run better. Even the horse seemed to find new energy, and when it lagged Mr. Clifford dug the point of his hunting knife into its flank. Gasping, panting, now one mounted and now the other, they struggled on towards that crest of rock, while behind them came death in the shape of those sleuth-hounds of Matabele. The sun was going down, and against its flaming ball, when they glanced back, they could see their dark forms outlined ; the broad spears also looked red as though they had been dipped in blood. They could even hear their taunting shouts as they called to them to sit down and be killed, and save trouble.

Now they were not three hundred yards away, and the crest of the pass was still half a mile ahead. Five minutes passed, and here, where the track was very rough, the horse blundered upwards slowly. Mr. Clifford was riding at the time, and Benita running at his side, holding to the stirrup leather. She looked behind her. The savages, fearing that their victims might find shelter over the hill, were making a rush, and the horse could go no faster. One man, a great tall fellow, quite out-distanced his companions. Two minutes more and he was not over a hundred paces from them, a little nearer than they were to the top of the pass. Then the horse stopped and refused to stir any more.

Mr. Clifford jumped from the saddle, and Benita, who could not speak, pointed to the pursuing Matabele. He sat down upon a rock, cocked his rifle, took a deep breath, and aimed and fired at the soldier who was coming on carelessly in the open. Mr. Clifford was a good shot, and shaken though he was, at this supreme moment his skill did not fail him. The man was struck somewhere, for he staggered about and fell ; then slowly picked himself up, and began to hobble back towards his companions, who, when they met him, stopped a minute to give him some kind of assistance.

That halt proved their salvation, for it gave them time to make one last despairing rush, and gain the brow of the poort. Not that this would have saved them, however, since where they could go the Matabele could follow, and there was still light by which the pursuers would have been able to see to catch them. Indeed, the savages having laid down the wounded man, came on with a yell of rage, fifty or more of them.

Over the pass father and daughter struggled, Benita riding ; after them, perhaps sixty yards away, ran the Matabele, gathered in a knot now upon the narrow, ancient road, bordered by steep hillsides.

Then suddenly from all about them, as it appeared to Benita, broke out the blaze and roar of rifles, rapid and continuous. Down went the Matabele by twos and threes, till at last it seemed as though but quite a few of them were left upon their feet, and those came on no more ; they turned and fled from the neck of the narrow pass to the open slope beyond.

Benita sank to the ground, and the next thing that she could remember was hearing the soft voice of Jacob Meyer, who said :

" So you have returned from your ride, Miss Clifford, and perhaps it was as well that the thought came from you to me that you wished me to meet you here in this very place."

CHAPTER XVI.

BACK AT BAMBATSE.

HOW they reached Bambatse Benita never could remember, but afterwards she was told that both she and her father were carried upon litters made of ox-hide shields. When she came to her own mind again, it was to find herself lying in her tent outside the mouth of the cave within the third enclosure of the temple-fortress. Her feet were sore and her bones ached, physical discomforts that brought back to her in a flash all the terrors through which she had passed.

Again she saw the fierce pursuing Matabele ; again heard their cruel shouts and the answering crack of the rifles ; again amidst the din and the gathering darkness, distinguished the gentle, foreign voice of Meyer speaking his words of sarcastic greeting. Next oblivion fell upon her, and after it a dim memory of being helped up the hill with the sun pouring on her back and assisted to climb the steep steps of the wall by means of a rope placed around her. Then forgetfulness again.

The flap of her tent was drawn aside and she shrank back upon her bed, shutting her eyes for fear lest they should fall upon the face of Jacob Meyer. Feeling that it was not he, or learning it perhaps from the footfall, she opened them a little, peeping at her visitor from between her long lashes. He proved to be—not Jacob or her father, but the old Molimo, who stood beside her holding in his hand a gourd filled with goat's milk. Then she sat up and smiled at him, for Benita had grown very fond of this ancient man, who was so unlike anyone else that she had ever met.

"Greeting, Lady," he said softly, smiling back at her with his lips and dreamy eyes, for his old face did not seem to move beneath its thousand wrinkles. "I bring you milk. Drink; it is fresh and you need food."

So she took the gourd and drank to the last drop, for it seemed to her that she had never tasted anything so delicious.

"Good, good," murmured the Molimo; "now you will be well again."

"Yes, I shall get well," she answered; "but oh! what of my father?"

"Fear not; he is still sick, but he will recover also. You shall see him soon."

"I have drunk all the milk," she broke out; "there is none left for him."

"Plenty, plenty," he answered, waving his thin hand. "There were two cups full—one for each. We have not many she-goats down below, but the best of their milk is saved for you."

"Tell me all that has happened, Father," and the old priest, who liked her to call him by that name, smiled again with his eyes, and squatted down in the corner of the tent.

"You went away, you remember that you would go, although I told you that you must come back. You refused my wisdom and you went, and I have learned all that befell you and how you two escaped the impi. Well, that night after sunset, when you did not return, came the Black One—yes, yes, I mean Meyer, whom we name so because of his beard, and," he added deliberately, "his heart. He came running down the hill asking for you, and I gave him the letter.

"He read it, and oh! then he went mad. He cursed in his own tongue; he threw himself about; he took a rifle and wished to shoot me, but I sat silent and

looked at him till he grew quiet. Then he asked why I had played him this trick, but I answered that it was no trick of mine who had no right to keep you and your father prisoners against your will, and that I thought you had gone away because you were afraid of him, which was not wonderful if that was how he talked to you. I told him, too, I who am a doctor, that unless he was careful he would go mad; that already I saw madness in his eye; after which he became quite quiet, for my words frightened him. Then he asked what could be done, and I said—that night, nothing, since you must be far away, so that it would be useless to follow you, but better to go to meet you when you came back. He asked what I meant by your coming back, and I answered that I meant what I said, that you would come back in great haste and peril—although you would not believe me when I told you so—for I had it from the Munwali whose child you are.

"So I sent out my spies, and that night went by, and the next day and night went by, and we sat still and did nothing, though the Black One wished to wander out alone after you. But on the following morning, at the dawn, a messenger came in who reported that it had been called to him by his brethren who were hidden upon hilltops and in other places for miles and miles, that the Matabele impi, having destroyed another family of the Makalanga far down the Zambesi, was advancing to destroy us also. And in the afternoon came a second spy, who reported that you two had been surrounded by the impi, but had broken through them, and were riding hitherwards for your lives. Then I took fifty of the best of our people and put them under the command of Tamas, my son, and sent them to ambush the pass, for against the Matabele warriors on the plain we, who are not warlike, do not dare to fight.

"The Black One went with them, and when he saw how sore was your strait, wished to run down to meet the Matabele, for he is a brave man. But I had said to Tamas—'No, do not try to fight them in the open, for there they will certainly kill you.' Moreover, Lady, I was sure that you would reach the top of the poort.

"HE LOOKED LIKE A PANTHER ABOUT TO SPRING"

Well, you reached it, though but by the breadth of a blade of grass, and my children shot with the new rifles, and the place being narrow so that they could not miss, killed many of those hyenas of Amandabele. But to kill Matabele is like catching fleas on a dog's back: there are always more. Still it served its turn, you and your father were brought away safely, and we lost no one."

"Where, then, are the Matabele now?" asked Benita.

"Outside our walls, a whole regiment of them: three thousand men or more, under the command of the Captain Maduna, he of the royal blood, whose life you begged, but who nevertheless hunted you like a buck."

"Perhaps he did not know who it was," suggested Benita.

"Perhaps not," the Molimo answered, rubbing his chin, "for in such matters even a Matabele generally keeps faith, and you may remember he promised you life for life. However, they are here ravening like lions round the walls, and that is why we carried you up to the top of the hill, that you might be safe from them."

"But are you safe, my Father?"

"I think so," he replied with a dry little chuckle in his throat. "Whoever built this fortress built it strong, and we have blocked the gates. Also, they caught no one outside; all were within the walls, together with the sheep and goats. Lastly, we have sent most of the women and children across the Zambesi in canoes, to hide in places we know of whither the Amandabele cannot follow, for they dare not swim a river. Therefore, for those of us that remain we have food for three months, and before then the rains will drive the impi out."

"Why did you not all go across the river, Father?"

"For two reasons, Lady. The first is, that if we once abandoned our stronghold, which we have held from the beginning, Lobengula would take it and keep it, so that we could never re-enter into our heritage, which would be a shame to us and bring down the vengeance of the spirits of our ancestors upon our heads. The second is, that as you have returned to us we stay to protect you."

"You are very good to me," murmured Benita.

"Nay, nay, we brought you here, and we do what I am told to do from Above. Trouble may still come upon you; yes, I think that it will come, but once more I pray you, have no fear, for out of this evil root shall spring a flower of joy," and he rose to go.

"Stay," said Benita. "Has the chief Meyer found the gold?"

"No, he has found nothing; but he hunts and hunts like a hungry jackal digging for a bone. But that bone is not for him; it is for you, Lady, you and you only. Oh! I know, you do not seek, still you shall find. Only the next time that you want help, do not run away into the wilderness. Hear the word of Munwali given by his mouth, the Molimo of Bambatse!" And as he spoke, the old priest backed himself out of the tent, stopping now and again to bow to Benita.

A few minutes later her father entered, looking very weak and shaken, and supporting himself upon a stick. Happy was the greeting of these two who, with their arms about each other's neck, gave thanks for their escape from great peril.

"You see, Benita, we can't get away from this place," Mr. Clifford said presently. "We must find that gold."

"Bother the gold," she answered with energy; "I hate its very name. Who can think of gold with three thousand Matabele waiting to kill us?"

"Somehow I don't feel afraid of them any more," said her father; "they have had their chance and lost it, and the Makalanga swear that now they have guns to command the gates, the fortress cannot be stormed. Still I am afraid of someone."

"Who?"

"Jacob Meyer. I have seen him several times, and I think that he is going mad."

"The Molimo said that too, but why?"

"From the look of him. He sits about muttering and glowering with those dark eyes of his, and sometimes groans, and sometimes bursts into shouts of laughter. That is when the fit is on him, for generally he seems right enough. But get up if you think you can, and you shall judge for yourself."

"I don't want to," answered Benita

feebly. "Father, I am more afraid of him than ever. Oh! why did you not let me stop down below, among the Makalanga, instead of carrying me up here again, where we must live alone with that terrible Jew?"

"I wished to, dear, but the Molimo said we should be safer above, and ordered his people to carry you up. Also, Jacob swore that unless you were brought back he would kill me. Now you understand why I believe that he is mad."

"Why, why?" gasped Benita again.

"God knows," he answered with a groan; "but I think that he is sure that we shall never find the gold without you, since the Molimo has told him that it is for you and you alone, and he says the old man has second sight, or something of the sort. Well, he would have murdered me—I saw it in his eye—so I thought it better to give in rather than that you should be left here sick and alone. Of course there was one way——" and he paused.

She looked at him and asked:

"What way?"

"To shoot him before he shot me," he answered in a whisper, "for your sake, dear—but I could not bring myself to do it."

"No," she said with a shudder, "not that—not that. Better that we should die than that his blood should be upon our hands. Now I will get up, and try to show no fear. I am sure that is best, and perhaps we shall be able to escape somehow. Meanwhile, let us humour him, and pretend to go on looking for this horrible treasure."

So Benita rose to discover that, save for her stiffness, she was but little the worse, and finding all things placed in readiness, set to work with her father's help to cook the evening meal as usual. Of Meyer, who doubtless had placed the things in readiness, she saw nothing.

Before nightfall he came, however, as she knew he would. Indeed, although she heard no step and her back was towards him, she felt his presence; the sense of it fell upon her like a cold shadow. Turning round she beheld the man. He was standing close by, but above her, upon a big granite boulder, in climbing which his soft veld-schoons, or hide shoes, had made no noise, for Meyer could move

like a cat. The last rays from the sinking sun struck him full, outlining his agile, nervous shape against the sky, and in their intense red light which flamed upon him, he appeared terrible. He looked like a panther about to spring; his eyes shone like a panther's, and Benita knew that she was the prey whom he desired. Still, remembering her resolution, she determined to show no fear, and addressed him:

"Good-evening, Mr. Meyer. Oh! I am so stiff that I cannot lift my neck to look at you," and she laughed.

He bounded softly from the rock, like a panther again, and stood in front of her.

"You should thank the God you believe in," he said, "that by now you are not stiff indeed—all that the jackals have left of you."

"I do, Mr. Meyer, and I thank you, too; it was brave of you to come out to save us. Father," she called, "come and tell Mr. Meyer how grateful we are to him."

Mr. Clifford hobbled out from his hut under the tree, saying:

"I have told him already, dear."

"Yes," answered Jacob, "you have told me; why repeat yourself? I see that supper is ready. Let us eat, for you must be hungry; afterwards I have something to tell you."

So they ate, with no great appetite, any of them—indeed Meyer touched but little food, though he drank a good deal, first of strong black coffee and afterwards of squareface and water. But on Benita he pressed the choicest morsels that he could find, eyeing her the while, and saying that she must take plenty of nutriment or her beauty would suffer and her strength wane. Benita bethought her of the fairy tales of her childhood, in which the ogre fed up the princess whom he purposed to devour.

"You should think of your own strength, Mr. Meyer," she said; "you cannot live on coffee and squareface."

"It is all I need to-night. I am astonishingly well since you came back. I can never remember feeling so well, or so strong. I can do the work of three men, and not be tired; all this afternoon, for instance, I have been carrying provisions and other things up that steep wall, for we must prepare for a long siege together ; yet I should never know that I had lifted a single basket. But while you were away—ah ! then I felt tired."

Benita changed the subject, asking him if he had made any discoveries.

"Not yet, but now that you are back the discoveries will soon come. Do not be afraid ; I have my plan which cannot fail. Also, it was lonely working in that cave without you, so I only looked about a little outside till it was time to go to meet you, and shoot some of those Matabele. Do you know—I killed seven of them myself. When I was shooting for your sake I could not miss," and he smiled at her.

Benita shrank from him visibly, and Mr. Clifford said in an angry voice :

"Don't talk of those horrors before my daughter. It is bad enough to have to do such things, without speaking about them afterwards."

"You are right," he replied reflectively ; "and I apologise, though personally I never enjoyed anything so much as shooting those Matabele. Well, they are gone, and there are plenty more outside. Listen ! They are singing their evening hymn," and with his long finger he beat time to the volleying note of the dreadful Matabele war chant, which floated up from the plain below. "It sounds quite religious, doesn't it ? only the words— no, I will not translate them. In our circumstances they are too personal.

"Now I have something to say to you, It was unkind of you to run away and leave me like that, not honourable either. Indeed," he added with a sudden outbreak of the panther ferocity, "had you alone been concerned, Clifford, I tell you frankly that when we met again, I should have shot you. Traitors deserve to be shot, don't they ? "

"Please stop talking to my father like that," broke in Benita in a stern voice, for her anger had overcome her fear. "Also it is I whom you should blame."

"It is a pleasure to obey you," he answered bowing ; "I will never mention the subject any more. Nor do I blame you—who could ?—not Jacob Meyer. I quite understand that you found it very dull up here, and ladies must be allowed their fancies. Also you have come back ; so why talk of the matter ? But listen : on one point I have made up my mind ; for your own sake you shall not go away any more until we leave this together. When I had finished carrying up the food I made sure of that. If you go to look to-morrow morning you will find that no one can come up that wall—and what is more, no one can go down it. Moreover, that I may be quite certain, in future I shall sleep near the stair myself."

Benita and her father stared at each other.

"The Molimo has a right to come," she said ; "it is his sanctuary."

"Then he must celebrate his worship down below for a little while. The old fool pretends to know everything, but he never guessed what I was going to do. Besides, we don't want him breaking in upon our privacy, do we ? He might see the gold when we find it, and rob us of it afterwards."

BENITA.

An African Romance by . . .
H. RIDER HAGGARD.

CHAPTER XVII.

THE FIRST EXPERIMENT.

AGAIN Benita and her father stared at each other blankly, almost with despair. They were trapped, cut off from all help; in the power of a man who was going mad. Mr. Clifford said nothing. He was old and growing feeble; for years, although he did not know it, Meyer had dominated him, and never more so than in this hour of stress and bewilderment. Moreover, the man had threatened to murder him, and he was afraid, not so much for himself as for his daughter. If he were to die now, what would happen to her, left alone with Jacob Meyer? The knowledge of his own folly, understood too late, filled him with shame. How could he have been so wicked as to bring a girl upon such a quest in the company of an unprincipled Jew, of whose past he knew nothing except that it was murky and dubious? He had committed a great crime, led on by a love of lucre, and the weight of it pressed upon his tongue and closed his lips ; he knew not what to say.

For a little while Benita was silent also ; hope died within her. But she was a bold-spirited woman, and by degrees her courage re-asserted itself. Indignation filled her breast and shone through her dark eyes. Suddenly she turned upon Jacob, who sat before them smoking his pipe and enjoying their discomfiture.

"How dare you ? " she asked in a low, concentrated voice. "How dare you, you coward ? "

He shrank a little beneath her scorn and anger, then seemed to recover and brace himself, as one does who feels that a great struggle is at hand, upon the issue of which everything depends.

"Do not be angry with me," he answered. "I cannot bear it. It hurts —ah ! you don't know how it hurts. Well, I will tell you, and before your father, for that is more honourable. I dare—for your sake."

"For my sake ? How can it benefit me to be cooped up in this horrible place with you ? I would rather trust myself with the Makalanga, or even," she added with bitter scorn, "even with those bloody-minded Matabele."

"You ran away from them very fast a little while ago, Miss Clifford. But you do not understand me. When I said for your sake, I meant for my own. See, now. You tried to leave me the other day and did not succeed. Another time you might succeed, and then—what would happen to me ? "

"I do not know, Mr. Meyer," and her eyes added—" I do not care."

"Ah ! but I know. Last time it drove me nearly mad ; next time I should go quite mad."

"Because you believe that through me you will find this treasure of which you dream day and night, Mr. Meyer——"

"Yes," he interrupted quickly. "Because I believe that in you I shall find the treasure of which I dream day and night, and because that treasure has become necessary to my life."

Benita turned quickly towards her father, who was puzzling over the words, but before either of them could speak Jacob passed his hand across his brow in a bewildered way and said :

"What I was talking of—the treasure, yes, the uncountable treasure of pure gold, that lies hid so deep, that is so hard to discover and to possess, the useless, buried treasure that would bring such joy and glory to us both, if only it could be come at and reckoned out, piece by piece, coin by coin, through the long, long years of life."

Again he paused, then went on.

"Well, Miss Clifford, you are quite right ; that is why I have dared to make you a prisoner, because, as the old Molimo said, the treasure is yours and I wish to share it. Now, about this treasure, it seems that it can't be found, can it, although I have worked so hard ?" and he looked at his delicate, scarred hands.

"Quite so, Mr. Meyer, it can't be found, so you had better let us go down to the Makalanga."

"But there is a way, Miss Clifford, there is a way. You know where it lies and you can show me."

"If I knew I would show you soon enough, Mr. Meyer, for then you could take the stuff and our partnership would be at an end."

"Not until it is divided ounce by ounce and coin by coin. But first—first you must show me, as you say you will, and as you can."

"How, Mr. Meyer ? I am not a magician."

"Ah ! but you are. I will tell you how, having your promise. Listen now, both of you. I have studied. I know a great many secret things, and I read in your face that you have the gift—let me look in your eyes a while, Miss Clifford, and you will go to sleep quite gently, and then in your sleep, which shall not harm you at all, you will see where that gold lies hidden, and you will tell us."

"What do you mean ? " asked Benita, bewildered.

"I know what he means," broke in Mr. Clifford. "You mean that you want to mesmerise her as you did the Zulu chief."

Benita opened her lips to speak, but Meyer said quickly :

"No, no, hear me first before you refuse. You have the gift, the precious gift of clairvoyance, that is so rare."

"How do you know that, Mr. Meyer ? I have never been mesmerised in my life."

"'HAVE DONE WITH THIS NONSENSE,' SHE SAID"

292

"It does not matter how. I do know it; I have been sure of it from the moment when first we met, that night by the kloof. Although perhaps you felt nothing then, it was that gift of yours working upon a mind in tune, my mind, which led me there in time to save you, as it was that gift of yours which warned you of the disaster about to happen to the ship—oh! I have heard the story from your own lips. Your spirit can loose itself from the body, it can see the past and the future; it can discover the hidden things."

"I do not believe it," answered Benita; "but at least it shall not be loosed by you."

"It shall, it shall," he cried with passion, his eyes blazing on her as he spoke. "Oh! I foresaw all this, and that is why I was determined you should come with us, so that, should other means fail, we might have your power to fall back upon. Well, they have failed; I have been patient, I have said nothing, but now there is no other way. Will you be so selfish, so cruel, as to deny me, you who can make us all rich in an hour, and take no hurt at all, no more than if you had slept awhile?"

"Yes," answered Benita. "I refuse to deliver my will into the keeping of any living man, and least of all into yours, Mr. Meyer."

He turned to her father with a gesture of despair.

"Cannot you persuade her, Clifford? She is your daughter, she will obey you."

"Not in that," said Benita.

"No," answered Mr. Clifford. "I cannot, and I wouldn't if I could. My daughter is quite right. Moreover, I hate this supernatural kind of thing. If we can't find this gold without it, then we must let it alone, that is all."

Meyer turned aside to hide his face, and presently looked up again, and spoke quite softly.

"I suppose that I must accept my answer, but when you talked of any living man just now, Miss Clifford, did you include your father?"

She shook her head.

"Then will you allow him to try to mesmerise you?"

Benita laughed.

"Oh, yes, if he likes," she said. "But I do not think that the operation will be very successful."

"Good, we will see to-morrow. Now, like you, I am tired. I am going to bed in my new camp by the wall," he added significantly.

*   *   *   *   *

"Why are you so dead set against this business?" asked her father when he had gone.

"Oh, father!" she answered, "can't you see, don't you understand? Then it is hard to have to tell you, but I must. In the beginning Mr. Meyer only wanted the gold. Now he wants more, me as well as the gold. I hate him. You know that is why I ran away. But I have read a good deal about this mesmerism, and seen it once or twice, and who knows? If once I allowed his mind to master my mind, although I hate him so much, I might become his slave."

"I understand now," said Mr. Clifford. "Oh, why did I ever bring you here! It would have been better if I had never seen your face again!"

On the morrow the experiment was made. Mr. Clifford attempted to mesmerise his daughter. All the morning Jacob, who, it now appeared, had practical knowledge of this doubtful art, tried to instruct him therein. In the course of the lesson he informed him that for a short period in the past, having great natural powers in that direction, he had made use of them professionally, only giving up the business because he found it wrecked his health. Mr. Clifford remarked that he had never told him that before.

"There are lots of things in my life that I have never told you," replied Jacob with a little secret smile. "For instance, once I mesmerised you, although you did not know it, and that is why you always have to do what I want you to, except when your daughter is near you, for her influence is stronger than mine."

Mr. Clifford stared at him.

"No wonder Benita won't let you mesmerise her," he said shortly.

Then Jacob saw his mistake.

"You are more foolish than I thought," he said. "How could I mesmerise you without your knowing it? I was only laughing at you."

"I didn't see the laugh," replied Mr. Clifford uneasily, and they went on with the lesson.

That afternoon it was put to proof— in the cave itself, where Meyer seemed to think the influences would be propitious. Benita, who found some amusement in the performance, was seated upon the stone steps underneath the crucifix, one lamp on the altar and others on each side of her.

In front stood her father, staring at her and waving his hands mysteriously in obedience to Jacob's directions. So ridiculous did he look indeed while thus engaged that Benita had the greatest difficulty in preventing herself from bursting into laughter. This was the only effect which his grimaces and gesticulations produced upon her, although outwardly she kept a solemn appearance, and even from time to time shut her eyes to encourage him. Once when she opened them again, it was to perceive that he was becoming very hot and exhausted, and that Jacob was watching him with such an unpleasant intentness that she re-closed her eyes that she might not see his face.

It was shortly after this that of a sudden Benita did feel something, a kind of penetrating power flowing upon her, something soft and subtle that seemed to creep into her brain like the sound of her mother's lullaby in the dim years ago. She began to think that she was a lost traveller among alpine snows wrapped round by snow, falling, falling in ten myriad flakes, every one of them with a little heart of fire. Then it came to her that she had heard this snow-sleep was dangerous, the last of all sleeps, and that its victims must rouse themselves, or die.

Benita roused herself just in time— only just, for now she was being borne over the edge of a precipice upon the wings of swans, and beneath her was darkness wherein dim figures walked with lamps where their hearts should be. Oh, how heavy were her eyelids! Surely a weight hung to each of them, a golden weight. There, there, they were open and she saw. Her father had ceased his efforts; he was rubbing his brow with a red pocket-handkerchief, but behind him, with rigid arms outstretched, his glowing eyes fastened on her face, stood Jacob Meyer. By an effort she sprang to her feet, shaking her head as a dog does.

"Have done with this nonsense," she said. "It tires me," and snatching one of the lamps she ran swiftly down the place.

Benita expected that Jacob Meyer would be very angry with her, and braced herself for a scene. But nothing of the sort happened. A while afterwards she saw the two of them approaching, engaged apparently in amicable talk.

"Mr. Meyer says that I am no mesmerist, love," said her father, "and I can quite believe him. But for all that it is a weary job. I am as tired as I was after our escape from the Matabele."

She laughed and answered:

"To judge by results I agree with you. The occult is not in your line, father. You had better give it up."

"Did you, then, feel nothing?" asked Meyer.

"Nothing at all," she answered, looking him in the eyes. "No, that's wrong, I felt extremely bored and sorry to see my father making himself ridiculous. Grey hairs and nonsense of that sort don't go well together."

"No," he answered. "I agree with you—not of that sort," and the subject dropped.

For the next few days, to her intense relief, Benita heard no more of mesmerism. To begin with, there was something else to occupy their minds. The Matabele, tired of marching round the fortress and singing endless war-songs, had determined upon an assault. From their point of vantage on the topmost wall the three could watch the preparations which they made. Trees were cut down and brought in from a great distance that rude ladders might be fashioned out of them, also spies wandered round reconnoitring for a weak place in the defences. When they came too near the Makalanga fired on them, killing some so that they retreated to the camp, which they had made in a fold of ground at a little distance. Suddenly it occurred to Meyer that although here the Matabele were safe from the Makalanga bullets, it was commanded from the greater eminence, and by way of recreation he set himself to harass them. His rifle was a sporting Martini, and he had an ample supply of ammunition Moreover, he was a beautiful marksman, with sight like that of a hawk.

A few trial shots gave him the range; it was a shade under seven hundred yards, and then he began operations. Lying on the top of the wall and resting his rifle upon a stone, he waited until the man who was superintending the manufacture of the ladders came out into the open, when, aiming carefully, he fired. The soldier, a white-bearded savage, sprang into the air, and fell backwards, while his companions stared upwards, wondering whence the bullet had come.

"Pretty, wasn't it?" said Meyer to Benita, who was watching through a pair of field-glasses.

"I dare say," she answered. "But I don't want to see any more," and giving the glasses to her father, she climbed down the wall.

But Meyer stayed there, and from time to time she heard the report of his rifle. In the evening he told her that he had killed six men and wounded ten more, adding that it was the best day's shooting which he could remember.

"What is the use when there are so many?" she asked.

"Not much," he answered. "But it annoys them and amuses me. Also, it was part of our bargain that we should help the Makalanga if they were attacked."

"I believe that you like killing people," she said.

"I don't mind it, Miss Clifford, especially as they tried to kill you."

CHAPTER XVIII.

THE OTHER BENITA.

AT irregular times, when he had nothing else to do, Jacob went on with his man shooting, in which Mr. Clifford joined him, though with less effect. Soon it became evident that the Matabele were very much annoyed by the fatal accuracy of this fire. Loss of life they did not mind in the abstract, but when none of them knew but that their own turn might come next to perish beneath these downward plunging bullets, the matter wore a different face to them. To leave their camp was not easy, since they had made a thorn *boma* round it, to protect them in case the Makalanga should make a night sally; also they could find no other convenient spot. The upshot of it all was to hurry their assault, which they delivered before they had prepared sufficient ladders to make it effective.

At the first break of dawn on the third day after Mr. Clifford's attempt at mesmerism, Benita was awakened by the sounds of shouts and firing. Having dressed herself hastily, she hurried in the growing light towards that part of the wall from below which the noise seemed to come, and climbing it, found her father and Jacob already seated there, their rifles in hand.

"The fools are attacking the small gate through which you went out riding, Miss Clifford, the very worst place that they could have chosen, although the wall looks weak there," said the latter. "If those Makalanga have any pluck they ought to teach them a lesson."

Then the sun rose and they saw companies of Matabele, who carried ladders in their hands, rushing onward through the morning mist till their sight of them was obstructed by the swell of the hill. On these companies the two white men opened fire, with what results they could not see in that light. Presently a great shout announced that the enemy had gained the fosse and were setting up the ladders. Up to this time the Makalanga appeared to have done nothing, but now they began to fire rapidly from the ancient bastions which commanded the entrance the impi was striving to storm, and soon through the thinning fog they perceived wounded Matabele staggering and crawling back towards their camp. Of these, the light now being better, Jacob did not neglect to take his toll.

Meanwhile, the ancient fortress rang with the hideous tumult of the attack. It was evident that again and again, as their fierce war-shouts proclaimed, the Matabele were striving to scale the wall, and again and again were beaten back by the raking rifle fire. Once a triumphant yell seemed to announce their success. The fire slackened and Benita grew pale with fear.

"The Makalanga cowards are bolting,"

"A FEW TRIAL SHOTS GAVE HIM THE RANGE, ... AND THEN HE BEGAN OPERATIONS"

muttered Mr. Clifford, listening with terrible anxiety.

But if so their courage came back to them, for presently the guns cracked louder and more incessant than before, and the savage cries of " Kill! Kill! Kill! " dwindled and died away. Another five minutes and the Matabele were in full retreat bearing with them many dead and wounded men upon their backs or stretched out on the ladders.

" Our Makalanga friends should be grateful to us for those hundred rifles," said Jacob as he loaded and fired rapidly, sending his bullets wherever the clusters were thickest. " Had it not been for them their throats would have been cut by now," he added, " for they could never have stopped those savages with the spear."

" Yes, and ours too before nightfall," said Benita with a shudder, for the sight of this desperate fray and fear of how it might end had sickened her. " Thank Heaven, it is over! Perhaps they will give up the siege and go away."

But notwithstanding their costly defeat, for they had lost over a hundred men, the Matabele, who were afraid to return to Buluwayo except as victors, did nothing of the sort. They only cut down a quantity of reeds and scrub and moved their camp nearly to the banks of the river, placing it in such a position that it could no longer be searched by the fire of the two white men. Here they sat themselves down sullenly, hoping to starve out the garrison or to find some other way of entering the fortress.

Now Meyer's shooting having come to an end for lack of men to shoot at, since the enemy exposed themselves no more, he was again able to give his full attention to the matter of the treasure-hunt.

As nothing could be found in the cave he devoted himself to the outside enclosure which, it may be remembered, was grown over with grass and trees and crowded with ruins. In the most important of these ruins they began to dig somewhat aimlessly, and were rewarded by finding a certain amount of gold in the shape of beads and ornaments, and a few more skeletons of ancients. But of the Portuguese hoard there was no sign. Thus it came about that they grew gloomier day by day, till at last they scarcely spoke to each other. Jacob's angry disappointment was written on his face and Benita was filled with despair, since to escape from their gaoler above and the Matabele below seemed impossible. Moreover, she had another cause for anxiety.

The ill-health which had been threatening her father for a long while now fell upon him in earnest, so that of a sudden he became a very old man. His strength and energy left him, and his mind was so filled with remorse for what he held to be his crime in bringing his daughter to this awful place, and with terror for the fate that threatened her, that he could think of nothing else. In vain did she try to comfort him. He would only wring his hands and groan, praying that God and she would forgive him. Now, too, Meyer's mastery over him became continually more evident. Mr. Clifford implored the man, almost with tears, to unblock the wall and allow them to go down to the Makalanga. He even tried to bribe him with the offer of all his share of the treasure, if it were found, and when that failed, of his property in the Transvaal.

But Jacob only told him roughly not to be a fool, as they had to see the thing through together. Then he would go away and brood by himself, and Benita noticed that he always took his rifle or a pistol with him. Evidently he feared lest her father should catch him unprepared, and take the law into his own hands by means of a sudden bullet.

One comfort she had, however: although he watched her closely, the Jew never tried to molest her in any way, not even with more of his enigmatic and amorous speeches. By degrees, indeed, she came to believe that all this was gone from his mind, or that he had abandoned his advances as hopeless.

A week passed since the Matabele attack, and nothing had happened. The Makalanga took no notice of them, and so far as she was aware the old Molimo never attempted to climb the blocked wall or otherwise to communicate with them, a thing so strange that, knowing his affection for her, Benita came to the conclusion that he must be dead, killed perhaps in the attack. Even Jacob Meyer had abandoned his digging, and sat about all day doing nothing but think.

Their meal that night was a miserable affair, since in the first place provisions were running short, and there was little to eat, and in the second no one spoke a word. Benita could swallow no food, she was weary of that sun-dried trek-ox, for since Meyer had blocked the wall they had little else. But by good fortune there remained plenty of coffee, and of this she drank two cups, which Jacob prepared and handed to her with much politeness. It tasted very bitter to her, but this, Benita reflected, was because they lacked milk and sugar. Supper ended, Meyer rose and bowed to her, muttering that he was going to bed, and a few minutes later Mr. Clifford followed his example. She went with her father to the hut beneath the tree, and having helped him to remove his coat, which now he seemed to find difficulty in doing for himself, bade him good-night and returned to the fire.

It was very lonely there in the silence, for no sound came from either the Matabele or the Makalanga camps, and the bright moonlight seemed to people the place with fantastic shadows that looked alive. Benita cried a little now that her father could not see her, and then also sought refuge in bed. Evidently the end, whatever it might be, was near, and of it she could not bear to think. Moreover, her eyes were strangely heavy, so much so that before she had finished saying her prayers sleep fell upon her, and she knew no more.

Had she remained as wakeful as it was often her fate to be during those fearful days, towards midnight she might have heard some light-footed creature creeping to her tent, and seen that the moon-rays which flowed through the gaping and ill-closed flap were cut off by the figure of a man with glowing eyes whose projected arms waved over her mysteriously. But Benita neither heard nor saw. In her drugged rest she did not know that her sleep turned gradually to a magic swoon. She had no knowledge of her rising, or of how she threw her thick cloak about her, lit her lamp, and in obedience to that beckoning finger, glided from the tent.

She never heard her father stumble from his hut, disturbed by the sound of footsteps, or the words that passed between him and Jacob Meyer, while, lamp in hand, she stood near them like a strengthless ghost.

"If you dare to wake her," hissed Jacob, "I tell you that she will die, and afterwards you shall die," and he fingered the pistol at his belt. "No harm shall come to her—I swear it! Follow and see. Man, man, be silent; our fortunes hang on it."

Then, overcome also by the strange fierceness of that voice and gaze, he followed.

On they go to the winding neck of the cavern, first Jacob walking backwards like the herald of majesty, then majesty itself in the shape of this long-haired, death-like woman, cloaked and bearing in her hand the light, and last, behind, the old, white-bearded man, like Time following beauty to the grave. Now they were in the great cavern, and now, avoiding the open tombs, the well mouth and the altar, they stood beneath the crucifix.

"Be seated," said Meyer, and the entranced Benita sat herself down upon the steps at the foot of the cross, placing the lamp on the rock pavement before her, and bowing her head till her hair fell upon her naked feet and hid them. He held his hands above her for a while, then asked:

"Do you sleep?"

"I sleep," came the strange, slow answer.

"Is your spirit awake?"

"It is awake."

"Command it to travel backwards through the ages to the beginning, and tell me what you see here."

"I see a rugged cave and wild folk dwelling in it; an old man is dying yonder," and she pointed to the right; "and a black woman with a babe at her breast tends him. A man, it is her husband, enters the cave. He holds a torch in one hand, and with the other drags a buck."

"Cease," said Meyer. "How long is this ago?"

"Thirty-three thousand two hundred and one years," came the answer, spoken without any hesitation.

"Pass on," he said, "pass on thirty

" 'GREAT HEAVEN!' SAID MEYER, 'IT IS PORTUGUESE,' AND FOR A WHILE THE TERROR OF THE THING
STRUCK HIM DUMB "

thousand years, and tell me what you see."

For a long while there was silence.

"Why do you not speak?" he asked.

"Be patient; I am living through those thirty thousand years; many a life, many an age, but none may be missed."

Again there was silence for a long while, till at length she spoke.

"They are done, all of them, and now three thousand years ago I see this place changed and smoothly fashioned, peopled by a throng of worshippers clad in strange garments with clasps upon them. Behind me stands the graven statue of a goddess with a calm and cruel face, in front of the altar burns a fire, and on the altar white-robed priests are sacrificing a babe which cries aloud."

"Pass on, pass on," Meyer said hurriedly, as though the horror of that scene had leapt to his eyes. "Pass on two thousand seven hundred years and tell me what you see."

Again there was a pause, while the spirit he had evoked in the body of Benita lived through those ages. Then slowly she answered:

"Nothing, the place is black and desolate, only the dead sleep beneath its floor."

"Wait till the living come again," he commanded, "then speak."

"They are here," she replied presently. "Tonsured monks, one of whom fashions this crucifix, and their followers who bow before the Host upon the altar. They come, they go—of whom shall I tell you?"

"Tell me of the Portuguese; of those who were driven here to die."

"I see them all," she answered, after a pause. "Two hundred and three of them. They are ragged and wayworn and hungry. Among them is a beautiful woman, a girl. She draws near to me, she enters into me. You must ask her—" this was spoken in a very faint voice— "I am I no more."

Mr. Clifford attempted to interrupt, but fiercely Meyer bade him to be silent.

"Speak," he commanded, but the crouching figure shook her head.

"Speak," he said again, whereon another voice, not that of Benita, answered in another tongue:

"I hear, but I do not understand your language."

"Great Heaven!" said Meyer, "it is Portuguese," and for a while the terror of the thing struck him dumb, for he was aware that Benita knew no Portuguese. He knew it, however, who had lived at Lorenço Marquez.

"Who are you?" he asked in that tongue.

"I am Benita da Ferreira. I am the daughter of the Captain da Ferreira and of his wife, the lady Christinha, who stand by you now. Turn and you will see them."

Jacob started and looked about him uneasily.

"What did she say? I did not catch it all," asked Mr. Clifford.

He translated her words.

"But this is black magic," exclaimed the old man. "Benita knows no Portuguese, so how comes she to speak it?"

"Because she is no longer our Benita, she is another Benita, Benita de Ferreira. The Molimo was right when he said that the spirit of the dead woman went with her, as it seems the name has gone," he added.

"Have done," said Mr. Clifford, "the thing is unholy. Wake her up, or I will."

"And bring about her death. Touch or disturb her, and I tell you she will die,' and he pointed to Benita, who crouched before them so white and motionless that indeed it seemed as though already she were dead. "Be quiet," he went on. "I swear to you that no hurt shall come to her, also that I will translate everything to you. Promise, or I will tell you nothing, and her blood be on your head."

Then Mr. Clifford groaned and said: "I promise."

"Tell me your story, Benita da Ferreira. How came you and your people here?"

"The tribes of Monomotapa rose against our rule. They killed many of us in the lower land, yes, they killed my brother and him to whom I was affianced. The rest of us fled north to this ancient fortress, hoping thence to escape by the river, the Zambesi. The Mambo, our vassal, gave us shelter here, but the tribes besieged the walls in thousands, and burnt all the boats so that we could not fly by the water. Many times we beat them back from the wall; the ditch was full of their dead, and at last they dared to attack no more.

"Then we began to starve and they won the first wall. We went on starving and they won the second wall, but the third wall they could not climb. So we died ; one by one we laid ourselves down in this cave and died till I alone was left, for while our people had food they gave it to me who was the daughter of their captain. Yes, alone I knelt at the foot of this crucifix by the body of my father praying to the blessed Son of Mary for the death that would not come, and kneeling there I swooned. When I awoke again the Mambo and his men stood about me, for now, knowing us to be dead, the tribes had gone and those who were in hiding across the river, had returned and knew how to climb the wall. "They bore me from among the dead, they gave me food so that my strength came back ; but in the night I, who in my wickedness would not live, escaped from them and climbed the pillar of black rock, so that when the sun rose they saw me standing there. They begged of me to come down, promising to protect me, but I said ' No,' who in the evil of my heart only desired to die, that I might join my father and my brother, and one who was dearer to me than all. They asked of me where the great treasure was hidden."

At these words Jacob gasped, then rapidly translated them, while the figure before them became silent as though it felt that for the moment the power of his will was withdrawn.

"Speak on, I bid you," he said, and she continued, the rich, slow voice dropping word after word from the lips of Benita in the alien speech that this Benita never knew.

"I answered that it was where it was, and that if they gave it up to any save the one appointed, then that fate which had befallen my people would befall theirs also. Yes, I gave it into their keeping until I came again, since with his dying breath my father had commanded me to reveal it to none, and I believed that I who was about to die should never come again.

"Then I made my last prayer, I kissed the golden crucifix that now hangs upon the breast wherein I dwell," and the hand of the living Benita was lifted, and moving like the hand of a dead thing, slowly drew out the symbol from beneath the cloak, held it for a moment in the lamplight, and let it fall to its place again. "I put my hands before my eyes that I might not see, and I hurled myself from the pinnacle."

Now the voice ceased, but from the lips came a dreadful sound, such as might be uttered by one whose bones are shattered upon rocks, followed by other sounds like those of one who chokes in water. They were so horrible to hear that Mr. Clifford nearly fainted, and even Jacob Meyer staggered and turned white as the white face of Benita.

"Wake her ! For God's sake, wake her ! " said her father. "She is dying, as that woman died hundreds of years ago."

"Not till she has told us where the gold is. Be quiet, you fool. She does not feel or suffer. It is the spirit within her that lives through the past again."

Once more there was silence. It seemed as though the story were all told and the teller had departed.

"Benita da Ferreira," said Meyer at length. "I command you, tell me, are you dead ? "

"Oh ! would that I were dead, as my body is dead ! " wailed the lips of Benita. "Alas ! I cannot die who suffer this purgatory, and must dwell on here alone until the destined day. Yes, yes, the spirit of her who was Benita da Ferreira must haunt this place in solitude. This is her doom, to be the guardian of that accursed gold which was wrung from the earth by cruelty and paid for with the lives of men."

"Is it still safe ? " whispered Jacob.

"I will look ; " then after a pause, "I have looked. It is there, every grain of it, in ox-hide bags, only one of them has fallen and burst, that which is black and red."

"Where is it ? " he said again.

"I may not tell you, never, never."

"Is there anyone whom you may tell ? "

"Yes."

"Whom ? "

"Her in whose breast I lie."

"Tell her then."

"I have told her, she knows."

"And may she tell me ? "

"Let her guard the secret as she will. Oh ! my Guardians, I thank you, my burden is departed; my sin of self-murder is atoned."

"Benita da Ferreira, are you gone?"
No answer.

"Benita Clifford, do you hear me?"

"I hear you," said the voice of Benita, speaking in English, although Jacob, forgetting, had addressed her in Portuguese.

"Where is the gold?"

"In my keeping."

"Tell me, I command you,"

But no words came; though he questioned her many times no words came, till at last her head sank forward upon her knees, and in a faint voice she murmured:

"Loose me, or I die."

CHAPTER XIX.

THE AWAKING.

STILL Jacob Meyer hesitated. The great secret was unlearned, and, if this occasion passed, might never be learned. But if he hesitated, Mr. Clifford did not. The knowledge of his child's danger, the sense that her life was mysteriously slipping away from her under pressure of the ghastly spell in which she lay enthralled, stirred him to madness. His strength and manhood came back to him. He sprang straight at Meyer's throat, gripped it with one hand, and with the other drew the knife he wore.

"You devil!" he gasped. "Wake her or you shall go with her!" and he lifted the knife.

Then Jacob gave in. Shaking off his assailant he stepped to Benita, and while her father stood behind him with the lifted blade, began to make strange upward passes over her, and to mutter words of command. For a long while they took no effect; indeed, both of them were almost sure that she was gone. Despair gripped her father, and Meyer worked at his black art so furiously that the sweat burst out upon his forehead and fell in great drops to the floor.

Oh, at last, at last she stirred! Her head lifted itself a little, her breast heaved.

"Lord in Heaven, I have saved her!" muttered Jacob in German, and worked on.

Now the eyes of Benita opened, and now she stood up and sighed. But she said nothing; only like a person walking in her sleep, she began to move towards the entrance of the cave, her father going before her with the lamp. On she went, and out of it straight to her tent, where instantly she cast herself upon her bed and sank into deep slumber. It was as though the power of the drug-induced oblivion, which for a while was overmastered by that other stronger power invoked by Jacob, had reasserted itself.

Meyer watched her for awhile, then said to Mr. Clifford:

"Don't be afraid and don't attempt to disturb her. She will wake naturally in the morning."

"I hope so for both our sakes," he answered, glaring at him, "for if not, you or I, or the two of us, will never see another."

Meyer took no notice of his threats; indeed the man seemed so exhausted that he could scarcely stand.

"I am done," he said. "Now, as she is safe, I don't care what happens to me. I must rest," and he staggered from the tent like a drunken man.

Outside, at the place where they ate, Mr. Clifford heard him gulping down raw gin from the bottle. Then he heard no more.

All the rest of that night, and for some hours of the early morning, did her father watch by the bed of Benita, although, lightly clad as he was, the cold of dawn struck to his bones. At length, when the sun was well up, she rose in her bed, and her eyes opened.

"What are you doing here, father?" she said.

"I have come to see where you were, dear. You are generally out by now."

"I suppose that I must have overslept myself then," she replied wearily. "But it does not seem to have refreshed me much, and my head aches. Oh! I remember," she added with a start, "I have had such a horrid dream."

"What about?" he asked as carelessly as he could.

"I can't recall it quite, but it had to do with Mr. Meyer," and she shivered. "It seemed as though I had passed into his power, as though he had taken possession of me, body and soul, and forced me to tell him all the secret things."

"What secret things, Benita?"

She shook her head.

"I don't know now, but we went away among dead people and I told him there. Oh! father, I am afraid of that man, terribly afraid! Protect me from him," and she began to cry a little.

"Of course I will protect you, dear. Something has upset your nerves. Come, dress yourself and you'll soon forget it all. I'll light the fire."

A quarter of an hour later Benita joined him, looking pale and shaken, but otherwise much as usual. She was ravenously hungry, and ate of the biscuits and dried meat with eagerness.

"The coffee tastes quite different from that which I drank last night," she said. "I think there must have been something in it which gave me those bad dreams. Where is Mr. Meyer? Oh, I know!" and again she put her hand to her head. "He is still asleep by the wall."

"Who told you that?"

"I can't say, but it is so. He will not come here till one o'clock. There, I feel much better now. What shall we do, father?"

"Sit in the sun and rest, I think, dear."

"Yes, let us do that, on the top of the wall. We can see the Makalanga from there, and it will be a comfort to be sure there are other human beings left in the world besides ourselves and Jacob Meyer."

So presently they went, and from the spot whence Meyer used to shoot at the Matabele camp, looked down upon the Makalanga moving about the first enclosure far below. By the aid of the glasses Benita even thought that she recognised Tamas, although of this it was difficult to be sure, for they were all very much alike. Still, the discovery quite excited her.

"I am sure it is Tamas," she said. "And oh! how I wish that we were down there with him, although it is true that then we should be nearer to the Matabele. But they are better than Mr. Meyer, much better."

Now for a while they were silent, till at length she said suddenly:

"Father, you are keeping something from me, and things begin to come back. Tell me, did I go anywhere last night with Mr. Meyer—you and he and I together?"

He hesitated and looked guilty; Mr. Clifford was not a good actor.

"I see that we did, I am sure that we did. Father, tell me. I must know, I will know."

Then he gave way.

"I didn't want to speak, dear, but perhaps it is best. It is a very strange story. Will you promise not to be upset?"

"I will promise not to be more upset than I am at present," she answered, with a sad little laugh. "Go on."

"You remember that Jacob Meyer wanted to mesmerise you?"

"I am not likely to forget it," she answered.

"Well, last night he did mesmerise you."

"What?" she said. "*What?* Oh! how dreadful! Now I understand it all. But when?"

"When you were sound asleep, I suppose. At least, the first I knew of it was that some noise woke me, and I came out of the hut to see you following him like a dead woman, with a lamp in her hand."

Then he told her all the story, while she listened aghast.

"How dared he!" she gasped when her father had finished the long tale. "I hate him, I almost wish that you had killed him," and she clenched her little hands and shook them in the air.

"That is not very Christian of you, Miss Clifford," said a voice behind her. "But it is past one o'clock, and as I am still alive I have come to tell you that it is time for luncheon."

Benita wheeled round upon the stone on which she sat, and there, standing amidst the bushes a little way from the foot of the wall, was Jacob Meyer. Their eyes met; hers were full of defiance, and his of conscious power.

"I do not want any luncheon, Mr. Meyer," she said.

"But I am sure that you do. Please come down and have some. Please come down."

The words were spoken humbly, almost pleadingly, yet to Benita they seemed as a command. At any rate, with slow reluctance she climbed down the shattered wall, followed by her father, and without speaking they went back to their camping place, all three of them, Jacob leading the way.

When they had eaten, or made pretence to eat, he spoke.

"SHE STOOD QUITE STILL, AFRAID TO MOVE"

" I see that your father has told you everything, Miss Clifford, and of that I am glad, as for me it would have been awkward, who must ask your forgiveness for so much. But what could I do? I knew, as I have always known, that it was only possible to find this treasure by your help. So I gave you something to make you sleep, and then in your sleep I hypnotised you, and—you know the rest. I have great experience in this art, but I have never seen or heard of anything like what happened, and I hope I never shall again."

Hitherto Benita had sat silent, but now her burning indignation and curiosity overcame her shame and hatred.

" Mr. Meyer," she said, " you have done a shameful and a wicked thing, and I tell you at once that I can never forgive you."

" Don't say that. Please don't say that," he interrupted in tones of real grief. " Make allowances for me. I had to learn, and there was no other way. You are a born clairvoyante, one among ten thousand, my art told me so, and you know all that is at stake."

" By which you mean so many ounces of gold, Mr. Meyer."

" By which I mean the greatness that gold can give, Miss Clifford."

" Such greatness, Mr. Meyer, as a week of fever, or a Matabele spear, or God's will can rob you of. But the thing is done, and soon or late the sin must be paid for. Now I want to ask you a question. You believe in nothing; you have told me so several times. You say that there is no such thing as a spirit, that when we die, we die, and there's an end. Do you not? "

" Yes, I do."

" Then tell me, what was it that spoke out of my lips last night, and how came it that I, who know no Portuguese, talked to you in that tongue? "

He shrugged his shoulders.

" You have put a difficult question, but one I think that can be answered. There is no such thing as a spirit, an identity that survives death. But there is such a thing as the sub-conscious self, which is part of the animating principle of the universe, and, if only its knowledge can be unsealed, knows all that has passed and all that is passing in that universe. One day perhaps you will read the works of my compatriot, Hegel, and there you will find it spoken of."

" You explain nothing."

" I am about to explain, Miss Clifford. Last night I gave to your sub-conscious self—that which knows all—the strength of liberty, so that it saw the past as it had happened in this place. Already you knew the story of the dead girl, Benita da Ferreira, and that story you re-enacted, talking the tongue she used as you would have talked Greek or any other tongue, had it been hers. It was not her spirit that animated you, but your own buried knowledge, tricked out and furnished by the effort of your human imagination. That her name, Benita, should have been yours also is no doubt a strange coincidence, but no more. Also we have no proof that it was so; only what you said in your trance."

" Perhaps," said Benita, who was in no mood for philosophical argument. " Perhaps also one day you will see a spirit, Mr. Meyer, and think otherwise."

" When I see a spirit and know that it is a spirit, then doubtless I shall believe in spirits. But what is the good of talking of such things? I do not seek spirits; I seek the Portuguese gold. Now, I am sure you can tell where that gold lies. You would have told us last night, had not your nervous strength failed you, who are unaccustomed to the state of trance. Speaking as Benita da Ferreira, you said that you saw it and described its condition. Then you could, or would, say no more, and it became necessary to waken you. Miss Clifford, you must let me mesmerise you once again for a few minutes only, for then we will waste no time on past histories, and we shall find the gold. Unless, indeed," he added by an afterthought, and looking at her sharply, " you know already where it is, in which case I need not trouble you."

" I do not know, Mr. Meyer. I remember nothing about the gold."

" Which proves my theory. What purported to be the spirit of Benita da Ferreira, said that it had passed the secret on to you, but in your waking state you do not know that secret. In fact, she did not pass it on because she had no existence. But in your sub-conscious state you will know. Therefore I must mesmerise you again. Not at once, but in a few days' time, when you have quite recovered. Let us say next Wednesday, three days hence."

" You shall never mesmerise me again, Mr. Meyer."

" No, not while I live," broke in her father, who had been listening to this discussion in silence.

Jacob bowed his head meekly.

" You think so now, but I think otherwise. What I did last night I did against your will, and that I can do again, only much more easily. But I had rather do it with your will, who work not for my own sake only, but for the sake of all of us. And now let us talk no more of the matter, lest we should grow angry." Then he rose and went away.

The next three days were passed by Benita in a state of constant dread. She knew in herself that Jacob Meyer had acquired a certain command over her; that a horrible intimacy had sprung up between them. She was acquainted with his thoughts; thus, before he asked for it, she would find herself passing him some article at table or elsewhere, or answering a question that he was only about to ask. Moreover, he could bring her to him from a little distance. Thus, on two or three occasions when she was wandering about their prison enclosure, as she was wont to do for the sake of exercise, she found her feet drawn to some spot—now one place and now another—and when she reached it there before her was Jacob Meyer.

" Forgive me for bringing you here," he would say, smiling after his crooked fashion, and lifting his hat politely, " but I wish to ask you if you have not changed your mind as to being mesmerised."

Then for a while he would hold her with his eyes, so that her feet seemed rooted to the ground, till at length it was as though he cut a rope by some action of his will and set her free, and, choked with wrath and blind with tears, Benita would turn and run from him as from a wild beast.

But if her days were evil, oh! what were her nights? She lived in constant terror lest he should again drug her food or drink, and, while she slept, throw his magic spell upon her. To protect herself from the first danger she would swallow nothing that had been near him. Now also she slept in the hut with her father, who lay near its door, a loaded rifle at his side, for he had told Jacob outright that if he caught him at his practices he would shoot him, a threat at which the younger man laughed aloud, for he had no fear of Mr. Clifford.

Throughout the long hours of darkness they kept watch alternately, one of them lying down to rest while the other peered and listened. Nor did Benita always listen in vain, for twice at least she heard stealthy footsteps creeping about the hut, and felt that soft and dreadful influence flowing in upon her. Then she would wake her father, whispering, " He is there, I can feel that he is there." But by the time that the old man had painfully dragged himself to his feet—for now he was becoming very feeble, and acute rheumatism or some such illness had got hold of him—and crept from the hut, there was no one to be seen. Only through the darkness he would hear the sound of a retreating step, and of low, mocking laughter.

Thus those miserable days went by, and the third morning came, that dreaded Wednesday. Before it was dawn Benita and her father, neither of whom had closed their eyes that night, talked over their strait long and earnestly, for they knew that its crisis was approaching.

" I think that I had better try to kill him, Benita," he said. " I am growing dreadfully weak, and if I put it off I may find no strength, and you will be at his mercy. I can easily shoot him when his back is turned, and though I hate the thought of such a deed, surely I shall be forgiven. Or if not, I cannot help it. I must think of my duty to you, not of myself."

" No, no," she answered. " I will not have it. It would be murder, although he has threatened you. After all, father, I believe that the man is half mad, and not responsible. We must take our chance and trust to God to save us. If He does not," she added, " at the worst I can always save myself," and she touched the pistol which now she wore day and night.

"So be it," said Mr. Clifford, with a groan. "Let us pray for deliverance from this hell and keep our hands clean of blood."

CHAPTER XX.

JACOB MEYER SEES A SPIRIT.

FOR a while they were silent, then Benita said:

"Father, is it not possible that we might escape after all? Perhaps that stair on the rampart is not so completely blocked that we could not climb over it."

Mr. Clifford, thinking of his stiff limbs and aching back, shook his head and answered:

"I don't know; Meyer has never let me near enough to see."

"Well, why do you not go and look? You know he sleeps till late now, because he is up all night. Take the glasses and examine the top of the wall from inside that old house near by. He will not see or hear you, but if I came near, he would know and wake up."

"If you like, love, I can try, but what are you going to do while I am away?"

"I shall climb the pillar."

"You don't mean——" and he stopped.

"No, no, nothing of that sort. I shall not follow the example of Benita da Ferreira unless I am driven to it; I want to look, that is all. One can see far from that place, if there is anything to see. Perhaps the Matabele are gone now, we have heard nothing of them lately."

So they dressed themselves, and as soon as the light was sufficiently strong, came out of the hut and parted, Mr. Clifford, rifle in hand, limping off towards the wall, and Benita going towards the great cone. She climbed it easily enough, and stood in the little cup-like depression on its dizzy peak, waiting for the sun to rise and disperse the mists which hung over the river and its banks.

Now whatever may have been the exact ceremonial use to which the ancients put this pinnacle, without doubt it had something to do with sun-worship. This, indeed, was proved by the fact that, at any rate at this season of the year, the first rays of the risen orb struck full upon its point. Thus it came about that, as she stood there waiting, Benita of a sudden found herself suffused in light so vivid and intense that, clothed as she was in a dress which had once been white, it must have caused her to shine like a silver image. For several minutes, indeed, this golden spear of fire blinded her so that she could see nothing, but stood quite still, afraid to move, and waiting until, as the sun grew higher, its level rays passed over her. This they did presently, and plunging into the valley, began to drive away the fog. Now she looked down, along the line of the river.

The Matabele camp was invisible, for it lay in a hollow almost at the foot of the fortress. Beyond it, however, was a rising swell of ground; it may have been half a mile from where she stood, and on the crest of it she perceived what looked like a waggon tent with figures moving round it. They were shouting also, for through the silence of the African morn the sound of their voices floated up to her.

As the mist cleared off Benita saw that without doubt it was a waggon, for there stood the long row of oxen, also it had just been captured by the Matabele, for these were about it in numbers. At the moment, however, they appeared to be otherwise occupied, for they were pointing with their spears to the pillar on Bambatse.

Then it occurred to Benita that, placed as she was in that fierce light with only the sky for background, she must be perfectly visible from the plain below, and that it might be her figure perched like an eagle between heaven and earth which excited their interest. Yes, and not theirs only, for now a white man appeared, who lifted what might have been a gun, or a telescope, towards her. She was sure from the red flannel shirt and the broad hat which he wore that he must be a white man, and oh! how her heart yearned towards him whoever he might be! The sight of an angel from heaven could scarcely have been more welcome to Benita in her wretchedness.

Yet surely she must be dreaming. What should a white man and a waggon be doing in that place? And why had not the Matabele killed him at once? She could not tell, yet they appeared to have no murderous intentions, since they continued to gesticulate and talk

"SHE HELD THE LAMP ABOVE HER HEAD, AND BY ITS LIGHT PERCEIVED A FIGURE STANDING BETWEEN
HER AND THE ENTRANCE TO THE CAVE"

whilst he stared upwards with the telescope, if it were a telescope. So things went on for a long time, for meanwhile the oxen were outspanned, until, indeed, more Matabele arrived, who led off the white man, apparently against his will, towards their camp, where he disappeared. Then, as there was nothing more to be seen, Benita descended the column.

At its foot she met her father, who had come to seek her.

"What is the matter?" he asked, noting her excited face.

"Oh!" she said or rather sobbed, "there is a waggon with a white man below. I saw the Matabele capture him."

"Then I am sorry for the poor devil," answered the father, "for he is dead by now. But what could a white man have been doing here? Some hunter, I suppose, who has walked into a trap."

The face of Benita fell.

"I hoped," she said, "that he might help us."

"As well might he hope that we could help him. He is gone, and there is an end. Well, peace to his soul, and we have our own troubles to think of. I have been to look at that wall, and it is useless to think of climbing it. If he had been a professional mason, Meyer could not have built it up better; no wonder that we have seen nothing more of the Molimo, for only a bird could reach us."

"Where was Mr. Meyer?" asked Benita.

"Asleep in a blanket under a little shelter of boughs by the stair. At least, I thought so, though it was rather difficult to make him out in the shadow; at any rate, I saw his rifle set against a tree. Come, let us go to breakfast. No doubt he will turn up soon enough."

So they went, and for the first time since the Sunday Benita ate a hearty meal of biscuits soaked in coffee. Although her father was so sure that by now he must have perished on the Matabele spears, the sight of the white man and his waggon had put new life into her, bringing her into touch with the world again. After all, might it not chance that he had escaped?

All this while there had been no sign of Jacob Meyer. This, however, did not surprise them, for now he ate his meals alone, taking his food from a little general store, and cooking it over his own fire. When they had finished their breakfast Mr. Clifford remarked that they had no more drinking water left, and Benita said that she would go to fetch a pailful from the well in the cave. Her father suggested that he should accompany her, but she answered that it was not necessary as she was quite able to wind the chain by herself. So she went, carrying the bucket in one hand and a lamp in the other.

As she walked down the last of the zig-zags leading to the cave, Benita stopped a moment thinking that she saw a light, and then went on, since on turning the corner there was nothing but darkness before her. Evidently she had been mistaken. She reached the well and hung the pail on to the great copper hook, wondering as she did so how many folk had done likewise in the far, far past, for the massive metal of that hook was worn quite thin with use. Then she let the roller run, and the sound of the travelling chain clanked dismally in that vaulted, empty place. At length the pail struck the water, and she began to wind up again, pausing at times to rest, for the distance was long and the chain heavy. The bucket appeared. Benita drew it to the side of the well, and lifted it from the hook, then took up her lamp to be gone.

Feeling or seeing something, which she was not sure, she held the lamp above her head, and by its light perceived a figure standing between her and the entrance to the cave.

"Who are you?" she asked, whereon a soft voice answered out of the darkness, the voice of Jacob Meyer.

"Do you mind standing still for a few minutes, Miss Clifford? I have some paper here and I wish to make a sketch. You do not know how beautiful you look with that light above your head illuminating the shadows and the thorn-crowned face on the crucifix beyond. You know, whatever paths fortune may have led me into, by Nature I am an artist, and never in my life have I seen such a picture. One day it will make me famous.

'How statue-like I see thee stand!
The agate lamp within thy hand.'

That's what I should put under it; you know the lines, don't you?"

"Yes, Mr. Meyer, but I am afraid you will have to paint your picture from memory, as I cannot hold up this lamp any longer; my arm is aching already. I do not know how you came here, but as you have followed me perhaps you will be so kind as to carry this water."

"I did not follow you, Miss Clifford. Although you never saw me I entered the cave before you to take measurements."

"How can you take measurements in the dark?"

"I was not in the dark. I put out my light when I caught sight of you, knowing that otherwise you would run away, and fate stood me in good stead. You came on, as I willed that you should do. Now let us talk. Miss Clifford, have you changed your mind? You know the time is up."

"I shall never change my mind. Let me pass you, Mr. Meyer."

"No, no, not until you have listened. You are very cruel to me, very cruel indeed. You do not understand that, rather than do you the slightest harm, I would die a hundred times."

"I do not ask you to die; I ask you to leave me alone—a much easier matter."

"But how can I leave you alone when you are a part of me, when—I love you? There, the truth is out, and now say what you will."

Benita lifted the bucket of water; its weight seemed to steady her. Then she put it down again, since escape was impracticable; she must face the situation.

"I have nothing to say, Mr. Meyer, except that *I* do not love *you* or any living man, and I never shall. I thank you for the compliment you have paid me, and there is an end."

"Any living man," he repeated after her. "That means you love a dead man—Seymour, he who was drowned. No wonder that I hated him when first my eyes fell on him years ago, long before you had come into our lives. Prescience, the sub-conscious self again. Well, what is the use of loving the dead, those who have no longer any existence, who have gone back into the clay out of which they were formed and are not, nor evermore shall be? You have but one life; turn, turn to the living and make it happy."

"I do not agree with you, Mr. Meyer. To me the dead are still living; one day I shall find them. Now let me go."

"I will not let you go. I will plead and wrestle with you as in the old fable my namesake of my own race wrestled with the angel, until at length you bless me. You despise me because I am a Jew, because I have had many adventures and not succeeded; because you think me mad. But I tell you that there is the seed of greatness in me. Give yourself to me and I will make you great, for now I know that it was you whom I needed to supply what is lacking in my nature. We will win the wealth, and together we will rule——"

"Until a few days hence we starve or the Matabele make an end of us. No, Mr. Meyer, no," and she tried to push past him.

He stretched out his arms and stopped her.

"Listen," he said, "I have pleaded with you as man with woman. Now, as you refuse me and as you alone stand between me and madness, I will take another course. I am your master, your will is servant to my will; I bid you obey me."

He fixed his eyes upon hers, and Benita felt her strength begin to fail.

"Ah!" he said, "you are my servant now, and to show it I shall kiss you on the lips; then I shall throw the sleep upon you, and you will tell me what I want to know. Afterwards we can be wed when it pleases me. Oh! do not think that your father will defend you, for if he interferes I shall kill that foolish old man, whom until now I have only spared for your sake. Remember that if you make me angry, I shall certainly kill him, and your father's blood will be on your head. Now I am going to kiss you."

Benita lifted her hand to find the pistol at her waist. It fell back again; she had no strength; it was as though she were paralysed as a bird is paralysed by a snake so that it cannot open its wings and fly away, but sits there awaiting death. She was given over into the hands of this man whom she hated. Could God allow such a thing? she wondered dimly, and all the while his lips drew nearer to her face.

They touched her own, and then, why or wherefore Benita never understood, the spell broke. All his power was gone, she was as she had been, a free woman, mistress of herself. Contemptuously she thrust the man aside, and, not even troubling to run, lifted her pail of water and walked away.

Soon she saw the light again, and joyfully extinguished her lamp. Indeed, the breast of Benita, which should have been so troubled after the scene through which she had passed, strangely enough was filled with happiness and peace. As that glorious sunlight had broken on her eyes, so had another light of freedom arisen in her soul. She was no longer afraid of Jacob Meyer; that coward kiss of his had struck off the shackles which bound her to him. Her mind had been subject to his mind, but now that his physical nature was brought into the play, his mental part had lost its hold upon her.

As she approached the hut she saw her father seated on a stone outside it, since the poor old man was now so weak and full of pain that he could not stand for very long, and seeing, remembered Meyer's threats against him. At the thought all her new-found happiness departed.

She might be safe; she felt sure that she was safe, but how about her father? If Meyer could not get his way probably he would be as good as his word, and kill him. She shivered at the thought, then, recovering herself, walked forward steadily with her bucket of water.

"You have been a long while gone, my love," said Mr. Clifford.

"Yes, father, Mr. Meyer was in the cave, and kept me."

"How did he get there, and what did he want?"

"I don't know how he got there—crept in when we were not looking, I suppose. But as for what he wanted—listen, dear," and word for word she told him what had passed.

Before she had finished, her father was almost choking with wrath.

"The dirty Jew! The villain!" he gasped. "I never dreamed that he would dare to attempt such an outrage. Well, thank Heaven! I can still hold a rifle, and when he comes out——"

"Father," she said gently, "that man is mad. He is not responsible for his actions, and therefore, except in self-defence, you must not think of such a thing. As for what he said about you, I believe it was only an empty threat, and for me you need have no fear, his power over me is gone; it went like a flash when his lips touched me," and she rubbed her own as though to wipe away some stain. "I am afraid of nothing more. I believe—yes, I believe that the old Molimo was right, and that all will end well——"

As she was speaking Benita heard a shuffling sound behind her, and turned to learn its cause. Then she saw a strange sight. Jacob Meyer was staggering towards them, dragging one foot after the other through the grass and stones. His face was ghastly pale, his jaw had dropped like that of a dead man, and his eyes were set wide open and full of horror.

"What is the matter with you, man?" asked Mr. Clifford.

"I—I—have seen a ghost," he whispered. "You did not come back into the cave, did you?" he added, pointing at Benita, who shook her head.

"What ghost?" asked Mr. Clifford.

"I don't know, but my lamp went out, and then a light began to shine behind me. I turned, and on the steps of that crucifix I saw a woman kneeling. Her arms clasped the feet of the figure, her forehead rested upon the feet, her long black hair flowed down, she was dressed in white, and the light came from her body and her head. Very slowly she turned and looked at me, and oh, Heaven! that face——" and he put his hand before his eyes and groaned. "It was beautiful; yes, yes, but fearful to see, like an avenging angel. I fled, and the light—only the light—came with me down the cave—even at the mouth of it there was a little. I have seen a spirit, I who did not believe in spirits, I have seen a spirit, and I tell you that not for all the gold in the world will I enter that place again."

Then before they could answer, suddenly as though his fear had got some fresh hold of him, Jacob sprang forward and fled away, crashing through the bushes and leaping from rock to rock like a frightened buck.

BENITA.

An African Romance by . . .
H. RIDER HAGGARD.

CHAPTER XXI.

THE MESSAGE FROM THE DEAD.

 "EYER always said that he did not believe in spirits," remarked Mr. Clifford reflectively.

"Well, he believes in them now," answered Benita with a little laugh. "But, father, the poor man is mad, that is the fact of it, and we must pay no attention to what he says."

"The old Molimo and some of his people—Tamas, for instance—declare that they have seen the ghost of Benita da Ferreira. Are they mad also, Benita?"

"I don't know, father. Who can say? All these things are a mystery. All I do know is that I have never seen a ghost, and I doubt if I ever shall."

"No, but when you were in that trance something that was not you spoke out of your mouth, which something said that it was your namesake, the other Benita. Well, as you say, we can't fathom these things, especially in a haunted kind of place like this, but the upshot of it is that I don't think we have much more to fear from Jacob."

"I am not so sure, father. Mad people change their moods very suddenly."

As it happened Benita was quite right. Towards supper-time Jacob Meyer reappeared, looking pale and shaken, but otherwise much as usual.

"I had a kind of fit this morning," he explained, "the result of an hallucination which seized me when my light went out in that cave. I remember that I thought I had seen a ghost, whereas I know very well that no such thing exists. I was the victim of disappointment, anxieties, and other still stronger emotions," and he looked at Benita. "Therefore, please forget anything that I said or did, and —would you give me some supper?"

Benita did so, and he ate in silence, with some heartiness. When he had finished his food, and swallowed two or three tots of squareface, he spoke again:

"I have come here, where I know I am not welcome, upon business," he said in a calm, matter-of-fact voice. "I am tired of this place, and I think it is time that we attained the object of our journey here, namely, to find the hidden gold. That, as we all know, can only be done in a certain way, through the clairvoyant powers of one of us and the hypnotic powers of another. Miss Clifford, I request that you will allow me to throw you into a state of trance. You have told us everything else, but you have not yet told us where the treasure is hidden, and this it is necessary that we should know."

"And if I refuse, Mr. Meyer?"

"Then I am sorry, but I must take means to compel your obedience. Under those circumstances, much against my will, I shall be obliged"—here his eye blazed out wildly—"to execute your father, whose obstinacy and influence stand between us and splendid fortunes. No, Clifford," he added, "don't stretch out your hand towards that rifle, for I am already covering you with the pistol in my pocket, and the moment your hand touches it I shall fire. You poor old man, do you imagine for a single second that, sick as you are, and with your stiff limbs, you can hope to match yourself

"NOW BEGAN BENITA'S TERRIBLE TIME"

against my agility, intellect and strength ? Why, I could kill you in a dozen ways before you could lift a finger against me, and by the God I do not believe in, unless your daughter is more compliant, kill you I will !''

"That remains to be seen, my friend," said Mr. Clifford with a laugh, for he was a brave old man. "I am not certain that the God—whom you do not believe in—will not kill you first."

Now Benita, who had been taking counsel with herself, looked up and said suddenly :

"Very well, Mr. Meyer, I consent—because I must. To-morrow morning you shall try to mesmerise me, if you can, in the same place, before the crucifix in the cave."

"No," he answered quickly. "It was not there, it was here, and here it shall be again. The spot you mention is unpropitious to me ; the attempt would fail."

"It is the spot that I have chosen," answered Benita stubbornly.

"And this is the spot that I have chosen, Miss Clifford, and my will must prevail over yours."

"Because you who do not believe in spirits are afraid to re-enter the cave, Mr. Meyer, lest you should chance——"

"Never mind what I am or am not afraid of," he replied with fury. "Make your choice between doing my will and your father's life. To-morrow morning I shall come for your answer, and if you are still obstinate, within half an hour he will be dead, leaving you and me alone together. Oh ! you may call me wicked and a villain, but it is you who are wicked, you, you, *you* who force me to this deed of justice."

Then without another word he sprang up and walked away from them backwards, as he went covering Mr. Clifford with the pistol which he had drawn from his pocket. The last that they saw of him were his eyes, which glowered at them through the darkness like those of a lion.

"Father," said Benita, when she was sure that he had gone, "that madman really means to murder you ; there is no doubt of it."

"None whatever, dear ; if I am alive to-morrow night I shall be lucky, unless I can kill him first or get out of his way."

"Well," she said hurriedly, "I think you can. I have an idea. He is afraid to go into that cave, I am sure. Let us hide ourselves there. We can take food and shall have plenty of water, whereas, unless rain falls, he can get nothing to drink."

"But what then, Benita ? We can't stop in the dark for ever."

"No, but we can wait there until something happens. Something must and will happen. His disease won't stand still ; he may go raving mad and kill himself. Or he may attempt to attack us, though that is not likely, and then we must do what we can in self-defence. Or help may reach us from somewhere. At the worst we shall only die as we should have died outside. Come, let us be quick, lest he should change his mind, and creep back upon us."

So Mr. Clifford gave way, knowing that even if he could steel himself to the deed of attempting to kill Jacob, he would have little chance against that strong and agile man. Such a struggle would only end in his own death, and Benita must then be left alone with Meyer and his insane passions.

Hurriedly they carried their few belongings into the cave. First they took most of the little store of food that remained, the three hand-lamps and all the paraffin ; there was but one tin. Then returning, they fetched the bucket, the ammunition, and their clothes. Afterwards, as there was still no sign of Meyer, they even dared to drag in the waggon tent to make a shelter for Benita, and all the wood that they had collected for firing. This proved a wearisome business, for the logs were heavy, and in his crippled state Mr. Clifford could carry no great burden. Indeed, towards the end Benita was forced to complete the task alone, while he limped beside her with his rifle, lest Jacob should surprise them.

When at length everything was done it was long past midnight, and so exhausted were they that, notwithstanding their danger, they flung themselves down upon the canvas tent, which lay in a heap at the end of the cave near the crucifix, and fell asleep.

When Benita woke the lamp had gone out, and it was pitch dark. Fortunately, however, she remembered where she had put the matches and the lantern with a candle in it. She lit the candle and looked at her watch. It was nearly six o'clock. The dawn must be breaking outside, within an hour or two Jacob Meyer would find that they had gone. Suppose that his rage should overcome his fear and that he should creep upon them. They would know nothing of it until his face appeared in the faint ring of light. Or he might even shoot her father out of the darkness. What could she do that would give them warning? A thought came to her.

Taking one of the tent ropes and the lantern, for her father still slept heavily, she went down to the entrance of the cave, and at the end of the last zigzag where once a door had been, managed to make it fast to a stone hinge about eighteen inches above the floor, and on the other side to an eye opposite that was cut in the solid rock to receive a bolt of wood or iron. Meyer, she knew, had no lamps or oil, only matches and perhaps a few candles. Therefore if he tried to enter the cave it was probable that he would trip over the rope and thus give them warning. Then she went back, washed her face and hands with some water that they had drawn on the previous night to satisfy their thirst, and tidied herself as best she could. This done, as her father still slept, she filled the lamps, lit one of them, and looked about her, for she was loth to wake him.

Truly it was an awful place in which to dwell. There above them towered the great white crucifix; there in the corner were piled the remains of the Portuguese. A skull with long hair still hanging to it grinned at her, a withered hand was thrust forward as though to clutch her. Oh, no wonder that in such a spot Jacob Meyer had seen ghosts! In front, too, was the yawning grave where they had found the monk; indeed, his bones wrapped in dark robes still lay within, for Jacob had tumbled them back again. Then beyond and all around deep, dark, and utter silence.

At last her father woke, and glad enough was she of his human company. They breakfasted upon some biscuits and water, and afterwards, while Mr. Clifford watched near the entrance with his rifle, Benita set to work to arrange their belongings. The tent she managed to prop up against the wall of the cave by help of some of the wood which they had carried in. Beneath it she spread their blankets, that it might serve as a sleeping place for them both, and outside placed the food and other things.

While she was thus engaged she heard a sound at the mouth of the cave—Jacob Meyer was entering and had fallen over her rope. Down it she ran, lantern in hand, to her father, who with his rifle raised, was shouting:

"If you come in here, I put a bullet through you!"

Then came the answer in Jacob's voice, which rang hollow in that vaulted place:

"I do not want to come in; I shall wait for you to come out. You cannot live long in there; the horror of the dark will kill you. I have only to sit in the sunlight and wait."

Then he laughed, and they heard the sound of his footsteps retreating down the passage.

"What are we to do?" asked Mr. Clifford despairingly. "We cannot live without light, and if we have light he will certainly creep to the entrance and shoot us. He is quite mad now; I am sure of it from his voice."

Benita thought a minute, then she answered:

"We must build up the passage. Look," and she pointed to the lumps of rock that the explosion of their mine had shaken down from the roof, and the slabs of cement that they had broken from the floor with the crowbar. "At once, at once," she went on; "he will not come back for some hours, probably not till night."

So they set to work, and never did Benita labour as it was her lot to do that day. Such of the fragments as they could lift they carried between them, others they rolled along by help of the crowbar. For hour after hour they toiled at their task. Luckily for them, the passage was not more than three feet wide by six feet six high, and their material was ample. Before the evening they had blocked it

"BEHOLD! BEFORE HER LAY THE BURST BAG"

completely with a wall several feet in thickness, which wall they supported on the inside with lengths of the firewood lashed across to the old hinges and bolt-holes, or set obliquely against its face.

It was done, and they regarded their work with pride, although it seemed probable that they were building up their own tomb. Because of its position at an angle of the passage, they knew that Meyer could not get to it with a pole to batter it down. Also, there was no loose powder left, so his only chance would be to pull it to pieces with his hands, and this, they thought, might prove beyond his power. At least, should he attempt it, they would have ample warning. Yet that day was not to pass without another trouble.

Just as they had rolled up and levered into place a long fragment of rock de-signed to prevent the ends of their sup-porting pieces of wood from slipping on the cement floor, Mr. Clifford uttered an exclamation, then said :

" I have wrung my back badly. Help me to the tent. I must lie down."

Slowly and with great pain they stag-gered up the cave, Mr. Clifford leaning on Benita and a stick, till, reaching the tent at last, he almost fell on to the blankets and remained there practically crippled.

Now began Benita's terrible time, the worst of all her life. Every hour her father became more ill. Even before they took refuge in the cave he was com-pletely broken down, and now after this accident he began to suffer very much. His rheumatism or sciatica, or whatever it was, seemed to settle upon the hurt muscles of his back, causing him so much pain that he could scarcely sleep for ten minutes at a stretch. Moreover, he would swallow but little of the rough food which was all Benita was able to prepare for him ; nothing, indeed, except biscuit soaked in black coffee, which she boiled over a small fire made of the wood that they had brought with them, and occa-sionally a little broth, tasteless stuff enough, for it was only the essence of biltong, or sun-dried flesh, flavoured with some salt.

Then there were two other terrors against which she must fight, the darkness and the dread of Jacob Meyer. Perhaps

the darkness was the worse of them. To live in that hideous gloom in which their single lamp, for she dared burn no more lest the oil should give out, seemed but as one star to the whole night, ah ! who that had not endured it could know what it meant ? There the sick man, yonder the grinning skeletons, around the blackness and the silence, and beyond these again a miserable death, or Jacob Meyer. But of him Benita saw nothing, though once or twice she thought that she heard his voice raving outside the wall which they had built. If so, either he did not try to pull it down, or he failed in the attempt, or perhaps he feared that should he succeed, he would be greeted by a bullet. So at last she gave up thinking about him. Should he force his way into the cave she must deal with the situation as best she could. Meanwhile, her father's strength was sinking fast.

Three awful days went by in this fashion, and the end drew near. Although she tried to force herself to it, Benita could not swallow enough food to keep up her strength. Now that the passage was closed the atmosphere of this old vault, for it was nothing more, thickened by the smoke of the fire which she was obliged to burn, grew poisonous and choked her. Want of sleep exhausted her, dread of what the morrow might bring forth crushed her strong spirit. She began to break down, knowing that the hour was near when she and her father must die together.

Once, as she slept awhile at his side, being wakened by his groaning, Benita looked at her watch. It was midnight. She rose, and going to the embers of the little fire, warmed up some of her biltong broth which she poured into a tin pannikin. With difficulty she forced him to swallow a few mouthfuls of it, then, feeling a sudden weakness, drank the rest herself It gave her power to think, and her father dozed off into an uneasy sleep.

Alas ! thinking was of no use, nothing could be done. There was no hope save in prayer. Restlessness seized Benita, and taking the lantern she wandered round the cave. The wall that they had built remained intact, and oh ! to think that beyond it flowed the free air and shone the blessed stars ! Back she came again, skirting the pits that Jacob Meyer had dug, and the grave of the old monk, till she reached the steps of the crucifix, and holding up her candle, looked at the thorn-crowned brow of the Christ above.

It was wonderfully carved ; that dying face was full of pity. Would not He Whom it represented pity her ? She knelt down on the topmost step, and clasping the pierced feet with her arms, began to

but she seemed to see the words written in the air before her. These were the words :—

" Clasp the feet of the Christ and draw them to the left. The passage beneath leads to the chamber where the gold is hid, and thence to the river bank. That is the secret which ere I depart, I, the dead Benita, pass on to you, the living Benita, as I am

" AS SHE STAGGERED BACKWARDS SHE SAW A HUGE AND LOATHSOME SHAPE RUSHING AWAY INTO THE DARKNESS "

..ay earnestly, not for herself but that ..he might save her father. She prayed ..s she had never prayed before, and so .raying, sank into a torpor or a swoon.

It seemed to Benita that this sleep of hers suddenly became alive ; in it she saw many things. For instance, she saw herself seated in a state of trance upon that very step where now she knelt, while before her stood her father and Jacob Meyer. Moreover, a voice spoke in her ; she could not hear the voice,

commanded. In life and death peace be to your soul."

Thrice did this message appear to repeat itself in the consciousness of Benita. Then, suddenly as she had slept, she woke again with every letter of it imprinted on her mind. Doubtless it was a dream, nothing but a dream bred by the fact that her arms were clasping the feet of the crucifix. What did it say ? " Draw them to the left ? "

She did so, but nothing stirred. Again she tried, and still nothing stirred. Of course it was a dream. Why had such been sent to mock her? In a kind of mad irritation she put out all her remaining strength and wrestled with those stony feet. *They moved a little*—then of a sudden, without any further effort on her part, swung round as high as the knees where drapery hung, concealing the join in them. Yes, they swung round, revealing the head of a stair, up which blew a cold wind that it was sweet to breathe.

Benita rose, gasping. Then she seized her lantern and ran to the little tent where her father lay.

CHAPTER XXII.

THE VOICE OF THE LIVING.

MR. CLIFFORD was awake again now.

"Where have you been?" he asked querulously in a thin voice. "I wanted you." Then as the light from the candle shone upon it, he noted the change that had come over her pale face, and added: "What has happened? Is Meyer dead? Are we free?"

Benita shook her head. "He was alive a few hours ago, for I could hear him raving and shouting outside the wall we built. But, father, it has all come back to me; I believe that I have found it."

"What has come back? What have you found? Are you mad, too, like Jacob?"

"What something told me when I was in the trance which afterwards I forgot, but now remember. And I have found the passage which leads to where they hid the gold. It begins behind the crucifix, where no one ever thought of looking."

This matter of the gold did not seem to interest Mr. Clifford. In his state all the wealth beneath the soil of Africa would not have appealed to him. Moreover, he hated the name of that accursed treasure, which was bringing them to such a miserable end.

"Where does the passage run? Have you looked?" he asked.

"Not yet, but the voice in me said— I mean, I dreamed—that it goes down

to the river-side. If you leant on me do you think that you could walk?"

"Not one inch," he answered. "Here where I am I shall die."

"No, no, don't talk like that. We may be saved now that I have found a way. Oh, if only you could—if only you could walk, or if I had the strength to carry you!" and she wrung her hands and began to weep, so weak was she.

Her father looked at her searchingly. Then said:

"Well, love, I cannot, so there's an end. But you can, and you had better go."

"What! And leave you? Never."

"Yes, and leave me. Look, there is but a little oil left and only a few candles. The biscuits are done and neither of us can swallow that biltong any more. I suppose that I am dying, and your health and strength are failing you quickly in this darkness; if you stop here you must soon follow me. And what is the alternative? That madman outside—that is, if you could find strength to pull down the wall, which I doubt. You had best go, Benita."

But still she said she would not.

"Do you not see," he added, "that it is my only chance of life? If you go you may be able to bring me help before the end comes. Should there be a passage the probability is that, although they know nothing of it, it finishes somewhere by the wall of the first enclosure where the Makalanga are. If so, you may find the Molimo, or if he is dead, Tamas or one of the others, and they will help us. Go, Benita, go at once."

"I never thought of that," she answered in a changed voice. "Of course, it may be so, if the passage goes down at all. Well, at least I can look and come back to tell you."

Then Benita placed the remainder of the oil close by her father's side, so that he could fill the lamp, for the use of his hands still remained to him. Also, she set there such crumbs of biscuit as were left, some of the biltong, a flask of Hollands and a pail of water. This done, she put on her long cloak, filled one of its pockets with biltong, and the other with matches and three of the four remaining candles. The fourth she insisted upon

"SPLASHING THROUGH THE MUD UPON THE UNKNOWN BANKS OF THE ZAMBESI, FLYING
FROM DEATH TO DEATH!"

leaving beside her father's bed. When everything was ready she knelt down at his side, kissed him, and from her heart put up a prayer that they might both live to meet again, although she knew well that this they could scarcely hope to do.

Had two people ever been in a more dreadful situation, she wondered, as she looked at her father lying there, whom she must leave to fight with Death alone

such fashion that it could not shut again behind her. Her idea was that it worked by aid of some spring, but now she saw that this was not so, as the whole mass hung upon three stone hinges beautifully concealed. The dust and corrosion of ages which had made this door so hard to open, by filling up the tiny spaces between it and its frame-work, had also rendered these cracks utterly imper-

"'BENITA! BENITA! HAVE YOU COME TO TELL ME THAT I MUST JOIN YOU?'"

in that awful place, while she went forth to meet him in the unknown bowels of the earth!

Mr. Clifford read her thoughts. "Yes," he said, "it is a strange parting and a wild errand. But who knows? It may please Providence to take you through, and if not—why, our troubles will soon be over."

Then once more they kissed, and not daring to try to speak, Benita tore herself away. Passing into the passage whereof the lower part of the crucifix formed the door, she paused for a moment to examine it and to place a fragment of rock in

ceptible to the eye. So accurately was it fashioned, indeed, that no one who did not know its secret would have discovered it if they searched for months or years.

Though at the time Benita took little note of such details, the passage beyond and the stair descending from it showed the same perfect workmanship. Evidently this secret way dated not from the Portuguese period, but from that of the Phœnicians or other ancients, to whose treasure-chamber it was the approach, opening as it did from their holy of holies, to which none were admitted save the head priests. The passage, which was about seven feet high by four wide, had been hewn out of the live rock of the mountain, for thousands of little marks left by the workmen's chisels were still discernible upon its walls. So it was with the stair, that had been but little used, and remained fresh as the day when it was finished.

Down the steps, candle in hand, flitted Benita, counting them as she went. The thirtieth brought her to a landing. Here it was that she saw the first traces of that treasure which they had suffered so much to find. Something glittered at her feet. She picked it up. It was a little bar of gold weighing two or three ounces that doubtless had been dropped there. Throwing it down again she looked in front of her, and to her dismay saw a door of wood with iron bolts. But the bolts had never been shot, and when she pulled at it the door creaked upon its rusty hinges and opened. She was on the threshold of the treasure-chamber!

It was square and of the size of a small room, packed on either side almost to the low, vaulted roof with small bags of raw hide, carelessly arranged. Quite near to the door one of these bags had slipped down and burst open. It was filled with gold, some in ingots and some in raw nuggets, for there they lay in a shining, scattered heap. As she stooped to look it came into the mind of Benita that her father had said that in her trance she had told them that one of the bags of treasure was burst, and that the skin of which it had been made was black and red. Behold! before her lay the burst bag and the colour of the hide was black and red.

She shivered. The thing was uncanny, terrible. Uncanny was it also to see in the thick dust, which in the course of twenty or more of centuries had gathered on the floor, the mark of footprints, those of the last persons who had visited this place. There had been two of them, a man and a woman, and they were no savages, for they wore shoes. Benita placed her foot in the print left by that dead woman. It filled it exactly, it might have been her own. Perhaps, she thought to herself, that other Benita had descended here with her father, after the

Portuguese had hidden away their wealth, that she might be shown where it was, and of what it consisted.

One more glance at all this priceless, misery-working gold, and on she went, she who was seeking the gold of life and liberty for herself and him who lay above. Supposing that the stairway ended there? She stopped, she looked round, but could see no other door. To see the better she halted and opened the glass of her lantern. Still she could perceive nothing, and her heart sank. Yet why did the candle flicker so fiercely, and why was the air in this deep place so fresh? She walked forward a pace or two, then noticed suddenly that those footprints of the dead that she was following disappeared immediately in front of her, and she stopped.

It was but just in time. One step more and she would have fallen down the mouth of a deep pit. Once it had been covered with a stone, but this stone was removed, and had never been replaced. Look, there it stood against the wall of the chamber! Well was this for Benita, since her frail strength would not have sufficed to stir that massive block, even if she had discovered its existence beneath the dust.

Now she saw that down the pit ran another ladderlike stair of stone, very narrow and precipitous. Without hesitation she began its descent. Down she went and down—one hundred steps, two hundred steps, two hundred and seventy-five steps, and all the way wherever the dust had gathered the man's and the woman's footprints ran before her. There was a double line of them, one line going down and the other line returning. Those that returned were the last, for often they appeared over those that descended. Why had these dead people returned, Benita wondered.

The stair had ended; now she was in a kind of natural cave, for its sides and roof were rugged; moreover, water trickled and dripped from them. It was not very large, and it smelt horribly of mud and other things. Again she searched by the feeble light of her candle, but could see no exit. Suddenly she saw something else, however, for stepping on what she took to be a rock, to her horror it moved beneath her. She heard a snap as of

"'WHO GAVE YOU AND YOUR BROTHER YONDER YOUR LIVES?'"

jaws, a violent blow upon the leg nearly knocked her off her feet, and as she staggered backwards she saw a huge and loathsome shape rushing away into the darkness. The rock that she had trodden on was a crocodile which had its den here! With a little scream she retreated to her stair. Death she had expected—but to be eaten by crocodiles!

Yet as Benita stood there panting a blessed hope rose in her breast. If a crocodile came in there it must also get out, and where such a great creature could go, a woman would be able to follow. Also, she must be near the water, since otherwise it could never have chosen this hole for its habitation. She collected her courage, and having clapped her hands and waved the lantern about to scare any alligators that might still be lurking there, hearing and seeing nothing more, she descended to where she had trodden upon the reptile. Evidently this was its bed, for its long body had left an impress upon the mud, and all about lay the remains of creatures that it had brought in for food. Moreover, a path ran outwards, its well-worn trail distinct even in that light.

She followed this path, which ended apparently in a blank wall. Then it was that Benita guessed why those dead folks' footprints had returned, for here had been a doorway which in some past age those who used it built up with blocks of stone and cement. How, then, did the crocodile get out? Stooping down she searched, and perceived, a few yards to the right of the door, a hole that looked as though it were water-worn. Now Benita thought that she understood. The rock was softer here, and centuries of flood had eaten it away, leaving a crack in the stratum which the crocodiles had found out and enlarged. Down she went on her hands and knees, and thrusting the lantern in front of her, crept along that noisome drain, for this was what it resembled. And now—oh! now she felt air blowing in her face, and heard the sound of reeds whispering, and water running, and saw hanging like a lamp in the blue sky, a star—the morning star! Benita could have wept, she could have worshipped it, yet she pushed on between rocks till she found herself among tall reeds, and standing in water. She had gained the banks of the Zambesi.

Instantly, by instinct as it were, Benita extinguished her lamp, fearing lest it should betray her, for constant danger had made her very cunning. The dawn had not yet broken, but the waning moon and the stars gave a good light. She paused to look. There above her towered the outermost wall of Bambatse, against which the river washed, except at such times as the present, when it was very low.

So she was not in the fortress as she had hoped, but without it, and oh! what should she do? Go back again? How would that serve her father or herself? Go on? Then she might fall into the hands of the Matabele whose camp was a little lower down, as from her perch upon the top of the cone she had seen that poor white man do. Ah! the white man! If only he lived and she could reach him! Perhaps they had not killed him after all. It was a madness, yet she would try to discover; something impelled her to take the risk. If she failed and escaped, perhaps then she might call to the Makalanga, and they would let down a rope and draw her up the wall before the Matabele caught her. She would not go back empty-handed, to die in that dreadful place with her poor father. Better perish here in the sweet air and beneath the stars, even if it were upon a Matabele spear, or by a bullet from her own pistol.

She looked about her to take her bearings in case it should ever be necessary for her to return to the entrance of the cave. This proved easy for a hundred feet or so above her; where the sheer face of the cliff jutted out a little, at that very spot indeed on which tradition said that the body of the Señora da Ferreira had struck in its fall, and the necklace Benita wore to-day was torn from her, a stunted mimosa grew in some cleft of the rock. To mark the crocodile run itself she bent down a bunch of reeds, and having first lit a few Tandstickor brimstone matches and thrown them about inside of it, that the smell of them might scare the beast should it wish to return, she set her lantern behind a stone near to the mouth of the hole.

Then Benita began her journey which, when the river was high, it would not have been possible for her to make except by swimming. As it was, a margin of marsh was left between her and the steep, rocky side of the mount from which the great wall rose, and through this she made her way. Never was she likely to forget that walk. The tall reeds dripped their dew upon her till she was soaked; long, black-tailed finches—saccaboolas the natives call them—flew up disturbed, and lobbed away across the river; owls flitted past and bitterns boomed at the coming of the dawn. Great fish splashed also in the shallows, or were they crocodiles? Benita hoped not—for one day she had seen enough of crocodiles.

It was all very strange. Could she be the same woman, she wondered, who not a year before had been walking with her cousins down Westbourne Grove, and studying Whiteley's windows? What would these cousins say now if they could see her, white-faced, large-eyed, desperate, splashing through the mud upon the un-known banks of the Zambesi, flying from death to death!

On she struggled, above her the pearly sky in which the stars were fading, around her the wet reeds, and per-vading all the heavy low-lying mists of dawn. She was past the round of the walls, and at length stood upon dry ground where the Matabele had made their camp. But in that fog she saw no Matabele; probably their fires were out, and she chanced to pass between the sentries. Instinctively, more than by reason, she headed for that hillock upon which she had seen the white man's waggon, in the vague hope that it might still be there. On she struggled, still on, till at length she blundered against something soft and warm, and perceived that it was an ox tied to a trek-tow, beyond which were other oxen and a white waggon-cap.

So it *was* still there! But the white man, where was he? Through the dense mist Benita crept to the disselboom. Then, seeing and hearing nothing, she climbed to the voorkissie and kneeling on it, separated the tent flaps and peered into the waggon. Still she could see nothing because of the mist, yet she heard something, a man breathing in his sleep.

Somehow she thought that it was a white man; a Kaffir did not breathe like that. She did not know what to do, so remained kneeling there. It seemed as though the man who was asleep began to feel her presence, for he muttered to himself—surely the words were English! Then quite suddenly he struck a match and lit a candle which stood in a beer bottle by his side. She could not see his face while he lit the match, for his arm hid it, and the candle burned up slowly. Then the first thing she saw was the barrel of a revolver pointing straight at her.

"Now, my black friend," said a pleasant voice, "down you go or I shoot. One, two! Oh, my God!"

The candle burned up, its light fell upon the white, elfish face of Benita, whose long dark hair streamed about her; it shone in her great eyes. Still she could see nothing, for it dazzled her.

"Oh, my God!" said the voice again. "Benita! Benita! Have you come to tell me that I must join you? Well, I am ready, my sweet, my sweet! Now I shall hear your answer."

"Yes," she whispered, and crawling forward down the cartel Benita fell upon his breast.

For she knew him at last—dead or living she cared not—she knew him, and out of hell crept to him, her heaven and her home!

* * *

CHAPTER XXIII.

BENITA GIVES HER ANSWER.

"YOUR answer, Benita," Robert said dreamily, for to him this thing seemed a dream.

"Have I not given it, months ago? Oh, I remember, it was only in my heart, not on my lips, when that blow fell on me! Then afterwards I heard what you had done and I nearly died. I wished that I might die to be with you, but I could not, I was too strong; now I understand the reason. Well, it seems that we are both living, and whatever happens, here is my answer, if it is worth anything to you. Once and for all, I love you. I am not ashamed to say it, because very soon we may be separated for the last time. But I cannot talk now, I have come here to save my father."

" Where is he, Benita ? "

" Dying in a cave up at the top of that fortress. I got down by a secret way. Are the Matabele still here ? "

" Very much so," he answered. " But something has happened. My guard woke me an hour ago to say that a messenger had arrived from their king, Lobengula, and now they are talking over the message. That is how you came to get through, otherwise the sentries would have assegaied you, the brutes," and he drew her to him and kissed her passionately for the first time, then, as though ashamed of himself, let her go.

" Have you anything to eat ? " she asked. " I—I—am starving. I didn't feel it before, but now ——"

" Starving, you starving, while I— look, here is some fresh meat which I could not get down last night, and put by for the Kaffirs. Great Heavens ! that I should feed you with Kaffirs' leavings ! But it is good—eat it."

Benita took the stuff in her fingers and swallowed it greedily ; she who for days had lived on nothing but a little biscuit and biltong. It tasted delicious to her—never had she eaten anything so good. And all the while he watched her with glowing eyes.

" How can you look at me ? " she said at length, " I must be horrible ; I have been living in the dark and crawling through mud. I trod upon a crocodile ! " and she shuddered.

" Whatever you are I never want to see you different," he answered slowly. " To me you are most beautiful."

Even then, wreck as she was, the poor girl flushed, and there was a mist in her eyes as she looked up and said :

" Thank you. I don't care now what happens to me, and what has happened doesn't matter at all. But can we get away ? "

" I don't know," he answered; " but I doubt it. Go and sit on the waggon-box for a few minutes while I dress, and we will see."

Benita went. The mist was thinning now, and through it she saw a sight at which her heart sank, for between her and the mount Bambatse Matabele were pouring towards their camp on the river's edge. They were cut off. A couple of minutes later Robert joined her, and as he came she looked at him anxiously in the growing light. He seemed older than when they had parted on the *Zanzibar* ; changed too, for now his face was serious, and he had grown a beard ; also, he appeared to limp.

" I am afraid there is an end," she said, pointing to the Matabele below.

" Yes, it looks like it. But like you, I say, what does it matter now ? " and he took her hand in his, adding : " let us be happy while we can if only for a few minutes. They will be here presently."

" What are you ? " she asked. " A prisoner ? "

" That's it. I was following you when they captured me ; for I have been here before and knew the way. They were going to kill me on general principles, only it occurred to one of them who was more intelligent than the rest that I, being a white man, might be able to show them how to storm the place. Now I was sure that you were there, for I saw you standing on that point, though they thought you were the Spirit of Bambatse. So I wasn't anxious to help them, for then—you know what happens when the Matabele are the stormers ! But—as you still lived—I wasn't anxious to die either. So I set them to work to dig a hole with their assegais and sharp tools, through granite. They have completed exactly twenty feet of it, and I reckon that there are one hundred and forty to go. Last night they got tired of that tunnel and talked of killing me again, unless I could show them a better plan. Now all the fat is in the fire, and I don't know what is to happen. Hullo ! here they come. Hide in the waggon—quick ! "

Benita obeyed, and from under cover of the tent where the Matabele could not see her, watched and listened. The party that approached consisted of a chief and about twenty men, who marched behind him as a guard. Benita knew that chief. He was the captain Maduna, he of the royal blood whose life she had saved. By his side was a Natal Zulu, Robert Seymour's driver, who could speak English and acted as interpreter.

" White man," said Maduna, " a message has reached us from our king.

Lobengula makes a great war and has need of us. He summons us back from this petty fray, this fight against cowards who hide behind walls, whom otherwise we would have killed, everyone, yes, if we sat here till we grew old. So for this time we leave them alone."

Robert answered politely that he was glad to hear it, and wished them a good journey.

"Wish yourself a good journey, white man," was the stern reply.

"Why? Do you desire that I should accompany you to Lobengula?"

"No, you go before us to the kraal of the Black One who is even greater than the child of Moselikatse, to that king who is called Death."

Robert crossed his arms and said: "Say on."

"White man, I promised you your life if you would show us how to pierce or climb those walls. But you have made fools of us—you have set us to cut through rock with spears and axes. Yes, to hoe at rock as though it were soil—you who with the wisdom of your people could have taught us some better way. Therefore we must go back to our king disgraced, having failed in his service, and therefore you who have mocked us shall die. Come down now, that we may kill you quietly, and learn whether or no you are a brave man."

Then it was, while her lover's hand was moving towards the pistol hidden beneath his coat, that Benita, with a quick movement, emerged from the waggon in which she crouched, and stood up at his side upon the driving box.

"Ow!" said the Captain. "It is the White Maiden. Now how came she here? Surely this is great magic. Can a woman fly like a bird?" and they stared at her amazed.

"What does it matter how I came, chief Maduna?" she answered in Zulu. "Yet I will tell you why I came. It was to save you from dipping your spear in the innocent blood, and bringing on your head the curse of the innocent blood. Answer me now. Who gave you and your brother yonder your lives within that wall when the Makalanga would have torn you limb from limb, as hyenas tear a buck? Was it I or another?"

"Inkosi-kaas—Chieftainess," replied the great Captain, raising his broad spear in salute. "It was you and no other."

"And what did you promise me then, Prince Maduna?"

"Maiden of high birth, I promised you your life and your goods, should you ever fall into my power."

"Does a leader of the Amandabele, one of the royal blood, lie like a Mashona or a Makalanga slave? Does he do worse—tell half the truth only, like a cheat who buys and keeps back half the price?" she asked contemptuously. "Maduna, you promised me not one life, but two, two lives and the goods that belong to both. Ask of your brother there, who was witness of the words."

"Great Heavens!" muttered Robert Seymour to himself, as he looked at Benita standing with outstretched hand and flashing eyes. "Who would have thought that a starved woman could play such a part with death on the hazard?"

"It is as this daughter of white chiefs says," answered the man to whom she had appealed. "When she freed us from the fangs of those dogs, you promised her two lives, my brother, one for yours and one for mine."

"Hear him," went on Benita. "He promised me two lives, and how did this prince of the royal blood keep his promise? When I and the old man, my father, rode hence in peace, he loosed his spears upon us; he hunted us. Yet it was the hunters who fell into the trap, not the hunted."

"Maiden," replied Maduna, in a shamed voice, "that was your fault, not mine. If you had appealed to me I would have let you go. But you killed my sentry, and then the chase began, and ere I knew who you were my runners were out of call."

"Little time had I to ask your mercy; but so be it," said Benita. "I accept your word, and I forgive you that offence. Now fulfil your oath. Begone and leave us in peace."

Still Maduna hesitated.

"I must make report to the king," he said. "What is this white man to you that I should spare him? I give you your life and your father's life, not that of this white man who has tricked us. If he were your father, or your brother,

"MEYER WAS DISARMED AND BOUND FAST TO A TREE"

it would be otherwise. But he is a stranger, and belongs to me, not to you."

"Maduna," she asked, "do women such as I am share the waggon of a stranger? This man is more to me than father or brother. He is my husband, and I claim his life."

"Ow!" said the spokesman of the audience, "we understand now. She is his wife, and has a right to him. If she were not his wife she would not be in his waggon. It is plain that she speaks the truth, though how she came here we do not know, unless, as we think, she is a witch," and he smiled at his own cleverness.

"Inkosi-kaas," said Maduna, "you have persuaded me. I give you the life of that white fox, your husband, and I hope that he will not trick you as he has tricked us, and set you to hoe rock instead of soil," and he looked at Robert wrathfully. "I give him to you and all his belongings. Now, is there anything else that you would ask?"

"Yes," replied Benita coolly, "you have many oxen there which you took from the other Makalanga. Mine are eaten and I need cattle to draw my waggon. I ask a present of twenty of them, and," she added by an afterthought, "two cows with young calves, for my father is sick yonder, and must have milk."

"Oh! give them to her. Give them to her," said Maduna with a tragic gesture that in any other circumstances would have made Benita laugh. "Give them to her and see that they are good ones, before she asks our shields and spears also—for after all she saved my life."

So men departed to fetch those cows and oxen, which presently were driven in.

While this talk was in progress the great impi of the Matabele was massing for the march, on the flat ground a little to the right of them. Now they began to come past in companies, preceded by the lads who carried the mats and cooking-pots and drove the captured sheep and cattle. By this time the story of Benita, the white witch-woman whom they could not kill, and who had mysteriously flown from the top of the peak into their prisoner's waggon, had spread among them. They knew also that it was she who had saved

their general from the Makalanga, and those who had heard her admired the wit and courage with which she had pleaded and won her cause. Therefore, as they marched past in their companies, singing a song of abuse and defiance of the Makalanga who peered at them from the top of the wall, they lifted their great spears in salutation to Benita standing upon the waggon-box.

Indeed, they were a wondrous and imposing spectacle, such a one as few white women have ever seen.

At length all were gone except Maduna and a body-guard of two hundred men. He walked to the front of the waggon and addressed Robert Seymour.

"Listen, you fox who set us to hoe granite," he said indignantly. "You have outwitted us this time, but if ever I meet you again, then you die. Now I have given you your life, but," he added, almost pleadingly, "if you are really brave as white men are said to be, will you not come down and fight me man to man for honour's sake?"

"I think not," answered Robert, when he understood this challenge, "for what chance should I have against so brave a warrior? Also this lady—my wife—needs my help on her journey home."

Maduna turned from him contemptuously to Benita.

"I go," he said, "and fear not; you will meet no Matabele on that journey. Have you more words for me, O Beautiful One, with a tongue of oil and a wit that cuts like steel?"

"Yes," answered Benita. "You have dealt well with me, and in reward I give you of my good luck. Bear this message to your king from the White Witch of Bambatse, for I am she and no other. That he leave these Makalanga, my servants, to dwell unharmed in their ancient home, and that he lift no spear against the White Men, lest that evil which the Molimo foretold to you, should fall upon him."

"Ah!" said Maduna, "now I understand how you flew from the mountain top into this man's waggon. You are not a white woman, you are the ancient Witch of Bambatse herself. You have said it, and with such it is not well to war. Great lady of Magic, Spirit from of old, I salute you, and I thank you for your gifts of life and fortune. Farewell."

Then he, too, stalked away at the head of his guard, so that presently, save for the three Zulu servants and the herd of cattle, Robert and Benita were left utterly alone.

Now, her part played and the victory won, Benita burst into tears and fell upon her lover's breast.

Presently she remembered and freed herself from his arms.

"I am a selfish wretch," she said. "How dare I be so happy when my father is dead or dying? We must go at once."

"Go where?" asked the bewildered Robert.

"To the top of the mountain, of course, whence I came. Oh! please don't stop to question me. I'll tell you as we walk. Stay," and she called to the Zulu driver, who with an air of utter amazement was engaged in milking one of the gift cows, to fill two bottles with the milk.

"Had we not better shout to the Makalanga to let us in?" suggested Robert, while this was being done, and Benita wrapped some cooked meat in a cloth.

"No, no. They will think I am what I said I was—the Witch of Bambatse, whose appearance heralds misfortune, and fear a trap. Besides, we could not climb the top wall. You must follow my road, and if you can trust them, bring two of those men with you with lanterns. The lad can stop to herd the cattle."

Three minutes later, followed by the two Zulus, they were walking—or rather, running along the banks of the Zambesi.

"Why do you not come quicker?" she asked impatiently. "Oh, I beg your pardon, you are lame. Robert, what made you lame, and oh! why are you not dead, as they all swore you were, you, you—hero, for I know that part of the story?"

"For a very simple reason, Benita: because I didn't die. When that Kaffir took the watch from me I was insensible, that's all. The sun brought me to life afterwards. Then some natives turned up, good people in their way, although I could not understand a word they said.

They made a stretcher of boughs and carried me for some miles to their kraal inland. It hurt awfully, for my thigh was broken, but I arrived at last. There a Kaffir doctor set my leg in his own fashion; it has left it an inch shorter than the other, but that's better than nothing.

"In that place I lay for two solid months, for there was no white man within a hundred miles, and if there had been I could not have communicated with him. Afterwards I spent another month limping up towards Natal, until I could buy a horse. The rest is very short. Hearing of my reported death, I came as fast as I could to your father's farm, Rooi Krantz, where I learned from the old vrow Sally that you had taken to treasure-hunting, the same treasure that I told you of on the *Zanzibar*.

"So I followed your spoor, met the servants whom you had sent back, who told me all about you, and in due course, after many adventures, as they say in a book, walked into the camp of our friends, the Matabele.

"They were going to kill me at once, when suddenly you appeared upon that point of rock, glittering like—like the angel of the dawn. I knew that it must be you, for I had found out about your attempted escape, and how you were hunted back to this place. But the Matabele all thought that it was the Spirit of Bambatse, who has a great reputation in these parts. Well, that took off their attention, and afterwards, as I told you, it occurred to them that I might be an engineer. You know the rest, don't you?"

"Yes," answered Benita softly, "I know the rest."

Then they plunged into the reeds and were obliged to stop talking, since they must walk in single file. Presently Benita looked up and saw that she was under the thorn which grew in the cleft of rock. Also, with some trouble she found the bunch of reeds that she had bent down, to mark the inconspicuous hole through which she had crept, and by it her lantern. It seemed weeks since she had left it there.

"Now," she said, "light your candles, and if you see a crocodile, please shoot."

CHAPTER XXIV.

THE TRUE GOLD.

"LET me go first," said Robert.
"No," answered Benita. "I know the way; but please do watch for that horrible crocodile."

Then she knelt down and crept into the hole, while after her came Robert,

So they toiled up the endless steps, a very strange procession, for the two Zulus, bold men enough outside, were shaking with fright, till at length Benita clambered out of the trap door on to the floor of the treasure chamber, and turned to help Robert, whose lameness made him somewhat slow and awkward.

"What's all that?" he asked, pointing

" 'NO LIE,' HE SCREAMED, 'NO LIE,' AS HE DRAGGED THE STUFF OUT AND SMELT AT IT "

and after him the two Zulus, who protested that they were not ant-bears to burrow under ground. Lifting the lantern she searched the cave, and as she could see no signs of the crocodile, walked on boldly to where the stair began.

"Be quick," she whispered to Robert, for in that place it seemed natural to speak low. "My father is above and near his death. I am dreadfully afraid lest we should be too late."

to the hide sacks, while they waited for the two scared Kaffir to join them.

"Oh!" she answered indifferently, "gold, I believe. Look, there is some of it on the floor, over Benita da Ferreira's footsteps."

"Gold! Why, it must be worth——! And who on earth is Benita da Ferreira?"

"I will tell you afterwards. She has been dead two or three hundred years; it was her gold, or her people's, and those are her footprints in the dust. How stupid you are not to understand! Never mind the hateful stuff; come on quickly."

So they passed the door which she had opened that morning, and clambered up the remaining stairway. So full was Benita of terrors that she could never remember how she climbed them. Suppose that the foot of the crucifix had swung to; suppose that her father were dead; suppose that Jacob Meyer had broken into the cave? Well, for herself she was no longer afraid of Jacob Meyer. Oh, they were there! The heavy door *had* begun to close, but mercifully her bit of rock kept it ajar.

"Father! Father!" she cried, running towards the tent.

No answer came. She threw aside the flap, held down her lantern and looked. There he lay, white and still. She was too late!

"He is dead, he is dead!" she wailed. Robert knelt down at her side, and examined the old man, while she waited in an agony.

"He ought to be," he said slowly; "but, Benita, I don't think he is. I can feel his heart stir. No, don't stop to talk. Pour out some of that squareface, and here, mix it with this milk."

She obeyed, and while he held up her father's head, with a trembling hand emptied a little of the drink into his mouth. At first it ran out again, then almost automatically he swallowed some, and they knew that he was alive, and thanked Heaven. Ten minutes later Mr. Clifford was sitting up staring at them with dull and wondering eyes, while outside the two Zulus, whose nerves had now utterly broken down, were contemplating the pile of skeletons in the corner and the white towering crucifix, and loudly lamenting that they should have been brought to perish in this place of bones and ghosts.

"Is it Jacob Meyer who makes that noise?" asked Mr. Clifford faintly. "And Benita, where have you been so long, and—who is this gentleman with you? I seem to remember his face."

"He is the white man who was in the waggon, Father, an old friend come to life again. Robert, can't you stop the howling of those Kaffirs? Though I am

sure I don't wonder that they howl, I should have liked to do so for days. Oh! father, father, don't you understand me? We are saved, yes, snatched out of hell and the jaws of death."

"Is Jacob Meyer dead, then?" he asked.

"I don't know where he is or what has happened to him, and I don't care, but perhaps we had better find out. Robert, there is a madman outside. Make the Kaffirs pull down that wall, would you? and catch him."

"What wall? What madman?" he asked, staring at her.

"Oh, of course you don't know that, either. You know nothing. I'll show you, and you must be prepared, for probably he will shoot at us."

"It all sounds a little risky, doesn't it?" asked Robert doubtfully.

"Yes, but we must take the risk. We cannot carry my father down that place, and unless we can get him into light and air soon, he will certainly die. The man outside is Jacob Meyer, his partner—you remember him. All these weeks of hardship and treasure-hunting have sent him off his head, and he wanted to mesmerise me and——"

"And what? Make love to you?"

She nodded, then went on:

"So when he could not get his way about the mesmerism and so forth, he threatened to murder my father, and that is why we had to hide in this cave and build ourselves up, till at last I found the way out."

"Amiable gentleman, Mr. Jacob Meyer, now as always," said Robert flushing. "To think that you should have been in the power of a scoundrel like that! Well, I hope to come square with him."

"Don't hurt him, dear, unless you are obliged. Remember he is not responsible. He thought he saw a ghost here the other day."

"Unless he behaves himself he is likely to see a good many soon," muttered Robert.

Then they went down the cave, and as silently as possible began to work at the wall, destroying in a few minutes what had been built up with so much labour. When it was nearly down the Zulus were told that there was an enemy outside, and that they must help to catch him if necessary, but were not to harm him. They assented gladly enough ; indeed, to get out of that cave they would have faced half a dozen enemies.

Now there was a hole right through the wall, and Robert bade Benita stand to one side. Then as soon as his eyes became accustomed to the little light that penetrated there, he drew his revolver and beckoned the Kaffirs to follow. Down the passage they crept, slowly, lest they should be blinded when they came to the glare of the sunshine, while Benita waited with a beating heart.

A little time went by, she never knew how long, till suddenly a rifle shot rang through the stillness. Benita was able to bear no more. She rushed down the winding passage and presently, just beyond its mouth, in a blurred and indistinct fashion saw that the two white men were rolling together on the ground, while the Kaffirs sprang round watching for an opportunity to seize one of them. At that moment they succeeded, and Robert rose, dusting his hands and knees.

"Amiable gentleman, Mr. Jacob Meyer," he repeated. "I could have killed him as his back was towards me, but didn't because you asked me not. Then I stumbled with my lame leg, and he whipped round and let drive with his rifle. Look," and he showed her where the bullet had cut his ear. "Luckily I got hold of him before he could loose off another."

Benita could find no words, her heart was too full of thankfulness. Only she seized Robert's hand and kissed it. Then she looked at Jacob.

He was lying upon the broad of his back, the two big Zulus holding his arms and legs ; his lips were cracked, blue and swollen ; his face was almost black, but his eyes still shone bright with insanity and hate.

"I know you," he screamed hoarsely to Robert. "You are another ghost, the ghost of that man who was drowned. Otherwise my bullet would have killed you."

"Yes, Mr. Meyer," Seymour answered. "I am a ghost. Now you boys, here's a bit of rope. Tie his hands behind his back and search him. There is a pistol in that pocket."

They obeyed, and presently Meyer was disarmed and bound fast to a tree.

"Water," he moaned. "For days I have had nothing but the dew I could lick off the leaves."

Pitying his plight, Benita ran into the cave and returned presently with a tin of water. One of the Kaffirs held it to his lips, and he drank greedily. Then, leaving one Zulu to watch him, Robert, Benita and the other Zulu went back, and as gently as they could carried out Mr. Clifford on his mattress, placing him in the shade of a rock, where he lay blessing them feebly, because they had brought him into the light again. At the sight of the old man Meyer's rage blazed up afresh.

"Ah," he screamed, "if only I had killed you long ago, she would be mine now, not that fellow's. It was you who stood between us."

"Look here, my friend," broke in Robert. "I forgive you everything else, but, mad or sane, be good enough to keep Miss Clifford's name off your lips, or I will hand you over to those Kaffirs to be dealt with as you deserve."

Then Jacob understood, and was silent. They gave him more water and food to eat, some of the meat that they had brought with them, which he devoured ravenously.

"Are you sensible now ?" asked Robert when he had done. "Then listen to me ; I have some good news for you. That treasure you have been hunting for has been found. We are going to give you your half of it, one of the waggons and some oxen, and clear you out of this place. Then if I set eyes on you again before we get to a civilised country, I shoot you like a dog."

"You lie !" said Meyer sullenly. "You want to turn me out into the wilderness to be murdered by the Makalanga or the Matabele."

"Very well," said Robert. "Untie him, boys, and bring him along. I will show him whether I lie."

"Where are they taking me to ?" asked Meyer. "Not into the cave ? I won't go into the cave ; it is haunted. If it hadn't been for the ghost there I would have broken down their wall long ago, and killed that old snake before her eyes. Whenever I went near that wall I saw it watching me."

"First time I ever heard of a ghost being useful," remarked Robert. "Bring him along. No, Benita, he shall see whether I am a liar."

So the lights were lit, and the two stalwart Zulus haled Jacob forward, Robert and Benita following. At first he struggled violently, then, on finding that he could not escape, went on, his teeth chattering with fear.

"It is cruel," remonstrated Benita.

"A little cruelty will not do him any harm," Robert answered. "He has plenty to spare for other people. Besides, he is going to get what he has been loo.ing for so long."

They led Jacob to the foot of the crucifix, where a paroxysm seemed to seize him, then pushed him through the swinging doorway beneath, and down the steep stairs, till once more they all stood in the treasure-chamber.

"Look," said Robert, and, drawing his hunting-knife, he slashed one of the hide bags, whereon instantly there flowed out a stream of beads and nuggets. "Now, my friend, am I a liar?" he asked.

At this wondrous sight Jacob's terror seemed to depart from him, and he grew cunning.

"Beautiful, beautiful," he said, "more than I thought—sacks and sacks of gold. I shall be a king indeed. No, no, it is all a dream—like the rest. I don't believe it's there. Loose my arms and let me feel it."

"Untie him," said Robert, at the same time drawing his pistol and covering the man, "he can't do us any hurt."

The Kaffirs obeyed, and Jacob, springing at the slashed bag, plunged his thin hands into it.

"No lie," he screamed, "no lie," as he dragged the stuff out and smelt at it. "Gold, gold, gold! Hundreds of thous-

ands of pounds' worth of gold! Let's make a bargain, Englishman, and I won't kill you as I meant to do. You take the girl and give me all the gold," and in his ecstasy he began to pour the glittering ingots over his head and body.

"'NO MORE SHALL THE WHITE WITCH STAND UPON THE PILLAR POINT'"

"A new version of the tale of Danaë," began Robert in a sarcastic voice, then suddenly paused, for a change had come over Jacob's face, a terrible change.

It turned ashen beneath the tan, his eyes grew large and round, he put up his hands as though to thrust something from him, his whole frame shivered, and his hair seemed to erect itself. Slowly he retreated backwards and would have fallen down the unclosed trap-hole had not one of the Kaffirs pushed him away. Back he went, still back, till he struck the further wall and stood there, perhaps for half a minute. He lifted his hand and pointed first to those ancient footprints, some of which still remained in the dust of the floor, and next, as they thought, at Benita. His lips moved fast, he seemed to be pleading, remonstrating, yet—and this was the ghastliest part of

it—from them there came no sound.
Lastly, his eyes rolled up until only the
whites of them were visible, his face
became wet as though water had been
poured over it, and, still without a sound,
he fell forward and moved no more.

So terrible was the scene that with a
howl of fear the two Kaffirs turned and
fled up the stairway. Robert sprang to
the Jew, dragged him over on to his back,
put his hand upon his breast and lifted
his eyelids.

"Dead," he said. "Stone dead. Pri-
vation, brain excitement, heart failure,
that's the story."

"Perhaps," answered Benita faintly;
"but really I think that I begin to believe
in ghosts also. Look, I never noticed
them before, and I didn't walk there, but
those footsteps seem to lead right up to
him." Then she turned too and fled.

Another week had gone by. The
waggons were laden with a burden more
precious perhaps than waggons have often
borne before. In one of them on a
veritable bed of gold slept Mr. Clifford,
still very weak and ill, but somewhat
better than he had been, and with a good
prospect of recovery, at any rate for a
while. They were to trek a little after
dawn, and already Robert and Benita
were up and waiting. She touched his
arm and said to him:

"Come with me. I have a fancy to see
that place once more, for the last time."

So they climbed the hill and the steep
steps in the topmost wall that Meyer had
blocked—re-opened now—and reaching
the mouth of the cave, lit the lamps
which they had brought with them, and
entered. There were the fragments of
the barricade that Benita had built with
desperate hands, there was the altar of
sacrifice standing cold and grey as it had
stood for perhaps three thousand years.
There was the tomb of the old monk who
had a companion now, for in it Jacob
Meyer lay with him, his bones covered by
the *débris* that he himself had dug out in
his mad search for wealth, and there the
white Christ hung awful on His cross.
Only the skeletons of the Portuguese
were gone, for with the help of his Kaffirs
Robert had moved them every one into
the empty treasure-chamber, closing the

trap beneath, and building up the door
above, so that there they might lie in
peace at last.

In this melancholy place they tarried
but a little while, then, turning their
backs upon it for ever, went out and
climbed the granite cone to watch the
sun rise over the broad Zambesi. Up it
came in glory, that same sun which had
shone upon the despairing Benita da
Ferreira, and upon the English Benita
when she had stood here in utter hopelessness, and seen the white man captured
by the Matabele.

Now, different was their state indeed,
and there in that high place, whence perhaps many a wretched creature had been
cast to death, whence certainly the Portuguese maiden had sought her death,
these two happy beings were not ashamed
to give thanks to Heaven for the joy
which it had vouchsafed to them, and for
their hopes of life full and long to be
travelled hand in hand. Behind them was
the terror of the cave, beneath them were
the mists of the valley, but about them the
light shone and rolled and sparkled, and
above them stretched the eternal sky!

They descended the pillar, and near the
foot of it saw an old man sitting. It was
Mambo, the Molimo of the Makalanga:
even when they were still far away from
him they knew his snow-white head and
thin, ascetic face. As they drew near
Benita perceived that his eyes were closed,
and whispered to Robert that he was
asleep. Yet he had heard them coming,
and even guessed her thought.

"Maiden," he said in his gentle voice,
"maiden who soon shall be a wife, I do
not sleep, although I dream of you as I
have dreamt before. What did I say to
you that day when first we met? That for
you I had good tidings; that though
death was all about you, you need not
fear; that in this place you who had
known great sorrow should find happiness
and rest. Yet, maiden, you would not
believe the words of the Munwali, spoken
by his prophet's lips, as he at your side
who shall be your husband, would not
believe me in years past when I told him
that we should meet again."

"Father," she answered, "I thought
your rest was that which we find only in
the grave."

"You would not believe," he went on without heeding her, "and therefore you tried to fly, and therefore your heart was torn with terror and with agony, when it should have waited for the end in confidence and peace."

"Father, my trial was very sore."

"Maiden, I know it, and because it was so sore that patient Spirit of Bambatse bore with you, and through it all guided your feet aright. Yes, with you has that Spirit gone, by day, by night, in the morning and in the evening. Who was it that smote the man who lies dead yonder with horror and with madness when he would have bent your will to his and made you a wife to him? Who was it that told you the secret of the treasure-pit, and what footsteps went before you down its stair? Who was it that led you past the sentries of the Amandabele and gave you wit and power to snatch your lord's life from Maduna's bloody hand? Yes, with you it has gone and with you it will go. No more shall the White Witch stand upon the pillar point at the rising of the sun, or in the shining of the moon."

"Father, I have never understood you, and I do not understand you now," said Benita. "What has this spirit to do with me?"

He smiled a little, then answered slowly:

"That I may not tell you; that you shall learn one day, but never here. When you also have entered into silence, then you shall learn. But I say to you that this shall not be till your hair is as white as mine, and your years are as many. Ah! you thought that I had deserted you, when fearing for your father's life you wept and prayed in the darkness of the cave. Yet it was not so, for I did but suffer the doom which I had read to fulfil itself as it must do."

He rose to his feet and, resting on his staff, laid one withered hand upon the head of Benita.

"Maiden," he said, "we meet no more beneath the sun. Yet because you have brought deliverance to my people, because you are sweet and pure and true, take with you the blessing of Munwali, spoken by the mouth of his servant Mambo, the old Molimo of Bambatse. Though from time to time you must know tears and walk in the shade of sorrows, long and happy shall be your days with him whom you have chosen. Children shall spring up about you, and children's children, and with them also shall the blessing go. The gold you white folk love is yours, and it shall multiply and give food to the hungry and raiment to those that are a-cold. Yet in your own heart lies a richer store that cannot melt away, the countless treasure of mercy and of love. When you sleep and when you wake love shall take you by the hand, till at length he leads you through life's dark cave to that eternal house of purest gold which soon or late those that seek it shall inherit," and with his staff he pointed to the glowing morning sky wherein one by one little rosy clouds floated upwards and were lost.

To Robert and to Benita's misty eyes they looked like bright-winged angels throwing wide the black portals of the night, and heralding that conquering sun at whose advent despair and darkness flee away.

THE END.